BLUE
BEECH
SERIES

JUST A FLING - JUST ONE NIGHT - JUST EXES

BOOKS 1 - 3

USA TODAY BESTSELLING AUTHOR
CHARITY FERRELL

Cover Designer: Opulent Designs

Just A Fling:

Editor: Jenny Sims, Editing 4 Indies

Just One Night:

Editor: Jovana Shirley, Unforeseen Editing

Just Exes:

Editor: Jovana Shirley, Unforeseen Editing

Proofreader: Bex Harper, Bex Harper Designs

Just a Fling

ONE

Hudson

"SAVE IT. That shit is your gig, not mine." I'm staring at my older brother, wondering when he lost his damn mind.

"You'll be doing me a huge favor," Dallas pleads.

"You want me to wash your panties? Sure. You need me to get rid of your old-school nudie mags so Lucy doesn't find out you were a little perv back in the day? I got you. *Those* are favors. What you're asking me is more than that, and you fucking know it."

"Come on. You're overreacting."

I shake my head. "I didn't withstand two tours overseas to come home and play bitch to some spoiled Hollywood princess."

I busted my ass in Marine training, slept in the shittiest conditions, and witnessed shit I'd give my left nut to un-see. No way am I moving on from that to following some high-maintenance chick around. "I've been gone for nine months, and this is the first thing you ask when I get home? Offering me some bullshit job you know I'd never take?"

"You'll be her bodyguard, not her bitch, Hudson."

"Either way, I respectively decline."

"She's not as bad as you think."

I snort.

"Do it for me. I'm going through hell right now. You taking this job will give me one less problem to worry about."

I hold up my hand. "Nuh-uh, don't you dare pull that shit."

"What shit?"

"The empathy hook you're attempting to sink into me that will make me look like a heartless bastard if I don't let you reel me in." I'd trade places with him and take his pain in a goddamn heartbeat if I could.

"Is it working?" He chuckles at my irritation. "Look, I was her security guard for five years. She's not only a damn good employer but also a friend who helped pay Lucy's medical bills and gave me paid leave to be with my family. I want to make sure she's protected, and last I heard, they haven't found anyone qualified enough to take my place. That's why I suggested you."

"How about you un-suggest me?"

He drags his hand through his shaggy brown hair. "What's your plan then, huh? The pay is better than anything here in Blue Beech. Make some fast cash, come home, and put a down payment on a house. You can quit as soon as they hire someone else."

I stay silent, and he stretches forward to punch my arm.

"You know I wouldn't ask if it wasn't important to me," he adds.

I lean back in my chair and focus on him from across his kitchen table. Dark circles ride under his sunken eyes, and stress lines that didn't exist when I left months ago stretch along his mouth. My older brother is hurting and in fear of losing the woman he loves. As his brother, it's my job to pull my shit together, put my pride aside, and help him.

His wife, Lucy's, breast cancer was caught too late and spread too fast. The doctors aren't sure how much time she has left. She's only thirty-one, and her diagnosis was a shock to us. Dallas quit his job as head security guard for Stella Mendes and returned home to be there for her.

"Fine," I groan, holding up a finger. "I'll do it but on one condition."

He raises a brow.

"It's only temporary. Two months max, so you tell them to get their asses on finding a replacement."

He blows out a ragged breath. "Thank you. Your flight leaves in the morning."

"The hell? You already booked my flight?"

He nods.

"What if I'd said no?"

"I'd have Lucy ask you."

"You play fucking dirty." It's one thing to argue with him, but no way can I say no to Lucy.

"This job will also get you out of town so shit can cool down for a minute. It's a win-win."

"I don't need shit to cool down." My muscles tense while I hold in my rage—the topic pissing me off more than the job offer.

He gives me a stern look. "Don't do something you'll regret."

"We're not having this conversation." I pinch the bridge of my nose. "It's off-limits right now, you hear me?"

"I understand, brother. I'd be one furious motherfucker, too."

THERE'S no missing the curious stares following me when I walk into the Down Home Pub, the hot spot in town if you're craving a beer, good time, or want to drown your sorrows.

Dallas forced me to go out for drinks—a pick-me-up for us both was what he called it. My dumb ass should've known it was more than grabbing a quick beer and shooting the shit.

A blue *Welcome Home Hudson* banner hangs at the front of the bar, and the pub is packed with familiar faces—people I've known all my life. Months ago, I would've loved this surprise.

Now? Not so much.

I've lived in Blue Beech, Iowa, all my life. It's a small town where everyone knows everyone's business. People say that about all small towns, but Blue Beech is the real deal. Everyone knew my fiancé was fucking around on me and planning a wedding with my best friend *on our scheduled wedding date* before I did. News doesn't travel as fast as word of mouth when you're overseas with limited communication.

Cameron sent me a bullshit Dear John letter. Every word was a stab to the gut. I ripped it up and burned the pieces. Crumbling relationships and marriages are a regular occurrence in military life. I'd become just another statistic.

Dallas hands me a beer, and I smile before chugging it in one go —savoring the bitter yet delicious malted barley. I slap my hand onto the bar and ask the bartender, Maliki, to pour us another round.

There's no missing the pity stares shooting in my direction, confirming everyone knows about Cameron. I spot a group of guys I played football with in high school huddled around the table and stroll in their direction. When I'm almost there, someone sticks their foot out in an attempt to trip me.

They fail, but I'm pissed.

What the fuck?

I turn around, ready to take my anger out on the jackass, but that outrage dissipates when I see her.

"Well, if it isn't the biggest asshat in the world. Sorry I'm late, but the hospital has been a madhouse," Lauren, my younger sister, says.

I laugh when she attempts to wrap her short arms around me in a hug and pat her on the head when she pulls away. "No biggie. I've only been here a few minutes."

She grins. "I've missed you. Guys aren't as scared to mess with me when you're gone. I've had to resort to my pepper spray and AK-47."

"You don't own an AK-47."

"True, but doesn't it sound badass when I say I do? You should probably buy me one for my birthday."

"I'm never buying you a gun. Hell, I wouldn't put it past you to shoot some poor bastard who said the wrong thing to you."

She laughs. "You know the tempers of the Barnes family aren't one to be reckoned with."

I debated on going home, but Blue Beech is all I've ever known. As I sit down and enjoy another beer, I'm happy I agreed to come instead of drinking my sorrows away in Dallas's basement.

That happiness lasts only twenty minutes and two beers in. I'm beginning to relax while Lauren divulges her latest dating fail when she stops mid-conversation and slams her drink down.

"I cannot believe that son of a bitch and hussy would show their faces here," she yells.

I look away from her fuming face to see what has her attention.

"Everyone in this godforsaken town knows your party is here tonight," she spats.

My hands turn numb, and I nearly drop my beer while the taste of bile swims up my throat.

The bar goes silent.

Even the jukebox cuts off for the ensuing shitshow.

I shift in my seat in an attempt to cool the fury crackling through me like a lit match.

There she is.

Cameron Pine.

The woman who decided I wasn't worth the wait is heading straight in my direction with the asshole she left me for at her side.

She's wearing a denim skirt and the same flannel top she wore the night I proposed. Her face is void of emotion, her curly blond hair swept back into a ponytail, and she's sporting her cherry red lipstick—a color she'd stained my dick with countless times. I used to love it when she marked me. She might've fucked me over, but that doesn't stop me from thinking she's breathtakingly gorgeous.

My gaze moves from her to something not so beautiful. A sight so fucking rancid it makes my stomach churn. Grady was my best friend who took my asking to watch over her too literal. I wanted him to make sure she was safe, not keep her pussy warm for me.

"Cameron better not come over here, or I will find an AK-47 and run her ass out of this bar," Lauren says.

My sister is loyal to a fault. Cameron was her best friend, but she burned all ties and threatened to kick her ass on multiple occasions when she found out about the affair. Even now, I'm not sure my baby sis will keep her cool and not choke slam Cameron *and* Grady.

"I had no idea they were coming," Dallas says, rushing to our table. He went outside ten minutes ago to call Lucy and check on her. "They obviously weren't invited."

"Unless I plan on moving out of Blue Beech forever, I'm bound to run into them," I reply. "Cameron wasn't happy with me and chose to be with someone who could be that nine-to-five, at the dinner table every night husband. I'm not that man."

The problem is, I still can't bring myself to hate Cameron.

Although, I'm fucking livid with Grady.

It takes two people to have an affair, I'm well aware, and it's wrong for me to place all the blame on him, but I can't put it on the woman I loved for over a decade.

The bar stays silent while everyone watches them grow closer.

"Hudson," Grady says when he reaches us. He looks stressed, scared, and I can't blame him. "Can we talk?"

Cameron stands behind him and rests her hand on his shoulder.

"You need to leave, asshole," Lauren demands. "And take that cheating skank with you."

"My sister is right," Dallas says. "You two have some nerve showing up here. Let's not make this uglier than necessary."

I hold up my hand to stop my siblings from going on. "It's cool." My eyes narrow in on Grady, and I can tell it wasn't his idea to come. "I'd love to have a chat and hear your pathetic ass excuse for stabbing me in the back over a goddamn chick." I tilt my head toward the back door, grab my beer, and he follows me to the exit.

I snatch his shirt collar and slam him against the brick exterior as soon as the door shuts behind us. "I told you to watch out for her, not fuck her!"

His lower lip trembles when I wrap my hand around his neck. "I'm sorry. I'm so fucking sorry, Hudson. It just happened!"

I tighten my hold on him and inch closer until we're nose to nose. "Having sex with someone doesn't *just happen*. You had time to stop. You could've walked away. Hell, not only did you fuck her behind my back but you also proposed to her while she was wearing my engagement ring. That sure as fuck doesn't *just happen!*"

It takes every bit of restraint in me not to smash my fist in his face. Cameron is vain enough that she would dump his ass if he weren't a pretty boy any longer.

Maybe I should.

"I love her, Hudson," he chokes out.

His words add fuel to my burning fire, and he grunts when I pull him closer, only to slam him back against the wall.

"She was mine!" I scream.

I release him and take a step back at the sound of the back door opening. Cameron steps out, and I hold my breath with a snarl. We haven't talked in months. I never replied to her pathetic letter. She said enough for the both of us.

My skin crawls as the memories of us and the plans we made for when I got home smack into me. She was supposed to be my wife, the mother of my children, and the woman I grew old with.

"Don't … don't do this, Hudson," she begs. "We came here to do the right thing and clear the air." Her voice lowers. "I'm sorry for hurting you. We both are."

I'm a tough guy who has withstood a lot of shit, but fighting back this hurt of betrayal from two people I trusted with my life kills me. Words neglect me while I stare into her baby blue eyes. It's not as easy to push my anger out on her like it is with Grady.

Tears fall down her cheeks. "He was there for me when you weren't. I begged you not to leave me again and told you how difficult it was being alone. I wanted a family, but you didn't care!"

"It was my fucking job, Cameron!" I scream.

"You're right, and the job of being a military wife isn't for me. I'm sorry."

"It is what it is," I mutter. "Stay the hell away from me. You deserve each other."

I turn around and walk away without another glance at them.

A few months away from this town might be what I need to clear my head and get my shit straight.

Let's only hope this chick is easy to deal with.

TWO

Hudson

I DEPART from the terminal after landing at LAX and stroll through the mob of people rushing around with phones in their hands. I'm not a fan of crowds. Solitude is more my thing, but I have a feeling I better get used to the contrary. Dallas has told me stories about working for Stella. Fans and paparazzi follow her around like a shadow.

Instead of going back to my party last night, I headed to Dallas's place and watched Disney movies with my niece, Maven.

I went from the plan of coming home to fuck my fiancé senseless to sitting on the couch with my niece watching a cartoon about a nitwit teen who traded her voice for legs in order to get laid by Prince Charming. Sleep wasn't my friend, and the cherry on top of my time home was Dallas waking me up at the ass crack of dawn to drive me to the airport.

I snag my luggage and sweep my gaze over the room. Dallas texted me directions of what to do when I landed. Stella's driver will be here to give me a ride to her place. I scan the signs being held up by people, waiting until I see the one with my name on it, and make my way over to the gray-haired man wearing a suit.

"You Jim?" I ask him.

He nods. "You Hudson?"

"Sure am."

I shake his hand and stop him from grabbing my luggage before he leads me out of the airport to a black SUV with windows tinted so dark they have to be illegal. I toss my bag in the back seat and sit in the front.

"Have you worked for Stella long?" I ask when he starts the car and leaves the parking garage.

Traffic is bumper-to-bumper.

Why would anyone want to live in this shit?

"Almost five years," Jim answers. "She hired me after your brother started, but unlike her bodyguards, I don't travel with her. I only drive when she's in LA." He glances over at me with pain on his face. "Dallas was damn good at his job, and I hope you're the same. I also hate to bring this up, but I'm sorry for what's happened to Lucy. I lost my wife to cancer last year and can't imagine the pain of losing her so young."

"Thank you, and I'm sorry for your loss. My sister-in-law is as tough as nails. She'll make it through this stronger than ever."

That's what I tell myself. My family is trying our best to stay positive.

I make small talk with Jim for the rest of the ride, and he punches in the passcode after we stop in front of a security gate. I stare at the lavish Spanish-style home in awe as he drives up to it. Homes in Blue Beech are nothing like this. Cameron and I rented a two-bedroom farmhouse that looked like a shack compared to this place.

"Hot damn," I mutter. "Some crib for a twenty-five-year-old."

Jim parks and cuts the ignition. "Working on a long-standing, Emmy-award-winning TV show gives you a pretty decent paycheck."

"I'd say so." It's too excessive for one person, in my opinion. "Does she live here alone?"

He nods. "Her sister stayed with her for a while but moved to New York six months ago."

The scent of vanilla hits me when I walk through the front door, and I take a look around, admiring the hardwood floors and cathedral ceilings before making it to the living room. A massive stone fireplace is the highlight of the room until you look through the floor-to-ceiling windows that give one of the most remarkable views I've ever seen.

I understand now why she bought the place.

That fucking view.

I could sit out there and think for hours.

My attention moves from the outside when two women walk into the room. Their mouths drop when they notice me, and I rudely stare as they come closer.

I recognize Stella immediately.

How could I not?

Stories and images of her are plastered on every magazine cover in grocery store checkout lanes, and she stays on TV with endless reruns. Cameron used to make me watch those stupid award shows with her, and Stella was a consistent winner.

Even with all that, I never expected her to be this beautiful. I can't take my eyes off her full-figured body. She's enthralling, flawless, fucking perfection. No wonder every cameraman wants a shot of her.

Stella Mendes is a woman who can bring a man to his knees with the slightest hint of a smile. Hell, she doesn't even have to smile. Just her presence makes you hungry for more.

Her straight hair, the color of coal, flows down her shoulders, framing her heart-shaped face with minimal makeup. Skintight white jeans show off her curves and stop a few inches from her ankles, and a black silk tank hangs loose on her shoulders, giving me a glimpse of her honey-colored skin.

Fuck me.

Good thing I'm only here until they find someone to take over the job.

Her attractiveness doesn't change my opinion of her. She might be gorgeous, but that doesn't mean she's a decent person. Cameron has told me stories about Stella being a spoiled diva who expects people to jump when she yells. There were times it was difficult for Dallas to come home for the holidays because of her hectic schedule.

That shit won't fly with me.

I'll work for her but won't be ordered around like a dog.

Stella holds out her hand to me. "Hudson, thank you for coming." Her voice is flat, and I can't tell if she's impartial or pissed that I'm here.

I shake her hand. It feels soft against my calloused skin. "No problem."

She jerks her head toward the petite redhead at her side that looks around the same age as her. "This is my assistant, Willow."

Willow smiles and gives me a friendly wave before clapping her hands. "Now that the introductions are out of the way, we have so much to do. You two will be spending a lot of time together, so I want to make sure you take care of my girl, Hudson."

Stella flinches at her remark and looks like she'd rather kick me out of her house.

Feeling is mutual, sweetheart.

THREE

Stella

OH FUCK.

Not good. Not good.

I'm so screwed.

My new bodyguard is …

I can't even think of the right words to describe him.

Mouthwatering?

I laugh to myself.

I can't come up with something more original and less lame than that?

Sexy. Masculine. Dominating.

Unfortunately, all humans with a penis are off-limits to me right now.

Hudson is built, muscles aplenty, but not like the men who spend forty hours a week lifting weights at the gym to score the perfect six-pack for their next Instagram post. He gives off a tough demeanor effortlessly.

Someone would be batshit crazy to mess with him, and that's exactly what I look for in a bodyguard. His ash-brown hair is short in the front and buzzed on the sides in your typical military cut. He didn't dress up for the occasion—wearing a pair of old jeans complete with worn holes, a white tee, and beat-up boots.

Even though we barely know each other, I already feel safe with him.

The downside to him being here is that I'm certain he's not my biggest fan. The grimace on his face made it clear he'd rather be anywhere but here.

Dallas has told me plenty about Hudson over the years. He's a small-town guy who spent the past eight years serving our country. He isn't into the whole Hollywood buzz and has called his brother a dumbass countless times for working for me.

He had to be desperate to take the job.

We say goodbye to Jim and head into my office. I get straight to business as soon as we sit down.

"Willow will keep you updated on my schedule," I tell him.

As if on cue, Willow hands him a folder and starts rambling off instructions. "Everything you need to know is in here, including all contact numbers, addresses, and emails. There's also a blueprint of the house, details of each stop during Stella's press tour, and a map of every hotel she's staying in."

Hudson listens and nods.

"How long have you been in the bodyguard business?" Willow asks. "Dallas didn't list any references other than the fact that you're his brother, and that's all that mattered."

He scratches his head, and his voice is rough when he answers. "This is my first bodyguard job."

"What?" Willow yells, looking at me in shock.

I expected her reaction, which is why I didn't tell her. I trust Dallas's word.

"So … you've never worked in this field *at all*?" Willow asks him.

I suck in a breath when he leans forward, plants his elbows on the table, and doesn't look fazed as he stares at Willow.

"I've never worked as a bodyguard, but I have plenty of experience fighting for my country, providing security at embassies, and putting my life on the line daily for the safety of others. That should be enough training for this job, don't you think? I pay attention to every movement around me, and my mind is always on the job. *Always*. And if it makes you feel better, I'm only here until you find a *more qualified* replacement."

We both stare at him, stunned and speechless.

Holy fucking hotness.

That's a damn good answer.

———

"HE'S CUTE," Willow says when we're alone in my bedroom.

We showed Hudson his room and left him to unpack his bag … and hopefully take a happy pill to get out of his cranky mood.

She holds up a finger. "Correction. He's not cute. *Cute* is how you describe a three-year-old freckled kid. That guy is a whole lot of man hotness. *All man* hotness."

Willow isn't just my assistant. She's also my best friend. I can count on her more than anyone. She always has my back and won't bullshit me when I'm being stupid. Frankly, she doesn't kiss my ass like most people.

I narrow my eyes at her. "Don't go there."

"It's time to move on from that douchebag."

"I *have* moved on from Knox. When I found out he bought a house and moved that pink-haired chick in, it was my reality check. He and I knew we weren't meant to be, but we were too comfortable with each other to cut the cord. He isn't the reason I'm saying don't go there. My situation is. I can't mess around with my security guard. You know mixing business with pleasure is a big no-no in my book. Not to mention, the dude looks like he can't even stand the sight of me."

She climbs onto my bed and sits across from me. "Yeah, I'm not sure what's up his ass, but maybe he'll warm up to you. And hey, just because he works for you doesn't mean you can't have a little fun." She wiggles her shoulders back and forth. "You need to get laid before cobwebs start growing down there. Lack of dick is also making you very irritable. Get some dick. Grow a smile. Just like he said he does his job, I'm sure he gives one hundred percent in the bedroom."

I throw my head back to stop myself from laughing. "Why am I friends with you again?"

"Because I'm Team Get Stella Laid."

"Don't get your hopes up. Last I heard from Dallas, Hudson is engaged to some longtime girlfriend. Guys meet their wives in like the third grade in their hometown."

She frowns. "Well, if you can't get a piece of him, we need to find you someone else."

"Reality check. Getting laid in my situation is not only doubtful but stupid."

She gives me an annoyed glare. "You can bitch about it all you want, but I don't feel sorry for you. I told you not to do it."

We've gone round and round about this.

"It was the best move for my future. My career trumps relationships and sex. I won't walk through my door one night and find my career sticking his cock into another chick."

She rolls her eyes. "Oh please, you'll always have work. You've had constant work for years because you're damn talented. Don't let them assholes tell you otherwise."

"It's a big deal migrating from television to movies. I want people to take me seriously and stop seeing me as only Clementine."

Clementine Storms was the character I played on my show. She was a geeky girl who found out she was a witch and spent her time experimenting and fucking up every spell and potion she tried.

She snorts. "People aren't going to take you seriously if word gets out about what you're doing. You'll be the joke of showbiz. They'll sever all respect, resulting in you becoming desperate and taking bad roles on the Lifetime channel where your husband plots to kill you."

I scowl. "I'll take my chances."

She's right. My credibility will be demolished, which was why I refused at first, but eventually, they broke me down. It was the best for my career is what they insisted. I question myself daily on whether I made the right decision.

———

"CAN I ASK YOU SOMETHING?" Hudson asks.

Willow left twenty minutes ago, so it's only the two of us. I hoped maybe he'd lighten up, but so far, all he's giving me is the cold shoulder. Hudson is more intense than his brother. I immediately felt comfortable with Dallas. He cracked a few jokes, told me stories about his family, and was an open book. Hudson is distant, glowering, and humorless.

"Shoot," I answer. It's about damn time he seemed interested in something.

He runs his hand through his hair. "I should've asked this earlier." He pauses and looks around. "What exactly are my duties here? What do I do all day?"

"Like Willow said, be prepared to spend time with me, *a lot* of time with me. You travel with me and stay here when I'm home."

His face shifts into a more guarded expression with my last statement. Dallas must have failed to inform him that tidbit of information.

I shrug. "I like to feel safe."

"I'll do my best to keep you that way." He leans against the doorframe and crosses his arms. "Have you ever had any situations?"

"Stalker wise?"

He nods.

"A few, but most of them were with my old bodyguard. It became less frequent after I hired your brother. He did a good job scaring off the creeps, so they never got close enough to cause me any harm."

I'm not sure how much Dallas told him about the responsibilities of this job. I've been stalked, harassed, and sent death threats. I do what I love, but that doesn't mean it doesn't come with risks.

FOUR

Hudson

"WHAT THE FUCK, DALLAS?" I ask as soon as he answers my call. "I'm living with this chick?"

I want to shove my foot up his ass. It was stupid for me not to ask more questions before hopping on a plane to take an unknown job.

Dallas chuckles. "I see you made it safe and sound. How was your flight?"

"Shitty. I gave away my first-class ticket to some pregnant gal who needed it more than I did. Now answer my question. What the fuck did you get me into?" I figured I'd be crashing at a hotel, not her house.

"Of course, you stay there. That's what I did when Lucy moved back home."

The only reason Dallas moved to LA and took the bodyguard job was because Lucy wanted to spread her wings and get a taste of life outside Blue Beech. The big city wasn't what she imagined, so she moved home after getting pregnant with Maven. Somehow, she and Dallas managed to keep a healthy long-distance relationship while he stayed in LA.

"Lucy was cool with that?" I ask.

"I hope you're not insinuating what I think you are. I'm a

married man who has the love of his life. There's no need for another woman. My relationship with Stella was strictly professional."

"How beautiful," I mutter.

"I got you a kick-ass job with great pay. A thank you would be nice."

"Thanks," I grumble. "What exactly am I supposed to do here? Hang out with this chick all day and night? I'll go fucking nuts."

"It's not all day and night. If you need time off, ask her. You'll be spending the next week attending promotional events and screenings for her new movie. Your lucky ass gets to travel and stay in the nicest hotels for free. Quit bitching and enjoy it."

"Do I have to paint her nails and braid her hair, too?"

"If you're into that shit, go ahead. She might not be too keen on your offer. This might surprise you, but she's a pretty private person."

I scoff. *Yeah right.* If you make the decision to be famous, you're choosing to give your privacy up and giving consent to all your dirty laundry being aired out to the world.

"What did you do with her?" I ask.

Dallas is more of a people person than I am. Maybe he'll have some decent ideas to get me through this.

"We watched movies. I read. Find something you have in common."

"We have nothing in common."

"Stay optimistic. You never know."

He changes the subject by giving me an update on Lucy. We talk for a good hour before I hang up to get ready for bed. It's after eleven, and I'm nowhere near tired, but I don't know what else to do with myself.

My bedroom is on the main floor in what I assume is the in-law suite. It includes a bathroom, a full kitchenette, and a desk filled with monitors giving me a view from every camera on the property.

I undress, turn on the TV, and slide into the world's most comfortable bed. My next three hours are spent tossing and turning until I get annoyed enough to go to my bag for an Ambien.

I go to the kitchenette for a glass, but the cabinet I open is empty.

I check another one.

Empty again.

I crack open the door and tiptoe down the dark hallway toward the kitchen. I make it around the corner at the same time a light flips on, and I collide with something ... or *someone*.

"Fuck!" a high-pitch voice shouts.

I stumble back to find Stella standing in front of me with her hand settled on her chest as she takes deep breaths.

"You scared the living shit out of me," she says between pants.

It looks bad, but I can't stop myself from sweeping my gaze down her body and appreciating the view she's giving me. My dick is enjoying it as well. Purple silk shorts small enough to be considered panties stop at the base of her thighs. A matching tank stops above her belly button, showing off her tan hips and belly button ring.

Stella has curves for days that I could explore for even longer. Every trace of makeup is gone from her face. Her hair is in a messy ponytail at the top of her head, a few tendrils sweeping in front of her wide eyes.

It's my first day on the job, and she's already trying to kill me.

"Shit," I finally stutter out. "I'm sorry. I thought you'd be asleep."

She's still startled but waves off my apology. "No biggie." She always seems to be on edge—like she's waiting for a killer to barge through the door with a chainsaw.

The room falls silent, and I start getting uncomfortable when her eyes drop down my body, not going any further than my cock. Her head tilts to the side as if she's studying my junk, and I don't understand why until I glance down.

I'm only wearing boxer briefs, and they're not regular boxer briefs.

It's the pair Dallas had given me as a gag gift.

Written across my cock are the words: *Take Me To Your Beaver.*

I clear my throat, and it takes a second to gain her attention. She's smirking when she finally looks at me.

"Take me to your beaver?" she asks, laughing. "*Nice,* and here I thought you had no sense of humor. Only on your underwear does your personality come out."

"They were a gag gift from my dickhead brother. I didn't get the chance to go through my clothes when I got home, so I threw random shit in my suitcase."

That's a lie.

The truth is, Cameron packed up my belongings while I was gone and dropped them off at Dallas's place when she moved Grady in. She conveniently forgot to also drop off the furniture, appliances, and electronics I bought.

She smiles. "Can't say I can complain about them."

My dick stirs. I need to reroute this conversation before I end up taking my cock to her beaver.

"There are no glasses in the cabinet," I say.

"The kitchen is always open. I'm pretty sure Dallas never used that kitchenette." She turns to flip on another light, and the kitchen lights up like the Vegas Strip. "Can't sleep?"

I shake my head.

"Me either. I'm putting on some tea. Want a cup?"

"The only kind of tea I drink is laced with sugar and served on ice. Not sure that'll exactly make me tired."

She grabs a teapot, fills it with water, and sets it on the stove. "It's herbal tea. Chamomile. My insomnia remedy."

We're standing in her kitchen both damn near naked, and she's offering me a cup of tea.

Can this get any more awkward?

I might as well make the best of the situation. She's not freaking out or rushing away in embarrassment, and I'll look like a dipshit if I do.

I shrug and sit down on a barstool. "It's worth a shot. Why can't you sleep?"

"I have a lot on my mind."

I raise a questioning brow, a silent plea to continue, and am surprised when she does.

"I'm making a significant career change. This is my first big role in a movie, and I want people to like it ... to like me. This is my chance to prove that I can do more than play some teenage witch."

"Do you like it?"

She nods.

"That's all that matters then." I throw my arms out to gesture to the kitchen. "You must have decent talent, considering you're able to afford a home like this at your age."

"Money doesn't equal talent."

"Good point."

"Do you not like me?"

The bluntness of her question surprises me. *Shit.* This isn't the conversation I want to have with her.

"What do you mean?" I ask, playing dumb.

"You have this wall up, and it seems you'd rather be anywhere but here. I mean, I'm not expecting you to be my biggest fan, but it's like I ruined your childhood Christmas or something."

"You want me to be honest?"

"I wouldn't have asked you if I didn't."

"I'm sure it comes as no surprise that I didn't want to take this job."

"Why? Because you think I'm a terrible person?"

"Never said that."

She leans against the counter and crosses her arms. "Actions speak louder than words, homeboy."

"I don't know you."

"Exactly, so you have no right to judge me so early."

"*But,*" I stress. "I've heard stories."

She snorts. "Didn't think you were one of those dudes. Stories from where?"

"Not from my brother," I rush out. I want to make that clear. Dallas has never said a bad word about Stella and has always kept her business private. "From magazines and shit." *And Cameron.*

She rolls her eyes. "Magazines and shit? Those are some credible sources, let me tell ya." She grins arrogantly. "It's okay. You don't have to like me. Not everyone has good taste."

Damn. Maybe she does have some spark in her.

I love me a smart-ass woman.

"Trust me, I have good taste," I correct. "And a good eye for character. So far, you haven't done anything too diva-like, but we've only known each other for a few hours. No one shows their flaws and bad side this early."

She stares at me blankly. "Does that mean you're hiding your flaws from me? You have some demon hidden away in there? Are you a psychopath or one of those men who like to be dressed up in a diaper and then changed as sexual foreplay?"

I can't stop a smile from flashing over my lips.

Spunk, yeah, she has it.

"The last two are a huge ass negative." *Internal demons? Possibly.* My stomach knots. "I'm sure you'll find qualities I have that you don't like. No one is perfect."

This conversation is taking a huge turn from where I wanted it to go. My plan was to drink this so-called miraculous sleep tea, have limited conversation, and get my ass some sleep.

"Have you ever watched my show?" she asks.

"Can't say I have. I tend to be an action more than teen witch fan."

Maven asked me countless times to watch Stella's show with her, but I was never interested. A hint of sadness stretches over Stella's face, and she turns around when the teapot whistles through our tension. Grabbing two tea packets, she places them in the mugs before pouring in the water.

"So … why can't you sleep," is her next question.

I scrub a hand over my face. "It's only my second night back in the States. It usually takes time to adjust to the different time zone."

She hands me a pink mug. "Where were you stationed?"

"Afghanistan, both times."

"Do you think you'll go back?"

"I promised my family I wouldn't, but I'm not sure now." There's nothing to keep me here now. The tea scorches the tip of my tongue when I take a drink. It's too bland for my taste but not terrible.

She puckers her full lips and blows into her cup. "Why aren't you sure?"

"Shit has changed. People changed. I changed. My situation is different than when I made that promise."

"I say do whatever makes you happy." She grins and holds up her cup when I yawn. "Told you it works." She slides across the kitchen floor in her socks. "Good night, Hudson. Hopefully, you'll like me tomorrow because we have a long day ahead of us."

I turn around in my chair to look at her. "What do you mean?"

"We're flying out in the morning to finish off the promotional tour. Didn't Dallas tell you?"

I shake my head. "Nope. Must've slipped his mind."

"Now you know. Get some rest."

I give her a small smile. "Good night, Stella."

I turn off the kitchen lights and take the tea with me to my room. Even though I'm growing drowsy, something is irritating me. I grab my laptop from its sleeve and open iTunes. When I find her show, I buy every season and make it through the first two episodes before dozing off.

FIVE

Stella

"YOU READY TO GET THIS party started?" Willow asks when she strolls into my bedroom.

Her red hair is pulled back in two tight French braids, and she's wearing a bright green maxi dress. Like me, Willow likes to travel comfortably.

I'm sitting on my bed in a similar dress, except mine is black, and double-checking I have my passport and everything I need for the trip.

"By the way," Willow goes on. "I saw your hot bodyguard downstairs in the kitchen making coffee. Someone needs to pull the stick from his ass."

I'm about to tell her about our conversation last night but stop myself. She'll only try to push him between my legs more.

"He's probably just tired," I say, suddenly feeling the need to defend him. "He's only been home a few days and is still adjusting to the time difference."

She grins and sits down across from me. "Dang, look at you Ms. Know-It-All. Did he tell you that?" Her face scrunches up when I nod. "I bet his girlfriend wasn't happy about him leaving to come here after only being home a few days."

"I think they broke up."

"Did your new bestie disclose that as well?"

"No, but he said he promised his family he wouldn't deploy again, but shit has changed now."

"Hmm … it sounds like both of you are in need of releasing some tension. You know what helps with that?"

"A massage? Oreo cookies?"

"A *massage* to your clitoris. Oreo cookies licked off your body."

I shove her arm. "Um, gross. You know I'd freak out if crumbs got in my bed."

She sighs. "One of these days, I'm going to find you a good man."

I sigh back more dramatically. "One of these days, I'm going to find you a good man, so you stay out of my love life."

Willow has a boyfriend, and he's not my biggest fan. Nor am I his. The guy is a loser, but she loves him, so all I can do is support her. That doesn't mean I always hold myself back from throwing jabs about him now and then. She can do so much better than a man she's caught cheating and sending dick pics to other women.

"If you don't start dating, you'll be eighty, wrinkly, and living alone with your sixty-something cats drinking whiskey and whining about how much men suck."

"As long as there's alcohol involved, it sounds like a promising future. Whiskey and pussies."

She rolls her eyes, jumps off my bed, and slaps my leg to do the same. "Until then, we have a plane to catch. Your luggage was brought downstairs by Muscled Marine, so as soon as you're ready, we can leave."

"Muscled Marine? You need Jesus."

"And you need some dick to get a better sense of humor."

Hudson is still in the kitchen when we make it downstairs. He's dressed this time, which makes me frown that I won't be getting another view of his finely sculpted chest that runs down to washboard abs.

Even with my tea, I didn't sleep well last night. I couldn't stop thinking about him being downstairs. I mentally made a list of questions to ask him and thought of different ways to show him I'm not who he thinks I am.

"Good morning, ladies," he says when he notices us and holds up a cup. "Coffee?"

"Dear God, yes," I say around a yawn. "Coffee before talkie." Coffee is my liquid heroin. I'm a caffeine aficionado.

Hudson chuckles. His laughter is what I expected it to be—deep, like it's coming from the pit of his stomach and forcing its way up his throat.

He pours me a cup and slides it across the island to me. "Coffee … because crack is bad for you."

"I took the road less traveled … that led to Starbucks, and that's made all the difference," I reply with a smile.

He looks impressed at my comeback. "Want to hear a joke? Decaf."

"Coffee, a liquid hug for your brain."

Oh my god.

Are we flirting?

Are we having a moment?

Over coffee puns?

Are we really flirting in this ridiculously lame way?

Our eyes are locked, his dark gaze impaling mine, and his mouth curves into a bigger grin. If it takes coffee and a lame joke to get him to crack a smile, I'll take it.

"I feel like I'm interrupting a moment," Willow says. "A coffee flirting I don't know what the hell is going on moment." She gestures back and forth between Hudson and me. "That's why I don't drink that shit. It makes people all weird and fidgety."

Hudson laughs while breaking eye contact with me. "It's a non-coffee drinker thing, Willow. You think we're crazy when it's really you."

And our moment has been shot down.

Thanks, best friend.

"Whatever," Willow mutters. "We have a plane to catch. Ready to go?"

Hudson finishes his coffee, rinses out his cup, and places it in the dishwasher. "I'm ready for whatever I'm getting myself into."

"I promise it's nothing as crazy as jumping out of planes and all of that other dangerous shit you did with your last job," Willow comments.

"I enjoy jumping out of planes. There's nothing that compares to that rush," Hudson fires back.

"No thank you on that," I cut in. "If God wanted me to fly, he would've given me wings."

"Correct me if I'm wrong, but we're about to board a plane that *flies*," he counters.

"Big difference."

"Yeah, your choice isn't nearly as fun."

"Maybe I'll have to try it sometime then."

I'm totally lying. This girl is not going to be hanging out in the air solo anytime soon, but I do want him to change his mind about me, to see that I'm not some spoiled diva who only eats pink Starbursts and makes my assistant go through bags of them to pick out all the other colors. Although, I do wish that rumor was true. Pink is the best flavor. Unfortunately, Willow would quit in a second if I told her to do something like that.

That's why my ex, Knox, and I connected so well. He knew this life and understood not to believe everything written in the headlines.

Real stories don't sell. Scandals do. Relationship rumors do.

Willow shoves my side in excitement and is practically jumping up and down when Hudson leaves the kitchen to grab his bag.

"I love being right," she squeals. "He totally has a thing for you. Fingers crossed he's single."

I give her a dirty look when she points at my vagina.

"I hope you waxed that kitty of yours."

SIX

Hudson

A GUY FALLS down in the seat across from me and stretches out his hand. "What's up, man? I'm Josh."

He's a built dude, a few inches shorter than me, and looks like he spends ample time at the gym. My money is on him being a boxer or a guy into MMA. His blond hair is tightly combed back into a man-bun.

I lean forward to shake it. "Hudson."

"You Stella's new bodyguard?"

I nod.

"I'm Eli's."

Eli is Stella's co-star and love interest in her new movie. During our drive to the airport, Willow filled me in on the cast, the movie title, and what we'll be doing.

"You have any tips for me?" I ask.

My brother's advice was to watch out for assholes and to always have Stella's back. She's had a few scary run-ins where Dallas had to tackle people to the ground. One guy even tried sticking a camera up her skirt. *Fucking creeps.*

"It's a decent gig if you don't work for an asshole," Josh says. "Eli isn't bad, and from what I've seen so far, Stella seems to be cool." He throws his arm out to gesture to the private plane we're on. "Another perk is the travel. There's no way I'd be living life like this if it weren't for my job." He pauses as a smile passes over his face. "And let's not forget about the ladies. It's a pussy magnet. Women sleep with me, hoping it'll bring them closer to whatever dude I'm working for. Although it might not be as easy for you since you're working for a chick."

"Yeah, I don't think women will be busting down doors to sleep with me thinking it might lead them into Stella's panties, and I'm not one to judge, but I don't bat for the other team."

"We'll be spending some time together, so if I have any extras, I'll send them your way."

Josh winks like his *favor* is equivalent to giving me a kidney or some shit.

My attention moves away from him when Willow moves past us in the aisle. She stops and turns around to look at us.

"Extras?" she repeats while giving Josh a cold glare. Her attention then moves to me. "Don't let this idiot corrupt you, Hudson. He's a bad influence."

"Ignore her," Josh argues. "Willow thinks I have cooties."

Willow stares at him in a look that resembles disgust. "Correction, I believe you have the adult version of cooties: STDs." She gives him a final snarl before leaving us and sitting by Stella in the row behind Josh.

Josh laughs, not realizing she's making fun of him and not flirting. "I've been trying to hit that for a while now."

"I take it you're failing?" I ask. *Of course, he is.*

"She's not giving it up, but I'll break her down soon. I'm sure of it."

"Good luck."

Willow seems cool so far. Josh ... not so much. I hope she doesn't fall for his cheesy shit. I'd hate to have to hear him brag about it.

I pull out my phone and open my Solitaire app. Sure, it feels good to have someone around that I can relate to, but there's no way in hell Josh and I will be friends. My douchebag radar is firing off at full speed. Hanging out with this guy would be like a giant contraceptive to any decent female.

———

I'M STANDING on the sidelines of a red carpet watching Willow situate Stella's dress until it's perfect. The black gown shows enough cleavage to make my dick stir but not so much that she might have a nip-slip if she makes the wrong move.

Willow explained my duties to me while Stella got ready for the show. My job is to stay by Stella's side yet remain unseen.

Stella runs her hand down her glossy jet-black hair, and the diamond bracelet around her wrist glistens. She struts the red carpet in her high heels like a pro, and it takes only a second for her to get into her perfect pose. The flash of cameras all going off at once hurts my eyes. They're afraid to miss a shot of her.

Paparazzi are squashed up like sardines behind a red rope that blocks them from her, and there are other security guards placed in every direction. Josh stops at my side at the same time I get a view of Eli.

Eli reminds me of a frat boy even though he's in his late twenties. Right now, he's sporting a cocky smile, his blond hair is gelled and combed to the side like a kid who stole his mom's beauty products, and he's wearing a black pinstriped suit that fits his skinny stature.

Josh slaps my back. "Let the madness begin, my friend."

I only nod in response.

I watch Eli pose for a few pictures and hold my breath when he moves into Stella's space. Stella's lips curve into a smile when he wraps his arm around her waist and drags her to his side. She tilts her hips toward him and rests her hand on his chest like a prom picture. The cameras go off like wildfire.

I cock my head to the side in confusion and scratch my cheek when Eli dips down and kisses her on the lips.

What am I missing here?

Stella and Eli barely exchanged three words on the flight. Eli sat next to Josh, and I tuned them out after they started arguing about what model was the most bangable on Instagram. Eli wasn't in her hotel suite when she got ready, and nobody mentioned him staying there tonight. Maybe they're in an open relationship type shit.

"Stella!" a woman screams when Eli grabs Stella's hand and walks her down the carpet. "How long have you two been dating?"

Neither of them answers her question.

"Eli!" another person blurts out. "Do you think your romance will continue when you finish promoting the movie?"

Stella and Eli make puppy eyes at each other before Eli leads her to the crowd of people waiting. "Our relationship will stay strong long after it ends," he responds before kissing Stella on the cheek. "I love her. She loves me, and that's all you need to know. Now, if you'll excuse us, we have a good ass movie to watch."

I force a smile when Stella and Eli reach me, and Willow rushes over to us with an annoyed look on her face.

"I hope it was worth it," she says to Stella, louder than I think she intended to.

"Don't start with me right now," Stella snaps.

"Whatever," Willow says, rolling her eyes. She looks at me while we file into the theater. "We're in the row behind the two lovebirds. I hope you have a thing for romance films."

I chuckle. "They're my favorite. Can't live without them."

"How'd I know you are a romantic at heart?"

"Definitely strikes me as the type," Stella comments, looking back at us and winking.

Stella sits next to Eli, and I take the seat behind her.

———

I'M NOT a romance film dude.

I fucking swear it.

The movie has my attention, and it's not because the storyline is kick-ass.

It's because of Stella.

I'm watching her every second, my gaze bouncing from the unreality of her on the movie screen to the reality of her in front of me. Eli's arm is settled on her shoulders, and I can't figure out why seeing him touch her *on- and off-*screen makes my blood boil.

I shake my head in an attempt to reason with myself.

There's no way I can be into this chick.

I'm only agitated because nothing is adding up.

I glance over at Willow next to me when her phone goes off again. It's been nonstop for the past ten minutes.

"You better answer that," I whisper. "It sounds important."

"Shit," she groans and roughly drags her phone from her pocket. "Everyone knows I'm here." She encloses her hand around the phone screen to block out the light and lets out a whimper. Her hand shakes as she types out a reply.

"Is everything okay?"

She keeps the screen covered but lowers her hand enough for me to read the text.

Mom: Brett got into a car accident. It's bad. You need to come home ASAP.

"Brett is my boyfriend," she says, close to tears. "This isn't good. I don't know what to do."

I give her a comforting look. "You go be with him."

"What about Stella?"

"I'll explain to her what happened and help out in any way I can in your place." I signal to the exit I scoped out when we walked in.

Willow squeezes my arm. "Thank you, Hudson. I'll do everything I can via phone and email until I figure out what's going on. Don't tell her why I left until the movie is over, okay? She'll freak out and try to come with me. That can't happen."

SEVEN

Stella

MY CHEST IS TIGHT. My jaw is tight. My muscles are tight.

"I can't believe you sat through the movie and didn't tell me," I yell at Hudson in the back hallway of the theater. He pulled me to the side minutes ago to tell me about Brett.

"I would've gone with her," I continue. "Call me a car. Hopefully, I can make it to the airport before her departure."

Willow has always been my rock. She was there for me during my breakup with Knox and when my so-called friends chose him over me. I wasn't good enough for them any longer. I hate that I can't be there with her now.

"Your reaction is why we didn't tell you," Hudson answers. "She didn't want you to get worked up like you are right now."

That's Willow—always putting my career before everything else.

"Of course, I'd get worked up! Something terrible happened to my best friend!"

His face softens.

"We need to figure this out."

"You make the call. If you want to fly to her, I'm game."

I stiffen when arms wrap around my waist from behind.

"You ready to head to the after-party?" Eli asks. "It's at this kick-ass exclusive club."

I peek back at Eli to see his face lit up in excitement.

Eli is a partier who goes through money and women like they're nothing. That's why they pressured me into playing his girlfriend. I'm looked at as the perfect role model. I'm the childhood star who didn't go wild and the perfect solution to the up-and-coming actor's bad-boy image.

I pull away from him and try to look disappointed. "Unfortunately, I have to bail. Willow's boyfriend got in a serious car accident, and I need to be with her."

"That won't be happening, Stella."

My heart races, and I groan at the sound of the high-strung voice that belongs to Tillie Armstrong, the pain in my ass with a stick up her ass who always seems to hit a nerve. She stops in front of me clad in a purple dress with her honey blond hair straightened to her shoulders.

"There was an agreement when you were given the movie part," Tillie reminds me. "Per your contract, you are required to attend all movie premieres with Eli *and* after-parties. In case you forgot, you signed the dotted line and must adhere to those obligations."

Tillie is the bitch … I mean *publicist* of the production company that funded our movie. Her favorite hobby is reminding me I'm contractually obligated to be their bitch. *Contractually obligated* makes up ninety percent of her vocabulary. I'm sure she says it in her sleep. She lurks, waiting to dispute my every move.

I'm contractually obligated to kiss Eli, to act like we're screwing, and declare my love for him. I wish I were contractually obligated to stick my stiletto up her ass.

"It's a family emergency," Hudson cuts in.

Tillie gives him an annoyed look. "I don't know who you are, nor do I care, but you're wrong. It's not a family emergency. It's someone else's family emergency. No relation. No excuses."

Hudson holds out his hand, his jaw clenching. "Then allow me to introduce myself. I'm Hudson, Stella's bodyguard. Now, you know who I am."

I bite into my lip and stare at him, loving how he's standing up to her.

"Pleasure," Tillie says, not bothering to shake his hand or introduce herself.

Hudson doesn't let her attitude stop him. He jerks his hand over to gesture to me. "You're going to make her stay here and do this shit when you can clearly see she's upset and wants to be there for her friend?"

"You must not understand contracts, Henry." Tillie looks over at me. "Show up to the party, or you'll be reaping the consequences."

"You must not have heard me. It's Hudson," he corrects.

Tillie snarls her lip. She's not used to people going to battle against her.

"Can't she miss one party?" Eli asks before Tillie decides to claw Hudson's eyes out. "I'll go with her to see Willow. It'll make me look like a supportive boyfriend."

Tillie shakes her head. "Neither one of you is going anywhere but that club. Period. This conversation is over." She gives us one last sharp look and leaves.

I fiddle with my bracelet. "Thanks for having my back and trying," I say to the guys, giving them a forced smile. I'm filled with devastation but trying to keep my cool. I'm an actress. I can do this.

Eli squeezes my shoulders in apology. "Sorry, babe. I'll do my best to get us out of the party as early as I can, if that helps?"

I nod. "Thank you."

"I need to find my manager and let him know what's going on," Eli says before disappearing down the hall.

"Who the fuck was that hag?" Hudson asks.

"That's the woman who holds my future in her hands and uses it as leverage anytime I don't fall in her line." I drop my arms at my sides. "She's the reason they gave me this role."

"Fuck her. That's bullshit." He stops to pull his phone from his pocket when it chimes. "It's Willow. She has fifteen minutes before her flight takes off. You want to give her a call?"

Tears fill my eyes, and I nod.

He hands me his phone, and I immediately hit Willow's name. She's sobbing when she answers. It hurts. I ask her over and over again if she wants me to come with her, but she refuses. She knows the hell Tillie will put me through if I bail. I make her promise to call or text when she lands and to keep me updated before hanging up.

"She good?" Hudson asks.

"As good as she can be," I answer. "Brett is in ICU, and her mom said it isn't looking good. She also said there are stories already floating around that he was drinking and driving and ran a stop sign."

"Fucking dumbass. How do they know that already?"

"A half-empty bottle of vodka was in the passenger seat. The hospital took a blood tox, but the results haven't come back yet."

"Shit. Poor Willow."

"That's not even the worst part."

His brows snap together.

"The car he hit was a mini-van with a family of four inside. They're not sure if one of the children will survive."

"Fuck. That has to be a lot for her to take in."

Brett drinking and driving doesn't surprise me. He's not a good guy, but Willow refuses to leave him. They've been on and off since high school, and she can't walk away because of their history, even though it's not a healthy relationship.

Something hits me when I look back at Hudson.

We're going to be alone in the hotel tonight.

Uh-oh.

Being in a hotel is different than my home, where thousands of square feet separate us. I didn't plan on drinking at tonight's after-party, but a stiff drink is sounding pretty damn good right now.

EIGHT

Hudson

"I'LL SUCK your cock if you let me through."

I stare at the half-naked girl who can't be any older than eighteen standing in front of me. "What did you just say?"

Another woman, a twin I'm assuming, comes to her side, and they both look up at me with innocent brown eyes.

Fuck.

I want to take them home to their parents.

How did they even get in here?

It's been one long ass day, and it keeps getting stranger by the second.

The after-party is in a club filled with dancers and women serving overpriced drinks. To be honest, it's giving me a damn headache.

When did I turn into an old man?

I enjoy having a good time, watching live bands, and drinking beers with my friends, but this shit is a madhouse. People are bumping into each other, screaming in faces, and girls are fighting their way into the VIP section like Stella and Eli are a fucking king and queen.

They remind me of roaches. I block one chick from sneaking in, and there's another one sliding into my left. No way are any of these groupie vultures going near my cock.

STD-free is the way I want to be.

Josh steps to my side with a disturbing smile on his face. "If he's not game, I am."

Of course, he is.

Dude will fuck anything if it means he doesn't go to bed alone with his sausage link in his hand. He's dumb to think these women actually want him. They look at him as a stepping stool to a better opportunity … Eli.

"How about you two make out and we'll consider if you're worthy of our time," he tells them.

My skin crawls at his creepiness.

I gesture to them. "Dude, they're fucking twins who look sixteen. Incest and pedophilia your thing?" *Sick fuck.*

He chuckles. "They're not *my* sisters, and obviously if they're here, they're old enough." He leans back on his heels, crosses his arms, and licks his lips. "I've always wanted to fuck twins. There's something so hot about it."

"Hot?" I repeat. "I think you meant to say fucking gross."

"Lighten up. We're all here to have a little fun."

The girls are staring at us with expectation and waiting for their golden ticket.

"We're eighteen," one says, grinning wildly. "Legal as can be."

I scowl at how pathetic they sound and look over at Josh. "Have fun with your cock-sucking sisters. I'll be over here doing my job and relishing in the fact I won't have to visit the clinic tomorrow."

He shrugs. "More pussy for me then."

I shudder. "Enjoy it while it lasts because I have a feeling your dick will be fall off in the next few years."

I walk away and lean back against a wall. I'm ready to blow this joint and hit the sheets. I glance over at Stella and Eli to find them whispering sweet nothings into each other's ears.

Why are these other women trying to get to Eli?

Stella has his full attention. It's obvious they'll be leaving together. Hopefully, they'll have their fun in his suite.

Their relationship confuses me. Stella didn't seem interested in him all day. She doesn't even look happy now as she chugs down drinks and stares into space. She rolls her eyes when Eli starts raining kisses down her neck but still tilts her head to the side to give him better access.

There's no enjoyment on her face.

He's not getting her all hot and bothered.

It can't be what it seems.

———

I LET OUT a breath of relief when Stella informs me that she's ready to leave.

My head is dying for some silence, and I swear if another chick offers me sex, I'm going to throw her out of the club.

I never thought I'd be bitching about being offered pussy. Yet, here I am. The worst part is that I have to wake up and do it all over again tomorrow.

Thankfully, the suite we're staying in is in the same building as the club. I have to help Stella walk back, and she wobbles in my hold. The alcohol hitting her doesn't surprise me. She spent her night competing against herself over how many drinks she could suck down.

I shut the door behind us and walk through the foyer of the decked-out suite. Stella lives a life of luxury. The suite is spacious and the décor expensive. I have my own bedroom and private bathroom, even though I'd prefer more privacy. I shared a bedroom and bathroom with dozens of other men for months. Some space would be nice.

I asked Stella several times if she wanted me to take her to Eli's room, but she only shook her head and muttered something along the lines of, "Over my dead body."

"Are you sure you don't want to stay with your boyfriend?" I ask again.

She collapses on the couch and starts fumbling with the strap of her sparkly heel, stumbling in the process. I should help her, but that's not my job. I'm here to make sure she's not kidnapped or murdered, not to help her do shit like that. She throws the heel down when she's successful, and it takes her a few seconds to gain control of herself to start working on the other.

"My boyfriend?" she says when she manages to get it off.

I recline against the wall and watch her. "The dude you were all over at the theater? The one you were tonsil scrubbing with at the club?"

How drunk is this broad?

"Eli?" Her face turns horrified when I nod. "Gross. He isn't my boyfriend."

"Fine, your fuck buddy."

"We sure as hell aren't *fucking*. We're fake dating."

The fuck? Who does that?

I rub the back of my neck, replaying her response like I misheard it. "Why would you fake date someone?"

It's the most absurd shit I've heard all day. Hell, maybe all year. And I've had one eventful year.

She leans back and waves her hand through the air. "It's complicated."

Complicated yet captivating.

I shove my hands into the pockets of my jeans and prepare myself for story time. This is something I can't wait to hear. "Sounds like it. I can listen to complicated."

"You're going to find out eventually," she mutters, looking anxious. "We're pretending to date to promote our movie. You know, drive up publicity and hype. His camp wants his reputation cleaned up because he's been somewhat of a loose cannon and man slut. They look at me as the perfect child star all grown up, so it was either I agree and get the role, or they find someone else to go along with it. I decided to advance my career."

I can't hold in my laugh, and her brows furrow at me.

"You're a rent-a-girlfriend?"

People actually do that shit?

It dawns on me now that was what that Tillie chick was referring to. She's in a contract to date Eli.

She grimaces at my comparison. "Don't say it like that."

"Why? It sounds better than me saying you're pimping yourself out for the success of your movie."

"Thanks, I appreciate you calling me a hooker."

"I didn't call you anything, Hollywood."

"You insinuated it."

"I guess so, but it's not exactly my business." I point at the door. "You sure you don't want me to leave? You can call Eli over, tip off paparazzi, and it'll look like you two are in here making sweet love when in actuality you'll be sexting other people from opposite ends of the couch." I grin. "Perfect relationship, if you ask me. Very romantic."

My crudeness surprises her. It surprises me, too.

She frowns. "Has anyone ever told you you're an asshole?"

I place my hand over my heart and lower my voice. "My feelings … stop."

I *am* acting like an asshole, but I'm mad at myself. I was changing my mind about Stella being a selfish brat after our talk in the kitchen and seeing her reaction to Willow's situation, but I was wrong.

She snatches her clutch and starts rummaging through it like a madwoman until she finds her phone. "I'm texting Willow and telling her to find a replacement for you immediately."

"Good riddance. My prayers have been answered. The sooner, the better."

"Why don't you quit then? Why even take the job if I repulse you so much?"

"My brother begged me to, and the last thing he needs at the moment is to be stressed about you being unprotected," I pause and tilt my head toward the phone in her hand. "And it's probably a bad idea to text Willow right now."

Some of her anger dissipates as her shoulders slump. "Good point. I'd be freaking out if something like that happened to my boyfriend."

"Your real boyfriend or a fake one? Can you be more specific so I can keep up?"

She flips me off. "You're an ass, and I'm speaking in generality. No boyfriend here. I'm officially on a break from dating."

"Unless you're getting a paycheck for it?"

"Go screw yourself. I'm fake dating for the sake of my career, and it's not the first time it's been done. I'm sure it won't be the last either."

"You might be right, but it's the first time I've known someone to. Where I come from, we don't date for paychecks. We tend to call those people hookers ... street walkers ..."

"I don't live *where you come from,* so how about that? *Where I come from,* we focus on our careers and people don't insult their bosses." She gets up from the couch to stomp to her bedroom and turns around to give me one last scowl before going in. "Keep your mouth shut about Eli. You can't tell your friends, girlfriend, anyone."

"You don't have to worry about that." I use my hand to form a zipping gesture across my mouth. "These lips are sealed."

NINE

Stella

I SLAM the door and dramatically collapse on my bed, pouting like a three-year-old whose blankie is in the dryer.

I'm drunk and overreacting but hearing the truth from Hudson hurt. He only confirmed what I've been afraid of from the start of signing off on this deal. I'm pimping myself out for the sake of my career and money.

I've tried telling myself it's not bad because I'm not screwing Eli.

Isn't it only hooking if you're fucking and sucking someone?

So, I'm in the clear, right?

Now, I need to convince my Hudson-altered conscience that.

Men are a pain in the ass.

Which is exactly why I've sworn them off.

They might come with a good penis, but there's always a side dish of problems.

A situation like this would usually warrant a call to Willow where I'd rant about how big of an asshole Hudson is. She'd tell me to kick him in the nuts or let it go depending on her mood.

I can't do that tonight. She's going through too much, and it would be selfish of me to bother her with something this petty. Unlocking my phone, I scroll down to Dallas's name. Maybe he can talk some manners into his jerk of a brother.

For a moment, I thought Hudson and I were moving in the right direction, maybe even starting to like each other. We had the whole late-night kitchen conversation, we flirted, and he stuck up for me with Tillie.

Apparently, I was wrong.

My finger hovers over Dallas's name, but I stop myself.

It'd be selfish calling him.

Well, damn.

Who can I call and complain to?

Who can I ask for advice?

I hit my sister, Antonia's, name. It rings several times before going to voicemail. She's probably busy. She signed a modeling contract six months ago and has been touring the globe for fashion shows.

I slap my forehead and know I've hit rock bottom when I call my mother.

Don't get me wrong. I love her.

The problem is I'm not sure if she loves me or only sees me as her meal ticket. We talked regularly, and she was my biggest fan until Knox and I broke up. She begged me to get back with him for the sake of my career and was furious when I refused.

My call goes straight to voicemail.

No *shocker.*

I contemplate calling an old friend but decide against it. I'm so out of touch with that circle. Most of them took Knox's side in the breakup. He's richer and has more connections than I do.

All invites and calls stopped coming my way after he told our friends he didn't want me around because he had a new girlfriend. Hollywood friends see you as disposable.

I toss my phone down and sigh. This should to be the peak of my career, but I feel so alone.

Tears fall down my cheek, and desperation leads me to grab my phone and hit the last name I should.

Me: YOU ARE AN ASSHOLE AND NEED TO WORK ON YOUR PEOPLE SKILLS AND MANNERS!

There.

I said what I needed to.

I put my phone down and pick up a magazine sitting on the nightstand. My phone beeps before I make it past the first article. I drop the magazine and take a deep breath before looking at the screen.

Hudson: Are you text-sulting me from the next room? Put on your big girl panties and stomp your spoiled ass out here if you want to scream at me. All caps aren't necessary. They don't do your entitled temper justice.

Ugh, the nerve of this jackass.

Text-sulting? Who even says that?

I swing my legs over the edge of the bed, jump off, and stomp my unspoiled ass back into the living room. Hudson is situated comfortably on the couch with not a care in the world.

Did our argument not even faze him?

"Temper?" I scream. "You want to see a temper?"

His arms are crossed, and a smile dances over his lips. "Go ahead, Hollywood. Temper away. Stomp your feet. Do whatever you feel is necessary to prove you're different than what the headlines say."

Why does he have a good comeback for everything?

I want to shock him, make him at a loss for words, and show him I'm a force to be reckoned with.

I point at him. "You need to start being nice, or I'll tell Dallas to inform your girlfriend how big of a dick you're being."

Yes, I suck at comebacks. I sound like a tattletale on the playground.

Hudson laughs while looking more entertained. "Let me know how that goes, will you? I have a feeling she'll be too busy fucking my best friend than worry about who I'm supposedly insulting."

My mouth slams shut.

His grin grows. "Not the response you were expecting?"

I was right about him no longer being in a relationship.

Embarrassment sweeps up my cheeks. "I thought you were engaged?"

Should this new information excite me?

It does.

"I was. Not anymore. Cameron decided she liked to screw my best friend, and I'm not one to share pussy. When I make someone mine, they're mine. Sharing is not always caring."

His answer sends shivers down my spine. My heart races over the way he talks about ownership.

"That sucks. I'm sorry," is the only response I can muster out after throwing a failed relationship in his face.

He shrugs. "Shit happens and you move on."

I walk farther into the room and sit down in a chair, wanting him to continue. *Give me more! Unleash your secrets!*

"How long were you two engaged?"

"We dated twelve years. Engaged three."

"Wow. That's a long time."

My final breakup with Knox crushed me. We dated on and off for almost a decade. I can't imagine how I'd feel if I found out he was sleeping with my best friend.

Friendship code 101: Don't fuck each other's exes.

Male or female.

Not even if the dude is young *Fight Club* era Brad Pitt.

They're off-limits.

If you do, you were never a true friend to begin with.

There are millions of cocks and vaginas in the world. It's not hard to find one that hasn't been with your best friend.

I take a deep breath and shove my hand out his way. "Can we call a truce?"

He looks at me skeptically. "You mean you're done calling me an asshole?"

"As long as you quit referring to me as a hooker."

"Fine, truce." He shakes my hand, and I'm disappointed at the loss of his touch when he releases me. "All hooker comments will be kept to myself."

"And stop *thinking* of me as a hooker, too. I'm not sleeping with Eli."

He taps his chin. "Do you know the definition of hooker?"

"Can't say it's something I've looked up before." I raise a brow. "Do you?"

I wait for him to spit out some Webster's Dictionary definition that confirms you don't have to sleep with someone to be defined as a hooker.

He laughs. It's deep and manly. "I'm only fucking with you, Hollywood. Consider all hooker-talk done. I promise."

I tip my head down. "Thank you."

"My hooker-ending talking pleasure."

I give him a hard look.

He laughs again while holding up his hands. "Last one, I swear."

I stand but stagger for a moment to gain my balance. "I need another drink."

The slight-buzz I have from the after-party is still drumming through me. That must be why I'm so emotional. Alcohol is like a therapist. It puts you in your feelings until eventually, you blurt out everything that's bothering you.

"You sure that's a good idea?" He sits up and scoots to the end of the couch like he knows he'll have to save me from busting my ass.

"Positive." I snag a pint of vodka when I make it to the minibar and mix it with a Coke before turning around and looking at him. I hold out my tongue and cough after swallowing down the first drink. *This stuff is not for the weak.* I hold up my drink. "What's your cocktail of choice?"

Alcohol drops my inhibitions. Maybe it will do the same for him.

He shakes his head. "I don't drink on the job."

"Then prepare to never drink while working for me since you'll pretty much always be on the job." I hold the bottle in front of me. "What if I said you're off the clock?"

His brows squeeze together. "I'm still good. It's three in the morning, and I'm exhausted."

"You're going to make me drink alone?"

My heart races when he stands up and advances my way. "Tell you what, Princess Peer Pressure, I'll have one beer if that makes you feel better. That's it."

It's no surprise he's a beer drinker.

I catch my breath when he walks around me to open the fridge and take him in while he's not looking at me. His hair smells like fake ocean breeze shampoo, and oddly, I find that attractive. I've been around so many men who pour on expensive cologne and use shampoo products so strong they give you a headache. It's nice for a man to smell like a man.

I jump and look at him in embarrassment when he pops off the cap of the bottle. He smirks, fully aware I'd been checking him out, and takes long strides to the couch like he's trying to get as far away from me as possible.

"What do we do now?" he asks, sitting down. "Drink and stare at each other?"

I collapse into the chair again. "I didn't think that far ahead. I can't sleep and need something to take my mind off my life."

"Your life that bad, huh?" His hand wraps around the neck of the bottle while gently tipping it against his lips.

"Don't patronize me. I'm not saying I'm impoverished."

"What will help take your mind off your *very* serious problems?"

I hold up my drink. "More alcohol. Mindless chatter." I angle my body toward him. "An *orgasm*." I shrug. "Maybe two."

I don't know who's more shocked at my response—him or me. I try to appear calm, but my heart is beating like crazy.

He points at me with his beer. "I'll take mindless chatter for four hundred."

That sucks. I was hoping for option three.

I throw my arms out. "Then let's chat away."

"Why don't we get to know each other since we'll be spending a lot of time together? It'd be nice to know I'm not hanging out with a serial killer."

I perk up in my seat and keep sipping on my drink. "How exactly do you suggest we get to know each other?"

He smirks. "Not like that, you little perv."

I put my hand over my heart, feigning offense. "Me? A perv?"

He chuckles. "Alcohol makes you more open. I like it."

"Hopefully, it's the same with you. You're like a sealed up, boring box."

"I'm not an emotional guy who expresses his feelings. Maybe that's why Cameron decided to cheat on me. She wanted some sappy dude who sang love ballads and shit. I'm not that guy."

I snort. "A man who sings love ballads doesn't mean they're sappy or even a good boyfriend. My ex is a master in songwriting and belting out love songs, and it didn't make our relationship stronger. It only made the fan girls want to suck his cock more and gave me insecurities. They don't tell you that love songs aren't made for love. They're made for money."

"The child star has quite the potty mouth."

"Profanity is my dominant language when I'm drunk. Don't judge me."

"No judging here. I like a girl who talks dirty."

My eyes widen, and he shakes his head when he realizes what he said.

Looks like we're both saying the wrong things to each other.

"Shit, I didn't mean it like that. I've never had a job like this, but I'm working on keeping it as professional as I can."

"Professionalism is dull." Yep, I'm officially getting drunker and braver with every sip.

"Consider our relationship dull then."

"You suck," I slur. The alcohol is making me dizzy, and I move back and forth in my chair.

He stands. "I think it's time for you to go to bed, drunkie."

"Oh come, on," I whine. "Your job is not to be a party pooper."

"My job is to take care of you."

"Oh, I know *plenty* of ways you can take care of me." I can't help but stare at his crotch when he stops in front of me. I lick my lips. "Plenty of fun ways."

I'm single. He's single.

The perfect situation for my abandoned vagina.

Maybe Willow was right.

I know I said all men are off-limits, but the appeal of Hudson getting me off tonight is changing my mind. My heart goes crazy when he helps me to my feet to stand on my own.

Okay, stumble on my own.

He grunts when I fall against his hard chest and circles his arm around my waist to stop me from busting my ass. For some idiotic reason, I take it as an invite to kiss him. I stand on my tiptoes and smack my lips into his briefly before he snags my wrists and nudges me away.

Big mistake.

Big freaking mistake.

He rests his hands on my shoulders, making sure I'm balanced but keeping distance between us, and stares at me with what looks like pity. I curl my arms around my stomach and dip my chin down to the floor.

He clears his throat before speaking. "It's time to call it a night." He forces a laugh in an attempt to make me feel less humiliated, but it doesn't work.

I run my hands down my dress. My embarrassment is erasing my intoxication.

"Can we act like this never happened?" I whisper, my voice cracking. I'm ready to go to my room and suffocate myself out of shame.

"We can definitely do that." Just like the first time we met, he looks like he'd rather be anywhere but here.

I want to stop the next words from flying from my mouth, but I can't. "I know it'd be so embarrassing for you to hook up with someone like me."

His jaw ticks, and his face shifts from apologetic to agitation. "The fuck you mean someone like you?"

"Someone like me," I repeat. "Don't think I don't see the way you look at me. You don't see *me*." I tap my hand against my chest while fighting back fresh tears. "You only see the headlines, the stories, what you think you know and feel as if it's beneath you to be attracted to someone so shallow."

His voice drops. "There's no way you can think I feel like I'm too good for you. I didn't stop you because of that. We can't cross that line. You're drunk. I work for you. I'm sorry if I gave you the wrong idea."

"It's fine. I'm sorry, and you're right." I finally gain the courage to look at him. "Can I ask you a question?"

He shoots me a guarded smile. "Go for it."

"Do you think what I'm doing is wrong?"

I know what his response will be. He expressed his disgust for it earlier, but *maybe* I changed his mind … even if just a little.

"Please be honest with me."

"I think fake dating someone sounds absurd, but we live in two different worlds. I know nothing about the Hollywood life. If you feel like that's what you have to do for your career, that's all that matters. I won't lie and say it doesn't sound desperate, but again, it's your life. That's me being honest with you. Now come on, let's get you to bed."

I nod, and he takes my hand to lead me down the hallway. I stay quiet while he lifts back the blankets on my bed and waits for me to get in before turning off the light and leaving.

I don't know what storm is suddenly brewing inside me, but I have a feeling Hudson is the force behind it.

TEN

Hudson

LEANING BACK against the door to my bedroom, I go over what just happened with Stella.

I walk to the side of the bed and hold my hands out in front of me, studying them and remembering how soft her skin felt against my calloused palms. It almost feels wrong for something so rough to touch something so delicate.

I close my eyes and remember her reaction to me touching her. I haven't been laid in so long. *Two hundred and seventy days to be exact, but hey, who's counting?* It killed me to walk away from something so damn tempting.

Most guys would call me a fucking idiot.

Hell, I'm calling myself a fucking idiot.

I drag my shirt over my head, throw it across the room, and peek down at the tent in my pants. I wanted nothing more than to push her onto the couch and give us what we both ached for. The attraction is there—there's no denying that—but I can't cross that line. I have a job to do, and I won't be able to concentrate on protecting her if all I can think about is how sweet her pussy tastes.

No drinking with Stella.

No hanging out with a drunk Stella.

No personal stories and opening up to each other.

We want different things.

There's no way I can sleep with her and then watch Eli touch her after. I can't sit to the side while they act like they're screwing if I'm screwing her. What confuses me the most is why I'm crushing on a liar who's fake dating someone to further her career.

I fucking hate liars.

I grab my laptop and mute the sound. Even though I want to listen, she can't know what I'm doing. Wearing headphones isn't an option either. *What if someone breaks in?* If something happens to her, it wouldn't be cool for people to find out I was jerking my dick to porn instead of doing my job.

I pull my cock from my shorts and slowly stroke myself.

Fuck. This feels so good.

Thank God for Porn Hub.

ELEVEN

Stella

REGRET POUNDS through my skull when I wake up.

Humiliation is riding at its side, pointing and laughing at me.

I'm embarrassed I offered myself up to Hudson, and he rejected me.

Insanity convinced me that us sharing a drink meant he wanted to screw me.

It's been so long since I've put myself out there like that to someone. It'll never happen again after his rejection. Not only is it a smack to my ego but it's also a slap to my senses for thinking it's okay to get involved with my bodyguard.

I want to be angry with him but can't.

Hudson did the right thing.

At least one of our brains was working last night.

I notice mascara streaks on my pillow. I cried last night and forgot to take off my makeup. *Here come the wrinkles to go along with my mortification.*

I enter the bathroom, wipe the mascara from my face, and climb in the shower. The steam helps to cleanse my pores of the extra alcohol and minimize my hangover. I run my fingers through the thick strands of my wet hair when I get out, wrap them in a tight bun, and start my walk of shame into the kitchen. Hudson is sitting at the table drinking coffee with a laptop open in front of him.

I don't look in his direction while heading straight to the coffee maker and jump when he speaks.

"Morning. How are you feeling?"

"Like I was living it up riding roller coasters all night," I mutter.

Maybe I can act like I don't remember last night. I gear up for the perfect *I did what?* look.

I'm an actress. I got this.

I pull out a mug from the cabinet with the hotel's logo, and my hands are trembling when I pour coffee inside it. I look around the room while taking small sips, not sure what to do.

He gets straight to the point. "About last night."

"What about last night?" I ask.

"I can tell by your face that you know exactly what I'm talking about."

I frown. "God, even bringing it up makes my head hurt. Can we not do this right now ... or say, maybe never?"

"Not talking about it will only make it more awkward."

"Fine, but you're going first."

He tips his finger toward the seat across from him. "Sit down."

"Seriously? You're going to make this all weird and personal?"

"You standing there looking uncomfortable as fuck is making it weird."

"Who decided you were the boss man all of a sudden?" I complain but do as told.

He sits back in his chair and clears his throat. "First things first. I hope you don't feel like I rejected you last night."

I scoff. "Too late for that."

"You're beautiful, and you have to know I'm attracted to you."

I raise a brow. *News to me.*

If this is his attempt to keep our relationship professional, it's not working. His admission makes me only want him more.

"You were drunk, and we're both lonely. I should've never allowed it to go that far."

"Speak for yourself. I'm not lonely."

His look causes me to slam my mouth shut.

He can read me like a damn script.

I perk up in my chair and settle my hands on the table. "I don't like where this conversation is going. It was a drunken mishap. Let's forget about it and move on."

"Fine with me. I only wanted to clear the air."

I swipe my hands together. "Consider it cleared." I pick up my phone. "Do you want anything from room service?" I forgot to order my breakfast last night. Willow usually does that for me, but I sent her a text telling her I'd have everything taken care of.

"Whatever you order is fine with me."

I order our food and start to answer emails and texts while he stays occupied with his computer. I open a message from Willow giving me an update on Brett's condition. His recovery isn't promising, and she's not sure how long she'll be gone.

My stomach drops at the resignation letter attached to the email. I message her back, insisting she take as much time off as she needs and her job will be waiting for her when she's ready to come back. Hudson allows room service in, and the sweet aroma of pastries and pancakes fills the room and causes my stomach to growl.

Hudson takes a bite of pancakes and groans. "Damn, this shit is good. I've missed food like this."

I nod even though I haven't touched my food. A question is eating at me. A question that's none of my business.

"How long has it been since you've been with a woman?" I ask.

Hudson nearly chokes on his food but doesn't hesitate to answer. "A little over nine months."

"You didn't screw someone the second you got home?"

"I was more interested in seeing my family than getting my dick wet. Not to mention, had I screwed someone, that news would've been all over our small town, given my situation with Cameron."

"I thought my drought was sad."

"Not a drought, Hollywood. It's lack of opportunity."

Lack of opportunity? There was opportunity with me last night.

"What are you going on?"

"Two months," I admit.

He grins and shakes his head. "Amateur."

Lord, give me courage for what I'm about to say and help a girl out if you can.

"Can I ask you something, and you promise to take me seriously?"

He cocks his head to the side. "Sure."

"I know only thirty minutes ago, you said you want to keep our relationship professional ..."

"I did."

"But what will throwing a little sex hurt?" I sound like a horny teenage boy who's the only one in gym class who hasn't had his cock sucked.

His voice deepens. "Bad idea."

"Why not have some fun? Haven't you ever had a one-night stand?"

His gaze closes in on me. "I've only been with one woman."

I nearly drop my coffee. Hudson continues to shock me.

What do they feed these guys in Iowa?

"You're lying."

He shakes his head. "I started dating Cameron in middle school and never touched anyone but her. Your proposition sounds nice, but I'm a selfish guy. I've never had to separate commitment and sex, and I'm not sure if I'd be okay touching you one night and then watching you suck face with Eli the next day."

"What if you can separate it? Why not try?"

"Dump the phony boyfriend, and maybe I'll broaden my horizons."

With that, he stands up, grabs his mug, and leaves the room.

———

"THIS SHIT FUCKING BLOWS," Eli says, plopping down in the seat next to me after boarding the plane. We're headed to London for the next premiere.

"What blows?" I ask.

I don't know Eli that well, which is weird, considering I've made out with him on-screen, and there are rumors we're screwing off-screen. He reminds me of my ex—nice guy but also a playboy eager to cross every Victoria's Secret model off his screw list.

Since agreeing to be his fake girlfriend, my life has been nothing but chaos. We've received backlash from not only fans but also mutual friends. Knox and Eli had been friends, and they saw that as a broken vow of bros before hoes. It's ridiculous, considering Knox gives two shits about who I'm sleeping with.

"Fake dating," Eli answers. "It's putting a damper on my sex life."

I roll my eyes. "Gee, thanks. I'm having the time of my life."

He chuckles. "It's not you. It's me."

I place my hand over my heart. "Tragic. I'm so heartbroken. Now, go tell Tillie about our breakup. I'm as ready to end this deal as you."

He smirks. "Or we can try a different route?"

"We kill Tillie?"

"I'm too pretty for prison, sweetheart." He shoots me a confident grin. "I was thinking more along the lines of us *actually* dating."

I smack him upside the head. "Not happening. Everyone knows your dating record is worse than Charlie Sheen's."

"Whoa, a little overboard there. I don't mean us dating-dating."

"That's what it sounds like."

"Consider it more as colleagues with benefits."

I cringe. "You've lost your damn mind."

"Have I? Think about it. Neither of us is getting laid. Why not take advantage of the crappy situation we're in? I've had blue balls for months."

I don't believe he's been abstaining from sex. "Not happening." I've already had one Hollywood bad boy break my heart—putting myself at risk again would be stupid.

"Why not? Everyone already thinks we're screwing, so we might as well make the best of it."

"How about this. You are more than welcome to have fun with other people *behind closed doors.* Don't make me look like an idiot allowing her boyfriend to cheat. As long as it's on the down-low, I don't care what or who you do."

"Risk a picture or story being leaked? I won't ruin my career for a one-night fling."

I nod in agreement. "I won't tell if you don't."

He raises a brow. "Is that what you're doing? Sneaking around behind closed doors?"

"Uh, no."

He snorts. "Yeah, right."

"What are you trying to say?"

"I'm saying if I was your bodyguard, you'd be more than happy to accept my offer of sex."

Am I that obvious?

I put on my best innocent face. "What?"

He throws his head back and laughs. "Don't try to bullshit me. You've been giving him bedroom eyes all morning. Deny it all you want, but something's going on between you two."

"You're wrong."

"If you haven't fucked yet, it'll happen. All I'm asking is you make sure no cameras or witnesses are around. I won't be humiliated either." He scowls. "I've kept my dick in my pants and held up my end of the deal. Do the same."

He gets up to leave, but I stop him before he moves into the aisle.

"I can't," I say.

He looks down at me in confusion.

"I can't keep my dick in my pants, considering I don't have one."

"Fucking attitude," he grumbles. "I'll clarify, keep dicks out of you."

I squint my eyes. "Only dicks?"

"Jesus Christ, what else do you put inside yourself?"

I shrug.

Messing with him is fun.

"Maybe you're not the prude I thought you were."

"The hell?"

He hunches when I shove my elbow into his stomach.

"You think I'm a prude in the bedroom?"

"Obviously. You aren't interested in fucking me."

I grimace. "Check your ego, amigo. Me not wanting to screw you doesn't make me a prude."

"I'm beginning to see that, violent one." He pats my head. "My offer still stands. Let me know if you change your mind."

I let out a long sigh.

Hudson made it clear he'll only touch me if I ditch Eli.

Is a fling with him worth my career?

TWELVE

Hudson

"HEY! YOU! BODYGUARD GUY!"

I turn to find the hag who'd given Stella shit last night marching toward me. Stella and Eli boarded the jet a few minutes ago while I stayed in the car and took a call from Dallas.

I contemplate answering her but finally do. "Yeah?"

Her hands rest on her hips as she narrows her eyes at me, and she taps her heel against the ground. She appears as if she's readying to lecture a child.

That child being me.

Not fucking happening.

"Let me give you some words of advice," she snarls. "You seem to be confused about how this industry works and the respect you need to give to keep your job."

I could give two shits about keeping this job.

I flash her a cold smile. "I'm not trying to make a mark in this industry, and sure as fuck don't need any advice from you. Appreciate your concern, though."

"How about this. Let me give you some tips on how to stay on my good side."

I smirk. "I don't want to be on your good side. I quite enjoy being on the opposite."

Her face pinches. She's used to barking demands and having people bow down to her. No doubt she'll try to convince Stella to fire my ass. "You should be."

I move in, not close enough to be intimidating but enough to convince her I'm not one to fuck with. "Being on your good side is at the bottom of my give a shit list."

Her eyes widen.

"And while we're sharing wisdom, I have a tip for you."

She clears her throat. "What's that?"

"Get laid and stop making everyone's lives miserable." I gesture to the plane. "You denied Stella to visit her best friend whose boyfriend is on life support. Have some compassion, grow a heart, be a good fucking human being."

She looks me up and down with disgust clear on her face. "Sorry, but I don't take advice from nobodies."

"News flash, you're also a nobody. You bully people and make sure contracts are fulfilled, but you're not the star." I grin. "Welcome to the club. Now, I believe we have a flight to catch."

I leave without another word and board the plane. Josh and Eli are deep in conversation, and I take the seat next to Stella, which results in her peering at me in surprise.

I stretch my legs out in front of me. "How many of these things do we have to go to?"

There are only so many premieres you can have before the movie is old news, right?

"Only one more to go," she answers, moving her neck from side to side like it's sore. "It's a short promo tour. My guess is they weren't sure how long Eli and I could fake being a couple."

I lower my voice and tilt my head toward Eli. "What's the plan with lover boy? How long do you have to participate in this dating scheme?"

The conversation I had with her this morning haunts me. I hate feeling this pull toward her *and* can't stop thinking about her.

She rolls her eyes. "I thought we were done talking about it?"

I hold up my hands. "I'm not trying to be a dick, I swear."

"That's a first."

"It's a valid question for someone who's involved."

"We have to attend all interviews and award shows together. There's a set date in the contract. I think we have eight months left."

"What if you decide you want out?"

"It will be a breach of contract, and they can sue me for more money than I made off the movie. Tillie will do everything in her power to destroy my career and reputation."

"Sounds like you signed a deal with the devil."

She shrugs. "It won't be that bad when we get back in LA. Eli is working on a movie being shot in a different state, so we won't have to fake it as much. My show is over, so I'll be auditioning for new roles. My life will be boring."

I nudge my foot against hers. "Hey, I like to think I'm a good time."

"Wrong. I *tried* to get you to be a good time, but you declined."

I bump my knee against hers next. "Fucking isn't the only way to have fun."

"Prove it then," she mutters.

Her challenging me only heightens my attraction, and I'm never one to back down from a challenge.

THIRTEEN

Stella

I WAS NEVER one of those kids who sat in front of the TV and dreamed of being on it one day. When teachers asked me what I wanted to be when I got older, it was never famous. Show business was more of my mother's dream that she never achieved, so she decided to live vicariously through me.

I hated doing commercials for toys and fast food restaurants. She once forced me to be in an ad for toilet paper. Instead, I wanted to be on the playground or at a sleepover with my friends, not attend every casting call in LA looking for a girl my age. The small roles changed when I turned fifteen and landed my first major gig on the pilot of a new show.

I loved my character, my castmates, and the production crew on the show. My mom didn't have to drag me out of bed and force me to go to work every day. It became my passion and what made me realize that maybe it was what I wanted to do with my life.

Unfortunately, we wrapped up our last season of the show a few months ago. Only so much time can pass before the kids get too old to live with their parents and storylines run out. The series ended with me finding the man of my dreams who also happened to be the head of the witching department at a prestigious school.

Too bad my life is the complete opposite.

Maybe that's why I liked it so much.

The cancellation of the show has me looking for the next role to fall in love with. I thought Sadie, the role I played in the movie with Eli, was it when I read the script. I was wrong. I see that now as I watch the movie for the sixth time that my heart wasn't in it.

We're at another screening, and I'm sure a migraine will hit me from smelling Eli's expensive cologne all night. I subtly look back at Hudson in the row behind us and wish I could replace Eli with him. I also wish I didn't want that.

Under no circumstances can I fall for my bodyguard.

That's so cliché.

So Heidi Klum after she divorced Seal.

I don't know of one celebrity–bodyguard romance that's worked out.

Why did Hudson have to slide into that open position?

He's loyal. Up-front. Real. Rare qualities in men as attractive as he is. Or maybe that's only in Hollywood. I should broaden my horizons.

Tillie will kill me. Eli will kill me. Dallas will probably kill me when things don't work out between his brother and me. I also don't see Hudson taking this job long term or staying in California. I can't give up my career and move to Cornfield Timbuktu.

I pinch myself, hoping it'll make me think more clearly. I'm daydreaming about moving to Hudson's hometown even though he's made it clear he wants nothing to do with me.

Willow is right. Lack of dick can make you delusional. When I get home, I'm dragging out my vibrator.

That will compensate enough, right?

It won't be as fun as a real cock and a hard body above me, nor can it eat me out, but hey, a girl has to get off some way.

Unless.

I can be persuasive.

My mind is toggling back and forth like two open internet tabs.

I want Hudson.

That's for sure.

But I *shouldn't* want him.

I *can't* want him.

I look up at the sound of applause, realizing I've zoned out for the entire movie.

———

"ARE we flying back to LA in the morning?" Hudson asks when we make it back to the suite from the after-party.

It's late, and I can't wait to take off my makeup and throw my ass into bed. You'd think someone my age would be excited to party all night, but I'm over it, especially now that I have to act like I'm obsessed with Eli the entire time.

Talk about a total buzzkill.

The buzzkill could've also been Hudson giving us a death stare the entire time we were playing boyfriend and girlfriend.

"We are," I answer. "Then we're taking a connecting flight to see Willow." Willow lives a few hours from LA.

"Any updates on her situation?"

"Brett is still on the ventilator. Other than that, nothing."

He nods.

We're standing in the living room only a few feet away from each other and having an awkward stare off. I tense at the sound of his throat clearing.

"We need to get to bed. We have a long day ahead of us tomorrow," he states.

I fiddle with my hands in front of me, still staring. In hopes I wouldn't make a fool of myself again, I chose to stay sober and only drink water tonight. Hudson clears his throat again, breaking me out of the weird trance I'm in. There won't be any late-night drinking or chatting tonight. It's going to end with me in my bed and him in his.

"Right, yeah," I whisper. "Good night."

He watches me walk to my room and waits until I shut the door before turning the lights off. I feel beat down while looking at the door.

What are we doing?

Why am I trying to play this game when he's withdrawn?

I don't go to the bathroom to change until I hear his door shut. I put on my pajamas and climb into bed with my phone in my hand to text Willow.

Me: How's everything going?

I'm not surprised when my phone beeps a few seconds later.

Willow: No updates. Results still don't look promising.

Me: I'm coming there tomorrow.

Willow: You don't have to do that.

Me: Yes, I do. You're my best friend.

Willow: Thank you. I love you.

Me: Love you more. Get some rest, girl.

I turn the ringer on high, in case she tries to call, and quickly fall asleep from exhaustion.

———

THE TEXT COMES before we board the flight to go back to LA.

Willow: Please tell me you haven't left to come here yet?

Me: No, we're scheduled to fly out in 20 minutes. What's up?

Willow: Don't.

My pulse spikes as I clasp my hand tighter around my phone in fear.

Me: What? Why? Did something happen to Brett?

I exit out of our text and try to call her, but it goes to voicemail.

Willow: Can't talk right now. Brett woke up.

I grin, jumping up and down while ignoring people's stares.

Me: That's great news! I'm so happy for you!

Isn't it? Because she sure doesn't seem happy about it. I would've expected a phone call from her beaming with excitement. Dread sinks into my stomach. Maybe he woke up, but that doesn't mean he's going to survive or be able to go back to his normal life.

Willow: It's crazy right now. Go home. Relax. I'll call you later and tell you everything. Love you.

Me: Love you. XO

I look over at Hudson, who's been giving me strange looks since my outburst of excitement. "False alarm. We're not going to Willow's."

"Is that good news or bad news?"

"I'm not exactly sure. Willow said he woke up, but there was no excitement, which is weird. It's like there's a void inside her right now, and I don't know what to do."

"Be patient with her. She's processing everything. Her world just tilted on its axis, and she's figuring out how to fix it."

"I guess you're right." This is unusual for Willow, but I'm going to give her time.

"So back to LA?"

"Back to LA."

FOURTEEN

Hudson

"WE MEET AGAIN," I say when I spot Stella stepping into the kitchen from the dark hallway. She's wearing something similar to what she had on the last time we were in this situation—lacy shorts and a tank top, sans bra.

I gulp, taking in the outline of her perky nipples underneath the tank.

Does she wear this shit every night?

Or is she still trying to break me down and convince me to give this casual sex offer a go?

"You can't sleep either?" I ask.

She's been slammed since we landed in LA this afternoon. We met with a friend of Willow's who's going to work part-time for Stella until she returns. The next stop was yoga class, which I thought would be a boring occasion, but surprisingly, I found it exciting. Seeing Stella in the downward dog position made my dick hard and showed me another one of her incredible traits. She's flexible as fuck, which is a plus in so many ways in the bedroom. We met her agent for dinner, and I listened to them talk about new show prospects.

A long day for Stella.

A boring as fuck one for me.

How did Dallas manage to go through this every day and not lose his mind?

"Unfortunately," she answers. "The stupid after-parties have my sleep schedule all out of whack." Her thick hair is pulled into two tight French braids that start at her crown and show off her high cheekbones.

I pat the chair next to me. "Good. Join the club."

Her full lips pinch together. "Good?"

"Yes, good, because not only can you keep me company, you can also make that weird, voodoo, puts you to sleep tea you swear by." I'm more excited about the company than the tea.

She throws her hands up in fake excitement. "Yay for me."

My eyes are trained to her as she moves around the kitchen to grab the teapot. I should offer to help, but I'm having too much fun watching her. Her top rises, giving me a glimpse of the bottom curves of her breasts, and my dick swells when she lifts up to grab the mugs from the top shelf of the cabinet.

I shift around in my seat, trying to talk my arousal down. She's here to make tea, not give me a boner. I promised myself to keep this professional, but the way she's swaying her hips while filling the pot is making me question my decision again.

I close my eyes and try to think of something else, but that only lasts a few seconds before they're wide open again, staring at her. I need to stop. I can't make our situation complicated because I'm going back to my normal life soon while she stays here in hers.

Normal life.

I laugh to myself. My life will never go back to the normal one I had in Blue Beech. There will be adjustments to make when I get home. I'm hoping another scandal has broken out that'll make people forget about Cameron fucking around on me. I don't want the stares of pity. I'm also going to have to pull in some of my anger toward Grady, so I don't punch him whenever we run into each other.

The perks of living in a small town.

I still prefer it to this LA shit. The traffic sucks. It takes hours to get anywhere, and the sidewalks are packed with women who look like they spent hours getting ready to get a kale smoothie. They had full faces of makeup *at the gym.*

"This might be completely out of left field," Stella starts to say, breaking me away from my thoughts. "But don't you think everything going on with us is weird?"

I have no idea what she's talking about. "What's weird?"

"Willow doesn't know if Brett is ever going to be the same. Dallas isn't sure how long he has left with Lucy. I feel like we have this cloud of death lingering over us, and we're waiting to see what tragedy happens first."

Thinking about losing Lucy is a punch to the gut. It won't only kill Dallas and Maven. It'll obliterate our entire family. She's been a constant in our lives for years. It's become an unnamed tradition that us Barnes boys tend to stay with our high school sweethearts and make a family. My parents did it. My grandparents did it. Dallas did it. Most of the other families in town do it. Those who do seem to be the happiest couples I know.

"I try not to look at it as we're waiting for Lucy to die," I say. "We're staying positive. Being a pessimist doesn't help the situation."

"I don't think I'm pessimistic. I'm just thinking about real life. It's never easy. Bad shit always happens. You'll never get through life unscathed."

Her answer hits a sensitive spot.

"Don't ever give up hope," I say. "You never know, both of them might make it through this standing tall. If there's one thing I've learned in my line of work, it's to never count anyone out until they're in a casket and someone is giving their eulogy. I've witnessed people lose their limbs. I've seen injuries so severe I thought they'd never see their families again, but you know what? They did. They survived because they were strong and badass fighters who knew they had an entire life ahead of them. Sure, their lives may never be the same, but they're alive. They're waking up with their family. They're seeing the sunshine. Anything is possible. Without hope, you have nothing."

I close my eyes, recalling the memories and flashbacks of all the good and bad things I've seen throughout my career. Some of them I'll never get over. You don't forget seeing someone take their last breath.

My eyes open to find Stella at my side with a look on her face much different than when I shut them. Her dark eyes are glossy as she pulls out the chair next to mine and carefully takes my hand in hers. I flinch at first but don't pull away, which is what I should do.

"Sorry, what I said was completely insensitive," she whispers. "I'm sure that was hard on you, never knowing what would happen day by day, or what you were walking into."

She has no idea. No one does unless you've lived it. Pain is building in the back of my throat, in my heart, in my mind. Memories can be the scariest motherfuckers to haunt you at night.

She blows out a tortured breath before going on. "You're brave. I could never do anything like that. I want to thank you from the bottom of my heart for taking that job ... and this one. No offense to your brother, but I've never felt safer than what I do with you." She holds our hands up and lightly brushes her soft lips against our connection.

It takes me a few seconds to regain control of myself. I don't want these wounds ripped open. I've tried my hardest to bury them, but somehow, Stella keeps digging deeper and deeper, forcing herself in. She's committed herself to discovering every component of me, whether I like it or not. This insane woman is getting closer and closer to my heart, and the harder I fight, the harder she does.

I clear my throat before bringing up our hands, pressing my lips to them just as she had. "Trust me, it's not easy. But I knew what I was getting into. I knew the possible outcome of going to another country and fighting. I think both of us knew the outcomes could've been bad when we chose our line of work."

She sighs when the teapot whistles through the air, and I place a hand on her arm to stop her from sliding out of her chair.

"Let me do it," I say.

I bring myself up when she nods and take the teapot off the heat. I've never made hot tea before, but it can't be that difficult.

"You're right about both of us knowing the risks in our jobs, but I'd say yours is much more intense. I get a lack of privacy, a few stalkers here and there, and people busting my ass about obligations. You get life or death, or possibly the loss of a limb. You do something so damn important, Hudson, and I wish they gave you more credit for it. I hate the way Tillie, Eli, all of them look as if you're beneath them, even though you're the real MVP."

I can't help but crack a smile, and she returns it in delight that she's hitting me where I never wanted to be cracked. She manages to bring out the light in me in even the worst times. Talking about this with someone is out of character for me. I've kept what I've seen, what I've gone through, to myself, allowing it to tear me apart from the inside.

Cameron grilled me with question after question when I got home from my first deployment. She wanted to know if I saw anyone die, if children actually walked the streets with homemade explosives strapped to their bodies, or if we spent our days doing nothing but playing around. She asked these questions as if I'd just gotten home from a banker's job.

I needed her to help me heal, but she only wanted to take me back down that road. She didn't understand. She only saw it as me shutting her out. I didn't want to release those internal demons on her or anyone else, so they stayed holed up inside me, burying themselves into my veins, where I'll live with them forever.

Stella gets up when she notices my hands start to shake while I pour the water into the mugs.

"Here," she says, taking it from me. She nudges her shoulder against mine. "I'm the tea master, so you better sit down and let the pro do her magic."

I give her a smile, one that's not forced, and do what she says. Stella is different. She cares. She respects me enough not to ask for the gruesome details. She's waiting for me to feel comfortable to release them on my own.

"Why did you join the military?" she asks, sliding my drink to me.

"You know, I'm not exactly sure. My grandfather served in Vietnam. My dad served. My family is big on tradition. One of my father's children needed to serve. I knew Dallas wasn't interested, and I'd never want to put that pressure on my sister, so I decided to take on the job. Another big push for me was what was happening in our country. I don't want to get political, but shit is fucked up. Innocent people have been dying for years."

She raises her cup. "I'll give an amen to that." She hops back on her chair and starts to sip on her drink, her full lips curving around the edge of the cup.

"Why did you decide to be Clementine?"

She squeals, grinning from ear to ear like I told her she won the lottery, and the mood has lifted. Tea splashes from my cup when she smacks me on the shoulder.

"Oh my god!"

I look around in confusion. "What?"

"You've been watching my show, haven't you?"

Fuck! I'm busted.

Stella had me too drowned in my feelings that I wasn't thinking about hiding that I've been secretly watching her show every night.

She smacks my shoulder again when I take a long drink without answering her. "Don't you dare lie to me."

I shake my head, my mouth still in my cup. "No. I've heard the name from Dallas."

"Oh, whatever, you've either been looking me up or watching. Which one is it?"

I set the cup down. There's nothing wrong with doing my research. "I was curious about who I was spending so much time with, so I watched a few episodes when I was bored."

She rests her hand against her chest and sways from side to side. "Hudson likes me; he really likes me," she sings out before pointing at me. "You shall never live this down. I'm beginning to think we might be getting closer than we thought we would. I have a feeling sex will be in our near future."

I decide to play along even though I'm thinking the same thing. "I must say Clementine grew out of her dorky phase into one fine as hell chick."

She laughs. "You are so lame."

FIFTEEN

Stella

MY PHONE RINGING interrupts our conversation. Willow's face pops up on the screen, and I try to answer so quickly I nearly drop it. As much as I want to continue this flirtatious conversation with Hudson, there's no way I'm missing her call. Something was wrong with her earlier, and I've been waiting to talk to her again. If she's calling this late, something is wrong.

I'm dreading whatever it is as I tap the Accept button.

"Hey girl," I answer, trying to sound upbeat.

"Hey," she says, sniffling.

Code Red. Code Red. Just what I thought.

"What's going on?" I rush out, my fake giddiness now disintegrated. I tuck the phone between my ear and shoulder.

There's a moment of silence, and I hold my breath for the news.

"Brett is awake and seems to be coherent," she finally tells me.

I exhale, confusion rushing through me. "That's great! It's a start, right?" I glance over to see Hudson's attention fixed on me.

"It is," she mutters. "I mean, I'm glad he's okay. He's recovering from a concussion, so he'll be in the hospital for a while. They're planning to perform facial reconstruction, but he's responsive and seems to have regained most of his memory."

Maybe her sniffles are sniffles of happiness.

"Good. I'm happy for you, Willow."

"He also decided he doesn't want to be with me anymore."

"What?" I yell louder than necessary.

Her sniffles turn into sobs. "He said his near-death experience woke him up." She scoffs. "*Literally.* Apparently, he wants to live his life and not be tied down. Settling is no longer an option for him." Her sobs turn into anger, and I wish I could wrap her in a tight hug and then take away Brett's cable TV in the hospital. "Disloyal son of a bitch. He's been *living his life* the way he's wanted for years. For fucking *years,* Stella! I stood by his cheating, no good ass every single damn day!"

I want to punch Brett in the balls and then elbow drop him for good measure. *How dare he do that to her?* Fucking asshole.

"Oh, and get this," she continues, huffing like she's exhausted every breath she has. "Some random chick showed up at the hospital the other day. His supposed side chick."

Damn side chicks. They always become a problem.

"I bet that went over well. Please tell me you're not calling me from jail and need to be bailed out for kicking her ass?"

"Hell no. She can have him. Let her see what a lying sack of scum he is."

"You deserve so much better. Everything will be okay, I promise. We'll find you a hot dude here, and you'll forget all about Brett's three-pump sex."

She sighs. "It's just a lot for me to take in, you know? I'm planning on coming back to work in a few days."

"Take your time. Do whatever you need to. Your job will be waiting for you whenever you're ready."

"Thanks. You seriously don't know how much I appreciate our friendship. I don't know what I'd do without you."

I wait to answer while she lets out a long yawn. "Get some sleep and call me in the morning, okay?"

"I will. Good night."

"Good night." I end the call and set down my phone before

looking over at Hudson. "Brett is still awake and seems to have regained most of his memory."

He whistles. "Shit. You had me scared for a sec."

I cock my head to the side. "What? Why?"

"I thought the dude died, and you were comforting her by saying she can do better, and his dick game was weak."

"No, *so not* the case."

He smiles. "Then help me with my confusion, will ya?"

I don't want to repeat what Brett did because I'm so irate about it. My anger might force me to show up at the hospital and knock him upside the head with a frying pan. Maybe he needs to suffer another concussion so he can wake up from the next one with more sense.

"He woke up and decided to dump her ass," I tell him, snarling my lip.

He scowls. "You're shitting me?"

I shake my head. "I wish I was. Douchebag wants to spread his wings like a pigeon and spread his bullshit to more of the female population."

Hudson sips his tea. "Sounds like a good man."

"Yep, even better news is that the chick he's been cheating with showed up at the hospital devastated."

He winces, his expression switching from resentment to pure hatred. He looks like he wants to be the next one in line to elbow drop Brett.

"I despise cheaters," he hisses. "They disgust me. Willow deserves better."

I nod in agreement. "It's not the first time he's been caught cheating. It happens all the time, and then he begs her to stay with him while giving some bullshit speech that he'll change. For some reason, Willow always falls for it. I pray it doesn't happen again."

His jaw muscles clench. "They never change. Once a cheater, always a cheater. Period."

"I ... I don't think that's necessarily true," I stutter out. "People make mistakes and learn from them all the time."

This is about his ex, and I hate that he's so angry about it. He's still in love with her. That's the reason for a reaction like that.

"Cheating isn't a mistake. It's unforgivable in my book. It breaks the bond of trust, and if I can't trust you, I can't be with you. It's not that difficult for someone to take a step back and realize that cheating on someone will tear them apart in every way possible. Make them feel like they're not good enough."

I gulp. This night had been going so well. He catches onto my uneasiness and snaps out of his frustration, his face apologetic.

"Shit, I'm sorry," he says. "You don't want to hear me whine about this shit. I shouldn't have acted like that." He finishes his tea. "It's probably time we get to bed." This seems to be a constant with him. We get somewhere, then he walks away. "Good night, Stella. Sleep well."

"Good night," I whisper.

I wait until I hear his bedroom door close before grabbing my phone and opening Instagram. I type Hudson's name, but my search comes up empty. I type Dallas's name next.

Jackpot.

There's nothing more satisfying than finding the person you want to stalk's profile is public.

Creeping here I come.

I scroll through his photos. Most of them are of him with Maven and Lucy. I spot the most recent one with Hudson. They're at his welcome home party. Hudson looks happy, a beer in his hand, and his arms around his brother and a short, dark-haired woman. I narrow my eyes at her but relax when I notice she's tagged in the caption as Lauren Barnes, their sister.

I proceed with my stalking until I'm well into weirdo territory and find one with Dallas, Lucy, Hudson, and a stunning blonde. I click on it and study the picture. Everyone is smiling, and she's tucked into Hudson's side, his arm around her.

It has to be the ex-girlfriend.

And she looks exactly like a woman I imagine Hudson with. Her hair is naturally blond and down in loose, effortless waves, and she's wearing cut-off shorts and a tee showing plenty of cleavage. The photo proves how deep Hudson loved her. There's a different light in his eyes than he has now.

I click on her tagged username to see more pictures of her and maybe the ex-best friend. It'd be hard finding someone better looking than Hudson. Someone who could compete with him.

Did she keep pictures of her and Hudson up or delete them?

Unfortunately, her profile is private.

Loser.

The only way I can advance further into my operation stalk Hudson mission is if I request to follow her, which will make me look like an insane person.

Game over for me.

I frown, pissed at my defeat, and decide to go to bed with Hudson on my mind.

SIXTEEN

Hudson

I ACTED like a douche lord in the kitchen.

I never meant to expose myself like that to Stella.

I'm not in love with Cameron anymore. I don't want her back. Once a cheater, you're always a fucking cheater in my playbook. What triggered my anger wasn't losing her. It was the lies and deception. I would've given my life for Cameron, sacrificed everything I had to make sure she was safe and happy, only to find out she'd turned her back on me when times got just *slightly* tough.

She should've come to me, told me she didn't want that life, and I would've gladly let her off the hook.

It only proves that pursuing a relationship with a friend you've known your entire life is a bad idea, which is why I'm taking a hiatus from dating. Whether I'm taking a break from fucking is still yet to be determined because my mind—my dick—can't stop thinking about dipping into some sweet pussy.

It's been too long since I've been intimate with a woman, and there's nothing more on your mind than getting laid when you come home from a long deployment. My problem is that my pussy-deprived mind is wrapped around tasting my new employer.

I snatch my laptop from the desk and power it up to start the second season of Stella's show. I shake my head at my stupidity of letting it slip that I've been watching it, but the excitement in her eyes told me she liked it. She's made it clear she's all in. She's mine temporarily if I make the move, and each passing minute with her is pushing me closer in her direction.

I blow out a breath.

I can't believe I'm about to say this.

"I'm bound to screw Stella Mendes," I whisper into the emptiness of my room. "And God help me, I think I'm falling for her."

———

"MORNING."

Stella's greeting is wrapped around a yawn. Her ebony hair is down and wild with tangles—my favorite look on her. I love seeing her unpolished, raw, untamed.

She's wearing different pajamas than she wore last night. The dark silk nearly blends in with her hair, and the tank is cut so low I'm sure I'll get a view of her nipples if she leans down far enough.

That'd be a good way to start the morning.

I lick my lips. *Fuck.* I need to smack some sense into myself with the whisk in my hand, but instead, I settle it on the side of the bowl and rub my hands over my sweats.

"Adulting fuel?" I ask, turning around to make her a cup of coffee without waiting for her response.

She yawns again. "Is that even a question?"

I pour her a cup, adding two teaspoons of sugar and a splash of coconut milk. I somehow have her coffee preference down, which further proves that I'm being an idiot and getting too close. I've even started making my coffee the same way. I never had coconut milk before coming here, but it's not too bad.

"Thanks," she says when I hand her the mug. She stands on her tiptoes to see what I'm doing. "You're making breakfast?"

I shrug. "I figured why not? You said your chef is on vacation, and I'm starving. It would've been rude for me to only make enough for one."

I grew up with a mother that always cooked enough to feed a football team. We seemed to constantly have a houseful of people—cousins, girlfriends, neighbors. People showed up, and we fed them.

"Always the gentleman," she says with a light laugh. "You need any help?"

I shake my head before tipping it toward the island. "Sit down and enjoy your coffee. You might be the master tea-maker, but I'm the breakfast expert."

She gives me a skeptic look. "Do you actually know how to cook? Or do I need to collect my valuables before you burn my house down?" She drags out a chair from underneath the island and sits.

"Sure do. When I was younger, my parents made us do the outside and inside chores, so we'd be a jack-of-all-trades. I can change your tire and then come home and bake you a scrumptious as fuck pecan pie."

She leans forward to settle an elbow on the counter, her chin resting in her cupped palm. "A jack-of-all-trades, huh? I like it. You fix shit, shoot shit, and cook shit."

I snap my fingers. "I think I'll make that my next pickup line."

"I expect royalties when it's successful and you get laid." She pauses, a smile growing. "Unless it's with me. I'll let you have a free pass then."

"You better quit trying to fuck me before I burn your breakfast."

"Eh, I wouldn't mind. To be honest, I've had my fair share of burnt food. Cooking is not one of my strong suits."

My shoulders relax now that she's changed the subject and isn't going to keep exciting my dick.

"Even when I try, I always seem to mess something up." She leans back, her manicured fingers wrapping around the handle of the mug, and keeps her eyes glued to me while I move around and do my thing. "But I have to say, I enjoy watching you in my kitchen. There's something sexy about a man putting in the effort to do something like this instead of calling room service or texting his chef what my favorite meal is."

"That's good to know." I can't believe she's never had a dude cook for her.

"*Although,* if you take your shirt off, it'll be even sexier." She grins, a flush creeping up her cheeks.

I hold up the whisk, batter dripping from it while trying to keep a straight face. "You keep trying to get me naked, I might have to file a sexual harassment charge against you."

She blows out a dramatic breath. "Why are you making it such a challenge? I thought all men like to get laid, especially when a woman is putting a no-strings-attached clause on the table. I feel like this should be the other way around."

"You might want to change your taste in men, Hollywood. Not all of us only care about getting our dicks wet. I think it would freak the hell out of you if I kept begging you to jump on my dick. I'd be like Eli's creepy bodyguard."

She shudders. "True story, but trust me, I wouldn't mind it from you." She licks her lips. "In fact, I'd encourage it."

"I'll keep that in mind."

"That's what you keep saying," she mutters. "Cock block."

I shake my head, laughing, and start to dip the bread in the batter.

"What's on the menu?"

"French toast and scrambled eggs."

"Sounds good."

She starts telling me stories of her cooking fails while I finish up our food. I hand her a plate, grab all the necessities for the meal, and pour her another cup of coffee.

She looks from my plate to my stomach and then to my plate again when I sit down next to her. "Question, how do you eat like this and look like *that?*"

"I work out," I answer, grabbing the sugar-free syrup, which is all she has, and pour it onto my plate. I do it to hers next. "Although,

I've been slacking on it since I've been here. Your gym consists of mostly cardio machines."

I wait for her to take the first bite, dying to see her reaction, and grin when she does.

She chews, swallows her bite down, and then stabs at her next one with a fork. "This is incredible. I wasn't expecting it to be this good."

We dig in, our conversation sparse as we stuff our faces, and she helps me clean up when we're finished. She's wiping her hands on a dish towel when she looks over at me with a grin. I know I'm in trouble.

"Back to the working out conversation," she says. "I have news that'll brighten your day."

I arch a brow. "Oh, really?"

"My yoga instructor is coming over for a morning session. Do it with me. We can burn off all those delicious carbs we just devoured."

Yoga?

I snort. "Thanks, but I'll have to pass on that."

She doesn't seem fazed by my dismissal. "Have you ever even tried it before?"

"Nope, and never plan to. Twisting myself into pretzel positions doesn't seem like a good time to me or my junk."

"It's not only twisting yourself into pretzel positions. Don't knock something until you try it. Plus, you said you've been slacking on your workouts."

I shake my head. "Still not happening."

She pouts her lips. "*Please,* for me."

I shake my head again.

"You're doing it, so get dressed, soldier. You're about to have your first yoga lesson."

I throw my head back, knowing damn well I'm about to cave. "How do I keep letting you talk me into shit I'd never do?"

She laughs and slaps my stomach as she walks by. "It'll be fun. I promise."

"If not, you better make it up to me," I yell to her back while getting a good view of her ass.

She whips back around. "I have no problem with that. I'm up for anything."

"*I'll* keep that in mind." We're playing a dangerous game.

She's laughing as she disappears into the foyer. I go to my room to change and grab my phone.

Me: What the hell does a dude wear to yoga?

Stella: It's nude yoga, so you don't have to worry about attire.

Me: You and your instructor are going to piss yourself when I show up in my birthday suit.

Stella: I dare you to do it.

Fucking with me seems to be her new favorite hobby. Stella will be the death of my morals. My momma will have a coronary if she sees me in some tabloid love triangle. People will think I'm the scum of the earth for messing with another man's woman, and I'll never be able to tell my truth because Stella will hate me if I let her secret out.

Operation Keep My Dick In My Pants is now in order.

I have a feeling I'm going to fail.

My phone rings. I snatch it up from the bed and balance it on my shoulder as I pull my shorts up.

"Hello?" I answer.

"How are things going?" Dallas asks.

"Good." I pause, debating with myself on whether to tell him. "About to have yoga class."

He laughs for a good thirty seconds. "You're shitting me?"

I stay quiet.

"You're doing yoga now?"

"No, asshat. I'm escorting Stella to yoga," I lie.

"Bullshit. You're going to climb up on that mat and Namaste the fuck out of your problems. Next time I see you, you'll be eating seaweed and hugging trees."

"Fuck off, what can I help you with?"

"Doing my daily check-in to see where your head is, and if you're done being a grumpy bastard yet."

"I think you know I'll always be a grumpy bastard, but it's getting better." That's an understatement. "It does get dull when I'm following her around doing mundane shit. How did you manage to do this for so long?"

"I don't know. I guess I got used to it. You will, too."

"No, I won't. I'm only here temporarily, remember?"

"I stand corrected. Get your yoga on and text me later. Maven is insisting I have a tea party with her."

"You're giving me shit about yoga when you're about to have drinks with stuffed animals?"

"The perks of having a kid, man."

I hang up and open my suitcase for a shirt. I haven't unpacked because *I'm not staying long.*

SEVENTEEN

Stella

HUDSON DOESN'T SHOW up naked to yoga, much to my dismay.

However, he does show, which gives me some optimism.

Today's yoga session will be interesting.

He might be wearing clothes, but there's not much to them. I slowly lick my lips, taking him in as he comes farther into the kitchen wearing athletic shorts that hang low on his hips and a T-shirt with the sleeves cut off that gives me the perfect view of his firm forearms and chiseled triceps.

I smile, lamely feeling special that I've convinced such a macho man to do this with me. He's beginning to surprise me more with every minute we spend together. I can feel him dragging me into his world, and I have a nervous feeling that if I get swept up, I'll never want to let go.

It's the calm before the storm.

It's going to happen, and I don't know how bad the devastation will be when it ends.

His mind is like a mystery book I want to read every page of.

Has he changed his opinion about me?

Does he think I'm a creep for hitting on him all the time?

Does he consider it sexual harassment?

Is he going to sue my ass because I want to get a piece of his?

His unpredictability is killing me.

It's also what's drawing me to him.

He's different.

He hasn't tried to sleep with me, even when I handed him my vagina on a silver platter. He doesn't only have a conversation with me in hopes it ends with my lips around his cock. The roles are reversed from anything I've ever experienced.

I'm the chaser this time, the beggar, the one who's throwing her panties at him and insisting he fuck me sideways … long ways … hell, any way, for that matter.

I want him. His cock. His tongue. His fingers. His touch.

Anything he's willing to give.

Just as long as it's *him*.

I'm a strong supporter of orgasms. I was always open to trying new things with Knox. We did the whole foreplay fun, experimented with our tongues and fingers for over a year before finally losing our virginities to each other.

What's surprising me is that I've never coveted someone's touch so powerfully before as I do with Hudson. I've never felt myself grow wet between my legs or had my heart rage out of control when I'm at the receiving end of someone's smile.

But I do with him.

I jump when the doorbell rings, and it takes away the opportunity for me to drill him on why he has clothes on. I'm wondering when I became this sex-crazed maniac as I spin around on my heels to answer the door and let Yolanda in.

"Good morning, sunshine," she sings out in her Dutch accent, strutting in with her yoga mat strapped around her shoulder. She gives me a peck on each cheek. "I saw the new movie. *Fabulous!* Absolutely fabulous."

Yolanda is the best yoga instructor in LA. She makes a killing off house calls because she's like some yogi expert. I met her when I attended one of her sessions at a friend's home about a year ago and was instantly hooked. I was still healing from my breakup with Knox and felt like a sad loser. She turned my depression into something positive. I walked out with a different perspective on life and hired her to come over two days a week when I'm in the city.

"Thank you," I say, leading her into the house.

"Are we doing in or out?" she asks.

"The weather is perfect, so let's go outside."

"I hoped you'd say that. Your view is one of my favorites. If you ever need someone to house-sit, I'm your girl."

"My bodyguard is also going to join us today."

Hudson steps forward at the mention of him when we reach the kitchen. "I'm a newbie," he says, shooting her a polite grin. "Be easy on me."

He winks, and I swear to God, Yolanda almost melts right in front of us. Let's add charmer to the list of Hudson's hot qualities.

"Of course," Yolanda answers. "What made you decide to join us?"

"It wasn't my idea." He points at me. "This one is hard to say no to."

Yolanda looks back at me with an arched brow and what I'm certain is a *you're so fucking him* look.

If only.

I open the French doors leading outside and walk outside to the patio by the pool in my backyard. I bought this house after my breakup with Knox. It was the first time I'd ever been on my own. I went from living with my mom to moving straight in with him when I turned eighteen. It's exciting to have something that only belonged to me. Having my own home gives me a sense of pride.

The backyard is what made me fall in love with the property. I put in an offer the same day as the showing. The infinity pool stretches out to the hills, plus a firepit and a hot tub and enough seating to entertain fifty people even though I've only had company a few times.

Yolanda strips off her shirt, showing off her black sports bra and a six-pack I'd kill for, and sets her mat down on the concrete. She's in her late forties but has the body of a woman my age.

I peek down at my stomach. It's flat, but my hips have a little too much *handle* in the love handle department. I'm not skinny, but I wouldn't say I'm overweight. I like to refer to myself as full of tits and ass. I inherited my mother's wide hips and large bust, but I try to keep my body in as good as shape as I can. That doesn't mean I'll turn down tacos.

I bend down to set my mat on the ground and hand Hudson my extra one.

He holds it up, raising a brow. "Pink?"

I smirk. "It brings out the color in your eyes."

He chuckles. "Good to know."

Yolanda starts us out in child's pose when we get ourselves situated and begins her mantra.

———

WE'RE thirty minutes into yoga, and I'm not feeling my Zen self, per usual. I'm not following along with any of Yolanda's instructions … because I'm turned on.

She directs us to go into downward facing dog, but I'm only catching onto bits and pieces of what she's saying. Her words are like background noise while I focus all my attention on Hudson, who is now shirtless and following Yolanda's orders.

He goes into the pose, his back arched and ass sticking up in the air, and I do the same. Sweat drips off his forehead and chest.

Is it gross that I want to wipe him clean with my tongue?

I shake my head in a failed attempt to focus on the task of getting my shit together, but my knees are trembling. My elbows are wobbly. I clench my fingers and toes, certain I'm about to fail at this pose even though I've done it dozens of times.

Think about peaceful shit, for God's sake.

You're in fucking yoga class.

Buddha.

Gandhi.

Not Hudson's penis.

Penis is not Zen.

No Zen is flowing through me right now.

No *Namaste bitches,* here.

I peel my attention away from Hudson when Yolanda gets up to adjust his pose. He glances over at me, and we make eye contact as he shoots me a playful grin that nearly causes me to fall. Yolanda comes my way next, most likely confused about why I'm fumbling around like a two-year-old who finally discovered she has legs.

My eyes don't leave his as Yolanda quickly corrects me and then goes back to her mat. Hudson's intense gaze impales mine, his rustic honey eyes drinking me in, and I can't look away. This only ratifies that I'm not the only one feeling this connection, this chemistry sparking between us.

Our connection is snapped a few minutes later when Yolanda has us move into the last position, and we finish our session.

Hudson stands and starts picking up our mats while I walk Yolanda to the front door, my feet slowly sliding along the travertine tile. A part of me wants to push her out of my house and race over to Hudson. The other part of me wants to beg her to stay because I don't know what's going to happen when she leaves.

She turns around and hugs me. "He seems like a keeper, that one."

"He's only my bodyguard," I say, trying to convince us both. "Nothing more."

"Nothing more *yet,* but I have a feeling there will be. I'm an instructor, which means I'm trained to watch. I saw the chemistry bleeding between you two. A spark that wants its final connection. The way your expressions altered while watching each other move into the next pose told me everything I need to know. There will be more. I can promise you that."

She gives me a final wave and disappears out the door.

I sigh. I'm usually relaxed when she leaves, but that's not the case today.

I'm on edge.

Is yoga supposed to trigger sexual arousal?

It brings out pheromones, dopamine, and all that good stuff, right?

It's never happened before, but I've also never done it with Hudson.

Never done it with *a shirtless and sweaty* Hudson.

I find him in the kitchen. He has his shirt back on and is pulling out two bottles of water from the fridge. I smile when he hands one to me.

"What did you think?" I ask, leaning against the island. "Are you ready to be the next yoga enthusiast?"

He wipes his forehead with the back of his arm. "It wasn't that bad."

I snort.

"Fine, it's not exactly my preferred type of exercise."

I lift my chin slightly. "What is your preferred type of exercise?"

"High-intensity shit. Loud music. Definitely no fucking chanting involved."

His answer doesn't surprise me.

"There has to be something you liked about it."

He smiles. "You're right. I enjoyed watching you."

Whoa. I almost drop my water.

I was on course to settle my hormones, but that response charges them back with the accelerator on high.

I straighten my stance, feeling brave. "What a coincidence. I enjoyed watching you."

A moment of silence passes through the air as we stare at each other. His breathing quickens, his chest moving in and out rapidly, and I prepare myself for rejection again.

"Fuck it," he mutters.

I'm too stunned to move as I watch him advance around the island with determination on his face. He cups the back of my neck and pulls me to him, our lips meeting, and nearly knocks the air from my lungs. My water bottle falls to the floor.

His lips are softer than I imagined. I'd watched him, studied the way he talked, laughed, and even grimaced, and wondered how they'd feel against mine if he ever gave in to temptation. He yanks me closer, his free arm curving around my waist, and gives me what I've been begging for.

Our breathing collides when his tongue slides against mine, and I stand on my tiptoes to better meet his mouth. His scruff brushes over my cheek, something I've never experienced before. Most men I've kissed have been clean-shaven. I'm positive I'll have beard burn on my cheek tomorrow and am hoping it'll also be between my legs.

My heart plummets when he pulls away. I squeeze my eyes shut, expecting him to stop, but he cradles my cheeks in his palms. I slowly open my eyes.

I'm panting. He's panting.

My back straightens while he holds me in place, and I wait for him to make the next move. It's taking forever.

"Look at me, Stella," he demands.

I stare into his eyes as he looks at me with a tenderness I've never experienced before.

He lowers his voice. "You're beautiful." He traces my lips with his finger. "You've probably been told that a million times, but there's no superior word to describe you."

It's my turn to initiate a kiss.

This time, we kiss with no hesitancy.

I suck on the tip of his tongue and savor the taste of him.

He picks me up, and I wrap my legs around his waist when he carries me to the living room. My hands shake when he carefully deposits me on the couch. Excitement shoots through me when he drops to his knees and tugs on my yoga pants. I lift my legs, assisting him in getting the job done faster, and my lungs are burning from breathing so hard.

My pants get tossed to the side, and he settles between my legs.

This isn't a fair fight.

He's calling the shots.

And surprisingly, I have no problem with it.

"Fuck, these are sexy," he says, tracing the edge of my panties where the lace meets my thigh. I throb between my legs when he skates his finger back and forth torturously. I push my hips up, a silent plea for more, and he takes the hint by hooking his fingers through the sides of my panties and tears them down my legs.

"Is this what you want?" he asks. "Tell me this is what you want."

Did he get fucking dementia?

I've been begging for this.

I decide against telling him that. Throwing around attitude when a man you're sure knows what he's doing is about to pleasure you isn't a smart idea.

"It's everything I want," I answer. "You're everything I want, Hudson."

My truth shocks the shit out of us both.

It also excites him.

His fingers dig into my hips, and he pulls me closer to his mouth. My legs are spread wide before he runs his tongue deep inside me.

The first lick has me craving more.

He uses the tip of his tongue to play with my clit and then shoves a finger deep inside me. My back arches as I moan, and he pumps his finger in and out of me, his tongue still working on driving me wild.

Fucking hell!

His tongue has me writing my vows.

Imagine what he can do with his cock.

He mercilessly adds another finger. I buck against his touch, my pussy walls tightening around his fingers like a glove, and he doesn't stop until I'm writhing against the couch while pleasure explodes through me.

"Let go, Stella," he says. "Let me see you get off."

I come alive and cry out as my orgasm shakes through me while he tells me how sexy I look. My legs shake as I sink my nails into the throw pillow next to me and try to catch my breath.

"Fuck me now," I order, coming down from the history-making orgasm but still not fulfilled.

He gives me one last lick before pulling away. I stare at him nervously while waiting for his next move. His jaw is tight, and he looks at me like he's on the edge of losing control. My head is level with his waist when he stands, and I take in the view of his erection showing through his shorts.

It would be so easy to reach out and touch him, but I resist. I need that same validation he wanted from me. I want him to tell me he's craving to have me as much as I am him.

He makes eye contact and peels off his shirt. I take in the sight of his chest and even though I've seen it before, it doesn't fail to turn me on.

"Drop them," I demand, my voice filled with authority.

He drops his shorts, and my pulse races.

His perfect cock twitches in front of me. It's swollen, thick, and I moan at the thought of how amazing it will feel sliding inside me. He doesn't waste another second before grabbing his erection at the base, and we both take a deep breath when he situates himself at my entrance.

I throw my head back when he slowly inserts the head.

Then I look back at him at the feel of him pulling away.

No! Why?

"Fuck," he hisses. "I don't have a condom."

Neither do I.

Since I was under the impression I wouldn't need them, I stupidly didn't bother restocking when I ran out.

"I'm on the pill," I blurt out, most likely sounding desperate.

Don't stop.

Don't walk away from this.

"I don't fuck without a condom." He scrubs a hand over his face and takes a step back.

A step that stomps on my heart.

I put my hands between my legs to cover myself and suddenly feel too exposed. "You never screwed your ex-fiancé without a condom?"

He snatches my pants from the floor and hands them to me before putting his shirt on. "Yes, on occasions."

"So, *you do* fuck without a condom." I don't know why I feel like this is a sucker punch to the stomach.

"I've never had sex with a stranger without a condom."

He's never had sex with a stranger, period. His insult makes me feel dirty in a way. Even though he's being responsible, I'm not a *stranger.* I'm not some chick he met in the club ten minutes ago.

"But you'll lick their vagina?" I argue.

He clenches his jaw. "Please don't take it the wrong way, Stella. It's not a diss to you."

How do I handle this situation?

What do I do now?

Do I shake his hand, thank him for his time, and then chat about the weather?

Storm Stella is about to roll through and punch him in the balls.

"Are you scared that you'll catch something from me?"

He winces. "Fuck no."

"Then what? Do you still have a problem with my so-called fake hooking?"

"No," he grits out. "Don't fucking put words in my mouth."

"Then correct me where I'm wrong."

My phone rings, and I roughly pull my pants up and rush into the kitchen to hide my embarrassment.

My shame.

My fucking stupidity.

I hold up my phone. "That's my reminder alarm. We have to go to my audition."

Yay. I get to spend an entire car ride with him.

He steps my way, putting his palms out in front of him. "Stella, please."

"Just stop, okay?"

Out of all people, why did I attempt to screw my bodyguard?

The guy who has to follow me and be around at all times.

EIGHTEEN

Hudson

I SIT down on the edge of my bed and rub my sweaty forehead.

My cock is still as hard as a rock.

Stella said she was going to change and rushed out of the room like she couldn't stand to look at me for a second longer.

Not that I can blame her.

I'm a disgrace to men right now.

A disgrace to everything I stand for.

I was careless and only thinking with my dick, not about what would happen if we crossed that line.

So much for keeping our relationship professional.

The way I ate her pussy was far from that.

The hunger to taste her everywhere was tormenting me, and I couldn't hold back any longer. Stopping us from having sex was one of the hardest decisions I've had to make.

I'm an asshole. I used the same mouth I pleasured her with to insult her. The words came out wrong. I could barely stutter out a decent excuse, and then she accused me of being scared she'd give me a damn STD.

That's not what stopped me.

Shit can happen, and birth control doesn't always work. Dallas and Lucy thought they were careful and then got pregnant with

Maven. I gulp. Cameron got pregnant when she was on the pill two years ago. Even though we hadn't planned it, we were excited. Then we lost the baby ten weeks later. I never want to feel grief that hard again.

It nearly killed us.

We spent months mourning our loss, and the fear of another miscarriage put stress on us.

Maybe that's what killed our relationship.

———

"I'M SORRY," I say when Stella gets into the SUV.

Jim has a few days off, so I've been driving her around.

I keep the keys in my hand. We're not leaving until she hears me out.

"What I said came out wrong," I continue. "I'm not experienced with this shit."

She shakes her head without looking at me.

"Say something, *please*. I feel like a fucking piece of shit."

She glares at me. "You had a girlfriend for nearly a decade. You're experienced. Hell, you're more experienced than men who have screwed dozens of women because you were there for your girlfriend not only physically but also emotionally." She shakes her head. "I get it. I'm not your type. You don't see me *for me*. You made that clear from day one."

"I'll admit I was wrong for judging you in the beginning, but I'm fighting with myself on what to do here. I explained why taking that step for us wasn't a good idea. I'm moving in two months. We'll never be able to have a relationship."

She crosses her arms. "Why does it have to be a relationship? Why can't we try something casual?"

"Do you think we can honestly do that? Only sex?"

Maybe she can, but I can't.

I've never been able to separate my feelings from sex because I've never had to.

"I don't know, but I feel like we need to do something. I can't stop wanting more with you. Why can't we try? If it doesn't work out, you can walk away without giving me a reason. I won't ask any questions."

Casual sex has never interested me.

She frowns when I shove the keys into the ignition.

"We should get going," I say. "Don't want you to be late."

"You are the most confusing person on this fucking planet," she groans.

She stays on her phone while I follow the GPS instructions. My thoughts roam with every passing mile. Maybe I should give casual sex a try.

I was monogamous for years. That didn't work out.

Maybe it's time for a change.

We can both use each other.

NINETEEN

Stella

I'M FORCING a fake smile while staring at the script in my hand.

I did my makeup and rode thirty minutes in traffic hell for this?

I hate it.

The character sucks.

The storyline sucks.

And the cherry on top is that my management company loves it and wants me to take it as my next gig.

Fuck my life.

Margot, the next damsel in distress, is not the role for me.

I took the role with my last movie to get my feet wet in the industry like my team advised, but I refuse to continue playing the naïve woman needing a man supporting her to survive. That's not the career path I want.

This chick stalks—*yes, freaking stalks*—a man she met in a coffee shop because he resembles her ex-boyfriend. She then proceeds to ruin his fiancé's life in order to get his attention, and they fall in love in the end.

This is a love story?

I can't play the role of a desperate and obsessed psychopath.

Sure, I've been crushing on Hudson since he moved in and have made sexual advances like a cat in heat, but I'm not standing over his bed at night and watching him sleep. I stupidly didn't do my homework and read the script before coming, but I was too busy. Not to mention, my management team made it sound mandatory.

"Stella."

The feminine voice startles me, and I look up at the producer and casting director as they stare at me in question.

"Huh?" I ask.

"I asked if Eli will have an issue with you having another man as a love interest," she answers with annoyance. "Some men don't want their girlfriends making out with other men."

I bite back my smart-ass comment for the sake of my career. Maybe if I tell her Eli is a possessive freak who will cut my toes off if I kiss someone else, they won't give me the role, and management won't be up my ass about it.

"Uh, no," I mutter. "He knows how the industry works. We both do."

Yes, I'm a chickenshit. Sue me.

She stacks her papers and presses them against the table. "Perfect. We'll be in touch."

I deliver another forced smile and exit the room, passing a row of other women auditioning to be Margot The Maniac.

Hudson jumps up from his chair when he sees me, and I follow him outside to the SUV. He's still on my shit list. I'm humiliated by what happened. I was there, completely bared to him, and he walked away as if it was nothing. If he thought his bullshit apology in the car would make it better, he's stupid.

"How did it go?" he questions, turning on the car.

I cross my arms and sulk in my seat. "I don't want to talk about it."

"You didn't get it?"

"I probably did."

"Then why does it look like someone told you your dog died?"

"Because I'm having a pretty shitty day, thanks in large part to you." I hold two fingers inches apart from each other. "We were *this* close to having sex." I stretch them out, emphasizing my aggravation. "Not only did I lose the opportunity to possibly have the best sex of my life because the orgasm-giver turned out to be a complete a-hole, I then had to leave and audition for the stupidest role in the world."

"Look, I'm sorry. What I said wasn't what I meant, and I'll continue telling you that until you forgive me. I can get annoying as fuck, too, trust me."

"If that's your plan to make me feel better, it sucks ass."

"Shit." He pinches the bridge of his nose, shaking his head. "I acted like an idiot. Not for the whole condom situation, but for how I treated you." He signals back and forth between us. "You and I both know it's not going to end well if we take this step."

"You didn't even give it a chance."

"I know, and I'm sorry. So damn sorry. I promise I'll make it up to you."

His apology doesn't help. The urge to call him a coward is hanging on the tip of my tongue, but it's no use. His mind was made up about me from the moment he landed at LAX.

I cross my arms. "Fine, and I'm going to keep you to that, by the way."

"I know I'm in the wrong, but can you at least give me credit for eating your pussy until you fell apart on my tongue?" His tone changes from apologetic to cocky.

He does have a point.

He didn't exactly leave me high and dry.

More along the lines of panting and soaked.

I sigh, not willing to let him win yet. "What orgasm? I was faking it so you wouldn't feel bad."

He throws his head back. "Oh Hollywood, you may be an actress, but that wasn't acting."

I give him a dirty look. "Whatever." My stomach growls. "I know you like to withhold me from life's necessities and all, but can you at least feed me? I've already been starved of another orgasm from you."

He grins. "A life necessity, huh?"

I can't hold back my laughter any longer.

"There's that smile."

My smile collapses into a frown. "Don't. I'm still fucking livid at you."

He chuckles, aware he's winning this round. "Where to?"

I give him directions to my favorite sushi joint a few miles away. I'm letting him off the hook too easily, but he's right. Sex without a condom would have been reckless.

I have no idea what's going on in his downstairs area. I mean, I don't think he has anything, but you never know. At least one of us was thinking rationally.

I can't get pregnant. My head aches at the thought of it. I can barely take care of myself, let alone be responsible for another human. I have someone who schedules my manicures, for Christ's sake.

He pulls up to the curb in front of the restaurant and unbuckles his seat belt. "Do you want me to grab you takeout, or are you meeting someone and want me to wait out here?"

"Give the keys to the valet," I direct him. "We're dining in."

"We're?"

I nod when he gestures back and forth between the two of us to clarify.

"Not a good idea, Hollywood."

"Am I that embarrassing to be around?"

"Yes. Look at you, all perfect and sexy. I'll get made fun of for days if I hang out with such a creature."

I unbuckle my seat belt and push his side. "Come on. I'm starving, and my sushi craving is killing me with every second we're having this ridiculous conversation."

He doesn't move. "Did you say sushi?"

"Sure did."

He shakes his head. "Nuh-uh, I don't eat that raw fish, seaweed shit."

"Who doesn't eat sushi?"

"Me, that's who. I already let you convince me to spend my

morning twisting my limbs into positions that my balls will never forgive me for. I draw the line at eating that shit. I like my fish fried, baked, anything but raw."

I roll my eyes but laugh. "Too bad. I'm not eating alone."

I open my door and jump out without waiting for his response. He curses under his breath as he joins me and hands the valet the keys.

"Pain in my ass," he grumbles while opening the door for me.

"Payback's a bitch."

———

"YOU SURE THEY don't have burgers here?" Hudson asks, turning the menu front to back a few times as though he's missing something. "There's a hidden menu you don't want me to see, isn't there?"

"Try the damn sushi and quit being a diva. I'm sure you've eaten worse."

"I absolutely have, but not when I've had the choice."

"How about you try this, and I'll let you choose dinner, deal?"

He smirks. "You plan to share another meal with me?"

I look down in an attempt to hide my smile. "Possibly." *I do! I do!*

He slides his menu to me from across the table. "Order me whatever you're having."

When the waiter brings our sushi, I make him take the first bite. Hudson stares at it with a scrunched-up nose and slowly picks up the chopsticks. He pinches the chopsticks together, picks up a roll, and examines it before shoving the sushi in his mouth.

"Admit it," I say when he starts chewing. "It's not bad."

"Fine," he groans, swallowing it down. "You win."

I clap my hands and squeal.

"Settle down. I'm not saying I want to eat it every day of my life."

With a smile, I grab my chopsticks and dig in. That's when they walk in, and I nearly choke on my food. Hudson's attention shoots to me in worry while I force myself to swallow down my bite.

"Just when I thought the humiliation of today couldn't get worse," I mutter, narrowing my eyes on the movement behind him. My stomach churns when the couple sits down at a table on the other side of the room.

Hudson turns around to see what's caught my attention. "I'd like to think you had a pretty good start to the day." He shifts back around. "Who's the dude?"

I haven't seen Knox in months, nor have I wanted to. His hair is grown out, and he's gained weight, but he looks happy. The smile on his face is a reminder of when we were young and in love—before the industry beat us up.

His new girlfriend is with him. I recognize her from the tabloids and have been questioned about her in interviews, when people ask for my autograph, or when the paparazzi just want to be assholes.

Everyone wants to know what I think about the woman who allegedly stole my boyfriend.

"My ex," I answer.

"Do you want to leave?" Hudson asks in a lowered voice.

I shake my head. "No, it's fine." I grab another roll. "I'm good."

He doesn't look convinced. "Do you still have feelings for him?"

I hate being asked that question. "God, no. Our relationship wasn't healthy. What bothers me is I'm scared I'll never have that."

"Have what?"

"Someone who looks at me like he does her. Real love. The shit they preach about in the movies they want me to star in." I rub at my eyes.

Don't cry. Please don't cry.

Hudson takes a sip of his water. "Why do you think you'll never have that?"

I shrug. "I don't know."

"You're young, Stella. Give it time. Don't give up."

"You haven't given up on love?"

"Fuck no. I won't let a cheating woman stop me from marrying, having kids, and ending up a happy man. Cameron's betrayal was only a speed bump in my life, and her behavior won't force me to live the rest of my life alone. Fuck that. I'll end up happier than I would've been with her."

I take a deep breath, feeling like it's my turn to share something personal. "My only dating experience is him and a fake boyfriend. I'm not sure I even know what love is. I thought I loved Knox, and it hurt like a bitch when we broke up, but maybe that's because it's all I ever knew. But after a while, it almost felt like a relief. We weren't meant to be, and it was time we quit wasting our time. You know what I'm saying?"

He smiles. "No explanation needed. My dating history is worse than yours. One girlfriend. No fake ones. I'm the wrong person to judge or offer advice on one's love life."

I give him a hard look. "I told you no more talk about fake relationships."

"Are you still in one?" He leans forward, resting his elbows on the table. "It would make me incredibly happy if you weren't."

"I think you know the answer to that."

The awkward silence returns.

His voice is the one to break the tension. "Was your ex also in the business?"

"You really don't know who he is?"

"I wouldn't ask if I did."

"He's Knox Rivers."

His nose wrinkles in disbelief. "You dated that dude?"

"Sure did." I can tell he's heard the stories about Knox. Most of them aren't good. "He wasn't always like that. People change. He was different when we were sixteen. He was monogamous and not the guy who only banged models."

"He cheated on you?"

"No." It's the truth, but people don't believe me. "We broke up and got back together a lot. Sometimes two or three times a week. It was during those times we'd hook up with other people. Never when we were together."

"Sounds like a stable relationship."

"Very stable. I think us going through the phases of stardom together gave us a bond we were afraid of breaking. We understood each other's lives and leaned on each other when people were making ours hell."

"Your parents weren't there for you?"

I shake my head. "That's another reason we clicked. Both of our fathers were absent from our lives … until we made it big, of course. Our moms were also similar: there every step of the way, taking money from us until they could survive on their own *with that money.* I haven't heard from my mom in weeks." I shake my head and release a bitter laugh when it hits me.

"What?"

"You have the picture-perfect family, and I barely have one."

"Every family has its problems. I'd never judge you for something you can't control."

"I wish I had what you do. A happy home." I stare at him, smiling at the thought. Whatever lucky woman who steals Hudson's heart is going to have a great life, and I'm already jealous of her.

"I was blessed with that, yes. Being a good man like my father is one of my biggest goals."

I smile. "That's adorable."

He looks almost offended when he leans in to whisper to me. "Don't refer to me as adorable again, Hollywood. I'm not a pretty boy or any of that shit that you're used to. I don't mind dirt underneath my fingernails. I don't wear tuxedos or do that black-tie bullshit unless it's for a wedding. I'm not adorable. I'm a fucking man."

TWENTY

Stella

I WALK into the living room and collapse on the couch in exhaustion.

It's been a long day.

I glance over at Hudson, sitting in a chair while texting on his phone.

"Alright, smooth talker," I say. "It's time for you to live up to your promise."

He slips the phone into his pocket and gives me his full attention. "Huh?"

"You promised to make up for your asshole behavior earlier. I expect you to honor that."

"How would you like me to do that?"

I smirk. "Preferably naked."

He chuckles, shaking his head. "There are plenty of ways to have fun other than fucking, Hollywood."

"You're right." I hold up my hand and start to count on my fingers as I list off my answers. "There's licking. Sucking. Kissing."

"With no fucking?" he cuts in. "Sounds like all your ideas end up with a bad case of blue balls."

He dodges a pillow when I toss it at him.

"Why do you have to be so complicated?" I groan. "Don't you want to get laid? Hasn't it been like what, a year for you?"

"Only nine months, thank you very much, and there's no disputing I'd enjoy getting laid. You saw my cock earlier, didn't you?"

Damn straight I did.

He was hard as a rock.

I rub my thighs together, remembering how his thick cock had twitched in excitement. "Why are you pulling away then? We want the same thing."

He snaps his fingers. "That's where you're wrong."

"How am I wrong? You playing for the other team now?"

"Pussy is the only field I play in, sweetheart. When I say we don't want the same thing, I'm not referring to sex. I'm in a bad place in my life right now and not sure a no-strings-attached and only fun sex relationship is the best way for me to pull out of it."

I gape at him. "You're in a bad place because of what happened with your ex?"

He drums his fingers against his chin. "She's a part of it, yes, but not all. Cameron cheating isn't the only bad shit that's happened to me."

"You want to talk about it?"

"I don't think a therapy session would be fun for either of us. Shit, it'd probably be a contraceptive more than anything. I'd scare you away."

"Nothing you could say would scare me away."

His gaze darkens. "Trust me on this one."

His face tells me he's finished with this conversation, so I decide to go a different route.

"So, no fucking. No heart-to-heart conversations. What's your plan of making it up to me then? And FYI, I have enough shoes." That's not technically true, but I'm trying to make a point here.

His mood changes from intense to laid-back as a smile builds on his lips. "How about dinner and a board game?"

The fuck?

"Your idea of redemption is feeding me and playing Monopoly? You're such a tease."

He's playing dick games, goddamnit.

"Sure is." He smacks his leg and brings himself up from the chair. "Now, what sounds good for dinner?"

Sex. His cock.

I get up and trail him to the kitchen, pouting the entire way. "How about you surprise me?"

He opens the fridge and starts moving things around. "Let's see what I have to work with." He looks back at me. "I want to give you a heads-up that this won't be my best meal, considering you don't have much in here."

"It will be better than anything I throw together." I stroll over to the wine fridge and grab a bottle before pouring us a glass. I leave his on the counter and take mine as I sit down behind the island. "I'll relax and enjoy the show."

He stops what he's doing to look up at me. "That'll work, but only on one condition."

"What's that?" I have a hateful relationship with conditions. Blame it on Tillie's condition-loving ass.

"You let me pick the game we play."

Is he actually for real about this whole game night thing?

I narrow my eyes at him. "Seriously? I thought you were joking about that."

He shakes his head. "The only way you're getting out of a game is if you put on an apron and start helping."

"Fine, one game."

He grins. "Scrabble it is."

"What's up with you Barnes boys and Scrabble?"

He stops to look up at me again, his brows furrowed. "You played Scrabble with Dallas?" He looks almost pissed off.

"Yes?" I answer, blinking. "The little shit is the most competitive person I know."

"Scrabble is the game of the Barnes family," he explains. "*We're all* competitive. We can't be beat."

I chug down the rest of my glass. "I don't know. I play a pretty mean game."

"Scrabble it definitely is then."

I slide out of my chair to pour myself another glass. "Then a repeat of what happened after yoga?"

He shakes his head. "Seven letters, one word."

"You suck?" I guess. *Not one word, but close enough.*

He laughs. "Nice try."

"Do you not like wine?" I ask, noticing his untouched glass.

He shrugs. "I'm more of a beer guy."

"I'll be sure to have the fridge stocked."

He grins. "Appreciate that."

TWENTY-ONE

Hudson

I'M BUSTING my ass to prepare the perfect meal for Stella.

I know my way around the kitchen, but it's been a while, so I'm a bit rusty. I decide on honey-glazed chicken because I have the recipe down pat. It might sound boring, but it's far from that. My chicken could win awards. It actually did in a Blue Beech cook-off. I'm not claiming to be Bobby Flay, but I can throw down.

My parents made sure we learned from both of them growing up. My dad took us under his wing to work in his repair shop, and my mom spent the weeknights teaching us how to cook and clean. Those cooking lessons paid off when Cameron and I got our own place. My ex's idea of a home-cooked meal was pouring a box of mac and cheese into boiling water. I'd get lucky sometimes, and she'd add hot dogs to her infamous pasta. Her specialty.

But I loved the woman, and when you love someone, you accept their flaws. Over time, you actually start to love them.

Stella sips her wine and keeps her attention on me as I move around the kitchen. I marinate the chicken, slide it in the oven, and start slicing veggies before tossing them in a skillet along with the seasonings. I don't have all the ingredients I need, but there's enough for me to work with.

I'm doing a lousy ass job at keeping our relationship professional already, and I doubt cooking her dinner and drinking together will help that. I consider myself a strong man, but the force of Stella Mendes is breaking me down.

We make conversation, talking to each other in excitement, and words jump from my tongue like fire as we throw out question after question.

We're both giving.

Both taking.

I want to know every detail of her life—every flaw, quirk, every-fucking-thing about her. In order to get that, I give her mine—convincing myself I'll put those bricks back up later. I'll only cave for tonight.

She rolls her eyes and calls me basic when I say my favorite color is green. I laugh when she declares hers is sparkles. Whether it's a real color is decided after a five-minute debate where I'm declared the loser. Her go-to food is tacos and guacamole. I'll remember that for the next time I cook for us. Mine is anything that pairs well with beer. She demands I clarify, and I finally cave in and admit it's burgers and ribs.

She talks me into having a glass of wine. My mouth waters as I load our plates with food. She grabs the bottle of wine, and I carry our plates outside to the patio. One thing I've come to love about Cali is the weather, especially in the evening. It's not too hot. Not too cold.

And the view is incredible.

Stella lights the candles on the table while I set down the plates. I pull out her chair before taking my seat across from her, and then something hits me.

I slide my chair out and get up. "Shit, we forgot glasses."

"Don't worry about it," Stella says, stopping me. She snatches the bottle and takes a drink from it. "It tastes even better this way."

I smirk. "I think I'm rubbing off on you, Hollywood."

"I agree." She leans in with a wild grin on her face. "I like it."

"Oh, really?'

"Yes, really." She looks around the yard. "Thank you for making me dinner and suggesting we eat out here. I've never truly been able to enjoy my backyard like this. I mean, I do yoga occasionally, but other than that, it's never used."

"You're not out here all the time? You couldn't get me to hang out anywhere else if I lived here."

"You do live here."

A smile tugs at my lips. "Good point."

"It's nice enjoying it without the stress. Whenever I entertained, I was always too worried to enjoy it. Everything had to be perfect because I was scared of people judging me. By the time it was all done, it was more of a headache for me."

"Tell me you've at least done something fun out here. Got wild? Skinny-dipped?"

"I wish, but no. I've honestly had such a great time hanging out with you in the kitchen and out here—the places I've never made use of." She picks up her fork but doesn't take a bite. "You make me feel so comfortable and allow me to be *me*. I can drink wine from the bottle and fuck cushions up without you gossiping behind my back."

She snags the cushion from the chair next to her and throws it across the yard.

Why do I feel so excited at her confession?

Why am I lighting up like a fucking firework knowing I make this chick feel good?

And why the fuck am I feeling the same way?

This California air must be fucking with me.

"That's where you're wrong. When you go to bed, I'm calling all my friends and telling them you're a monster for drinking out of the bottle."

She snorts. "I'm so sure."

Our food is getting cold, but I don't care.

I want this conversation.

"This has been an exciting night for me, too," I say.

"Yeah, right." She flips her hair behind her shoulder. "Says the guy who's spent his life protecting people and shooting firearms. You do all kinds of crazy stuff, and Dallas has told me plenty of stories about the trouble you caused when you were younger. I doubt making me dinner and watching me drink is fun for you."

"Not saying it's the best entertainment I've had, but I've never enjoyed getting to know someone as much as I have you, and I've never been so happy about someone proving me wrong."

"Proving you wrong how?"

"About who you are. I was a dickhead for judging you at first."

"At least you have the balls to admit it."

"I'm not afraid to admit I'm not always right." I can write a book of everything I've done wrong in my life, including stopping us on the couch earlier. I should've hunted for a condom.

"Glad I proved you wrong."

Our conversation is interrupted by the sound of her stomach grumbling.

I point at her plate with my fork. "You take the first bite."

"Why?" She narrows her eyes at me. "You trying to poison me?"

I throw my head back. "Jesus, no. It's rude for the chef to take the first bite."

"All right, but FYI, if I'm taking the bite to my death, I stuck a note somewhere in my room that says if I die, you did it."

"Damn, you're untrusting. Taste my food before I take it as an insult."

She cuts off a piece of chicken, takes a bite, and immediately goes in for another. A moan escapes her while she chews, and I shift in my chair. I've never enjoyed watching someone eat.

Maybe it's because she's eating my meat.

Fuck, that was lame.

"Holy hell," she finally says. "This is unbelievable. You weren't kidding about your kitchen skills. Your breakfast was good, but this dinner is incredible. I'll forever be asking you to cook for me. Consider that your new j-o-b."

I hold my hand up. "Whoa there, don't be getting too excited. This won't happen too often."

I go in for my first bite while she takes her third. She wasn't exaggerating to pump up my ego. Even with a few ingredients missing, it's good as fuck.

I'm slower in clearing my plate than she is because I can't stop watching her.

My cooking is good, but it's not the best part of this meal.

It's her. Her company. Her conversation.

I'll never forget my time with Stella. The memories will stay with me as I board a flight to Iowa when it's time to leave and live my life —remembering this as one of my favorite pit stops.

I'll never forget her sipping wine so dark it stains her lips the perfect crimson red, or the view of her taking long breaths between her laughs when she's excited. No matter what, I'll forever remember my time in California with the woman who was out of my league.

I'll always have that *what-if* in the back of my mind.

What if we weren't living in two different worlds?

What if I was willing to give up everything and move here?

What if she was willing to do the same?

———

"I HAVE A CONFESSION TO MAKE."

I take my last bite and look up at Stella. "Go on."

She sips on her wine, looking guilty. "I'm not exactly a Scrabble master."

I set my napkin down next to me and slide my chair out from under the table. "That's my cue to go. I can't hang out with Scrabble imposters." I gesture to the wine in her hand. "I'm okay with you chugging from that bottle, but lying about Scrabble is where I draw the line."

She rolls her eyes. "The first time I played was with your brother."

"Did you not have a childhood?"

"If by childhood, you mean my mom dragging me from audition to audition and then forcing me to get my hair lightened, then yes, I had the perfect childhood."

My stomach drops at her answer. "Shit, I'm sorry." Her response pisses me off. My parents made us work around the house and do chores, but they never stopped us from going out and having fun.

"It's fine. I eventually had my fun when I started making my own money."

"I take it Scrabble wasn't at the top of that bucket list?"

"Can't say it was. I tried getting Willow to play it with me once, but that girl is the queen of short attention span. We lasted two rounds before she decided we needed to catch up on *Teen Mom*."

"Priorities."

"You know it. Therefore, game night never became a thing for me."

"Surely, you have friends other than her?"

She used to hang out in the clubs with people all the time, at least that's what Lucy told me when Dallas first took the job. She was nervous he'd fall under the seduction of the women around him.

"As of lately, no. I lost most of them in my breakup with Knox."

"What? Like a prenup? You got the curtains and fine china, and he got the crew upon going your separate ways?"

"Something like that. They had to choose, and they chose him." She shrugs. "I'd rather keep to myself now anyway. The last thing I need is someone finding out about this whole Eli scheme and blabbing about it." She's acting like it's nothing, but there's no doubt it bothers her to lose people she thought had her back. Maybe money and fame don't buy happiness.

She scrubs her hands over her face and takes another sip of wine. "I have an idea."

I arch a brow. "Your ideas are never good."

"Let's make a wager."

"Do proceed."

"Scrabble winner gets to choose how we end the night."

"In other words, the winner gets to decide if I spend the entire night fucking you in that pool or not?"

She flinches, my answer catching her off guard, and warmth swims over her cheeks. "Exactly."

"That doesn't make me want to win."

She winks. "Be a gentleman and lose."

"I wouldn't count on it. I told you us Barnes men are competitive about our board games."

"Bring it."

———

"AROUSAL?" Stella screeches around a fit of laughter so loud I'm sure she woke the neighbors.

We're still outside finishing off our second bottle of wine and battling over Scrabble.

"How the hell did you get those letters?" She reaches over the table, grabs the box, and starts searching through it for evidence I'm cheating. "That can't happen in real life."

I hold up my hands. "Playing fair and square over here, Hollywood. Don't be pissed because the Scrabble gods are in my favor."

"The Scrabble gods must be trying to tell you something if you have the letters to spell arousal."

She has a point.

My mind is still blown that I'm trying to win when the outcome of losing means we have sex.

I point at the board. "Your turn."

She runs her manicured hand over her chin and dramatically debates her next move. Her eyes squint before a sly smile spreads across her plump lips. I run a finger over my mouth and remember how delicious she tasted this morning.

I scoot forward while watching her spell out her word, and my mouth drops when she finishes.

"Balls deep?" I question, going back over the letters as if there's a mistake.

And she thinks my ass is cheating?

"That's two words."

"Says who, Webster?"

I signal down to my lap. "Says the guy with balls."

She rolls her eyes. "Okay, well says the girl who's had her fair share of working with balls, I get some say." Her hand flies to her lips as her face turns red. "Dear God, can we act like those words never left my mouth? This is what happens when I drink too much wine. I start talking about my experience with balls." She smacks her forehead. "See! There I go again!"

I can't help but burst out in laughter, and she gives me a look that falls between dirty and annoyance.

She's right about the alcohol. It's getting to us. I never imagined I'd play Scrabble so damn kinky. Add Stella and booze to the equation, and this is the best damn game night I've ever had.

"Care to share some of those working experiences?" I ask but then stop her before she answers. "Scratch that. I don't want to hear about any of your past experiences. I'd rather you show me about how you work with them and let me experience it myself." I glance down at my now-stirring cock growing more excited from this *balls talk.*

She jumps up from her chair. "Excuse me while I go drown myself."

I stand, meeting her at the pool, and spin her around to face me. "Come on, it'll look bad on my resume if my employer drowns while I'm on the job. Don't be embarrassed. My dick likes your balls talk."

She attempts to pull away to block her face, but I stop her. "I appreciate you trying to make me feel better and all, but that so did not turn you on."

I move my hand to hers and bring it straight to my aching erection. She doesn't flinch or move her hand.

This action right here seals our fate.

"Still think I'm lying?"

She massages me. "Possibly, but all the evidence hasn't been seen. Remove the pants."

"Let me convince you with Exhibit B then."

Her eyes widen and follow my every move when I take a step

back. Nervousness drives through me like a bullet when I unbuckle my jeans. Anticipation rises at the sound of my zipper going down. Any thoughts I've had about not touching Stella again are long gone.

Nothing will cure this sexual tension but sex.

I've been jacking off for days in an attempt to get over my attraction to her, but it hasn't helped. I'm harder than I've ever been, and I haven't even touched her yet.

She gasps when I drop my pants and boxer briefs, and I stand in front of her in all my naked glory. The backyard is secluded, and I'm hoping none of her stalkers are creeping around and get a shot of my dick ... or one of Stella when I pound into her pussy soon.

She stays quiet, her eyes glued to me, and I glance down at my pulsating cock.

The fuck?

It's hard as a rock—not flaccid or any other weird shit, so what's going on? She's been up-front about wanting my dick, but now that I'm handing it to her, she's mute?

Maybe she's rethinking this.

Maybe her plan was to get me all worked up and then walk away like I did her.

I'd deserve it.

I clear my throat. "A little quiet over there."

"Just taking in the view," she says.

"And?"

"Not bad."

"Just not bad?"

She chews on the tip of her nail. "I mean you know what they say about cars. It can look nice, but what really matters is the acceleration and speed behind it. What's under the hood. What do you have for Exhibit C?"

"How about I show you?"

From the shit-eating grin on her face, it's clear she wants my dick, but there's something more mischievous on her agenda. I lift my shirt over my head and throw it down before getting closer.

I thank the good man above that I have kick-ass reflexes, in large part to Dallas picking on my ass for years until I learned how to defend myself, because as soon as she goes to push me in the pool, I grab her arm, taking her with me. Holding in a breath, we go under and gasp for air while resurfacing.

"I show you my dazzling cock, and that's what I get in return?" I ask, catching my breath and shaking my head. "So ungrateful."

She's laughing. "You didn't have to throw me in with you."

"Oh, yes, I did."

Because we're about to have some fun.

TWENTY-TWO

MY BREATHING DRAGS, my lungs working on overdrive, while we stare at each other underneath the bright moonlight.

Hudson's perfect, hard, his hard cock making my mouth water. His hand is cold when he reaches out to capture my waist, and he pulls me into his muscular chest. Our eyes meet when he stares down at me with a sin-filled grin. I moan when our eye contact breaks, and his erection brushes my thigh.

I'm terrified but eager for his next move.

Our lips are only inches apart.

"Looks like you won, Hollywood."

He's so damn close I can feel his heart beating against mine.

I tilt my head to the side, licking my lips. "What do you mean?"

"The wager. You won. Tell me what the loser needs to do to redeem himself."

I don't give him an answer.

Well, *I do* ... but not with words.

It's with my lips crashing into his with urgency and desperation.

He groans into my mouth, slipping his tongue through, and guides us to the shallow end of the pool, our connection never parting. I moan when I'm pushed against the wall, and his strong arms cage me in, one going to each side of my body.

His tongue plunges farther into my mouth, skillfully massaging it against mine.

This kiss is aggressive. Abrasive. We're devouring an act denied for too long. He pulls at the hem of my top before ripping it right down the middle.

Yes, he fucking rips it.

And throws it on the ground like it is last season's Gucci.

I break away to give him a dirty look. "That's my favorite shirt." It was also expensive as fuck.

"*Was* your favorite shirt," he corrects. "It looked expensive, and I didn't want it to suffer more water damage. I heard that's bad for fine silk. Which is why this is the next to go."

He unsnaps my bra and tosses it next to my shirt. I'm about to praise him for caring about my precious lingerie, but all words stop when he traces my nipples with his tongue before latching onto it, sucking hard.

I'm screaming at myself when I push at his shoulders to stop him. "No condom again," I whisper, my voice trembling. My vagina and brain are having a showdown. One wants to stop this before it ends terribly. The other doesn't care as long as he keeps doing that thing with his tongue. "If that's still your rule, stop now. Don't lead me on and do that shit again, or I might take my dinner knife and castrate you."

My threat might be a little overdramatic, but whatever.

Getting someone worked up and then walking away is quite possibly the most overdramatic thing you can do, right?

"You need to make a decision." It's not a request. It's a command.

"I won't stop," he softly assures me. "If that's okay with you?"

He moves in closer while waiting for my answer.

"I'm clean, and I trust you are," he goes on. Water flies from his hair when he shakes his head. "What I said earlier came out wrong. I have shitty delivery, and I'm sorry."

He puts some distance between us and tilts his head forward to run his tongue between my breasts.

Hell yes.

How the fuck is everything he does so damn hot?

He pushes into my touch when I reach down and start stroking his shaft. I love the sound of him moaning in my ear while he slides his hands down my sides and hitches my legs around his hips, giving me a better sense of how hard he is for me.

Another gasp leaves me at the temperature change when he walks us up the pool steps and straight to the outdoor furniture area. My heart is hammering so hard I can feel it against my throat when he carefully lays me down on the couch and takes a step back.

He licks his lips, drinking in the sight of my half-naked body on display for him.

I hold in a breath when he leans down and unsnaps my shorts, dragging them down my legs and tossing them to the side. A burst of energy rushes through me when he drops to his knees at my side and teasingly rubs me through my panties.

I arch my back, begging for more, and loving the stimulation of the lace caressing my clit.

He's not even directly touching me where I want him yet has me on the top of the orgasm ladder. He doesn't let up until I'm almost to my brink, *almost right fucking there.*

That's when he pulls away. It wouldn't be a moment with Hudson if he didn't start fucking with my mind and orgasm in some way.

"What the hell?" I scream. "I told you to let me know if you were going to change your mind!"

I narrow my eyes but take the time to admire the view of his cock close-up. The tip glistens with pre-come, and I almost fall off the couch when he slowly strokes it once.

That's my job.

What I'm supposed to be doing.

"Hollywood, there's no way I'm walking away from you tonight. I'm only getting started."

"Then get started! Why are you still standing there?"

I'm not a virgin, nor am I worried about him making it

romantic. All I need is an orgasm, and this girl is good to go. That's probably why I've had such a great relationship with handheld electronics lately.

He glances from side to side. "You sure you're okay with us doing it here?"

I can't help but laugh at how ridiculous we probably look. He's standing in front of me with a massive boner while giving me a damn questionnaire. Meanwhile, I'm spread out on my pool furniture wearing only panties.

"Yes. Now, fuck me," I demand.

He grins and strokes his cock one last time before moving to the end of the couch. My panties are off in a flash—flying through the air at the same time he slides up my body and hovers over me.

We do one of our infamous stare downs.

The horniest stare down in history.

Our lips meet again, igniting a passion stronger than anything I've ever experienced. I break away, my lips roaming down his neck to his hard nipple, and I tug at it with my teeth.

It's hypnotic the way we move together so effortlessly. His fingers and tongue seem to know all my sensitive spots.

I'm sweaty, and my heart is racing by the time he sweeps my hair back, meets my gaze, and slowly pushes inside me. I tilt my hips up to take every inch of him while adjusting to his large size.

I've never had sex with anyone without a condom before. Knox and I never had sex without protection. Besides being terrified of having children, our managers provided us with every birth control method known to man.

Hudson doesn't break eye contact when he withdraws and slams back inside me. My breasts bounce while he pumps into me, and his hands travel up to squeeze them. I spread my legs wider, and his balls smack against my ass. His tongue is cold when he sucks on my nipple, and I nearly lose it when his mouth returns to mine. He slows his pace, which isn't how I want it tonight.

I need rough and hard.

Like earlier, he thinks he's running the show.

One thing I need to teach Hudson Barnes is that I like being in charge, too.

"I want to be on top," I moan, writhing underneath him.

I gasp when he pulls out, helps me up, and then falls down on the couch in a sitting position, his legs spread apart.

He grins while I nervously stand in front of him and starts stroking himself. I inhale a breath and straddle him, shuddering as I sink down on his erection. He drops his head forward to stare at our connection. I run my fingers through his wet hair and pull at the roots while slowly starting to ride him.

"Fuck yes," he moans. "Ride me just like that."

I've taken the control from Hudson—a man who likes to have it at all times. But he doesn't seem to care as I take every inch of him.

He's abandoning his dominance.

I'm abandoning my gracefulness.

"Does that dick feel good, Hollywood?" he hisses through clenched teeth.

"Yes, so damn good," I groan around other words that I'll blush tomorrow.

I'm trembling, my legs tangled and shaking against his, but nothing is holding me back.

It's as if I'm on top of the world.

Well, on top of the world's best cock.

He palms my ass and rocks his hips up, our movements at the perfect pace until we're both moaning and sweating. I bite into my lip when my orgasm hits before collapsing against him. Hudson shudders while coming inside me and rests his head on my shoulder as we catch our breath. My stomach knots as I avert my gaze, sweeping over the yard, and I hesitate before looking down at him.

I'm nervous.

Terrified.

Did we get caught up in the moment?

Does he regret this?

His hand glides up my back, and he strokes my skin while smiling up at me.

I can't help but laugh at myself for being so worried. Hudson isn't that kind of guy. He won't give me a pat on the back and then walk away.

"I think I won the game tonight," I whisper. My pitch embarrassingly rises like I have a sore throat. That's most likely not the only part of my body that's in for a sore morning.

He brushes my hair away from my sweaty face. "No, Hollywood. You riding my dick like that made me win at life."

TWENTY-THREE

I HAVE A NEW FAVORITE.

Shower sex.

More specifically, shower sex with Hudson.

That's how I started my wonderful morning.

We stayed in the shower until the water turned cold, and Hudson helped me dry off. He went to his room to change and have his daily checkup call with his family. I love how close he is with them.

I grab my phone from my nightstand and collapse on my bed, my feet hanging over the edge, and notice a missed call from Willow.

My phone rang earlier, but I was on my knees with Hudson's cock in my mouth, so unfortunately, she got sent to voicemail. I love my friend and all ... but sex.

Again, *shower sex.*

Wet bodies.

Wet everything.

I can't stop grinning when I hit her name.

"It's about time you called my ass back," she says. "I've been calling you for hours."

"It's been *twenty minutes,*" I correct. "Calm your tits."

She laughs. "My tits are very calm over here ... and very much neglected as well. It sucks being single."

"You know what that calls for," I sing out.

"Benny, my lovely vibrator, who never seems to let me down. By the way, that was the worst birthday present. I told you I wanted a unicorn. Not an orgasm generated with double A's."

"You'll be thanking me for it as you venture into singlehood. Trust me, nothing cures the heart of a bad breakup like some good self-induced orgasms."

"Eh, you're probably right. Now, on to more important things. How bad do you miss me?" She's taking this breakup better than I thought she would. That ... or she's putting up a front.

"You've been gone?"

"Funny. Are you almost dead over there? Are you feeding yourself? Bathing? Taking your multi-vitamin?"

"You do know I'm twenty-five, not three, right? Although I do miss your help."

"Anything new? How did your audition go? I haven't heard anything back, but I know Susie said agents have been calling about you because of the hype from *Forever Ago*."

Susie is my manager, who mostly communicates through Willow unless she has a new part or a possible deal she wants me to look at.

"The script was an absolute nightmare. Fingers crossed I don't get the part."

"There's my optimistic best friend. I didn't get a chance to read it. That bad, huh?"

"Yep." I study my fingernails and blow out a long breath. "I hooked up with Hudson." My mouth blurts out the words. The need to tell *someone* has been killing me.

Is this a bad idea?

Am I stupid?

I need some advice here.

I've never had a no-strings attached relationship, so I'm not sure how to go about doing this.

Am I allowed to tell Willow?

Is he going to tell Dallas?

A moment of silence passes.

"What do you mean hooked up?" she finally asks.

"You know … *hooked up.*"

What the hell?

Saying you hooked up is like saying peanut butter goes with jelly.

Do I need to whip out dolls and show her what parts went where?

"What's your definition of hooked up? Like you guys made out for a minute or did anal?"

"Oh my god, Willow!" I yell, nearly rolling off my bed as she breaks out into a fit of laughter.

"You have to be more specific, girl. I never know with you."

"You never know with me? I'm not the anal sex queen. Jesus!"

"Now, give me all the details."

"Well, the first time—"

"Hold up, girlfriend," she interrupts. "There's been more than one time, and you're just now telling me this? What the hell?"

"I didn't know I needed to report to you when I get laid."

"You do when it's with your hot bodyguard—who you've sworn you're staying away from. I need *every detail.*"

"You're going through a breakup. I don't want to be insensitive."

"That's not insensitive. It actually makes me feel better hearing my best friend is getting some good dick. Just because I'm down doesn't mean I want everyone around me to be down and sex-deprived."

This is why Willow is my best friend. She'll ask about your day when hers was hell, and cheer for you from the sidelines when you're falling in love, even when she's going through a breakup.

I make myself comfortable and tell her everything. I've had more orgasms in the past few days than I've had in months. Hudson might not have been intimate with a list full of women, but he definitely has plenty of experience.

"What are you going to do now?" she asks when I finish. "Date him? Is it casual? I mean, won't it be complicated with the Eli situation?" Willow begged me not to agree to the Eli deal, but I didn't listen to her.

I play with my hair, twirling strands around my finger. "I don't know. I like him and enjoy spending time with him. He gets me."

"Are there feelings?"

"Yes, and that scares me."

"Why?"

"He's going back to Iowa as soon as we hire someone else. What happens then? Will we shake hands, say thanks for the sex, and never speak again? I insisted it'd be a no-strings-attached fling, but he's told me plenty of times he's never been into an arrangement like that."

"Long-distance relationships can work. My situation isn't the best example, but you and Knox were good for a while."

There's optimism but also concern in her voice. In this industry, so many long-distance relationships have fallen apart.

Shoot, it's not even just in this industry.

Distance ruined Hudson and his fiancé's relationship. They say the heart doesn't notice miles, but I call bullshit. It notices when you're going to bed alone, the insecurities, and the panic that pumps through you when you haven't heard from them for hours.

Are they hurt?

With someone else?

Distance is hard on the heart.

"Knox and I were good at faking," I say—the excitement of my morning fading.

"Don't pull away while he's there. Give it a chance. If things don't work out, look on the bright side. You won't have to worry about running into him again."

"Good point." I've been dodging anywhere Knox hangs out, and if Hudson weren't with me yesterday, I would've stormed out of the restaurant the moment they walked in.

"Promise you'll give it a chance. Do it for me and my broken heart."

"*Fine,* I'll do it for you."

She snorts. "I know you love me and all, but you're doing this more for yourself and your vagina."

"*Onto* the next subject. How are you doing?"

"I haven't been back to the hospital and moved my shit back to my mom's. My biggest issue is Brett's bitch sisters. They're pissed I burned his sneakers before leaving. I took pictures and sent them to his phone, so he'd know they were gone. It'd be rude for him to stress finding the perfect shoes for his next date."

I chuckle, shaking my head. "How did I know you'd do something to make him pay? You're having too much fun with this."

"Burning shit mends a broken heart. The flames bring out a whole new you. I'm ready to find myself, change my hair, do all that *new me* crap they talk about in self-help books. My mom's been sending me Pinterest quotes about moving on."

"Is it working?"

"The Pinterest quotes? Hell no. I don't want to be that sad girl who looks on the bright side. I want to be the bitch who goes on a revenge spree. Burning his shit, writing he's a cheater on his car, maybe hunt down one of his friends and sleep with him … or all of them."

I laugh. She's so lying. Willow has only been with Brett, and I don't see her going on a one-night stand binge.

"You do know he's in the hospital right now? Don't you feel kind of bad for him?"

"Yes, which is the only reason I haven't kicked his balls into his stomach."

TWENTY-FOUR

Hudson

I HAVEN'T SPENT much time with Stella today.

It fucking sucks.

I went from dreading the days with her to looking forward to them.

Now that I've had a taste of her, I can't get enough. If I woke up every morning with the taste of her on my tongue, I'd be one happy motherfucker.

We slept in our own beds last night. I could see she wanted me to stay with her, but I'm not ready for that yet. I can't scare her off. When she asked to join her in the shower this morning, there was no saying no.

Her schedule has been jam-packed, and people have been in and out of the house all day. She made conference calls with her agent, and her stylist came over with a shit ton of clothing. My free time has been spent hanging out in my room and searching for new job prospects.

My father took over my grandfather's business after he passed and wants me to work for him. I grew up in the repair shop that specializes in engines and large farming equipment and has been in my family for over sixty years. Like Grandfather did, our dad expects Dallas or me to take over when he retires.

That'd been my plan after promising Cameron I wouldn't deploy again. I've worked on equipment ten times my size since I was fifteen, and I'd enjoy it. But first, I have to get my shit together. My dad made it clear he wasn't handing the company over to anyone not settled.

Growing up, we were given a checklist in life. Find a wife, have children, and work hard until retirement. Live life to the fullest. Be happy. My mom would say this every night before bed without fail. Having fun is cool but only after our responsibilities are met.

My phone beeps at the same time I shut my laptop after sending my final email.

Stella: I'm having a pizza delivered in 5 minutes. Will you answer the door and bring it up to me in the gym?

Me: Only if you share.

Stella: Duh.

My stomach growls at the thought of pizza. The majority of Stella's food is health-nut bullshit. Gluten-free this. No high-fructose syrup that. I've forgotten what real sugar tastes like.

When the alert goes off that someone is approaching the gate, I glance at the video screen in the corner of my bedroom. I buzz the delivery guy through, and the delicious scent of greasy cheese hits me when I open the door. My stomach growls when I tip him, and I grab plates and drinks from the kitchen before going upstairs.

"Pizza delivery," I call out, walking into the gym.

Stella smiles and hops off the treadmill without bothering to turn it off. I size her up as she struts toward me in a sports bra and workout pants. Her hair is in a loose ponytail, and sweat trickles down her chest and between her breasts. I lick my lips, craving her more than the pizza.

"Finally," she moans. "I'm starving."

Her moan matches the one she makes when we're having sex. I guess my sex game is on the same excitement scale as pizza.

She opens the box while it's in my hands and pulls out a slice. After taking a bite, she moves back to the treadmill, the slice still in her hand, and goes back to working out.

I set the pizza box on a weight bench. "What are you doing?"

Her forehead creases together while she looks over at me, keeping her pace. "Eating dinner?" She plucks off a pepperoni and pops it in her mouth.

"On the treadmill?"

She nods.

"You're eating pizza on the treadmill?"

This woman is a nutjob.

"Sure am." She points at the box. "You better get yourself a slice before I eat it all."

I keep staring at her.

"Are you not hungry?"

"My mind is too busy trying to figure out why you're eating pizza on the treadmill."

"Haven't you ever heard of multitasking? My agent was up my ass *about my ass* today. I looked heavy in a few bikini pictures that were leaked, so I need to tone this up." She smacks her ass. "My problem is that my soul mate is carbs. Therefore, in order for me to give in to my one true love, I have to work out."

The fuck?

"Sweetheart, you are not fat and are being too hard on yourself. And fuck your agent for making you feel less than perfect." I scrub my hand over my jaw and level my eyes on her. "That ass is perfection. Your hips, fucking flawless, especially when I grip them while you're riding my cock."

Hollywood is a bunch of sugar-hating, green smoothie-drinking dickheads.

She almost loses her step at my response but manages to correct herself. "Thank you. I'm glad you appreciate this ass. I only wish your opinion was the same as everyone else in the business."

"Someone else's opinion of your body shouldn't define how you feel about yourself. You're beautiful."

Bitterness fills my mouth, and I wonder how many people have tried to change her. From her mom forcing her to color her hair to the people who work for her complaining about her weight.

She flashes me a shy smile and holds up the last bite of pizza before popping it in her mouth. "If I want to eat like this, I have to work it off."

I beckon her with my finger. "Come here."

She shakes out her arms while staring at me skeptically. I stand quietly until she does what I asked. She jumps off the treadmill, and I plant my hands on her hips. She gasps when I turn her around in my arms and guide us to the mirrored wall. We stare at our reflection as I hold her in place.

"You know what I see?" I whisper into her ear.

She shivers but stays quiet.

"A beautiful woman—inside and out. Don't fucking listen to anyone who tells you otherwise."

Her eyes meet mine, and her plump lips curl into a smile. "Who would've thought underneath that tough exterior was a man so comforting? There's a spot of understanding in you that I've never found with anyone else. No matter what happens to my career, my money, or my appearance, I have a feeling it'll never change the way you look at me."

I gulp. "Never."

She shifts in my hold, turning to face me, and clasps her hands around my neck. When her lips meet mine, I kiss her softly.

"I think you were sent to California for a bigger reason than to be my security guard."

"You're right." I kiss her again. "That reason was you."

A connection this strong doesn't just happen. We were pushed together to prove we're capable of love, receiving and giving it, and to show us there's a light at the end of the tunnel of our broken hearts. We're two heartbroken souls looking out for one another.

My breathing hitches when she releases me to fall to her knees at the same time as my shorts are pulled down. My cock is already hard at the sight of her innocently staring up at me while biting her lip, and it springs forward in front of her.

I wrap her ponytail around my hand, and her locks spill forward when I undo it from the band. I rake my fingers through her soft strands when she wraps those beautiful lips around the tip of my cock, sucking hard. There's no taking my eyes off her while she slowly draws me into her mouth. I tighten my grip on her hair and guide her just how I like it, even though it doesn't seem she needs my help. I hardly blink while I take in the breathtaking sight in front of me. Her head bobs on my cock, and the sensation of her moans vibrating against my shaft is killing me.

My muscles tense, and before I come, I warn her in case she wants to pull away. She doesn't. I release her hair and stroke her cheek as she swallows my come.

"How do I taste?" I ask.

She runs her tongue along her bottom lip. "Better than any pizza or dessert in the world."

I'm light-headed while coming down from the high of my cock being in Stella's sweet mouth. I help her up to her feet and guide her straight to a seated weight bench. A gasp leaves her when I retreat a step and pull down her pants and panties to her ankles—not bothering to have her kick them off. My cock is hard again when I twist her around and bend her over, her ass in the air. Her back arches at the same time I slide inside her.

She rests her palms on the front of the seat and throws her head back to look at me. "I have a feeling I'm about to work that pizza off."

———

"I'VE DEFINITELY WORKED up an appetite now," Stella says.

We're sitting on the floor, panting, and trying to catch our breath after the best workout of my life. Hands fucking down, I'll never see a view as hot as Stella bent over a weight bench taking my cock.

I drag the pizza box to us. "You deserve this, babe. No doubt you burned every calorie you've eaten this month from fucking me so hard."

She grabs a slice and takes it with both hands. "I'm almost too exhausted to feed myself."

I set my piece on the floor and grab hers—positioning it at her mouth while she opens and takes a bite.

She laughs after swallowing it. "We're sitting on the floor, sans pants, and stuffing our faces with pizza."

"I have a feeling this is the most romantic post-sex situation there's ever been."

We spend the next five minutes finishing our food and chugging water. I'm chewing my last bite when Stella's mood shift into something that resembles nervousness.

"Tell me what's on your mind," I tell her.

She waves off my question. "It's nothing."

"Tell me what's on your mind."

She crosses her legs, and her nervousness morphs into shyness. "Will you sleep in my bed tonight?"

I grin. "Are you ready to take this relationship to the next level, Hollywood?"

She pushes my shoulder. "I'm serious."

"I'd love nothing more than to share your bed with you."

She looks up at me with a smile.

"Only because I'm sure it's a lot more comfortable than mine."

She rolls her eyes. "You're so damn annoying." She pauses. "I mean … is that taking a step too far in a *casual sexual relationship*? This is all new to me."

"You do remember I've only fucked one other chick in my life? It's new to us both. How about this: we make our own rules since neither one of us knows what's in the sex only relationship playbook? Sound good?"

She nods. "Sounds good."

TWENTY-FIVE

I HAVEN'T BEEN this happy in so long.

My bed has never felt so comfortable as it does when I'm wrapped in Hudson's arms. His legs are tangled in mine, and the heat of his chest is perfection against my back.

All night, I've been swept into a cheesy-happy phase. I'm scared to shut my eyes and sleep.

What if I wake up and it's not real?

Now that Hudson is opening up to me, I'm terrified to lose him.

I was on an orgasm high when I invited him into my bed, and surprisingly, the casual sex talk didn't have me running for the hills. It cleared up so much of my confusion … but not *all* of it. What's in his head is a mystery.

Are his feelings as deep as mine?

He's letting me in—something he hasn't done with many people and is hard for him. That tells me I'm edging myself inside him.

Will he allow me to stay?

Or am I only a pit stop in his journey?

My head aches at the thought of him leaving me and falling for a woman from *his world*. A woman his mom loves and who enjoys similar things. A woman who'll build a life with him in his hometown.

Me?

I've discovered I don't need a man who blends in with my lifestyle anymore.

It hasn't worked out well for me in the past.

All I care about is being happy.

Finally, I've found a good man, and I don't know how long he's staying.

I'm startled when his lips go to my ear, and he whispers, "Everything okay? I'm not squeezing the life out of you, am I?"

I shake my head as goose bumps crawl up my arms. "No ... just having trouble sleeping. You're still awake?"

"There's something I need to tell you." Nervousness is laced along his words. "I'm only telling you this *in case* it happens. The last thing I want to do is scare the shit out of you ... or for you to think there's something wrong with me."

I gulp. "Go on."

"It's embarrassing."

"What? Do you piss the bed or something?"

He chuckles. "I wish it were as easy as controlling my bladder. I have dreams."

"I think almost everyone does."

"Let me rephrase it for you. They're more along the lines of nightmares ... flashbacks ... of shit that I've witnessed but never want to think about again."

I shift in his arms.

I need to face him for this.

He can't see my face, but I want him to know I'm here for him.

No matter what, dreams or no dreams, I'll never ask him to leave my bed.

"Like PTSD?" I ask.

"Yes. It's the worst the first few weeks I'm home, but over time, they decline. It took six months to get rid of them last time."

His confession sends a bolt of pain through me. I can't imagine being afraid to fall asleep ... scared of what will haunt you when your eyes close.

"Have you had any since you've been home this time? Since you've been here?"

"Every night."

There's a moment of silence.

"Cameron would wake me up and tell me to stop. According to her, I tossed and turned and made weird sounds. I wanted to give you a heads-up, just in case."

I rub his shoulder. "You'd never scare me. You make me feel safer than anyone." I grab his hand. "Do you want to talk about it?"

"I don't want to burden you."

"You can tell me. I want to know anything you're willing to give. I'm all ears, Hudson. I'm all yours."

Give me anything.

Give me it all.

Open your heart.

Open your wounds.

Let me try to heal them.

Those words are on the tip of my tongue, but the fear of him leaving my bed stops me from releasing them.

"I've seen stuff I wish I didn't. I've eaten breakfast with men, they've shown me pictures of their families, their pregnant wives, babies, and then saw them die hours later. I've dragged children …" His voice cracks, and his pain bleeds through the room. "I've dragged children out of rubble … some of them … dead. Some alive. Their faces … they haunt me." He kisses my forehead. "Maybe with you in my arms, I'll sleep better."

I sigh dramatically. "I guess I'll have to do it then."

He chuckles in my ear. "You're amazing. Thank you."

I smile.

TWENTY-SIX

Hudson

THE SHRILL of my phone ringing wakes me, and the sheets moving tells me it did the same with Stella.

It's early, nowhere near sunrise, and I release her to scoot to the edge of her bed. I grab my phone, and fear rips through me when I see Dallas's name on the screen.

This isn't a call to chat.

It's a call that's going to wreck my world.

I hurriedly answer, shoving the phone to my ear, and my heart pounds against my chest so hard I can feel it in my ears. "What happened?"

"It's Lucy." His voice breaks. If he goes on, he's going to lose it.

"I'm on my way."

"Thank you, brother."

The call ends.

I roll out of bed and start to shuffle around the room as quietly as I can, hoping Stella can fall back asleep. I snag my pants and attempt to shove my foot through the leg, but it's difficult to do.

Maybe it's the nerves.

I freeze when the light turns on. Stella yawns as she pulls her hand away from the lamp and situates herself with her back against the headboard.

"Hudson," she whispers.

"Yeah?"

"You're trying to put my pants on."

I look down and realize I'm trying to squeeze into white skinny jeans. I pull them off my foot and lay them over a chair.

"What's going on?" she asks in concern.

"That was Dallas."

We exchange nervous looks. She knows but isn't going to insinuate anything.

"What did he say?"

"Lucy is gone." My voice sounds almost lifeless.

Her hand flies up to her mouth. Even though she suspected it, it's still a shock. "Oh my God. I'm so sorry."

I run a hand through my hair. "I hate to do this since Willow is gone, but I have to find someone to cover for me. I'm sorry, Stella, but I need to go home."

She nods. "I understand. There's no way I'd let you stay."

"Do you have any idea how fast we can get a replacement? Is there an agency or something we can go through?" I grab my pants when I spot them on the other side of the room and have no trouble getting dressed this time.

"There's no need for that. I'm coming with you."

I stop mid-zip of my fly. "I'm sorry, what?"

"I'm coming with you to Iowa."

I'm staring at her, my mouth gaping.

"Dallas is my friend. I want to be there for both of you." She shyly looks down and studies her hands. "I mean … if that's okay with you."

"I'm always okay with having you around, but are you sure it's a good idea? Won't Tillie have your ass?"

"I don't give a shit what she thinks is a good idea at the moment. I'll get my bags packed and ask Willow to book us a flight."

"Thank you for this." It's a big step for her … for us. She's coming to Blue Beech as a support system for me … for my family.

"You don't have to thank me for being there for you, Hudson.

You've been doing it for me since the moment you walked into my home."

TWENTY-SEVEN

Stella

WILLOW BOOKED us the first private flight she could, and I threw everything I needed in my suitcase before rushing to the airport with Hudson.

Our flight won't take us straight to Blue Beech since it's in the middle of bum-fuck-Egypt, so we'll take a car the rest of the way.

"Willow wanted me to tell you that she's sorry for your loss," I say after the pilot informs us that he's ready for takeoff.

Devastation has taken over Hudson. It's everywhere—on his face, the way he moves, how he's barely spoken ten words since we left the house. And those words were only telling me how grateful he was that I'm doing this for him.

He gives me an artificial smile. "Tell her thank you."

Dallas told me stories about Lucy. They started dating in the days of recess, and his family saw her as their family.

"Have you ever been to Iowa?" he asks.

My stomach settles at his push for conversation. I've never lost anyone close to me, so I can't connect with him in that way. The only loss I've ever dealt with is a relationship, and that's not shit compared to death.

"No," I answer. "But Dallas has described it pretty well. He said it's one of those small towns where people are in their own little world. Ones people think only exists on TV shows. You borrow sugar and milk from each other and leave your doors unlocked."

I shudder. That shit would never happen in LA.

Robbers. Rapists. Fucking psychopaths.

It'd be a cold day in hell before I left my bedroom unlocked, let alone my front door.

"That's Blue Beech," he says with a hint of a smile. "Living in a small town has its ups and downs, but I wouldn't trade it for anything. There's always something that feels good about going home."

"You would never move away or live anywhere else?" I ask the question casually but am dying to hear his answer.

He shakes his head. "All I need in life is family and a good place to come home to. That's Blue Beech for me."

His answer is sweet, but that doesn't stop it from plunging pain through me. My naïve dream that Hudson would pack up and move into my house is nothing but that—a dream. He'll never be mine because I can't be that girl for him. There aren't career opportunities in Blue Beech.

The career or the man.

Which one would be harder to lose?

My phone beeps with a text.

"Willow wants to know where to book my room," I read out loud.

I want to stay with Hudson but can't assume that's an option.

"This will make me sound like a bum, but my ex kept the place we were renting. I haven't had a chance to look for anything else. You have three options: We can crash at Dallas's or my parents' house, you can stay at the bed and breakfast in town, or there's a hotel an hour away from town, but trust me, it's not anywhere you'd want to stay."

That's somewhat of an invite to stay with him, right?

Unfortunately, he laid the decision at my feet. Inviting myself into someone else's home feels uncomfortable, especially since I've already invited myself to Iowa in the first place.

"I can stay at the bed and breakfast. I'll have Willow book it for me. Do you know the name of it?"

He cups his hand over my knee and squeezes it. "I do, but I was hoping that wasn't the decision you'd make."

I suck in a breath. "You want me to stay with you?"

His face softens, like he's now more at ease. "Of course, I do."

I stare down at his hand—something about it screams ownership. "Do you think Dallas will be okay with that? Having me there while he's grieving?"

Maybe I can convince him to stay at the bed and breakfast with me.

"I think he might enjoy the company, but if you don't feel comfortable, it's okay. You'll have to stay at the bed and breakfast by yourself, though."

I'm caught off guard. "What? Why?"

"If I sleep there with you, people will know something is going on between us, and we can't let your dirty little secret out, can we?"

His voice changes with those last words.

The mood shifts.

My decision to fake date Eli haunts me again.

———

HUDSON'S SISTER, Lauren, picks us up from the airport. To say I'm a nervous wreck to meet his family is an understatement. The entire flight was spent debating with myself on whether I made the right decision in coming.

Willow never questioned me when I asked her to book us a flight. No one has told Tillie, but I have a feeling she'll throw something when she finds out. Hopefully, she's too busy making someone else's life miserable than to worry about mine right now.

Hudson carries our bags when we land as I follow him through an airport that's definitely not LAX. A petite, dark-haired woman wearing scrubs is leaning against a pink Mustang. I recognize her from Dallas's Instagram.

"Flying private, huh?" she asks, pushing herself off the car. "Small-town boy is turning into Mr. Big Shot."

"Nice to see you too, baby sister," Hudson replies, giving her a hug. "I told you not to drive the Pink Panther and take Mom's car. It's too small for three people."

She squints at him. "First off, her name isn't Pink Panther, and had I driven Mom's car, I would have been late picking your ungrateful ass up. My work hours are nuts, and I couldn't even get off early when I found out about Lucy."

We all flinch at her last statement.

Hudson's hand tightens around the handle of my Louis Vuitton luggage. "You need to quit that fucking job then. That's bullshit."

Color rises in her cheeks. She looks almost sleep deprived.

"I can't quit my job because I have bills and an ass-load of student loans to pay off for the half Mom and Dad aren't paying." She walks to the back of the car and pops the trunk. "Unless you hit the lottery and want to pay them?"

"We both wish," he mutters, placing our bags in the trunk.

Her face is blank when she shoves her hand my way. "I'm Lauren."

I shake it. "Stella. Thank you for picking us up."

Her lips tilt up into a fake smile.

Is she upset about Lucy or mad I tagged along?

Hudson slams the trunk closed. "I'll take the back seat. Stella, you can have the front."

"No," I rush out. "I'll take the back. You two probably have a lot to talk about."

"We're going to be in the same vehicle. I can talk to her from the back."

The next five minutes is spent arguing about who will take what seat until Lauren threatens to leave us at the airport.

I lose.

"FYI, you look like shit, Hudson," she says.

Hudson smacks the back of her seat. "You're so sweet. How are you holding up?"

I look over at her as a tear slips down her cheek.

She wipes it away as though it never happened. "As good as I can be. Lucy was so young. It's unfair."

I nod in agreement but don't feel comfortable enough to join the conversation.

"And Dallas?" Hudson asks.

"Not good. He's holding in the hurt to be strong for Maven, but it won't help him in the long run. You need to talk to him."

"You know how Dallas is. Us Barnes boys don't like to talk about feelings. We feel like pussies."

"Don't undermine pussies. They're very powerful," Lauren argues. "If he'll open up to anyone, it will be you."

Hudson runs his hand over his puffy face. "I'll try."

Lauren looks over at me. "Did you ever meet Lucy?"

I nod. "She was very sweet."

She smiles at my answer.

Lauren's attention goes to the road, but I can tell she's skeptical of my presence.

―――

THE RIDE IS LONG, and I yawn when I see the welcome sign to Blue Beech.

"Holy shit, you weren't joking about it being in the middle of nowhere," I comment.

"Welcome to Blue Beech," Lauren replies. "Where there's no fancy coffee shops or malls to buy designer handbags."

Definitely skeptical.

Perfect.

"Lauren," Hudson scolds.

She rolls her eyes and goes silent.

Hudson's attention turns to me. "There's not much when you first get to town, but it gets better. The circle is where people hang out, and the excitement happens."

Lauren scoffs. "It sounds like you're trying to sell Blue Beech to her."

Hudson ignores her while I keep my thoughts to myself and stare out the window. Buildings come into view. People are walking around downtown and sitting on benches. Quaint shops and restaurants line the streets. We drive out of town and onto country roads until she pulls into the drive of a ranch home. The landscaping boasts bright flowers with dozens of gnomes arranged between them.

"This is my parents' house," Hudson tells me.

———

"MOM AND DAD, THIS IS STELLA," Hudson introduces.

Their house is as adorable inside as it is out.

It's cozy. Family pictures are everywhere. The furniture is worn but still cared for.

"And Stella, these are my parents," he goes on. "Rory and John."

I give them a shy wave.

Me shy?

That's unusual.

"It's nice to meet you," I say. "I'm sorry for your loss."

Rory gives me a small smile. I have a feeling I'll be seeing a lot of those here. They don't want to be rude but are mourning.

"Thank you," Rory says. "We appreciate you coming and giving Dallas time off so he could be with Lucy."

You can tell Rory is a nice woman by just looking at her. Her brown hair is pulled back into a chignon, and she's wearing a purple tunic and black leggings.

John resembles an older version of Dallas and Hudson. He's tall, his hair similar to his sons, with speckles of gray throughout the strands. I have no doubt he was as handsome as them growing up.

"You're welcome. I was happy to help," I answer.

My financial advisor suggested against me covering Lucy's medical bills. I make good money, but I'm not loaded. Maybe to other people I am, but in the world I live in, I'm just comfortable.

You decide what you want to spend your money on, and I decided I wanted to help the guy who looked out for me for years. I didn't want him worrying about finances during this difficult time.

"What's happening with sleeping arrangements?" Rory asks.

Hudson and I exchange a look.

"We're staying at Dallas's," he answers.

"*Both of you?*" Lauren questions.

"Yes, both of us. She's comfortable with us." Hudson arches a brow. "Unless you want to give up your bed? I wouldn't mind sleeping in your apartment."

"You can have the couch," she fires back.

"It will be good for Dallas to have company," John cuts in. Wrinkles crease his forehead when he frowns. "I hope he doesn't take it as hard as I think he will. There's no coming back from losing the woman you love. I pray to God I go before your mother does."

Rory reaches down and grabs his hand.

Oh, hell. I'm witnessing a love story.

People really act like this in real life?

TWENTY-EIGHT

Hudson

DALLAS'S front door is unlocked.

Stella stayed at my parents' while I took the eight-minute drive to his house. I want to see where he's at in his head before anything else.

He's sitting on the leather couch with his head bowed when I walk into the living room. He doesn't look up until I beat my boots against the wood floor. He stares at me blankly with loose shoulders. His eyes are red and underlined with dark circles. He's been waiting for this moment. The moment to release his pain in privacy.

I feel like shit for interrupting.

"Where's Maven?" I ask.

He rubs one eye and then the other. "Taking a nap."

"Have you told her?"

He nods. "This morning. We've been in here all day watching her favorite movies." He squeezes his eyes shut. "The ones she and Lucy watched all the time. It seems to be helping her take her mind off it temporarily, but I know it won't fix it." His voice breaks. "My girl lost her mother, and I don't know how I'm going to raise her alone."

"You know all of us will be here to help you every step of the way. You're an amazing father." I sit next to him and wrap my arm around his shoulders. "Lucy will never be replaceable to Maven, but Mom and Lauren will do everything they can to help."

"You don't understand," his voice falls into a sob. "I thought I prepared myself to lose her, but I was so damn wrong. I was never ready for this. Nothing can stop this pain. I loved her more than I loved my own life."

I fight back my tears. "None of us were ready to lose her."

"Lauren was working at the hospital when it happened."

"Were you there?"

He nods. "I've been there every minute of the day. Mom has been watching Maven for me. Without my family, I couldn't have even made it this far."

"We'll always be here for you. You call, I'll come running."

He glances over at me with his shoulders still slumped. "You staying here while you're home?"

"You know I am." I pause. "Is it okay if Stella does too?"

He flinches. "She couldn't find someone to cover your job?"

"We didn't bother trying. She asked to come with me."

He tilts his head to the side. "That's nice of her. I know Lucy appreciated everything she did for us."

"I can have her stay at Mom and Dad's if you want."

He raises a brow. "Does she want to stay here with you?"

I shrug. "She'll probably feel more comfortable here with us, but if you want privacy, Mom and Dad won't mind her crashing in my old bedroom."

"She can stay here. Maven likes her. She thinks she's a big shot for hanging out with someone on TV, so maybe it'll get her mind on something else. She can have the guest room, so you can either sleep on the couch up here or on the one in the basement."

"You know I'm a gentleman."

He scoffs. "That's not what Grady has been going around saying after your little alley talk."

I flinch hearing that bastard's name. "He deserved that and more."

"I hear ya."

———

DALLAS WAS right about Stella helping Maven.

Maven has spent the evening showing Stella her bedroom and doll collection. They then watched TV until Maven crashed out on the couch, and Dallas carried his daughter to her bed.

"Everything good?" I ask Stella, guiding her down the stairs that leads to the basement.

She sighs. "Yes, I just hate how bad I am with people who are sad. I feel shy around your family, like an outsider, and I don't want them to think I'm bitchy."

"Don't think like that. It takes a lot for my family not to like someone, let alone call them bitchy. They appreciate everything you've done for our family and have liked you since before you even got here."

"Your mom asked me to help bake for the reception. I've never baked anything in my life and will definitely be the joke of the town when she tells people I don't know the difference between flour and sugar. They'll tell you to kick me to the curb."

I grab her waist and pull her to me. "My ex couldn't cook for shit. As long as you make me happy, and *definitely* as long as you keep riding my dick like you do, I could give two fucks if you know how to bake a pie. You don't have to be anyone else to get the approval of me or my family."

"What about your sister? She's not my biggest fan."

It looks like I wasn't the only one to notice Lauren's apprehension toward Stella. I make a note to talk to her.

"Lauren means well. She just doesn't want to see me get hurt again."

"I won't hurt you," she whispers. "So please do the same for me."

I grab her chin with the tip of my finger and drag it up. "Stella, I have no idea what the fuck is going on between us, or where it will go, but I'll do everything in my power never to hurt you."

TWENTY-NINE

LUCY'S WAKE IS TODAY.

I've never been to one before and wasn't sure what to expect when I got dressed this morning. I want to make a good impression on Hudson's family in case they ever find out about us.

We're at the funeral home, and I'm standing next to Hudson while receiving every odd look known to man. Nosy stares. Dirty looks. Friendly smiles.

I introduce myself as Dallas's friend, and a few parents have scolded their children for asking for my autograph. I don't mind it. The only times I have is when they do it to sell it online and make a profit.

Dallas and Maven have sat next to Lucy's casket all day, and my heart breaks for them. You can see the love he had for his wife everywhere on him.

"Heads-up," Hudson says. "My ex just arrived."

He tilts his head toward a blonde walking in with a cute guy.

"The cheating ex?" I ask.

It's a stupid question since he's only had one ex, but her showing up takes me by surprise.

"Yep," he clips out.

"And the best friend?"

"That would be him."

I wish jealousy wasn't creeping through me like a bad drug as I study her. She's pretty, in shape, and I'm sure doesn't have an unhealthy relationship with carbs like I do. Cameron has the all-American girl look complete with the blond hair, large bust, and tan, toned legs.

I should walk over and thank her, maybe slip her a hundred, for letting Hudson go. If she didn't cheat on him, he wouldn't be with me. She would be the one receiving the attention I'm growing addicted to. I force myself to move my focus from her to the dickhead friend. Dude is attractive with blond hair, decent-size muscles, and a cute smile, but he's no Hudson.

"FYI, you're so much hotter than him," I whisper, looping my arm through Hudson's. "Talk about a downgrade."

He peeks down at our connection. "Appreciate it, Hollywood."

We've never touched like this in public. He waited until everyone was asleep before getting in bed with me last night.

I wait to see if he pulls away and smile when he doesn't. Hudson has no problem showing ownership with me. I'm the one who's scared … and stopping it because of my Eli situation.

"You don't think she's going to come over here, do you?" I ask.

"Doubt it. The last time she and Grady came around me, my hand ended up around his neck."

"Yeah, let's hope they stick to their side," I mutter.

———

I'M WASHING my hands when I hear the bathroom door slam shut after Hudson's ex walks in.

"Stella, right?" she asks.

She smiles and waves. It's not a genuine smile, more along the lines of one that says she wants to kill me and hide me in these cornfields kind of smile.

It won't make a good impression on Hudson's family and the

good people of Blue Beech if I have a girl fight in the bathroom at a funeral.

I grab a paper towel and dry my hands. "It is."

"Everyone keeps saying how nice it was for you to come all this way for Dallas. I mean, you were only his employer. Are you this nice to everyone who works for you?" She blows out a breath. "Must be exhausting."

Really? This is the route she's going?

"Dallas was my bodyguard for years, and I got to know him and his family, so yes, I care about the people who work for me."

She straightens her stance, and her glossy lips slip into a hard line. "How do you and Hudson know each other?"

Chick is trying to trap me.

Like me, she's wearing a dress and heels, so if she does try to fight me, I might have a chance. I've managed to master living in heels. I can squat in these bad boys, run from men with cameras, and I've even boxed in them a few times for a commercial. I'll be able to hold my own on this one.

Hopefully.

"Hudson is working for me now," I answer, giving her a satisfied smile. "He took Dallas's job."

Yep, he's with me every night.

"How kind of him." She lets out a bitter laugh and moves away from the door. "You want to know something hilarious? Hudson used to give Dallas so much shit for working for you and constantly told him to quit. I recall him calling you a spoiled diva once, but he's a good brother, so I'm sure he'll do the job until he comes home. You do know he will always come home, right?"

Her words make me light-headed, and I'm thankful she's no longer blocking the door.

Who starts shit at a funeral?

I shrug. "I guess he changed his mind. He seems to be pretty good at it. Maybe it's his calling."

She scowls. "Doubt it."

I give her a forced smile, turn around, and leave the room.

———

"CAN I SHOW YOU AROUND TOWN?" Hudson asks when we walk out of the funeral home. His hand goes to my back as he guides me down the sidewalk. "We can grab a cupcake from Magnolia's Bakery or a sandwich at the diner?"

I look around. "Are you sure that's a good idea, given all the curious eyes?"

"They'll think I'm being a gentleman and keeping you company."

"What about Dallas?"

"He and Maven are meeting with the pastor. Dallas is unsure of the best approach to explain everything to Maven. She knows her mom is gone, but he wants to make sure she knows Lucy is in heaven."

"Poor thing. I can't even imagine what she's going through right now."

"Maven is strong like her mother."

There's a pause of silence.

It's broken when he claps his hands. "So ... how about that cupcake?"

I smile. "Only if you help me work off the calories later."

"You fucking know it."

People stop us to hug Hudson and welcome him home when we walk down a sidewalk lined with beautiful flowers. They express their sympathy for his loss and then introduce themselves to me. They're all friendly. Blue Beech is nothing like LA.

Hudson points out all the landmarks and the spots where he and his friends caused the most trouble. He tells me about his bright idea to toilet paper the gazebo for their senior prank that resulted in him being busted. His punishment was giving manicures at the local nursing home. We end our tour by stopping at a shop with a bright yellow door.

A bell rings when we walk in, and the small space is crowded with tables. It smells like heaven and calories. You walk in and know you'll be leaving the place ten pounds heavier.

"Holy shit," I say as we make our way toward the glass counter filled with cupcakes galore. "I want one of everything."

Hudson laughs. "I can make that happen."

A middle-aged woman wearing a bright pink floral apron with streaks of icing on it grins from behind the counter. "I knew you couldn't come home and resist one of my red velvet cupcakes. Now, honey, I know you've been hearing condolences all day, so I'm going to let my sweets do the talking for me." She turns around and grabs a large box of cupcakes. "I planned on dropping these off at your brother's after I close, but I might as well give them to you while you're here. Give these to Dallas and that angel of his. I don't mind if you snag a few for yourself."

Hudson takes the box from her with a smile. "Will do, Maggie. Appreciate it. You know how much Maven loves your shop."

Maggie looks over at me. "And what can I get you, sweetie?"

There are so many options.

I wasn't hungry ten minutes ago, but my stomach suddenly growls.

"What do you suggest?"

She points at Hudson. "The Barnes men seem to have a weakness for my red velvet, but I have a new strawberry cupcake that's been quite the hit lately."

"Strawberry it is then."

Hudson pays for our cupcakes, and we sit at a table next to the window.

"Why is everyone so nice around here?" I whisper.

He chuckles, looking proud. "It's Blue Beech. We have each other's backs, know what kind of cupcakes our friends like when they're having a bad day, and are always up for giving a helping hand."

"It's so different than what I'm used to."

"You grew up in LA, right?"

I nod. "My mom knew she wanted me to be famous before I left her womb, and where else but California can that be accomplished?"

"California is all you know. Blue Beech is all I know. You become familiar and comfortable with your surroundings."

"I wish I'd grown up in a place like this."

He winks. "We accept newcomers of all ages if you ever want to make a life change. It's a good place to raise a family."

His response is my cue to dig into my cupcake. Maggie was right. The strawberry is to die for.

"It's where you want to raise your family, isn't it?" I ask, licking frosting from my thumb.

"Wouldn't want to be anywhere else. You want to raise yours in LA?"

"I never really thought about having kids."

"You don't want to be a mother?"

I shrug. "I'm not sure I'd know how to be one." I lower my voice. "I'm scared I'll be a terrible one."

He looks shocked at my admission. "Why would you think that?"

"I never had a good example."

"So? Trust me, when that day comes, you'll have that maternal instinct. I know it. You will be one incredible mom, Stella."

"Let's hope so."

I realized my mother wanted me only as an opportunity years ago. I saw the way Knox's mom used him for money. The same thing happened to countless friends of mine in the business. Our parents don't care. Some, like my mom, saw us as meal tickets, and others threw money at their kids as an excuse to get out of parenting.

He reaches over and brushes his thumb over my lip to wipe away the frosting. "Goddamn, I wish I could've used my tongue to clean that off instead."

THIRTY

Hudson

DALLAS LEANS BACK in his chair and rests his arms behind his neck. "When were you going to tell me you're sleeping with Stella?"

We're back at his place, and our family left an hour ago. Maven is spending the night with my parents. Stella is in the shower. And we're in the kitchen reminiscing about the good times we had with Lucy over beers.

I take a long drink before answering, "I have no idea what you're talking about."

"Don't bullshit me. I'm a grieving man. I deserve the truth. You took her around town—"

"That means I'm fucking her?" I interrupt.

"No, but the way you look at each other does. For fuck's sake, you brought her home with you, she has you doing yoga, and who knows what else. You're fucking her."

I rub my temples. "You have too much shit going on right now to worry about my sex life. Hell, I'm more worried about you being okay than my sex life. My concern right now is you, how you're doing, and what I can do to help you through this. We can talk about who I'm sticking my dick into another time."

Preferably never.

Kissing, or fucking, and telling isn't my thing. I lost my virginity before all my friends. Hell, before Dallas, but no one knew because I don't have a big-ass mouth. I would listen to the guys in the locker room bragging about getting to third base when I was hitting home runs. I've never felt the need to brag and never wanted to disrespect Cameron.

"Appreciate it, brother, but I feel like all I've done today is talk about my feelings and thank people for their condolences. I don't want fucking condolences. I don't want pity. I don't want fucking cupcakes. I just want my wife back." He looks up at the ceiling, shaking his head, and tries to hide the tears I know are impending. "She was perfect. The best wife a man could ask for. An amazing mother, beautiful, caring. Why? Why, Hudson? Why did God have to take her away from me? Why? I needed her! I loved her!"

I rub my eyes to stop my tears. I wish I was better with words, but I'll give it a shot. "I know you loved Lucy, and she loved you. You had a love stronger than anything I've ever seen. She had love before she passed. Her heart was full because you gave her a great life. She was happy and knew you'd be a great dad to Maven." My heart slams against my chest. "I'm glad we're talking about this. Everyone has been afraid of you holding it in."

He scoffs. "Who are you now? Counselor Hudson?"

"You can't always be the strong one." I pull myself up from my chair and grab us another round of beers before handing him one. "More to take the edge off."

He draws in a deep breath and uses the back of his hand to wipe his eyes. "Thanks, man." He takes a drink and sighs. "You and Stella, huh?"

I rub my hands down my pants. "You pissed about it?"

"No, more along the lines of surprised."

I raise a brow. "Surprised she would mess around with someone like me?"

"Fuck no. I'm surprised you opened up your mind to see her for who she really is." He tips his beer toward me. "I told you it was a good idea to go there. You owe me."

"Yeah, yeah, I'll do a load of your laundry or some shit."

"You still quitting when they find someone else to take the job?"

I run a hand through my hair. Stella and I haven't had this conversation yet, but I know I don't want to stay in California. "That's my plan."

"What are you doing then?" His voice turns harsh. "You're just going to leave her? Why are you leading her on if you're not staying?"

"We're *fucking,* Dallas. Having fun. Not getting married. She's not going to give up her life. I'm not giving up mine."

His eyes harden. "You've had that talk then? You've explained that under no circumstances are you staying there?"

"Kind of."

I've told her I'd never leave Blue Beech. Isn't that enough?

"Fucking liar."

———

I GO DOWN to the basement in search of Stella when Dallas goes to bed.

I find her standing in front of the bathroom vanity looking in the mirror with her back to me. She's running her hands through her wet hair. I sneak up behind her, circle my arms around her hips, and slowly dust kisses along her neck. She tilts her head to the side, and I take that as an invitation for more.

I'm wrong.

My hands fall to my sides when she pulls away and leaves the bathroom.

"What's wrong?" I ask, following her into the bedroom.

She starts looking through her suitcase. "Nothing." She picks up a shirt, then drops it.

"Don't bullshit me, Stella. If I did something to piss you off, tell me so I can fix it."

I don't do the whole beating around the bush shit, and I think Stella had a habit of doing that in her last relationship. I want us to be up-front, open, and personal.

I grab her hand and turn her around to face me, and her attention goes to the floor.

"This isn't the right place to have this conversation, Hudson."

I get that. She wants to be respectful and not argue in Dallas's home. I respect her for respecting him.

I tug on her hand and start walking toward the stairs. "Come on, then."

"What?"

"We're going for a drive."

"Now?"

I nod. "My truck is here. I'll even buy you an ice cream cone if we make it to the shop in time."

A tiny smile breaks through her lips. "Jesus, you and your sweets. If I stay here any longer, my ass will get even bigger."

"I like that."

———

I KILL the engine to my truck when we make it to our destination— Blue Beech Edge River. It's my favorite spot in town to come and think. It's also the choice spot for horny teenagers who have nowhere else to go to get laid.

I flip on the overhead light and look at her. "Tell me what I did."

She sighs, waving her hand through the air, and a light blush passes over her cheeks. This isn't a conversation she's ready to have. "You know what? It's not even that important. Let's get that ice cream, and we'll talk about it another time."

She's shutting down on me.

"It is fucking important if you're upset about it. Tell me if I did something wrong, so I won't do it again."

"I overheard your conversation with Dallas," she whispers.

I pause and go through what we talked about in the kitchen, but I'm drawing a blank on what could've offended her. "And you're pissed at me why?"

Her gaze drops down to her lap before she starts to answer, but I interrupt her.

"We're not talking about shit until you look at me. Don't hide. Tell me how to fix this. If I did something stupid, don't let me get away with it."

She glances up at me, and my stomach twists when I see the sadness in her eyes.

"You told him we're pretty much fuck buddies and you're bailing as soon as your time is up." She shakes her head, and her voice breaks. "What are we doing, Hudson? Am I only a good time to you? Some rebound to mend your broken heart?"

Fuck.

This is all my fault.

I slap the steering wheel. "No, Stella. You aren't a rebound or a fling that doesn't mean anything to me. Am I confused? Hell yes. You know I don't like to share, and if you say the word, I'll make you mine right now. If you say you're mine, we'll figure out a plan to make it work with us. Until then, I'm sorry, but I can't plan a future with a woman who won't even claim me. That's why I fought this in the beginning because I was scared of this happening."

"So am I!" she screams. "I never expected to fall for you like this. I'm scared your feelings aren't as strong as mine and terrified of dropping my career and risking everything only for you to walk away from me. You recently got out of a long-term relationship that lasted over a decade. How can I be certain I'm not a rebound … a fuck buddy …"

"I have the same uncertainties, Hollywood. We've had long-term relationships that failed and are scared of getting our hearts shattered again. I won't deny I'm afraid, but that also doesn't mean I'm against falling in love again." I make sure we have good eye contact before continuing. "In fact, I know I'm not." I press my hand to my chest over my heart. "I can already feel you inside me, repairing the parts Cameron broke, and I'm afraid you'll do even more damage."

I'm shocked at my honesty. I don't open up. I'm not an emotional dude.

She swipes a tear from her cheek. "I'm so afraid of getting hurt. I told myself I was anti-relationship because the heartache, the loss, it's just too much for me."

"Looks like we're just two complicated souls looking for love."

She keeps crying.

"Come here, Hollywood." I grab her arm to drag her onto my lap and start brushing away the tears until there's none left. "I don't want to make you cry. I told you, I'll do everything in my power never to hurt you, but I want the same from you. Take this step with me. Go all in. Stop pretending to be with another man."

She shivers, her body shaking, when I run my hands down her arms.

"I want you to be mine. It killed me yesterday when I couldn't hold your hand—couldn't touch you in fear of what your consequences would be. Goddamn, you have no idea how hard that's killing me. I'm over here falling for a woman I can't claim."

She's breathing heavily while staring down at me with dilated pupils and starts trembling in my arms.

"I want that too," she whispers.

"Promise me you'll do something about it … that you'll do whatever it takes to be mine. Tell me you're ready to be all in."

She nods repeatedly. "I promise. All in."

I can feel her heart beating as she presses her chest into me and rests her lips on mine.

"Now claim me, Hudson Barnes."

THIRTY-ONE

Stella

I ASKED him to claim me.

That's what he does.

His hand curls around the back of my head, and I waste no time devouring his mouth. This is the most intimate kiss we've shared. Something about confessing our feelings and telling each other we don't want to walk away seems to have made everything so much hotter.

Every touch more exciting.

I tilt my head to the side, exposing my bare neck and silently pleading for more of anything he's willing to give.

Touch me. Kiss me. Love me.

I shiver when his lips hit my neck, sucking hard on my sensitive skin, and I know I'm going to be covering up the evidence of his mouth there with makeup tomorrow.

He's so addictive.

"Say you're mine," he gasps. "All fucking mine."

"I'm yours," I moan. "Only yours."

The space is small, but I manage to get his pants down far enough to pull his cock free. I scoot back to get a good grip and slowly stroke him. He pushes my dress up past my breasts, massaging them and pinching a nipple that nearly sends me over the edge, and swipes my panties to the side before slowly lowering me onto him. The rough texture of the steering wheel bites into my back when I grind down on his lap and take in his length.

I lose control as soon as I start riding him, giving him my all, and he grabs my hips, slamming me into him with more power.

The sound of our heavy breathing and skin slapping takes over the silent cab. The aroma of our sex fills up the small space.

I've made up my mind by the time my orgasm shakes through me.

I'm willing to take the risk.

I'm ready to make Hudson Barnes mine.

I just have to figure out how.

———

I STRETCH my arms out against the crisp sheets and feel the emptiness in the spot next to me.

I decided to stay behind for Lucy's funeral today. It's too intimate for an outsider and would make people curious. I've been followed for the past decade and had friends sell stories on me to make a quick buck, so I'm not the most trusting person. Trust isn't just given. It has to be earned.

I stretch my arm out to grab my phone from the nightstand, and there's a Post-it note stuck to the screen.

Coffee maker is on.

All the necessary ingredients to make it your own are in the kitchen.

Call or text if you need anything.

Later, you're mine.

Hudson

He must have gone to the grocery store early this morning while I was sleeping and got coconut milk because I don't recall seeing any yesterday. He has to be exhausted. We went for round two when we got back last night, and I couldn't feel my legs by the time he rolled off me, took me in his arms, and we fell asleep. He didn't have one nightmare.

I get out of my bed to brush my teeth and head upstairs to the kitchen in search of the coffee maker.

It's on.

Thank God.

It's embarrassing, but I have no idea how to make coffee. I give myself a mental note to watch a YouTube video on it. You can learn how to do anything on the internet—cook, clean, steal cars, make coffee. Ah, modern technology.

I'm about to start my coffee-making research when a close-up of Willow's face pops up on my phone screen. My stomach tenses for some reason. I'm scared it's bad news, and bad news before your first cup of coffee is the worst way to start the day. I'm not ready to adult or have conversations until at least my second.

Please be a checkup call or an update on a new audition.

Not something that's going to turn my life upside down, or Tillie's reaction to my mini-vacation with another man.

I put the call on speaker. "Hello?"

"What the hell is wrong with you?" she yells on the other line. "Are you trying to commit career suicide, you lunatic?"

"Huh?" is the only response I can muster out while I run through the possible scenarios of what she could be mad about.

"Everyone and their mama are calling you a cheater right now. It's everywhere. Someone sold a video of you dry humping *or possibly fucking* Hudson, you can't really tell from the angle, in the front seat of a pickup truck. The internet is blowing up!"

Fuck me. Fuck me. This is the end of my career.

My throat tightens, my stomach revolts, and fear snakes through me. I never thought news would travel like that here, or that someone would follow us in order to sell a story. Hell, I thought we were in the boondocks of fucking nowhere.

"Tell me you're joking," I stutter out, my throat tightening as tears build at my eyes. "Tell me this is some prank you're playing on me."

"Tough shit, Stella. It's not a joke. It's code red. Code fucking red."

"Who … who could've done this?"

"I'm assuming paparazzi got word that you took a flight there and decided to meander to good ole Iowa to see if they could stalk you and find a story."

The tears start to fall. I was too careless, acting too free, and not thinking about the damage that kissing Hudson would do to my career.

"What do I do, Willow?"

I cringe when I see a call beeping in from Tillie. I hit ignore. The witch is going to have to wait to rip my head off.

"You need to come clean. Tell the truth about Eli."

"Do you know the damage that'll do to my reputation?"

"Uh, probably nothing near as bad as looking like an unfaithful tramp."

"I have to talk to Eli … to Hudson … before I do anything."

"Do that and get back with me ASAP. I need to put out a statement before this snowballs. In the meantime, quit being so damn dumb."

"You're the one who told me to start banging Hudson!"

"Really? I also told you to bang Justin Timberlake when he was single, but did you try to jump on that shit? I'm all for you being happy, girlfriend, and this little selling your soul deal isn't making you happy. The problem now is saving your ass. They can sue you. It's breach of contract." She pauses. "There's more."

As if this day couldn't get any fucking worse.

"What now?" I burst out.

"Spencer Marcum is also making headlines."

"I should care why?"

"Not only are the headlines blazing with pictures of you and Hudson but they're also talking about you and Spencer. He did an interview with Howard Stern and said you cheated on Knox with him."

My head starts spinning, and my heart drops to my stomach. I'm going to lose the two most important things in my life in one day.

My career and Hudson. I run to the bathroom and start to dry heave, but nothing comes out.

"I'm going to lose him," I whisper when I gain control of myself, tears blinding me.

"What?" she asks.

"Hudson. I'm going to lose him. He'll hate me when he finds out I cheated on Knox."

"Why? It was before him."

"He hates cheaters, despises them, and thinks once a cheater, always a cheater."

"Explain the situation. He'll understand." Her voice is tight. She's pissed at me but still has my back.

"He won't," I sob. "He won't understand."

Hudson

FUNERALS.

I hate them.

And I fucking hate the fact that I've gone to my fair share of them. They never get easier. What makes them even worse is when they're for someone who was taken too soon.

When someone dies at ninety-five, people go on about their victory of making it so far.

She almost made it a century. She was badass. What was her secret?

When someone dies at thirty, it's a tragedy.

The only question is why.

Why were they taken away so soon? Why couldn't we have them longer?

The world is not fucking fair. Death isn't fucking fair. The grim reaper always seems to come for the good ones—the ones with hearts of gold who are supposed to stay with us until their skin wrinkles, until they get dentures, until they get the chance to spoil their grandchildren.

Sadness gnaws at me stronger with every passing tear. I peek over at Dallas sitting a few seats down from me with Maven settled on his lap. His arms are enveloped around her like a shield, and they stare at the purple casket topped with flowers and lined with gold trim, both of their eyes swollen. He's still fighting to hold it together for Maven and to be a strong father. I think back to what Lauren said. She was right. It's all an act.

This is a reminder that I need to grab life by the balls and take advantage of every day I'm given. Every single fucking second of my life needs to matter because I don't know how many more I'll get. I can't keep burying parts of me away from Stella in fear of the future because hell, who knows how long mine will be.

Dallas takes Maven up with him when he gives the eulogy. He squeezes her hand, and the words slip from his mouth slowly. He's composing himself the best he can while reminding us what a good woman Lucy was. Even though none of us need reminded.

My mother is crying next to me. She's lost a daughter. Her son lost a wife. Her granddaughter is now motherless. Every person in this room is losing a sliver of their heart today.

I wish Stella was here, but I understand her reasoning. I tip my head down as tears fall from my cheeks while silently asking God not to take anyone else from me.

———

I THROW my arm around Dallas's shoulders as people clear out of the funeral home. "I'm here for you, brother. You and Maven, whatever you need, you let me know."

He wipes his dark eyes. "Lucy's death has forced me to give up on having any certainty in this life except for one—that I can rely on my family every minute of every day, no matter what. All of you are the only reason I'm standing today and not breaking down in front of my daughter. I'll never be able to thank you guys enough. And what you did, taking that job so I could spend Lucy's last few weeks by her side, I'll never be able to repay you for that."

I squeeze his shoulder. "Family doesn't ever need to repay family for helping them. We'll always be here, come hell or high water … or Hollywood."

I get a small chuckle from him.

"I'll be at your side every step of the way. You can count on that."

I don't know where we'll go from here, but I can't hang out with Stella in clubs when my family is broken thousands of miles away.

I have a decision to make.

And it won't be an easy one.

———

I'M THE SUGAR-RUNNER.

Not only does my mother love to bake, she loves to emotional bake. If she's having a bad day, she's in the kitchen making something. It's her happy place.

The reception is being held at my parents', and I know it will smell like the Pillsbury Doughboy's ass crack when I get there. The kitchen was already loaded with pies, cakes, and cookies this morning. No doubt there will be more.

My mom left the funeral home as soon as the service ended without making small talk or thanking people for coming like we did. She wanted everything in order so Dallas wouldn't stress about it. She stopped to pick up Stella before going home, and I'm meeting them at her house.

Thinking back to the conversation I had with Stella last night brings a smile to my face. She's going to end that bullshit agreement with Eli. We'll figure out a way to make our relationship work.

I toss every item on my mom's list into the shopping cart and head to the only open checkout lane. People stop me on my way to express their condolences. Everyone loved Lucy. She didn't have a bad bone in her body. She was a pharmacy tech at our local drug store and always went out of her way to help people. She even dropped prescriptions off at people's houses if they were too sick to pick them up. Everyone is going to miss her.

Mrs. Pipes shoots me a friendly wave while the cashier finishes helping her, and I begin loading my groceries on the belt. When I finish, I grab my phone to check for missed calls, and something catches my eye before I turn the screen on.

The air grows thin.

My vision grows blurry, and I feel like I've been punched in the stomach.

Stella has graced tabloid covers for as long as I can remember. I never paid attention before—only briefly noticing her name because my brother worked for her.

Until now.

My muscles painfully tick underneath my skin as I read the headline again, just in case my mind is fucking with me. I blink, giving myself one more opportunity to act like I didn't read it correctly. I lose again and clench my jaw while taking in the words written above a photo of Stella kissing me while straddling my lap in my pickup.

Stella Mendes busted cheating on Eli with bodyguard! It's not the first time it's happened! See her many scandals with other men, including actor Spencer Marcum!

What fucking creep spied on us to take this picture?

This headline has to be bullshit, right?

They need catchy yet false headlines to make sales.

My fingers twitch with desperation to pick up the magazine and buy it, but word will be all over town if someone catches me. I snatch it from the holder and flip through the pages until I find the story about Stella ... and me. I take pictures of each page with my phone and put the magazine back as soon as Mrs. Pipes wheels away her cart.

"I take it your mother is on a baking spree?" Jojo asks when she starts to ring me up.

I graduated with her, and her dad owns the grocery store. She's also one of Cameron's friends.

I force a smile. "How could you tell?"

"Poor Dallas. If you guys need anything else, call me and I'll drop it off after my shift, okay? It's no hassle."

"I'll let her know. Thanks."

I pay, grab the bags, and am about to walk out when Jojo stops me.

"Hudson, I want you to know I had no idea what was going on with Cameron and Grady."

I shrug. "It happened. I'm over it."

I could give two shits about Cameron right now. All that's on my mind is Stella.

I throw the groceries in the passenger seat and pull my phone from my pocket as soon as I slam the door shut. I can't believe I'm reading tabloid stories about my girlfriend ... or the girl I'm screwing ... because I'm not sure what she is to me. I *really* can't believe they have pictures of me in there.

Damn, how my life has changed.

I don't like it one fucking bit.

Don't like my business out there like this.

I sit in my truck for a good fifteen minutes reading the article about us having some sordid affair behind Eli's back. That's not the worst part. There are also claims that our affair isn't the first one she's had.

Spencer Marcum, another actor, let it slip that he slept with her when she was with Knox. He has the texts to prove it, and they're posted on the next page.

She asked him not to say anything to Knox or anyone else and said it could never happen again. She texted him again a week later with a heads-up that she told Knox out of guilt, and Knox said he better not see him around.

Who was this woman? It's not my Stella.

I shake my head, gritting my teeth. I've fallen for another liar. Another fraud. *Another cheater.*

I close out of the pictures and open my browser to search for other stories about her and Spencer online. There are pages of them dating back to over a year ago. It's been a while since their supposed hookup happened, but I hate the fact that she never told me about this after knowing how I despise cheaters.

She's just like Cameron.

I can't have my heart broken again by someone who doesn't cherish commitment.

Me: What do you know about Stella and Spencer Marcum?

I'm an asshole for even bringing this up to him today.

Dallas: Not my story to tell, man.

I want to tell him it is because he's my brother, but the last thing he needs to worry about is my relationship problems. He would've told me if it wasn't true, and he didn't.

Not my story to tell means it happened, but he doesn't know all the details, or doesn't care to share Stella's business.

THIRTY-THREE

Stella

"IF YOU'LL SET the timer on the oven for fifteen minutes, we can start on the next batch," Rory instructs while handing me the pan of unbaked cookies we made from scratch.

She also showed me how to make a cherry pie and chocolate chip cookies.

All in a two-hour span.

I haven't baked this much in my entire life.

She left the funeral early and stopped to ask if I'd like to help her get everything prepared for the reception. Even though I'm a nervous wreck on the verge of losing everything I love and have been dodging every phone call coming through for the past few hours, I couldn't say no to her. So here I am, baking cookies while on the edge of falling into a full panic attack at the thought of Hudson leaving me. I'm playing Betty Crocker while my career is going up in flames.

Just wonderful.

Hudson doesn't read the tabloids, so there's a chance he might not find out that not only is my career going down the drain but his name is also being dragged into the gutter with it. It's wrong for me to even consider hiding this from him, but I'm not sure what else to do.

Rory is helping take my mind off my problems while she tells me story after story of how she and John fell in love in high school and raised their children in this house. They've been married for over thirty years, yet it seems like they're still in the honeymoon phase.

I want a love like that someday.

I slide the tray into the oven, shut the door, and turn back around at the sound of the back door that leads into the kitchen opening. I can't help but smile at the sight of Hudson walking in with an armful of overflowing grocery bags. My smile drops when I see the look on his face.

He knows.

"Let me help you with those," I rush out, a pain in the back of my throat.

"I've got it," he mutters, setting them on the counter. He kisses Rory on the cheek and then looks over at me. "Can I talk to you for a minute?"

I scrape my hands together and nod. "Sure."

"Don't take too long now," Rory says. "Your father called to tell me people are on their way over. I need all the help I can get."

He tilts his head toward the basement stairs, and I lead the way, gulping with every step.

"What's up?" I ask, turning to look at him.

He pulls his phone out to show me the screen. "Care to explain this?"

I draw in a nervous breath as I read the headline in the photo.

I'm terrified. I'm nervous. I don't want this to be real life.

It's a story about me. About me being a cheater, a liar, everything Hudson hates. It's the same story Willow called me about this morning.

I'm. So. Fucked.

It's worse than I thought.

My hands start shaking. "It ..." I pause, scrambling for the right words.

I push myself to fight back the tears. I want to yell that the person in that article isn't me anymore, but I can hear the footsteps upstairs.

People are here.

I take a deep breath. "It happened *one time,* once, with Spencer, and that was before you. It was forever ago. You can't get mad at me for something I did in the past."

He jerks the phone away and slides it back into his pocket in what seems like slow motion.

"I'm not mad that you had sex with him," he replies calmly.

"Yes, you are." I try to match his cool demeanor, but it's difficult.

He's holding himself back. He doesn't want to lose his shit where other people can hear him.

He rubs a palm over his forehead. "You're right. Maybe I am judging you, but it's not because you had a sex life before me. I'm pissed that you had sex with him when you were still with Knox. *You cheated.* You know how I feel about that shit."

I suck my cheeks in. "I … I didn't think it was necessary to tell you about my past screwups."

"You sat there and made me believe you weren't happy with him and that he wasn't a good boyfriend. Not once did you say you weren't a good girlfriend. Not once did you say you cheated on him. Fuck, you even agreed with me that cheaters are terrible people. Meanwhile, you knew you were guilty of the flaw I hate most in people."

I technically never *agreed* with him. Silence isn't agreeing with someone, but I let that go.

"I was lonely and confused," I whisper. "He was never around."

He shakes his head in agony, his eyes cutting down to me. "Jesus Christ, you sound exactly like Cameron."

I wince at his insult. "I'm nothing like her. I would *never* do something like that to you."

"You did it to a man you dated for *years.* A man you were in love with. Why should I think I'd be any different?" He gestures back and forth between the two of us in frustration. "This was all one big mistake."

Tears shimmer in my eyes. "What do you mean?"

"You and me. Why are we wasting our time with something we know isn't going to last?"

I throw my arms up in defeat. "You've barely even given us a chance!"

"Look at the big picture, Stella. We come from two different worlds. Do you plan to move here to be with me? Can you keep your career living here?"

"Well … no."

"Exactly! And your Hollywood life isn't for me! This is my home, where I belong, and California is yours."

"Long-distance relationships can work. I did it with Knox for years."

He scoffs. "News flash, Stella, it didn't work. You cheated, and you guys broke up! That's the worst possible answer you could've given me."

"Fine, I'm a screwup! Is that what you want to hear? That I did something you think so terrible of? It was years ago. I was young, dumb, and lonely."

He runs his hands through his hair in frustration. "You're right, and I understand people make mistakes."

"Thank you." I go to grab his hand, but he recoils at my touch. I should've known it wasn't going to be that easy. "I promise you I will never do anything like that to you. You and me, we're different than how it was with Knox."

"You can't guarantee that," he rasps.

"Yes, I can."

His upper lip curls. "You're doing it to me right now by lying about dating another man. The world thinks I'm screwing you behind his back. We're in a relationship where we can only touch each other behind closed doors. People think you belong to someone else." He grits his teeth. "When you're supposed to be mine. We agreed to go all in, Stella. Now's the fucking time."

"Just give me more time," I plead, my heart racing. "Give me a few weeks."

I promised him that I would end things with Eli, but I can't just do it right now. These things take time. I need to meet with my attorney to look for possible loopholes in the contract and talk to my management company to get them on board. This decision will have consequences.

He flinches. "Does that mean you're going to continue playing pretend with him? You're going to stand there and tell me that you're willing to throw me under the bus and not tell the truth?" He looks at me in disgust. "Unbelievable."

"It's my job, Hudson. What do you expect?"

"What do I expect? Maybe for the girl I'm falling in love with to come clean. To tell them I'm not this terrible man fucking someone else's girl. I expect you not to be ashamed that you're with me."

"Shame? It's not shame. If there's anyone I want to tell the world I'm in love with, it's you!"

Love.

We've both thrown out the word in the past five minutes. You're usually in a good place when you say that to someone for the first time. It ends with kisses, sex, and good feelings.

This is anything but magical. It's a goddamn nightmare. I have no time to relish this moment of him confessing his love because the sadness that he's about to leave me overcomes that.

"Then prove it!" We both flinch at how loud his voice rises, and he controls his breathing before going on, his tone turning soft. "Have Willow put out a statement." He begins to pace in front of me. "This isn't only about us anymore. It'll destroy my family. It'll kill my mother. We're already having a tough time with Lucy's death."

I shut my eyes in embarrassment. I'm selfish. I never even thought about his family. "I'm sorry. I will go up there and tell them the truth about everything."

He stops his pacing and gawks at me. "Just them?"

I look around, unsure of what he's asking me.

"Either you step up and tell everyone the truth, or you need to leave."

His response is like a smack in the face.

"What? You can't … you can't be serious?"

"Two options, Stella. Me or your contract."

"My career is on the line."

"So am I."

I swallow hard. "I can't yet!"

"Then leave. I won't be a man in the shadows." He scrubs his hand over his face, and I notice his eyes are glossy when he pulls it away. "I hate ultimatums and never thought I'd be someone who had to give them to the woman I love, but I have no other choice. You need to make a decision, and there's only one that will keep me."

"*Please*," I whimper. "Give me a few weeks."

He stares at me in disbelief, his eyes cold. "You can stay at Dallas's until Willow finds a bodyguard to fly home with you. Consider this my resignation."

He gives me one last look, one last chance to change my mind, and I do nothing but stare at him with tears in my eyes.

"Have a nice life," he says.

My entire world falls apart at the sight of his back. I stumble to the couch and cry for I don't know how long until I see Lauren tiptoeing downstairs to ask me if I'm ready to go.

I glance around the crowded room for Hudson when I make it upstairs but don't see him. Lauren barely looks at me during the drive to Dallas's and doesn't say a word until she parks in the driveway.

"Look, my brother has been through a lot, and he's a good guy," she says, scowling at me. "If you're not serious about being with him, walk away. Don't hurt someone because you want to have some fun."

I nod and step out of the car at the same time as the tears return.

He begged me for a chance, and I walked away, even after promising him I wouldn't last night. I'm a coward who deserves to be alone, and Hudson deserves someone better than me.

I'm relieved to find Dallas's front door unlocked and the house empty. I left my phone here so it wouldn't go off like wildfire when I was with Rory.

Running downstairs, I start throwing all my shit in my suitcase. I cry as I pick up my phone and notice all the missed calls. I'm going home with a broken heart and a PR nightmare.

When I call for a taxi, I know I'm making the wrong decision.

————

WILLOW MANAGED to snag me a private flight after we argued back and forth over texts for ten minutes about me traveling without a bodyguard. We fought for another ten minutes after that when I demanded she not tell Hudson about it. I'm no longer his problem.

I don't start opening my texts until I'm on the plane with a glass of wine in my hand.

Eli: What the hell? You said if you did anything, you'd keep it under wraps. I look like a goddamn idiot. Thanks a fucking lot.

Tillie: You need to get back to LA and meet me in my office ASAP.

Willow: Call me please. We need to talk about this. I need to know what you want me to do.

I call Willow. She's been trying to call me for the past hour, but I kept sending her to voicemail. I didn't want to break down in the middle of the airport.

"Jesus, Stella," she blurts out upon answering. "What do you want me to tell all of these people blowing up my phone?"

"Tell them to get fucked," I reply.

"*Whoa,* that's something I've never heard you say, but I'm down with that." She pauses. "What's going on with Hudson?"

I gulp. "He gave me the ultimatum of him or fake dating Eli."

"I'm guessing by the sound of your voice you didn't choose him?"

"I asked for time."

"What if things were reversed? Put yourself in his position. What if you had to sit back and watch him prance around with another woman for months?"

I frown at her valid point. "You're making me feel even more like shit."

"Good. It was my intention. Is your career worth losing him?"

"I told you. My career will never leave me." The tears come back for their next appearance. "You and I both know it'd never work out with him living in BFE and me living in LA."

She sighs. "Looks like we're going to be two bitches going through heartbreak together. I'll pick you up from the airport with new onesies, ice cream, and the sappiest romance movies ever made."

I pull my phone away from my face when it beeps to see the caller. It's what I've been doing since Hudson walked away from me. I get my hopes up, and then they fall when I don't see his name.

He's not calling.

I made that choice and severed everything we built.

———

"BREAKUPS BLOW DILDOS," Willow says, handing over the tub of ice cream we've been eating from for the past thirty minutes.

"Tell me about it," I mutter with the spoon in my mouth. "So long, good dick; hello, self-induced orgasms. At least the memories stayed with me. I can still imagine Hudson doing it to me every single time. Is that bad? I have a feeling if I saw a therapist, she'd tell me I'm going down the wrong road in my path of trying to get over him."

She slumps down on the couch. "I agree. Men are assholes. Enough said."

I hold up my spoon. "Hear, hear."

She grabs the ice cream from me. "Although I don't feel *that* sorry for you, considering yours is an easy fix. You can have the man you're in love with at the snap of your fingers ... or the click of a social media post telling the truth." She shakes her head. "That poor guy is being labeled a bad person when he's actually a pretty chill dude."

I snatch the ice cream back from her and take a bite. "Can it before you're cut off," I say, my mouth full.

It's been twenty-four hours since I landed in LA, and Willow has made it her mission to repeatedly tell me it'd be easy for me to get back with Hudson. I guess she doesn't care about possibly being unemployed because that's what will happen if I do that right now.

"Trust me, misery loves company, but I'd much rather see you happy," she rambles. "And that Muscled Marine makes you happy." She snags the bottle of wine from the coffee table and drinks straight from the bottle. "How was the sex, by the way?"

The wine is the next thing I grab while giving her a dirty look. "I'm in depressed, breakup mode. Do you think I want to talk about Hudson's amazing sex skills?"

"I'll tell you about Brett's."

"Couldn't care less," I sing out.

"Two-pump chump is all I have to say."

I drop my spoon. "You're kidding."

"Nope. The guy couldn't use his fingers to save his life either. Half the time, I thought he had paralysis of the hand when he tried."

"Fuck him and his lame fucking self." I hold up the bottle of wine. "And fuck the men who break our hearts."

THIRTY-FOUR

Hudson

MY LAST PAYCHECK was electronically deposited into my bank account.

I'm drinking away almost every penny of it at Down Home Pub.

I've been the depressed drunk guy sitting in the corner of the bar for the past three hours. People have noticed me but steered clear of approaching. I'm sure I look like a maniac right now. Everyone has been walking on eggshells around me. In pity, I'm sure.

Surprisingly, no one has questioned me about the Stella affair. I'm certain by the stares they give me that they've heard about it. I went to every store in town and bought every magazine with my face on it. The last thing I need is my mom seeing them.

"Fancy seeing you here," Cameron says, pulling out the stool next to me and sitting down.

Perfect.

Just the person I didn't want to see.

"What do you want, Cameron?" I ask, snarling.

"Attitude," she mutters, flipping her hair over her shoulder. "You've changed since you started screwing Little Miss Superstar. I never pegged you for a guy who went for someone like that. Doesn't seem your type."

I scowl. "I never pegged you for the type to cheat on me with my best friend. I guess we're surprising each other."

Cameron sighs. "I was lonely and confused. Grady was there as a shoulder to cry on. Things escalated. I never meant for it to happen."

I turn to get a good look at her for the first time in a long time. "If you were lonely and confused, you should've talked to me about it. Not jump into bed with someone else, especially my best fucking friend." I swing out my arm, gesturing to the nearly empty bar. "Speaking of Grady, where is your little fiancé? Don't you need a man at your side at all times?"

She blows out a noisy breath. "I'm still in love with you."

"Nice try." I snort and chug the rest of my drink. I'm going to need another if I have to deal with Cameron's shit. She can beg and plead on her knees, but I'll never take her back.

"I tried with Grady. I really did, but I couldn't fight back my feelings for you. He finally couldn't take it any longer. You're embedded inside my soul, Hudson. *You and only you.* I did something terrible, something unforgivable, but I'm begging you to dig into your heart and remember how much you loved me. How happy we were together."

The bartender hands me a whiskey neat, and I take a drink before telling her how ridiculous she sounds.

"How happy we were together?" My voice rises. "You weren't happy, Cameron. You were so damn unhappy that you ran into another man's arms!"

Tears fall down her cheeks. "Please believe it was a mistake. You have to believe me."

"A mistake? So what? You used him until I was ready to give you the life you wanted? Who cares about mine ... or even Grady's feelings ... just as long as you're getting what you want?"

"It's not like that," she stutters out.

"Yes, it is. You had me, Cameron. You had every single damn piece of me, and you threw it away because you're selfish. Your selfishness cost me my best friend and my trust in love. I will never forgive you for that. I'm sorry, but I can't open myself up to you again. I've realized you're nothing I thought you were. You're not someone I'd ever want to marry."

"But some spoiled television brat is?" she fires back with a sneer. "You know that's not the life you want, and you sure as hell know she's not going to move to Blue Beech and settle down here. Are you going to leave your entire family and move into her mansion while she's making out with other men on TV?" She lets out a childish laugh. "And let's not forget, she cheated on her boyfriend with you. What makes her better than me?"

"You don't know what the fuck you're talking about," I grind out.

"It's all over the internet. You were screwing her behind her little boyfriend's back." She crosses her arms. "What's the difference between her being a cheater and me being one? We did the same thing. Is it different because you weren't the one who got cheated on?"

My stool goes flying backward when I jump up from it. "She was never with him! It was a publicity stunt for their new movie together. They never touched each other behind closed doors. They never shared a bed! *Nothing!* She did all of that with me!" I slam my fist down on the bar. "Me!"

Her tears fall faster as she looks up at me in desperation. "I'm sorry. I didn't know. I thought …"

"Yeah, you spoke before you fucking thought. For someone who's in love with me, you sure don't seem to know me if you'd think I'd do something like that."

"Please," she begs. "Let's go talk somewhere private about this."

I run my hands over my face. "I can't. Sorry. I wish you the best, Cameron, and I hope you find whatever happiness you've been searching for."

THIRTY-FIVE

Stella

"OH FUCK," Willow says, staring at her phone as though she got a notification we're about to be murdered. "Fuckity fuck!"

She and I have spent the week sulking and holding daily *we got our asses dumped* meetings. I won't let her go back to her apartment because I hate being alone.

We go shopping. We do yoga. We try everything to keep our minds off the men we loved and lost.

Some days it works. Some days it doesn't.

The nights are what tears me apart. Thoughts and memories of Hudson haunt me, keeping me up until the morning, and tell me I'm an idiot for not trying to get in touch with him. I haven't even washed my sheets because they smell like him. I'm well aware it's gross.

I haven't called because I'm scared he'll reject me.

He's the one who asked me to leave.

The one who broke things off.

Who didn't want to wait until I could figure out a way to get out of my contract.

But I can't help but feel most of the blame. I was selfish to pursue him when I knew my situation.

"What are you freaking out about over there?" I ask, shoving another bite of ice cream in my mouth while walking on the treadmill.

It's three in the morning, and this is what we're doing.

We're officially losers.

She steps off the bicycle to hold her phone my way and hits the play button. "You're going to want to see this."

A video starts. I trip on my feet, my delicious ice cream falling to the floor, and stare at the screen unblinking when I see Hudson. He's sitting in what looks like a bar arguing with a woman. A woman who looks like Cameron.

"She was never with him!" he screams. "It was a publicity stunt for their new movie together. They never touched each other behind closed doors. They never shared a bed! *Nothing!* She did all of that with me!"

The image is blurry, but there's no doubt it's him. I'll never forget his husky voice. My hand flies to my mouth, and I'm sure that rocky road is about to come up. I jump off the treadmill before I fall and try to control my breathing.

Oh. My. Fucking. God.

Hudson's word vomit just ruined my career in thirty seconds.

"I'm just going to throw this out there," Willow says with a smile. "But I'm pretty sure he's talking about you."

"You think?" I snap.

"I'm also pretty sure the world knows who he's talking about given that it's all over the internet right now." She pulls the phone away, so I can't watch it again. "You're even a trending hashtag."

Fuck me.

I pull my phone from my pocket and open Twitter.

"Seriously?" I yell.

It's #StellaDoesntShareBeds.

"Who comes up with this shit?" I ask.

"It's the internet. A guy banging a McChicken went viral. Your hashtag is lame compared to other ones."

"People have way too much time on their hands."

"Who's the chick in the video?"

"The ex." I hate that she was there with him. That video is going to haunt me for the rest of my life, and I'm going to think about her every time I have to hear about it.

Willow scrunches up her nose. "I wish she were uglier."

"You and me both."

Why was he hanging out in a bar with her?

I know we broke up, and I know I'm still fake dating Eli, but it still hurts.

"He did something you didn't have the balls to do for weeks. Make a public statement and stand up for your relationship."

"He was drunk. If he were sober, it would've never happened."

I slump down on the floor, and she sits down across from me.

"What do I do?" I ask.

My phone starts ringing before I get an answer.

I hold it up to show her the call. "And it gets worse. Tillie is already calling to rip my head off."

"That troll always seems to know everything as soon as it happens. I think she has a tap on our phones. She's like the NSA. Fucking psychopath."

"What do I do?" I repeat.

She perks up and rests her hands in her lap. "First things first. You need to decide if you love the dude or not."

I go silent. I can't seem to form the words to answer her question. They're stuck in my throat as I try to come down from my freak-out. My head is pounding so hard it's making me light-headed.

Am I pissed at Hudson for doing that?

Or more relieved?

I'm not sure.

Willow snaps her fingers in front of my face. "Earth to my best friend. Are you in love with the dude or only missing his sex organ?"

"Do you think I'd be freaking out this much if I wasn't?"

She scoots in closer to give me a hug.

"I'm scared, Willow."

Her face softens when she pulls away. "Scared to love him?"

I nod.

"Sweetie, don't be afraid to love someone. Love is one of the biggest risks we take because we don't know if it's going to thrive or burn to the ground and take us along with it. But the risk is worth the sting. I promise you that."

I start to fan my face with my hand to fight off the tears. "I know."

She rubs her hands together. "So ..."

"I don't want to keep waking up without him."

THIRTY-SIX

Hudson

I WALK INTO MY PARENTS' house with a blasting headache and a hangover from hell. My bright idea of washing my feelings for Stella away with whiskey didn't work out in my favor.

That old pal made me a fucking idiot for the entire world to see. I never wanted to be in the spotlight, never wanted people to know my business, and now I have my phone and email flooded with people offering me money for the inside scoop on Stella's life.

Fucking scavengers.

Dallas sent me the link to the video this morning, and I had to refrain from throwing my phone across the room. My temples throb. I want to put the blame on Stella for this mess. It would've never happened if we didn't start fucking around, but I know the truth. It's unfair for me to blame her for my dumbass getting drunk and opening my big mouth.

"Good morning, idiot," Lauren says when I walk into the kitchen. She narrows her eyes at me in disapproval and slides her plate of half-eaten eggs to the middle of the table. "I saw your obliterated ass on TMZ. Way to keep our family name classy. We were like the Kennedys of Blue Beech, but your behavior has moved us to the lines of the Kardashians. People want to know all of our business, but the respect is gone."

"Don't start your shit," I grumble, making myself a cup of coffee.

I snuck out of Dallas's to avoid his interrogation. Plus, Maven started off her morning living it up with her karaoke machine. Kid's Bop and hangovers don't go well together. And I need to talk to my mom before the mother gang here bombards her on how terrible her son is.

"Oh, I'm just getting started. If you didn't want to hear my mouth, maybe you should've used your pint-sized brain before getting wasted off your ass and bringing attention to our family like this. I swear on everything, if you give Mom a heart attack, I will cut you."

"Chill out. Mom isn't going to have a heart attack. You're overreacting."

She snorts.

"This shit will blow over when the next scandal of a cheating celebrity breaks out. Trust me, I might be popular here, but I'm irrelevant in Hollywood."

"Irrelevant? Is that why we've had several phone calls from reporters? Mom took the phone off the hook and is in the other room reading the Bible so she doesn't have another child breaking people's vows."

"They aren't married. Hell, they aren't even dating."

"Let's add liar to your homewrecker title."

I sit down. "Lauren, I was telling the truth in that video. They were never dating."

"They really were faking a relationship?"

I nod.

"Why the hell would anyone do that?"

"For their career. Publicity. Hype."

She scrunches her face up in disgust. "Sounds like a hooker move to me."

I sigh, remembering the similar conversation I had with Stella about her arrangement.

"You have bad luck in relationships," she goes on. "You might want to change your type or switch teams."

"Says the girl who's also single."

"Hey! My current relationship status is trying to get out of student loan debt and make enough money to survive."

I get up to grab some ibuprofen from the cabinet and fill up a glass of water. "Don't you have a home?"

"Yes, but Mom always makes me breakfast."

"What are you, twelve?" I ask, swallowing down the pills.

"Says the guy crashing in his brother's basement."

I rub the back of my neck to remove some of the tension. Lauren's ass sure as hell isn't helping in the hangover healing. She might be worse than Kid's Bop.

"I have a great idea. How about you eat in silence?" I tell her.

"You've already turned into quite the bossy diva for your short time in Hollywood." She laughs. "You didn't choose the starlet life. The starlet life chose you."

"Enough!" I yell, slamming my glass down, my anger getting the best of me. "Just let it go."

She holds her hands up. "Shit ... sorry. I was only trying to make light of the situation."

"I know. I'm sorry." I collapse in the chair next to her again. "I feel like I'm going nuts, and I don't know what to do. I wish I would've never taken that goddamn job."

"Are you in love with her?"

"With Stella?"

She nods.

"No."

"Don't lie to me."

I stay silent.

"I swear I won't give you shit for it."

I snort.

"I want you to find love, especially after what Cameron did to you. If you think this chick is it for you, then I'm all for you fighting for her. But if it's not, if it was only about sex, walk away. Our family can't go through any more stress right now. Only proceed if your feelings are real."

I scrub my hand over my face and groan. "It doesn't matter anymore."

"Why doesn't it matter if you're in love with her?"

"Our lives are complete opposites. All of that being in magazines and people shoving cameras in your face isn't what I want in my life. I want to stay in Blue Beech. She doesn't."

"Have you even asked her if she does, or are you just assuming?"

"It's over. She made her choice. Now, drop it."

"Hudson …"

I can't handle this conversation right now. I'm growing more nauseated with every second.

"Drop it," I say, my voice stern. "If I don't hear the name Stella again for the rest of my life, I'll be a happy man. I worked for her temporarily. We screwed a few times. It was nothing serious. We were both bored and looking for a good time."

"Keep trying to convince yourself of that, but I know you. You don't do casual sex. You don't screw a girl you don't care about. That's not my brother."

"Maybe it is now."

―――

"YOU LOOK LIKE SHIT," Dallas says when I walk in.

The sucky thing about being close with your siblings is that they're all under the impression they can jump into your business and tell you what to do. It's annoying as fuck even though I know they have my best intentions at heart.

I debated with myself on whether to drink away my sorrows for the second night in a row, but after what happened last night, it'll be a while before I show my face at the pub again.

"Really?" I ask. "Because I feel fucking fantastic."

He slides a beer across the coffee table to me when I collapse onto the couch. If I can't go to the bar, at least I have him here to bartend and get me hammered.

I hold the bottle out in front of me and take a good look at it.

"How come whenever the brain and the heart fight, it's always the liver that suffers?"

"Because it's the easiest one to take our anger out on," Dallas answers, kicking his feet up on the table. "Have you talked to Stella?"

I shake my head.

"She didn't reach out about the video?"

"I wouldn't know even if she did. I turned my phone off to ignore the endless calls. I'm changing my number tomorrow."

"Maybe you should call her."

"She made her choice."

"Did she? Or did you see a stupid magazine headline and push her away because of it? Didn't you give her the ultimatum of you or her career?"

"No, it was *me or Eli.* I'd never force her to give up her career. I only told her I wouldn't be the other man. Don't sit there and act like you wouldn't have done the same thing. Yes, I gave her an ultimatum, which shouldn't be used in relationships, but this situation was different. I'd never force her to do anything she doesn't want to do. She knew they'd rip me apart for that article. She knows how I felt about cheating." I look up at him. "Did you know?"

"About her and Spencer?"

I nod.

"I was there."

I tighten my fingers around the beer bottle.

"Not in the room, but they were at a club, both of them wasted. Stella got into an argument with Knox. She ran into Spencer, one thing led to another, and he came to our suite with us at the end of the night. Then I went to bed."

"Did he join her in her room?"

"I didn't follow them, but I'm assuming so."

"Why didn't you tell me?"

"It's not my story to tell, and if I recall correctly, you sat in my kitchen saying it wasn't anything serious between you two. If you weren't in a relationship, why does it matter? It was in her past, Hudson. She was young, drunk, and desperate for affection. Her ex was off touring the world and flirting with thousands of women every night. There was a different story about him cheating on her every other day, and she could barely get him on the phone sometimes. Don't hold one mistake over her head. Talk to her. Fix this. You two seemed happy together."

"I could never make her happy."

"Shut the fuck up and quit wallowing in your self-pity."

"I can't give her what those other men can. I don't have access to jets. I can't buy ten-thousand-square-foot homes or extravagant gifts. That's Stella's type, and that will never be me. I was a fuck toy while she couldn't have a real boyfriend."

I'm whining like a little bitch.

His voice lowers. "Stella isn't like that. She won't expect that from you. Do you love her?"

I shrug. "I don't know what I feel anymore."

"Don't bullshit me."

"Would I be this upset if I was trying to bullshit you?"

"Brother, take my word, wasting time on love because of fear is a mistake. You never know how long you have until it's gone. Do it for me. Do it for Lucy. Let love into your heart again before you end up losing it." He wipes tears from his eyes. "All I have to say is I'm encouraging love for everyone around me because I know what it makes you feel. Even in the short time I had with Lucy, it was like a dream come true. My dream life that ended up in a nightmare. I wouldn't change it for anything, though. Time isn't something that's promised to anyone—no matter how rich, how young, or how healthy you are. You can lose everything in the blink of an eye. Don't let it hold you back."

I finish off my beer to give me courage. "I'm having dreams again. They stopped when I was with Stella for some reason, but now they're back."

Dallas sits back to look at me with hooded eyes. "Shit, brother. Why didn't you tell me?"

"It's embarrassing. I'm a twenty-seven-year-old man having nightmares."

"There's nothing embarrassing about PTSD, Hudson. Not one damn thing. You want to talk about it?"

I shake my head. "I'll get through it. Just know I have your back, and I know you've got mine. No matter what bullshit life throws us, we've got this."

THIRTY-SEVEN

I GRAB my phone from my lap.

"Should I text him?" I stammer out. "I should text him."

I'm in New York for an awards show. Not only is our film nominated in three categories but Eli and I are also up for best couple.

Ha. Best couple.

My stomach has been in knots all day. Per the contract that is ruining my life, I have to walk the red carpet with Eli and act like we're in love. Even with all the shit that went down, the pictures of Hudson and I being leaked, the production company still didn't grow enough balls and put out a statement that we're not an item. We still have to partake in this charade.

Nominated or not, I'm not looking forward to this.

Each day I'm locked into this disaster proves that getting the role wasn't worth it. I turned my back on someone who made me his top priority. No one else has ever done that for me.

And in return, I chose that contract over him.

Joan, my makeup artist, grabs my chin and holds it in place. "What you should do is stay still before he gets a call from a one-eyed chick because she can't stop moving while I finish her eyeliner."

"No, you shouldn't text him," Willow says in a disapproving

tone. "You should *call him.* Texting is cowardly in situations like this. Words can be misinterpreted. Texting is for late-night booty calls or telling your asshole ex he was the worst sex of your life. Not for confessing your love and apologizing. Put your big girl panties on. Hit his name. Tell him how you feel before it's too late and he finds some cowgirl out there with honeysuckle straw hanging out of her mouth."

I roll my eyes at her. "How can you sound so smart yet like an asshole at the same time?"

She grins. "It's one of my many talents."

I've been battling with myself on how to fix things with Hudson —if that's even possible.

Is it too late?

I know one thing for sure. I can't live this fake life anymore.

I broke down last night. I missed him. My heart ached to hear his voice. My skin missed his touch. I decided I needed to find a way to make everything right with him. The problem is *how* can I do that?

I sigh, my shoulders slightly slumping, which results in another annoyed look from Joan. "What if he shuts me down? He thinks I'm a cheater, a liar."

"Your behavior and silence make you look like one," Willow argues.

"I want to give you a dirty look right now, but Joan will kick my ass."

"Damn straight," Joan says, adding glue to a false eyelash.

"Call him," Willow demands. "Try. You reaching out will convince him you're not any of those things."

I scoff. "Like it's that easy."

"It really is."

I take a deep breath of courage before hitting his name and then frown at the response. I end the call. "Too late. He changed his number."

"Dickhead," Willow says. "How do you know?"

"That's what the recording just told me," I reply.

Willow points at my phone. "Text Dallas and ask him to give you his new number."

"Isn't that stalkerish?"

"We all stalk people when we're in love."

Joan takes a break from me to look over at Willow. "Pretty sure stalking is illegal whether you're in love with the person or not."

I nod in agreement. "We need to find you a boyfriend stat before you end up in the looney bin."

"Says the girl who doesn't have one either."

I open my mouth for my next smart-ass comment but stop when I hear the sound of the suite's front door slamming shut.

"Fuck that shit!" an irate voice yells.

Eli comes storming into the room with Tillie on his heels, fury blazing off the both of them. His manager, a quiet guy I've never even had a conversation with, walks in a few seconds later, worry clear on his face.

"Eli," Tillie says cautiously.

He points at me with a snarl. "I'm not walking the red carpet with her. I refuse to look like a desperate man okay with his girlfriend fucking around on him. This dating deal is over. I played my part. Paid my dues. You want someone to sue, sue her ass. She's the one who got busted fucking another dude."

I can't blame Eli for his animosity. I would've reacted the same way if photos leaked of him with another girl. No one wants to look like the idiot who stayed with the cheater.

"What if I release a statement denying her affair with the bodyguard?" his manager asks. "They're friends. That's it. The picture was taken at a weird angle."

Willow snorts.

Joan laughs.

"People aren't fucking dumb," Eli snarls. "Any angle will show them sucking each other's faces off and fucking."

"Why do you even care?" I ask. "You got what you wanted. You can go out and have your fun now."

"No, I fucking can't." He tilts his head toward Tillie. "*This bitch* …"

My mouth, along with everyone else's except for Tillie's, falls open. Eli is as over it as I am. Thankfully, he's doing the talking for me. Tillie doesn't seem fazed at his name-calling. I'm sure it's not the first time she's been called that and worse.

"She's threatening to sue me if we don't continue this lie," Eli goes on. "Not happening. I will jump my ass on stage and tell everyone the truth."

"And risk your reputation?" Tillie asks.

"New plan. We'll tell them you decided to go your separate ways," Eli's manager says. "No one needs to know about the agreement."

"How about we don't go?" I suggest.

"Not happening," Tillie says. "Nice try, though."

I'm still on her shit list and also positive she wants to suffocate me in my sleep.

"See what you caused because you had to go screw around with the bodyguard, for God's sake," Tillie says to me before leaving the room.

I flip her the bird.

"That chick needs some dick herself," Joan comments. "She's in one hell of a bad mood." She brings her attention back to me. "You better not ruin this face I spent thirty minutes working on with tears."

I look up in the mirror and realize I'm crying. "Shit," I say, wiping away tears.

"I hope you're not shedding tears over that bitch," Joan goes on. "She isn't shit. Don't let her control your life. If you like a guy, be with him. Why is that such a problem?"

Willow hands me a tissue. "That's what I've been saying. What are you going to do?"

Tillie being mad isn't why I'm upset. These are tears of regret for letting other people control my life and causing me to lose someone I love.

"I hope it's to stop fucking crying," Joan says. "Think about something happy before you ruin my artwork over here. It's disrespectful."

I roll my eyes. "Happiness isn't something I'm capable of right now."

"How can we help?" Willow asks.

"Bring him back to me," I answer."

She throws a makeup brush at me. "Then what the hell are you doing, Stella? I can't fix that. Joan can't fix that. *You* have to do something. You have to go to him."

"I have responsibilities here that I can't walk away from," I argue.

"Uh … yes, you can."

"Don't be funny," I mutter.

"I'm being honest. You have no obligations right now. You aren't working on a project. You have nothing holding you back. *Nothing.* You have enough money that you could retire tomorrow if you wanted to. Take time off. Find yourself."

"I'm still obligated to go to this stupid ass award show."

"What if I tell them you got food poisoning and puked all over your dress?" She jumps up from her chair as if it's the best idea she's ever had. "You can't show up naked."

I shake my head. "That's not happening. I'll go to the awards show and figure out what to do with my life when it's over."

THIRTY-EIGHT

Hudson

I PEEK up from furniture shopping on my laptop when I see Dallas walk into his guest bedroom. I'm still crashing here until I move into the house I signed a lease for yesterday. Starting over will be a bitch, but I won't be asking Cameron for my furniture back.

I shudder, thinking about the fact she brought another man into our bed.

Thank fuck I dodged that bullet.

"You. Me. Guys' night in," he declares. "We've been some depressing ass dudes on the brink of singing Taylor Swift songs if we don't get our shit together. Lauren kidnapped Maven for the night, so we can drink all the alcohol we want."

"What's wrong with Taylor Swift?" I question. "'Shake It Off' is a good jam. Maven is making me a fan."

He laughs, shaking his head. "Oh hell, he's growing a heart again."

I flip him off. "Guys night sounds good to me."

I'm up for anything that'll keep my thoughts off Stella. I've been trying to *shake her off* by staying busy, but it's not working. It's worse at night. I stay up thinking about her, and then when I finally do doze off, I'm woken up by another flashback.

Shit sucks.

Even though our time was limited, there's something about her I can't let go.

We were both lost and fell right into each other's laps at the time we needed somebody the most.

Love can build up over time, or it can tear into you like a storm —sweeping you off your feet—and you have no idea what happened. You have no time to prepare yourself for surviving or for the devastation of heartache. That's what I experienced with Stella. I fell for her and crashed into her waves before I realized I even stepped outside.

I never believed in instant love until her.

I never thought I'd crave someone I'd only known a month until her.

I was brought up with the notion that love assembles with time. That's what happened with Cameron, with my parents, with everyone I know. But that wasn't the case with Stella. Love can assemble with conversations, with sweet gestures, with making the other person feel as though they're perfect in your eyes.

And fuck do I miss her ... miss that rush.

And the world isn't helping me move on.

She's everywhere.

Every-fucking-where.

In real life.

In my dreams.

Even Maven is finding it crucial to watch reruns of her show that are now streaming on Netflix.

New rule: no dating anyone who's on TV.

———

I WALK into the living room with a beer in each hand and plop down on the couch before handing one to Dallas.

I'm making myself comfortable when he changes the channel.

"What the hell, dude?" I snap. I'm not pissed that he changed our regular programming of sports. It's what he turned it to. "Guys' night involves drinking and staying the fuck out of our feelings. Next channel please."

Seeing her will tear me apart, and I sure as fuck won't put myself through hell if I don't have to.

He looks at me from the other side of the sectional while trying his best to look innocent. "What are you talking about? I've been waiting for this all week."

I throw my arm out toward the TV and narrow my eyes. "You've been counting down the days to watch *The Teen Choice Awards*?"

He nods.

"Something you've never taken an interest in before. Not even when we were teens."

"It looked good. Maven asked me to watch to tell her everything when she gets home tomorrow."

"Fucking liar. What it looks like is you setting me up."

He grins. "You have two options. *The Little Mermaid* or this."

"The fuck? Last time I checked, you had every single damn channel known to man."

"True, but I'm hosting guys' night, which means I get to choose what we watch."

I settle back in my seat. "Screw it. Whatever your plan is, it's not going to work."

He holds up his hands. "No plan here."

I stop myself from calling him out on his shit. He's having fun with this, something he hasn't had in a long ass time.

Might as well give him what he wants.

THIRTY-NINE

Stella

MY HEART IS close to bolting out of my chest.

I've never done anything like this before.

This decision could obliterate my career even more than it has since the whole Eli-Cheat-Gate. It's not like it's at its highest point right now anyway.

Eli's shoulder bumps into mine when he leans in from his seat to bitterly whisper in my ear. "We better not win this shit. You can bet my ass I won't go up there and accept that award with you."

Tillie eventually convinced—well, threatened—Eli to come. He drew the line at walking the red carpet or participating in any interviews, and surprisingly, she agreed. And even more shockingly, she allowed me to do the same, which most likely only happened because she didn't want me to be interrogated.

News has been slow these past few weeks, so our so-called cheating scandal has been a shitstorm with Eli being the brunt of the jokes. Humiliation is destructive to a career in this industry. Tabloids and the internet will never let you live it down.

We're in the front row of the awards show that's thirty minutes in. Thirty minutes too long. I can't wait to get out of here. I run my hand down my dress when the presenter starts naming the nominees in our category. Winning the award isn't what's important to me.

It's the opportunity I want.

The moment.

I lose my chance if we lose.

Unless I pull a Kanye.

The presenter, a girl I've worked with on my show before, opens the envelope and squeals before screaming our names for best movie couple.

"You've got to be fucking kidding me," Eli mutters, covering his face to hide his aggravation from the cameras.

He stands up, which goes against what he said he'd do, but doesn't bother helping me out of my chair. His manners do come through when he waits for me before going on stage. He helps me up the stairs, so I don't bust my ass in my eight-inch heels.

The crowd is clapping.

Fan girls who post Instagram photos of us with #relationshipgoals are squealing in excitement.

Relationship goals.

Ha. We're nothing but phonies.

Eli stands back, his arms crossed, and gestures for me to go ahead. All eyes are on me when I stand in front of the microphone. My stomach knots so tight it physically hurts, but I have to do this. I close my eyes and take a calming breath before I let my confession slip through my lips.

"I want to start by thanking our fans who watched the movie and voted for us," I begin. "You have given me so much in my career —showed me compassion and honesty. I've let you down by not giving that honesty back."

Eli's chest hits my back as his lips go to my ear. "Don't fucking do it, Stella," he hisses, grabbing my elbow.

I jerk myself from his hold and continue. "For as long as I can remember, there's been speculation about my life. I grew up in the public eye—everyone witnessing the best and worst times of my life —whether I liked it or not. The negative stories, they hurt, and I faked who I was to prevent them. Acceptance is all I wanted in this merciless industry. I put other people's approval before my happiness and believed my happiness and that approval was dependent on what I was wearing ... who my friends were ... who I was dating." I start to choke up but force myself to push through, even when the tears start. "I wasn't following my heart." My hand presses to my chest. "I'd like to apologize for not doing that, for being dishonest to myself and you. I never cheated on Eli. We were never a couple."

Eli is walking off the stage when I glance back to silently apologize.

I inhale another breath before continuing. I've already started digging my grave—might as well jump in. "I can't continue choosing my career, my reputation, over my happiness. You'll never get the best of me if I do. I was hurting myself and the man I love to make everyone else happy. I can't do that anymore."

Jaws are dropping, and phones are up, recording me, no doubt. My vision grows blurry from my tears.

I've never felt so free.

I swipe a fresh tear from my face as applause erupts around the room.

I whip around in my heels, and the cameras follow me as I flee backstage, where Willow is waiting.

"I am so fucking proud of you," she squeals. "Now, we have to get you out of here before the rest of the mob shows up. I have a car waiting for us."

"Thank you," I breathe out.

My new bodyguard follows me through the hallway while I keep my head down and ignore the camera flashes and questions about my relationship with Hudson. A rush of cold air and relief hits me when we walk out the exit doors.

Willow shoves my phone in my hand as soon as we slide into the back seat of the SUV with tinted windows.

I immediately text Dallas.

Me: Did you get him to watch it?

I fan myself with my hand. My heart is in the grips of a man I'm not sure even wants anything to do with me.

I took the risk.

I hope he does the same.

"Calm down before you have a heart attack," Willow orders. "Dallas has your back and wants his brother to be happy. Let's hope he hog-tied him, or whatever those country people do, to a chair and made him watch."

"Even if he did, that doesn't mean it'll change Hudson's mind about me."

I almost drop my phone when it vibrates.

Dallas: I did. His reaction wasn't pretty. I'm sorry, Stella.

No. No!

Why did I wait so long?

Why did I hold back on something that made me feel whole?

Hudson isn't one for grand gestures. He's simple. All he asked for was honesty and commitment. He gave me so many chances to give it to him, but I was too stubborn. I walked away and tore down everything we built.

My hands are shaking as I type out my response.

Me: It's fine. Thank you for trying.

"Tell me it's good news," Willow says.

I can tell she already knows from the crestfallen look on her face.

"It's over," is all I can whimper. My hands are still shaking. My legs are shaking. I'm shattering everywhere. "I need to accept that."

She scoots in closer to pull me in for a hug. "He'll come around."

I shake my head. "No. He's too headstrong. You should've seen his face when I chose to leave. It was a mixture of disgust and regret. He lost all feelings for me when I told him I wasn't going to tell the truth."

I start to scrape away at my fresh manicure in an attempt to calm myself. She squeezes me one last time and pulls away when her phone goes off. Her eyes grow wide as she reads a text and then frantically starts smashing her fingers against the screen.

"Who are you talking to?" I ask. "In case you forgot, I'm over here having a crisis."

"You're having a pity-party before you've even given him time," she argues, still concentrating on her phone.

"Fine." I cross my arms and pout. "Tell me who you're talking to."

"Damn, nosy." She rolls her eyes. "It's Brett's cheating ass. He wants to get back together."

"Vomit. Please tell me you're not considering it?"

"Hell no." She's still typing like she's writing a farewell letter before dying.

"Stop entertaining him then."

She laughs. "I enjoy watching him squirm."

"Like he squirmed his pint-size wiener into vaginas that weren't yours?"

"Pretty much."

"How about I help you out with that and stop you from doing something stupid." I attempt to snatch her phone, but she's faster than I am.

"Nice try. Let me have my fun. Don't blame a girl for enjoying breakup revenge. They seem to always come back sniffing around when they realize you're done playing their games and have moved on."

"If only Hudson were a douchebag like Brett."

She darkens her screen and slips her phone into her bag. "If that were the case, you wouldn't be sacrificing your career for him. That was a big step, and I'm proud of you."

"Glad I have your support for being unemployed and single the rest of my life." I moan out in irritation. "I need carbs. I need alcohol. I need carbs mixed with alcohol."

I TURNED my phone off after reading the text from Dallas, handed it to Willow, and made her promise not to give it back under no circumstances until tomorrow—even if I threatened to cut her hair off while she's sleeping.

I'm avoiding all forms of communication in fear of what people are saying about my speech.

"When I declared I was going off the grid, I assumed you'd do the same," I whine.

We're back in the hotel and lounging in bed wearing our pajamas. It's been three hours since I humiliated myself in front of millions of people. It's felt like three hundred days. Willow has been on her phone nonstop since we got back to the room and refuses to let me read the texts from Brett.

She looks over at me, raising a brow, while sitting cross-legged across from me. "You know what they say when you assume."

I roll my eyes. "Whatever. You officially suck at being a heartbroken wing-woman."

Her face turns serious. "I'm your assistant. I have to make sure people aren't talking too much shit about you. My mother is also texting me about your drama. I swear, that woman is more interested in your relationships than my own." She holds her phone out to me. "If you're so bent out of shape about it, you can text them back."

I wave my hand through the air when her phone beeps again. "Forget it. Go right ahead. Make that thing useful and order some food while you're at it. I'd like alcohol and ice cream to be our guests of honor."

"Don't you think you have enough here?" She jerks her head toward the bottle of vodka sitting on the nightstand.

I opened it about an hour ago after throwing my shoes across the room and declaring I was swearing off men for the rest of my life. What's better than being a heartbroken hot mess? Being a *drunken* and heartbroken hot mess.

I jump up on my knees. "Oh my god! Speaking of ice cream, don't they make some with alcohol in it now?" *That's my kind of dessert.* "If you find it and get it delivered, I'll give you a raise."

"If I do, you'll stop bitching about me being on the phone?"

"Stay on your phone all you want, and I'll enjoy my alcohol and sugar."

"Challenge accepted."

"ARE YOU DEAD?" I stutter to Willow's voicemail. I searched the place for my phone and found it hidden in a bathroom cabinet. "It's been twenty-five minutes since you said you were meeting the delivery guy in the lobby. Where did you find it? Craigslist?" I slap my hand against my mouth and hiccup. "I'm a terrible person. I got my best friend murdered over ice cream desperation."

I continue to ramble how I'll make sure she has a good funeral but stop when I hear the door open. I end the call, and the phone bounces on the mattress when I drop it. I slide off the bed and nearly face plant in the process of rushing into the living room.

"Fuck, Willow, why aren't you answering your phone? I thought I was going to have to identify your body," I screech. I'm throwing my arms in the air and dramatically stomping my feet.

I skid to a sudden stop.

My breathing restricts like all the air has been sucked out of the room.

Hudson stands only a few feet away from me in a wide stance. His hands are pushed into the front pockets of his ripped jeans, and his whiskey-colored eyes stare into mine with uncertainty. I rub my eyes—certain the alcohol is toying with my mind.

"Your new bodyguard needs fired," is his icebreaker.

I relax at the sound of his gentle voice. He's not angry or here to yell at me for wronging him. He's here to be the Hudson I fell in love with—the rough on the outside man who opened up his softer side to me.

"It's hard finding someone as skilled as you," I whisper, stumbling over my words.

What does this mean?

Is he here to ask me not to talk about him in public … or did my speech change something?

I run my hands through my tangled hair. It's not how I'd planned on seeing him in our moment of reconciliation, but it's how he prefers me, so no need to stress about it. He appreciates the real me, not my money, my fame, or how I look after an hour with my glam squad.

I don't move when he takes a step closer.

"I had a guys' night tonight," he tells me.

I look around in confusion. "Okay?"

"We ended up watching some awards show."

I cover my face in humiliation. "Please tell me you turned the channel before they announced best couple?"

He grins wildly. "But that was my favorite part, Hollywood."

I move my hand to reveal a timid smile. "So, it worked?"

He takes another step. We're only arm's length away from each other. "It brought me here."

"Is that a yes?"

He takes that last stride, stopping in front of me, and grabs my hand. I stagger a bit when he leads me over to the sofa and sits us down so we're facing each other.

"I know you're probably pissed at me, and you have every right to be," he says.

I flinch. *Me pissed at him?*

I was the one who chose my career over us.

"It was killing me to watch you pretend to be with another man. *Fucking killing me,*" he stresses, his face turning grim. "Even though it was one of the hardest decisions I've ever had to make, there was no choice for me but to let you go."

I clutch at my chest. "But I was yours. I told you that. I wanted nothing more than to be yours! I didn't want Eli. I wanted you!" My eyes start watering, and I can feel the tears ready to unveil.

"Actions speak louder than words, and your actions were playing the fake girlfriend of another man. I couldn't even touch the woman I loved in public. When those pictures of us leaked, even though I never wanted it to happen, I thought that maybe it was a good thing —maybe you'd be honest and choose us. But you didn't. Instead, you fled and left me hanging out to rot like the bad guy treading on some other dude's woman, when, in actuality, it was my heart getting stomped on."

"I know, and I'm so sorry! I had too many people wanting too many things from me." My buzz is beginning to wear off.

"All I wanted from you was to choose me. You can have your career. You can have the life you want. I want you to be happy and to be part of what's making you happy. I wanted to hear you say those words, Stella! I wanted to hear, *to feel*, that you were falling in love with me as much as I was you."

Whoa. My heart starts racing.

"I do fucking love you!" I tell him. "I realized I couldn't lose you, and in case you missed it, I did in front of millions of people. If you don't believe what I said was true, turn on the TV, log onto the internet, and watch it again. You can hear you're the only one I want."

"I saw it. It's not that I don't believe you. What I'm trying to say is that even though I appreciate the gesture, that's not what I needed."

"What do you need then?"

"For you to choose me and not make me share." He shakes his head. "Maybe I should've given you more time. I don't know where we went wrong or what could've changed the outcome. All I know is I'm here to say I'm sorry."

I take his hand in mine. "I'm sorry for everything. I've been doing some soul-searching."

He chuckles. "With the help of alcohol, I see."

I narrow my eyes his way. "Hey! I'm not perfect."

He squeezes my hand and brushes his thumb along the edge. "I'm not expecting you to be. I mean, technically, you're perfect in my eyes. But in reality and relationships, perfection is unrealistic. All I'm asking from you is honesty and loyalty. I can deal with any other bullshit thrown our way. I promise to give you the same." His other hand reaches out, and he uses his thumb to wipe my tears away. "And I sure as fuck don't want to make you cry."

I point at my face. "Tears of joy. I promise."

He brushes a tangled strand of hair away from my face. "And drunkenness, which is why I think we need to stop any other serious conversations for tonight. I want you sober when we figure things out."

I perk up. "You're going to stay?"

"I'm not going anywhere."

I grin.

He grins.

I'm drunk and lovestruck. Nothing else matters at this moment but the two of us. Not what other people think. Not the consequences of my speech.

Nothing.

He pulls me closer, and I turn, making myself comfortable with my back against his hard chest, and relax.

He feathers his fingers down my arm. "You want to know one of the biggest things I've missed about us?"

"The blowjobs?"

He chuckles. "Yes, I've definitely missed those, but what I miss the most is sharing a bed with you. I loved waking up next to you in the morning. I don't know how, but you shine a light on my flashbacks and nightmares. I don't feel anything but happiness when you're in my arms."

I tilt my head back, and he moves in to press his lips against mine. Our mouths linger before we separate. I've missed this so much. Nothing compares to being in his arms.

"I feel nothing but happiness when I'm there. You make me feel like I'm enough, like no matter what mistakes or decisions I make, I won't lose you," I tell him before something hits me, and sweep my eyes over the room. "Uh, have you seen Willow?"

"She and Dallas are grabbing a bite to eat," he answers. "I booked her a room so we could talk."

Thank God.

I raise my brow. "Talk, eh?"

"Trust me, there will be much more than talking in the morning. I'll be giving you speeches with my tongue between your legs as breakfast."

I shiver. "I have something to look forward to. Hopefully, it cures hangovers."

He chuckles. "If not, we can try other ways."

"I like the sound of that, and before I forget to ask, you said Willow *and Dallas* are grabbing a bite to eat. He's here?"

"He decided to come with me. It'll be good for him to get out of town. I know people mean well, but they're still dropping off condolence pies and flowers. It's tearing him apart."

"I agree. Willow is probably giving him a tour and forcing him to visit every food truck. She loves this city. I take it this was planned, and everyone was in on it but me?"

"After I saw your speech, I texted Willow telling her I needed to see you. I asked her not to ruin the surprise."

Hell, this was a setup. She wasn't texting douchebag Brett. Her sneaky ass was texting Hudson. I can't believe she didn't hide the alcohol if she knew he was coming. I'm sure it would've looked very suspect had she taken the liquor. Her sneakiness has made me goddamn happy, so I guess she'll get a raise and a new puppy or something.

———

"TILLIE, Tillie, Tillie, my mom, my sister." I'm reading off the list of voicemails on my phone.

It's morning, but the sun isn't blessing me with its presence thanks to the thick curtains. My brain is playing ping-pong with my skull.

"Reporter," I continue. "TMZ. Reporter. Buzzfeed. Tillie. My manager." I sigh, tossing my phone on the floor. "It might be time to change my number."

"Or block Tillie," Hudson says, lifting himself up with his elbow and resting his chin in his palm, smiling down at me.

I love waking up next to him. His hair is a tousled mess, and his gaze on me is gentle. Tilting his head forward, he brushes his lips along the tip of my nose.

"That crazy ass woman is most likely searching the streets for you and punching people in the face when they tell her they have no idea where you are," he adds. "We need to come up with a plan on how to handle her."

Kill her?

"Willow emailed my attorney in case she tries to sue me and take my firstborn."

My perfect assistant not only has my back personally but professionally as well. She jumped with glee when I told her my speech idea. She pulled out her phone and immediately began drafting an email to my attorney and publicist, waiting to hit send until it actually happened. Willow might be little, but the chick gets shit done.

"Don't you mean our firstborn?" he corrects.

That sentence shoots a spark right through my veins, waking my ass up. Bring on the sunshine. I suddenly feel rejuvenated, at the top of the world, and am on the verge of getting up to perform a happy dance. I no longer think I'd be a bad mom with Hudson at my side. I'll be fine, and there's not a doubt in my mind he will be an amazing father. He's great with Maven.

I can already imagine it.

I stare up at him, our gazes meeting, and I can feel my smile growing. "Let me correct myself. *Our* firstborn."

"Just wanted to clarify," he says, his grin matching mine. I shudder when his fingers dance over my arm. "Now that we've had the children talk, how about we rewind and have the pre-baby talk?"

He stayed true to his word last night. We didn't have a big relationship conversation. He made me drink plenty of water, told me to make myself comfortable in his arms on the couch, and we watched TV until I dozed off. He then carried me to bed and tucked me in.

Yesterday started out in hell and ended up in heaven.

Heaven is about to cloud when we bring up plans, compromises … and the miles that separate us.

Why can't we skip the serious relationship questions?

Love … that's why.

It always seems to make everything so damn complicated.

He laughs when I groan. "We held off until you were sober, so where should we start?"

I sit up. "I can change that. I didn't get a chance to finish the vodka last night."

He stops me from sliding out of bed. "Nice try."

I frown, and his tone turns serious. Not stern-like, but more like a straight to business voice. "What's the next step?"

"I want to take some time off," I answer, timidly looking at him. "I thought I could maybe stay in Iowa with you?"

My idea catches him off guard, and his response does the same to me.

"You don't have to do that."

"What do you mean?"

"I don't want you to change and completely uproot your life for me. You love acting. It's in your heart. I can't ask you to give it all up and move to Blue Beech. You wouldn't be happy."

I hold my hand out to stop him. "I'm not saying I want to retire or start raising cattle. I've been thinking about taking a break for a while now because I haven't found a role I've liked. I'll have my manager keep an eye out for anything that might catch my interest." I snuggle in closer to him. "Meanwhile, I'd like to get out of the spotlight until everything dies down."

"You promise? I don't want you to make this decision because you think it's what I want. We can work something out. California isn't my ideal home, but I would move there if it meant being with you. Hell, I'd be happy anywhere if you're by my side."

"Me too, which is why I want us to try Iowa out. Just for a while … a test run."

He leans down and nudges my nose with his. "Privacy does sound pretty damn good."

I grin against his lips. "Doesn't it?"

"Just promise me one thing."

"What's that?"

"If you don't like it, you'll tell me."

"I promise." I scoot in closer, tangling my legs with his. "Now, I believe you also made some promises last night. Something about helping me with my hangover. How about you let me clear my head by giving me some?" I shiver when his hand sweeps down my thigh and slides between my legs.

"How about I make you orgasm that hangover out of you and then let you suck my cock until you feel hydrated?"

"Sounds like the perfect remedy."

FORTY

Stella

Six Months Later

"I HAVE A SURPRISE FOR YOU," I sing out, swinging my hips in the kitchen while making a cup of coffee.

I shiver when Hudson comes up behind me to sweep his arms around my hips and brushes his soft lips along my neck.

"Oh, really?" He chuckles in my ear. "How about you give me a clue?"

I twist in his hold and circle my arms around his neck before kissing him. "Nuh-uh, that would ruin everything I have planned."

He plants his lips back against mine, taking the opportunity to slide his tongue inside my mouth. He tastes like fresh mint. "I'll work for it."

"Gross! Chill out, tonsil scrubbers," Willow says.

I glance over Hudson's shoulder to find her pulling out a chair at the kitchen table and sitting down.

"Be considerate of those who aren't exactly love's biggest fans at the moment." She narrows her green eyes and gestures back and forth between Hudson and me. "This kind of cheesy behavior will not only ruin my breakfast, but it will also wreck your argument of convincing me to move to this godforsaken town that consists of a total of five square miles."

Her mouth drops open when I start slicing my finger across my neck in warning repeatedly until Hudson looks down at me in confusion. I straighten my stance and shrug, trying my best to appear clueless.

He pulls away. "You're considering moving here ... permanently?"

I can see the excitement dancing in his eyes.

I'm also giving Willow the dirtiest look I can manage.

"Not *permanently*," she rushes out, answering for me while trying to save both of our asses. "Don't get your balls all up in a bunch, country boy. That came out all wrong. *What I meant* is that she's trying to get me to stay here *when she is.*"

I love California. It's been the place I called home since I was in diapers, but these six months I've spent in Blue Beech have been a breath of fresh air. I've never felt so free.

After the awards show and Hudson's surprise visit, we spent the next two days in New York before flying to Iowa. The first few weeks were hectic. The paparazzi continued stalking me, but they eventually gave up when they figured out I wasn't giving them anything regarding Eli-Cheat-Gate. They moved on to search for the next celebrity scandal.

Willow went back to LA, packed some of my things, and mailed them to Hudson's rental. She's been staying in California since I haven't needed her for anything, but I will now, so persuading her to make this her new home is my goal while she's visiting this weekend. She's not into the idea yet, but I'm going to make her fall in love with Blue Beech like I did.

Hudson chuckles and kisses me on the cheek before grabbing his travel mug. "Don't keep me clueless for too long." He winks and signals back and forth between Willow and me. "I'm headed to work. You two maniacs stay out of trouble and let me know if you need anything."

He and Dallas are working for their dad's company and trying to expand the business. They've been attending auctions to buy farm equipment, then fixing them up to sell to local farmers.

Willow salutes him. "Aye aye, captain."

He gives me another cheek kiss and leaves while a cheesy smile spreads across my face.

"Have I told you how much I like that dude?" Willow asks. "Who would've thought once you pulled that stick out of his ass, he would be hilarious and fun?"

"It's the environment," I say, grinning wildly. "Everything is more exciting in Blue Beech."

Her eyes sharpen my way. "Don't even try it. I told you I'd give you this weekend for your whole surprise party thing, and then I'm back to the city where I can get takeout sushi on every corner."

―――――――

"I CAN'T BELIEVE you pulled this off without me finding out," Hudson says as he looks around Magnolia's.

The bakery is packed with a mixture of people from Blue Beech and out-of-towners. It was the perfect place for me to throw a party. I haven't seen some of these people in nearly a year, and I'm sure most of them are going to break my kneecaps when they realize they'll be surrounded by baked goods all night.

Carbs. Sugar. Butter.

All of the things I'd once tried my best to steer clear of are now something I treat myself to at least once a week.

"It's been hard," I reply. "But so worth it."

"You ready to spill the beans?"

I jump up and down in excitement. "Let me introduce you to someone first." I snag his hand and lead him over to an older man wearing a polo and dark jeans.

"This is Max," I introduce. "He was the executive producer for my old show."

Hudson shakes his hand. "It's nice to meet you."

I take a deep breath. *Here goes.* "I didn't say anything, in case I was getting my hopes up, but I pitched an idea to him about filming a show here in Blue Beech a few months ago."

"You're shitting me?" Hudson bursts out. He points at Max when I shake my head. "And you ... you bought it?"

"Sure did," Max replies.

I jump again, adding a squeal this time. It's been hell holding on to this information for the past month. When something good happens, the first person you want to share it with is the one you love.

"They not only bought it. They *love it*," I yell. "I'll be playing an actress who moves to a small town when her career fails after a publicity crisis."

He runs his hands through his hair, every trace of excitement vanishing from his face. "Jesus, let's hope it's not based on a true story."

Max chuckles. "I can promise you it's not." He tilts his head my way. "I've known Stella for years. Talent like hers can never fail."

Max then goes into the details. We've already found the perfect location thirty minutes out of town to film at and plan to start shooting in three months. I've never been so thrilled about a project.

"You don't feel that way, do you?" Hudson asks when Max leaves to talk to one of the writers. "That you're becoming a failed actress? I don't want you to stay here if it's not what you want. I know you love to act, and I don't want to hold you back from that."

"Absolutely not," I affirm. "It's *loosely* based on my life with the experiences of this change. I'll learn that there's more to love in a small town than I imagined. I never thought I'd feel this way about a place like this and the people here. My dream is to act and be happy. I'll have both of them here." I take his hand and squeeze it. "I swear to you. This is what I want."

It's the truth. Once word got out that I wasn't having an affair with Hudson, Blue Beech greeted me with open arms. They see me as *me* now. Not the celebrity. They don't snap pictures when I'm shoving a cupcake down my throat, or when Hudson slips me a kiss in the town circle after a parade. There hasn't been a photo of us leaked in four months.

He steps in closer, lowering his voice. "We're going to do this, huh? Settle here and make a life?"

I grin. "Damn straight, we are."

He clasps his hands on my cheeks and brushes his lips against mine. "I'm not sure what I did to deserve someone who keeps making me the luckiest man alive. I love you."

"I love you."

———

"WHERE ARE WE GOING?" I ask when I notice Hudson doesn't turn down our street on the way home from Magnolia's.

We came. We conquered cupcakes. Then the bakery slowly started to clear out as people left to crash into their sugar-induced comas.

Hudson looks over at me, his hands on the steering wheel. "You thought you were the only one who could keep a surprise?"

"Sneaky ass," I mutter. I rub the back of my neck while trying to think of what his surprise could be.

Holy shit, is he going to propose?

I play with my hands in my lap as my nerves go batshit crazy. Surprises aren't as fun when you're not the one keeping them.

I crank my head to the right when he turns down his parents' street and up a dirt drive. He jumps out of the cab and circles the truck to open my door. He grabs my hand, snags a flashlight from the bed, and walks us into the middle of the field.

I take a look around. "I'm a little confused here."

He chuckles. "I've been talking to my parents. They have so much land here, more than they know what to do with, so I offered to take some off their hands." He drops my hand and turns in a circle. "What do you think about building Casa Barnes-Mendes here?"

I'm staring at him, bug-eyed and silent.

He scratches his cheek. "If it's not something you want, tell me. It's not set in stone yet."

I jump up into his arms and wrap my legs around his waist. He holds me up as I stare down at him with a smile.

"Yes!" I yell. "Yes!"

"You had me terrified for a second."

I brush my lips against his. "I enjoy watching you squirm." I run my hands down his chest as I slide back to my feet. "This is the perfect plan."

"Now, how about I take you to our temporary home and show you how much that excites me?"

"I like the way you think, but first, we need to find Willow."

"Ah yes, Lauren texted me and said she took Willow under her wing tonight. The Down Home Pub is having a live band play, and when I told Lauren about your new show, she decided to sign up for the Operation Get Willow to Move Here Team. She's going to drop Willow off later tonight. They thought we needed some solo-celebrating time."

"I love friends who care about their friend's sex lives. Let's get home before our company gets back."

FORTY-ONE

Stella

I CAN DECLARE last night as being one of the best of my life.

I want to replay it over and over again.

Hudson's eyes flutter open when I lift myself to straddle his waist in bed. I shiver, the chilly air hitting my back after leaving the heat of our sheets, but I have a feeling he'll warm me up.

His promise to show his excitement for all the progressive steps we took last night continued well into the morning. The scent of sex wavers through the room, reminding me of all the dirty things we did to each other last night. I'm running on only a few hours of sleep, but I'll never be too exhausted for him.

A low groan escapes his throat when he clasps his hands onto my waist, his fingers biting into my bare hips. "Damn baby, good morning to you, too," he growls out, rocking his hips up so I can see just how *good* my surprise is.

I moan at the friction of his erection rubbing in *almost* the right spot. His hand climbs forward to cup my breast, and I throw my head back when he uses a single finger to tease my nipple.

I'm wide-awake now.

I torture him back by grinding my hips and sliding his cock between my thighs.

"Our sex was so good last night that I thought we'd celebrate by having more sex this morning," I breathe out.

His hand slides down my waist straight to my clit, and that's the next place he teases me. I rise up to grab his thick erection and slowly sink down on it.

We both gasp.

Sex with Hudson seems to always get better.

The whole it gets boring with time theory has yet to be proven in our bedroom.

"That's it, ride that cock," he mutters, his eyes shutting.

I shift my hips, rolling them in a circle so I can feel every inch of him.

Then it happens.

I stop at the sound of the doorbell ringing.

And ringing. And ringing.

Then there's a bang on the door.

My phone starts ringing.

His phone starts ringing.

"Ignore it," I plead, dropping my hands down to rest on his chest and rotating my hips into a circle. His groan convinces me he's obliging, but instead, he grips my waist and stops me.

"You riding my cock is the last thing I want to interrupt, but they're blowing our shit up." He starts to get up after I slowly climb off him with a murderous look on my face. "You stay here. I'll get it."

I stop him before he makes it out of bed and point at his lap. "You have an erection the size of the Eiffel Tower. I better get this."

He looks down at his cock that's coated with my juices. "*Fuck,* I promise I'll make it up to you."

I pull on my robe and head downstairs, cursing the air and the person interrupting. Willow rushes in barefoot when I throw the door open. Her hair looks like a rat's nest. Her dress is wrinkled, and her makeup looks like she got into a fight with the sprinkler.

"What the hell?" I mutter. "Where have you been?"

Last night was a blur to me—thanks to all of the celebratory alcohol we drank after getting home and the mind-blowing sex that followed. I gave Willow a key, so I figured she slipped in quietly and went to bed after leaving the bar with Lauren.

"You look like hell," I continue.

Way to bring a girl down, Stella.

"It doesn't matter," she cries out. "All that matters is I need to leave right fucking now. Can you take me to the airport?"

I follow her as she dashes up the stairs to the guest bedroom.

She drags her suitcase from the closet and starts throwing all her shit inside. "I can take a cab if it'll take you a while. I need to get out of this fucking town as soon as fucking possible."

I grab her arm, turning her around to look at me. "What is going on? What happened?" *Who do I need to kill?*

"I need to go home! That's all you need to know."

"What. Is. Going. On? Did something happen to you last night?"

My stomach sinks.

Did someone hurt her? Was I choosing dick over my best friend's safety?

She sniffles, wiping away the tears. "Do you promise not to tell anyone?"

"It depends on if I need it as justification for murder."

"I slept with Dallas last night."

Whoa. I stumble back.

"What?" I slap myself on the forehead a few times to wake myself up if I'm dreaming.

She didn't just say what I think she did, did she?

"I slept with a man who lost his wife only six months ago. I can't even imagine how much he regrets it." She pauses and holds her finger up. "Wait, I can because he woke up and freaked out when he found me sleeping in his bed."

"Holy shit sticks."

"Tell me about it. I can't face him again. I can't move here. I promise I'll do all of your work from LA. If you need someone closer, you'll have to replace me."

As badly as I want to tell her I'll never be able to replace her, I can't think about work right now. My priority is my best friend.

I run my hand down her hair and pat her shoulder. "It's cool. I get it. We'll figure something out."

"Thank you," she chokes out.

"Let me get dressed, and then I'll take you to the airport."

She nods, and I kiss her on the cheek before leaving the room. My heart is hurting for her.

Hudson is out of bed, his erection gone, and tugging on a shirt when I walk back into the bedroom.

"What's going on?" he asks. "I heard Willow crying but wasn't sure it was my place to go out there."

I shut the door behind me and lower my voice. "Uh ... I don't know if I should say."

He stops mid-zipping his jeans. "Is it something serious?"

"Dallas, uh ..."

"Dallas?" He grimaces. "Dallas what?"

I'm still trying to find the right words. I have to tell him. As much as I don't want to break my word with Willow, Hudson will find out anyway.

"They slept together last night." The words come out in a rush of breath.

"You're fucking shitting me?"

"I wish I was," I whisper. "She's freaking out. I need to take her to the airport."

"Fuck!" he hisses. "Shit is about to hit the fan."

I shrug. "Maybe it's not such a bad thing. Neither one of them is in a relationship. There's no reason they can't chalk this up as a one-night stand."

"It is a bad thing. Dallas will never forgive himself for this. He had to have been drunk."

"I'm sure Willow was as well ... or that it was a mutual attraction. She's not one to date-rape men." If he's trying to insinuate that Willow took advantage of Dallas, we're about to have an argument.

"Hell, that's not what I meant by that, I swear. What I meant was he's probably beating himself up over it right now."

"Go talk to him. See what he's thinking."

He kisses me. "Be careful. Call me when you're on your way back home from the airport."

FORTY-TWO

Hudson

DALLAS IS SITTING in his living room when I walk in. A bottle of whiskey hangs from his fingers. His face is drowning in regret—his eyes red-rimmed and glossy.

We stare at each other for a moment before I move farther into the room and take the seat on the other side of the sectional. I stopped in the guest room to see Willow before I left my house. I wanted to tell her goodbye and assure her that I'll talk to him. She looked like a hot mess, and I have no doubt they're both struggling with this.

"Where's Maven?" is my first question. Not only can we not have this discussion if she's here but he also can't be drinking like this around her. "I can have Stella come get her for a while."

He shakes his head. "She spent the night at Mom and Dad's." His voice shakes. "You know, don't you?"

I rub my hand over my face when he takes a drink. "Do I know that Willow just fled our house like there's a plague outbreak here because something happened between the two of you last night?"

"I feel like the biggest piece of shit in the world, Hudson." His voice cracks. "It's only been months since I lost Lucy. She was my life. *My fucking life.* How could I touch another woman like that? How could I fuck someone else?"

I pause as a brief silence falls between us while struggling to come up with the right words that he won't take the wrong way.

"Eventually ..." I stop and take a deep breath. "Sooner or later, you're going to have to move on, brother."

Was that the best thing to say? I don't want him to feel bad about touching Willow. He did nothing wrong.

"Not that fast!" he yells. "I was hers for over a decade! You can't throw that away in six months. *Fuck!* Everyone in this town is going to hate me."

"No one is going to hate you for moving on."

He snorts, the bottle going back to his lips.

"Do you like Willow?"

He stares down at the floor. "Nuh-uh, don't you dare start that shit. I'm not dating anyone for a long ass time. Dating isn't what I need. It sure as hell isn't what Maven needs."

"You're going to stay single and celibate for the rest of your life?"

He looks back up at me. "I haven't decided that yet." He gestures to the house. "I brought her in here. I took her to our bed. Jesus Christ." He throws his arms out in frustration. "I don't know what I'm going to do."

"You're going to be a strong man for your daughter, that's what you're going to do, you hear me? Don't beat yourself up over this. If it was a onetime thing, then so be it. If you like Willow and want to explore shit with her, go for it. It's your choice, and no one is going to look down on you for your decision. There's been plenty of women who've approached me about trying to get close to you, so they have no right to judge for something they're trying to participate in."

"I don't even want to talk about this right now. I feel like complete shit."

I grab the bottle from him. "This isn't going to help."

He frowns. "You suck."

"You need to call Willow."

His skin bunches around his eyes. "And say what? Sorry I freaked out when I woke up and saw you in my bed? There's no way she doesn't hate me right now."

I point the bottle at him. "Make shit right. Stella will kick my ass if Willow quits."

———

"YOU TALK TO HIM?" Stella asks.

"Yeah. He looks like shit, feels like shit, and doesn't know what to do," I answer.

"You might want to explain to him that you don't talk about how big of a mistake sleeping with someone is *in front of them*. I almost had Willow convinced to move here. There's no changing her mind now. She said I could either hire someone else or let her work from LA." She plops down on our bed. "Everything was going so well. We're building a house. I just got my dream show, and I need my assistant here, not states away. Not to mention, I want to be there for her. She's gone through too much this year with men."

"We'll deal with whatever happens, okay?" I sit down and wrap her in my arms. "You can always visit Willow in LA until she feels comfortable coming here again. We got this."

FORTY-THREE

Hudson

Two Months Later

HER SHINY, ink-black hair lays in a tangle on the pillowcase, and I prop myself up with my elbow to watch her with sleepy eyes.

It's what I do every morning. I wake up and admire the woman in my bed, wondering how I managed to get so damn lucky to have her.

It's not considered creepy doing that, is it?

It's okay if the person you're watching is who you're in love with, right?

I can see that being a stalker's justification, so yes, I guess it is creepy, but I'm not sneaking into her house and watching her sleep.

I'm watching the woman I'm proposing to next month.

I never imagined I'd be here.

I came back to the States devastated after losing the woman I thought I'd spend the rest of my life with. That heartache brought me to the woman who actually deserved my heart and that title. Cameron shitting on me made me realize that no matter what obstacles are thrown my way, or how many miles separate us, my heart will always belong to Stella. I hate the lame-ass cliché—but everything does happen for a reason.

When I took the job with Stella, I thought I was hitting my rock bottom, but I was really smacking face-first into the foundation of who I was and what I wanted. I opened my mind, opened my heart, and moved outside of my small-town boy marrying the small-town girl plan.

Did I think that'd lead me to falling in love with a TV star?

Fuck no.

But hey, shit happens.

Construction has started on our new home on the property I bought from my parents, and Stella decided to keep her house in LA. We travel back and forth when she has promotional events or if we're in need of a quick getaway. I've come to realize that you can make a home anywhere when you're with the one you love.

They've started filming her new show, which results to her being gone as long as fifteen hours a day. Since it's not too far out of town, I get to bring her dinner and watch her work sometimes.

It's one of my favorite parts of my day.

My lips curve up when her eyes shutter open and then narrow my way.

She yawns. "I told you I hate it when you watch me sleep."

I smirk. "It makes my day to know I can be put through anything and no matter what, I still come home to something so damn beautiful. I let you have my side of the closet. Let me enjoy my few seconds of staring without you making a fuss."

She rolls her eyes. "That sounds even creepier." She yawns again. "You all packed?"

I nod, and she snuggles into me, whining.

"I'm going to miss you."

I kiss the top of her head and drag myself out of bed. "I'm going to miss you more."

"I just don't want them to start again," she whispers, concern etched on her face.

"I haven't had them in months, Hollywood. If they do, I'll call you."

I've only had a few flashbacks and nightmares since we've been back together, and those are when she's working late or out of town. Stella is the light to my darkness.

She pouts her lips. "You promise?"

"Promise. I think this retreat will not only help others but it'll benefit me as well."

"I'm so proud of you for making it happen. You're such a sexy badass."

I got some of the guys in my old battalion together, and we started a group that helps soldiers dealing with PTSD. Our first retreat is this weekend in North Carolina, close to where most of us trained. I've been busting my ass this past month to ensure everything will be perfect.

Stella licks her lips when I grab my clothes. "Is it weird how much seeing you naked turns me on?"

"Just as weird as it is me watching you sleep."

"Good thing we found each other." She wiggles around in the sheets and pats the space next to her. "Surely, us creeps have a few minutes to say goodbye to each other properly?"

"You know damn well it'll last more than a few minutes, and as much as I'd love to get some morning sex, I can't. Dallas will be here in about ten minutes." My dick twitches as I pull on my boxer briefs and grab my jeans. "You had me up all night, woman. Your stamina is unbelievable."

Even though Dallas isn't a Marine, he helped me plan this, so I wanted him to be there.

She laughs. "I had to get three days' worth of sex in." Her head tilts to the side when something hits her. "Why is Dallas on his way here? I thought we were picking him up, and then I was dropping you guys off because he didn't want to leave his truck at the airport?"

"Change of plans," I say, not looking at her.

"And that change is?" she asks suspiciously.

"Dallas had to pull out because Maven is sick."

"What?" she screeches. "I told her Dallas would be gone. That was the only way I could convince Willow to come to town this weekend. She's going to think I lied."

"It'll be okay."

She scoffs. "You better say goodbye to me now because it won't be okay. She's going to murder me if she has to face your brother."

"She probably won't even see him. If she does, tell her shit changed at the last minute."

"I'll fly out there."

I've never brought up Willow to Dallas since that morning. It's a she-who-shall-not-be-named situation.

I grab my duffel bag. "I'll text you when I get there, and we'll FaceTime before bed."

She raises a brow. "Are you okay with that?"

"Why wouldn't I be?" We have a nightly ritual where if one of us is going to bed before the other is home, or we're out of town, we FaceTime so we can tell each other good night. It's cheesy, I know, but I fucking love it.

"You're going to be in a cabin with twenty other men."

"And?" I walk back to the bed where she's sitting up on her knees and swipe her tangled hair from her face. "I don't care who's around. I'll always take your call."

She blushes, her lips tilting up in the corners. "I love you, Hudson Barnes. More than you can ever imagine."

I touch my mouth to hers. "I love you, Stella Mendes. The best thing that's ever happened to me."

I kiss her one last time before pulling away. She smacks my ass, laughing, and tells me to have fun.

My nightmares are gone.

My dreams are real.

Stella Mendes is mine.

I'm hers.

My life couldn't get any fucking better.

Just
ONE NIGHT

PROLOGUE

"WHAT THE FUCK HAVE I DONE?"

I've never had a one-night stand, but I'm positive those aren't the first words you want to hear the morning after.

I twist in the warm yet unfamiliar sheets and can taste last night's whiskey in my mouth.

I lick my lips—*wrong move*—and regret it when the flavor of him hits my tongue.

Him.

The man pacing in front of me with his head tipped down while wearing only boxer briefs that show off his bulge.

I've lost count of the number of times the word *fuck* has fallen from his mouth.

I don't know what to say.

Don't know what to do.

"How the fuck could I have done this?" he continues.

My heart rams into my rib cage, just as hell-bent on escaping this situation as I am.

I'm stupid.

So damn stupid.

I drag the sheet up until it hits my chin, and he runs a hand through his thick bedhead hair, tugging at the roots the same way I

did last night when he went down on me. He doesn't know I am
awake and can hear him, but that doesn't make the wound any less
severe.

His head rises when I jump out of bed and start scrambling for
my clothes. The sheet drops from my body at the same time I
frantically pull my dress over my head.

I have to get out of here.

Our eyes meet as I yank my panties up my legs. Apology and
torture spill across his clenching jaw. The tears are coming, warning
me to look away so that he won't see my humiliation, but I can't. I
stare and silently beg him to change the outcome of this morning.
The string to our stare down is cut by the sound of my name, a mere
whisper falling from his loose lips.

I dart out of the bedroom, snag my purse I drunkenly threw over
the arm of the couch, and rush toward the front door, not even
bothering to search for my heels.

I refuse to glance back, but I hear him. No, I *feel* him
behind me.

"Willow, please," he pleads to my back with a strained voice
while I fight with the lock.

I slam my fist against it. *When did they start making these things so
damn difficult?*

"Don't cry." He blows out a stressed breath. "Just give me a
fucking minute, okay?"

Relief hits me when the lock finally cooperates, and I slam the
glass door in his face at the same time he repeats my name. I nearly
trip on my feet when I jump down the porch steps.

I pause when I make it to the last one.

One more.

Against my will, I turn around for one last glance.

He's staring at me in agony with the door handle gripped in his
hand. For a split second, I'm stupid enough to think he'll fix this.
Stupid enough to believe he'll say something, do something to make
this right.

But he doesn't.

He drops the handle, spreads both palms against the glass, and bows his head.

That's my cue to get the hell out of here.

Fuck him.

Fuck whiskey.

Fuck my stupid decisions.

This is what I get for sleeping with a man mourning his dead wife.

Willow

CHAPTER ONE

THREE MONTHS LATER

I SHOULD'VE NEVER ANSWERED his call.

"Have you been smoking crack?" I screech into the phone. "I'm telling Stella to break up with you. I can't have my best friend screwing a dude who does crack." I'm deleting him from my Contacts as soon as the call ends. I can't associate myself with someone this batshit crazy.

Hudson sucks in what sounds like an irritated breath. "No, Willow, I'm not smoking crack. It'll be the icing on the cake if you show. She misses you."

"You know I can't come back there." My throat tightens, the memory of that night crashing through my mind like a horror movie that keeps you up late at night. Hell, he does keep me up at night.

"It's not like you're fucking blacklisted. You've chosen not to come back. I emailed you your flight information. See you in a few days."

The line goes dead.

Asswad.

I grip my phone, ready to call him back and tell him to shove that ticket up his ass, but I can't.

I can't because he's proposing to my boss/best friend at her surprise birthday party. Stella deserves this—deserves love, happiness, and her best friend in attendance for one of the most important nights of her life. So, I'll put my hate of the small town aside and risk seeing him—the jackass whose bed I fled from after our very drunken and very regrettable one-night stand.

He'll be in attendance, given it's his brother doing the proposing, which means I have to put my big-girl panties on, keep them on, and refrain from smashing a wine glass over his head.

All while keeping the biggest secret of my life.

While staying sober.

This will be interesting.

———

SOME PEOPLE BELIEVE in soul mates.

I believe in champagne and cupcakes.

The problem tonight is that I can only binge on one of the above, and it's not the one I prefer.

I get a whiff of Stella's signature rose perfume before she cages me in for a hug. I squeeze her tight, a silent sorry that I've been a sucky friend, and we're both nearly gasping for breath by the time we release each other.

Damn, I've missed my best friend and how I could always confide in her without judgment. That's changed now. My secret will destroy her relationship.

"I can't believe you came," she cries out with a red-lipped smile. "How did Hudson convince you? Buy you a mini pony? Promise to kick Dallas in the balls?"

I laugh. "Two horses actually. And I didn't consider the second option, so thanks for the idea. I'll add it to my list of demands next time."

I snag her manicured hand to admire the glistening princess cut diamond sitting beautifully on her finger. It's perfection and so Stella —nothing too exuberant or obnoxious but still flashy.

"I have to give it to the corn-fed, small-town boy," I go on. "He did a kick-ass job in the ring department."

She stares down at her finger, her smile now nearly taking over her entire face. "He did, didn't he?"

Hudson threw her a great party. He invited the few family members she talks to, his family, and everyone on the cast and crew of her show. There's food galore, confetti sprinkled all over the white-tableclothed tables, and a *Happy Birthday* banner hangs in front of the empty DJ booth.

Stella is not only my boss, but also childhood star turned Hollywood's princess. I'm her assistant. That's how I met Mr. Wrong One-Night Stand. We worked together for years until he quit to move back home, and Hudson took his job.

Hudson couldn't give Stella mansions or fancy cars, but he did shower her with enough love and happiness to make up for it. She moved from LA to Blue Beech, Iowa, after convincing a producer to shoot her new show here. I tried to resign, but she wasn't having it and agreed to let me do all my work from my apartment in LA.

Her hands rest on her hips over the black designer dress. "Are you staying with us tonight? I just put a new smart TV in the guest room, and we know how much you like your classic movies."

I grimace. "That's a giant *hell no*. The last thing you need around on the night of your engagement is Willow, the giant contraceptive. I'm crashing at Lauren's."

Lauren is Hudson's and Mr. Wrong's sister.

She groans. "Fine, I'll settle for that because you showed up. That's a big deal, and you did it for me."

I crack a smile. "I also came for the cake." That comment results in her pushing my shoulder.

Her face turns serious. "Have you seen him?"

The mention of him gives me a nasty taste in my mouth. "Who?" She crosses her arms at my response, and I scoff, my heart racing, "Oh, you mean the bed evacuator? Nope."

That's a lie. He was on my radar as soon as I walked in—for precautionary reasons, of course. I saw his back first, the one I assaulted so much, I ruined my manicure, and worry snaked through me. I cowardly fled the scene when he spun around and saw me.

"Hopefully, he's ducking underneath tables, so we don't have to face each other," I say.

She smirks. "We both know Dallas is not a man who ducks underneath tables."

"Looks like I'd better start then."

"Don't you think it'd be a good idea if you talked? Cleared the air?"

"I need to talk to him like I need anal bleaching. Both of them would be a pain in the ass and are never happening."

She laughs, snagging a bubbly glass of champagne from a waiter walking by, and thrusts it toward me. "Here's some liquid courage. Just don't drink too much that you land in his bed again."

I swat the drink away. "Not happening, and no, thank you."

She stills and studies me. "Since when do you turn down champagne? Alcohol is always mandatory in these situations."

"I'm trying out a new diet."

"You might want to wipe the icing off the side of your mouth if you want to keep up with that lie."

I scrub away the remnants of my sugar binge and lick my finger. Thou shall not waste buttercream frosting. "It's this new craze diet where sugar is the main source of nutrition and alcohol is bad. *Very bad*. It's called the good decision-making diet." I start fake picking lint from my dress, so she doesn't see the untruth in my eyes. The black dress is ugly and shapeless, and I bought it specifically for tonight to hide my body and secrets.

"So, you're not drinking because he's here?"

Shit. That would've been a more believable excuse than a damn diet. I nod, feeling bad for lying to her, but I can't break the news here. It'd ruin her night.

"Does that mean, the chances of letting him rip off your panties for round two is likely?" She sets the glass down on the table behind her and bounces in her heels, like me banging Dallas again would cure world hunger.

"Calm down, matchmaker. Studies show that alcohol gives you shifty eyes." I point to my hair. "Shifty eyes don't look good on redheads."

"Bullshit. You can't deny you had a connection. Neither one of you is the casual banging type. Talk. Maybe there's a spark that'll lead to a firework."

More like a wildfire breakout.

"The only *connection* we have is that he stuck his penis inside me once. That's it. Nothing more. Now, it's time to move on."

She pushes my shoulder when I go back to my fake lint-picking. "Okay, what the hell is going on with you?"

"Nothing," I blurt out, shifting my neck from side to side like I'm sore. "Jet lag is a bitch."

"Liar."

I wave off her accusation. "It's your engagement party. Tonight is all about you."

"If that's the case, then I want answers."

I chew on the edge of my lip while her dark eyes study me. I get the opportunity to look away when music starts to blare through the room. I glance at the DJ booth and then to the makeshift dance floor in front of it and almost gag at his first song choice.

Boyz II Men? Really, dude?

Looks like we're getting served cheese with these cupcakes.

The sight of Hudson hurrying over to us relieves me. He wraps his arms around Stella from behind and squeezes her hips, his mouth going straight to her ear.

"Dance with me," he attempts to whisper, although I'm sure everyone in the state heard him.

Stella melts at his touch, like it's the first time they've ever had physical contact, and my heart hurts. This is what real love is. This is something I'll never have. She groans, and I know my best friend well enough to know she's going to turn him down to continue our conversation.

"Go dance with your *fiancé*," I insist. "We'll talk later."

A smile accompanies her next groan. "*Fine*, but you're not leaving this town until you spill the tea."

"I wouldn't imagine it any other way."

Hudson kisses her cheek, snags her hand in his, and sweeps her toward the dance floor. The crowd cheers, and people jump up from their seats to join them.

I release a deep breath, happy I dodged that conversation, and decide to reward myself with another cupcake. I grab a chocolate one with strawberry icing and huddle myself into a corner at the farthest end of the room. Shame sinks through me when I do another once-over of the party to search for the man who screwed me in more ways than one.

One more glance. That's it.

One more view of the man who gave me the best night of my life and the worst morning.

My throat tightens when I spot him sitting at a crowded table in the middle of the room with the entire Barnes family. His daughter, Maven, has his full attention as she grins wildly and dramatically throws her hands up in the air while telling him a story. His head tilts back in laughter, causing my knees to weaken. That's the smile I longed for that morning.

God, he looks sexy.

More delicious than these cupcakes.

Too bad he isn't as sweet.

Dallas Barnes is tall, dark, and handsome but also scarred, rough, and broken down by burdens. He's the man of your dreams who has been through hell and hasn't risen above it yet.

Tingles sweep up my neck as flashes of our night together come crashing through me harder than this sugar rush. I drink him in like the glass of champagne I can't have while he runs his strong hand over the stubble of his dominant jaw. The same hand that ignited nerves in my body I never knew existed. His hair, the same color as the whiskey we threw back, is freshly cut on the sides and grown out on top.

I rub at the sudden ache in my neck while begging my mind to forget, to stop feeling *something* every time I see him. Hell, every time I think about him. It's always hate laced with desire.

We were two lonely and heartbroken souls who connected over a night of drinking our pains away. When the alcohol proved not to be potent enough to heal, we tried to fuck it away.

Fucking and feelings do not go together like macaroni and cheese.

I used him. He used me. I thought I was okay with that until reality smacked me in the face when he kissed me for the first time. That was the moment I turned greedy and wanted more than just a quick fuck. The problem is, he didn't.

As if he senses me watching him, his deep-set charcoal eyes move in my direction, and my back stiffens. I hold in a breath when he scoots out his chair, gives Maven a quick peck on the top of her head, and walks toward me.

Oh, shit.

Shit. Shit. Shit.

The first few buttons are undone on his chambray shirt, exposing the top of his broad chest, and the sleeves are tight around his muscular arms. He's not fit from spending seven days a week at the gym. No, he's naturally buff, and the manual labor he does now only amplifies it.

Was driving me crazy his goal tonight? No doubt Hudson told him I'd be here.

I move my gaze from one side of the room to the other, desperately searching for the nearest exit, as he gets closer. I'm his chosen target. I bite my lip at the realization that I'll have to walk past him to leave. The determination on his face assures me that I'm not going anywhere until he gets what he wants.

I shove the remainder of the cupcake in my mouth and silently give myself a pep talk to make it through this conversation without plowing my heel into his balls. I stupidly run my hands over my dress after swallowing down the last bite and then cringe at the pink frosting smear.

Real smooth.

So much for appearing cool and collected.

This hot-mess look won't make him regret kicking you out of his bed.

I tense when he reaches me, and he shoves his hands into the pockets of his jeans, staring at me with affliction. The thread around his shirt buttons stretches when he leans back on his heels and waits for my response.

"Willow." He releases my name like an announcement, and the familiar scent of him drifts up my nostrils, a mix of regret and whiskey with small notes of cedar.

It's comforting at first since I've always felt a sense of security when he is around, but then I remember what he did.

I settle my hand against the wall to keep me from falling on my ass. "Dallas," I reply with a sneer. "Fancy seeing you here."

"It's my brother's engagement."

My mouth slams shut, and my gaze drops to the floor at my stupidity. "Oh, yeah ... right."

Silence passes.

I don't look at him when I lift my head back up. Instead, I avert my attention to the people dancing, laughing, and having a good time in the room, wishing it were me.

Hell, three months ago, that would've been me. I cast a glance to his mom and dad. *Do they know what we did? That he screwed my brains out one night?*

He clears his throat to gain my attention again. I give in and focus on his broad-jawed face. He's staring at me in gentleness, almost pity, which surprises me.

"How long are you in town for?" he asks.

"Two days." My initial plan was to fly in and out within the same day, but Hudson begged me to stay longer for Stella.

"Get breakfast with me in the morning."

His question startles me. The breakfast offer is a little too late. That should've happened on our morning after.

"I'm not much of a breakfast person."

He scratches his cheek. "Grab coffee?"

"I don't drink coffee." This is the truth. Never been a coffee fan. Never will be.

"What the hell do you do in the morning then?"

"Sleep." *Get sick. Roll around in my sheets, wishing I could turn back time.*

He pulls his free hand from his pocket and slides closer into my space.

Way too close.

His steadfast eyes meet mine. "*Please.* I want to make shit right. My brother is marrying your best friend. I'm the best man. You'll no doubt be the maid of honor. We need to be civil and stop dancing around each other if we don't want everyone to know something happened between us."

There's the answer I was looking for. I wince, unsure if he's more worried about our tension ruining the wedding or that people will find out about our one-night stand.

I wave my hand through the air, careful not to hit him in the face. "Consider that night forgotten. I already have."

"Don't bullshit me. We've known each other long enough for you to be honest with me."

I hold up my hand in anger, the need to spew out something terrible snapping at me. I want to strike him with pain that consumes him like he did me. "In case you've forgotten, *you* kicked me out of your bed. What do you want from me? A friendly hug? A casual conversation with fake smiles? Not going to happen, so quit wasting both of our time. You stay out of my way. I'll stay out of yours. Agreed?"

"I didn't kick you out of my bed," he hisses. "You ran out my front door faster than a speeding bullet."

I forget we're not alone and edge closer until my chest hits his. "You jumped out of bed like *you* were dodging a speeding bullet." I grit my teeth to gain control of myself. "That was before you said that what we did was a mistake, *over and over again*, like your lips were a broken record."

His face burns like I didn't just hit him with the verbal truth, but also a physical one. He lets out a hard sigh, giving me a small sampling of the whiskey and frosting lingering on his lips. Tightness forms in my throat, and I clutch at my stomach. Just like his cologne preference, I'm sure the taste of him hasn't changed.

"I'm sorry. I overreacted," he replies. "I tried calling to apologize, but you wouldn't take my calls."

"Nor will I ever."

"Fuck, Willow, how many times do I have to say this until you forgive me? I was in a dark place and was out of line." His voice lowers even more, and I barely make out his next words. "I didn't regret that it was *you* in my bed. I was pissed at myself for even letting it happen, for putting you in that situation."

His answer doesn't make me feel any better.

I slide against the wall to move away from him. "It's done. I'm over it."

"Twenty minutes and a pastry," he pleads. "Give me that, and I promise I'll never bring it up again."

I take a deep breath. This is Dallas Barnes. A man I worked alongside for five years. A man whose job was to protect Stella and me. Tragedy changes a man. Loss changes a man. This isn't the Dallas I knew. This is a new man, a man who lost himself when he lost his wife.

I sink my teeth into the inside of my cheek. "I'm sorry, but I can't. I'll be civil for Stella's sake, but I won't spend a minute longer with you than I have to." This is for the best. I want him to hate me. I want him to want nothing to do with me in case he ever finds out what I'm keeping from him.

The anger in my words shocks him, and he runs his hand over his face.

"Daddy!"

He stumbles back at the sound of his daughter's voice. She's barreling our way, and her brown pigtails soar through the air. She runs right into his leg with a *humph* and giggles when he catches her.

"Come dance with me!"

Affection fills his face when he peeks down at her with a smile and twirls a pigtail around his finger. "Give me a second, sweetie. I'm talking with Willow, and then I'm all yours."

"But this is my favorite song ever." She pouts.

I force a laugh, seeing my perfect escape plan. Dancing seems to be my savior tonight. "You can't deny a dance with a girl that adorable," I say, shooing them away. "Go. I need to make a call anyway."

Maven jumps up and down, clapping her hands in excitement, and Dallas stares at me with concern before leaning forward.

"I never had any intention to hurt you," he whispers.

But you did, I mouth back.

Damn, did he.

"Daddy!" Maven whines. "The song is going to be over!"

He gives me a nod before walking away.

I don't let the tears fall until I see his back.

The fuck?

I'm not this overly sensitive chick.

These hormones are messing with my hard-ass persona.

I brush them away, sniffling, and dash toward the exit. I need to get out of here and away from these people. I need silence, a moment to sulk about how I made a stupid decision for the millionth time.

I'm almost out the door when I nearly trip on my feet. My arm is grabbed, and I'm pulled down a dimly lit hallway. I attempt to swat the connection away, but it doesn't work, and I'm not released until we land in a small utility room.

"What in the flying fuck is going on with you?" Stella demands, crossing her arms. "And don't you dare try to feed me some new diet bullshit. Diets don't make you cry."

"Nothing," I stutter out, wiping my warm cheeks in an attempt to rid myself of the evidence.

"Bullshit." She pauses, waiting for me to let out my secret, but I stand my ground. "I'll keep us in here all night." She narrows her smoky eyes my way. "Do you want to be blamed for keeping a girl away from her engagement party?"

Guilt trips. Stella excels at giving them.

"I'll tell you later. I promise."

She shrugs, pops a squat on the carpeted floor, and stretches out her legs.

I let out a dramatic breath. "*Fine.* But you have to promise, it won't leave this room."

"All of your secrets are safe with me. Always have been."

"This is bigger than hacking into Brett's phone or when I pissed myself after we drank too many Skinnygirl margaritas."

"You could've killed Brett, and I wouldn't blab."

"Promise me."

"Jesus, Willow, *did* you kill the bastard?"

My heart thunders in my chest. I'm on the verge of passing out, so I sit down across from her. I can't take these words back. The secret won't be mine any longer, and she'll be thrown into a difficult position.

"Someone you care about will get hurt if I tell you."

Her voice fills with worry as she hunches forward. "Is it about Hudson?" She relaxes when I shake my head. "Then, what is it?"

"I'm pregnant." The words feel heavy when they fall from my lips for the first time.

She silently stares at me, stunned at my response, and then her face brightens with fake excitement. "That's great! Congratulations." She's won an Emmy, but even she can't fake enthusiasm about this. "I didn't know you were back with Brett."

Brett. My asshole of an ex who's out on bail and awaiting trial after driving drunk and hitting a family of four.

"We're not. I haven't seen him since we broke up."

"Then, who's the father?"

I wait for her to come up with the answer, so I don't have to give it to her.

Her mouth drops open, a gasp escaping her. "Holy shit. Dallas is the father?"

"Yep, and I don't know what to do."

"I take it, you haven't shared the news with him?"

"Nope."

Her gaze lands on me in expectation. "But you're going to before you leave, right?"

"Not exactly. I was, uh … thinking about, say, never?"

"What?" she screeches. "Have you lost your mind?"

"It's for the best."

"You can't do that." She leans forward to take my hand in hers. "Don't see this as me being unsupportive, but that's fucked up. And that's coming from a girl who faked a relationship with a douche bag for months."

"It's for the best. I'm going to raise this baby on my own."

"Why?" She shakes her head, rolls her eyes, and sighs at the same time. "And I suppose you want me to keep quiet?"

My voice cracks. "Yes. *Please.*"

"If I do what you're asking, I'll be hurting Dallas. I'll be hurting the man I love. It'll ruin my relationship with everyone in their family if they ever find out." Her eyes start to water.

This is the first time I've ever doubted my trust in her.

"What they don't know won't hurt them. If the truth does come out, I'll tell them you had no idea."

Stella turns around at the same time my attention goes to the door when it opens. Hudson is staring at us with a bloodthirsty expression on his face.

"Excuse me for interrupting," he huffs out. "I was searching for my bride-to-be."

Did he hear our conversation? The look on his face confirms he heard *something,* but how much?

"I wasn't eavesdropping … at least, not at first," he goes on. "Some words of advice: when you have a conversation about fucking someone's life up, you might want to lower your voices."

My heart thuds in my chest. "Hudson, please," I beg. "Please don't tell him."

He moves into the room, closing the door behind himself, and thrusts his finger my way. "Don't you fucking dare ask me to keep this from my brother." His piercing stare goes to Stella. "And please tell me you weren't going to agree to it."

Stella's eyes swell as she throws her arms out toward me. "She's my best friend!"

"And he's your soon-to-be brother-in-law who deserves to know!" he yells. "That'll be my niece or nephew. Did you even wonder how keeping this to yourself would hurt me and my family?"

Talk about a fucking loud mouth.

"Keep your voice down," I hiss in warning.

His face hardens, almost appearing sinister, and sweat builds along his forehead. "I swear on everything that I will hate you if you do this. You don't pull shit like this on a man, especially one who is as good of a father as Dallas. He's not some piece-of-shit, deadbeat dad."

I squeeze my eyes shut in an attempt to not only stop the tears, but to also block out the view of Hudson's disgust. "It has nothing to do with him. It's what's best for me."

"Bullshit. It's you being selfish."

"Hudson," Stella snaps. "Enough!" She pulls herself up from the floor and helps me to my feet. She doesn't release my hand until I'm stable. "What are you so afraid of, Willow? What's the worst that could happen?"

Fear does the Macarena in my stomach. I can't tell them the truth. "Everything," I release. "He's a grieving widower who regrets touching me."

Stella's face softens. "This secret will add to his hurt when he finds out later."

"That's *if* he finds out." I peek over at Hudson, the anger still manifested everywhere on his body.

He locks eyes with me and shakes his head. "Un-fucking-believable. You fucking do this to him, Willow, and I will never speak to you again." His glare goes to Stella. "Good memories of our engagement night, huh?" He turns his back on us and slams his hand against the wall before opening the door and storming out.

"He's going to tell him, isn't he?" I ask.

"I'm sorry," Stella replies. "I shouldn't have pushed you, but you have to tell Dallas before Hudson does. Maybe this baby will bring some joy into his darkness."

"I'll tell him. Just give me a few days, okay?"

She nods. "As much time as you need. I can't say the same for Hudson though. You know how close they are."

"Fuck!" I scream, grabbing the ends of my hair and pulling it.

"That's what put you in this situation." She smiles when I flip her off.

"I need another fucking cupcake."

Dallas

CHAPTER TWO

I OPEN the fridge with more force than necessary and snag a beer. My brain pounds when I pop the cap off, take a long yet unsatisfying drink, and set it aside for something stronger.

Nothing will be potent enough for me tonight.

But that won't stop me from trying.

Maven is at my parents', so I have no responsibilities tonight.

To say surviving the party was a challenge is an understatement. I wasn't sure I'd be able to make it through and good thing I didn't have to do it sober. I should be glad my brother found happiness, but I'm an asshole living in a dark hole, avoiding the sunlight. I'm only happy I managed not to stand up and object to him asking Stella to marry him.

Marriage isn't the answer, I wanted to scream out. *Don't let yourself get wrapped up in someone so much, you don't know who you are when they're gone.*

I pat myself on the back for keeping my mouth shut. The glass bottle feels chilly when it grazes the bare skin of my neck.

Then, I saw Willow. Hudson gave me a heads-up that she was coming, and even if I had tried to argue about it, nothing would've changed. She's Stella's best friend … and the only other woman I've slept with since Lucy died. Hell, the only woman I've slept with other than Lucy.

I decided I was going to talk to Willow and make things right between us. The problem was, I wasn't expecting my chest to ache at the sight of her walking in ... or my hands to grow sweaty as I wondered how her skin felt underneath that black dress.

Is it still as soft as it was that night?

Does she still smell like strawberries?

Taste as sweet?

My plan to make shit right went out the window. All I thought about was asking her to come home with me and let me make up for my asshole behavior. I haven't touched anyone in months, haven't had the desire to, but seeing Willow made my heart race and my dick stir. Hell, it was a full-time job stopping myself from staring at her every three seconds.

I asked her to breakfast, and she looked at me like I was scum beneath her shoes. I had done a shitty thing, but I've tried to man up to it on more than one occasion, and she keeps shooting me down. So, I'm still a lonely asshole who only gets turned on at the thought of his dead wife and a woman who hates him.

I reach up to the tallest cabinet above the fridge and pull out the bottle of Jameson, my good friend who doesn't judge me when we hang out too much. I owe this motherfucker thousands of dollars in therapy. The liquid burns but feels almost euphoric, seeping down my throat.

Lately, all I've done is pretend—pretend that I'm okay in front of my family. I put on a brave face and make it through the day for my daughter ... and then I go to bed, wanting nothing more than to rip myself out of my skin.

I flinch when I hear my front door slam and take the bottle with me to investigate. I stumble back at the sight of the last person I expected to show up at my door tonight.

"Yikes, what the hell are you doing here?" I ask. "Stella decide to leave your ass already?"

Hudson snatches the bottle from my hand with a snarl. "We need to talk."

I put my hands in the air. "If it's about me cornering Willow, I only did it, so we'd be civil during your wedding festivities."

He lifts the bottle to his lips and takes a sip. "I, uh …" He takes another. "I have a feeling the two of you are going to have to learn to be civil long after my wedding."

His response doesn't make sense, but I'm blaming it on the alcohol. "I won't be an asshole again, okay? I tried to apologize, but the chick wasn't having it." Not that I blame her. I pulled the biggest dick move out of all dick moves … because all I was thinking with was my dick.

"Willow is pregnant." He grinds the words out, the air in the living room shifting to something I don't recognize.

I blankly stare at him. "Okay?" My heart sinks that she's found someone else. No wonder she wanted nothing to do with me. She's found a man who isn't a broken asshole. Good for her. I would've only ruined her.

"Willow. Is. Pregnant," he stresses.

I'm not catching his drift. What does he want me to do? Throw her a baby shower? "I'll be sure to buy her a gift."

The coffee table shakes when he pounds his fist against it. "Willow is pregnant with your goddamn baby, you fucking dumbass. I thought you'd be smart enough to put two and two together."

Good thing he grabbed the bottle from me. This would've been the moment it crashed on to my hardwood floor. "You're fucking with me."

His straight face answers my question. He can't give a DNA test with his eyes, but I believe him.

"Why would you assume it's mine? We slept together once."

"I overheard her telling Stella."

I digest his news and swallow a few times before grabbing my keys. A picture cracks when I throw them across the room as I realize I'm in no condition to drive.

"I need a ride."

"The fuck you do. In case you forgot, I got engaged tonight. I've already missed a few good hours because I couldn't think of pussy when I knew I was keeping this from you."

"How very noble of you," I mutter, wincing when he slaps the back of my head. "Stella's vagina doesn't have a curfew. Take me to Lauren's."

"Hell no. Stella will bite my dick off the next time I ask for a blow job."

"Take me to Lauren's, or I'll walk."

"Get in my fucking truck."

CHAPTER THREE

BANG! Bang! Bang!

I'm having a nightmare where a psychopath is pounding on the door of Lauren's apartment. I'll be murdered, and my skin will be worn as a coat. I don't realize I'm awake until I hear the familiar, masculine voice.

"Willow!" he screams on the other side of the door.

Bang! Bang!

"I know you're in there! Open up!"

My heart races, and I slap my hand over my mouth, not sure if it's because I don't want to make a peep or I'm close to puking.

"Lauren!"

Bang! Bang!

"One of you had better open this door before I break it down!"

Oh, shit.

Shitty-shit-shit!

I should've known Hudson couldn't keep his fat mouth shut. He probably went and tattled as soon as he got the chance.

I rub my eyes when the lights turn on. Lauren comes rushing into the living room, tying a purple robe around her waist in frustration.

"I hope blood doesn't make you queasy," she bites out, stomping her feet.

I raise a brow.

"Because I'm about to castrate my brother."

If only she had done that sooner.

I pull myself into a sitting position, resting my back on the couch, and shrug like the shitshow about to happen isn't my fault.

Curse words fly out of her mouth with every step she takes while he continues his tantrum on the other side of the door.

"Jesus, fuck, Dallas!" she yells, swinging the door open. "You'd better be getting a bedroom ready at your place for when I get evicted."

He bursts into the living room without paying her a glance. His sharp eyes cut straight to me, demanding answers, and his pain-stricken face confirms what I was afraid of. He's as terrified as I am.

"Is it true?" he blurts out.

Lauren slams the door and storms into the living room. "Is what true?"

His attention doesn't leave my face. "Are you pregnant?"

I have no words. I'm frozen in place—unable to move, unable to talk, unsure of where to go with this.

"I'm confused as to why that's any of your business and why you felt the need to show up here like someone is about to blow the place up," Lauren replies for me.

He doesn't answer her. His attention stays fixed on me, as if Lauren weren't even in the room.

"Answer me," he demands.

I clear my throat, about to cave in and tell him but chicken out and nod instead.

The anguish on his face amplifies. "Is it mine?"

This is the moment.

This is where I have to decide not only my future, but also my baby's.

"Wait … what?" Lauren screeches.

Dallas

CHAPTER FOUR

MY HEAD SPINS like I've been beating it against a wall all day.

Not one rational thought has climbed through my brain since Hudson broke the news. He'd been thrown into a tough spot. He either had to betray the woman he loved or his blood.

He chose me. He chose the truth. Instead of fucking his fiancée senseless the night of his engagement, he came over and spilled her best friend's secret. I would've never forgiven him had he kept it from me. Pure ice sinks through my veins as I just think about it.

Lauren is behind me, firing off question after question, but my attention is pinned on Willow. Her green eyes, filled with confliction and scorn, narrow my way.

I take a calming breath as an attempt to help us both relax. "Is the baby mine?" I ask again.

All eye contact shatters when her gaze drops to her lap, and she fidgets with her hands. Sure fucking sign of lying. I stupidly pull out the pregnancy test I forced Hudson to buy at the pharmacy before coming here from my pocket. I can't decipher if the gasp coming from her is from surprise or anger.

The snarl of her upper lip answers my uncertainty.

"You brought a freaking pregnancy test?" she shrieks. "Have you lost your fucking mind?"

A reaction. Finally, I get *something* from her.

Hudson warned me she'd go Muhammad Ali on my ass when she saw the test, but as I mentioned before, my brain isn't functioning at its finest.

I stumble forward when Lauren pushes my back to gain my attention.

She signals between Willow and me. "Why would you assume the baby is yours if she's pregnant?" Her hand flies to her mouth. "Holy mother of God, you two are banging?"

"No!" Willow yells, as if the thought horrifies her.

That puts a damper on a man's ego.

I grit my teeth. This isn't a conversation I want to conduct in front of my baby sister. "Lauren, some privacy, please."

She scrunches up her nose. "In case you've failed to notice, this is my apartment. Where do you expect me to go at three in the morning?"

"Your bedroom."

She rolls her eyes. "Whatever. You suck."

"And be sure to put on earplugs," I call out to her as she heads down the hallway.

She twists around on her heels with a smirk. "And miss this conversation?"

I give her a look, one that tells her I'm not fucking around, but that only grants me another eye roll. Her bedroom door slams shut, and I know she's not going for her earplugs.

The air is heavy.

I'm staring at Willow.

She's staring at me.

A scarlet flush rides up her high cheekbones.

I've never had a staring contest last so long.

Willow has the face of an angel with light freckles scattered along her nose and cheeks. Her personality-matching fire-red hair is pulled back into a ponytail with loose strands flying in every direction. I've never had one negative thought about her until tonight. She has a huge heart and bends over backward to help others, often putting them before herself. She smiles as if she's never been hurt, but I know she has from the many times I saw her dip out of rooms with tears in her eyes after an argument with her ex-boyfriend. She acts hard but is a softie.

She's also cautious with letting people in. This is going to be a challenge.

"Put that pregnancy test away before I shove it up your ass." Her cold tone startles me.

It takes me a few attempts before I manage to push it back into my pocket. She flinches when I move in closer and drop to my knees in front of her. Pain coats my throat as I clear it.

"If you're pregnant," I say, blowing out a breath. It takes me a second to continue. "If you're pregnant and I'm the father, we need to come up with a plan."

There.

That's me stepping up and being a man even though I want nothing more than to throw myself out the window. No matter how broken I am, no matter what hell I'm going through, I could never turn my back on my child.

Willow shakes her head, swatting her hand through the air, as if dismissing what I said. "Dallas, don't worry about this, okay? You're going through a lot. I can do this on my own."

"If there's one certainty I have for you, it's that, that's not fucking happening, do you hear me?"

She sighs, rubbing her forehead. "*Fuck.*" An annoyed laugh leaves her full pink lips. "You storm over here at the ass crack of dawn after one of the most exhausting days of my life and demand I make a plan?" She snorts. "That's not what's happening right now, *do you hear me?*" She lies back down on the couch and pulls the blanket up her body. "I'm going to sleep, and you can go back to doing whatever it is you were doing … as long as it's not drunkenly waking up the entire building while waving pregnancy tests through the air."

Fuck. She has a point.

Lauren interrupts us by walking back into the living room and holds both hands in the air. "Don't get pissed at me, but, Willow, take my bed. I can't have a pregnant chick crashing on my couch."

A slight smile hits Willow's lips. "I appreciate the offer, but I'll be fine." The smile collapses when her attention goes to me. "As long as it's quiet."

That's Willow—accommodating everyone else and always putting herself last in line.

"You sure?" Lauren asks, and Willow nods. "Okay, let me know if you change your mind or need anything." She tells us good night and goes back to her bedroom.

"What are you doing?" Willow asks when I grab a blanket and pillow from a closet.

I throw them on the floor next to the couch. "You're exhausted. I'm exhausted. Let's get some rest and talk in the morning."

"You have a bed *at your home*. Go sleep in it."

I squat down and fluff the pillow. "I'm crashing here. End of discussion. I can't risk you sneaking out on me in the middle of the night and flying thousands of miles away before talking. We'll be having a conversation about this tomorrow."

She sends me one last glare before shifting on her side and giving me a view of her back. I switch off the light and make myself as comfortable as I can, resting my arms behind my head and staring at the ceiling.

A baby.

A baby with another woman.

I fight every day to hold Maven and myself together. How am I going to do this?

It'll be a struggle, but I'll figure it out.

I made Lucy a promise to be a good man, and I plan on keeping it.

Dallas

CHAPTER FIVE

THREE MONTHS AGO

THE GOOD PEOPLE of Blue Beech visit the Down Home Pub for three reasons:

#1: To forget.

#2: To feel alive.

#3: A live band is playing, and they don't have shit else to do.

I'm number one.

It's a hole in the wall, the only bar in the county, and it has been here longer than I've been alive. It's not fancy, and it doesn't carry top-shelf shit, but I feel more comfortable here than any upscale club in LA.

I've been a regular since my twenty-first birthday, but in the past ten months, I've become almost a part-time resident the two days a week I don't have Maven. My parents demand they get plenty of time with their only grandchild. I tend to come during the week when the people who don't like conversation are here.

It's a full house tonight, which is why I didn't want to come. I hate crowds. Hate the flashes of pity men give me after sucking down another shot of cheap whiskey. Hate the women who take turns coming over with the belief that food and attention will heal me.

A fucking casserole isn't going to restore this empty soul of mine.

I walked into the bar to find Lauren and Willow sitting at a table in the back. Lauren ordered a round for everyone and did her best to get us to get up and socialize, but neither one of us was having it. Willow eventually convinced her to bail on us and have fun on the dance floor.

Thank fuck.

My sister goes overboard when she tries to pep me up and give me a good time.

How Willow ended up here is a mystery to me. Pubs aren't her thing. She sips champagne, does yoga, eats chocolate with fancy-ass names. She flew in for Stella's crew party, so the only reason I can come up with is, she's trying to stay away from Stella and Hudson's lovefest.

I lean back in my chair, balancing the neck of my beer bottle between two fingers, and stare at her as she gives the bar a once-over. The pendant light above us shines over her head like a halo when she starts peeling paint off the table. Her weariness surprises me. I've always thought of her as a chameleon—someone who adapts to any situation she's thrown into.

I set my beer bottle down and wipe my sweaty palms against my jeans. "What's Tinder?" *Really? This is what I say to break the ice? It's all I could think of.*

My question surprises her, and she lifts her gaze to me. "Tinder?" She scrunches up her face like she didn't hear me correctly.

"Yeah, what is it? Lauren has been up my ass all week, insisting I join it."

She laughs, a smile cracking at the side of her lips. "Really? You've never heard of Tinder?"

"Trust me, I wouldn't be sitting here, feeling like an idiot, if I had." I grab my beer and take a long draw, finishing it off. "Looks like I'm the only one lost on the Tinder subject."

"It's a dating app." She pauses. "Let me correct myself. It's a booty-call app. Swipe right; swipe left. Let's bang; let's not."

"A booty-call app." I snort. "It's sad when your sister cares more about you getting laid than you do."

"I seem to have the same problem with everyone *but me* worrying about my vagina getting the business." She laughs again, the sound of it putting me at an unfamiliar ease—something I haven't felt in a long time.

I want to hear that laugh again. A woman this beautiful doesn't deserve to be sitting in the back of a run-down pub with sadness in her eyes.

"Hudson told me about the bullshit your boyfriend pulled," I say.

Her ruby-red lips frown, and she runs a nervous hand down her dress. I pinch the bridge of my nose, regretting my words. Bringing up her douche-bag ex isn't going to get me another laugh.

"Hudson has a big mouth," she mutters. "And *ex*-boyfriend."

"Sorry 'bout that. Hudson told me what your *ex* did."

"What he did was fucked up and the final straw of our relationship."

"Did the kid die?" I pause, the question hitting too close to home. I have a daughter. That could've been Maven. I can't imagine what those parents are going through.

"Fortunately, no. Unfortunately, he has severe brain damage and will never be the same."

Fucking jackass. Shows how one stupid decision can impact the lives of others. I only met her ex a handful of times, but I instantly knew he'd never be a friend of mine.

"And him?"

"He's out on bail, and his trial has been postponed until he completes physical therapy."

"You shitting me?"

She shakes her head. "The perks of being the son of the town mayor."

"I'm sorry," I whisper.

"It makes me sick that I loved someone who did something that bad."

She snatches the drink Lauren ordered her and downs it. My lips slightly turn up when her face twists into something that resembles disgust.

She sticks out her tongue and points to the glass, like it's poison. "Is your sister trying to kill me? What is this shit?"

"Jameson," I answer, feeling my lips tilt up again—something they haven't done with anyone other than Maven.

She stares at me, blinking.

"Whiskey."

She pushes the glass up the table with both hands. "Well then, that's my first and last time drinking whiskey. I'm more of a wine-slash-champagne-slash-give-me-something-fruity kind of girl."

"Whiskey is stronger on the heart than champagne. You can't go wrong with trying to forget with whiskey. I promise you that."

"In that case, order me another." She pauses to wag her finger at me. "Wait, if it's such a heart-mender, why aren't you drinking it?"

I shrug. "I planned on being good tonight with beer."

She holds her empty glass up. "I planned on champagne. If I'm drinking it, so are you."

I smile for what feels like the first time in months and hold my hand up to tell the bartender, Maliki, we need another round.

"This'd better work," she says when Maliki drops off our drinks. She knocks the whiskey down like a pro, inhales a deep breath, and squints her eyes when it's gone. "Shit, that one was even stronger."

"It'll help. I promise." I tap the table before draining mine. It burns as it goes down.

"Do you miss her?" she asks out of nowhere, as if the question had been on the tip of her tongue all night.

My jaw flexes. I'm surprised at her question. "Every fucking second of the day." My honesty shocks me. I've shut down every conversation my family has tried to have with me about Lucy. "Do you miss him?"

"Every fucking second of the day, and I hate myself for it. I can't stop missing the parts of him that weren't terrible."

Maliki, like he can read my mind, brings us another round. She takes another long drink, and I still in my chair, all of my attention on her while I wait for her to go on.

She scoffs, "This is *not* a conversation I thought I'd be having tonight. No one brings him up, for fear I'll want him back if they mention his name."

I nod, a cloud of grief passing over me. I want to be mad that she's complaining about losing someone she can take back at any second because I don't have that option. I'd be irate, pissed, and ready to spit out fire if anyone else had said that to me.

But not with Willow.

I grip my glass and watch her take another sip of her drink. The strap of her green dress hangs off her shoulder, giving me a glimpse of the light freckles sprinkled along her pale skin. I've never looked at her, *really seen her*, until tonight. Her red hair is pulled into two tight buns at the top of her head, a few spirals of perfect curls falling out of them.

"How about we make a toast?" she asks.

I hold up my glass. "To what are we toasting?"

"To getting wasted. To going numb. To forgetting."

I like the way she thinks. "To drinking the pain away." I tap my glass against hers. "Let's drown our sorrows."

We drink our pain away. We forget our troubles. Hell, we forget everything and everyone around us.

My brain isn't functioning when I ask my next question. It would've never happened if I were sober.

"So, have you tried it out? Had a booty call with this *Tinder*?"

Willow

CHAPTER SIX

I HAVE TO PEE.

The bathroom is across the hall, only steps away, but I can't go. I'm fake sleeping, and I have been for what feels like days. My muscles hurt. My head aches. As soon as Dallas leaves, I'm off Lauren's couch, out of this town, and on my way back to California.

Even though my back is to him, I can sense him watching, his eyes slicing into my skin, hoping to cut answers out of me. He'll end up empty-handed because I have nothing for him. My goal is to exhaust him with silence until he gives up.

What happened last night runs through my mind. I've never seen Dallas so angry and intense.

In an attempt to go back to sleep, I close my eyes, but my plan is ruined when it hits me. I nearly trip over him when I jump off the couch and race down the hall, straight to the bathroom.

Un-fucking-believable.

Why now?

I make it to the toilet just in time as everything I shoved down my throat last night comes up. It's disgusting. I'll never get used to this morning-sickness hell. I flinch when a cold hand moves along my neck to attentively grab my hair and hold it behind my shoulders. He silently kneels next to me and keeps his hand in place until I finish.

"Good ole morning sickness?" His voice is soft and comforting —the complete opposite of what he gave me last night. He must've slept off the asshole.

I flush the toilet and slide away from him, my butt hitting the cold tiles, and I rest my back against the bathtub. He waits until I get comfortable and hands me a bottle of water.

"Thank you," I say, taking a long drink. "It seems morning afters aren't our thing."

"I'd have to agree." He slumps down against the closed door and stares at me, doing what I knew he'd do—wait for answers. His foot brushes against mine when he stretches his legs out. He's in the same clothes as he was last night, his jeans unbuttoned, and his hair is messy.

I cock my head toward the toilet. "You want a go at it now?"

His thick brows squish together. "Huh?"

"I figured it was your turn to puke your guts out. You had to have been wasted off your ass to tell yourself that showing up last night was a sound idea."

He chuckles. "I'll admit, that was a stupid decision. I'd been drinking, but I wasn't wasted, and I'm sure you understand the shock I was feeling."

"No," I reply sarcastically. "I can't relate at all."

He found out I was pregnant. I'd found out I was carrying a physical being in my body by someone I couldn't stand.

He scratches his cheek. "How long were you planning on keeping this from me?" And he jumps right in.

Eighteen years. My entire life if I could've gotten away with it.

"To be honest, I have no idea."

He links his hands together and holds them in front of his mouth, trying to come up with the right words. He blows out a ragged breath. "You don't like me. I get it. And, to be honest, you're not exactly my favorite person right now either for keeping this from me. But I have to get over it, just like you have to get over what happened between us." He points to my stomach. "Because that? *That* changes shit."

"It doesn't change anything. I'm not expecting anything from you. I can do this on my own."

He holds his hand out, looking shocked. "Let me get this straight. I'm an asshole because I had a minor freak-out after we had sex? What does that make you for your secret? You've known you're pregnant for who knows how long, and you didn't think it'd be right to let me in on that tidbit of information?"

"You have a halfway good point," I mutter.

Okay, it's a full good point, but I won't give someone credit when I don't like them.

He clicks his tongue against the roof of his mouth. "Make yourself comfortable, sweetheart. Looks like we're about to have that talk."

I snort. "Not happening. I can still taste puke in my mouth. I'm not doing anything but brushing my teeth and getting in the shower." I narrow my eyes at him. "So, don't make yourself comfortable. We're postponing the talk."

"Okay, *princess*. Tell me when it's convenient for you. This afternoon?"

"Tomorrow."

"You'll be on a flight tomorrow."

"And? Lucky for you, they've invented this thing called a phone. I'll call you when I get home."

"I'd rather do it face-to-face."

"Then, we can FaceTime."

He pulls out his phone. "What time is your flight leaving?"

"Why?"

His eyes are on his phone as he starts typing and scrolling his finger down the screen. "Lucky for me, Hudson booked your flight and sent me the information this morning."

"Fucking snitch," I mutter.

"Looks like I'll be joining you. Hopefully, I can pay off the poor soul who's stuck next to you, and we can talk about it all the way back to California." He gives me a cold smile. "It'll be fun."

If he thinks his behavior is going to make me *work with him*, he has another thing coming.

"You're joking."

"Do I look like I am?" He holds his phone out, so I can see his screen. "Would you look at that? They have seats available."

"Don't you think that's creepy? Following me around? Stalking me?"

"Not stalking you. Asking for answers. This conversation will happen whether you like it or not. I'd prefer not to chase you around the goddamn country, but if that's what it takes, I will."

I cross my arms with a snarl. "Fine, I'll talk to you later."

His dark eyes level on me. "Promise you won't bail."

I force a smile. "I promise."

He hesitates before getting up and taps his knuckles against the door. "I'll be seeing you soon, *Baby Momma*."

"I hate you!" I yell to his back.

——————

"I'M PISSED at the both of you for keeping me in the dark about this," Lauren says, placing her glare on me before switching it to Stella, who ditched Hudson this morning to show up here with muffins and a list of everything she wanted to know about what had happened with me and Dallas last night. "I have so many questions right now."

Lauren hasn't let me do anything since she woke up this morning. She's a nurse, so you'd think she knows that carrying a baby doesn't make you disabled.

"Questions I won't be answering," I mutter. "No one, except for Stella and Hudson, knew about that night. I was hoping it'd stay that way."

"One question, and I'll shut up," Lauren pleads.

"I'm not talking about having sex with your brother," I argue.

Her face pinches. "Gross. Not where I was going with this, creep."

I lean back in the barstool. "You'd better make it a good one because that's all you're getting."

She settles her elbows on the counter and eagerly stares at me from across the island. "How did it happen?"

I wag my finger at her. "I'm blaming it on you."

She takes a step back and shoves her finger into her chest. "Me? I might get messy drunk sometimes, but I don't recall telling you to take your panties off and give my brother the business."

I frown. "Fine. Let's blame it on the whiskey and lack of entertainment in this town's only bar."

Her mouth drops, satisfaction twinkling in her eyes as she puts two and two together. "The night at the pub?"

I stubbornly nod.

"Holy shit. I am to blame."

Stella scoots in closer. "They're the last two people I imagined screwing."

"Screwed," I correct. "A one-time thing."

"Have you decided what you're going to do?" Stella asks. "You do know, Dallas isn't going to let you freeze him out."

"No." I was so hell-bent on keeping this a secret, I never thought about what would happen if the truth came out. "We're talking later."

Stella perks up. "Like, a date?"

Lauren cracks a smile. "Survey says they've surpassed dating. She's carrying his baby."

I flip her off, and my throat tightens while I prepare myself to ask her a question I've been trying to avoid. I stare at Lauren. "So, you're not mad at me?"

Dallas's family's reaction is another reason I wanted to keep this private. They loved his wife, Lucy, like she was their own, maybe even more than Dallas. He'd started dating her before he even knew his dick could get hard, and I'm some random one-night stand crawling in to replace her.

"Why would I be mad?" Lauren questions. "As long as you're not screwing the same man as me, I couldn't care less, and inbreeding isn't my thing." She skips around the counter to wrap me in a hug. "It's no secret that I loved Lucy, but I understand the circumstances. I want my brother to be happy. He *needs* to move on." She pulls away and settles her hands on her hips. "Now, my answer would be different had you kept this from him."

She's acting cool but also letting me know where her loyalty stands. If she has to pick a side, it won't be mine. If she thinks I'm the one Dallas needs to move on with, she's out of her mind, but like so many other times, I choose to keep my mouth shut.

Dallas

CHAPTER SEVEN

"NOW, there's a sight for sore eyes."

Hudson's voice sends a rumble through my skull. I had too many drinks and bombs thrown at me last night. The way he sluggishly climbs up the stairs and collapses into the red rocking chair next to me tells me he didn't get much sleep either. Hopefully, for a better reason than mine.

"You're on my shit list," he grumbles.

I point to his rib cage that's exposed by his cutoff T-shirt. "Those scratches of anger or pleasure?"

He holds up his arm and inspects the skin with an amused, almost boyish smile. "Pleasure. Most definitely pleasure."

I never thought I'd see him happy again after his ex dumped him for his best friend while he was stationed overseas, but Stella came along and changed everything.

"Then, I beg to differ that I'm on your shit list. Had you slept on the couch, I'd feel sorry for you, but from those marks, I'm positive you didn't. End of discussion." I hand him the extra cup of coffee I poured while waiting for him to show up, certain he'd make an appearance this morning.

"Not end of discussion. Stella ran off at the ass crack of dawn to gossip at Lauren's because you knocked up her best friend."

"Fine, I owe you one. I'll mow your grass. Work one of your shifts."

"You going to tell me what went down?"

I snort. "I see Stella isn't the only gossip enthusiast in your home."

He scratches his unshaved cheek. "She's rubbing off on me."

I drum my fingers against the wooden arm of my chair. "Willow didn't deny she was pregnant, so I'd say that confirms it."

The words *I'm pregnant* never left her mouth, but she would've been hell-bent on denying it if it weren't true. She's spent years working with Stella's publicist, making up stories to clean up gossip about Stella. She would've had a good-ass comeback if it weren't true. Hell, I'm surprised she didn't have an excuse already laid out, waiting for when shit hit the fan.

"And?" he pushes.

"There's a possibility I'm the father."

"A possibility? She seemed pretty damn sure about it last night."

She still does.

"What if it's not mine though?"

"You and I both know, Willow isn't like that or a liar. Stella swears Willow hasn't slept with anyone but you in months." He chuckles. "Trust me, from the look on her face, she wishes it were someone else's."

I scrub my hand over my face, hoping it'll help clear my head. "That's what I'm afraid of."

He laughs. "Get prepared, brother. This is happening whether you like it or not."

"We're talking today, figuring shit out."

"The first shit should be, figuring out the living situation. That was my biggest struggle with Stella. Blue Beech was out of her comfort zone, and LA was out of mine."

LA was once my home. I didn't mind leaving Blue Beech years ago when Lucy asked, but that's no longer an option. Maven needs to be here with my family. *I* need the support from them. Willow, on the other hand, is stubborn. I can't picture her packing up her life and moving away from the chaos of the city life.

"Stella changed," I argue, trying to convince myself that it could work.

"She did, but that doesn't stop Willow from begging her to move back every time they talk."

"Fuck," I hiss. I'm going to have my work cut out for me.

Hudson slaps my shoulder and gets up. "Good luck. Let me know if you need anything, but try to wait a few hours, okay? I have a beautiful fiancée waiting at home for me, hopefully wearing nothing but her engagement ring."

"WHAT DO YOU MEAN, she's not here?" I ask, standing in Lauren's doorway and feeling a sense of déjà vu from last night. It seems like I've done nothing but chase Willow around since Hudson broke the news.

"I mean, she's not here," Lauren repeats, shuffling backward to let me in.

"Goddamn it," I mutter, rushing into her apartment like a madman.

My first pit stop is her bathroom to pull back the shower curtain. All clear. Next is Lauren's closet. Then, underneath her bed. No sign of Willow.

"She promised," I repeat over and over again while checking the linen closet. "She fucking promised."

Lauren meets me in the living room with an apologetic face. "I'm guessing she called a cab and bailed while I was in the shower."

I collapse on her couch and drop my head back. Lucy never fought me like this. Our relationship was always easy. She was mine. I was hers. No power struggles existed.

"Maybe she went for a walk?" I ask.

The couch dents when Lauren sits down next to me. "Her bags are gone, and I doubt she's taking a walk with them."

I slowly lift my head, and she bends forward to snag her phone from the coffee table.

She sucks in a breath a few seconds later and ends the call. "Straight to voice mail."

"Same with me. That's why I came over."

Willow promised.

Promised we'd talk.

Promised she'd stay.

She's nothing but a goddamn liar.

I'm not letting her run.

I won't let her shut me out.

Willow

CHAPTER EIGHT

I'M A RUNNER.

Not one who runs 5Ks for fun.

A runner from situations I don't want to face.

I shut my phone off when it rings for what seems like the hundredth time and slip it into my bag. I'm not ready for this—for the reality of what's about to become my life. I don't want to engage in conversations about childbirth, epidurals, and midwives. And definitely nothing about moving.

Call me selfish, but I refuse to move thousands of miles for a man in love with another woman. A man who'll *always* be in love with that woman. A man who, even though he irritates me to no limit, made me feel beautiful and wanted one night.

He gave me an intimacy I'd never had. All I'd gotten in the past was a boyfriend who lied and cheated like it was his job. The more time I spend with Dallas the more those memories of how he made me feel that night will pop up.

I check the time on my watch and relax in my seat, my shoulders drooping. It never fails that I choose the worst in the penis pool. Millions of men in this world, and somehow, I manage to always pick the screwed up ones who see me as nothing more than a disposable fuck.

"Did you think it'd be that easy?"

I tense at the sound of his sharp voice. It's as if a knife has been jabbed into my throat. I'm terrified to face him. I can sense his eyes tearing into my back, feeling the pain as if they were breaking flesh.

I should've taken the Greyhound or hitchhiked. I probably shouldn't have headed straight to the most obvious place—the fucking airport.

"You had enough balls to run away. Don't be a coward now. Turn around and look me in the eyes," he demands. "Tell me you're not only selfish, but a liar as well."

His bossiness and cruel words set a match to my already shitty mood.

How dare he judge me. How dare he act like he understands what I'm going through.

"Willow." My name sounds like a threat, assuring me he's not leaving until I give in.

I pull myself up from my chair with a dramatic moan and jerk my purse over my shoulder. The airport is no LAX, but there are plenty of people around with curious eyes.

Dallas's face is challenging, like he's ready to close a business deal. He did nice, and I took advantage of it. Now, he's giving me something else.

I made a promise and broke it. He has every right to be pissed.

I'm ashamed it takes me a minute to square up my shoulders, to show him I'm not someone who can be scolded like a child.

"We're not doing this here," is all I say.

He sweeps his arm out. "After you, your highness."

Since I'm not that familiar with the airport, I head to the women's restroom, uncertain if he'll follow me.

He does.

"This is a better place to do it?" he questions, locking the door behind us and leaning back against it when I nod. "Suit yourself."

I throw my arms down to my sides with a huff. "What do you want from me, Dallas?"

"What do I want from you?" He lets out a mocking laugh. "I

want you to act like a responsible adult. It might be hard for you to realize, but this isn't only about you."

"I know."

"So, why run?"

"I'm scared!"

"And I'm assuring you, there's no reason to be." He comes closer as a long breath releases from his broad chest. "I know your trust in me is shit." He signals between the two of us. "I'm not asking you to marry me or be with me or, hell, even like me. I'm sure we can both agree that a relationship is out of the question. You can think I'm a shit person all you want, but I'm not a shit dad, and you fucking know it."

He's hitting me with all the truths. You'd think someone would break entirely when the love of their life died. Lucy's death shattered Dallas, but she left scattered pieces, so he'd be able to take care of Maven. She knew their daughter would be Dallas's savior when she was gone.

He goes to grab my bag. "Come on. Lauren has a twelve-hour shift. We'll talk, and then you can have her apartment to yourself for the night."

I hold my hand out to stop him. "I'm getting on that plane."

His lips press into a white slash, and he tiredly rubs his face.

"Scooby is waiting for me."

He blinks. "I'm sorry, *who* is waiting for you?"

"Scooby."

He folds his arms across his chest and kicks his legs out. "You two hanging out in the Mystery Machine with Velma?"

"Scooby is my cat, smart-ass," I snap, jutting my chin out.

"Why you named your cat Scooby is a conversation for another time, but we'll be having some serious talks about the name of our child. I won't have a Shaggy Barnes running around."

My hand falls to my chest at the sound of a knock on the door. Dallas holds a finger to his mouth. The knocking stops, and I open my mouth to tell him that I'll see him later when it starts back up again. The person on the other side must really need to go because the knocks get louder and faster.

"Out of order!" Dallas finally yells. "Go somewhere else."

The knocking subsides, and I narrow my eyes his way. "You do know, this is the women's restroom? They're probably going to security."

I shrug. He can't badger me if he's in jail.

"Then, let's make this quick."

"My mom is watching Scooby for me. I told her I'd be back by tomorrow. I also need to tell her about the whole becoming-a-grandma thing."

Family—Dallas's weakness.

I realize I chose the right words when his face falls into an apology.

"Why didn't you tell me that?"

I wrinkle my nose. "If you haven't figured it out by now, I'm not the most open person."

"That makes two of us. What a pair." He gives me a gentle smile. "Go home, Willow. Tell your mom, but keep in contact."

My shoulders slump. "I will."

"Promise me." I open my mouth to do what he asked, but he stops me, scowling. "Actually, don't bother. Promises don't mean shit to you." He unlocks the door. "If you don't answer my calls, the next time you see me will be when I'm standing on your mom's doorstep, introducing myself."

———

"I DON'T KNOW why you won't let me keep him," my mom whines while running her fingers through Scooby's thick white hair.

A few strands stick to her hand because he sheds like no other. We have the whole let-me-keep-Scooby talk every time she cat-sits.

I flew into LA, got my car from my apartment, and then drove to my mom's house. She lives in the same house I grew up in, in a small suburb three hours out of LA. The ride gave me time to figure out how I was going to break the news to her.

"Mom, you bought him *for me* as a present."

After Stella moved away, he was a birthday gift to keep me company, but I think she used me as an excuse to buy herself an animal.

"You're out of town so much, and you don't give him the attention he deserves," she goes on.

She's right. I'm not much of a cat person, but I couldn't ask her to return him to the animal shelter. Scooby came from a good place. I only wish she'd chosen something that needed less upkeep—like, say, a goldfish.

"You seem to enjoy spending time with your grandcat," I reply. "I'm doing you a favor by traveling so frequently."

She lifts her chin. "When are you going to move home, find a good man, and settle down? Stella is doing it. Maybe you should follow her example."

Here we go again.

This is why the majority of my visits with her are when she's Scooby-sitting.

"Men and I aren't on the same page right now." *I have a feeling we'll never be.*

"If you'd quit looking in all the wrong places, they'd be. Come to church with me tomorrow, honey. They expanded, and traffic is booming! God-loving young men are scouring the place for a good wife to start a family with."

I can't stop myself from scowling. "Men scouring the place for a wife? Not my type, Mom. That sounds not only desperate, but also scary." I'm sure those men wouldn't approve of me carrying someone else's baby out of wedlock.

I drag my phone from my pocket when it beeps. I turned it back on when my plane landed but have yet to reply to the seventy-eight text messages from every citizen in Blue Beech.

Dallas: You make it to your mom's okay?

I set my phone to the side, ignoring it, and then pluck it back up. His threat wasn't empty, and the last thing I need is him showing up here.

Me: Just got here. Talking to her.

Dallas: You break the news yet?

Me: I need to loosen her up with a glass of wine first.

Dallas: Good luck.

Me: I should be the one telling you good luck. She'll probably take it better than your parents.

Dallas: I haven't told them yet. I'm waiting for you to be here. Consider your mom practice.

Me: Not happening.

He's eating bath salts if he thinks I'll be attending that shitshow. Dallas's family is as traditional as it gets. They're nice people, don't get me wrong, but super old school.

Dallas: We'll talk about it.

We'll talk about it?

The hell kind of answer is that?

I toss my phone onto the pillow next to me on the couch. "How about we go to dinner at La Vista tonight?"

———

MY PLAN of liquoring my mom up, so I could spill the beans wasn't as bright as I'd thought it was an hour ago.

She wisps her hair, the same color as mine, away from her eyes to better stare at me. She's been eyeballing me since our drink order was placed five minutes ago. I'm doing my best to avoid direct eye contact with her, scared she'll read my mind.

The restaurant is packed. It always is on Saturday nights, given it's the nicest place in our suburb. A few of my mom's friends stopped to talk to us while we waited for our table, their eyes scrutinizing and judging me for the wrongs my ex-boyfriend did to a young kid who was the star of his little league baseball team.

"I take it, you have something to tell me," she says.

A knot ties in my belly. "Huh?"

"You've been nervous since you got home today. You then bring me to La Vista and order a glass of wine for me before the waiter even got the chance to introduce himself. You bring me here whenever you have news you don't want to break to me."

Come to think of it, she's right. I brought her here when I decided to move to LA, when I got back with Brett, and then when I told her I'd officially broken things off with him.

I lower my head in shame and blurt out my confession, "I'm pregnant."

She takes a long drink of wine before giving me a response. Her brows pull in as she carefully chooses her words. "This isn't some April Fool's Day joke, is it?"

"It's June."

I'm trying to read her, but I can't pinpoint what's going on in her mind. She's not happy, but she's not unhappy.

"How do you feel about this?"

My heart thrashes in my chest, and my chin quivers. "Like an idiot." An idiot for not using protection. Go figure, my ovaries are the .01 percent that gets pregnant while taking the pill.

"Do I know the father?"

"It's not Brett's."

A rush of relief releases from her lips. "Thank Jesus."

"It's Dallas Barnes."

"Stella's old bodyguard?"

I nod. "And Hudson's older brother."

Mortification floods her face. "Isn't he …" She grabs the glass of red wine and chugs the remainder of it down, her emerald eyes wide. "Isn't he married?"

Oh, fuck. She's afraid I'm a homewreckin' ho.

"His wife passed away almost a year ago."

She nods slowly, digesting my answer, the familiarity of it flashing across her face like a burn. "You didn't tell me you two were dating."

I can't distinguish if she's asking a question or giving a warning. My mother knows the nightmare of never getting over your first love —a memory that bites at every inch of your body until your last breath.

"We're not dating," I answer. "It was a one-time thing. Too much whiskey, not enough thinking."

I take a sip of water, a breath of courage, and proceed to tell her everything minus the details of the actual baby-making, and I am unable to stop the tears from falling from my eyes ... and hers.

She stretches her arm across the table to grab my hand in hers. "If Dallas wants to be in the picture, give him a chance." Her voice is soft, caressing, a vocal hug. "He's a father, a single one at that, who knows the responsibility of taking care of a child."

"I'm strong, Mom." My throat is dry, causing my words to come out raspy. "I can do this on my own."

"Honey, I'm not denying you can, but I know from firsthand experience, it isn't easy, doing it alone. No mother can replace the void of a father. We can both agree on that."

A knife slashes through my heart. The reality of what I did smacks me in the face, like I've been unconscious this entire time.

I was that child, the one without a father. It was by choice for the first fifteen years. He didn't decide he was ready to be a dad until he was diagnosed with stage five colon cancer. My mother welcomed him with open arms. I didn't.

He passed away at the young age of forty-one when I was sixteen. My mother forgave him at his deathbed. I didn't. I couldn't. The bitterness was still wrapped in my heart. I couldn't forget all the times I'd been a jealous-filled child when I watched my friends have fathers.

Everyone has choices in their life. He chose to leave. You can't take that shit back when you find out your time is limited, and you have no one to help you through it.

She drops my hand and sits back in her chair, the wine now relaxing her. "Your father always wanted grandchildren."

I want to tell her that I don't care what he wanted. My mom has gone through hell since he left her ... both times.

"I doubt that dream included a love child," I mutter.

"A grandchild is a grandchild. A blessing. No matter what the situation."

CHAPTER NINE

DALLAS: **You break the news yet?**

The text was sent two hours ago. My phone stayed in my purse throughout dinner, and when we got home, we spent the rest of the night bingeing on popcorn and Matthew McConaughey movies.

Me: Sure did.

I change into my pajamas and slide into bed. My mom kept my room how it was when I moved out. The same sponge-painted yellow walls and pictures of me at different school events on the dresser. I zero in on the prom picture of Brett and me and tell myself to toss it and any others with him into the trash tomorrow.

The phone rings, and I freeze up and stare at the screen for a few seconds when his name flashes across it. We've talked on the phone before, for business, so why am I terrified of answering?

I inhale a breath of courage before accepting the call. "Hello?"

"How'd she take it?" Dallas asks.

Hello to you, too.

I chew on my nails. "Not bad. I did crush her hopes on if I'd decided to move home and find a husband though."

"You dream crusher, you."

I smile.

"Did she ask about me? About who the dad is?"

"She knows who you are."

A brief silence passes.

He met my mom at Stella's Christmas dinner one year. I brought her as my plus-one after Brett went missing for forty-eight hours on a drinking binge. He and Lucy were there, and Mom talked about how their relationship was beautiful on our way back to my apartment.

"She's happy I at least got knocked up by a decent man."

"Good." He pauses for a few seconds. "I need to ask for a favor."

"If it's being present and accounted for when you tell your parents, that's gonna be a hard no."

"Let me correct myself. I need to ask you for *favors.*"

"You're really pushing it, you know that?"

"Come to Blue Beech."

"I was just in Blue Beech, remember? Hudson having a big mouth, three a.m. wake-up call—all of that jazz."

"Damn, Ms. Difficult, *stay* in Blue Beech. Give it a try. A trial run, if you will."

"Didn't we have this talk in the bathroom?" I ask, exasperated. *No way in hell is that happening.* "We decided we're not moving in together, getting married, or any of that forced nonsense."

"Whoa, whoa. Pump your brakes, sweetheart. I promise, this is *not* a marriage proposal. It's a moving proposal, so we can do this as a team."

"Why can't we do it as a team in LA?"

It's his turn to let out an exasperated breath. "I have a daughter here who adores her friends and family. My business is here. Hell, *your* job is here. Any other points I need to throw out? You belong here, Willow."

I grow quiet, and he lets out an irritated groan.

"Fine, I'll come to you if I have to, but prepare to explain the reason to my family. I won't be pushed away from this, and I am not a man you can play games with. I'm a man who will fight for what he wants and the people he loves. You might not have given birth to our baby yet, but that doesn't mean I don't care for it."

He has a point. Maven has already lost her mom. It'd be greedy of me to ask Dallas to move her away from her home and the family she has left.

"Where am I supposed to stay? On the streets?"

"You can stay at my place. I have a guest room."

"Not a chance in hell."

"Stella's?"

"Shack up with the lovebirds? Again, not happening."

"We'll find you a rental then."

I yawn. This conversation is getting too dangerous, sounding too final. "Let me sleep on it. I'll talk to you tomorrow."

———

I'M READING another article of what having a baby does to your vagina when the doorbell rings. My mom left for church an hour ago, so yelling for her to answer it isn't an option. I throw the covers off me before slipping out of bed with a groan. It rings again as I trek down the stairs.

I'm cranky. Heartburn and headache made an appearance and decided to stay all night. Heartburn was the consequence of overeating pasta, and the headache was from the regret of possibly agreeing to move to Blue Beech.

I swing the front door open, and my temples throb at the sight of the world's biggest asshole standing on the porch with white roses in his hand like he's picking me up for prom.

"Nuh-uh, not today, Satan!" I yell before slamming the door in his face and locking it.

Someone must've spotted me at La Vista last night and told him I was in town.

Brett bangs on the other side. "Willow! At least talk to me!"

"Fuck you!" I yell back. "Go give those to one of the fifty women you fucked behind my back."

"I have a key," he warns. "Don't you make me use it!"

"I have a baseball bat. Don't you make me use it!"

He knocks a few more times. "I'll be back. Don't think I won't. Every fucking day until I break you down."

"That's what they make restraining orders for!"

He knocks again. "I'll be back."

And then silence. Not surprising. Brett is one of the laziest men I know. He doesn't like to work for anything, but he'll try to sweet-talk me like he did every time I took him back in the past. Dealing with him is the last thing on my to-do list. Actually, not even on the list. He's lazy but also irritating when he's not getting his way. I'm guessing the woman he was cheating on me with got a glimpse of the real him and bailed. That means, he's ready to run back to me.

Maybe I do need to get out of California, get some fresh air, and clear my head. I lean back against the front door as frustration builds in my head. I'm mentally cursing myself when I head back to my room.

I snatch my phone from the nightstand, nearly ripping it from my charger, and hit Dallas's name, praying to God I don't regret this tomorrow.

Me: Blue Beech. A trial run. That's me compromising.

My phone beeps seconds later.

Dallas: Thank you. You have no idea how much I appreciate this.

I exit from his name and hit Stella's.

Me: Hello, new neighbor!

Stella: YES! Team Stella for the win! You're staying with me, BTW.

Me: Not happening, BTW.

Stella: Why? Don't tell me you're crashing at Dallas's? How romantic.

Me: Are you nuts? I'm renting a place.

Staying with Dallas is not an option.

What would he tell his daughter? That I'm homeless and then— surprise!—I'm carrying your sibling?

Dallas

CHAPTER TEN

"BUT … but Auntie Lauren lets me have it," Maven whines.

I snatch the coffee cup from my six-year-old, who is under the impression she's a grown-up, and replace it with an organic apple juice box. "I'll be having a conversation with Auntie Lauren."

My sister's idea of a well-balanced diet is iced coffee, margaritas, and deli sandwiches from the hospital's vending machine.

She sits down at the table with a un-caffeinated frown at the same time I place a bowl of strawberry oatmeal in front of her. I promised Lucy that Maven would be taken care of, and that means making her eat balanced meals.

My days have gone from traveling the world with Hollywood's elite to packing nutritious lunches, attending dance recitals, and reading the same bedtime stories for months on end.

But I wouldn't trade it for the world.

Time is valuable. Hug your children. Kiss your wife. Make life your bitch because you never know when it's going to turn on you.

I grab my phone and sit down next to Maven.

"What are you doing?" she asks before taking a bite of her oatmeal.

"Texting your aunt."

"Tattletale," she mutters with a frown.

Me: Mom and Dad paid for four years of nursing school, and you don't know that kids shouldn't have coffee? Your license needs to be revoked.

My phone beeps a few minutes later.

Lauren: Relax, old man. Unbeknownst to your caffeine-fiend spawn, I give her decaf. She wants to be my mini me, which I approve of.

My family has been the key to my survival. Lauren stepped up to be a mother figure to Maven when Lucy passed.

Me: That's scary. Is the apartment underneath you still vacant?

The struggling musician who lived underneath her got evicted last month for playing music all day and night. She threw a party in celebration when he left.

Lauren: Depends on why you're asking. If it's for a dude in a band, then no.

Me: Give me your landlord's number.

Lauren: WHY?

Jesus, they might be my backbones, but they are damn nosy.

Me: I need to find a place for Willow.

Lauren: Holy shit! She's moving here? The apartment is open. I can't wait to have a front row seat to your guys' drama!

Me: Send me the damn number.

I grab Maven's backpack, and she gets into my truck at the same time Lauren sends me the number. I wait until I drop Maven off at my parents' before calling Lauren's landlord, Fred. He gives me the good news that the apartment is vacant but is unwilling to put a hold on it for me, so I drive to his office and pay the security deposit.

The apartment comes fully furnished, but I decide to take a peek at it before Willow moves in. I'll do anything in my power to make sure she's comfortable here.

It's a damn good thing I did.

"I need help," I tell Hudson when he answers my call.

"With what?" he asks.

"Getting Willow's apartment together. I'll also need some input from Stella."

He takes a deep breath, almost sounding surprised. "So, you're really doing this, huh? Moving Willow here?"

"Did you think I wouldn't?"

"No, I thought *she* wouldn't. I'll believe it when I see it."

Willow

CHAPTER ELEVEN

LAUREN POPS the trunk and steps out of her over-the-top pink Mustang when I walk out of the airport. The car is hideous yet has a certain appeal to her.

"You know, I'm confused," she says, helping me with my bags and then throwing her hands on her hips in question, as if I can read her mind as to what she's confused about.

One thing I admire about Lauren is her inability to bullshit. She might just barely be grazing five feet, but she'll ask you straight up instead of gossiping behind your back.

I slam the trunk shut. "Confused about what?"

She doesn't answer my question until we're in the car. "On why you'll screw my brother but refuse to let him pick you up from the airport."

It's a three-hour drive to Blue Beech, and I asked Lauren to pick me up instead of Dallas, so I wouldn't have to spend hours alone with him, answering questions. I have the impression it might not be much different with his sister.

I fix my glare on her. "Haven't you ever had a one-night stand?"

"I live in a town with a population of six hundred. Half of the men were married off before their balls dropped. There's no one to have a one-night stand with." She pauses to give me a side-eye. "I guess I can't speak for everyone."

"Oh, kiss my ass," I grumble, rubbing my eyes.

Sleep hasn't been my friend lately, and I had an early flight. I doubt I'll be able to unwind when I get to Blue Beech either.

"Did he do that, too?" She laughs when I flip her off. "You kinky kids, you."

"I wish you had never found out," I grumble.

"*Secrets don't make friends,*" she sings out, gearing the car in drive.

"They sure can keep them though."

She tips her thumb toward my growing belly. "That, *my friend*, would be a mighty hard secret to keep."

I made a list of lies when my first pregnancy test came out positive. IVF treatment. Secretly adopted a baby. A one-night stand, and I didn't get the guy's name. The last one is technically only a half-lie.

I slump down in my seat. "I can't believe I'm doing this."

"Doing what? Moving to the best place in the world and being surrounded by delightful company? We're going to be neighbors. That, my dear, will be the highlight of your life."

"No, I can't believe I packed up and moved to a town void of takeout sushi but also where I'll be labeled a widower-chasing tramp. Might as well pin a scarlet letter to my chest and call it a day."

"You can't be serious." She peeks over at me, her amused smile fading into concern. "Willow, no one is going to call you a widower-chaser. I mean, not to your face at least." She pauses to give me a cheesy grin. "Although it does have a nice ring to it. Willow the Widower-Chaser."

"That's it. Turn this pink puss car around."

I yelp at the sound of the door locking. "Prepare for a three-hour drive filled with prying questions and nineties hip-hop. I hope you're a Snoop Dogg fan."

———

"WOW, THIS IS A NICE PLACE."

I drop my bag onto the mahogany wood floor and explore my new apartment. It's an older building with a floor plan similar to Lauren's, except mine is a two bedroom and has more space. Something like this would cost a kidney in LA. My mom told me I was choosing to live in rich-people poverty when I moved there.

A fresh coat of taupe paint covers the walls, and an exposed brick fireplace is at the front of the living room with a flat screen TV mounted above it. The furniture is new, and decorative touches are scattered throughout the living room and kitchen. A red-and-black-checkered throw is thrown over the back of the couch, and succulents are placed on the end tables to each side of it.

"Thank you for talking to your landlord, putting down the deposit, and getting everything in order on such short notice," I say to Lauren, pulling my purse up from the floor by the strap. I rummage through it in search of my wallet. "How much do I owe you?"

Her hand goes up, stopping me. "Put your wallet away. Thank Dallas. This was all him."

I give the apartment another once-over. "What? How?"

Blame it on the loser I dated for nearly a decade, but my mind can't wrap around a man doing this for me. I guess Stella wasn't lying when she said small-town guys were a different breed.

"Ask him. In the meantime, get yourself settled in. I have a double shift in a few hours and need to hit the shower. Text me if you need anything, *neighbor*."

I smile. She made a six-hour round trip to pick me up and then has to pull a double. "Have fun. Thank you for the ride. I owe you one."

"I got you, girl," is all she says before winking and waving good-bye.

I scoop up my bags and take them into the bedroom when I hear the door shut. Just like the rest of the apartment, the bedroom is spacious. Settling my suitcase on the cream-upholstered king-size bed, I start to unpack.

I let my mom watch Scooby for a few weeks, so I could get settled in and check with the landlord if pets were allowed. Only a few bags came with me on the flight, and I'm having my other stuff and car shipped. I have a baby on the way and am not handing an airline my savings to have a few extra bras.

I drop the shirt I'm hanging up at the sound of the doorbell.

"You forget something?" I ask, opening the door. I stumble back when I don't see Lauren.

Dallas is standing in front of me, shoulders broad and square, wearing a red-buffalo-plaid flannel that nearly matches the throw on my couch, dark jeans with holes in both knees that hug his legs, and brown boots. My heart races, and I can't stop myself from running a finger over my lips.

Shit. Pregnancy hormones are making an appearance. They seem to be well acquainted with him.

Dallas has the efficacy to pull off attractiveness with this casual demeanor better than any man wearing an expensive suit. My ex was a hipster wannabe who regularly sported holey jeans, beanies, and flannels. He was a generic version of the real thing—Dallas. He's no wannabe. He's this rugged, down-to-earth man who has no idea how wet he makes my panties.

I smooth down my hair and shyly smile. "Hey," I say in nearly a whisper.

Tension bleeds through the air like an open wound. Our last face-to-face conversation wasn't exactly pretty.

His thick lips curl up. "If it isn't Blue Beech's newest resident."

"*Temporary* resident," I correct, scooting to the side. My back brushes against the wall as I give him enough room to step into the apartment and shut the door.

His scent, a light evergreen that reminds me of a vacation lodge deep in the mountains where you never want to leave, hangs in the air like smoke as he skims the living room. "You getting settled in okay?"

A few inches separate us, and I play with my hands in front of me, nervousness climbing up my spine. We haven't been alone like this since that night with the small exception of the women's restroom at the airport, which has the privacy that's equivalent to one in prison.

"I haven't had a chance to find a place for everything yet, but the apartment is gorgeous. I can't believe you did all of this. Thank you."

He stares over at me, his eyes flashing with victory and satisfaction. "Thank you for moving here."

I draw in a sharp breath when he edges closer into my space, standing in front of me, as if he's geared to tell me a secret. Being too close for comfort seems to be his thing, which I find completely unnecessary. This isn't L.A. *The square footage is out of this world, dude.*

"You have no idea how much I fucking appreciate it."

I shrug off his gratitude and laugh. "I needed a getaway for a while anyway. Nothing like a vacation before delivering a baby."

He chuckles lightly. "Just a vacation, huh?"

I nod.

He runs his boots back and forth over the hardwood floor. "I stopped by to make sure you showed up and weren't planning on bailing again."

I hold out my arms. "I'm here, in the flesh, breathing and everything."

"I also wanted to see what you might be doing tomorrow night."

Like I have big plans here?

"Most likely, unpacking."

"Perfect, you're free. I'm taking Maven to the fair tomorrow. Come with us."

Is he nuts? He wants me to hang out with not only him, but also his daughter?

"The fair?" I scrunch up my face. "Like vomit-inducing, spinning rides and honky-tonks?"

"No." He pauses. "I mean, yes to the rides, no to the honky-tonks. You watch too many movies."

"I work for movie stars. Watching their movies is part of my job."

"I'll pick you up at six."

"I'll have to pass."

"Come on, who doesn't like the fair?"

"I've never been to one."

His lips tilt into a half-smile, and he opens the front door, patting the inside of it. "I'll pick you up at six."

"Wait!"

"Have a good night, Willow."

The door slams shut behind him.

Willow

CHAPTER TWELVE

THREE MONTHS AGO

"WANT TO DANCE?"

Dallas and I both flinch at my question.

Did those words leave my mouth?

This whiskey shit is messing with my insanity. I shouldn't want to dance with Dallas. I definitely shouldn't be feeling this weird pull between us after only a few hours of drinking together.

Lauren stopped by our table earlier to give me a ride back to Stella's, but I wasn't ready to end my time with Dallas. Turned out, neither was he. He offered to walk me back to Hudson's on his way home. Surprisingly, Lauren didn't find it weird and took off.

The place is close to empty, except for the few lone rangers at the end of the bar, and the band left with their armful of groupies. The music has been downgraded to static-infused country songs coming from an old jukebox in the corner of the room.

He stares at me with hooded eyes, and I wave my hand in the air as rejection slaps me in my stupid, drunken face.

"Forget it," I rush out, beating him to the punch. "Of course you don't." This will mortify me when my senses come back in the morning.

He holds his fist to his mouth and lets out a shuddering breath. "I'm not really up for dancing."

He jumps up from his stool, and I avert my eyes to the tabletop. *This is where he bails. Do they have Uber around here?*

His tall frame towers over me, and I jump when his strong hand grabs my chin to tilt it up.

Our gaze meets, latching on to each other's in a strong hold, and he lowers his voice. "But I will for you."

His fingertips smooth over my chin as he waits for my answer, and my brain goes fuzzy. Every person and every noise disappears around us.

"Never mind," I stutter out, not sure if my words are even audible. "It's okay. I'm a terrible dancer anyway."

His hand disappears, and he bends down, so his lips are at my ear. "Get up, Willow."

I shudder at the feel of his breath against my skin, goose bumps popping up my neck.

"You've been answering my Tinder questions and listening to me be a miserable bastard all night. I owe you a dance."

"Are ... are you sure?"

"Positive. Hell, I need it as much as you."

I take his hand and slide off my barstool. "Lead the way."

His grip is tight. Secure. I keep my eyes downcast, so I don't see the expressions on people's faces when they see him dancing with someone who's not *her*.

Judgmental eyes won't ruin my night.

My heart races when his hand leaves mine, and he swoops his arm around my back, looping it around my waist. His hand settles on the arch right above my ass, and he starts moving us to the beat of the music.

"What song is this?" I ask.

"'Hurt' by Johnny Cash."

He shuts his eyes, holding me closer, and I take in the lyrics. Dallas didn't choose this song, but God, does it fit his life right now.

The jukebox is giving me a warning. *Run! Run! You naive girl. This man will only end up hurting you.*

A sharp pain fills his eyes as he stares down at me. "You have no idea what you brought out of me tonight." He blows out a ragged breath. "What you gave me tonight, Willow. I've never opened up like this to anyone."

Even Lucy? is the question I want to ask, but I bite my tongue. *Me either* are the words I want to say next, but again, I don't, for fear he'll run away.

Almost a decade with Brett, and never did emotions drum through me like this.

Is this what it feels like—falling for someone? Is this why people who've experienced love crave it so much?

Love.

I gulp down a thousand feelings. I'm overthinking this.

I can't fall for a man after one night of conversation and a dance.

"I've never danced with anyone like this," I admit.

Instead of pulling away, he draws in nearer, pressing his mouth to my ear. I shiver as his crisp breath hits my sweaty skin. "Like what?"

"Without grinding my ass against someone while Lil Jon plays in the background."

Proms. Frat parties. Clubs. Those are the only places I've danced with men. Never so slow, so personal, so gentle. Never like *this.*

He chuckles—not only surprising me, but also making me smile. "I'm taking your virginity of how a real man dances with a woman."

My response is resting my chin on his shoulder and losing myself to the music as he takes me into another world. We stay silent in our moment, but it's a comfortable silence, something that feels necessary right now. I expect him to pull away when the song ends, but he doesn't. We dance into the next one with my arms nestled on his rugged shoulders as we feed something we shouldn't.

"Last call!" a voice yells in the distance, snapping me out of my powerful trance. I'm unsure of how many songs we've danced through. "Five minutes until closing time!"

I attempt to pull away, but Dallas tightens his hold, silently asking me not to let go yet.

"Give me that five minutes," he pleads.

"Of course," I whisper, slipping my hands down his back. "I'll give you however long you need."

He nods his thank-you. Time slows. These five minutes feel like a lifetime. Our embrace grows tighter, our sway to the music slower and the connection sharper.

"Dallas, man, I hate to do this, but I have to shut this shit down," the guy who screamed out the last call warns.

I lose our connection when he retreats a step, my arms splaying down his sides and then falling to mine, and he gives me an apologetic look.

"Sorry," he whispers to me before turning his attention to the bartender. "You're good, man. Enjoy your night."

The bartender, the same man who was making our drinks, gives him a thumbs-up and a smile. "It was good seein' ya!"

His gaze lowers to mine. "You ready to go back to Stella's?"

No! No!

I'm debating on asking the bartender how much he wants for this bar, so we can stay longer.

I force a smile. "I have to be, considering we're getting kicked out."

He grabs my hand, interlacing our fingers, and holds them against his shoulder. "It's beautiful out tonight. How 'bout we take the scenic route? Might be a good idea to show you the beauty of Blue Beech since Hudson says you hate it and refuse to move here with Stella."

I tilt my head to the side. "Hey now, did he tell you to give me a good time in an attempt to change my mind?"

"You know me better than to think I'd take commands from my baby brother. *But*"—I knew that *but* was coming—"that doesn't mean I won't try to convince you Blue Beech is a good place, and you should really consider moving here."

"I'll keep that in mind." *Especially if I can get another night like this.*

He bows his head. "Thank you."

"I didn't make any promises."

"Not thank you for allowing me to show you around. Thank you for making me forget I'm a miserable man missing half of who he is. Thank you for not treating me like a broken fucking object that needs fixing."

I hide my face on his shoulder to conceal my smile. "You've done the same for me." With my mouth pressed against his denim shirt, my face hidden, I take a risk that could go horribly wrong. "You know somewhere I haven't seen in Blue Beech?"

"What's that?"

"The home of Dallas Barnes."

Don't judge me.

I know what I'm doing is wrong, but bad ideas sometimes lead to good things, right?

Willow

CHAPTER THIRTEEN

ONE OF THE biggest things I've learned about Blue Beech so far is real-life county fairs are nothing like the movies.

Dallas texted me this morning to remind me of the time he was picking me up and told me to have an appetite. The impulse to decline spilled through me, but the thought of experiencing something new prevented it.

I mean, who doesn't want to find out what the fair hype is all about?

Dallas parks his truck in a grassy field converted into a parking lot. The amount of cars surprises me. *This many people live here?*

He helps Maven out of the truck before circling to my side. "Thank you for coming," he says when he opens my door. He grabs my hand and assists me out of the lifted truck. "It's all Maven's been talking about today."

I nervously laugh. "Guess it was time to pop my fair cherry." I grimace at my word choice. *No, Willow. No flirting with the widowed asshole.*

He smirks. "Honored to be the one to do it."

I nod, relieved he didn't shut down on me but scared it'll happen sometime tonight. Like me, Dallas is a pro at freezing people out at the snap of his fingers.

Maven is spinning in circles with her arms out in the air. Her hair is pulled back in two French braids that are finished off with furry pink bands holding each one in place. *Did Dallas braid them for her?*

I swing the strap of my cross-body bag over my shoulder while Dallas scoops Maven up and spins her around one last time. He takes her hand and leads us toward the flashing lights and white tents. When we hit the dusty pathway, I peek down at my feet, wishing I'd chosen different shoes. Everyone is in boots or sneakers while I'm sporting studded black flats that are going to be ruined by the end of the night.

"I want to ride that one!" Maven exclaims, pointing at rides as we make our way through the crowd. "Then, that one. And that one."

"Dinner before rides," Dallas replies, casting a glance my way. "What's your fair poison?"

"My what?" I ask.

He peeks down at Maven with a smile. "This is Willow's first time at the fair," he explains, as if I were the only person who hadn't done such a thing.

Maven giggles, her face lighting up. "Really?"

I nod, and she reaches out to connect her hand with mine. My chest tightens when I squeeze my hand around hers, a sadness sinking through me. We resemble the other families here—mom and dad treating their eager daughter to a night full of games, candy, and fun.

"My absolute favorites are elephant ears and cotton candy!" she says.

"Hey, I've had cotton candy," I argue.

"But have you had *fair* cotton candy?" Dallas counters, causing Maven to burst out into more giggles. "*Blue Beech* cotton candy?"

I glance over at him. "Wasn't aware there was a difference."

His dark brows rise. "Oh, there most definitely is."

We stop at a table underneath a blue tent, and Dallas insists on getting our food. Maven takes the seat next to me, her legs bouncing up and down in excitement.

"Did you know Daddy said I get to ride big-kid rides this year?" she asks with a burst of energy I wish I had every morning. "Last year, I wasn't tall enough, but I've grown *lots and lots!*"

"No way!" I reply before holding my hand up in the air. "I had to wait until I was *this* big before I got to do that."

Her head tilts to the side. "I thought you'd never been to a fair?"

Girl is smart for a six-year-old.

"I've been to Disney."

She bounces in her seat. "Me, too! Mommy and Daddy took me for my birthday. I had lunch with Princess Jasmine!"

I place my hand over my heart and gasp. "Princess Jasmine? That's so cool. Is she your favorite princess?"

She nods repeatedly. "Who's yours?"

"Ariel." I point to my hair. "Have to support my fellow redhead."

"She's my second favorite!" She claps her hands. "Maybe, next time, you can come with Daddy and me and meet Princess Jasmine!"

I nod timidly. "Yeah, maybe."

Our conversation stops when Dallas gets to the table with drinks in his hands and plates lined up his arms, like an experienced waiter. I slide out of my seat to help him set everything down.

"Are you feeding the entire town?" I ask.

"I promised to give you the full fair experience," he says, sitting down across from me. He points to the plates the same way Maven did with the rides. "Tenderloins are Maven's and my favorite. I also grabbed some fried chicken, shish kebabs, and pizza in case you wanted to play it safe. Then, we have some elephant ears and cotton candy. Drinks are an option of a lemon shake-up, water, or soda."

I snag a lemon shake-up. "So many healthy choices."

He chuckles. "We're splurging tonight."

Maven sticks out her tongue. "It's better than broccoli. Daddy makes me eat gross broccoli."

Dallas points his fork at her. "Give a man some credit for adding cheese to it for you."

Maven picks up a shish kebab and waves it through the air. "Not better than cotton candy! Pink is the best!" she sings out.

The nauseating smell of meat smacks me in the face, causing my stomach to churn, and she sets it back down on her plate. I close my hand over my nose and mouth—not only to block out the stench, but also to stop myself from vomiting in front of a crowd of people.

Dallas drops his sandwich. "Everything okay?"

"The meat," I choke out underneath my hand, shaking my head. "None of that."

He gets the hint, grabs it from Maven's plate, and tosses it in the trash. "Sorry, honey," he tells her. "Bad meat."

She nods and moves on to a tenderloin.

I move my hand and take a deep breath, whispering, "Thank you," to him.

His lips tilt up in a smile, a real one, something I haven't seen from him since I've been here. My breathing hitches. My heart skitters.

"Any weird cravings yet?" he asks.

"Cupcakes. Cake. Brownies. Sugar in general."

He laughs, another authentic one, making me happy I came. "I'll remember that."

My lips curve into a smile, meeting his, and I snack on a slice of cheese pizza while Maven takes over the conversation of how excited she is to leave for summer camp in a few days. She shoves her plate forward after the last bite and focuses on Dallas in determination that is too intense for a kid whose age hasn't reached the double digits yet.

"Time for rides, Daddy!" she declares. "And don't you forget, I get to ride the *big-kid* ones. No more kiddy zone for me."

Dallas holds his hand up. "Hold it, youngster. Only the ones you meet the height requirement for, remember?"

"Is she trying to talk you into letting her bungee jump again?"

Hudson's voice catches me off guard, and I turn around to see him and Stella coming our way. The sight of her eases me. Hudson

… not so much. I'm not sure how he feels about me. Stella insists he holds no grudges against me, but I don't believe her.

"I'm not old enough for that *yet*," Maven says.

"Or ever," Dallas corrects. He stares down at Maven, shaking his head. "You, my dear child, are going to give me a heart attack before forty."

"Hey, brother," Hudson cuts in. "Which will be worse—the day she wants to bungee jump or date?"

"Dating," Dallas answers without hesitation. "I will bungee jump at her side before I agree to dating."

"Gross, I don't want to date," Maven chimes in with disgust.

Dallas taps the top of her head. "That's my girl."

"You want to ride roller coasters with me, Uncle Hudson?" Maven asks. "Willow is coming!"

Pregnancy and carnival rides don't go together.

"Oh no," I moan out. "I get motion sickness."

I'm not sure when Dallas is going to break the news that she's going to be a big sister, but I most certainly don't want to be in attendance. Lord knows the questions she'll have.

Maven's smile morphs into a pout. "My mommy did, too, but she was always okay."

I regret looking at Dallas at the mention of Lucy. His body goes still, and I'm confident his heart is beating faster than anyone on a roller coaster here. The lightness of our time together has been extinguished, a whirl of unease stepping through. He scratches his neck, and I notice a vein popping out from it.

"How about I go with you? I love roller coasters!" Stella quickly offers up, lying to the poor girl.

"Thank you," I whisper to her while Maven waits for Dallas's permission.

His eyes are vacant, his face cloaked with pain. He's checked out.

"I'll make sure the two of them stay out of trouble," Hudson says. "You keep introducing Willow to coma-inducing foods and sell Blue Beech to her."

Dallas pinches the bridge of his nose and nods. I grab my lemon shakeup and suck it down without even bothering to argue with Hudson about the "sell Blue Beech to her" comment. The thought of Dallas showing me around makes me queasier than the meat.

Stella grabs Maven's hand, and the three of them take off through the pack of people. I'm struggling to find the right words. I want to console Dallas, but I'm not sure if it's a good idea. It might push him away more.

Isn't that what I wanted when I found out I was pregnant?

Now, I'm thriving for more from him.

For as long as I can remember, I've admired his love for Lucy. His commitment to her, even when half-dressed women threw themselves at him in hopes of seeing Stella.

Seeing their relationship made you believe in love again.

And that's why I can't get close to him.

He'll never give me that.

You don't get love like that twice in a lifetime.

You can't awaken those emotions back out of a broken man.

I need to back off and quit trying to make strides with him that'll only end up stomping on my heart when I'm forced to face the devastation that he's just around me because I got knocked up by him.

I don't realize I'm staring until his hollow eyes meet mine. His Adam's apple bobs while he piles the plates on top of each other and disposes them into the trash.

He fraudulently smiles down at me. "You ready for your Blue Beech pitch?"

I grab a bag of cotton candy. "I'll listen, but I'm not someone easily convinced."

"Oh, Miss Andrews, I can be a very persuasive man." He must've given himself a pep talk on his way to the trash because his excitement meter has risen a few notches.

I shove a handful of cotton candy into my mouth before getting up. We walk in silence, side by side, passing annoyed parents yelling at their children and people spending their paychecks on games that are scamming them.

Everyone stops and stares when we walk past them, like we're the show animals. A few women have pulled out their phones to record us. We appear as platonic as it gets. Hell, maybe more like strangers, considering we're not saying a word to each other.

No story here, people.

Don't twist it into something it's not.

Because it's way more complicated than us having sex.

"How about a game?" Dallas asks, breaking my attention away from the crowd of women pointing our way.

I throw them a dirty grimace and set my eyes back on him.

We've stopped in front of a ring-toss game with giant animals hanging from the roof of the tent.

"The chances of me winning that small stuffed animal is one in a gazillion, and it will cost me a couple of hundred bucks. I'd rather save my money and buy a new handbag." *Or a crib.*

"I like your style." He laughs, shaking his head. "I've blown so much money on those stupid things. Lucy loved them." He tilts his head toward the flashing lights and spinning rides. "Ferris wheel?"

"I see you live on the wild side."

"Risky is my middle name. Be right back."

I combatively stare at him while he jogs over to the ticket booth without waiting to hear my answer.

How do I tell him I'd rather blow my life savings on a game than be stuck in the air with him?

As bad as I want to, I can't. It's hard for me to give him shit when it looks like someone ran over his dog.

So, I wait in line.

He hands the bored attendant our tickets and helps me into the car. It's cramped as we sit across from each other. I blush each time our knees brush in the tight space.

"You make a doctor's appointment yet?" he asks when the wheel starts to move.

I sigh playfully. "This was your plan, huh? Get me hundreds of feet in the air, so I can't bail when you ask me complicated questions?"

He holds his hand up, a smile cracking at his lips. It's not as real as the one he gave me at the beginning of the night, but it's better than the artificial one earlier. "Convenient timing, I swear." He pauses, the smile still flickering at his lips. "Subconscious smart move on my part, considering your history of being a runner."

His jeans rub against my bare leg when I situate myself on the metal seat. Like my flats, shorts weren't the best fashion choice.

"Awkward conversations aren't a favorite pastime of mine," I mutter.

"You mean, making adult decisions aren't?"

"I'm twenty-six." I mentally slap myself. *That's my argument?*

"Last time I checked, twenty-six was an adult."

"I mean, I don't have much experience in making adult decisions that don't only impact my life."

When I graduated from high school, I moved to LA for college and have lived my life without answering to anyone. I travel regularly for my job and don't have to worry about anyone other than my boss controlling what I do. My personal decisions have never impacted anyone else's life before.

"You'd better get over that shit *fast*. We're about to be making some big decisions together," he says.

My chest feels tight. I haven't come to terms with having a long-term relationship with Dallas, and I don't feel like diving into the reality of it now. "I haven't made a doctor's appointment yet. I have no idea where to go, but I'd prefer an office not close, considering the town doctor probably delivered you." *And Maven.*

"That's true."

I throw my arms out. "Exactly!" *Does it make me a sucky person that I don't want the same doctor Lucy had? God, I sound like a jealous brat.*

"Dr. Riley's son recently graduated from med school and moved back to work at the practice. He said he'd see us on the low until you're ready to tell people."

On the low? Like I'm going to be pushing a royal baby out of me?

"You're positive he won't tell anyone?" I ask.

"Positive. I have plenty of dirt to easily blackmail him."

"Good. Blackmail away. I'd rather not have any more attention brought to us."

He chuckles and leans forward to scan the crowd below. "I take it, I wasn't the only one noticing all the prying eyes?"

"Sure weren't."

"Ignore them. Something new will come up, and they'll forget about us."

"Doubt it. You're like the bachelor of Blue Beech, and I'm sure they want you to give a rose to a *local girl.*"

"Other people don't decide whom I spend my time with."

They might not decide, but that doesn't mean they won't talk shit about it.

I point to my stomach. "In other news, I need to find more creative ways to hide this. I'm showing more, and I don't want people to find out."

"We're having a baby, Willow. It's eventually going to come out. You're struggling with the reality of it, and that's why I'm holding back on saying anything, but you'd better come to grips with it soon. I need to tell my daughter and parents before you go into labor."

Dallas isn't a bullshitter.

He shoots it to you straight. Been that way for as long as I've known him, which is something I'm not used to. The guys I date tend to be liars who whisper sweet nothings into your ear and then do the opposite. I've never had a guy ... a *man* like Dallas.

He clears his throat. "And, since I have you hostage, I'd better ask the question that's been bugging me."

Oh God. What now?

"Tell me the truth. Why did you hide this from me?"

I look around. *How long does it take for us to get back to the ground?*

"Willow," he says, practically growling my name. "Give me a clear answer, not something half-assed. I want real. The truth."

I lean in and take a deep breath. *Here goes. He wants it. I'll give it. He's not going to like it.*

"I remember every second of our night together." My pulse races like a freight train is about to hit me. "You made me feel special, like I could have someone other than a cheating scumbag. You made me feel alive." *Am I really going to do this?* I want to sound strong, but my voice cracks. "At least temporarily." I stop to inhale another breath, chickening out.

"What happened that makes you question our night wasn't special?"

His gaze is fixed on me, intense, and he settles his elbow on his knee. His free hand rests on my thigh.

"You called me her."

I thought I had his attention before, but my admission kicked it into overdrive.

His head jerks to the side. "What?"

"You called me her ... *Lucy.*" Tears bite at my eyes, breaking the hold I've been trying to keep. *There. I said it. I gave him the truth.*

His face contorts with a mix of pain and disbelief. "What? No way. You're lying."

"I'm not lying."

I regret it every day. Regret not slapping him in the face or screaming when it happened, but I couldn't blame him. I couldn't blame him because my intention of having sex with him was the same—to forget the person I longed for. I wanted to erase Brett. He tried to erase Lucy.

He scrubs his hand over his face. I've spent the last decade reading a man who lied for years, and Dallas isn't lying about not remembering.

He scoots in closer to clasp my chin in his hand. "Fuck, Willow. I'm sorry. No wonder you hate my fucking guts and can barely stand to look at me. I'm sorry. God, I'm an asshole."

He runs his hand over my cheek while apologizing repeatedly. I draw in the trace of cotton candy and cinnamon on his breath.

The end of our ride is getting closer, and I wish I had a panic button to freeze us in place.

"You're the only woman I've kissed other than Lucy," he says, his lips inches from mine. "The only woman I've touched. The only woman I've ever had in my bed."

I relax into his touch, into his words. *Should this admission turn me on? Should it make me want to straddle him and get a public indecency arrest?*

"And it's not for lack of trying," he goes on. "This will make me sound like an arrogant jerk, but I've had women knocking on my door daily, but I've never given them a second look. Replacing Lucy with a quick fuck wasn't my intention. I could've done that with anyone. I might've said her name, but I swear to you, I knew who I was inside of, and it wasn't her."

I breathe heavily and take in the callous palm roaming over my cheek.

"We were both missing other people that night. We can agree on that."

I nod at the truth. "What do you want from me?" I whisper, my lips nearly hitting his.

"I want you to move here permanently. I want you to raise our baby here. I don't want you to leave."

His eyes soften, and I dart my tongue over my lips without even realizing it.

God, the desperation of wanting to kiss him, of wanting to screw him, of wanting his touch anywhere on my body is all I'm feeling right now.

"What do you want from me, Willow?"

To wrap my hand around your cock again. To feel you inside me one last time. To love me like you loved her.

"I ... I don't know," I answer breathlessly. I can't concentrate on anything but us.

He takes in a sharp breath. "Why can't I stop thinking about you?"

I make my move, unable to stop myself, and crash my lips against his. He tastes more like cotton candy than he smells. He groans while moving his hand from my face to the back of my neck, diving into my hair and drawing me in closer, opening his mouth so that our tongues meet.

His mouth is soft and forbidden. Him only kissing me is going to send me over the edge. He scoots in closer to use his knee to separate my legs more and slides his hand up my thigh, stopping where my shorts end.

"What are you doing to me?" he mutters, taking me deeper into his mouth and inching his hand underneath the fabric, his fingers spreading apart.

I moan and tilt my hips up, permitting him to keep going. His fingers crawl to my middle, right over my panties, and he rubs his thumb across it.

"Fuck," he groans. "You're soaked."

I close my eyes as he moves my panties to the side.

"Okay, who's next in line?" the operator yells.

Dallas's hand disappears in seconds, and his back hits the seat, his breathing labored. "Fuck. I'm sorry. That shouldn't have happened."

I straighten my shorts, rub my hands over my hair to fix it, and curl my arms around my stomach. No doubt I would smack him in the face if we weren't in a public place.

"You're right. It won't happen again," I whisper.

The operator winks at us when the car stops, and we get out.

"It happens all the time, man," he says, smirking. "Figured you wouldn't want to keep up your show in front of everyone."

Oh, hell. He saw us.

I stumble forward, my legs feeling weak, and Dallas rests his hand on the small of my back to stabilize me. We're back to silence, like he didn't have his hand in my shorts only minutes ago, like he wasn't about to get me off in a Ferris wheel car. He guides us straight to Stella, who's waiting on Hudson and Maven to finish up a ride.

Our conversation ends.

Our connection ends.

My hope for him ever touching me again ends.

I can't get attached. I can't let Dallas Barnes in again.

In my head. In my vagina. In my heart.

Dallas

CHAPTER FOURTEEN

MY HOPES of taking Willow to the fair, so she'd change her mind about staying here blew up in my face.

All because me and my dick.

All because my lack of being laid.

And the fact that she looked so delicious, so damn sexy, sitting there, that I couldn't stop myself. I nearly lost it when I felt how wet she was for me. I wanted to prove to her that I wasn't an asshole whose mind was on my dead wife when I slept with her. I fucked up. I'll be the one to blame when she packs up and leaves.

We'd started to break ground, begun building something, and then my dumbass took a wrecking ball to it. My night with her had been incredible. Touching her had been incredible. What I had done that morning was fucked up and is one of my biggest regrets.

I called her Lucy.

Humiliation and stupidity crack my core.

I don't blame her for hating my ass and keeping her distance.

Had the roles been reversed, had a woman called me another man's name in bed, I would've stepped away … and most likely kicked her out of my bed.

I want to change. To be the man who can rise through the flames stronger than ever, but I can't.

That's why what happened tonight scares the shit out of me.

My goal at the bar had been to drink away the pain, the memories. I hadn't been searching for someone to talk to. Nowhere in my mind was the idea of having a one-night stand. It all took a turn when Willow spoke to me. My attention was all hers as soon as we had our first drink together. I wasn't going to leave that bar unless it was with her.

Tonight has proven it wasn't only a drunken attraction that brought us to my bed.

That fucking terrifies me.

Maven is passed out in the backseat, exhausted from going on every ride multiple times, and Willow hasn't said one word since we got in my truck.

Man, I wish my daughter would wake up and start rambling about random shit like she usually does. I gear my truck into park when we arrive at Willow's apartment and unclip my seat belt to open the door for her, but she's faster than I am.

"Well, uh … good night," is all she says before opening the door and jumping out of the truck like it's on fire. "You don't need to walk me up." She slams the door, races up the steps, and goes inside.

I shut my eyes. "Good night, Willow," I whisper even though she can't hear me.

I wait to pull away until I see the light come through her windows.

I get Maven changed when we get home, tuck her into bed, and start to pick up around the house. If I slack on the housecleaning, my mom comes over and not only plays maid, but detective as well. She checks the fridge to make sure we're consuming all the food groups and goes through my mail and underwear drawer.

I grew out of letting my mom make my bed over a decade ago— the reasons different now than before. I'm not stashing porn and condoms underneath my mattress. It's more her searching for evidence that I'm getting laid or seeing someone. She's resorted to leaving information about online dating and schedules of all the social functions happening in town.

No fucking thank you.

I finish cleaning up the aftermath of Maven's sleepover with her stuffed animals last night. It happens when I go into my bedroom. I tried to hide all the pictures once. Picked them up and shut them away in the attic. Ten minutes later, I returned them.

I like to see Lucy when I'm having a bad day, when I need someone to understand me, when I need to tell her about all the crazy stuff our daughter does. I grab the picture from my nightstand and trace my fingers over her wedding dress, her tan face, her blonde hair, and then her pink lips.

"You always were the best at giving advice," I whisper, setting the frame down to twist my wedding ring. "Tell me what I should do."

I shut my eyes and remember her last words. Lucy knew what I needed before I knew it myself.

"Find someone to love," she demanded.

"That's not … that's not possible," I whispered.

"It is. I promise you, the day will come." I opened my mouth to argue, but she placed her finger against the crack of my lips. "You might not see it now, but it will. Your heart will make the right choice to move on with someone who loves you and Maven. Don't be scared, my love. Give it a chance. Heal and let her help you do it."

I kiss my fingers, press them to her picture, and turn off my lamp.

Sleep doesn't come to me.

Dallas

CHAPTER FIFTEEN

MAVEN GRINS at me with her gap-toothed smile, a clear sign she's up to no good. Two bags are set at her feet, waiting for me to load them into my truck. "Daddy, I need your phone this week. Pretty, pretty please."

"For what?" I ask.

"In case I need anything," she answers in annoyance, as if it were a reasonable request for a six-year-old.

"Nice try. You're not taking my phone to camp."

She huffs and stomps her feet. I've already vetoed her iPad making the trip. *Damn kids and electronics.* They act like it'll kill them to spend a weekend in the wilderness without Wi-Fi.

"What if I get lost in the woods and can't find my way back?"

"I've pointed out the North Star to you several times."

She frowns. "What if I see a big ole mean bear?"

I laugh. "Having a phone will be the last of your worries. If you see a bear, slowly back away, and don't make eye contact." *I thought I wasn't supposed to deal with this shit until her teenage years.*

She crosses her arms and gives me her best pouty face. She knows how to pull at my heartstrings. Her perfected pouty face has landed her a gerbil, a goldfish, and the iPad.

"Don't act like you won't miss me," I tease.

Her pouty face turns into an annoyed one.

"Now, grab your sleeping bag, and let's get going," I instruct.

This will be the longest we've been away from each other since Lucy passed. It was different when she was here. I lived states away, traveled frequently, and only came home a few times a month. I regret having that long-distance relationship. I thought I'd have more time, but it just goes to show you that time is never guaranteed. Live each moment and hug the ones you love because you don't know what can happen tomorrow.

"What are you going to do when I'm gone?" she asks as I strap the seat belt around her.

"Work. Do grown-up stuff."

I shut the door and jump into the driver's seat. The camp is about an hour drive, and I made a playlist for us to enjoy during the trip since we have the no-electronics rule. Maven is going to hate it ... at first because I usually let her listen to her teenybop bullshit, but I want to introduce her to something new today.

"One Direction, Daddy!" she yells as soon as we pull out of the driveway.

"Oh, man, I forgot to tell you."

She scrunches her face up. "Forgot to tell me what?"

"Now that they broke up, their music can't be played anymore. It's banned."

"Since when?"

"Yesterday. It was all over the news." I peek back at her silence to see tears running down her face. *This can't be for real?* "What's wrong, May-Bear?"

"They're gone," she cries out, her pouty face intact.

Jesus Christ. "Let me double-check. It might have changed."

I switch to Maven's favorite station and groan when a One Direction song conveniently comes blasting through my speakers.

So much for Bob Dylan.

My little girl always wins.

———

KIDS ARE JUMPING out of cars, backpacks strapped to them, and running toward the group of others congregated in front of the clubhouse. Maven has already said her good-byes and taken off with her friends.

I lean back against my truck and slide my hands into the pockets of my jeans. My parents sent us kids to Camp Maganaw, and I never failed to have a blast. My attention goes straight to Bear Claw Cabin. It's been updated with a fresh slab of paint and a new door, but the memories I have in that cabin will always be there. Lucy and I had our first kiss behind Bear Claw after sneaking out one night.

"Dallas, how are you holding up?"

I briefly glance over when Cindy stops at my side and copies my stance. Cindy and I went to high school together, and she was Lucy's hairdresser. She married the quarterback, had a baby, and then divorced the cheating drunk a few years ago.

I move dirt with the toe of my boot. "As good as I can be, I guess."

A breath bursts from her lips. "I get it. It's hard. I never thought I'd be with anyone other than Phil, but I've learned that the best way to heal is by moving on."

I ram my heel into the ground as anger flushes through me. "A divorce and death are not fucking worthy of comparison," I grind out.

I bite my tongue to stop myself from telling her what wants to come out. Cindy was one of the casserole-and-muffin-making chicks who checked up on me daily in the weeks after losing Lucy. I finally had to put a stop to it after the third week.

If she believes finding someone else with help, more power to her, but I won't be the man to do it … and she sure as hell isn't replacing Lucy.

"You know, you're a jackass. I'm sorry if my concern for you and your daughter eating makes you so rattled," she snaps.

"I told you I appreciated the meals, but they weren't necessary. I don't need help feeding my daughter. We both know your *concern* wasn't making sure we had hot meals twice a day."

She slumps back against the truck. "So, it's true then?"

"What's true?"

Her *concern* has switched to annoyance. "You and the new chick in town have something going on?"

My eyes stay pinned to her.

"Stella's friend," she clarifies, annoyed.

"The hell you hear that?" I ask with a scoff.

"We all saw it at the fair—to my surprise, considering, months ago, you made it clear you weren't interested in dating, *period.*"

"I'm not dating anyone." I pause and pinch my lips together. "Not that it's anyone's fucking business."

A rush of red storms her cheeks. "Asshole," she mutters before turning around and stomping to her car.

———

TWO DAYS HAVE PASSED since the fair fiasco, and communication with Willow has been limited and vague. Phone calls go unanswered. Text messages consists of one word. I've never received so many *K* and *Cool* responses.

That's changing today.

It's our first doctor's appointment. I texted Willow the details after scheduling it and waited for the argument I knew was coming, but surprisingly, she agreed … with a fucking *K.*

I park my truck and wait until she walks out of her apartment before jumping out and joining her on the sidewalk.

"Nuh-uh," she says. "I'm driving myself."

"No one is driving," I reply. "It's a five-minute walk. I thought we'd enjoy the stroll."

She pinches her lips together, and her shoulder smacks against mine when she bursts past me and down the sidewalk. "I'll pass."

She pushes when I pull.

I pull when she pushes.

One of us is always resisting when the other comes forward.

I speed-walk to keep up with her. "Come on. The weather is

perfect. Let's save the environment and conserve gas, not pollute the air. Walking with me will save the world."

My humanity-saving argument doesn't stop her, and I nearly miss her mocking me, an uneven smile on her lips. I don't hold back my shit-eating grin when she passes her car and keeps walking. I stay a few steps behind and let her believe she's getting her way until it happens.

I rush forward when she trips on her feet, falling forward, her knees almost hitting the concrete while her lips are close to kissing the sidewalk. I stretch my arm out to capture her around the waist, and she yelps as I steady her. Instead of breaking my hold when she's stable, I tighten my grip, my fingers sinking into the cotton of her *Girl Power* T-shirt, and stare down at her.

I wait for her to pull out of my hold and tell me never to touch her again. She does none of that. She stays still, catching her breath, and shakes her head.

"Really?" she mutters. "So damn cliché. I fall, and you catch me."

I can't help but chuckle at the actuality of her words. "Just like in the movies."

I release my hold on her waist but move my hand to her elbow just in case.

"You're nervous," I say.

I run my hand up and down her arm in an attempt to calm her nerves. I don't know what has her riled up more—her almost fall, us touching, or this appointment.

She pulls out of my hold with a grimace and runs her hand down her long hair. "No shit, Sherlock."

"Anything I can do to help?"

"Not come."

"Anything I can do *but* that?"

Her hands start shaking, and I turn so that I'm standing in front of her. She attempts to maneuver around me, but I take a step over. She tries the other side. I do the same thing.

"Breathe. Relax." I inhale and exhale a few times in hopes that she'll follow my lead. She does. "Everything is going to be okay, I promise. If you feel uncomfortable, we'll leave."

We do this for a good five minutes, and she sniffles while calming down. "These damn pregnancy hormones are going to be the end of my sanity."

I smile. "I wish I could say they get better, but from what I've witnessed, they don't." I move out of her way and settle my hand on the arch of her back when she starts walking again.

"Then, I'd be careful not to piss me off."

"That's been my goal since day one."

I've been sucking ass at it though.

She sniffles again. "You need to work harder."

Thought confirmed.

I move my arm up and wrap it around her shoulders, bringing her to my side, hoping she doesn't pull away. This isn't sexual. It's something you do to a friend having a bad day.

"Come on, I can't have you showing up to the doctor in tears. My mom would have my ass if she found out. Give me something I can do to calm you down."

"Punching you might work."

I break our connection to move back in front of her and start walking backward. "If being your punching bag helps, then have at it." I throw my arms out and gesture for her to take a swing.

I'm the one stumbling this time when she pushes me back. "God, you piss me off."

"What? Why? I'm giving you what you want."

I've never had complications like this with a woman. Granted, my experience is limited to one woman, so that doesn't say much in itself. I don't remember learning Lucy's quirks because I grew up with them. They were instilled in me before I knew how to spell my name.

She scowls. "What I want is for you to stop being so damn nice."

"What? Why?" I repeat, confused as fuck.

If I'm an ass, she's pissed. If I'm nice, she's pissed.

"Because you're making it difficult to hate you right now."

"That's a bad thing?"

"Yes!"

I'm doing everything in my power to fix this, to make her feel comfortable, so she doesn't run away again, but it's killing me. I'm very rarely the fun guy. My role has always been the serious and overprotective brother. Hudson was the Marine who thrived on having a good time, and Lauren was the mischievous one I caught sneaking out on too many occasions. I was the big brother who made sure everyone was okay and protected.

I stop us in front of the restored yellow Victorian home. "And we're here." Perfect timing before we get into another argument, and my goal of distracting her has somewhat succeeded.

She assesses the building and glares at me like I'm fucking with her. "This ..." She does another once-over. "This is a house. Where's the office?"

I point to the sign with the doctor's name.

"This isn't some midwives shit, is it? Not to be judgmental, but I'm not having my baby in some old home's bathtub."

"We'll go to a hospital when you give birth, and so will the doctor. Give Dr. Riley a chance. If you hate him, we'll go to the city."

Compromise. Compromise. Fucking compromise. Marriage taught me that compromise is what keeps you going when the tides get rough.

She sighs. "Let's do this then."

Willow

CHAPTER SIXTEEN

THE DOOR CHIMES when we walk in, and the nurse behind the counter jumps up from her chair to greet us. Her smile collapses when she notices Dallas behind me. She has the perfect sun-kissed blonde hair and a summer tan. She reminds me of Lucy. Dallas's type.

She tucks a strand behind her ear. "Dallas … I didn't see you on the books today."

"Hey, Fiona. I'm with Willow Andrews. We have an appointment with Aidan," he explains, keeping his focus on me.

Dallas wasn't lying about there being an office inside. It's not modern, like the one I went to for my first pregnancy test. First professional one. I'd taken fifteen at-home tests and then finally gone to the doctor because I was in denial and determined they were all defective.

A few chairs sit in the waiting room across from the wooden front desk A photo of an older man with his name underneath it is centered on the wall, and a corkboard covered with flyers is hung next to it.

Get your flu shot!
Join the bowling league!
Fire department fundraiser this Friday!

The nurse's red lips dip in surprise as she stares at me in curiosity the same way everyone did at the fair. "I see. Let me collect the paperwork your doctor sent over this morning, and then I'll show you to your exam room."

Dallas tucks his hands into the pockets of his jeans. "Is Rick in today?"

"No, he's out hunting. Won't be back until the weekend. We have a light schedule today, even with Aidan here." She laughs. "Everyone remembers all the trouble he got into when you guys were younger, and they aren't sure if they trust him with needles yet."

I jerk my head to glare at Dallas. *The hell? Is he bringing me to some quack?*

"Aidan knows what he's doing," Dallas says, reassuring me. "We can't all stay the kids who drank behind my parents' barn or nearly lit the town square on fire."

Fiona slaps his shoulder. "I miss those days." She taps it next. "How have you been doing?"

He nods, scraping a hand through his hair, and his face tightens. "Fine."

"You let me know if you need anything, all right?"

"Thanks," he replies flatly.

Well ... this sure is fun.

"So, where to?" he asks.

She leads us to a room at the end of the hallway. The door isn't numbered but does say *Dr. Aidan Riley* across the top glass.

I sit on the exam bed while Dallas scoots his chair next to me. I don't realize I'm tapping my feet until he rests his hand on my thigh, causing me to flinch. I surprise myself by not moving it. He might piss me off, but his touch relaxes me. That still doesn't stop me from scowling at him though.

There's a knock on the door, and Dallas moves his hand like a kid caught with it in the cookie jar when the doctor walks in.

The first thing I notice shouldn't be how attractive he is, but he's definitely a looker. Blond hair cut short in almost a frat-boy style but more sophisticated and an oval face with perfect features. I was expecting a dude in overalls. Now, I'm stuck in a room with two men I wouldn't have a problem screwing. My OB-GYN and the off-limits man who knocked me up.

He holds out his hand with a smile. "Willow, pleasure meeting you. I'm Dr. Riley, but call me Aidan, considering my father has the same name, and I'm not an old goat."

I smile back, and his attention goes to Dallas next, worry crossing his features.

"Dallas, you doing okay, man?"

My smile collapses. I feel bad for Dallas. His loss follows him everywhere. He will forever be known as the man who tragically lost his wife too soon. And I'll forever be known as the woman who screwed the heartbroken widowed man and got knocked up.

Dallas's attention stays on me as he answers, "Sure am, Doc."

Aidan sits down on the rolling stool and comes closer. "The doctor who gave you your initial pregnancy test sent over your records. It appears, you're around twelve weeks. Good timing for your first ultrasound."

"Right ... right now?" I ask. I knew he'd want to run tests but figured he'd want to ask more questions before diving straight in.

"We can do it another time if you'd like," Aidan replies.

"No." I clear my throat. "Today's fine." I want to see my baby. I peek over at Dallas. "You probably don't want to be in here for this."

He kicks his legs out and makes himself comfortable in the chair. "I'd like to be. That cool?"

Fuck no.

Aidan opens a cabinet and pulls out a cup before handing it to me. "You think about it. Meanwhile, I need a urine sample." He tips his head toward the other side of the room. "Bathroom's right there."

I shut the door behind me and am washing my hands when I hear their conversation.

"Your mom know about this?" Aidan asks.

"No," Dallas answers. "Just Hudson, his girlfriend, and Lauren."

"Is she ..." Aidan pauses. "Are you two ..."

"Are we dating? No. It was a one-time thing."

Aidan chuckles. "Oh, man. Good luck, my friend, and congratulations on the baby."

———

MY HEAD FLIES UP, nearly colliding with Dallas's, and I'm struggling to keep my breath.

"Twins?" I yell. "Did you ..." My gaze flicks to Dallas, who looks in as much shock as I am. "Did he ... did he say twins?"

"Sure did," Aidan answers with a wide grin. "My first prenatal patient, and we're having twins. *Yes!*"

"Don't take this the wrong way, Doctor, but you're new at this, right? Are you sure you know how to read these correctly? They're probably more ancient than what you worked with in med school."

Aidan is still smiling, not offended. "I read these things for years when I shadowed my father. I clearly see two fetuses." He puts his finger on the screen. "Here's baby one." Then, he moves it over. "And baby number two."

Holy shit. Holy shit.

Dallas is sitting up straight, mouth open, and staring at the screen like he has to memorize it for a test tomorrow.

I can't think straight. I was scared shitless when I thought I was having one baby. Now, I'm having *two?*

Double the responsibility. Double the diaper-changing. Double the expenses. Double the help I'm going to need from Dallas. Double the time we'll be spending together.

———

"LET'S GET LUNCH."

I stop in my tracks and coldly gape at him. From now on, I'll be placing all of this pregnancy blame on him because it's too much for me to carry two babies in my body along with the responsibility of our choice on my shoulders.

He knocked me up. I'm the one who has to push the babies out, so he can deal with the blame for the pain and fear I'm experiencing. It only makes sense.

"Lunch?" I repeat. "Don't you mean, let's find a safe, pregnancy-approved Xanax? Or let's go to yoga? Or find a stress-management class? Did you hear what Aidan said? I have two babies inside me."

We found out we're having twins, and he wants to get fucking lunch? Surely, I can't be the only one in shock.

Lucky for me, Fiona was on break and unable to witness the panic in me when we left the exam room.

He stares at me with unease. "I heard him loud and clear. Two babies make feeding you even more important."

"Are you not fucking terrified?" I shout.

We're on the sidewalk outside the doctor's office, which isn't too far from the town square where most of the people hang out and gossip. There's a chance someone might hear us, but I don't care right now.

He takes a deep breath. "Nervous? Yes. But it's nothing I can't handle." He takes the step separating us and runs his hands over my arms. "You can do this. *We* can do this. You're going to be a great mother. When the babies come, your instincts will kick in, and you'll have it figured out. Hell, I've seen you do shit for Stella that's more demanding than children. So, yes, I'm nervous and surprised as fuck, but I'm relieved, knowing our twins will have a kick-ass mother. I trust you. I have faith in you. It won't be easy, but we'll make it work."

I scrunch up my face when he snorts. "What's so funny?"

"I bet you're glad you didn't hide this from me now. Admit it. You're going to need my help."

"You're changing all the diapers, by the way. That's your daddy duty."

"Whatever you need, I'll be here." He rubs his hands together. "Now, how 'bout that lunch?"

"Lunch together? Like, in a public place?"

He chuckles. "Yes, together. There's a diner down the street that serves the best sandwiches and pies you've ever had."

I fake a yawn. "Thanks for the invite, but I'm pretty exhausted."

I used to feel comfortable with spending hours with Dallas. We traveled together for weeks straight at times and ate meals together, and it never felt weird. *So, why does it seem like such a big deal now?* We slept with each other, for God's sake.

"Come on." He places his hands together. "*Please.*"

"Fine, but a quick meal, and that's it." It's hard to turn down this man.

He grins in victory. We pass small shops and bakeries before stopping in front of Shirley's Diner. Large windows line the front, and I see the prying eyes before we even step foot inside. My anxiety triples when I follow him to a booth at the front of the diner sitting along the window.

"You okay?" he asks when we sit down.

I lean in and lower my voice. "They're staring at me like I'm from a different planet."

"They're just curious." He rests his hands on the table. "Say the word, and I'll get up from this table and tell them to stop."

"You'd do that?" I grab his arm when he starts to get up and let my fingers linger around his muscle before slowly peeling them away. "No!" I spread my napkin across my lap in an attempt to calm my nerves. "Forget I said anything."

An older, dark-skinned waitress comes to our table. "Dallas, it's nice to see you. I was afraid you'd been cheating on me with a new diner."

Dallas chuckles. "You know I'd never betray you, Shirley. I've just been busy."

She waves off his response with a grin. "You know I'm only giving you a hard time." Her lips form a sincere smile when she glimpses at me. "And I see why you've been busy. What can I get for you, sweetie? Iced tea? Lemonade?"

"Lemonade." I hold the menu up and set it back down. "And whatever today's special is."

"I'll have the same," Dallas tells her.

Shirley grabs our menus. "Coming right up."

"She's nice," I comment when she scurries over to the booth across from ours.

"Blue Beech is filled with nice people," he replies.

"I'm assuming you meant to say nosy people." *How bad will it get when news about my inhabited uterus gets around?*

"Yes, they're nosy, but they'll lend you a helping hand without asking for anything in return, feed you, take care of your pets when you're out of town, and always make sure you're doing okay when something tragic happens. They're only staring because they want to get to know you."

"Or because they're not used to seeing you with someone who's not Lucy."

A hint of a frown hits his lips, and his shoulders stiffen. "You could say that. I've been the town's brooding bachelor for a minute now, who's never been seen with another woman."

"They see you as a traitor. You're finally seen with a woman, and she's an outsider." I stop when I catch my words, my brain scattering to backtrack them. "Not that we're, uh … more than friends. Just *friends* sharing a meal."

"They're well aware we're more than friends sharing a meal." He relaxes in his seat. "They're really going to find out when you start to show and wear clothes that don't swallow you up."

"I'll tell them I got fat."

"And then lost all the weight, and we suddenly have two babies?"

I shrug. "Sounds legit to me."

Shirley interrupts us and winks while dropping a turkey bacon club and our drinks in front of us. "You two enjoy."

"You ready to come up with a plan yet?" Dallas asks when I take my first bite.

"Nope," I answer after chewing.

He nods, telling me the conversation isn't over but that he'll save it for later. "What's your favorite food?"

I look up from my plate. "What?"

"Your favorite food. We can't sit here in silence, and I figure we'll ask each other questions we never did when we worked together."

I tell him it's a tie between sushi and tacos. His is his mom's carrot cake. We throw questions at each other back and forth while we eat. Having a normal conversation with him feels right. It's comfortable. It doesn't feel like first-date awkwardness because this is definitely not a date.

My dream vacation is staying in one of those tiki huts in Bora Bora. His is Yosemite. Black-and-white movies are my thing. He's not much of a movie buff, but we both agree that anything with Tom Cruise is overrated.

Shirley collects our plates and comes back to set a delicious piece of blueberry pie in front of me.

"Oh no, I didn't order this," I say.

She smiles. "It's on the house, honey. First slice for a newcomer is always free."

"Thank you." I take a bite and groan at the deliciousness. "Shirley is officially my favorite person in this town."

He smiles in amusement. "She's bribing you. The first piece is never free."

"What do you mean?"

"Don't think I'm the only one hoping you stay in Blue Beech."

Willow

CHAPTER SEVENTEEN

"GUESS WHO'S BACK, back again. Willow's back, tell a friend," Stella sings when I slide into the passenger seat of her BMW SUV.

My best friend might've shut the door on the celebrity lifestyle, but that doesn't mean she gave up her love of expensive handbags and foreign cars or that she doesn't stop gifting those cars to her favorite personal assistant.

She's grinning, her eyes pinned on me, and her charcoal-colored hair is pulled back into a high ponytail that shows off her Spanish features.

I buckle my seat belt while groaning. "I'm officially putting my two-weeks' notice in."

It's my first day back at work since moving to Blue Beech, and it feels good being around Stella again. We went from spending endless days side by side to communicating through video conferences and text messages.

Her lips curl into a smile. "You'd miss me too much, but you can bet your ass I'll be giving you maternity leave for as long as you'd like, and then you can bring the cute munchkin to work."

No one knows we're having twins yet, and Dallas promised to keep it that way until I was ready. I need time to wrap my head around everything in my life being multiplied.

"Paid leave, right?" I ask.

"Duh." She wiggles in her seat before shifting the car into drive. "So ... does this mean, you're staying?"

I've lost count of the number of times Stella has asked me to move here—before and after the Dallas situation. I would've been fired for refusing to relocate if I worked for anyone else.

"Undecided. I'm giving it a chance, but I can't make any promises. I still need to come up with my single-mom plan."

We don't leave the parking lot because she puts her car back in park to give me her full attention.

Her face fills with worry. "You're not a single mom, Wills. You have Dallas."

I'm single. I'm going to be a mom. Hence, single mom.

"Not sure that makes a difference," I mutter.

Her hand tenderly brushes against my arm. "If you're worried about that, I can assure you, Dallas will be there for your baby ... *for you.* He'll change diapers and wake up when the baby is screaming bloody murder in the middle of the night. He'll help financially. If that's not someone supporting you, I don't know what is."

I snort. She has a point, but I still want to see him as the jackass I thought he was that morning.

"Why are you so uneasy about a man being a *good man?* If I recall correctly, you were jumping my ass when Hudson and I were going through a rough patch. It's your turn to listen."

I hate when my actions come back to bite me in the ass. "Different circumstances."

"How are they *different circumstances?*"

"Hudson had cheating fiancée baggage. He wasn't a single dad who lost his wife. What's Dallas going to do? Have sleepovers with Maven at my apartment? I won't be stepping foot into his house after what happened there."

She rolls her eyes, her understanding moving into aggravation. "Grow up. He was going through a rough time."

"He didn't seem to have a problem with me in his bed when we were screwing—only when it was time to face his mistake."

"He doesn't see you as a mistake."

"You didn't see his reaction. The way he still looks at me."

"I'll pay better attention today."

"*Today?*"

She shrugs casually with a mischievous smile. "We're bringing them lunch."

"We?" I turn around to view the backseat. "Do you have someone shoved in your trunk?"

"You and me. *Us.* We're bringing the guys lunch."

"They're grown men. Can't they feed themselves?"

I've texted Dallas a few times on the phone, but I haven't seen him since the diner. I'm still in the process of getting comfortable with him when we're alone. Hudson and Stella breathing over our shoulders won't make it any easier.

Dallas

CHAPTER EIGHTEEN

I WIPE my hands on a shop towel and toss it to the ground when my stomach growls. "Shirley's for lunch?" I ask Hudson. "I'm fucking starving."

I've been here since five in the morning, finishing up an engine on a tractor for my father's friend who needed it done yesterday. One of our biggest battles of working with agriculture and construction customers is that they're seasonal. They want their equipment done the moment they drop it off, or they're losing money.

Good for our pockets.

Bad for our stress levels.

He shakes his head. "Nah, Stella is bringing me food."

"Ah, yeah. Forgot about your little lunch dates." I smirk. "Cute kids, you. Reminds me of when I was in third grade, trying to convince Lucy to kiss me by bringing her pieces of Mom's pie on the playground."

"Asshole." He throws his towel at me and slides off a stool. "Want to join us? She brings enough to feed an army."

"I'll pass."

He returns to putting all of his tools up, and I snap my fingers to gain his attention.

"And don't forget, we have the auction tomorrow. What time do you want me to pick you up?" I ask.

That gets his full attention. "Shit, I forgot about the auction." He narrows his eyes at me. "Now that you bring it up, I told you I couldn't go."

"Nice try, jackass. I would remember you trying to bail because I wouldn't have let you. They have an excavator going through that I know we can get a kick-ass deal on."

We're in the process of expanding the family business my grandfather started decades ago. Our dad is ready to retire after twenty-five years and wants us to take over.

"I have plans with Stella."

He runs a hand through his hair, which is lighter and longer than mine. All of us Barnes children look alike with a few exceptions. I don't sport as much facial hair as Hudson. I'm convinced he does it to hide his jaw since mine is stronger than his, but he won't admit it. He argues that the few inches he has on my height counts for more than good bone structure.

"Your fiancé will be fine without you for a day."

"She'll be fine ... because I'll be with her. Go alone. You're a big boy."

I frown. "It's an eight-hour round trip."

"It'll give you time to reflect."

"Reflection and I aren't a good match. Trust me." I fucking hate being in my head.

He winces, shocked at my response, and I'm positive I've won this discussion. "Ask Willow to tag along."

And I'm wrong.

"She can hardly stand spending twenty minutes around me at a doctor's appointment. I doubt she'll be jumping at the idea of a road trip."

He shrugs, his mouth curving into a sly smile. "Looks like we're about to find out."

"The fuck does that mean?"

I whip around at the sound of a door slamming. The shop is

twenty minutes out of town. The only people who come around are employees, customers, and us. I like it—the quietness, the peace.

I follow Hudson out of the garage to find Stella coming our way while holding up a bag.

"Lunchtime!" she yells, stomping across the gravel parking lot.

Willow circles the car, slowly dragging her feet in our direction, making it clear she'd rather be anywhere but here.

Hudson slaps me on the back. "Would you look at that, brother? Perfect timing." He jogs forward to meet Stella halfway and plants a kiss on her lips.

I follow his lead but trail a few feet behind in hopes of sparing myself from their lovesick hellos.

I'm a miserable bastard, but that doesn't mean I'm not happy for my baby brother. He went through a messy-ass breakup. His ex fucked him over by screwing his best friend and used their scheduled wedding date to marry the so-called friend. Hudson ditched town, took over my job as Stella's bodyguard, and somehow convinced her to fall in love with him.

"I'm starving, babe," he tells her with another kiss. "Did you bring enough for my pain-in-the-ass brother?"

Stella throws me a look with a smile. "Sure did. I also brought a friend." Her chin tips toward Willow when she makes it to us. "Do you two know each other?" She slaps her knees. "My bad, you knocked her up."

"Funny," Willow grumbles, throwing her a dirty look. "You remember that two-weeks' threat?"

"You have anything going on tomorrow, Willow?" Hudson asks.

She peeks over at Stella. "No. Stella said I have the day off." Her green eyes flash between the couple in confusion.

"You do," Hudson replies. "You're probably going to be pretty bored, so I have good news for you. Dallas has to go out of town for work and needs some company. You feel like tagging along?"

She bites her lip and shoves dirt around with her shoe, dirtying them up. "I have a busy day. I need to unpack."

"Weird. You told me you were finished unpacking yesterday,"

Stella says, exchanging a glance with Hudson, confirming this isn't some last-minute idea.

Willow shoots her a death stare. "I have baby books to finish reading."

"Read them on the way," I suggest.

She sucks in a breath at the sound of my voice and finally acknowledges me.

"As a matter of fact, how about you read them to me?" I go on.

My jump into the conversation has shocked everyone, including myself. Making an eight-hour round trip alone sounds like a fucking nightmare.

Willow's mouth presses together in a grimace. "You can't be serious."

"Sure am. I'll bring the doughnuts. You bring the baby lit." I grin. "I'll be there at eight."

Willow

CHAPTER NINETEEN

I SPENT last night drafting texts to Dallas that I never sent.

The keeping-my-distance plan I made at the first positive pregnancy test is backfiring in my face. I can't stop myself from reaching out and clasping on to every hand he holds out even though I know he'll do nothing but drop me at the end. My heart is begging for a repeat of that soul-to-soul connection we shared.

Dallas gets me in a way no one else seems to. He understands what it feels like to have your heart ripped out and torn to shreds. He understands the way love can throw you into a pit of denial. He wouldn't come to terms that Lucy was sick until it was too late, and I couldn't grasp that my boyfriend since high school had been cheating on me for years.

Our hurt is the polar opposite. I know losing someone is nothing compared to a breakup. My pain doesn't even register on the scale of his. His hurt snuck up on him, wearing him down on short notice, and I'm terrified he'll drag me into the dark place with him.

We run from the truth because it's easier to live a lie than face the monster. I was content with living with my struggles ... until that positive test. I won't allow my babies to be raised by two broken people. One of us has to be strong, and I can't do that with Dallas Barnes playing with my heart.

The doorbell rings at eight sharp. Like me, Dallas is punctual. You learn to be that way when you're working with tight schedules and dealing with celebrities who have no regard for time. I've had to drag people out of bed, brush their teeth for them, and even buckle them up in their private jets.

"I'm surprised you didn't run off this morning," he says when I open the door.

Me, too, buddy. Me, too.

Three red travel cups are stacked in one hand, and a white paper bag is clutched in the other. A pair of heels is tucked underneath his armpits. I reach out to help him with the cups when he slides past me to get into my apartment. I inhale his woodsy scent while following him into the kitchen.

He drops the bag on the counter and then holds up the familiar black peep-toe heels. "These belong to you."

The shoes I left at his house.

The ones I thought I would never see and didn't care to see again. He'd be on my mind every time I slipped them on. *Where did he keep them? Did Maven see them?*

I grab them from him and toss them onto the floor. "Thank you." I take in all of the cups. "Someone joining us today?" I sound more disappointed than I should about having a third-wheeler on this trip.

He shakes his head. "All I know about your morning drink of choice is coffee is a no-go, so I had to get creative and bring options."

"By creative, you mean …"

"Asking the woman behind the counter at the doughnut shop."

I lean against the wall. "And what did she suggest?"

"Hot chocolate, decaf green tea, and passion fruit something." He counts off the list with his fingers. "I have no damn clue what the last option was, but she said health nuts have been going crazy over it. Thought I might as well give it a go."

His answer is so Dallas.

"Green tea for one then, please."

He frowns. "Well … fuck."

"What?"

"I didn't take you as a green-tea lover, so I chugged it down on the way here."

"*A green-tea lover?* I don't see you as one either, considering you once told me not liking coffee was an abomination."

"It truly is." I keep staring at him until his lips crack into a smile. "I'm only fucking with you. Green tea is in the middle cup." He snags the doughnuts. "We'll eat on the way. Let's hit the road."

———

"I LIKE THE SHIRT TODAY," Dallas says.

We've been on the road for about an hour and have covered the weather, the latest news, our ideas for where Stella and Hudson should get married, and what the best movie that came out this year was.

Everything but baby talk.

Which I'm totally okay with.

I pull at the bottom of my *You Had Me at Tacos* tee. Graphic tees are my thing. "I thought I'd give you a hint of what we're having for lunch."

"Can we delay that until dinner? There aren't that many stops on the way, and I doubt any of them serve quality tacos."

I nod. "I can settle for dinner."

It's not like I have anywhere to be. It's either hang with him or sit, bored, in my apartment. You can only watch so much Netflix before you're ready to pull your hair out.

"I'll find you the best damn tacos you've ever had for tagging along today." He grins while peeking over at me. "I woke up this morning, expecting a text from you, bailing."

I cast a curious glance from my seat. "Disappointed I didn't?"

"Hell no. I told you I'd enjoy the company."

I study his driving position. He's leaned back in the seat, right arm stretched out and steering. It comes across so casual, so laid-back, and I never thought I'd be so turned on by the way a man drove.

"What made you change your mind?"

His question smacks me out of my eye-fucking-him moment. "A change of scenery sounded nice."

He chuckles, faking offense. "Not the company?"

I bite the side of my lip. "I haven't decided on that yet."

"I admire your honesty and pledge to give you the time of your life, so you can make that decision at the end of this trip. The drive is beautiful. We won't hit any of that bullshit LA traffic you're used to."

"How long are we talking?"

Now that I think about it, I should've asked more questions before jumping into his truck. It seems I have a habit of jumping into things with this man without considering what could happen first.

"Eight-hour round trip. We'll be at the auction for an hour or two. My eyes are only on one piece of equipment, which will be at the front of the line. I bid and fill out the paperwork, and then we'll be back on the road."

"Sounds like a whole process. How often do you do this, and why do you do it?"

"Once or twice a month, depending on what they have for sale. Hudson and I buy machinery that needs to be updated. We fix it up, modernize it—that kind of stuff. Then, we sell it to farmers and construction companies around the area."

Interesting. I knew he and Hudson did some type of machinery work but never knew what exactly it was.

Stella's explanation consisted of, "They fix stuff and sell machines," which wasn't as thorough as his answer.

"How did you get into it?" I want to draw out every detail of his life that I can.

"My grandfather started the business decades ago. My dad ran it after he passed and while I was in LA and Hudson was in the military. He's ready to retire, so he asked us to take over. Since we're home for good now, we figured it was the perfect time. We've already expanded the business and doubled our clientele."

"So, you bid on the machines you want and then take them to the shop if you win?"

"Most of the time, I bring a trailer and tow the machine with my truck, but today, I'll have a contractor pick it up and deliver it to the shop."

I squint my eyes at him. "Why not tow it today?"

"It's not only uncomfortable, but also a longer trip when towing a piece of heavy machinery. I want you to be comfortable."

Dallas might have had parts of his heart shattered, but fragments are still shoved in there, beating. He's kind even though he's heartbroken. He's miserable, but he manages to consider other people.

"I've been on eighteen-hour flights and gone straight to work without sleeping for another twenty-four," I tell him. "It's nothing compared to traveling with Stella."

"You get paid for that. You're not getting paid for this, and quite frankly, even if you were, I'd still want to make it comfortable for you." He shakes his head and whistles. "I sure don't miss traveling with Stella."

I nod in agreement. "At first, it was a blast, but it's not always glitz and glam, working for Hollywood's finest."

His fingers close around the steering wheel, and he stares at the road. "Seemed like a good idea then, but I have my regrets."

"Regrets about working for her or not moving back when Lucy did?"

"Both, to be honest." The ease of his laid-back mood evaporates. We've moved from the weather to an intimate conversation. "Moving to LA was Lucy's idea. I was fine with staying in Iowa, but she wanted a change."

I've been curious about Dallas's story since he started working for Stella. She filled me in on small details, and I picked up information here and there, but we never ventured into personal conversations, never let our real life seep through the cracks of our professional one.

"You moved for her?" I ask.

"I loved her." So much was said in those three words.

"Why did you stay when she moved back?"

Dallas had been working for Stella for three years when Lucy moved back home. Stella was a stressed mess, worried about finding a new bodyguard as good as him, but he decided to stay, relieving us both.

Sadness. Regret. Tension. All of those emotions pass over his face. "I offered, sometimes even begged when the loneliness of missing my family barreled through, but Lucy insisted I stay. The money was too good to pass up. Our plan was to save enough money, so I could move home after a few years. We'd be able to live more comfortably." More waves of sadness smack into him, and he pauses. "Fuck it."

I stay quiet, not sure if he's going to shut down or break down.

He expels a long breath before going on, "I've never told anyone this, not even Hudson. We …" He hesitates again. "We were trying for another baby. Maven was unplanned, so we wanted to do things the right way. Expand our family. Funny how life works. We could conceive when we weren't ready but couldn't when we were. Her doctor suggested IVF, which costs a fucking fortune, so we decided to save money and try it in a few years."

Wow.

My heart breaks at his confession. He was desperately trying to have another baby with his wife and failed. Then, I got pregnant after a one-night stand with him. His wish for more kids has been granted but with the wrong woman.

"You regret not coming back," I say, my voice thick, my throat hurting.

"Every fucking day of my life."

I wanted his reality, his secrets, but I now wish for a dead end. This road is too heartbreaking, and I'm roaming along the sidewalks of guilt. He has to go through all of the motions with me now even though he wanted to do them with someone else.

"You don't expect to lose your wife that young," he continues. "You don't expect your daughter to be motherless at six. We were fucking robbed, and I didn't take advantage of spending all my time with her, protecting her, until life broke in and took her from me."

His vulnerability shocks me. It's comforting to see a flash of something other than anger spark out of him. His hurt opens up emotions in me, and I'm holding myself back from bursting into tears at the sight of this broken man. I'm fighting back the urge to reach out and console him. To let him know everything will be okay.

But I can't, for fear of falling harder for a man who's unavailable. When I fall in love, I fall hard, and that's my weakness. People that love as deep as I do get their hearts shattered harder when it all falls apart.

He blows out a stressed breath and focuses on me in pain. He tilts his lips up into a forced smile. "And here I said I'd give you a good time."

"You're fine. I like this Dallas," I answer, honestly.

He rubs the back of his neck. "You like me being a miserable bastard?"

"I like you being real," I correct. I've never evoked emotions like this out of anybody.

"This is as real as it gets. This is me, and I wish I could be someone better for you."

"What you're giving me is enough." *He wants to be a better father, not a better lover, not a better man for me.* I repeat that to myself over and over in my head, hoping it'll drill the reality through. "I mean … what you're giving the babies."

"I hope that never changes."

Dallas

CHAPTER TWENTY

"WOOHOO! WE WON!"

I can't stop my lips from breaking into a smile, watching Willow jump up and down in excitement after the auctioneer yells, "Sold," and points to me.

The men around me are either staring at her in annoyance or desire, and I want to slap all their thoughts from their heads.

I've managed to snag the excavator and got a better deal than I planned. An overweight man wearing a business suit had me worried for a minute when he started driving the price up, but lucky for me, he gave up early.

I know his kind. The men who are only in business for profit and for retail-fucking people with no concern about how they bust their asses every day to keep food in their families' mouths. Barnes Machinery and Equipment isn't like that. We give a shit about people, about their checkbooks, never high gross.

Willow insisted on tagging along with me at the bidding yard. I offered to let her wait in the truck or hang out in the coffee shop across the street since there's a lot of standing and waiting around for your item to come up. She wouldn't have it and refused to decline a ticket into my world.

She hasn't complained once, which doesn't surprise me. She's a hard worker, who scored a job with one of the most prestigious celebrity PR and assistant firms in LA at twenty-one. She worked with Hollywood's elite and impressed Stella so much, she hired her full-time. Even though Stella isn't as hard on her, Willow works her ass off to make things easier for her boss.

Hell, most of the time she goes above and beyond what is asked of her. She works long hours, does the shit no one else wants to do, and fixes any problems that come along.

"How about some jams?" Willow asks when we get back into the truck.

I paid for the machine, filled out all the necessary paperwork, and scheduled the delivery. We'd gotten lunch before the auction started, and now, my goal is to find her some kick-ass tacos for being such a good sport.

"You be the DJ," I answer.

Music comes blaring through the speakers when she turns the radio on. I haven't used it since dropping Maven off at camp and cringe at the same time she bursts out into a fit of laughter. Since her laugh is contagious, I can't stop myself from doing the same.

"Whoa," she says when she catches her breath. "Didn't peg you as a Bieber fan, Barnes."

I turn down the volume a few notches. "I'm not. *Maven* is a Bieber fan."

"Blaming it on the kid, huh? How convenient." She smacks her palm against her forehead. "Oh. My. God."

I lift my chin. "What?"

"My baby daddy is a Belieber."

"A what?"

"A Belieber. A member of Justin's fan club."

For fuck's sake.

Not only do I have to listen to this shit, but now, Willow also thinks I'm his biggest fucking fan with posters of his mug splattered all over my bedroom wall.

"I'm not, let me repeat, I'm not a member of his fan club."

"I believe you." A smile still dances on her moist lips.

"Appreciate it."

"You're the President of it."

I can't stop myself from smiling as a light chuckle echoes from my chest. "Oh, come on, you honestly can't believe I listen to this shit."

"The evidence is clear, counselor. His music is on your radio."

Thunder roars through the sky so loud, I can't hear Bieber, and rain smacks into my windshield. *Fuck.*

"And look at that. God knows you're lying, too."

"Or the weather predicted a seventy percent chance of thunderstorms, but I hoped it'd be in our favor."

At least it waited until after the auction to pour hell down.

The windshield wipers squeak when I shift them to high, and Willow turns down the music, reading my mind so that I can focus better on the road. My headlights shine brightly as the sky turns a deep shade of black even though it's only after six.

I lower my speed and get better control of my view on the road when a loud pop rings out, and my steering wheel starts to shake. The ride gets bumpy, and Willow hangs on to her seat belt for stability.

I pull the truck over and park it before slamming my hand against the steering wheel, causing the horn to blare out.

"Motherfucker," I mutter.

"What?" Willow asks.

"We have a flat."

She stares at me as if it's not a problem. "You know how to change a tire, right?"

I nod. "It helps if you have a spare though."

Her jaw drops. "You're kidding me."

"I wish I were." I feel like a defeated asshole.

This puts a damper on our almost perfect day. We're stranded in the rain, and instead of tacos, I'll be giving her Maven's fruit snacks as the final course.

"No big deal. We'll call a tow truck. I've been in bigger messes than this in my sleep."

"One problem with that." I pull out my phone to show her the screen. "No service. Tell me you have something."

She snatches her purse from the floorboard and rifles through it before finding her phone.

Horror takes over her face when the screen comes to life.

"For real?" she shrieks, throwing her hands up in the air. "We're in the ass crack of no-man's-land stranded with no spare tire. This is straight out of a horror movie." She turns around and lays her gaze out the back window. "Swear to God, if a meat-truck-driving serial killer pulls up, I'm making a run for it."

I grind my teeth, my heart crashing with anguish and guilt from putting her in this situation. I gave my dad my spare last week and forgot to replace it.

Her face softens when she peeks over at me. "Shit, sorry," she whispers over the pelting rain hitting the windshield. "That was too dramatic for this situation. I tend to do that at times."

"You're fine. I'll take dramatics over you wanting to kill me." I turn around in my seat and snatch a jacket from the backseat. "I'm going to see if I can manage to get service in the field over there."

She points out the window. "It's pouring. There are no streetlights. We should wait until the storm calms before going out."

I put the jacket on. "What if it storms all night?"

She starts to unbuckle her seat belt. "Then, I'm coming with you."

I stop her and snap it back in place. "The fuck you are. Stay here, and I'll be back in a flash."

I jump out of the truck despite her protests and hold my phone in the air while sprinting toward the field. The rain comes at me sideways while I wait for the service bars to light up on my phone.

Come on! Come on!

I jump, nearly losing my phone, when a crack of lightning bites through the dark sky. I can barely make out the truck in the downpour and am still messing with my phone when I notice the bright shine of headlights getting closer.

My attention snaps away from the car to the truck at the sound of a door slamming. I scream her name and race toward her when she starts running to the side of the road, waving her hands in the air. The car flies by, splashing her with water, and her shoulders slump in failure.

Fear and anger splinter through me like the storm.

"Have you lost your mind?" I scream, snatching her by the waist from behind and swinging her into my arms. I hover my body over hers to protect her from getting more soaked and tighten my hold on her shivering body while walking us from the street back to my truck. "They could've run you over!"

My breathing halts, dying in my throat, and a chill colder than the rain zips down my spine when she rotates herself in my arms. My hands stay on her wrists as she glares at me before jerking out of my hold with a huff.

"I was flagging them down for help!"

"You running out in the street, waving down some stranger, does not fucking help me. You keeping your ass in the heated seat in the safety of my truck is what helps me."

"It was worth a try!"

The way her voice cracks makes me feel like shit. We lock eyes. She's staring at me like she's searching my soul, assessing the situation in my eyes, unsure of what my next step will be.

I suck in each breath she expels, inhaling her sweet scent, nearly panting at the sight of her dripping wet in front of me, neglecting the shitty situation we're in. Her shirt is soaked to her skin, her hard nipples peeking through the thin tee, and I lick my lips, mentally tasting her.

My next step should be getting her inside the truck, out of this chilly ambush of rain, but goddamn it, I can't break away. I run a hand through her hair and smooth it down before lowering my fingers to her cheek. She shuts her eyes and relaxes into my touch.

I inch forward, my chest brushing against hers, and she lets out a soft moan. The sweet sound runs straight to my dick.

"Dallas," she whispers, eyes still closed, "what are we doing?"

I can't stop myself from chuckling. "We're standing in the rain."

"No," she croaks out. "What are *we* doing?"

Dallas

CHAPTER TWENTY-ONE

WILLOW'S QUESTION shakes me back into reality, and I drop my hand from her face.

She wants to have this conversation now.

In the pouring rain.

I chuckle.

This situation sums up our relationship.

Bad timing. Unexpected. Not sure what the next move is.

I run my hands down her arms when her teeth start to chatter. "We need to get you in the truck," I say, squeezing her shoulders.

I move around her to open the door. She nods timidly, her front teeth biting into her soft lip, and turns her back to me to climb in. I stand behind her, helping her up, and make sure she's secure.

"I managed to get one bar in the middle of the field. I'm going to try to get in contact with a tow company, so I need you to refrain from leaving the car. I don't give a shit if a parade starts coming down the street." I nod my head toward the dashboard. "Turn the heat on high. I have clothes in my gym bag in the backseat for you to change into."

"Got it. No getting out of the car." I go to close the door, but she stops me. "What if a serial killer is running toward you with a knife?"

This woman and her fucking questions. *Where does she come up with this shit?* "You lock the doors and let me deal with it."

"I'm trained in martial arts, you know. I was a junior green belt. I would be a great help."

"Look at you, badass. Keep your eyes out for killers and promise me you'll stay in here." I can't believe I'm standing in a fucking storm and taking the chance of getting struck by lightning to entertain this conversation. Willow gets me swept up into her world, her words, and I can't seem to walk away. "Promise me you'll stay in here."

"My promises don't mean shit, remember?"

"Make them mean something."

I slam the door shut and let out a sigh before jogging back to the field. I ignore the rain as I hurry back to the same spot and dial the number as fast as I can, hoping that not only the service stays connected, but also that Willow keeps her ass planted in the truck.

I make it through and give the tow company our location. Then, I shove my phone into my pocket. I stop to search the dark sky and twist my wedding ring while rain drips from the tips of my fingers to the mud underneath my boots.

I don't move. I only think.

My mind hasn't been fighting back the painful thoughts of missing Lucy today. I haven't felt like a failure of a husband since I knocked on Willow's door this morning. I haven't cursed the world for my loss. The constant guilt and anger didn't seep through me when I saw the happy family in the booth across from us at the small diner we ate lunch in.

The presence of Willow blocks out that dark tunnel in my brain and gives me a way toward the light and out of my hole.

I open the back door when I get back to the truck, toss my mud-covered boots in the backseat, grab my tennis shoes from the floorboard, and slide into the driver's side.

My attention shoots straight to Willow. She's still in her wet clothes and slipping her fingers through the strands of her dripping hair. She sighs, grabs her purse, and digs through it until she scores a hair tie.

I gulp as she lifts her hair up, exposing her long, sleek neck.

Fuck, she's breathtaking.

"You good?" I finally ask.

She bashfully runs a hand along her pale cheek. "Sorry about that. Minor freak-outs tend to be my thing during stressful situations."

Her answer is a shot of relief. Relief of not scaring her away. Relief she's not broaching the conversation she started outside.

"Don't worry about it. Tow truck will be here in ten to fifteen minutes."

"They'll take us back to Blue Beech or fix the flat?"

"Depends. If he can change it in the rain, he will. If not, he'll take us to the closest repair shop. Flats typically are a quick fix."

Minutes of silence pass through the cab until Willow says something. "We missed you when you left, you know." She snorts, and I'm unsure of where she's going with this conversation. "The temps they sent when you left were terrible, and Hudson was a total asshole for the first month."

I perk up in my seat. She's talking about when I quit working for Stella. I didn't give much notice. I left a day after Lucy told me the diagnosis.

"He was mending a broken heart," I say, sticking up for my brother.

"Hmm, so is that what happens when men are *mending a broken heart?* It justifies them acting like assholes?" Her face is playful, but her tone isn't. It's built up in hurt, betrayal, and also confusion.

Fuck. Where is this tow truck? I should've offered more money to get it here sooner.

"You trying to insinuate something?" I brace myself for the impact she's about to give me.

"Damn straight I am."

I swallow down my guilt. "Care to elaborate?"

"People get their hearts broken. People lose people. No offense, but it happens every day. Every minute. That's no excuse to act like a dick. You were a dick to me. Hell, *all* men are dicks if you're not letting them give you theirs. That's when they're nice and comforting."

"I'll apologize again for my dickdom. Hurt people don't always intend to hurt other people. That's not my intention. Trust me, I'd never want anyone to go through the hell I'm going through."

Her attention moves to the back window as headlights pull up behind us. Perfect timing to end this conversation. Intimate conversations with Willow are high risk for me. I'm a man of few words, and it seems I always choose the worst ones with her.

I grip the door handle. "Don't get out of this truck, headlight-chaser."

I meet the man in the middle of our trucks. He's sporting a parka and black boots.

"Nice day out here, huh?" he asks, thrusting his hand my way.

"For a duck," I mutter back, shaking his hand.

"It's about to get worse for ya."

Of course. The day goes more to shit.

Instead of asking why, I wait for him to elaborate.

"I can't work in this weather," he says. "It's dangerous, and they're talking about possible tornados." He whistles. "Half of the town's power is out due to the storm. Our mechanic went home to his family 'cause of it, but I'll ask him to come in first thing in the morning to fix this."

"Fuck. You've got to be kidding me."

He takes a step closer while chewing on a toothpick. "Wish I were. If it helps, I can give you a ride to the motel a few blocks down from the shop."

I slap him on the shoulder. "Appreciate it." I nod toward his truck. "You happen to have an umbrella in there?"

"Sure do."

"Thanks, man."

I jump back into my truck with the umbrella in my hand, ready to hear Willow rip my head off when I tell her we'll be having a sleepover tonight. I open my mouth when reality cuts through me. *How am I going to handle a sleepover?* I grind my teeth. This is a small town. They'll no doubt have more than one room available. I jumped the gun with the thought that we'd be sharing.

She's relaxed in the leather seat with her bare feet resting on the dashboard. I can't stop myself from giving her a once-over. Her soaking T-shirt has been replaced with a rose-colored lace tank top that showcases her cleavage. Her breasts are small, but that doesn't mean they don't excite my dick. They fit perfectly in my hands that night.

"Everything okay?" she asks.

I jerk my chin up, my throat tight. "He's giving us a ride into town."

"Perfect. How long will it take them to fix it?"

"Till tomorrow."

Her legs drop from the dashboard faster than Maven comes running when I mention ice cream. "What?" she shrieks. "Where are we supposed to sleep?"

"There's a motel a few blocks down from the repair shop."

"Can't we take an Uber back home and then pick it up in the morning?"

I smirk. "Ubers don't go to Blue Beech, babe."

———

"SORRY, but we only have one room available."

Go fucking figure.

Stranded. Check.

Having to share a room. Check.

What else can happen that's not going to make Willow wish she'd never stepped foot into my truck?

"We're always booked up on auction days. It's even worse today," the woman with steel-gray hair says in a hoarse, cracked voice while shaking her head at us like we're in the principal's office. "People don't want to travel in this mess. Here's a piece of advice for next time: book in advance."

"Thanks for the tip." I don't give two shits about her advice. She's our last resort. "We'll take it."

I grunt when Willow edges into my side to push herself in front of me. She faces the woman with a *Harriet* name tag.

"That's a room with two beds, right?" she asks.

"Sorry, honey. All we have is one queen." Harriet releases a bland smile. "Again, book in advance next time."

Sharing a bed. Fucking check.

Willow shoots me an innocent smile. "This will be interesting."

Willow

CHAPTER TWENTY-TWO

IF DALLAS BELIEVES I'm calm, I'll be asking Stella for a job tomorrow because I deserve an Emmy.

I'm doing everything in my power not to freak out right now.

We've shared a bed before.

Granted, we fucked each other, but no alcohol will be present tonight. We'll keep our hands to ourselves and build a pillow wall to separate us, and everything will be okay.

No touching. No sex. Fingers crossed he won't freak out tomorrow morning and leave me stranded.

On the bright side, we can't do anything stupid enough to make a baby again.

Shit. Babies. My mind still hasn't wrapped around that.

Dallas plays with the room key in his hand, circling it around his thick fingers, while we stand in front of room 206.

"What are you thinking?" he asks.

This seems to be our go-to question.

"That we have no other choice," I answer, signaling to the door in a hurry-it-up gesture. "This is our only option unless we decide to be a pain in the ass and have someone pick us up, and then they'll have to drive you back tomorrow to get your truck." I scowl at the door like it's my worst enemy. "Open sesame. Let's do this."

He obliges in what seems like slow motion while I look around. It's not exactly the Ritz, but I don't see any vermin running about, so that's a plus.

As Harriet pointed out with her stupid, smug smile, which I wanted to slap off, there's only one bed. What she failed to mention was that she's a liar because the bed is not a queen. It's a full, which means I have even less room to build my cockblocking fort. I briefly wonder if Dallas would be opposed to sleeping in the bathtub.

It's a standard room with a fake-wood-paneled bed topped with a generic comforter, a desk complete with a Bible and phone, and an older flat screen TV. I shuffle into the room, as if I were on my way to lethal injection, and Dallas stands in the doorway, his hypnotic eyes trained on me.

I sit on the edge of the bed and chew on my nails. "Oh, shit," I say. "Where's, uh ... Maven?"

This is only now hitting me. *Jesus, am I going to be one of those mothers who forgets her kids at the supermarket?*

He chuckles while stepping into the room, and I tense at the sound of the door clicking shut. It's official. We're slumber-partying it up.

"I didn't forget about my daughter, if that's what you're thinking. She's spending the week at summer camp," he answers.

"Camp? Like on *The Parent Trap*? That's a real thing?"

"It looked real when I dropped her off." He tosses the key on the desk.

What hotel still uses actual keys these days?

"Which side of the bed do you want?" he asks.

"It doesn't matter."

He points his chin at where I'm sitting. "I'll take that side. It's closer to the door, and you'll be closer to the bathroom."

He opens up the desk drawer, shuffles a few papers around, and shuts it. His next destination is the nightstand. He does the same thing and drags out a piece of paper ripped on both sides.

He blows out a breath. "Room service menu is tempting."

My stomach growls at the mention of food. I'm eating for three, and my appetite hasn't done anything to make me doubt it.

"I'm apologizing in advance for not feeding you quality tacos, but you have some superior choices here."

I bet. "And what would those be?"

He starts to read them off while fighting to keep a straight face. "Ramen noodles—"

"There's no way it says that," I interrupt.

"I'm not shitting you." He holds out the wrinkled piece of paper for me to read. Sure enough, ramen noodles is on there. "The other world-class options include grilled cheese, corn dogs, tomato soup, and sloppy joes." He frowns. "I'm not a picky person, but none of these sound exactly appetizing."

I agree. "So many options, such a small stomach." That's not *exactly* true.

The bed descends when he sits next to me. "Again, I'm sorry about this."

"Don't be. This will be a good story to tell our kids one day."

He smacks the paper. "So, what'll it be?"

"A corn dog might be my safest option."

"I owe you plenty of taco nights after this," he mutters, shaking his head. "Fucking corn dogs."

"Hey now, I have nothing against corn dogs."

He doesn't need to feel guilty about this. Shit happens that's out of your control sometimes. It's not like he planned to get a flat in the middle of nowhere.

He hands me the paper. "Anything else you want?"

I skim my finger down the page. "Might as well add some French fries while you're at it."

"Got it." He gets up from the bed and picks up the phone connected to the wall with a cord. "Room service, please." He orders my food and throws in ramen noodles for himself.

My stomach grumbles again, and I throw a pillow to get his attention, smacking him in the head. "I'll take some of those, too!"

He nods, rubbing his head. "Make that two ramen noodles." He hangs up. "Dinner is ordered. Get comfortable. I'll grab some drinks from the vending machine I spotted on our way in."

He snatches the keys from the desk, and I pull my phone out of my purse to see three missed calls and texts from Stella, asking how things are going and when I'll be back in town.

Me: Not until tomorrow. This is me officially calling in late. We're stranded because of a flat.

My phone beeps seconds later.

Stella: Stranded where?

Me: Neverland, for all I know. I'd say thirty minutes from the auction. Doubt it's on a map.

Stella: You need us to pick you up?

Me: No. Dallas got us to a motel. We're okay for the night.

My phone abruptly rings.

"Hello?"

"You're staying the night together?" she shrieks. "This is the best day ever."

"You damn liar!" I hear Hudson yell in the background. "You told me the same thing last night when I made you orgasm four times in a row."

"Ignore him," she mutters. "*Sooo* ... what are you guys doing?"

"Dallas is raiding the vending machine, and I'm sitting on the bed. No excitement over here." My response is along the lines of pathetic.

"You can always make it exciting."

I sigh. "I'm hanging up now."

"Call us if you change your mind and need a ride."

"I will. See you tomorrow."

"Damn straight you will. I'll be sitting on your doorstep, waiting to drag every detail out of you."

As I'm ending the call, Dallas walks in with drinks in his hand and a duffel bag draped over his shoulder. He sets the cans on the desk to hold up the bag on display.

"You didn't take me up on my clothes offer earlier, but I keep my gym bag in my truck. You need something to sleep in?"

"Are they dirty or clean gym clothes?" Not that it matters. I'll gladly sleep in anything that smells like him—dirty, bloody, stained, you name it.

"Filthy. Dirty. Sweaty." He chuckles, and I fake a horrified look. "I'm kidding."

I blush at the thoughts running through my head. "I know."

He drops the bag next to me on the bed and starts to rummage through it. "What's your preference? Pants? Shorts?"

"Shorts, please."

He holds up a pair of blue shorts with a red stripes down the sides. "These okay?" He pulls out a T-shirt next.

"They'll work." I play with the fabric in my hand when he hands them to me. "I'll go, uh … change in the bathroom."

I'm getting my pervert on when I shut the door behind me and smell his shorts. Fresh linen. I never knew what that smell was until my mom bought me the scented candle for Christmas. It was my favorite scent until I got a whiff of Dallas's *fresh linen*.

Even with my growing stomach, I have to tie the drawstring tight around my waist to keep the shorts from falling to my ankles. I grab the shirt and contemplate taking off my bra. It's usually the first thing I dispose of when I walk through the front door, but I'm not alone.

I unsnap it, snap it back, hesitate, and decide to leave it on. I pull the shirt over my head and pause to take in my reflection in the mirror before going back out. I grimace and smooth my hands over my hair. Rain turns it into a frizzy mess.

"Dinner is served," Dallas announces when I walk out. "It didn't take them long to microwave it."

I laugh. "Gourmet ramen at its finest."

He scoots out the desk chair, so I can sit down, and he places the corn dog, French fries, and the Styrofoam bowl of noodles in front of me.

"I lived off this stuff when I moved to LA and was looking for a job. Hell, even after I found a job, I ate it more than I should have because I was lazy." I grin and kick his foot when he sits down on the bed. "Meanwhile, your lucky ass got to live in Stella's guest suite that was complete with a gourmet chef."

He hooks his thumb toward his bowl. "This might be giving him some competition, and don't act like Stella didn't invite you to move in every month."

"That's true, but I wanted my own place, you know? My own space. Believe it or not, I'm an introvert at heart."

Stella also despised Brett, and they couldn't be in the same room for five seconds without wanting to rip each other apart.

"Makes two of us. Lucy was the extrovert to my introvert. She could make conversation with anyone in the room. Me? I was cool with standing to the side and people-watching."

I stiffen in my seat. *Lucy.* Her name always sends a bolt of mixed emotions through me.

Guilt from sleeping with Dallas. Jealousy that she was the one he adored, the woman he loved and shared a bed with without freaking out in the morning.

I nod and slurp a noodle into my mouth, attempting to appear relaxed. Dallas sets his bowl on the nightstand and slides to the edge of the bed until he's only inches from me. I slurp my noodles louder and faster, sounding obnoxious, and act like I don't notice how close he is.

He stays quiet until I swallow down my bite. "I was in a dark place then."

I drop my spoon into the bowl. "What?" *Why is he bringing this up? Abort mission. Please.*

"That morning. Hell, for months."

I fish the spoon out of the bowl, and my heart sinks at the pained expression on his face.

"Sometimes, I still am." He scrubs his hand over his face. "Sorry for sneaking this shit on you after the nightmare of a day we've had, but I can tell it bothers you when I mention her."

It's only fair I'm honest back. "Hearing her name makes me feel guilty."

He pats the space next to him, and I take the invitation, sliding between the small space between us and sit down next to him.

"If anyone should feel guilty, it's me," he says.

"I obviously played a part in it."

He didn't fuck himself.

"And today was not a nightmare. I enjoyed myself," I add.

"You don't have to lie to make me feel better."

I smack his arm. "You know I wouldn't lie about that. I'll take every chance I can to bust your balls."

"Point made. I enjoyed myself, too. To be honest, lately, the only time I seem to be in a happy place is when I'm with you." He lets out a heavy breath. "You took me out of my stressed out, broken world and gave me a good day. Same with the night we spent together. I like myself when I'm with you. I forget about the loss and the hurt. You make me feel alive again."

I nod. He misses Lucy and will always miss her but is opening up a portion of himself for me to discover.

Keep going.

No, stop. Red light. Don't drag me down this tunnel if it ends in hurt.

Keep going.

Why can't I think straight? I need to think with my head, not my heart.

"If I could take it back, I would," he goes on.

"Take us back, sleeping together?"

"No, take back my behavior. I might've not been all there, but I didn't bring you to my home for a simple fuck. I promise you that."

I bump his shoulder with mine. "It's my turn to say you don't have to lie to make me feel better."

"Babe, no bullshit. The opportunity for a quick fuck has been open to me several times, but I've never succumbed to any advances. Not one. Drunk. Sober. Horny as hell. It wasn't only my dick that felt a connection with you. I didn't want to admit that to myself that morning." He shakes his head. "I'm still having trouble with admitting that you pulled something out of me."

I wring my hands together. "Yes, there's an attraction between us, but that's as far as our relationship can go." I refuse to be second best to another woman.

He rests his hand on my knee and sucks in a breath. "I know. We'll stick to staying friends and co-parents. I didn't say that in hopes of having sex again. I said it, so you'd know I never meant to disrespect you, and what happened that night seems to be what makes us uncomfortable most of the time. I don't want that."

"Me either," I whisper.

"Good. Then, it's settled." He wraps his arm around my shoulders. "We're new besties."

———

IT'S ALMOST MIDNIGHT.

Even though we had the no-more-awkwardness conversation, it has yet to leave the building. Everything was fine while we finished eating, when we had to share a toothbrush because there was only one in the vending machine, and even when we watched endless episodes of *Cops*, which I learned is his favorite show.

Our problem now is going to bed.

We have to make ourselves comfortable and slip underneath the sheets. The lights will go off. There's intimacy involved in this whether we like it or not.

"You ready to admit, you're tired?" Dallas asks when I'm on my eleventh yawn. He chuckles. "Come on, go to sleep. You're not going to miss anything exciting here."

"Fine," I groan out. "If you insist." My shirt rises when I slide down until my head hits the rock-hard pillow. The air in the room grows thinner when I peek up and notice his eyes pinned to my exposed stomach.

He lifts his hand. "Can I?"

I nod in response since I'm struggling for words. My stomach flutters at the same time he presses his steady hand against it. It dawns on me that he's never touched my stomach like this before. Not even during the ultrasound.

His touch comforts me, the opposite of what I thought would happen, and I settle myself on my elbows to watch him. He's gentle, treating me like I'm expensive china, and he cradles my skin with his hand in awe.

"I can't believe we have two babies growing in here," he whispers. I smile when he shifts, so he's eye-level with my stomach.

"It's beautiful." He lifts up to focus on me with compassionate eyes. "You're fucking beautiful." He lowers his head and places his lips against my stomach. "Fucking perfection."

I miss his touch as soon as he pulls away and makes himself comfortable on his side. The smile that's been plastered to his lips since I gave him the okay is still there while he stares down at me.

He's waiting for me to tell him not to call me beautiful, to make a sarcastic comment, because that's what I do when conversations get heavy.

"What are you thinking?" he finally asks.

That your touch calms me more than a lavender bath and an expensive massage. That I wish we hadn't agreed to keep things platonic because the things I want to do with you right now are far from that.

"I'm thinking …" It takes me a second to come up with something. "I'm thinking today is officially the weirdest day of my life."

He cocks his head to the side. "That's what's heavy on your mind?"

I gulp. "Yep."

"You seemed to be in deep thought about that," he argues, running a finger over his chin.

"It's a deep subject." *Oh, hell. Let's put our attention back on people getting arrested, please.*

"Fuck, I wish I could read your mind right now, but I'll run with your answer."

I scrunch up my brows in question.

"I'll act like I'm convinced with the weirdest-day-of-your-life lie." A grin plays at his thick lips. "Today was weirder than the time one of Stella's stalkers broke into her house, dressed as a housekeeper, and begged her to wear black lipstick while going down on him?" He chuckles. "And, if I remember correctly, you tasered him before I even made it into the room."

"Asshole deserved it," I mutter.

He bursts out in laughter. *Real laughter.* I feel like I've hit the jackpot every time I get that from him.

"I'll have to call it a tie between the two."

"I'll take that and agree that getting stranded with you has been eventful. The plus is, I'll always remember this. We've formed a stronger relationship and learned more about each other in a day than we did throughout years of working together. So, thank you for the good memories and not bailing on me. Eating ramen noodles and watching a *Cops* marathon all alone wouldn't have been nearly as much fun."

I lower my head to hide the cheesy smile biting at me. He needs to stop talking like this if he wants to stay on the just-friends level. I lift my gaze when he scoots in closer, wiping out the small distance between us, and his eyes soften as he drinks me in.

I play with the chain of my necklace. "What are you thinking?"

It's my turn to ask the questions. Hopefully, he won't lie like I did.

His jaw flexes. "You want to know the truth?"

"Of course."

"What I'm thinking is, how bad I want to kiss you right now," he answers with no hesitation.

Anticipation drives through my body and straight between my legs, but I keep a calm face. "Then, what's stopping you?"

Adios, platonic, co-parenting plans. Hello, making shit complicated. At least it'll come with an orgasm. Hopefully.

He grins. "Good point."

My tongue darts out to wet my lips at the same time he presses his mouth to mine. He sucks on the tip of my tongue before dipping his into my mouth. I've never found the taste of generic toothpaste so delectable. Our lips slide against each other, as if we'd been doing this for years.

My heart pounds when he lifts up to move over me, keeping our lips connected, and I open my legs to allow him enough room to slide between them. I take in a deep breath when his mouth leaves mine to trail kisses down the curve of my neck.

He's slanted over me, careful of my stomach, and all I'm staring at is his erection straining through the thin gym shorts. My pulse races when I remember how big he is and how electrifying he felt inside me last time. No time is wasted before he rubs his fullness against my core to hit my most sensitive spot. I'm close to having an orgasm before we've even started.

It won't take much. I haven't been touched in forever, and if he's telling the truth, neither has he. We need to take this slow if we want it to last.

Unfortunately, what I need isn't what my body wants.

I need to get off.

I need this to last longer.

Why does this man constantly seem to drag out mixed emotions?

"More," I beg and squirm underneath him. *So much for wanting this to last longer.* "I need more."

More touching. More kissing. More of him everywhere.

My back arches when his mouth returns to mine. This kiss is different than the soft one before. It's greedy. Untamed. Eager.

"Where do you want more?" he asks against my lips.

"Everywhere," I moan out.

He groans deep from his throat when I run my foot up and down his leg and start moving into him more aggressive than what's appropriate. I shift until his cock hits me in the perfect spot, and then I grind against him.

He uses a single finger to untie my shorts, and I wiggle out of them in seconds, desire blazing through me. He doesn't bother removing my panties. Doesn't see them as a challenge.

Instead, he pushes the lace to the side and gives my clit the attention I've been dying for, rubbing it with the pad of his thumb.

I gasp when he slowly slips a finger inside me while still giving me the feel of his cock. His thick finger gracefully moves in and out of me. Not how I want it. I move against him harder to tip him off on how I need it.

"Slow down, baby," he says with a laugh. "You keep doing that, and my dick is going to explode. You probably want this to last longer than a few minutes."

"I don't care how long it lasts if I get what I want," I mutter.

He chuckles and shoves another finger into me without warning. He gives me rough. "That better?"

"God, yes," I moan out in response.

"I have something you'll enjoy even more."

He dips his fingers out of me in order to grab the strings of his shorts.

Finally. This is what I need.

The sound of a phone ringing startles me.

His hand drops from his shorts, and he curses under his breath. My heart beats wildly when he places them in his mouth and sucks on them on the way to his gym bag. I can't stop staring at the outline of his swollen cock when he opens the bag and grabs his phone.

We were right there.

Right freaking there.

My vagina does not deserve this.

He checks the caller before answering.

"Hello?" He drops down in the chair and expels a stressed breath. "Hey, honey. How's camp?" he croaks out. "What's wrong? You're feeling homesick? That happened to me my first time there, too." He pauses. "I promise."

I catch my breath when he falls quiet again.

"You know what helped me? I wrote my parents a letter, telling them all the cool stuff I was doing there. I'll ask your counselor to mail it out for you, and I should get it before I pick you up."

I pull my shorts up at the next pause. We won't be finishing this.

"Good. I'll be waiting for the postman every day."

I sit up on the bed.

"Call me if you need anything, okay? Good night. I love you."

He ends the call and tosses the phone on the desk. His eyes are pinned to the floor while he sits there, looking tortured. His chest heaves in and out, and the only sound is coming from the police sirens on the TV.

"Dallas," I finally whisper.

He lifts his head, and my chest aches at the unease on his face.

"Shit, Willow. I'm fucking sorry."

He pushes out of the chair, his erection not as visible as before when he was about to screw me but still there, and then he storms out of the room.

Tears slip down my face.

Another rejection.

I'm done lying to myself.

I'm done thinking he'll change.

Fuck Dallas Barnes.

Dallas

CHAPTER TWENTY-THREE

I DESERVE the rain pouring down on me in front of our hotel room. I deserve to get sucker-punched in my fucking face, mugged right here on this sidewalk, and stabbed in the back for how I treated Willow *again*.

My cock is hard. The taste of Willow's sweet pussy is on my tongue. My head is not only blasting with thoughts of how turned on I am, but also of how terrible of a man I am.

I did it again—treated her like shit and walked away while in the moment.

Willow deserves someone better than me, someone who isn't a mess. But why does it kill me to picture her having that someone? Why can't I get her out of my head and stay in this miserable place, as I promised myself I would months ago?

I shake my head in agony. What would it look like to Lucy if I fell for someone else? That would hurt her memory, show I was a shitty husband, make it seem like she was replaceable in my eyes.

I bang my palms against the motel's brick wall. *But, Jesus, fuck, what about me?*

I clench my hands and stalk back and forth, depicting a serial killer.

Would it hurt Lucy if I moved on?

She's gone.

Hell, knowing Lucy, she's probably smiling down at me. She begged me to find someone else to love and made me promise I'd eventually move on, for my daughter's sake and mine. I agreed, lying to her on her deathbed.

But who wouldn't when time was running out and you didn't want to waste your last words arguing about giving your heart to another woman?

I never thought it was possible. The thought of touching another woman made my skin crawl.

Until Willow.

Can I stay confined in my miserable bubble? Keep my heart in reserve because I'm terrified of losing someone I care about again?

I tilt my head up to stare at the dark sky.

"Lucy, baby, tell me what to do. Am I making a wrong move or being a fucking idiot?" I whisper while a million thoughts rush through my mind.

The bed is empty when I walk back into the motel room. I look at the window first, like a dumbass, considering the window is right next to the door, and I would've seen her leave. The bathroom light shines through the bottom of the door, and I hear the shower turn on.

Lucky for me, the door isn't locked. My hand is shaking when I open it while taking a deep breath. I make out her breathtaking silhouette through the thin shower curtain at the same time I hear her crying.

Damn it! I'm a fucking asshole.

I take a step into the room and say her name.

She doesn't reply.

I repeat it, louder this time.

Silence.

I strip out of my wet clothes, and when I climb in across from her, she pushes me back.

"What the hell, Dallas?" she shrieks. "You scared the shit out of me."

"I'm sorry," is all I can muster. Sorry for scaring her, for turning her down, for acting like an asshole. *Why am I always fucking up with her?*

Her tears get lost in the water. "I'm sick of your *sorrys*. I'm done, Dallas." She throws her hands up. "Done with your bullshit games. I refuse to be some toy for you to play with when it's convenient for you."

She winces when I stretch my arm out to move her fiery-red hair from her face, so I can see her beautiful green eyes better.

Today was a good day. We had fun. I told her shit no one else knows. I felt our babies in her stomach for the first time. We kissed. I had my hand in her panties and fingers in her pussy.

Then, I fucked it all up.

"No more bullshit," I whisper. "I promise."

"Your promises don't mean shit," she says with a snort, throwing my words back at me. "It only makes you look like more of a jackass each time."

I am a jackass.

"Tell me what you want me to do. How can I make this right?"

"Let yourself live!" she shouts. "Get it through that thick skull of yours that it's okay to move on, for your sake!" She stabs her finger into my chest. "For your daughter's sake!" Her finger moves to my stomach. "For my fucking sake!"

I cup her cheeks with both hands. "I've tried," I ground out. "I've tried telling myself I shouldn't do this with you, but maybe that's where I'm going wrong. I'm not supposed to be fighting it." I caress her soft skin. "Neither one of us is supposed to be fighting it because the only thing that feels natural is this. Us together."

"No," she breathes out. "You only fight shit that you don't want to happen."

"Trust me, fighting it means, it's *all* I want to happen." She shakes her head, and I wipe away her tears. "Say the word. Tell me you don't want me. Tell me you want me to leave this shower."

She breathes in deep breaths and stays quiet.

"Do you want me to leave?" I stress.

She pinches her lips together and won't answer.

"Or would you rather I did this?"

She gasps when I fall to my knees and inch her feet apart. I run my hand up her leg and straight to the opening of her pussy.

"Answer my question," I demand.

Instead of pushing me again, she slips her hand into my hair and moans. "That. I'd rather you did that." Her nails dig deep into my scalp before I make another move. "Keep going."

And that's what I do.

I situate one of her legs on the edge of the bathtub, and her body trembles at the first swipe of my tongue.

The taste of her is sweet.

Fucking heavenly.

I could eat her out for the rest of my life and never go hungry.

I apologize with my tongue.

Own her with it.

Beg her not to turn her back on me and plead to her to give me another chance.

If my words aren't convincing enough, I hope my tongue can do the trick.

"Shit, that feels so good," she mutters when I drive two fingers into her pussy and flick my tongue at her opening at the same time.

My dick stirs when I peek up at the image I'm getting. I'm on the verge of combusting from the view of Willow grinding her pussy into my face. I don't stop until I know she's on her way to falling apart.

"I'm close," she chants over and over again. Her foot arches off the edge, and she holds the back of my head in place as she lets go, her juices running onto my tongue while she moans out her final release.

So fucking gorgeous.

So fucking delicious.

My cock is hard as a rock. I'll be taking a cold shower and jacking off to thoughts of what happened in here when Willow goes to bed.

"Does that at least make up for some of my dickness?" I ask, looking up at her.

She spreads her fingers a few inches apart and massages my scalp. "A little. You still have some making up to do. I can take payment with your tongue a few more times."

I stand up, rub my hands down her sides, and then squeeze her hips. "Lucky for you, I don't mind paying interest."

She laughs. "Good to know."

I jerk my head toward the outside of the shower. "You ready to hit the sheets? It's late, and I know you're beat."

She nods. "You did just lick all the energy out of me."

I grunt when she wipes her mouth, and my hands are shoved off her hips. This time, she's the one dropping to her knees.

I stop her when she opens her mouth and bobs her head toward my dick. "No, this was about you."

I've turned down blow jobs on more than one occasion, but my body has never physically ached when I did, like it is doing now. I eye her full lips, the way she's licking them and staring at my cock like she can't wait to taste it.

"Trust me," she says. I tense and moan when she licks the pre-cum from the tip. "Me sucking your cock is just as much for me."

Her lips wrap around me before I can even come up with a response. My cock twitches, growing even harder, and I let her set the pace even though I want to plow my cock in and out of her mouth, fuck it until she can't breathe.

She takes me in, sucking me hard, and adds her hand to stroke me.

I throw my head back. "Shit, Willow. This is amazing."

She devours my cock, not stopping to catch her breath once, as water pours down over us. I thought the sight of pleasuring her with my tongue was my favorite, but her on her knees, sucking my cock, is running in close second.

I can't wait to fuck her again.

I know that'll be number fucking one.

"So fucking good."

My plan of not controlling her speed annihilates when I feel it coming. I jerk my hips up, and she moans against my cock, exciting it more.

"So good." I swipe the hair away from her face, so I can see every inch of her and give her a warning when I come, but she doesn't pull away.

The water turns cold at the same time she swallows my cum with a smile.

Willow

CHAPTER TWENTY-FOUR

"AND THEN WHAT HAPPENED?" Stella asks, nearly jumping off the couch in eagerness.

I'm back at work, and we're hanging out in her over-the-top trailer while she's making me do *another* rundown of what happened last night. She knows everything but the part where we dry-humped each other and had an oral face-off.

She'll get that story another time. It's still fresh in my mind, and I don't want questions to ruin the image yet.

Nervousness is an understatement of what I felt when I woke up this morning. The bed was empty. A bad sign. I grabbed my phone, and my heart settled when I heard the shower running. Joining him crossed my mind, but I'm not as gutsy as him.

When he got out, he said the truck was ready to pick up, and a shop employee would give us a ride there.

An hour later, we were back on the road.

No more kissing, hugging, or talks of what went down, *literally,* last night. It gave me relief yet also fried my brain at the same time. I'm concerned. Scared. Terrified.

We made light conversation. He told me about Maven's call last night. She was homesick and wanted to hear his voice. We listened to the radio, and I let him choose the music. It was *not* Justin Bieber.

"You know what happened," I answer.

Stella gives me a puppy-dog look. "No, I don't," she whines. "More happened than what you're telling me. I know you better than you believe."

I throw my arms out and fall back on the couch. "You've pulled every detail out of me. What more do you want? I can start making stuff up if it helps your weird imagination. We got married. Adopted kids to go with the baby on the way. Bought a house with a four-car garage. Surprise!"

She rolls her eyes. "No one copped a feel while you were sleeping *together?* Surely, the two of you are horny as hell, considering you've both been celibate for a minute. There you were, stranded in the rain, cold and lonely. How romantic."

"Now, you're making shit up. We weren't cold and lonely."

She clips a dark strand of hair behind her ear. "Work with me here." She narrows one eye at me, studying, like the answer she wants is marked across my skin. "You have every side effect of an orgasm."

"Side effect? Since when did you get into the pharmaceutical business?"

"I haven't seen a smile that bright on your face in a long time. Your skin is glowing. You look like you've been wandering around Wonderland all day."

"Pregnancy gives me mood swings. I could get crazy angry in three seconds."

She jumps up from the couch to lock the door, and I squirm in my seat when she joins me again.

"Uh, what are you doing? Keeping me hostage until I give you what you want?"

Her lips curl up. "How'd you know?"

I rub my hands together. "You have to promise you won't tell Hudson."

"Jesus, Willow," she moans out, her smile collapsing. "Do you not trust me anymore?"

My cheeks burn. "The whole scenario at your party scares the crap out of me."

She sucks her cheeks in before answering, "The only reason Hudson found out was because he was eavesdropping, not because I told him. I would've kept your secret."

She rises from the couch again. I'm afraid I've pissed her off when she unlocks the door and sticks her head out the door.

"Hudson?" she yells, looking around before slamming it shut, the lock clicking back. "No fiancé in sight. Half of the cast and crew have left for the day. You have my word that my lips are sealed."

I inhale a long breath before giving her the real rundown of what happened. She squeals, claps her hands, and is on cloud nine with every word.

———

I SNAG my phone from the nightstand when the doorbell rings. No missed calls or texts, and I didn't make plans with anyone.

Dallas texted earlier, asking me to go out for tacos, and I declined. Getting stared down while eating isn't on tonight's agenda. It's getting more difficult, hiding my baby bump. I'm going to have to get more creative.

I throw my post-shower wet hair into a sloppy ponytail and peek through the peephole when I reach the door. Dallas didn't give me a heads-up that he was coming, which is irritating because my baggy gray sweatpants and three-sizes-too-big T-shirt isn't the most attractive outfit to greet the guy who gave you a fantastic orgasm the night before.

He moves into my apartment with grocery bags covering half of his face. His muscular arms are securely wrapped around the bags, and he nearly runs into me when I stand in the middle of the doorway because I can't take my eyes off them.

"What are you doing?" I ask when he sets the groceries on the kitchen counter.

"You didn't want to go out for tacos, so I brought the tacos to you." He winks. "I promised tacos, so they're coming your way, and you can bet your ass that they're better than anything you'd get at a restaurant."

Shit. Fingers crossed he's not expecting me to help him.

We'll be eating grilled cheese by the end of the night. Burned grilled cheese.

I watch him while he digs out the groceries and starts moving around my kitchen as if he were my roommate. He sifts through the cabinets before pulling out pans and bowls.

"You know how to cook?" I stupidly ask.

He cuts open the hamburger, drops it in the pan, and turns a burner on low. "I'm a single dad."

"Good point," I mutter.

This soon-to-be mom had better take some notes. Takeout has always been my main food group, but that doesn't mean I eat like shit. I get healthy takeout—at least, I did before, but there's not a big market for that here.

"I cook dinner every night. Come over and eat anytime you want."

That's a big hell no. Any appetite I build up will be lost when I step into his house, and the memories of his freak-out flood me.

I take in my T-shirt and pull at the bottom. "I wish you had told me you were coming over."

He snags a cutting board and starts cutting the bell peppers. I slide into his spot, pushing him away and causing him to grin, and take his place. I start slicing the peppers, the simplest task for me to take over, without saying a word.

"You would've bailed," he replies.

"No, I wouldn't have." That's the truth. I bailed on going out to dinner but would've been up for his company. "I would've made myself not look like a train wreck."

"You look gorgeous." He nods toward my belly. "You've been hiding it well. Anyone know about the twins yet?"

I shake my head. "You spill the beans to anyone?"

"I'm waiting for you to give me the green light. You do know, we have to tell everyone sooner or later, right?"

"I do, but why does it feel like it's shock after shock? Guess what?" The knife waves through the air when I dramatically throw my arms up. "I'm pregnant. Guess what? It's with twins!"

"Put the knife down, Mike Myers." He laughs while peeling an avocado and then mashing it in a bowl. "You realize, life is full of surprises as you get older. You grow wisdom with age."

I click my tongue against the roof of my mouth. "Appreciate the insight, *old man.*"

"Whoa, who are you calling old?" He smirks and bumps his hip against mine. "You want to be on dish duty tonight?"

I slide the peppers off the board and into a glass bowl. The lettuce is my next victim. "I'm calling *you* an old man."

"Sweetheart, we're six years apart."

"Six years is a long time. You were in kindergarten, learning how to write your ABCs, when I was born."

"You seemed to find this *old man* attractive enough to sleep with."

"Eh, let's blame it on the alcohol."

"I'll keep waiting for you to admit it."

I drop the knife. "Admit what?"

"Admit this so-called *old man* made you feel better than any *boy* you've been with your age." He rests the spatula on the stove, and his eyes fix on me. "You lose a taco for every lie you tell, so I'd suggest you stick with the truth if you have an appetite."

Fucking tacos.

Are they worth honesty?

My stomach growls.

Hell yes.

"I don't have much to compare since I've slept with only two men. Brett cared about pleasing me in the beginning." I sigh. "That changed in the end. He'd get off, slap my ass, thank me, and then go back to his video games."

"Shit, you dated a fucking loser," he grumbles. "LA is saturated with men, and you stuck around with him? I never understood that."

"That's what everyone says."

"Why'd you stay with him then?"

"I don't know. Convenience?"

"That's a piss-poor excuse to stay in a relationship."

"You're telling me, you've never stayed with someone because starting over sounded too rough?" My voice is filled with defensiveness. I'm not alone on this.

"Fuck no. I'd never be with someone I didn't love. I stayed with Lucy for so long because my life would've been a nightmare without her. I loved her more than my own air. I would've given my life for her, taken her cancer, given her my health."

"It might not be with Lucy, but you're doing it now." I shift around him and go to the fridge for a bottle of water.

My response *really* catches his attention.

"What was that?"

I take a drink and slowly swallow it while he stares at me in confusion.

"Nothing," I mutter. I place my water on the counter and go back to my chopping duty.

He plucks the knife from my hand. "Not so fast. Tell me what you mean."

Here goes nothing. "You're doing the same thing!"

He raises a questioning brow and reaches back to turn the stove off.

"You've accepted being alone because the thought of starting over without Lucy seems too rough. *Convenience.*"

My eyes pierce his, and I wait for him to turn around and leave me with a half-cooked dinner. I should feel guilty about what I said, but I don't.

His shoulders draw back while he takes a pained breath. "She was my wife. You're not supposed to get over the love of your life."

My mention of Lucy has put a damper on taco night, but it

needed to be said. His answer will tell me if last night was just sex or if he's ready to open his heart and try something with me.

"I'm not saying you have to get *over* her but more of coming to terms that she's gone. I stayed with Brett because the thought of something new scared the living shit out of me, and you're doing the same. Don't throw stones at glass houses."

He wipes his hands down his jeans. "How'd you do it then?"

The fact that he's still standing here shocks me. "Do what?"

"Let your heart move on."

"It wasn't easy. It was one of the hardest decisions I'd ever made."

His jaw twitches, and his eyes are downcast on me. I suck in a breath. "I'm trying, trust me. I'm fucking trying for you." We're so close, I can feel his heart beating against my chest. "You've opened up what I feared for months. It doesn't seem as fucking scary, exploring with you."

———

I POINT my fork at my plate. "This is delicious." Screw those fancy taco joints. Dallas Barnes kills anything they serve. "Seriously, the best guacamole I've ever had."

He showed me how to make it step by step. I'm in charge of taco night next time.

"Told you I knew my way around a kitchen," he says proudly and then takes a drink of water.

I offered to run upstairs and grab a beer from Lauren's fridge for him. Tacos always taste better with beer. He wouldn't let me because it wasn't right for him to drink when I couldn't.

"How was work today? Stella drill you about our trip?" he asks.

Yep, drilled me as hard as his tongue did in the shower. I give him my best *duh* impression, and he laughs.

"Hudson pulled the same shit with me."

"They're more invested in our relationship than their own." I scrunch up my face. "I can't blame them though. I did the same thing with them."

"I'll admit, it's fun when you're on the other side." He tilts his water glass my way. "Did I thank you for the company the night we got them back together?"

A while back, Stella and Hudson broke up after the tabloids went after their relationship. I called Dallas, and we set up a plan to get them back together. It worked, and Hudson and Dallas flew to New York to surprise her.

I didn't want to be a cockblock during their making up, so I hung out in the lobby. That was where Dallas found me. We spent the night tasting food at every food cart, and I showed him my favorite spots in Times Square.

"You gave me my first good night in a while," he says. "No matter how shitty I'm feeling, you seem to always bring me back to the light." He runs his hand over his jaw. "Since we're talking about fixing relationships, about last night ..."

"I know, I know. It was a mistake," I rush out, sensing his regret. *Did he make tacos to soften up the blow?* "We were tired, not thinking clearly, horny *again* because we hadn't been laid in months."

"Whoa, hold up. I wasn't tired, and my mind was crystal clear." He stretches his shoulders back and grins. "Although you hit the nail on the head with the horny part."

What's he saying?

"I didn't eat your pussy last night just to get off. I don't do pity sex or pity *oral* sex." His tone turns serious. "In fact, I thought my sex life was over, but then you sat your perky ass across from me at the bar with your sexy-as-hell red hair pulled back to show off your contagious smile." He chuckles and leans in to rest his elbows on the table. "So, let's quit using the horny-and-not-thinking excuse."

Why do my words always come back to bite me in the ass? I'm judging him for pushing me away yet doing the same.

"In case you forgot, I was there in the morning," he continues.

"'Cause you were stranded."

Why can't I stop pulling away? Rejection still scares me.

"That was part of the reason, yes, but the other was you."

"Good. So, we can confirm we're both sexually attracted to each other. Maybe we should explore that and leave our feelings to the side for now."

"You want this to only be about sex?"

I nod.

"You sure about that?"

"Positive."

We'll screw for now and get each other out of our systems. In my head, I want to believe the only reason I'm pursuing him is that he gives me the best orgasms I've ever had. I want sex, and then we can worry about a relationship later. The opposite of what I was taught as a kid, but whatever.

He wipes his mouth, throws the napkin on his plate, and gets up from the chair. "Let's see if I can change your mind." He holds his hand out to me.

I stare at him in shock. I wasn't expecting this to go down now. "What?"

His eyes grow wilder every second he stares at me. "A warning, sweetheart. Don't challenge me and then be surprised when I rise to it."

I take his hand and let him pull me up. He doesn't give me a chance to take another breath before he hungrily captures my mouth with this. I moan when his tongue slips into my mouth. The kiss makes it clear that he's going to make me regret saying that all I wanted was his cock. It explains he'll make me beg for it until I admit that I want more.

I gasp for those lost breaths when he grabs a handful of my ass and draws me in closer. I waste no time in pushing his shirt up and over his head. I didn't have the chance to thoroughly appreciate his body last night in the shower. His tongue between my legs consumed my every thought.

My mouth waters at the sight of his firm chest, muscles galore, the six-pack finely sculpted. He's right about one thing. He might be older, but his body and his cock outweigh Brett in every way. He tenses when I run my lips down his chest and flick my tongue against his nipple. His cock swells under his jeans, him *rising for the challenge*, if you will, and I drop to my knees to frantically pull it out.

I'm taking control before he gets the chance to.

Blow jobs have never been my thing. I saw them as a chore with Brett, but everything is different with Dallas. The thought of his hard dick inside my mouth excites me. Pleasing him pleases me.

I wet my lips, drinking in the sight of his large erection twitching in front of me, pre-cum dripping from the tip. His head falls back when I take the full length of him in my mouth. He's so big, it stabs me in the back of my throat. I bring my mouth back, drawing his dick out to catch my breath, and then eagerly suck him back in.

"Fuck, that mouth, Willow," he croaks out when I sink my nails into his ass to blow him better.

His hand dips down to wrap around his cock, and he jacks off in sync with my mouth. The hottest fucking thing I've ever experienced. I take him in, more excitedly.

He's close, I can tell, and I can't wait to taste his cum again.

Can't wait to swallow him down but still have the taste of him lingering there.

I wait for it, my mouth moving faster, but he pulls away right before we reach the finish line.

The hell?

His face burns with desire as he stares down at me on my knees. "I'll never get the sight of this out of my mind. It's better than anything I've imagined while jacking off."

Chills climb up my spine. "You think about me when you're jacking off?"

His hand is still wrapped around his cock, and he goes back to slowly stroking it. "Every fucking time," he grits out.

"Let me finish the job then," I say with a pout.

He shakes his head. "I'm going to finish the job in your tight pussy. I know you enjoy sucking my cock, but that'll be nothing compared to sliding inside you." He catches my chin between his thumb and forefinger. "Now, stand up, so I can put you on this table and eat you as my dessert."

I shyly bite my lip. "How can a girl deny that?"

"You'll never want to deny me when I give you this dick again. You'll be coming back for more."

He picks me up underneath my elbows and settles me on the table. I open my legs the second my ass hits the edge. I'm ready for this. I *need* this.

"Put your hand over my mouth before you start," I breathe out.

He cocks his head to the side. "Didn't know you were into that."

I shake my head and laugh. "We have to be quiet. Your sister lives right above me, and the walls are thin."

"I don't give a shit. I want to hear you scream my name."

My sweatpants and panties are off in seconds, and he disposes of my bra and T-shirt. He licks his lips when he takes in my breasts. He cups them and leans down to draw a nipple into his mouth. He sucks hard and releases me, and not another word leaves his mouth before he drags my legs over his shoulders. My breathing hitches when he falls to his knees.

The first lick sends jolts through my body, and I would fall off the table if he wasn't holding me in place. His tongue is an expert, dipping in and out of me, before he slips it out to suck on my clit. When he uses it to separate my folds for a better angle, my toes arch toward the ceiling.

Ache blossoms through my chest, and the need for an orgasm pushes at me even harder. His hands move up and down my legs as he pleasures me, and I make sure I'm balanced well enough before reaching down and pushing a finger inside myself. I work in sync with his tongue the same way he did when I was sucking him off earlier.

Our connection is what ends me. My back comes off the table, my legs buckling against his shoulders, and I never want to come down from this orgasm as it shoots through me.

"Say my name," he groans, still working his tongue in me.

I do as I was told—not screaming it at the top of my lungs, but repeatedly gasping it out.

He slowly releases my legs with a shit-eating grin on his face. "Damn, I love the sound of that when my face is shoved in your pussy."

He gets up and goes to help me down from the table, but I stop him.

"I want to fuck you."

He's shocked at my outburst. "Don't worry, sweetheart. I fully plan on doing that—*multiple times*—but let's save the table sex for another time. I want you in your bed."

I grunt when he picks me up in his arms, newlywed-style, and he races to the bedroom. As badly as I want this, I still have nervousness riding through me like a hurricane. We're taking a big step here.

This isn't a quick blow job in the shower.

This is *sex*—something so intimate for the both of us. Neither one of us sleep around, so this is a big deal, especially for him.

I don't want him to freak out this time and feel like he's betraying Lucy by sleeping with me.

"Are you sure about this?" I ask when he carefully lowers me onto the bed.

He doesn't respond until I give him full eye contact. "I've never been surer." He situates himself between my legs, and his cock impales me with no warning.

I constrict around him while he gives me time to adjust to his size. I know the situation I'm getting into with his first thrust. His first moan tells me I'm not making the wrong decision.

He starts out slow, which frustrates me. This is something I've wanted for months. I tilt my hips up to give him a better angle, excite him, and hint that I want more.

Harder. Faster. More.

It works.

He pounds into me rougher, sweat building up along his forehead, and groans with every stroke.

"Say my name," I whisper. "Tell me who you're in bed with." It's my turn to show ownership.

"Willow," he says, his eyes drinking in my face ... my body.

We slow down when he stretches forward to take my lips with his, and he devours my mouth.

"I'm in Willow's bed, fucking Willow, and Willow is about to make my dick explode."

I kiss him until he pulls away to fuck me harder. That's when I place my hands over my stomach to hide it. I've never been an insecure person, but I've gained weight. *A lot of weight.* My stomach is no longer flat. I see myself as less attractive.

"Don't," he demands in a raspy voice. "Let me see what we did together."

I slowly drag them away, and he grasps my hands in his, placing them over my head and tightly holding them.

I shudder underneath him, coming undone, and scream out his name again.

There's no doubt everyone in the building heard that one.

He jerks and gives me two more thrusts before releasing himself inside me.

"Fuck," he grunts, breathing as hard as I am. "That was fucking amazing."

I'm still catching my breath when he collapses next to me. We're a sticky and sweaty mess. Pretty sure I've burned off every calorie of those tacos.

I turn my focus on him. "You work an appetite back up?"

He smirks. "I had a very filling dessert."

His answer makes me tingle. *Tingle.* This is the first time I've ever felt myself do that.

"I'm starving, and I don't like eating alone if I don't have to. Lucky for you, I have a pantry full of ramen noodles."

He chuckles. "Fucking ramen noodles."

I'm falling for this man who is broken, a little ruined, a bit of a disaster ... and who gave up on love.

Willow

CHAPTER TWENTY-FIVE

I TENSE when the bed shifts behind me.

He yawns.

Then, he heads to the bathroom.

What happens now?

God, why am I so paranoid every morning after?

We went back to the kitchen last night and didn't have ramen noodles. Instead, we had ice cream, and then he did fuck me on the table after licking our dessert off my chest. We were exhausted, and I'd reached my exercise goal for the month, so he suggested a movie. I introduced him to my favorite black-and-white film, *Casablanca*, and we passed out before reaching the end. He carried me to bed, kissed me good night, and wrapped his arms around me. It felt good to be held, relaxed me, and I was back to sleep in seconds.

His next move this morning will tell me everything I need to know about our relationship—or possible lack thereof. Him not bailing at the hotel doesn't count, doesn't ease my mind, because he had an obligation to stay with me. He didn't have a working car, and Stella would've kicked his ass if he'd left me stranded.

I brace myself for whatever is about to happen when he comes around the bed and drops to one knee, so we're eye-level.

His lips curl up as he edges closer. "I didn't want you to assume I was sneaking out. I have to pick up Maven from camp."

I smile. "Do you mind if I come along?"

What the hell am I thinking?

"You up for another road trip with me?"

"Why not?" I want to spend all my time with him.

My smile grows when he kisses my forehead.

"All right, get dressed, and we'll be on our way. I'll grab my clothes from the truck."

I hop out of bed like I'm ten and it's Christmas, and I scurry to the bathroom.

Our relationship shifted into something last night—something that exceeds friends but isn't quite into the whole relationship thing yet.

Friends with benefits?

Co-parenting with benefits?

Sex, not love?

———

"OH MY GOSH, this is so cute," I say when we pull into the camp parking lot. "It's not like the movies but still cool."

Dallas cocks his head toward my stomach. "Can't wait for our little ones to join Maven here in a few years."

"A few years? You mean, six?"

"I started coming here in Pampers."

I slap his shoulder. "You are such a liar."

Maven comes running our way as soon as we get out of the truck.

"Daddy!" she screams. "You brought Willow! This is the bestest day ever!"

I lose a breath when she rushes into me and wraps her tiny arms around my waist.

"Hey now," Dallas says, coming up behind her and peeling her away from me. "What am I, chopped liver? You haven't seen your dad in a week, and you roll right past me."

She giggles and jumps into his arms. "You know I missed you, Daddy!" When he releases her, she pulls a stack of papers from her bag. "I made all of these for you and wrote letters like you said!" She snatches the top piece from Dallas's hand and holds it out like she can't wait for me to see it. "This one is for you."

"Wow, thank you," I say with a smile. It's a hand-drawn picture of her and a tall redhead holding hands and walking around what resembles lights. "It's so pretty."

Her eyes sparkle with pride, and she bounces on her tiptoes. "It's us at the fair. I had *sooo* much fun and can't wait to do it again next year!"

I squat down and give her another hug. "Me either. Maybe, next time, I can gain some courage and join you on the rides."

"I would love that so much!" She turns around. "Daddy! Willow said she'd get on the big-kid rides with me next year!"

Dallas smiles and winks at me. "Oh, really? We'd better hold her to that."

"Dallas, I thought that was you," a feminine voice calls out.

Maven loses my attention when I see a woman walking our way. A pretty blonde dressed similar to what Lucy used to wear, and she gives me a once-over, sizing me up to see if I'm competition.

Sure am, sweetie.

She thrusts her hand in my face when she reaches us, and I can't stop myself from rolling my eyes. Her face scrunches up into a sneer to assure me it wasn't missed.

"You must be Willow. It's nice to finally meet you. You're all everyone in town has been talking about."

Her eyes drop down to my stomach, and I pull my arms around it to block her view.

Really? I cross my arms. *Let's see her squirm.*

"Like what?"

I've only gone to the fair and the diner for lunch once. The only other times I've left my apartment is to go to work, and Stella's show is filmed thirty minutes out of Blue Beech. I've kept to myself, but I'm sure she's heard about me from the videos taken at the fair.

My question surprises her. I don't mean to be rude, but the way her eyes scrutinize me is rude in itself.

She signals between Dallas and me. "That you two have been spendin' an awful lot of time together." Her smile is bright and phony. "You're from the big city, like Hudson's little fiancé, right?"

"Sure am. I'm her best friend and assistant."

"I see," she clips. "How long do you plan on staying here? You probably miss LA. It's pretty boring around here."

"Cindy," Dallas warns.

She whips around to smile at him. "What? I'm only introducing myself to the town's newest ..." Her attention moves back to me. "Visitor? Resident?"

"Resident," he growls to her back. "Willow is a new *resident* of Blue Beech, so you march on and relay that to your gossip club and quit interrogating her."

She throws me a flat smile, turns around to give him her attention, and slides her hand across his chest. He jerks away.

"You want me to make y'all dinner tonight? I can bring that fried chicken of mine you love so much." She glances down at Maven with a faker smile than she gave me. "Didn't you say it was your favorite, honey?"

Maven shakes her head. "My grammy's fried chicken is my favorite."

Dallas glares at Cindy. "As much as I'd love to chat and deny your company, we have places to be. Enjoy our day."

"Call me," she sings out to him.

This time, she wraps her arm around his, and he pulls out of her grip, narrowing his eyes on her.

"Stop." He gives her his back and grabs Maven around the waist. "You ready to go, sweetheart?"

I throw *Cindy* the dirtiest look I can manage before getting into the truck.

She brings him dinner? He said he cooks every night.

Dallas gets into the truck and leans into my space. "Don't let your head go there. Give me the benefit of the doubt, and we'll talk about it."

I nod. My heart aches with jealousy, terror, and betrayal.

Dallas starts the truck with fire in his eyes.

———

"WALKERS! WALKERS! WALKERS!" Maven chants twenty minutes into the drive home. "Daddy, you promised!"

Dallas pats my thigh. "You hungry?"

"The waiters are rude to you at Walkers!" Maven says. "It's *so, so, so, so* funny! They told Daddy he had a nose bigger than a rhino's horn one time."

I laugh and twist in my seat to smile at her. "No way." I fake lower my voice and place my hand on the side of my mouth. "I totally see what they're talking about though."

Maven bursts into a fit of laughter.

"Hey now," Dallas cuts in. "That's supposed to be the part where you stick up for your dad and argue that I don't have a nose like a rhino." His hand moves to rest on my leg this time when I turn back around. "You cool with stopping?"

"I'm not passing on this, rhino man."

———

MAVEN AND DALLAS sit across from me in the booth.

Walkers is an old-fashioned diner where the waiters wear ridiculous uniforms with unusual, most likely made-up names.

The waitress tells me I'm cheap when I order a water. Maven cracks up.

She says Dallas isn't man enough for real beer when he orders a root beer. Maven cracks up.

She gladly takes Maven's order for a milkshake without saying a word. Maven still cracks up.

At least they're nice to kids.

Not only does Maven take over all the conversation, telling us everything she did at camp, but she also takes my mind off what happened with *Cindy*.

Fucking Cindy. I can't be pissed at Dallas for hanging out with another woman when we're not officially anything. I can't call dibs on him just because I'm carrying his babies.

Wait … yes, I can.

I can because, last night, he was in my bed.

I'm calling dibs.

————

I'M STUFFED AFTER LUNCH, but Maven insists we share a dessert.

"My birthday party is next weekend," she tells me, scooping up a bite of the brownie sundae. "Will you come? Pretty, pretty please with cherries on top?"

I swallow my bite down. "Sure." My attention goes to Dallas. "I mean, if that's okay with your dad."

"I'd love for you to come," he answers.

"It's at my grammy and grampy's," she continues. "They have a giant yard, and Daddy promised to get me a princess bounce house, so all my friends can play in it. Didn't you, Daddy?"

Dallas ruffles his hand through her static-filled ponytail. "Sure did."

"A princess bounce house?" I say with high enthusiasm. "I can't say no to that."

Maven bounces in her seat. "Yay! I'm so excited!"

We finish our dessert, and Dallas leaves the table to pay the bill.

"Do you have any kids?" Maven asks as soon as he's out of earshot.

I nearly spit my water in her face and cough a few times before managing to swallow it down. It takes me a second to get over the shock and tilt my lips into a smile.

"I don't," I croak out.

Dallas

CHAPTER TWENTY-SIX

FUCK, it's been a day.

After I dropped Willow off, I helped Maven unpack her bags. We went through all of her painted pictures, letters, and worksheets she'd created. There were several she had drawn with her family doing activities she enjoyed. I flipped through them with a smile, and my heart crashed into my chest when I got near the bottom of the stack.

She and I are standing together, holding hands, and a blonde angel is flying above us. *Lucy* is flying over us.

The next one was a picture of us with Willow.

My daughter is confused.

Willow is confused.

Shit, I'm confused as a motherfucker.

Cindy's comments when I picked up Maven didn't help. Dinner went well until I went to pay the check. After that, Willow froze me out.

I can't wait to collapse on the couch and go over all the shit I need to fix. I need to clear up the Cindy situation with Willow before shit falls apart.

My day gets even more complicated when I finish Maven's favorite bedtime story and tuck her in.

"Willow is nice," she says. "I'm glad she's coming to my birthday party."

I kiss her forehead. "Me, too, honey."

"And she's really pretty."

I nod, hoping I can make it out of the room before she starts her favorite game of a million questions.

"Is she your girlfriend, Daddy?"

She never fails to catch on to something.

I shake my head and fake a laugh. "Now, that's a silly question."

She frowns. "It's not a silly question."

"Your daddy can't have a girlfriend."

I need to tread lightly here. I can't get her involved in something that could break her heart. I'm already growing attached to Willow, constantly thinking about her. *But can I throw my daughter into the mix?* I'm more worried about her heart getting broken than my own.

"Why not? Mommy told me, when she was gone, you'd someday get a new girlfriend who'd be a good mommy to me. Willow would be a good mommy, don't you think so?" She sighs. "Maybe I'll ask her."

Oh, fuck. Holy fuck. This is heading into territory I'm not ready for. Territory Willow isn't ready for.

I squeeze her sides over the blanket. "Honey, Willow is just Daddy's friend."

"*And* my friend," she corrects.

"And your friend."

"She rubs her belly a lot. Marci's mommy did that all the time when she had a baby in there. Does Willow have a baby in there?"

And shit just got even more complicated.

Willow

CHAPTER TWENTY-SEVEN

"YOU'RE OVERTHINKING THIS," Stella says on the phone. "You can't seriously believe Dallas is messing around with some other chick named fucking Cindy. I've never heard of a Cindy, which means she doesn't get thought of around here."

I thought the night at the hotel was a crazy one.

That's nothing compared to today.

I spent a morning with Dallas. We hung out with his daughter. A woman told me he'd been hanging out with her. Maven asked me if I had kids, and I somewhat lied to her. I don't have kids … *yet.*

"She said he's been eating her food. Fried chicken, to be exact," I argue.

"And?"

"And?" I shout. *Why does she not agree that this is a problem?*

"Does eating her food mean eating her vagina or something? Is fried chicken a code phrase I don't know about?"

I slump down on the couch and groan. "I don't know. I just …" *Just don't want him falling for another woman.* I'd better start whipping up some food Betty Crocker–style to compete with this chick's fried chicken. Time to call KFC for their secret recipe.

"Trust me, you're the only woman I've seen Dallas hanging out with. Shit, even talking to."

"You not seeing it doesn't mean it's not happening. You don't see me witnessing you screwing Hudson, but I know you guys are."

"Holy shit," she bursts out.

"Holy shit what?"

"You're falling for him, aren't you? This isn't about your hook-up the other night or about you wanting to get along for the baby. You're into him."

"What?" I yell. "No! Absolutely not!" I'm getting good at this whole lying/denying-my-feelings thing.

"Oh, come on. It's obvious. You've been hanging out, having dinner, giving each other oral before having sex, and picking up his daughter from camp. All that is falling-for-each-other stuff."

"It's not *obvious*." I take a deep breath to change the tone of my voice to sound more self-contained. "Don't take me making sure my baby daddy isn't a psychopath for me falling for him."

She sighs dramatically. "You owe me a hundred bucks when you two become official. I can take it out of your paycheck. I'll ask Hudson if anything is going on with Dallas and fried-chicken chick."

I snort. "Like he'd tell you. Dallas is his brother. Bro code."

"I can be very persuasive with my man. Trust me."

I stretch my legs out and measure my stomach—something I've been doing every night to track my progress. "I'm beginning to second-guess my decision of forcing the two of you to get back together. All this lovey-dovey crap makes me sick."

She laughs. "It's the morning sickness making you sick. I can't wait until you and Dallas admit you're in love, and I can throw all of this back in your face. I'll be the one rolling my eyes at your lovey-dovey shit."

"Whatever. Dallas is in love with his wife, who passed away." I'm acting like a brat, feeling sorry for myself, but this is where I start to push him away again. My heart is ready to go back into solitude. You can't have your heart broken if you don't give it out. "He'll always be in love with her, and I doubt that's going to change anytime soon."

She expels a long breath. "People move on. He can still love her *and* you."

"People can move on, yes, but a man in love as deep as Dallas was? No." A call beeps through, and I pull my phone away to check the caller ID before she keeps up with her argument. "Let me call you back. I have a call coming through."

"Is that call from Dallas?"

"Good night, best friend."

She's laughing when I end the call to answer his.

"Hello?" I throw my hand over my mouth, regretting taking the call. I haven't prepared myself for this conversation yet. I have to get myself together.

"Hypothetical situation," he breathes out, sounding stressed. "What would you say if I told you Maven knew you were pregnant?"

I don't even have time to *think* about what I would say before I screech out my reply, "I'd say you were out of your mind, and there was no way she'd know unless someone—say, her *father*—told her."

"Another hypothetical situation. What would you say if I told you Maven knew we were having twins?"

"What?" I shriek. *Him and his big mouth.* "You've lost your mind!"

He groans. "I couldn't help it! My six-year-old is apparently the damn baby whisperer. She asked me if you were pregnant because you rubbed your belly like fucking Marci's mom."

"Marci's mom? Who's that?"

"Another pregnant woman, I'm assuming."

"Let me get this straight. She asked if I was pregnant because I rubbed my stomach like another pregnant chick?"

"Correct."

"And you felt it was important to confirm it?"

"Correct again."

"Are you nuts?" I scream.

"I didn't know what to do. I can't lie to my daughter."

The hell he can't. I'll be lying to my children all the time about stuff they have no business knowing yet.

"Oh, really? So, you've told her Santa Claus isn't real and the Easter Bunny is you?"

He chuckles but tries to keep his voice serious. "You know what I mean."

"Well, you could've maybe, I don't know, changed the conversation to fucking Barbie dolls or something? Asked her to have a tea party? Talked about anything but my uterus."

"We can't have tea parties before bedtime," he explains.

"That fake caffeine is bad for children and their stuffed dogs after the streetlights come on, huh?"

"Smart-ass," he mutters. "I don't see why you're pissed. You should be thanking me. This saves you from having to be there when I planned on telling her."

"At least one good thing to come out of this." My heart stammers, and confusion flickers through me. Why am I upset that I wasn't there? Why am I sad I didn't get to see her reaction?

"You still pissed?" he asks a few seconds later.

"Not pissed. Shocked."

"If it makes you feel better, I made her promise she wouldn't tell anyone until I told her it was okay."

"I'm not sure how much I trust a promise coming from a six-year-old."

"It helps when you add an extra birthday gift as a hush bribe. Some parenting advice to a mommy-to-be—nothing works better than bribery with extra doll clothes."

"Bribery is okay, but lying is off the table? Makes sense. I'll have to keep that in mind." *While mine is going fucking crazy right now.*

"Now that I know you're not pissed, *just shocked,* I need to ask for a favor."

Seriously? This co-parenting relationship with benefits is getting demanding.

"Haven't you thrown enough at me tonight?"

"This one will be a fun one."

"Shoot." I cross my fingers that it doesn't involve any more pregnancy announcements.

"Will you go shopping with me for Maven's birthday present? Lauren planned on going with me, but she's been pulling double shifts to save up for a house. I don't want to put more stress on her."

"Maybe you should ask *Cindy*. You can go shopping, and then she'll feed you some fried chicken casserole." I'm acting petty, but this is how I bring up my problems. I use my sarcasm to tell people how I feel.

"What?"

"The smiley chick who came over when we picked Maven up." *Is clarification needed?* "The one who thought her fried chicken was the best thing since sliced bread."

"Wow," he says with a laugh.

"What?".

"Surely, you don't believe I'm hanging out with her?"

"No," I stutter out. "I mean, I don't know."

He sounds like he's enjoying this now. "Would you be upset if I were?"

"Nope. Not at all. Eat her fried chicken. Get heart disease. It's all good."

"Willow," he draws out in warning, "would you be upset if I were?"

"Would I upset? Nope. Pissed? Yes. Will I have sex with you again if you are? Definitely not."

"I'm not hanging out with her, I swear. She came around and dropped off food when Lucy passed but hasn't been around in months. Even then, it was nothing. I accepted the food, so my daughter wouldn't starve until I got my shit together. When I managed to perfect grilled cheese, I put a stop to it."

I roll my eyes. "Whatever."

"You're the only woman I'm hanging out with. Hell, other than my sister and mother, you're the only woman I even talk to. So, now that that's done, when do you want me to pick you up for shopping?"

"We're not going anywhere in town, are we?"

"No. I figured we could take a trip into the city. She asked for an

American Girl doll?" He says it like he's unsure if that's the right name.

"Oh, I had one of those, growing up. Which one does she want?"

"Uh ... one that looks like her? They have a store in the mall near the airport."

"Another road trip, huh?"

"Seems to be our thing. My mom is taking Maven to her bake sale, and then they're going shopping for her party decor on Saturday. That okay?"

"My Saturday looks open." Like almost every day.

Stella is on break from filming and hasn't been asking much of me, so getting out of my apartment sounds refreshing.

"Then, it's a date."

I grin. "It's a date."

Dallas

CHAPTER TWENTY-EIGHT

"DO you remember the doll I want, Daddy?" Maven asks for the umpteenth time.

I tap my finger on the side of my head. "Sure do." I have it written in my phone notes. I pulled up the doll website last night, and there's a shit-ton of options. I pause and cock my head to the side. "And you don't even know if you're getting a doll."

Yes, she does.

She bounces from foot to foot. "I *really, really, really* hope so." She skips up the steps to my parents' porch to meet my mom standing outside. "Grammy, don't I need an American Girl doll?"

My mom draws her into her side. "Of course you do, sweetie."

Maven wags her finger my way with a smile on her lips. "You have to listen to your parents, just like you tell me."

"Oh, honey, your daddy was not a good listener when he was your age," my mom replies with a laugh. She squeezes Maven's shoulders. "Now, go wash up for lunch, and we'll go to the bake sale and then shopping for your party decorations."

"Yay! Princess Jasmine all the way!" she shrieks. She pulls the door open and disappears into the house.

"Thank you for watching her, Ma," I say.

She nods. "Anytime. You going to the city to get the doll?"

I scrape my boot against the steps. "It's what she wants."

She can't contain her loving smile "And her daddy always gets her what she wants."

"It's the least I can do. She lost her mother. She deserves the world."

Her smile drops. "You're getting her a doll in the hopes that she won't be sad every day?"

I grew up with parents who refused to sweep shit under the rug. If there was a problem, we talked about it. If they wanted to know something, they asked and expected honest answers. I grew up, facing my challenges, but this isn't a problem easily fixed. No amount of parenting or life lessons could've prepped me for losing Lucy.

"That's not the ultimate reason, but it has something to do with it," I answer. "I want her to heal and enjoy her childhood. If that means spoiling her right now, then that's what I'll do. Whatever my daughter needs to put a smile on her face, I'm willing to do it."

A tear slips down her cheek. I hate seeing my mother upset. I take the few steps up to wrap her in my arms. She sniffles for a second before she continues her impending lecture.

"It'd help her much more if her father started working on the healing process as well," she says when she slips out of my arms.

I clear my throat to bring out my kindest warning voice. "Ma …"

She wipes her eyes and then places her hand on my shoulder. "Dallas, honey, I loved Lucy. We all did. We all miss her, but she's gone."

"She was my *wife*." I'm using all my power not to get pissed with her. "You'd be lost without Dad."

"I would. The difference between you and me is, I'm in my sixties. I have thirty years on you, son. A whole life is waiting for you. Happiness is out there, but you're never going to find it if you're blocking it out. Find someone for Maven. Find someone for *you*."

My mother is the best person I know. She's beautiful. Selfless. Caring. There will never be another woman with a heart as kind and nurturing as hers. She raised us to be strong, fearless, and independent.

Her age doesn't show, and Lauren is the spitting image of her. They're both short and have long brown hair. Lauren keeps hers down most of the time while my mom's stays in a bun. They also have a personality with enough spark to light up a city. Mom doesn't make it easy to get upset with her.

"Can we talk about this another time?" I ask.

"Of course." A smile plays on her lips. "Are you going shopping by yourself?"

I shake my head. "Willow is coming with me."

"Stella's assistant?"

I nod, and her lips form a sly smile.

"Word on the street is, you've been spending an awful lot of time together. Beautiful girl, I must say. The few times I met her, she was such a sweetheart."

"I see the Blue Beech gossip is still alive and kicking," I mutter.

"You go have fun, honey. If it gets too late, stay there, and have a nice dinner. I've already told Maven she could spend the night, so we have plans."

"You spoil her too much."

"That makes two of us." She pulls me in for another hug. "Now, I'm ready for some more grandchildren. I don't know why my children are taking so long to give them to me."

Oh, shit.

She's about to be surprised.

———

THE AMERICAN GIRL store is packed with moms and daughters, and I have no idea where to make my first move.

Willow cracks up before grabbing my hand. "Come on. I'll try to lead the way the best I can. It's been about two decades since I had one of these dolls, but surely, not that much has changed."

We don't lose our connection and dodge people while migrating through the loud crowd.

"We're looking for one that resembles her!" I yell over the noise, as if it were normal to be hunting for the incarnation of your child.

I scan the aisles and stop her each time I think I've found it, but Willow shakes her head and continues her search.

Good thing she came with me, or I would've grabbed the first doll I saw and bolted out of here. Lauren most likely wouldn't have had the patience to deal with this crowd either. She didn't play well with dolls. She drove my mom crazy because she popped all the heads off them, so she could play outside with Hudson and me.

Unlike us, Willow is thorough. She'll assess every doll until she finds the perfect fit.

We've been in the store for thirty minutes when she spots the one and clutches the doll to her chest for me to see. "What do you think?"

It eerily resembles Maven. The dark brown hair, a bow clipped to the side of it, bright purple sunglasses, and a checkered dress.

I tilt my head toward the doll. "Sold."

"Now, we need to find clothes for her."

I point to the doll. "She has clothes."

"She needs more than one outfit. *Geesh.*" She pulls on my shirt. "Do you live with only one outfit?"

"No, but unlike this doll, I'm a living, breathing human."

"She needs outfits." She pivots around, and I follow her into another section.

Willow picks out three outfits for the doll, and a sense of happiness jerks through me when she demands to pay for the clothes. I've been terrified of letting someone else around my daughter. I didn't want her to feel neglected or jealous. I didn't think another woman could make Maven feel as loved as Lucy did. But Willow thinks of my daughter, smiles with my daughter, enjoys her company. And my daughter enjoys hers.

"One more stop, and then we'll head home." I snag her hand

after paying for the doll and hope I'm taking her in the right direction. I haven't been here since Lucy was pregnant.

"I'm in no rush." She's more at ease in this crowd than she's ever been in Blue Beech.

She stills when we reach our destination, and I'm not sure if it's a good or bad thing. It's a baby store, the largest one in the state, and it has everything you need from clothes to furniture to supplies.

"I thought we could look around. See if there's anything we like," I tell her. She nods in hesitation, and I throw my arm out. "After you."

"Are you sure we're ready for this?"

"One hundred percent."

———

"IS it bad that I have no idea what some of this stuff is?" Willow asks. "I've read every baby book I could get my hands on. Researched for hours and made lists of every necessity needed, but this all seems too overwhelming."

I still have Maven's nursery furniture in the attic. We kept it in hopes of having another baby and saw it as a good-luck token. As much as I want to pull it out, along with the memories, it wouldn't be right for me to do that to Willow.

"It is at first. I Googled everything of Maven's to figure out how to use it." I point to the cribs on the other side of the store. "One thing we know our little tykes will need for sure is somewhere to sleep. Let's start there, and we'll work our way through the store."

She grins. "Sounds good."

Willow

CHAPTER TWENTY-NINE

DALLAS LEANS against the doorway to the guest room I'm converting into a nursery. "There's still time to change your mind and set the cribs up at my place."

"Yes, you've mentioned that several hundred times," I reply.

Our shopping adventure ended with bags of baby items. We spent three hours shopping and had to get two of everything. Dallas shoved my card away when I tried to pay and nearly threw my wallet out the window when I tried to give him half of it in cash when we got in the truck.

He wraps his arms around my waist from behind and drags me into his firm body. "I'll give you the master and crash in the basement. I'll be the nanny. I'll get up in the middle of the night and change diapers. Feed them. Bathe them. Whatever you want."

"Give you the master."

The room where he freaked out on me.

No freaking thank you.

It'd help me physically with the babies but not emotionally. It'd obliterate my heart. Two babies is hard work, but I'd rather risk being sleep-deprived than take him up on that offer.

I'll fuck him but not walk through his front door.

I'm a hot mess.

He scrapes his hands together. "You want to start setting everything up?"

"Can we leave that for another day? I'm exhausted, my feet hurt, and I'm sore everywhere."

"You want me to give you a massage?"

"Can you do it with your tongue?"

He smirks. "I'd love to."

———

STELLA SITS DOWN NEXT to me with a plate of cake in her hand. "Hudson said Dallas spilled the baby beans to Maven."

We're at Maven's birthday party, and she's started opening gifts. I showed up early, sat down so that the table would hide my stomach, and haven't moved since.

Maven's face lights up with excitement as she opens each gift, and she thanks the gifter before moving on to the next. Dallas is saving ours for last. I peek over at him and smile at the happiness on his face as he watches her.

He's a good dad.

He might be broken, but he managed to repair part of his heart and opened it up for her. I'm hoping he'll do the same with our babies.

Half of Blue Beech's population is here, eating the food Rory, Dallas' mom, made—which is enough to feed the entire NFL—chasing their screaming children around, and staring at me like I have a nip slip. Maven has attempted to drag me to the bounce house dozens of times, and it looks like Disney vomited everywhere.

"She figured it out herself," I answer.

"No shit?"

"Apparently, I rub my stomach like some other pregnant chick around here does. She put two and two together." I laugh. "Dallas broke the news because he couldn't handle fibbing to a six-year-old."

"Damn, kids are getting smart these days. I was still under the impression storks dropped babies off on doorsteps when I was her age."

Maven squeals and jumps up and down when she opens Dallas's gift. She screams again when opening mine, and then she runs over to give me a tight hug. "Thank you!" she yells, still jumping up and down. She sits down next to Stella and starts ripping open the doll box and all of the accessories.

Stella bumps my shoulder with hers. "You sure you don't want to take a run in the bounce house? It'll be a first time for me."

"You've never been in a bounce house?" I ask, looking horrified. *Who hasn't been the kid who fell down and tried to get up while the others bounced harder to stop them?*

"Nope. My mom considered having a childhood was an abomination, and all I needed to do was work." She puts her hands together. "So, *please.*"

I point to my stomach. "No sudden movements, remember?"

"Oh, crap, I keep forgetting about"—she pauses and nervously looks around—"*that.*"

"She can't go into the bounce house, Aunt Stella!" Maven shouts with a gasp. "She has to be very, very careful because there is a baby in her tummy." She stops to correct herself and holds up two fingers. "I mean, two babies in her tummy because she and Daddy are having twins!" She slaps her hand over her mouth. "Uh-oh." Her gaze sweeps over to Dallas with wide eyes. "Sorry, Daddy. I broke our secret. I'm so, so sorry!"

The noise in the backyard comes to a halt, and Rory's cup falling to the ground is the only sound I hear before I freak the hell out.

Dallas

CHAPTER THIRTY

HOLY FUCK.

This isn't how I imagined this going down.

Willow looks like she's about to vomit. My mom looks hurt. My dad looks like he's ready to lay into my ass. Hudson is grinning like a motherfucker.

I clear my throat, ignoring every set of eyes on Willow, and bolt her way. I kiss my daughter on the top of her head. "It's fine, May Bear. Why don't you go show your new doll the bounce house, okay?"

"I'm sorry, Daddy," she says again. "I've just been so excited." She throws her hands out. "It just blurted right out of my mouth."

I kiss her forehead. "It's okay."

Willow jumps out of her chair when her eyes start to water. She doesn't want anyone to see her cry. "If everyone will please excuse me for a second." Her voice breaks. "Or a few minutes. Possibly a few hours … or days."

She turns and dashes into the house. Stella jumps up to follow, but I stop her.

"Let me have this one, okay?"

She stares at me with a hard look and hesitation before nodding.

As soon as I leave the crowd, I can hear the voices erupt into chaos. Question after question is being fired off, one after the other, to my family. I feel sorry for leaving them to the Blue Beech gossip wolves, but I have to make sure Willow is okay.

I find her sitting on the bed in my childhood room with tears in her eyes. I shut the door and bend down in front of her. I take her chin in my shaky hand and lock eyes with her.

"I'm so fucking sorry, do you hear me?" I whisper. "I made a mistake."

She tries to pull away from my touch, but I don't let her.

"Please," I hiss. "Please don't fucking run from me because of this."

Willow is a pro at helping other people with their problems but terrible at facing her own. It's easy for her to turn her back on situations she doesn't want to deal with.

She sniffles. "This is humiliating. Did you see their faces? All the jaws dropping?"

"They were surprised, which we expected. I mean, we haven't exactly been forthcoming about your pregnancy or *this*." I signal between the two of us. To be honest, I'm relieved it's out there. I wish it had happened in a better situation, like us sitting my parents down and spilling the news, but at least the secret is off my chest now.

"This?" she questions, scrunching up her face and reenacting my movement. "What do you mean, *this*?"

I get up and sit down next to her on the bed. "We're doing something here. I'm as confused as you are about it, but we are. You're the only woman I've looked at since I lost Lucy. I can't ..." I pause. "I can't stop thinking about you. Whenever I leave your apartment or drop you off, the excitement from when I get to see you next keeps me high. Hell, I can't wait until the next time I even get to talk to you. You're something I look forward to every day. The thought of seeing you, talking to you, and spending time with you gives me so much fucking happiness." My revelation only makes her cry harder. "What can I do to make this better? Anything. I'll do anything."

Except let you walk away.

Please don't fucking walk away.

"Turn back time to months ago," is all she whispers.

Fuck. I want to beg her not to go there.

"Tell me you don't mean that. You might've thought that at first, which I don't fucking blame you, but tell me, after all this time we've spent together, after seeing the beautiful babies we made on that monitor, that you don't mean that."

She sighs. "I ... I don't." She covers her face with her hands. "I thought I would. Sometimes, I wish I still felt that way. I thought it was the end of my happiness when I found out I was pregnant after our night together, but now ... now, I can't think of a time when I've been happier. A time when I thought I was doing something so right." She rubs her stomach. "These past few months have changed my life, too."

"These past few months have dragged me out of the darkest hole I thought I'd never escape." Not all the way. I'm still there, and I'll never be the same man, but Willow has brought out parts of me I thought would never come out again. And I can feel myself healing as the sun rises each day.

I drop down to my knees to take in the sight of her and show her the honesty in my eyes. "You brought me to the light. We might not have expected this, but it's somehow made us stronger, brighter, happier."

I cringe at the knock on the door that interrupts us. Stella pokes her head in, apology on her face, and takes in the scene in front of her.

Me on my knees in the begging position, and Willow crying.

Willow wipes away a tear and nods her head, silently permitting Stella to come in and shut the door behind her.

The door opens again seconds later, this time without a knock, and Hudson appears with brows knitted in concern. "I know this is bad timing, brother, but Maven is in the bounce house, crying, and insists on only talking to you or Willow."

"Fuck," I snap, averting my attention to Willow. "Will you be okay for a minute?"

She nods. "Go ahead. I'll be fine." I get up, but she grabs my arm to stop me. "Actually, I'd like to come with you, if that's okay?"

"I'm not sure you'll be ready for eyes on you," Stella says.

"How about I try to get her to come in here?" Hudson asks, leaving the room before waiting for our answer.

Willow sniffles again. "That's a good idea."

Stella starts to go toward the door but stops and darts over to Willow. "I love you," she says with a hug. "Know that I'm here, no matter what, and I love you."

This brings a small smile out of Willow. "I love you, too."

Stella pokes her shoulder. "And you know you have some explaining to do. *Twins?* You couldn't even let a girl know she's having two godchildren now?"

"I was waiting for the right time," Willow replies.

The door opens again, and a sobbing Maven comes running into the room and crashes into my arms. "Daddy, I'm sorry!"

I keep my arms around her and rub her back. "It's okay, May Bear."

She turns around, still in my arms, and shyly peeks over at Willow. "Are you mad at me?"

Willow's eyes go soft, and her tone turns soothing. "Of course not, honey. Just shocked, is all."

She composes herself, gets up, and runs a hand down her dress. I can't stop myself from grinning at the sight of her stomach showing through. Fingers crossed, she'll let it be on display more now. "I need another slice of cake."

I grab her elbow to make sure she's stable and dip my mouth to her ear. "You sure you're okay with going back out?" I ask. "We can leave, if you want?"

"We'll have to face them sooner or later," she says.

"We'll be out in a few minutes," I tell Hudson. "Tell people no questions until we're ready."

Maven wraps her hand around my leg. "I know you promised extra doll clothes if I kept our secret." She pushes her lower lip out. "Do I still get to keep them?"

Willow snorts before bursting out into a fit of laughter. "God, I needed that."

Willow

CHAPTER THIRTY-ONE

"I KNOW my son demanded no baby talk, and I respect that, but can I give you a hug?" Rory asks.

I nod, and she pulls me into her tight, patting my back. "Congratulations, dear. I am incredibly grateful for you. So is John, who's around here somewhere, waiting to corner his son and lecture him on keeping secrets from his mama." John is Dallas's father.

The majority of the crowd has ventured home, but a few people are still hanging around. Since we came back, Dallas stayed by my side until minutes ago when I finally convinced him to go to the bounce house with Maven and her doll. Some people have been pretending not to stare at me, others have refused to acknowledge me, and the rest have shamelessly watched every move I make.

"Don't worry about them," Rory says when she pulls away. "If anyone asks too many questions, you let them know they'll have to deal with me." She grabs a slice of cake and hands it to me. "You deserve this. I told Dallas to give you my number. Don't hesitate to call if you need anything."

I nod. "Thank you."

She throws me another smile, pats my shoulder, and then walks over to a table of women hunched over while talking in hushed voices. Most likely about me.

CHARITY FERRELL

"Holy shit," Stella gasps, wrapping her arm around my shoulders. "That was seriously something out of a movie. I need to use that in a script."

"No benefiting from my problems for your career," I mutter, leaning into her.

"How are you feeling?" she asks when we sit down at a secluded table.

"A million things at once. Mortified that this is how everyone found out. Relieved that we no longer have to hide it."

She smirks. "He's a good dad, Willow. He'll be good to you and your baby." She winces and pouts. "I mean, *babies*. Why do I feel like I'm not your first call anymore?"

"Sorry. It's just been so overwhelming. I'm still digesting it myself. There hasn't even been a call to anyone else." I shake my head. "Hell, all of these people found out before my mom did."

"You'd better call her. Blue Beech news makes national news."

I laugh. "I saw the town's newspaper. The front page was about some ribfest cook-off. I'm sure my mom subscribes because who can go about their day without finding out Sandy May's special recipe?"

"Sandy May makes killer ribs. I'd never even had ribs until Hudson dragged me to that festival."

"I'm sure there's a plan in Dallas's head to drag me to the next one."

"It'll be fun." She pokes my side. "Now, if you get any more baby news, you'd better let me know. If I find out you're having quintuplets from another six-year-old, I won't be happy."

"Maven didn't tell you? It's actually sextuplets. We're waiting for another party to shock everyone."

"Very funny." She glances around. "By the way, I'm pretty sure Rory is over there, planning your baby shower."

"God, her reaction was dramatic. Her fruit punch fell to the ground in slow motion. I thought she wanted to kill me for not telling her."

"Oh, that was just the shock. You didn't see the bright-ass smile on her face after you left. She's not pissed. She's fucking elated." She laughs. "The only people who weren't over the moon were the women who wanted to be the one Dallas had knocked up. You got knocked up by Blue Beech's finest bachelor. You go, girl."

"SO, THE NEWS IS OUT," Dallas says.

"The news is out," I repeat slowly.

Maven is passed out in the backseat, snoring like a man in a nursing home, and it's almost eight o'clock. She apologized to me countless times for her outburst, but I couldn't be upset at a girl sporting a *Birthday Girl* tiara and sash.

"You want to come over?" he asks. "Hang out for a bit? I have leftover cake."

Jesus, does everyone think all I eat is cake?

The thought of spending more time with him excites me, but the problem is, going to his house doesn't. It terrifies me. The memories from our night together might slash a hole in the connection we've been making. We've already been through enough today. Reliving those memories isn't something I want either one of us to do.

"Not tonight," I answer. "I'm exhausted."

"You sure?"

I nod at the same time he pulls up to my apartment building, and I stop him from unbuckling his seat belt. "Don't wake her up. I can walk myself in."

"Okay. I'll wait out here until I see your light come on, and you call me to let me know you made it in okay."

And that's what he does.

IT'S seven in the morning, and someone is banging on my door.

"What is up with your family knocking people's doors down at the butt crack of dawn?" I ask when Lauren walks in.

"Good morning, my future sister-in-law," she sings out while walking into my apartment. "I brought doughnuts and green tea."

Seriously?

"What do you want?" I mutter in my best cranky voice.

"You didn't believe it'd be that easy to dodge me, did you, neighbor?" She plops down on a barstool at the island. "I was upset enough that I got called into work and missed my niece's birthday party, and then I find out you're having *twins*, and you didn't tell me." She crosses her arms. "As the girl who lives above you, I am extremely offended."

I take a gulp of the green tea. *Yummy.* "We were waiting. No one knew."

"Except the six-year-old."

"Except the six-year-old," I mutter. "Your brother apparently can't lie to his daughter."

"Yeah, he sucks at saying no to her. She's got him wrapped around her finger. Now, if it's a girl, I'd like her name to be Lauren."

I side-eye her. "It's too early to argue about baby names."

"It's never too early to hash it out over baby names. *Trust me.* I've heard stories from the maternity ward nurses about the kind of drama and chaos families have over baby names."

"I'm naming them after my pet goldfish—Goldie and Nemo."

She rolls her eyes. "Now that we've got Lauren Junior covered, what's going on with you and my big bro?"

My brows lift. "Other than the fact that we're having twins together, nothing."

"His truck was here the other night when I got home at *four in the morning*. It seems to be here pretty frequently, if you ask me. Since we know you weren't discussing *baby names* at four in the morning, what were y'all doing?"

"Discussing nursery decor."

"You suck," she grumbles.

I perk up. "You love me."

"I do. But can I say something serious?"

"I don't think I can stop you."

"Don't hurt him."

This really catches my attention. "Huh?"

"You know exactly what I'm talking about. Don't hurt my brother. He's been through too much to lose someone else he loves."

Deflection time. "I've made it clear, I won't ever keep the babies from him."

"I'm talking about *you*, girlfriend." She annoyingly shakes her shoulders while drinking her smoothie through the straw.

"Your brother most certainly does not love me."

She grins. "Not yet. From what my mother tells me, it's getting pretty damn close, and my mama knows everything."

Dallas

CHAPTER THIRTY-TWO

THE EXCAVATOR I bought from the auction is kicking my ass. Even though I do my due diligence the best I can, you never know what you're going to get when you buy an item as is.

It's an easy fix but fucking time-consuming, and Hudson ran off for a staycation with Stella for the day—whatever the fuck that is—at the local bed-and-breakfast. I tried to fight him on it, telling him they could eat Cheerios at their kitchen table, and then he could come into work, but he agreed to give me as much time as I needed off when Willow had the babies.

Almost a week has passed since Maven's birthday party, and I've talked to Willow on the phone a couple times a day but not in person.

The machine loses my attention when the music is cut off.

I look down and grin. "This is a nice surprise."

Willow holds up the cooler in her hand. "Thought I'd bring you some lunch."

Good. I'm fucking starving, and I was planning on skipping lunch, so I wouldn't have to spend time driving into town and then back today.

I carefully move down the ladder and wipe my forehead with the back of my arm while coming her way. I laugh when she licks her lips while brazenly eye-fucking me at the same time I'm eye-fucking her.

She's not wearing her usual baggy clothes today. I'm not sure where she got the maternity clothes, but she's breathtaking in her jean shorts and T-shirt that says *Tacos for Two, Please*.

Her and her tacos.

I run my hand down my sweaty chest. I have the air on high, but I get hot, no matter what, when I'm working on machine engines. "You like what you see?"

She lifts her gaze back up my body and grins playfully. "Oh, I *love* what I see."

"You know, I'm more than just a hot, lean body."

I curl my arm around her shoulders to pull her into me and plant a kiss on her lips. She doesn't even flinch. Us touching has become so natural. Not only does it feel good, having her here, but she also showed up without my asking. She took the time to make lunch and came to surprise me. She can deny it all she wants, but she's falling for me.

"I'm starving. What did you whip up for us?"

She glances around the room. "It's a surprise."

I gesture toward the other side of the garage. "We have a table and shit in the office, if you want to eat in there, or we can go outside?"

"Outside. I've been quite the hermit lately. I could use some sun."

"You know the remedy to that problem?"

She wrinkles her cute nose in annoyance. "Funny. I'll start venturing out of my apartment when the time is right."

"I hope it's before our kids turn sixteen."

She shoves my side and pulls away when we reach the picnic table underneath two weeping willows. My grandfather built the table decades ago for when my grandmother would bring him lunch.

I rub my hands together when we sit down. "So, what have we got?"

Her eyes widen in reluctance. "They say it's the gesture, not the gift, right?"

Did she bring cheese and crackers? A Snickers bar and Sunny Delight?

"I'll enjoy whatever you brought."

She draws in a breath when I open the cooler and start dragging out its contents. There are plastic bags with sandwiches in them.

"I love me some peanut butter and jelly," I say upon further inspection. The next item is a bag of tortilla chips large enough to feed Maven's entire preschool and then a covered bowl. I open it and can't stop the cheesy smile from hitting my lips. "And guacamole."

"I'm giving you a run for your money on the best guac in Blue Beech."

"Let's taste-test it, shall we?" I open the bag of chips and dip one into the guacamole.

It's good, definitely not as good as mine, but I can tell she worked hard on it. She analyzes me chewing it likes she's a contestant on *Top Chef.*

"You killed it. I'll bring over my trophy for you later this evening."

She raises a brow. "You're just saying that because we're having sex."

"There are better things I could say to you to get laid than"—I stop to fake a smoldering gaze I saw on *The Bachelor* once—"*Hey, girl, you make excellent guacamole. Let's fuck in a bed of guacamole, have it served at our wedding, and name our children Guac and Mole.*"

She throws a chip at me while trying to contain her laughter and then slides the sandwich in front of me. "Now, eat your PB and J and shut up. I slaved all day, making this."

I scarf down the two sandwiches she made me and make sure I moan with every bite of her guacamole.

She looks from side to side. "So ... is there anyone else here?"

"No. Just me today. I'm sure you know, Hudson is feeding Stella strawberries in bed."

She laughs. "I booked the room for them. Stella's been coddling me since our secret came out. I couldn't handle it any longer."

"What secret?"

She leans forward. "You know."

"Which one? I believe we have a few."

She narrows her eyes my way. "You know exactly which one I'm referring to."

"The one where we're having twins?" I give her a shit-eating grin. "Or the one where I've been eating your pussy?"

She blushes. "You've been doing that? I think I'm in need of a reminder."

I smirk. "Oh, I see what's going on here. You thought you could come here and butter me up with PB and Js to get laid?"

She shrugs. "Just a little."

I point to my chest. "You do know I'm sweaty as fuck?"

"Let me make you even sweatier," she whispers with a wink.

I surge to my feet. "You don't have to ask me twice."

Willow slips off her seat and speed-walks to the garage. Her mouth crushes to mine as soon as I lock the shop door behind us. Adrenaline speeds through my blood as she demands more of me, pressing her tongue into my mouth. I'll never be disappointed to come to work again. This memory will hit me every time I walk in.

I grunt when I'm pushed back against the wall, and she kisses me harder, owning me, as our tongues slide together. She consumes me. The need of wanting her takes over every thought in my mind. I seethe at the loss of our connection when she runs her lips over the line of my jaw.

She's running the show.

She needs this.

And I'm a willing participant—anytime, any-fucking-where, any way.

My hands trail down her body to cup her perfect ass and lift her off the floor. I spin us around, so I have her against the wall now. She wastes no time in grinding against my cock. I do the same against her pussy.

"God," she whispers. "Please fuck me. I need it."

"Where do you want it?" I grit out.

She jerks her chin toward the parked car on the other side of the garage. "There."

We don't usually work on cars here, but I'm doing it as a favor for a buddy.

He's the one doing the fucking favor now.

"You want me to fuck you on that car, baby?"

Her breathing is labored, and she has to speak between breaths. "Yes"—inhale—"right"—exhale—"there."

"You want it hard or soft?"

"Hard. Really hard," she says against my mouth.

Heat radiates through my chest when her teeth graze my tongue, and she bites it.

Oh, yeah. She wants it hard. Rough. Dirty.

We fumble around until we're both naked, and I race across the garage and lower her bare ass on the '67 Chevelle.

I brush her hair back from her face and don't make another move until her eyes meet mine. "Willow, you're beautiful."

A bright grin spreads across her mouth when she hears her name, and I tense when her soft hand wraps around my aching cock. My heart hammers against my chest when she guides me into her. My head throws back as a roar rips through me.

The first move is made by her tilting her waist up, slowly taking in the length of me, and I'm close to losing it when my gaze drifts down to our connection.

Her pussy juices cover my cock. Her legs are open wide as she takes me in again and rolls her hips in the process. Nothing describes the feeling of watching the girl of your dreams lying on the hood of a car and taking your cock like she owns it.

"Fuck, you feel good," I grind out.

No more taking it slow. I grab her ankles, pull her down the car until she's on the edge, and slam inside her. She clings to my shoulders and rests her weight on me.

"I'm there," she says, her body going weak. "Oh God, I'm there."

I keep my focus on her to watch her face. Her mouth opens, a loud moan escaping her, and she clenches around my dick.

The view of her getting off sets me off.

My body shakes when I bury my face between her breasts and release inside her.

We stare at each other, breathing heavily, and she cracks up laughing.

"Not the best reaction after someone gets you off," I say, unable to hold back my smile.

"I so buttered you up with my guacamole."

I join her laughter.

Willow Andrews isn't just working her way inside me. I'm also falling in love with her.

Willow

CHAPTER THIRTY-THREE

TWO PAINT SAMPLES are in my hand as I hold them against a wall in the nursery.

Red or yellow?

I want to go with a neutral theme since we don't know the sex of our babies yet. I drop them onto the floor when my phone rings.

"Hello?" I answer.

"Hey," Dallas says on the other line. "You busy?"

"Nope, just unpacking the rest of the stuff we bought for the babies and trying to decide what look I'm going for in the nursery." I balance the phone between my shoulder and ear. "What's up?"

"Maven's preschool called. She's sick. I'm swamped at the shop, and my parents aren't available until this evening. Any way you can pick her up and hang out until I get a break from here?"

"Sure, that's no problem."

He lets out a relieved sigh. "Thank you. I shouldn't be any later than five. There's a spare key under the planter on the porch. Make yourself comfortable. There's plenty of food in the house. Let me know if you need anything, okay?"

"Okay."

I throw my hair up in a ponytail, change into shorts and a T-shirt, and hop into my SUV. I don't realize what I'm about to do until I pull into the parking lot of Maven's preschool.

I'm going to his house.

Holy shit. I should've told him I'd bring her back to my place.

Stepping foot in his house again is something I've been putting off even though he's invited me countless times.

I take in a breath. *I have to get over this fear, right?*

There's no way I would've gotten away with it for too much longer. At least it won't be in front of Dallas in case I have a panic attack.

———

"HELLO. YOU MUST BE WILLOW," the older woman behind the desk greets me when I walk through the front door and into the lobby. "Dallas said you'd be picking up Maven." She picks up the phone and tells the teacher I'm here.

I look up at the sound of heels coming down the hallway. I recognize the woman from Maven's birthday party but don't recall seeing her again after the pregnancy outburst.

She stops in front of us and rests her hands on Maven's shoulders. "Hi, Willow." She gives me a red-lipped smile and holds out her hand. "I'm Mrs. Lawrence, Maven's teacher."

"She's my aunt Beth," Maven corrects.

I freeze up and blink a few times, noticing the similarities between her and Maven ... and Lucy. Mrs. Lawrence—*Beth*—squeezes Maven's shoulders.

She nods. "That I am." Her voice turns soothing. "I'm Lucy's sister."

I shake her hand. "It's nice to meet you."

Damn, Dallas has thrown me so many curveballs today, I'm dizzy. I'm meeting the sister of his dead wife *and* going to the house he shared with said wife.

"She's had a fever for the past hour. Thank you for picking her up. It seems everyone is busy or out of town today, and I couldn't find a sub to come in for me."

"It's fine. I was, uh …" *Getting a nursery together for my babies with Dallas.* "Off work today."

"I feel no good, and I'm sleepy," Maven whines, rubbing her eyes.

Beth kisses her cheek before releasing her. "Get some rest, sweetie." Her attention moves to me. "Please ask Dallas to keep me updated, and don't hesitate to call if she needs anything."

I nod, pressing the back of my hand against Maven's forehead. She's warm.

"Of course."

I help Maven into the backseat of my car, and she falls asleep the first few minutes into the short drive to Dallas's house. Even though I haven't been back inside of the house since that night, I know where it is. We've driven by it dozens of times, and Maven has pointed it out to me.

I admire the large white farmhouse he restored years ago. There are large gray shutters on each side of the windows and planters under the ones next to the front door. It's perfectly landscaped with bright pink roses and daisies. It's a beautiful home.

The key is under the planter, like he said, and I follow Maven through the front door.

"Mommy and Daddy always let me sleep in their big bed when I no feel good," she says, stomping down the hallway. "It's right down here."

Oh, honey, I know where it is.

I gulp when she opens the door. This is the moment of truth where I find out if I can go forward with Dallas or if I can't get over him loving another woman. This is where I find out if I'm a quick screw because he's horny. You don't have to love someone. Hell, you don't even have to like them to fuck them.

The familiar whitewashed wood bed sits in the middle of the large master bedroom. The plaid comforter is the same as it was that night. The scent in the room smells like him. Nothing has changed. My hands are on the verge of shaking as I help Maven into the bed.

That's when I see it.

The picture of him and Lucy on the nightstand. There's another of Lucy by herself on the other nightstand. Her ... or another woman's perfume is sitting on the dresser next to a white jewelry box with her name branded on the front. There's a chair in the corner with a woman's sweater draped over it.

Was that Lucy's?

Or is it Chicken Chick's?

"Will you put on cartoons for me?" Maven asks with a yawn.

"Sure." I snag the remote from the nightstand and flip through the stations until I find her favorite cartoon.

She slides underneath the blankets and relaxes against the pillows.

I tap the bed as my heart thumps against my chest. My throat grows tight, and the room feels warmer than Maven's forehead. "You let me know if you need anything, okay?"

"Will you stay?" she asks. "And watch with me?"

I nod even though all I want to do is abort mission and hang out in my car until Dallas gets here. I take off my shoes and sit down next to her, over the covers. That night haunts me as the opening of the cartoon lets out some annoying song. Maven snuggles into my side.

"Willow," she whispers, hesitation layering her voice.

"Yeah?" I ask.

"Will you be my new mommy?"

I blankly stare at her, fighting off the desire to flee the room, and try to give her the most comforting smile I can manage.

"You're going to be my brother or sister's mommy, so maybe you can be mine, too, since my mommy is in heaven."

A knife digs into my heart, and I take in a deep breath to stop the tears. Maven looks just as upset as I feel.

I kiss the top of her head and then smooth my hands over her hair. I don't know what to say. I don't know what to do. I don't even know my name at this point because my brain is spiraling out of control. "We'll talk about it when you feel better, okay, honey?"

"Okay," she whimpers.

She only lasts five minutes into the show before she dozes off. I slowly and quietly pull away from her and get out of the bed to grab my phone.

I catch my breath when I make it into the kitchen and drop onto a chair. I glance around the kitchen. More pictures of Lucy on the refrigerator. Another one by the coffeemaker. A grocery list that's not in Dallas's handwriting is stuck under a magnet on the fridge.

Will I always think everything is Lucy's here? That Dallas wants to keep and display every part and memory of her, so he won't forget … so he won't move on?

It's petty of me to think these things. He wants to keep those memories of her alive because he was a good husband.

But I can't stop myself.

That's why I need to take a break from him. Why I need to consider the consequences before throwing myself into a situation this serious. His daughter asked me to be her new mommy. That's big. *Huge.* A little girl's heart is on the line, and I can't break it if everything doesn't go well with Dallas.

I grab my phone and text Stella.

Me: You busy?

She got home from the bed and breakfast yesterday, and nothing was on her schedule for the day.

Stella: Nope. Just going over some scripts. What's up?

Me: I picked up Maven from school for Dallas because she was sick, and now, I'm not feeling so hot myself. Would you be able to watch her until Dallas got home, so I could get some rest at my apartment?

Stella: I'll be there in 15. You need anything?

Me: I'm good. Thank you.

Her answer slows down my heart rate. Now, I need to make sure she doesn't notice anything is off with me. I need to put my actress face on and hope the actress herself doesn't find out I'm a fraud.

I'm still in the kitchen when Stella walks in. She rushes into the room and falls down in the chair across from me.

"You feeling any better?" she asks with concern.

"Not really," I mutter. "I just need to lie down. I've been working on the nursery all morning, and I think I overdid it. That, or the twins are pissed that I fed them a healthy breakfast this morning."

She laughs and gets up to wrap her arms around my shoulders. "You take care of yourself, girlfriend. Call me here soon."

Dallas

CHAPTER THIRTY-FOUR

IT'S BEEN a hell of a day.

The shop's phone has been blowing up all day with people wanting maintenance on their machines that weren't scheduled in. I took them, of course, but I'm feeling overwhelmed.

I can't wait to get home to my girls. Willow texted me a few hours ago when she picked up Maven, but I haven't heard anything from her since even though I've tried calling. I'm guessing they fell asleep when Maven made her put on cartoons.

I wasn't sure how Willow would react when I asked her to take Maven to the house, but she didn't seem to have a problem, which is a fucking relief. I don't want her to feel like she can't step foot through my front door. I don't want her to feel uncomfortable in my home. I want her to feel so fucking good there that she decides to move in.

I start my engine and then kill it a few seconds later.

Fuck. She's going to see them.

She's going to see all of Lucy's stuff. I haven't built up the courage to move anything related to Lucy. Her toothbrush is in the holder, her clothes are in the closet, her touch is everywhere. I haven't moved anything because it's comforting, knowing there's a part of her there. I can't forget about her if her bracelet is still on the kitchen counter. I can't forget her if I see her favorite pink top when I open the closet.

I don't want that to change. I don't want to forget the woman I loved. I don't know if I can move her things yet, but I have a feeling that Willow won't be comfortable until I do.

I call her again. No answer. I text her next.

Me: You doing okay over there?

I start my truck again and head home. She still hasn't answered when I pull into the driveway, and instead of parking next to her car, I see Stella's red BMW. I walk in, check in on Maven sleeping in my bedroom, and then meet Stella in the kitchen. She's at the table going over scripts.

"Hey," I greet, tossing my keys onto the counter.

She presses a finger to her lips. "We don't want to wake her up. She's been knocked out for a few hours."

I nod, lowering my voice. "Where's Willow? I've tried calling her a few times but no answer." Anytime Willow goes MIA, I go into nervous-wreck mode.

"She texted me and asked me to come hang out because she wasn't feeling well. She wanted to go home and lie down."

I lean back against the counter, resting on my elbows. "Huh. I wonder why she didn't mention anything to me."

She chuckles. "You know Willow. She doesn't want to inconvenience anyone."

"You heard from her since she left?"

She shakes her head. "She seemed like she couldn't wait to get out of here. I wish I had more for you, but she's been distant with me lately. It most likely has something to do with her fear of sharing anything with me since it will get back to you because my fiancé has a big-ass mouth."

"Fuck, sorry 'bout that. I don't want to come between the two of you. If it helps, I don't expect anything from you. Your loyalty is to her."

They've been close for years, and I hate that she has no one to turn to right now.

She gets up. "No worries. She's used to dealing with shit on her own. Brett made her that way. She kept all of their problems inside because she was sick of us telling her to break up with him every day. It's hard to vent to people when they agree the guy you're venting about is an asshole."

"I get it."

"I have to head out. I have a reading for the new season of my show in an hour." She kisses my cheek. "Let me know if you hear from Willow, okay? And I'll do the same for you. I'll call her on my way to set and ask if she wants to come with me. Maybe I can get something out of her."

I hug her. "Thank you for watching Maven. Be careful, and keep me updated."

"You're welcome, and of course."

Maven is sound asleep and snoring when I go to check on her again. She insists on sleeping in my bed if she coughs the wrong way. Some might find it annoying, but I enjoy that she considers my space a healing place.

I turn off the TV and do a once-over of the room.

Then, a twice-over.

Willow didn't run because she was sick.

I was right.

She ran because Lucy was everywhere.

Willow

CHAPTER THIRTY-FIVE

EVEN THOUGH I don't know where I'm going, I packed an overnight bag. All I'm sure of is, I need to get out of Blue Beech for a minute and clear my head.

Is it sad that Lucy's stuff upset me?

I've been second best to Stella for years. Her assistant. The second choice to hang out with and only when someone wants to get closer to her. People have looked past me to see the celebrity. I can handle not being the star in the spotlight, but being second place in someone's heart isn't an option.

My SUV's sunroof is open. The music is up while I drive down a deserted road. I didn't turn on my GPS. I'm just driving. I'm blurting out the words to my favorite song when a sharp pain shoots through me, causing me to buckle forward. I swerve to the side of the road when another one hits me just seconds later. Tears well in my eyes, and the pain overtakes me. This isn't a baby kicking or morning sickness.

It's something else.

Something I haven't been expecting.

Something I haven't read about.

Something not normal.

I dump the contents of my purse out in the passenger seat to find my phone and then power it on.

Please have service. Please have service.

One bar. All I have is one bar.

I dial the three digits as tears start crawling down my cheeks.

"Nine-one-one, what's your emergency?"

"My name …" My voice trembles, and I struggle to come up with the right words. "My name is Willow Andrews. I was driving." I stop and double over, holding my stomach and groan. "I'm pregnant and having severe abdominal pain."

"Okay, ma'am," the woman says on the other side. "Do you know your location?"

I urgently search for a street sign, mile marker, anything that can help them. *Nothing.*

"I … I'm not sure. There's hardly any traffic." I open the Maps app on my phone to get the exact location and recite it to her.

"Thank you. We have an ambulance on the way. Stay with me, okay? Take deep breaths, Willow. Are you experiencing any bleeding?"

I'm sobbing louder. "I'm not sure." I'm not proud of this, but I dip my hand into my panties and gasp when I drag it back out. There's not much of it, but it's there. And it's bright red.

Tears fall down my face faster.

"You doing okay, Willow?" she asks.

"Yes," I croak out, the words barely audible. "Yes, I'm bleeding."

I should hang up and call Dallas. Call Stella. Call my mom. *Somebody.*

But I can't move. I'm frozen to the spot, imagining every nightmare that could happen.

Please let everything be okay with my babies.

Please let everything be okay with me.

Please. Please. Please.

Dallas

CHAPTER THIRTY-SIX

I'VE BEEN PACING the floor in my kitchen for what seems like hours. I fed Maven dinner, and she passed back out an hour ago. Her fever has gone down, which is a relief.

I've tried calling Willow countless times. At first, it was going straight to voice mail. It's ringing now, but she's not answering, so I get her voice mail again.

When my phone rings fifteen minutes later, I quickly hit the Accept button without even looking at the caller ID. "Hello?" I rush out.

"Dallas!" Lauren screeches. "You need to get to the hospital right now."

"What?" I stutter out. "What's going on?"

"Willow is here. They brought her in about ten minutes ago."

My stomach drops. "How do you know? Did she call you?"

"Oh, gee, I don't know, maybe because I work here. Get here fast, and I'll explain everything. I've got to get back to my patients."

"I'll be there as soon as I can."

I hang up, and my hands are shaking when I dial Hudson. "You busy?"

"Nope, just parked on the couch, watching sports and waiting for Stella to get home. You want me to come hang out with you and my sick niece?" He must've not heard the urgency in my voice.

"Can you come watch Maven for me?"

He catches on now. "What's going on?"

"Lauren said Willow got admitted to the ER."

"Fuck," he hisses. "What for?"

"I don't know. Lauren wouldn't tell me over the phone." *That means, it's not fucking good.*

"I'll be there in five, sooner if I can."

"Thank you."

I call Willow's phone again. It rings. Then, voice mail. A million reasons why she's there flash through me. If it were contractions or something small, Lauren would've told me to ease my mind.

Why didn't Willow call me? Why didn't she let me know what's wrong with our babies? It's just as much my information as it is hers.

Because she's fucking selfish, and I'm fucking pissed.

———

THIRTY MINUTES LATER, I'm pulling into the hospital parking lot. A bad taste fills my mouth as I run through the sliding glass doors. The last time I was here was when I said good-bye to Lucy.

I nearly collide with the front desk and ignore everyone standing in line, cutting straight to the front. "Willow Andrews," I blurt out. "I'm looking for Willow Andrews. Redhead. She's pregnant."

The middle-aged woman stares up at me in annoyance. "You family?"

"The father of the twins she's pregnant with. My sister is a nurse here and will vouch for me. Lauren Barnes." Never thought I'd use that to my advantage of getting in somewhere.

The way her face falls confirms it's not good news. She picks up the phone. "Will you please tell Nurse Barnes her brother is here?"

The doors open, and Lauren comes sprinting into the waiting room. "Dallas!" she calls out, nearly out of breath, and waves her hand. "Come with me."

We speed-walk through the crowded hallway, and she knocks on a door before opening it. Willow is lying in the bed, tears and mascara running down her face, while the nurse checks her vitals. Her eyes are puffy from crying. She's exhausted. Broken. Worn out. Like she's been through hell. I'm positive I'm about to go there, too.

I rush over to her side, take her shaking hand, and slowly massage it with my thumb when she starts to cry harder.

"I don't know what happened. I was driving down the road, and all of a sudden—" Her free hand flies to her mouth, stopping any words from exiting.

"All of a sudden what?" I ask, swallowing hard, my voice breaking, my heart breaking.

The nurse hits a few buttons on the monitor and scurries out of the room. Lauren shuts the door and leans back against it.

Willow moves her hand, so I can understand her. "All of a sudden, I got these sharp pains in my stomach." She plays with her admittance bracelet over my hand and glances at Lauren in torture. "Can you … will you …"

Lauren takes a step forward with a pain-stricken face. "They did an ultrasound. It's the first thing we did when the EMTs brought her in."

My eyes pierce hers. "The EMTs. An ambulance brought you in?" I've already heard more than I want to, but I know it's only going to get worse.

"There was only one heartbeat," Willow whispers.

A knot forms into my stomach, tightening every muscle, and I gag, positive I'm about to vomit. I squeeze her hand before pulling away to sit down.

"One heartbeat? What do you mean, one heartbeat?" I ask, practically begging for the answer I want even though I'm not going to get it. "We have two babies. *Twins.* I saw them with my own two eyes at our ultrasound!" My lip trembles, and I lock eyes with Lauren. "Tell them to do it again." My tone is demanding.

"I already had them do it again. They showed me ten times!" Willow cries out. "I begged them to keep doing them, so I could prove them wrong. There were two heartbeats during our last ultrasound. I swear there was!"

"There was," I gulp out.

"They did multiple ultrasounds," Lauren says, wiping her eyes. "Trust me when I tell you, they wouldn't put an expecting mother through this unless they were positive about it." She moves across the room to rest her hand on my shoulder. "I'm sorry, but the second baby is gone."

"The fuck you mean, the second baby is gone?"

There's a knock on the door that gains our attention, and Lauren tells whomever it is to come in. I've been to too many doctor visits and had too many hospital stays with Lucy to know when a doctor is about to deliver bad news, and the doc that walks in is about to deliver some bad news. I prepare myself for the blow.

He shoves his glasses up his slender nose. "Hello, I'm Dr. Jones." I stand up, and he holds his hand out for me to shake. "I'm deeply sorry for your loss. I've talked to Willow, but I wanted to come back when you arrived in case you had any further questions for me."

"Sure do," I reply. "Where's my other baby?"

He doesn't seem surprised at my aggression. No doubt, he was expecting it. "We performed an ultrasound on Willow. She immediately told us she was pregnant with twins when she was brought in, but we could only find one heartbeat. I double-checked. Another doctor did, too." He looks over at Lauren. "Your sister did also."

Lauren's face falls.

"Willow experienced symptoms of a miscarriage. She lost one of the fetuses from what appears to be vanishing twin syndrome."

She lost a baby.

One of our babies is gone.

Gone. I'm so sick of that word.

If I could set that word on fire and kill it, I would. Risk doing time. Risk going to hell. Risk anything not to hear that fucking word again.

Everything good in my life gets taken from me.

"What about the other baby? There's a heartbeat?" I rush out.

"Yes, there is a heartbeat for the surviving fetus."

"And everything is okay with that one?"

"So far, yes. The prognosis of the surviving twin is hopeful, but it can be more difficult since she's in her second trimester."

"So, what do we do now?"

"The ultrasound didn't show any remains of the lost fetus, so we won't have to perform any additional procedures. Again, I'm sorry for your family's loss." He hands me a card. "If you have any additional questions, please feel free to call anytime. Day or night."

I grip the side of the bed from my chair and stare down at Willow when the doctor leaves. "How did this happen? Where were you?"

She hesitates before answering me, looking deflated and hugging herself. "Taking a drive."

Lauren moves to Willow's side to kiss her on the forehead. "I'm going to give you some privacy. Let me know if you need anything."

"Taking a drive?" I ask. "I thought you didn't feel well. Why were you taking a drive when you were sick?"

This stops Lauren from leaving, and she whips around to stare at me. "Dallas, none of this is Willow's fault, so don't you dare go there. There was nothing she could've done to stop the miscarriage."

"I'm not blaming her," I hiss.

I'm blaming myself. I'm fucking blaming everyone and everything.

"Well, you're not convincing me of that," Willow fires back. "Sure sounds like it."

"All I asked was, why you were out driving in who the fuck knows where when you knew you were pregnant, and you told Stella you were sick!" I reply.

Her face lights up with anger, and she jabs a finger in my direction. "Don't talk to me like that. Don't you think I'm hurt about this? I lost a baby, too!"

"Okay, *now*, I'll give you two some privacy," Lauren says. She points to me before leaving. "Don't be a dick."

When Lauren shuts the door, I stare at it for a few seconds to calm down. Arguing with Willow isn't going to help either one of us. It'll only make shit worse.

"What happened?" I ask softly. "Why did you leave my house? I could've been there for you."

She blows out a breath. "I needed to clear my head. Get some air."

My voice starts to break. "Why?"

"I just did. It was all too much. Too much was happening, and I couldn't keep up. Stella said she could watch Maven, and I needed to get out of there."

I can tell she didn't mean to say that last sentence.

"You needed to get out of there?" I repeat.

She nods.

"Are you going to tell me why?"

"It doesn't matter."

I rub my eyes to fight back the tears. "It was because of Lucy's stuff, wasn't it?"

"That was one of the reasons, yes." She's not shocked I knew what it was. She knew I'd know.

This is my fault. If I had picked up Maven myself or taken down Lucy's stuff or told Willow to take Maven to her place, this might've never happened.

"Fuck. I'm sorry. It didn't even cross my mind before I asked you."

She shrugs. "It's fine. She's a part of your life. She was your wife. I get that now."

"What do you mean, you get that now?"

"I understand the loss of someone you love. I now understand, sometimes, you can't get over it." She rubs her stomach as the tears fall. "I know I'll never get over this, just like you'll never get over Lucy. I don't blame you for it. I'm not mad."

"What are you saying?" I ask, simmering with fear.

Her eyes are vacant. Dull. She's here physically, but she's not *here.*

"I'm saying, we should spend some time apart."

I feel my pulse in my throat. "Are you ... are you saying you're done with me?"

She shakes her head and rubs her forehead, like I'm stressing her out. Like it's the last conversation she wants to have.

Me, too.

"I can't be done with you. We're having a baby together, but we should take a step back from everything else."

I can't be hearing her right. I lost Lucy. I lost one of my babies. Now, I'm losing her.

"Take a step back from the relationship we've been building? Take a step back from feeling happiness? Take a few steps back from making love?"

She cringes. "Don't call it that."

"Don't call it what?"

Her jaw clenches in anger. "Making love. We don't *make love,* Dallas, because we don't love each other. We fuck. That's it. You and I both know it."

"You know that's not true!" I grind out, fighting the urge to raise my voice. "If I were only interested in *fucking* someone, do you think I'd do it with the most complicated woman in the world?" I shake my head and lean in. "I do it because I'm falling in love with you. Not for a quick fuck!"

"Oh, shit!"

I stumble back at the sound of Stella's voice and look at the doorway to find her standing there with my parents.

"Bad timing?" Stella asks regrettably, tears lining her eyes. "Sorry, I suck at knocking."

Tears are falling down my mom's cheeks. My dad has his fist against his mouth to fight his own hurt.

They know before even asking questions.

I stride across the room to hug my mother, rubbing her back as she lets out her hurt, and then move to my dad next. He's not much of a hugger, but he keeps a tight hold on me, understanding my pain.

I lean back on my heels. "Will you give us a moment?"

They nod, and I'm back at Willow's side when they're gone. I scrub my other hand over my face and try to control my breathing. "You honestly can't believe I'm not in love with you. I've been trying to show you how damn good we are together."

Her chin trembles as she prepares herself to break my fucking heart. "I might be younger than you, but I'm not stupid, Dallas. We have fun together. We like each other. We're attracted to each other. But your heart isn't ready for anyone else. And my heart isn't whole enough to give someone a piece I'm not sure I'll get back. We were caught in the moment, moving too fast, even though we told each other in the beginning that a relationship was off the table."

"That was before I brought you into my life, before you showed me how wonderful you were with my daughter, before you showed me what it was like to be happy again."

She stares down at her stomach without saying another word. She said what she needed, and now, she's done.

"So, this is it, huh? Where you want us to go? I've lost two people in my life that fucking meant something. No, make that three if you walk away from me."

She keeps her head bowed and grimaces.

"Please, look at me. Goddamn it, look me in the eyes and tell me you don't want me."

She appears almost frail while slumping down on the bed. "I understand you're upset about our baby, but please don't try to act like you're hurt because I'm asking for space. We would've never worked because you're not ready to open your heart to me."

"Glad I know where I stand with us." I push off the railing on the bed. "I need some air."

I speed out of the hospital without stopping to talk to anyone else, get in my truck, and slam my fist against the steering wheel, taking all of my anger out on it. The pain hits me like a brick. I let the tears fall freely, and I'm certain my heart is dying in my chest.

My tears were finally starting to dry from losing Lucy.

I'm back at square one.

My life keeps falling apart.

Dallas

CHAPTER THIRTY-SEVEN

ELEVEN MONTHS AGO

YOU DON'T KNOW what you have until it's gone.

It's a bullshit cliché.

But fuck me if the reality of those nine words isn't smacking me in the face.

I knew what I had.

I cherished what I had.

But I sure as hell didn't plan on it getting ripped away from me at thirty-one years old.

The beeping of the machines next to Lucy is the only noise in the room. I have a love-hate relationship with them. They're her helping hand, her strength, but they won't be here much longer.

And neither will she.

A relentless surge of panic rips through my veins like a drug when I grip my hand around hers. Watching someone you love die is like your flesh torturously being stripped from your bones, inch by agonizing inch, baring the most vulnerable parts of yourself.

I wipe away my tears with the back of my arm, pissed at them for blurring my limited view of her. I haven't cried like this since I was in Pampers.

I'm a Barnes boy. We're known for our resilience, for our strength in the most desperate times. Emotions don't bleed through our skin. We hide them underneath and let them eat us alive.

At least, that's what I thought until I had to shoot myself with the truth. She is going to die, and there is nothing I can do. No one I can fight. No amount of money I can pay to stop it.

That shit does something to a man.

I tilt my head up to painfully stare at the tiled ceiling and wish it'd cave in on me. Her lips are a bruised blue when I bore my eyes back to her.

Metastatic breast cancer.

It spread fast, too fast, and was caught too late. There was nothing we could do. Chemo didn't work. Praying didn't work. Her liver is failing. Her body is shutting down.

I've followed her wishes. This is where she wanted to do it—not at our home where our daughter lays her head. Here, with just the two of us, so that's what I'm giving her.

"Take me," I plead to the good man above. "Take me, goddamn it!" My chest aches, my lungs restricting airflow, and I pound my fist to my chest. "Let her fucking stay! Take my last breath and give it to her!"

My throat is scratchy and sore, like I've been screaming my pleas, but they've merely been coming out as a whisper.

I tighten my grip on her, wishing I could be her lifeline, as she starts to let go. I gulp down the urge to beg her to hold on, beg her not to leave me, but the thought of her enduring more pain kills me just as much as losing her. I have to let her go in peace even if I selfishly don't want to.

I don't know how to live without her.

I sob as the radiant eyes I fell in love with dim.

No!

Take my light! Take it all from me!

Let her keep shining!

I slump down in my chair like a fucking coward when the machine starts to fire off.

And, with her last breath, she takes me with her.

Dallas

CHAPTER THIRTY-EIGHT

GONE.

I was on the verge of a panic attack when they brought me to the hospital. I cried. Man, did I cry. I'm shocked I have any tears left. I didn't know what was happening—if I was miscarrying, if it was something serious, if I was overreacting. The pain told me something was off, and I was hoping that it wasn't the something that happened.

I shrank into my bed, a cry escaping my lips, when they couldn't find the second baby's heartbeat. They checked it once. Checked it twice. Nothing. Blame wrapped around me like a blanket when Dallas walked in. I shouldn't have been on the road in the middle of nowhere. I shouldn't have been stressing myself out over a man when I had babies to worry about.

At first, I blamed myself.

Then, that blame shifted to Dallas.

He shouldn't have asked me to go to his house.

It's not my fault we lost the baby.

It's not his fault we lost the baby.

But, sometimes, you want to blame someone because you can't handle knowing they're just gone. Even though I haven't been pregnant that long, I've already started to fall in love with my babies, and now, one of them has been taken away from me. My heart is hurting, like someone stuck a knife inside and is twisting it until every part of me has ruptured.

I still have a baby relying on me. I'm not going to put myself into any other stressful situations. I won't be worried about Dallas's heart because I'm only going to focus on keeping mine sane for the baby, and trying a relationship with him isn't going to do that.

I need space. I need to step away. I stare at the door, wondering if he's going to come back or not, and tense up when a knock comes.

Stella peeks her head in. "Cool if I come in?"

"Yes," I answer. I need someone right now.

She smiles and sits down in the empty seat next to me. "Have you called your mom yet?"

I shake my head. "I honestly don't want to tell anyone. She'll want to fly here and take care of me, which is what I don't want. I need time to breathe on my own, to accept this, to take it in." I rub my stomach. "Can you give me a ride home when they release me?"

She squeezes her hand over mine. "Of course." She opens her mouth and then shuts it. She wants to talk about Dallas, most likely wants us to patch things up, but that's impossible right now.

Like I told Dallas, I understand now. I know how it feels to lose someone you love so much, someone you thought you'd spend years with.

And I understand never wanting to let them go.

———

THREE DAYS HAVE PASSED since Stella brought me home from the hospital.

I'm sore. Exhausted. Hopeless.

Calls and texts have gone ignored, and the only reason I've seen Lauren is because she has a spare key to my apartment and lets herself in, uninvited. I'm selfish because they're worried about me, but I want to be left alone. I asked Dallas to give me some space, and except for a few texts, he has. But no words, no lecture, nothing will stop me from feeling some blame in this. I was too stressed. I wasn't eating right. I should've been resting more. The guilt that my body is the one that lost my child kills me.

I called my mom the day I got home. We cried. She prayed. She begged to fly out here to be with me, and I begged her not to.

I'm reading another article on vanishing twin syndrome when I hear my front door open. I turn around on the couch and shut my laptop at the same time Lauren walks in, wearing her scrubs, going straight to the kitchen like she owns the place.

"Hey, girl," she calls out when I meet her. "I hope you have an appetite." She starts the oven and begins pulling out containers of prepared food. "Tacos are on the menu for tonight."

I do a scan of all the items laid out on the counter. Meat. Lettuce. Cheese. Salsa. Guacamole. "You made all of this?" I ask. "Didn't you have to work?"

She laughs, removing the lid from the meat and pouring it into a pan. "Sweetie, you know my cooking is shit. Although my reheating game is pretty good." She turns the burner on. "Dallas did all of this last night before going to work and asked me to bring it over."

I snort. "Why? Is he scared I'm not feeding myself well enough, and we'll lose the other baby?" The words come out before I can stop myself.

She narrows her eyes at me. "No. And we both know he doesn't think that, so quit acting like a brat."

"Excuse me?" I snap.

"You heard me," she says, her attention going back to the stove. "Quit acting like a brat."

I huff. I puff. I want to kick her out of my apartment, but she keeps going, "I get you're going through pain, but don't forget you're not the only one experiencing this loss. So is my brother."

I press my finger to my chest. "He's the one who tried to blame me for losing the baby."

"Did he say those words?"

"Well … not exactly."

"The only thing that's exact about your argument is that he never said you're to blame. Not once. You're pissed at him because you have no one else to be mad at—because no one is to blame. *No one.* You heard the doctor. The miscarriage would've happened, no matter what."

"I don't blame him for the miscarriage."

"But you blame him for what occurred before the miscarriage. You need something to blame for losing the baby, so you're blaming it on Lucy's stuff at his house."

"Don't do this, Lauren," I mutter. "I'm not talking to you about this."

"Then, don't talk to me. Talk to him. *Please.*"

"I have. We've texted a few times."

"Maven has a sleepover tonight. Let him come over."

"I can't," I whisper, and my voice starts to crack. "It'd be too hard."

"Going through a hard phase in life is a lot more difficult with no one at your side. It starts getting softer, gentler, when you have someone else with you. Trust me."

———

DALLAS KNOWS food is the way to my heart. The tacos and the slice of blueberry pie he sent over are making me reconsider seeing him. Lauren's right. We've barely said a few words to each other since our argument at the hospital. I've run our exchange through my mind hundreds of times, staying up late because I can't sleep, and I've tried to dissect every word that fell from his lips.

I shut my eyes and remember what he said.

"Take a step back from the relationship we've been building? Take a few steps back from making love?"

He said *making love.* I corrected that and said we were only fucking.

I'm the only one being honest with myself, with our relationship. We were both in a sensitive place the night of our one-night stand,

and I'm afraid we're only pulled to each other because of that and my pregnancy.

But bad days, bad months, don't last forever, and eventually, we'll get over our bad times and realize we were only using each other as a Band-Aid until we healed. He'll go back to being a widower mourning his wife but still be getting laid. And I'll go back to being a woman who doesn't want anything to do with love but still getting laid.

We're having sex for the need of it, the connection of it, for desire. Not for love, like he said. I gulp. Not for love on his part because the more time I spent with him, the more I knew I was falling into the pit of somewhere I didn't want to go. A hole of falling for a man not interested in falling for me other than in the sheets. I'm afraid to admit, I'm in love with this broken, beautiful, loving man.

There's a knock at the door when I'm taking a tray of cookies out of the oven. Dallas cooked for me, so I wanted to return the favor. Making the cookies has also helped keep my mind off everything I'm going through. Granted, I used a premade box mix, but a girl has to start somewhere.

Dallas said he'd be over after dropping Maven off for her sleepover. I take a deep breath and don't bother looking through the peephole before answering the door.

"What the hell are you doing here?" I yell.

Brett is standing in the doorway with flowers. *Yes, fucking flowers again.*

His blond hair is swept back in a baseball cap, and a T-shirt and jeans cover his tall and scrawny body.

My asshole ex has a history of bad timing—having a girl in our bed when he thought I was out of town, sending dick pics without putting a password on his phone, being on a date with another woman when I ran into him at the frozen yogurt shop.

I stumble back when he takes a step forward and shuts the door behind himself.

"I heard about what happened to our baby."

"I'm sorry. What did you just say? Our *what?*" I'm dreaming. I have to be dreaming. This isn't happening.

Brett is out on bail. He shouldn't even be leaving the county, let alone the state.

He tilts his shoulder in a half-shrug and walks into the living room, placing the flowers in the middle of the coffee table and sitting down. "I've gotta say, I'm unhappy you kept this from me, but I'll forgive you … for the sake of our family."

"Have you lost your mind?" *Does jail make you imagine things?* I take a step closer to look him in the eyes. He has to be high to consider this to be a good idea. "Are you on drugs?"

"No, Willow, I'm not on drugs," he mocks in annoyance.

"You need to leave."

"I'm not leaving until we talk about our dead baby."

"There is no *our* baby, dumbass."

My breathing labors, and my fist itches to connect with his face. He just referred to my baby as *dead.* He gets up and struggles to grab my hand, but I fight him off.

"Leave before I call the cops. You know this baby isn't yours. I haven't touched you in almost a year."

"I don't care. I'll take on the responsibility if it's another man's because I love you." He arrogantly looks around the room. "I don't see anyone here to help you. What'd you do? Get knocked up by some random dude while traveling with Stella?" He clicks his tongue against the roof of his mouth and shakes his head. "You know, that's why I said I didn't trust you working with her. You'd get mad at me for cheating when I knew you were doing the same."

That's a lie. He was always jealous of my job.

"Fuck you. Do you honestly believe I'd ever have a baby with you? You almost killed a child."

He points to my stomach. "I want a paternity test on the one that's still alive."

God, could his words be any more horrible?

"Excuse me? You admitted the baby wasn't yours seconds ago."

"No, I didn't."

I don't have the time or the patience to deal with this asshole today. Or ever. "Screw you. I just had a miscarriage, for fuck's sake, and you thought it would be a good idea to fly thousands of miles and harass me?"

We look at the door at the sound of a knock. Brett goes to answer it before I can stop him. I make it at the same time Dallas walks in, bumping into Brett on his way, and his attention bounces between Asshole and me.

"Did I miss something?" he asks.

"Stella's old bodyguard?" Brett spits with a bitter laugh. "The fuck is he doing here?"

"The better question is, why are you here?" Dallas fires back, moving into his space.

"Stop!" I hiss. "I have neighbors!" I gesture for Dallas to close the door behind him. I can't lose my apartment because of this.

Brett points to my stomach again. "This is my baby, and I've come to take care of my family."

Dallas looks straight at me. "What is he talking about?"

"How do you even know about the baby?" I finally ask Brett.

"My father told me after your mom asked the church to pray for you. Your mom wouldn't tell me where you were, so I took matters into my own hands. I figured you were still working for Stella, stalked her social media, and found you." He shrugs like that's not creepy at all and then throws his arm out toward a fuming Dallas. "You never answered my question. What are you doing here, bro?"

"Don't fucking call me bro," Dallas snarls.

He smirks. "Jesus, fuck, this is the dude you're banging? This is the dude trying to take you and my baby away from me?"

Dallas takes a step closer. "You better get the fuck out of here before I throw you out."

"So, you were cheating on your dying wife with her? You guys have been fucking around this entire time." He laughs. "This is fucking perfect. You're not such a good man, are you? You walked around like you were this perfect husband who then left his job to take care of his dying wife, but you were cheating on her and fucking my girl." He glares at me. "You're nothing but a lying cunt."

I jump when Dallas punches Brett in the mouth. Brett pushes him back. Dallas wraps his hand around Brett's neck and traps him against the wall.

"What the fuck, dude?" Brett struggles to breathe out, wiggling to get free. "I'm pressing charges!"

"You're not even supposed to be here!" I yell. "Call the cops, please. Let them take you back to where you belong—behind bars."

We don't have to call the cops because they knock on my door seconds later.

"Blue Beech Police Department!" one yells.

Dallas moves his hand from Brett's throat to open the door, and Brett dramatically collapses on the floor, holding his throat and fake choking.

Two officers step in. A young guy and an older gentleman.

"Hi, I'm Officer Barge," the older man says.

The younger cop tips his head forward. "Officer Layne." He surveys the room. "We received a noise complaint about two men fighting." His eyes cast a look straight to Dallas. "What's going on, man?"

"He punched me!" Brett screams, stumbling to his feet and sticking out his chest. He's a badass now that there's protection. "I want him put in jail."

"I punched him," Dallas says. "Because he was harassing her. She's pregnant with my baby, and he was giving her trouble. He's out on bail, and he shouldn't even be out of California."

"That true?" Officer Barge asks.

"No," Brett lies.

Officer Layne holds out his hand. "Let me see some ID."

Brett flinches. "Are you going to ask him for ID? He's the one who assaulted me!"

"Already know who Dallas is," he answers and then tilts his head my way. "I know who she is. Now, how 'bout you let me get acquainted with you?"

"I'll tell you who I am. I'm the son of a mayor in a very affluent California town."

"Cool story, man," Officer Layne replies. "But this ain't California, hipster boy. I don't care if your father is the president. Let me see some ID, or I'm going to have to bring you in for failure to cooperate."

Brett pulls out his wallet and reluctantly hands his driver's license over.

"I'll go run this," Officer Layne says while Officer Barge keeps his eyes narrowed on Brett.

The officer and Dallas make small talk until Officer Layne comes back.

"It appears you broke the stipulations of your bail. We're shipping you back to that *affluent* town of yours where you can enjoy your time in a cell." His upper lip snarls in disgust. "I can't believe they even gave you bail for what you did."

Brett throws every name at me while they cuff him and force him out of my apartment. "He doesn't love you!" he screams before the door shuts. "He'll always love that dead bitch!"

Dallas stalks out of my apartment, ready for round two, but the police officer stops him from getting to Brett.

"Let it go, man," Officer Layne says. "He isn't worth it." He looks at me. "Congratulations on the baby, you two."

Dallas slaps him on the back. "Thanks, man."

He hands me a card. "Willow, you let me know if he gives you any more trouble."

Dallas's defeated gaze focuses on me after he shuts the door, and his jaw twitches. "That fucker telling the truth?"

"Huh?" My brain is so exhausted, I don't catch the severity of his question.

"Is he telling the truth about him being the father?"

My heart races. "Are you kidding me? You believe him?"

"I don't know what to believe. He seemed pretty damn adamant about it."

"If you want to believe him, be my guest. Leave. I planned on doing this by myself from day one, and I have no problem going through with that plan. I don't need you or Brett. I'm a woman who has her shit together. I have a good job and don't need to fucking baby-trap a guy." I shake my head. "Fucking trust me, it would've been much easier to do this on my own."

"Don't say that," he growls.

I cock my head toward the door. "Leave. I'll take care of this supposed illegitimate baby on my own."

"Don't." He grabs my hand in his. "Don't say that. You can't be pissed at me for asking. I asked, you told me the truth, I believe you."

I release his hold and shove him away from me. "The fact that you even doubted me is bullshit."

This is too much to handle right now. My hands are shaking in anger. I should've punched Brett in the face.

Dallas throws his arms in the air. "I'm sorry. It's been a rough fucking week. I came over to make things right with you, and that asshole was here."

"He showed up, unannounced! It's not like I invited him."

He grabs my hand, leads me across the room, and situates me on the couch. I hold my breath when he falls next to me and then drags me into his chest. I relax against him, and my heart calms when he starts massaging my neck.

"Why does it seem like the world's against us?" I whisper.

"It's not." He places a kiss on my neck. "People go through trials and tribulations, but we'll be okay. We can get through this because we have each other to lean on. It fucking killed me for you to think I blamed you for losing our baby. I was hurt. Upset. Expressing my emotions isn't something I excel at." He chuckles. "Those words came from Lauren, not me."

"That makes two of us."

I drop my head back on his shoulder to see him, and my body relaxes when he kisses away the tears hitting my cheeks.

"How about we start the night over?" he asks. "Let's act like your douche bag of an ex with bangs longer than yours didn't come here."

I reach up to circle my hand around his neck and bring him down for a kiss. "You have no idea how great that sounds."

I planned on telling him we needed to stick to being friends tonight, but that's all changed. Brett slapped some reality into me. I could turn my back on Dallas and have to deal with more men like Brett because I'm too scared to get close to someone capable of love, or I could spend my time with a man who has a heart.

Things might not work out with us.

Things might go wrong.

But being with him feels much better than being alone.

We stay on the couch and talk about everything that's happened since we last saw each other. Maven is feeling better and is back to her usual self. She's been asking hundreds of questions about where I am.

Dallas tucks me into bed and turns around to leave.

"Are you not staying the night?" I ask, disappointed.

He smiles. "Hell yes, I am. But I need to get rid of those ugly-ass flowers first."

I can't help but laugh. I needed that.

He comes back with an even brighter smile on his face, and I arch my brows in question.

"You baked me cookies," he states.

"Tried to." I frown. "They're a little burned."

"You do like me."

We spend the rest of the night eating burned cookies in bed.

———

"MAVEN MISSES YOU," he whispers in my ear.

It's morning, and the faint ray of sunlight peeks through the windows as we lie in bed. My hand is in his. My legs are a wild mess across his. It feels good to have him back here.

I shut my eyes. "I miss her. Tell her I'll be seeing her soon." His hand tightens around mine, and I sigh. "So, this is what grief feels like."

No wonder Dallas was so miserable when Lucy died. This pain is what he was feeling. This void in my heart is what he was going through.

"Losing someone isn't fun." His breathing slows. "I just wish we could've met him even if it was for only a minute."

His eyes are on me when I shift to rest my chin on his warm chest and smile up at him. I sag against his body when his arms wrap around my back, and he settles me next to him, his fingers tracing my spine.

"Him?" I ask.

He chuckles. "Is it bad I was convinced we were having a boy?"

I can feel his thick breathing when I stroke his chest. "I was so convinced we were having a girl, I had a name picked out."

"Is it Daphne?" he asks, and I can feel his laughter through his chest. "She can hang out with Scooby, and they'll chase ghosts together."

An even bigger roar of laughter comes from his chest when I pinch his nipple. "No!" I follow his lead, feeling it coming from the bottom of my stomach, and damn, does it feel good for something other than pain to consume me. "Can I ask you for a favor though?"

He nods.

"Let's wait until we have the baby before choosing a name. I don't want to get my hopes up and then have something happen."

His arm tightens around me. "Nothing will happen."

I reach up and run my fingers over the stubble on his cheeks. "Just in case."

"We'll wait. And, when you have our baby and it's a girl, we'll go with the name you choose. If it's a boy, we'll go with mine."

I smile. "I like that idea."

"Now, can I ask you a favor? You don't have to answer right away. Think about it and get back with me when you decide."

Damn it. Him and his favors.

"What?"

Sincerity takes over his features. "Consider moving in with me.

I'll do anything to make you comfortable there. Sleep on the couch. Crash in the basement. Sleep in my truck if I have to."

"It didn't end well the last time I was at your house. I feel like too much of an outsider."

"I'll make things right. Make you happy there. Give me a chance."

I slowly nod. "I'll think about it."

"And ..." he draws out. "Just one more serious question."

"What more can you want?" I ask, faking annoyance.

"Why did you name your cat Scooby? Letting you name our child worries me."

"My grandfather had a cat named Scooby. No one understood why, and he never told us." I narrow my eyes at him with a smile. "So, consider yourself lucky to hear my reason."

"And what would that be?"

"Because my grandfather named his Scooby."

He nods. "Let's keep the cartoon names to our animals."

Dallas

CHAPTER THIRTY-NINE

I REMEMBER the day I told Maven that Lucy had died.

I sat her down and broke the news, and she didn't take it well. For weeks, she cried and lashed out. Trying to explain death to a six-year-old isn't easy. All I could tell her was that Mommy had gone to heaven, but she took that as Mommy had left because she was mad at her. We went to counseling with our preacher. I stayed at home for days, built pillow forts, and had tea parties with stuffed animals.

Telling her about losing one of the babies terrified me, thinking that she'd revert to that sadness. We'd lost too many people. Gone through too much hell. Maven had started suggesting names from her favorite books. Everyone we passed on the street, at the grocery store, at her preschool had heard her boast and brag about how she was going to be a big sister.

I took advice from my family and set her down last night. As badly as I wanted Willow at my side, she'd been through enough. Maven cried but is more understanding of death now. She said her mommy was taking care of the baby in heaven.

It's been a week since I asked Willow to move in. She hasn't brought it up again, and I know what I need to do before she does. And today of all days is when I decide I have to do something that will hurt me.

I didn't want to get out of bed today, but I had to pull my shit together and do it.

Today is a day I used to celebrate. Now, it's a day of darkness. My mom offered to watch Maven before I even told her my plans.

I take the drive I haven't made in a few weeks. I haven't told her the news, I've been afraid to tell her, but I can't be anymore.

I sit down in front of her gravestone and place the pink tulips, her favorite flower, in front of it.

"Hey, Lucy-Pie," I whisper. "Happy birthday." I chuckle, sitting back. "Big thirty-two."

I sigh. "I know I haven't been here in a while. I'm sorry. And I know you like me to be honest, so that's what I'm going to give you. I've been consumed with guilt, feeling like a trader, a bad husband, like you'd be disappointed in me. It was a dumbass thought because I know your heart. You'd probably want to slap me right now and tell me to get it together. You'd lead the way for me when I didn't know which way to turn. Tough love is what you called it."

My eyes water. "I'm having a baby. We were supposed to have two, but we lost one. It was like going through hell again. Maven wants you to watch over her baby brother or sister. Can you do that for us?"

The sun beats down on me, and a tear falls down my cheek. "I lost the baby like I lost you, and I was so mad. So damn mad. I felt sorry for myself. I was pissed at everyone … at everything. But my anger and fear is only going to make me keep losing people."

I sigh and slip my wedding ring off my finger. I stare at it one last time before digging a small hole in the dirt with my fingers. My hands shake while I bury it next to the tulips. "I realize now why you made me promise. I had no problem promising to be a good father, and that's what I'll do to both of my children. I reluctantly promised to find love again, and I hope you'll be proud of me when I say I have." I tell her about Willow, about our babies, about how excited Maven is to become a big sister.

I wipe my nose. "And, while you're up there, will you give our baby a hug for us?"

I won't forget about Lucy.
I won't try to replace her.
But I will let myself move on.

Dallas

CHAPTER FORTY

IT'S BEEN a month since we lost the baby.

A long and gruesome month.

There hasn't been a day that's gone by that I haven't gone over the things I should've done differently to stop the miscarriage from happening. I've read article after article and talked to Aidan about it at every appointment.

So, I've been doing everything I can to take it easy, attempting to stay on bed rest, like the doctor suggested, but I'm going stir-crazy.

The uncertainty of another miscarriage has been the only thing on my mind.

Dallas hasn't brought up his offer for me to move in with him. I don't know if it's been retracted or if he's scared of the rejection.

Stella insisted I do most of my work from home, and when I do visit her on set, she practically caters to me like I'm her boss. Lauren stops by before every shift. Rory and my mom regularly check in with me, and Dallas and Maven are here nearly every day.

Lauren is right. Having a good support system helps.

I sit on the couch and stare at the doorway to the nursery. Something I do every day. I haven't been back in it since I lost the baby. Dallas keeps asking if he can put the crib together or start painting, but I can't bring myself to say yes.

It's not that I don't want this baby to have a nice nursery.

It's that I'm terrified I might lose this baby, too.

The front door opens, and Maven comes running into the living room. Dallas is behind her with a bag of takeout.

Her smile beams when it lands on me. "Can I ask her now, Daddy? Can I *pleeease* ask her now? I can't wait any longer!"

I tried to stop it, Dallas mouths to me.

She plops down next to me on the couch, and I play with her hair.

"Ask me what?"

"Um …" She opens her mouth but chickens out and slams it shut.

Well, that's new.

She whips around to look at Dallas. "Will you do it for me, Daddy? You say it much better."

He slowly nods, and I know what he's about to ask isn't going to be easy on me.

"Maven will be starting kindergarten soon. Tomorrow is Parents' Night."

"Will you please come with me?" Maven chimes in. Her spunk is back. "Pretty, pretty please? It'll be *so, so* much fun. They'll have snacks, and you get to meet my teacher! I'm going to big-kid school!"

I don't know if Maven told him she'd asked me to be her new mommy, but he hasn't mentioned it. And I don't plan to tell him. That's a secret between the two of us.

Dallas leans back against the wall and fights a smile on his lips. "There was no way I was going to stop her from asking you. You know she doesn't take no for an answer very well. Plus, I could use the company."

"Please," Maven continues to plead. "Everyone else is going to have their mommy there."

The air leaves the room.

"Maven," Dallas says, his voice almost sounding shaky, "you know Willow isn't your mom."

"I know, *but* she'd be a good second mommy." She closes her eyes in sadness. "She doesn't even have to be my new mommy. I just want her there, so I won't feel left out."

Dallas rubs his hands over his face. "I'm sorry. I wasn't expecting all that."

I wave off his answer, seeing the hurt on Maven's face, recognition hitting me. I was the girl without a father at everything. I understand her hurt, the pain she's going through.

"Maven, I'd love to go," I answer, shocking myself and Dallas.

She springs off the couch. "I told you she'd say yes, Daddy!" She wraps her short arms around me and jumps up and down.

My heart warms. I'm doing the right thing. Going to her Parents' Night will help me just as much as her.

———

WE DEVOURED OUR DINNER, and Maven fell asleep on the couch while watching cartoons.

"Want to talk?" Dallas asks.

I'm not reluctant this time. I'm not going to blow him off. I lead him to the kitchen.

He blurts out his apology as soon as we sit down. "I don't know where the hell the mommy thing came from. I'll break the news to Maven and tell her you had something come up."

"I'm going," is all I reply, but so much is said in those words.

"You don't have to do it if you don't feel comfortable. You looked like she'd asked for a kidney."

"It surprised me, is all. I want to go. I know what the need feels like to have two parents at functions because I was the little girl whose father never showed up. It was heartbreaking, and if me doing something as small as showing up makes that little girl feel better, I'll be there."

He leans forward and presses his lips to mine. "Thank you. You have no idea how much this means to me."

———

"YOU'RE GOING to love my school!" Maven squeals when we pull into the parking lot of the elementary school.

I run a hand down my stomach. No more hiding the baby bump. No more hiding my affection for Dallas and his little girl.

Maven's class is small, and we take a table in the back. Parents fill the room, greeting each other and spewing off question after question.

Everyone knows everybody.

Except for me.

But that doesn't mean they don't know *of* me.

"Oh, you're that actress girl's friend, right?"

"So, Dallas, this is the woman you've been spending all your time with?"

"I heard about what happened at the birthday party. That sounds so tragic to have the news come out like that."

If they're not asking ridiculous questions, they're staring.

There are a few exceptions though. Not everyone is nosy and rude. A few have introduced themselves without fishing for gossip, and they seemed genuine.

Dallas took Maven up to select her cubby, and my body tenses when someone sits down next to me.

"I was hoping you'd come," Beth says in a soft voice. "My daughter and Maven are in the same class this year. They're going to have a blast together." She smiles. "This is the first time I've seen you since you picked her up from preschool, so I haven't had the chance to congratulate you on the baby, and give my condolences on your miscarriage."

I flinch.

"I hope you don't mind that Maven told me, but I promise, your business is not mine to tell."

"Thank you," I whisper.

"How far along are you?"

This isn't an interrogation. She's not asking me this question out of spite. There is not a doubt in my mind that she's truly happy I'm having this baby.

"About five months," I answer, giving her a smile back.

"I remember the anticipation as the date gets closer. You're nervous the baby is going to come anytime."

I smile and nod. *I'm more nervous of losing my baby.*

Our attention is caught at the sound of Maven laughing. Dallas is down on one knee, helping her decorate her cubby with stickers and stuffed animals.

Beth tilts her head toward them. "He's a good man. A broken one, yes, but still a good one."

"He's been a good friend to me."

"Just a friend?"

I shrug. "Our situation is … complicated."

She pats my shoulder. "I hope I'm not overstepping my boundaries here, but there's something I want to give you." She opens her purse, and I notice the water in her eyes as she places a folded piece of paper in my hand. "My sister wrote this before she passed and asked me to give it to the woman Dallas fell in love with." She closes her hand around mine as a tear passes down her cheek.

I jerk it back to her. "You're mistaken. Dallas isn't in love with me."

"Read it. It'll help you understand how he loves you."

————

I DON'T MENTION the letter to Dallas.

I keep it tucked in my pocket and constantly check to make sure it hasn't fallen out all evening. The meeting doesn't last much longer after Beth leaves, and Dallas and Maven convince me to go out for dessert before going home.

Other than doctor's appointments, which Aidan started sneaking us through the back door for, this is my first time stepping out with Dallas since the miscarriage. I've been so terrified of getting judged, of people staring, of hearing vicious things coming out of their mouths, but I'm done with that now.

Tonight has made me feel comfortable.

Tonight hasn't made me feel like such an outsider.

Maven doesn't hesitate in unbuckling her seat belt when Dallas pulls up to my apartment. They've been here more than their house lately. She heads straight to the couch and drags out the crayons and coloring books I leave for her in the coffee table drawer. Her tongue sticks out as she colors, and Dallas makes each of us a cup of tea.

We watch a movie until she falls asleep with a crayon still in her hand. He kisses me good-bye, and they leave. I'm picking up the mess when I remember the letter. I take a deep breath, not knowing what I'm getting myself into, and lie back on the couch before opening it.

To the lucky woman who reads this.

Hello,

My name is Lucy. I'm sure you've heard about me. Possibly seen my pictures, my belongings, traces of me in the home we shared. You might've even known me.

I was Dallas's wife. And, since you're reading this, I'm no longer here.

Dallas is a difficult man. Always has been. He'll be even more difficult after my death, but please don't give up on him. If he's opened up his heart enough for you to receive this letter, you have something extraordinary. Receiving this letter means he's in love with you. I'm sure he's fighting it because he wouldn't be a Barnes boy if he didn't fight the reality that's right in front of him.

Watch his actions. Those are what speak his love. He's not the best at words, but the more you let him in, the more he opens up for you.

Don't be afraid. We've all had other loves. Don't think he can only have one because you've proven that wrong.

Please don't give up on him because he won't give up on you. When you make your way into his heart, he'll fight to keep you there. He's the strongest man I've ever known.

Thank you for loving my family and give Maven a kiss for me.
Lucy
I'm in tears when I finish, and I hold the letter to my heart.

Dallas

CHAPTER FORTY-ONE

WILLOW: **We need to talk.**

Her text isn't the only thing that worries me. She sent it at three this morning. The early hours of the morning are when your brain is working the hardest, going over important choices, the shit you want to forget but can't.

Is this a good or bad we need to talk?

Should I be heading to the airport?

After I drop Maven off at school, I call Hudson and let him know I'll be late today, and then I drive straight to Willow's apartment. Fingers crossed it's not empty when I get there.

I take the stairs three at a time and find her sitting on the couch. My chest gets heavy when I notice the moving boxes scattered everywhere. Some flat, some put together, some taped up with scribbled words on them.

She nervously glances back at me while I trudge across the room. I don't take my eyes off her–like it's the last time I'll get to see her. Her naturally plump lips that fit perfectly around my cock are puckered as she watches me. The hair I love twirling my fingers around is down in loose curls. The woman I've fallen in love with is going to walk away with the remaining pieces of what's left of me.

"Hey," she says. "You never texted me back. I wasn't sure if you got my message."

Why? Was she trying to get out of here before I showed up?

I snatch a half-filled box and dump out the contents. I need physical evidence that my life is going to change. That I'll be going back to the miserable asshole I was before she took me over.

"What the hell?" Willow screams, sliding off the couch in frustration.

I scowl at the items on the floor. Clothes. Shoes. My eyes zero in on the shoes she left at my house that night. Her gaze goes to me, then to the pile on the floor, and back to me.

Where did this sudden change come from?

We spend all of our free time together, and from what I believe, we've been enjoying it. No arguments have occurred. Every prenatal appointment has gone well.

What happened? Where did it go wrong?

"You going somewhere?" I ask.

Her brows scrunch together. "The moving boxes give it away?"

"Sure did." I struggle to keep my voice calm.

Stress is bad for the baby. We can't risk another miscarriage. I won't argue. Won't fight it. She's calling the shots. I'll move if that's what she wants, get a job bussing tables in LA if I have to, turn my life upside down to keep her.

Her head cocks to the side. "I thought this was what you wanted?"

I grit my teeth. "That's never what I wanted. Not once have I told you to pack up and ditch us. Just so you know, what you're doing is going to leave my daughter and me broken. Do you understand? You're not supposed to turn your back on us because we fell in love with you. I fell in love with you." I shake my head, my voice breaking. "And we don't want another person we love to leave us."

She blows out a breath and smiles.

The fuck?

"Did you bump your head? These boxes are for me to move in *with you.*"

Her answer melts the burden off my chest. "What did you say?"

"I said, I've been packing my stuff because I'm accepting the offer of moving in with you, dipshit."

Damn, does my girl have a mouth on her.

Stupidity rails through me. So much time has passed since I asked her to move in, I figured it wasn't an option.

She's staying. Halle-fucking-lujah.

I crack a smile while she blankly stares at me.

"So, now that you know I'm not leaving your ass, promise me you won't do that anymore," she says, her tone turning emotionless. "If you want me to move in with you, you can't go around, saying things you don't mean."

I cock my head and stare at her in confusion. "What don't I mean?"

"That you love me." She throws her hands down to her sides. "We get along great, the baby will have two parents, but don't get my hopes up. I've made my mind up to move in, so you don't have to lie to me."

Oh, shit.

The L-word hasn't left my mouth again since we lost the baby. In fear of her running away, I've stopped myself every time. Now, my dumbass has blurted it out and ruined any chance of her moving in with me.

I draw nearer before she kicks me out, and I walk her back until her back hits a wall. I press a hand to her cheek, and hers wrap around my neck, massaging the built-up tension. I look down, searching for eye contact, but she's not giving it.

"Look at me," I whisper. My voice turns raw. Raspy. My breathing falters when she does. "I'd be lying if I said I didn't love you."

I didn't bring her home with me that night, expecting to fall in love. I never thought that having surprise babies, going on road trips, getting stranded, and then surviving a miscarriage would bring so many emotions out of me. That it would warm my cold heart. That'd it bring me closer to her.

She's managed to do that.

She makes me want to be a better man.

A man who believes in love again because he's in love with her.

She's a strong woman with a heart of gold, who brought a flashlight in my darkness to show me the way to happiness when I was fighting not to find an exit.

I won't lose her.

"Tell me you feel it, too," I say.

Worry is evident on her face. The hesitation tells me she's insecure about getting hurt again if she says it. My pulse quickens. The same feeling is driving through her. She wouldn't have agreed to move in if it wasn't.

"I'm scared of feeling it," she finally replies. "I'm scared that loving you is reaching for something that'll never be mine. A lifeline I can't reach because you're in love with someone else."

I look down at her, unblinking. "I'll always be your lifeline. You'll always be able to reach me because you have my heart. No matter what you're going through, I'll be at your side, helping you hold on."

Tears fill her eyes. "You can't love me like you loved her."

"You're right. The way I love you is different than the way I loved her. I've fallen in love with you in different ways, for different reasons, than I did with Lucy. I've fallen in love with finding love, learning your tics, how to make you smile, hearing your fears, and getting to know the deepest parts of your soul. I loved Lucy. I'll never stop loving the memory of her, but I can love you right along with it."

I grew up with Lucy. I loved her for as long as I can remember, but I don't remember *falling* in love with her because I knew everything about her. This is something new to me. A different love but still love. You don't love the same every time.

I squeeze Willow's hips and hope my next question isn't pushing the limit. "You ready to admit you love me yet?"

She shakes her head.

"Then, why are you crying?"

"Hormones," she croaks out. "Fucking hormones."

"You can blame it on that for now." My mouth finds hers, giving her a long kiss, before pulling away and pecking the tip of her nose. "But I'll be asking again later."

"What are you doing?" she asks when I move across the room and pick up a box.

"Helping you pack your shit. You can keep the apartment for as long as you want, but I'm going to take as much time with you under my roof as I can get."

Willow

CHAPTER FORTY-TWO

DALLAS AND HUDSON are moving the few boxes I packed for my trial run at Dallas's.

I'm doing this.

Really doing this.

I stop on the porch before walking through the front door. I jumped down these stairs, barefoot, with tears running down my face. I stare at the door, remembering my last look of Dallas that day. *Let's hope history doesn't repeat itself.*

I haven't been back in the house since Maven was sick. Maybe I should've taken a tour, made sure I was emotionally stable to handle more than three hours here.

I'm going to walk in there, be strong, and do what's right for my heart.

For my baby. For *us.*

The excitement of spending more time with him and Maven is what keeps me walking. I love spending time with them. I'd go to bed, wishing Dallas were there to hold me, to kiss me, to share the moment when the baby kicked.

Dallas is still a man who struggles, but that only makes me fall more in love with him. Lucy's note sparked something inside me, an insight I never thought about when I shut myself down after considering a future with him. Dallas might be a little broken, but he knows what love is. He sacrifices for love, for his family—something Brett never did with me.

I'd rather have a broken man who knows how to love than a man with no scars who's never loved anyone but himself.

Dallas squeezes my elbow when I walk through the front door. "If you're not cool with this, let me know, okay? I'll call a realtor, and we can look for another property."

I stare at him, unblinking. "Are you talking about buying a new house?"

He practically built this house with his own two hands. He loves this home.

"If that's what makes you comfortable." He slides in closer and gently pushes a fallen strand of hair from my ponytail out of my eyes. His hands then rest on my hips. "This is your home now, do you hear me? *Our* home. I want you to be able to relax, to be able to touch me, to feel okay with having sex with me here." He chuckles. "Because we know that's going to be happening a lot as soon as our little one is born."

I smile. "You have no idea how much I've missed that." Especially with him. It's hard to go from having sex with fuck boys to Dallas and then being told you're on bed rest and that you need to refrain from sex. It's like tasting an expensive cupcake for the first time after years of eating cheap candy, and then it gets taken away from you.

His hand moves down to brush between my legs. "I might not be able to fuck you yet, but I promise I'll do something for you tonight."

I rest my hand on his chest. "I have something to look forward to."

"You most certainly do."

"All right, kids, take it to the bedroom," Hudson says, walking in. "And, speaking of bedroom, is that where you want me to put this stuff?"

I take my time while Dallas waits for an answer. "Yeah," I stutter out. "Sure."

I follow them down the hallway and into the bedroom, not sure if I'm truly ready for this. I take in a heavy breath and wait for the blow of bad memories and heartache to hit me, but nothing does when I walk in.

The furniture and bedding is new. I try not to make it too obvious that I'm searching for the signs of Lucy I saw last time I was in here, but they are now missing. The perfume bottle, the pictures, the clothes—it's all gone.

Hudson sets the box down on the floor and leaves the room.

"You got rid of her stuff?" I ask Dallas, guilt seeping through me. Forcing his hand to do this wasn't what I wanted. "I swear, my intentions weren't for you to erase her."

"I didn't erase her."

He holds his hand to his heart while mine pounds. He's no longer wearing his wedding ring. Hasn't been for a few weeks, but I haven't questioned him about it. I wasn't sure if he did it to make me happy, or because he wanted to for himself.

Now I know it's because he wanted to.

"No matter what, Lucy will always have a spot in my heart," he goes on.

I nod. I don't want him to lose that either.

"It was time I did it. I can't keep living in the past, especially when it was destroying my happy future. It was hell, don't get me wrong, pushing myself to do something I should've done months ago. I waited until I was ready, so thank you for giving me time to do that. I went through everything with Maven. She chose the stuff she wanted to keep, and then Lucy's family came over for their own keepsakes."

I sit down on the bed and trace my fingers over the new white bedspread. "Just don't kick me out of this bed, okay?"

He smirks. "Sweetheart, the only reason I'd kick you out of this bed is to fuck you on the floor."

I stand up to wrap my arms around his neck. He did all of this for me. Opened his heart back up for me. He wants to make a home with me and have a family together because he loves me.

I love him.

I'm tired of running from it. Tired of fighting. I have to be strong and honest for our baby, for ourselves, for the six-year-old girl who made me a *Welcome Home* sign, which is displayed on the front door.

"I love you," I whisper into his mouth.

"There it is." He grins. "And I love you."

Dallas

CHAPTER FORTY-THREE

FOUR MONTHS LATER

THE EAR-BLASTING cry is music to my ears.

A sound I was afraid I wouldn't hear. I put the sadness that there should be two in the back of my mind. I won't let that loss interfere with the bliss of this moment.

No surprise to me, Willow was a fucking trooper. She spent ten hours in labor and didn't complain once. All that was on her mind was the excitement of meeting our baby mixed with worry that it might not happen. I stayed by her side the entire time, not moving once, because I didn't want to miss a thing. She needed to know I was with her on this all the way.

Our life has turned into a whirlwind of changes. Willow has moved in, but nothing has changed in the Barnes' household. It feels like she's been there forever. I was anxious at the beginning, given our history there, but losing our baby has taught us to cherish every moment.

Fuck the petty shit.

Fuck running.

Fuck being afraid.

His wails calm when Aidan hands him, wrapped in his blanket, to Willow. My breathing halts when she situates him in her arms, already comfortable with how he likes to be cradled, and she plays with his tiny hand while whispering to him.

I stare at them with compassion. With happiness. With love.

As much as I want to have my turn, I wait until she's ready. She deserves this.

My heart thrashes against my chest when she stares up at me with wet eyes. She moves her arm, shifting toward me, and I waste no time in scooping him up. He's perfect—from his full head of dark hair to his button nose—and he's squirming like a fish out of water.

I'm ready to take him home. To show him the nursery we've been working on for months. To give him love every day.

Aidan heard a heartbeat during every ultrasound, but the thought of losing our baby still hung over our heads daily.

The chance of another miscarriage was high. There could have been problems at birth.

Those burdens have fallen off me. That worry is gone. He's here, healthy, and staring up at me with sleepy, dark eyes that resemble Maven's.

He owns my heart already.

It's been a rough journey, but like our road trips, we've seemed to make them enjoyable, memorable, crazy. Our turns and detours made us stronger, made us love deeper, made us appreciate each day.

We name him Samuel.

After my grandfather.

Willow and Maven love his name just as much as I do.

Samuel Logan Barnes.

Eight pounds and four ounces of fucking adorableness.

My son. My new sidekick. More happiness brought into a life I thought was over.

I didn't know what I was going to get when we walked into the hospital this morning. My heart surged with fear with every step I took. Bad news had been a constant for me here. I'd experienced so many losses within these walls.

That ended today.

This place will no longer be a reminder of loss.

I lost people I loved here.

And I've gained someone I love just as much.

Willow

CHAPTER FORTY-FOUR

I AM A MOTHER.

I whisper those words to myself again. *I am a mother.*

This job, this role, means more to me than any I've ever had.

I tried to stay positive before Samuel was born, but it was hard because the doctor telling me there was a chance I'd never be able to hold him was a constant worry.

"Jesus, someone had better give me some Tylenol to cure this baby fever," Stella says while rocking Samuel back and forth, cooing.

Our friends and family have piled into the room, all of their attention on Samuel.

Samuel. I've only known him a few hours, but he already has my heart gripped in his tiny fingers.

My mom flew in a few days ago and has been staying in my apartment along with Scooby. She's fallen in love with Dallas and Maven, and we're already in talks of her moving here. I've caught the Blue Beech initiation bug.

Samuel has taken his first selfie and had his first diaper changed by me, and people rock-paper-scissored over who got to hold him first.

Hudson throws his hands up. "I'm all for making a baby. Tell me when and where, babe." He slaps Dallas on the back. "Congrats, big brother. You might be one ugly dude, but you make some cute kids."

Dallas laughs and punches him in the arm.

That gorgeous smile hasn't left his face since I handed him Samuel for the first time. Stella gives Samuel back to him as the baby-holding circle starts again from the top.

Dallas cradles him and rocks from side to side. "That's my boy."

Maven tugs at his shirt. "And my little brother!" she announces. "I'm a big sister now!"

We've had to nearly pry Samuel from her arms every time she's held him. She made a list of requests, and the top one was him sleeping in her bed. There's some explaining to do when we get home. Samuel can't be thrown into strollers and tossed on the floor after changing his diapers, like she does with her toy babies.

I'm exhausted by the time the room clears out, and Dallas is sitting on the edge of my bed. He gently climbs in next to me and laces our fingers together.

I close my eyes and sigh when his lips hit mine.

"We did it," he says. "We made a healthy baby."

I lean up for another kiss, making it last longer, and hold my hand against his cheek. "We did it." I stretch my legs out and drum my fingers along his skin. "A year ago, this is so not where I thought I'd be."

He chuckles. "Oh, sweetheart, it's a hell of a lot better than where I imagined I'd be." He situates himself to look at me better. "You saved me, Willow. You saved my daughter. And not only did you save us, but you also gave us Samuel as a bonus. I've been lifted from fires I never thought I'd escape because of you." He disconnects our hands to circle his around my wrist. "And, someday, you're going to let me put a ring on this finger." His lips graze my ring finger.

"Oh, man, did we go backward on that one," I tease. "First does not always come marriage."

"We do our own thing at our own pace."

"That we do."

Willow

EPILOGUE

TWO MONTHS LATER

I STRETCH out in the sheets and yawn when Dallas comes walking back into the bedroom with Samuel in his arms. I watch the silhouette of him with the help of the sunrise creeping into the morning sky. He's shirtless, wearing only a pair of loose gym shorts, and I lick my lips when he climbs back into bed.

"Dirty diaper," he explains with a grin. He pokes Samuel's belly. "You know our little man can't handle a dirty diaper."

Dallas is the only man ... hell, the only person I know who enjoys changing diapers.

"Thank you," I whisper.

We agreed to take turns in getting up with him at night, but that hasn't happened. Dallas is a lighter sleeper and never wakes me up when it's my turn. He does whatever Samuel needs and comes back to bed without uttering one complaint.

Moving in with him was the right decision. My initial worry that it'd hurt our relationship is gone. It's only fueled more attraction and love between us.

Our bond is tighter, our love stronger.

"Daddy?"

Maven's voice catches me off guard. She's standing in the doorway with her blankie. Dallas or Samuel must've woken her up. She rubs her eyes and sluggishly stomps into the room. I scoot over and pat the space between Dallas and me, and she climbs right in. I smile when her head rests on my shoulder, and she snuggles into my body.

The cartoons come on.

We eat breakfast in bed.

This is my family.

One night changed my life.

One night gave me life.

JustEXES

Gage

PROLOGUE

I JUMP out of my car, the menacing downpour coming at me sideways, and sprint into a home I frequent more than my own.

Her door is unlocked.

No shocker.

She's expecting me.

My shoes squeak against the hardwood floor as I charge down the hall and find her in the bedroom. She's parked on the edge of the bed, her frail body motionless, while a dangerous storm brews in her ice-cold blue eyes.

Eyes pointed in my direction.

"Where is he?" I scream. My voice cracks at her detached facade.

"Gage." Her tone is calm. Controlled. Not what any sane person would have in this situation. "Let me explain."

"What did you do, Missy?" My voice grows louder, angrier, more venom flowing with every sharp, nervous word spit out. "What the fuck did you do?"

"It's all your fault, you know," she fires back. "If you had loved me right, none of this would've happened!"

"You did this out of spite for me?"

I move closer at the sound of sirens in the background.

Determination thrums through me to get to her before they do, and I drop to my knees, prepared to plead if need be.

"Where is he?" I stress, tears biting at my eyes.

Her smile is wicked. "You'll never know." Those four words kill me yet satisfy her as she sings them out.

Seconds later, footsteps grow louder, and the police start filing in.

"Be prepared to rot in a cell for the rest of your life," are the final words I say before they haul her away.

ONE

Lauren

FOUR MONTHS **Later**

"I didn't set my apartment on fire!"

At least, I don't think I did.

My nails press into my palm, an attempt to stop myself from smacking the smirk off my asshole of a landlord's arrogant face.

Ronnie—said asshole—widens his grin. "Tell that to the police."

"The police?" I shriek. "You called the cops?"

"Sure did."

He gestures toward what's left of the burned-down complex I'd called home this morning. Thankfully, the firefighters extinguished the flames and are loading their supplies back into the truck while my neighbors watch. My apartment has been reduced to rubble and ashes, my belongings scorched, and Ronnie the Dick found it necessary to point the blame at me.

He chuckles. "Perfect timing. They've arrived."

His threat doesn't alarm me as much as it should, and I force a smile before swinging around. This will be cake. Flirting has saved me from countless speeding tickets. They'll take one look at me and know I'm not some pyromaniac.

That confidence shatters when I spot the officer stepping out of the police cruiser across the street. My breathing falters, my grin collapsing faster than panties drop after prom, and an ache plummets through my chest.

Am I dreaming?

I smack my cheeks. Squint my eyes. Pinch myself.

There's no questioning it.

It's him.

Years have passed, but his handsome face has been etched into my memory since age six. There will never be a time I won't recognize the sun-kissed, gorgeous man headed in my direction. More scruff covers his strong cheeks than when we were teens, and his chest is broader, his muscles larger.

His almond-shaped carbon-black eyes are pinned my way, attempting to outstare me, as if I'm a target he can't wait to hit. Vindication rides along with his all-business attitude. He remembers our history—how he begged me not to leave him and then told me I was dead to him when I walked away.

No amount of flirting will save me today.

I am so fucking fucked.

My father will kill me when I call for bail money.

I'm frozen in place, watching him grow closer, his partner behind him. My brain tells me to make a run for it, but my legs aren't agreeing. Instead, I use this time to take in this new man.

Everything—from the way he walks to his body—has changed. The navy uniform envelops his solidly built frame, advertising every modification on him. His jet-black hair has grown out from his boyish cut in high school. Hard lines fill his stunning face, and his strong jaw is clenched—a silent admission his life hasn't been a fairy tale since our breakup.

This familiar yet unfamiliar man no longer looks at me with love.

It's hate. Pure, unadulterated hatred.

Gage Perry—*Officer* Gage Perry—towers over my small frame like a high-rise when he reaches me.

"What … what are you doing here?" I stutter out. *Fucking A.* I can't even form a complete sentence without failing.

Don't let him sense your nervousness.

The expression on his face switches from hateful to winning, like a guy who hit the lottery. "Oh, little hell-raiser, you didn't hear the news? I moved home. Disappointed you weren't my first call?"

Oh, yeah, still hates my ass.

"Why didn't anyone tell me?" It's more of a question to myself than him.

"Why would they?" His voice is deep, sharp, like daggers stabbing through my chest. "What I do is none of your business, is it, Lauren? You made that clear years ago." Our eye contact is broken when he glances over to Ronnie and points at me. "This your arsonist?"

Ronnie puffs out his chest. "I believe the fire started in her apartment."

Gage's attention flashes back to me. "That true?"

I can't stop myself from rolling my eyes. "That doesn't mean I was in there playing Boy Scout. I have no idea how it happened." My voice rises as the reality of the trouble I could be in hits me. *Now entering freak-out mode.* "I wasn't even home!"

"She's been harassing me for weeks to break her lease," Ronnie cuts in, nodding with each lying word.

"That means I thought scorching the place was a better option?" I wave my finger in Ronnie's direction. "In case you failed to notice, *liar,* my stuff went up in flames, too. It would've been simpler for me to write a check for a few thousand bucks than lose all my belongings."

Gage shoots a glance toward his high school best friend/I'm assuming now partner, Kyle. "I think she's guilty. You?"

Kyle smiles in entertainment and narrows his green eyes at me. He's the co-chair of my hate club. "I concur with you, partner."

"I'll take her in for questioning," Gage tells them. "I know from personal experience that she enjoys seeing shit go up in flames." His attention turns back to me, giving me a warning that I'm in for a ride from hell. "She's an expert on obliterating shit."

Ronnie rubs his hands together. "Appreciate it, Officer."

"You've got to be kidding me," I shout when Gage pulls out the stainless steel handcuffs from the back of his belt. "Handcuffs, really?"

His amusement is gone, replaced with the look of a cold and calculated man.

He takes a step closer. "Turn around. I'll read you your rights."

I scoff, "Not a chance in hell."

He looks to Kyle in question. "Should we add failure to cooperate to her charges?"

"Damn you," I hiss, my stomach rolling while I do as I was told. The cuffs are cold when Gage slowly tightens them around my wrists. "I take it, you still hate me."

Shivers run down my spine when the solid wall of his chest brushes against my back, and he leans in to whisper in my ear, his lips sliding along the lobe, "I'll hate you until the day I die." He grips my shoulder, turns me around, and jerks me forward. "Kyle, take the landlord's statement. I'd better split, so we can get this pyro to the station before she does any more damage."

Kyle chuckles while saluting him. "Sure thing."

I throw out every curse word known to man and nearly trip over my own feet while he leads me to his car. "You sure you can handle being alone with such a criminal?"

A harsh laugh leaves his throat. "Oh, I can handle you just fine, sweetheart."

Everyone's attention stays on me during my profanity show. Gage opens the back door with one hand, pushes my head down for me to slide in without bumping it, and slams the door in my face. I scope out my audience, their phones recording my episode, and shift around in a seat that had to have been made from the same material as my childhood Barbie dream car.

"I hate you," I hiss when Gage slides into the driver's side.

He starts the car. "Good. I fucking despise you."

I slump back against the seat. "You seriously don't believe I started that fire, do you?"

"Intentionally, no. Although, knowing your crazy ass, it wouldn't surprise me."

"Then, why am I back here? At least let me ride passenger."

"Nah, it's more enjoyable, watching you throw your tantrum through the rearview mirror."

I fight with the handcuffs. "This is abuse of power! I'll be filing a complaint."

"Don't get me started on *abuse of power,* sweetheart."

I sigh and shut my mouth. An argument is what he wants. There will be no falling victim to his game.

Yeah, that'll really one-up him, Lauren. He won the jackpot in ex revenge today.

Silence takes over the ride, and my back stiffens when I notice we're heading out of town.

"Wait ... where are we going?"

"Taking the scenic route."

The fuck?

"Let me out, okay? You can hate me, stick pins in the voodoo doll I'm sure you have of me, toilet-paper my new house when I'm no longer homeless. My mom will flip her shit if you turn me in. I could lose my job!" I slam the cuffs against the seat while he ignores me. "Let me out of here, Gage Perry, or so help me God, you'll regret it. Don't think I won't make it my life's mission to make yours a living hell."

I yelp, and my body slams against the steel cage in front of me when he swerves to the shoulder of the road and brakes to a hard stop.

"You want out?" He kills the engine and steps out of the car.

Seconds later, my door flies open, nearly causing me to fall out of my seat.

"Then, get out."

I scoot my butt against the seat and slowly slide out. I square my shoulders up as soon as my feet hit the pavement and shake away the loose hair from my face, blowing at the strands that aren't cooperating. The handcuffs clink when I spin around and hold my arms up behind me.

"Cuffs need to be taken off," I tell him.

Silence.

I peek over my shoulder at his failure to move. His cold stare is replaced with amusement.

"Not happening, sweetheart." He tips his head toward the street. "Enjoy your day, pyro."

"What?" My voice rises when I scan my surroundings, and he walks back to the car. "It's twenty minutes back to town *in a car*. It'll take at least an hour to get back on foot!"

He pauses, his hand clutching the door handle, and fixes his gaze on me. "I did what was asked of me—to let you out. Enjoy your walk. Maybe it'll give you time to think about your actions."

I shake my arms in a sad attempt to rid myself of the cuffs, like I'm damn Houdini. He slips into the cruiser, and the engine starts.

Screw him.

I won't allow him the pleasure of witnessing me upset. My breakdown will have to wait until he's out of sight. The car stays running in neutral while I straighten my shoulders and walk along the side of the road.

It's no easy feat, walking with your hands clasped behind your back. Pride kicks inside me when I pass the cruiser, and shock fills his face at the realization that I'm not playing his games. His not pulling away confirms his plan wasn't to leave me stranded. It was a ploy to hear me beg.

The passenger window rolls down.

"All right, fuck, I feel bad," he yells. "Get in."

I walk faster and force myself not to look back when he steers onto the street. "Fuck off."

For a brief moment, the thought that he might leave me stranded passes my mind. The old Gage would've never done something so cruel, but this isn't the man I loved in high school. This man is different, someone I recognize yet don't at the same time.

Instead of speeding off, he cruises beside me, the car not going any faster than what I'm walking. Gage might hate me, but he'd never leave me in a possibly dangerous situation. He's been that way for as long as I can remember. It's one of the reasons I fell in love with him.

"Jesus, I forgot how goddamn stubborn you are," he shouts.

"And I forgot how big of an asshole you are. Good thing I dumped your ass."

An ache rocks through my chest in regret as soon as the words leave my mouth. I look over at him, knowing they hit him harder as he goes stiff in his seat, memories and anger flashing across his face as a reminder of how much I hurt him.

It was a low blow.

Gage hadn't done anything wrong when I broke up with him. I didn't leave because I was unhappy. His begging for me to stay broke my heart as much as it did his, but my reason for walking away wasn't for me. Rather, it was for someone else. I ignored his calls for weeks and had my roommate lie when he'd show up at my dorm room to talk to me.

After three weeks of rejection, he left me a voice mail telling me to never contact him again. I listened to it on repeat, hot tears rolling down my swollen cheeks, and the severity of what I'd done clung to my heart with regret.

"Get in the fucking car, Lauren."

I don't stop. "No."

We go back and forth with our argument, and it's not until I notice the bottom of my feet are as black as the soot covering my apartment that I stop. No way in hell can I take more of this walk in my flip-flops *and* make it to the hospital in time for my shift. I also have to find a family member to let me crash with them until I get a new place to live.

"Fine," I groan. "But, before I do, I want to make it clear that I'm doing it only so I don't lose my job."

He doesn't say a word when he pulls over to stop. The door slams behind him, and he circles around the car. His touch is cold when he releases me from the cuffs, and I shake my hands out, a sigh of relief leaving my chest. *I shall never take these babies for granted again.* No conversation is made while I settle into the seat or when he drives back into town.

It's been years since I've seen him. In the past, there were no moments of silence between us. We were loud, rambunctious, lovesick teens who never shut up or got enough of each other.

"Where do I drop you off?" he finally asks.

I peek at him in confusion. "You're not taking me to the station?"

"Fuck no." A hint of a smile plays at his lips. "It'd be too much paperwork, and I hate paperwork."

I perk up in my seat in victory.

"You'd better spit out an address and calm your arrogant ass down before I change my mind," he warns at my response.

"My parents." I raise a brow when he snorts. "What?"

"I'm back in town. You're staying at your parents'. A bit of nostalgia is creeping in."

The same feeling is bursting through me. "I guess so."

I want to punch him in the face.

I want to apologize.

I want him to know I regret what I did and that my heart beats only for him.

But it wouldn't change anything.

No amount of apologizing will reverse the betrayal and pain I caused.

TWO

Gage

I DON'T FIND enjoyment in arresting people.

That changed when it was the woman who smashed my heart with her small fists. It changed when it was the person I'd thought I'd spend the rest of my life with who bailed on me. I grew up loving Lauren Barnes, and so help me God, I'll die loving her.

I'd been careful since arriving back in our hometown, Blue Beech, Iowa, avoiding all the places Kyle said she frequented. In the back of my mind, there was the reality that, eventually, we were bound to cross paths. This town is small, and the gossip is heavy.

Although I couldn't have planned our reunion better myself. It stung, seeing her, touching her, and when I pulled out the handcuffs, I wished I could've been using them for a different reason—preferably in my bed.

She'd ruined the chance of that happening years ago. Lauren made her choice to leave me, and my life has been shit since.

I struggle with myself on what to feel about today's events. Relief clung to me when she told me to drop her off at her parents', not a boyfriend's. No diamond graced her finger. It was the first thing I'd looked for when handcuffing her. I won't lie. I feel some satisfaction in knowing she hasn't found love again either.

I rub away the knot of tension in my neck.

Why do I give a fuck?

She's not why I came home. It was for my dad … for my fucking sanity … so I wouldn't charge into the Department of Corrections every time I got drunk and demand Missy pay more for what she did.

My keys hit the kitchen table next to the stack of decade-old *Time* magazines. My father is seated next to them with a newspaper in his hands, and his oxygen tank is at his side.

"She knows I'm back," I say.

He folds up the paper and places it in front of him. "How'd it go?"

"I arrested her."

His sunken chestnut-colored eyes study me before he responds, "Son, I understand you're upset with her, but was that necessary?"

"Absolutely. She set a building on fire."

He rubs his chin. "I think we both know you weren't doing it for the safety of the town."

"Of course I did it for that reason." I cock my head. "I can't say it didn't give me pleasure though."

He sighs. "Forgiveness is a brave thing, son. A man becomes strongest when he bears no malice."

"I don't want your words of wisdom. I'm not ready to bury that hatchet."

———

"JESUS CHRIST, Dad, what the hell are you doing up there?"

My head is tilted back to gain a better view of him on the roof, tinkering with the satellite dish. It looks almost comical when I eye his oxygen tank following behind him while he moves the dish in different angles and directions.

He grunts and catches a deep breath before answering, "Dang satellite dish is actin' up again. I've already missed fifteen minutes of the game."

"And you thought it was a killer idea to climb on the roof with your tank?"

How he managed to pull it off is beyond me.

He shoots me a stony stare—the same one he gives when I stop him from doing physical work that is too hard on his body. "I'm a grown man who's climbed atop rooftops and buildings taller than this. I'm capable of fixing stuff myself."

Accepting his limitations on doing manual labor has been difficult for him. His health is deteriorating, and his chronic obstructive pulmonary disease is progressing. The COPD makes it harder for him to complete his daily tasks.

"You're a *sick* grown man," I correct, hating that I have to remind him and hoping he doesn't see it as an insult. I stalk over to his old, rusted ladder settled on the side of the house and wiggle it, double-checking it's at least halfway steady before I climb up. "Let me help you down, and then I'll take a look at it."

He stomps my way, wheeling his tank behind him, and stumbles in front of me when I make it to the top of the ladder. "I got this. Stop treating me as if I were a child!"

I grit my teeth. "No, you don't *got it*. Now, let me help you down."

He teeters forward at the same time I reach for him. My arms fly out in an attempt to catch him, but it only sends me down with him, taking the ladder with us.

THREE

Lauren

"NURSE BARNES, treatment room three, patient fell off a ladder," Natasha, the nursing director, tells me when I stroll into the ER after my brief dinner break.

The hospital has been short-staffed since I started three years ago, and I work more than I sleep. Not that I mind it, especially now, given that I'm homeless and I need all the overtime hours I can manage.

"How serious?" I ask.

Ladder falls can range from minor to pretty damn ugly. You can walk in to find a patient suffering from a broken arm or one needing facial reconstruction surgery.

Welcome to ER life. You never know what will be thrown at you each shift.

"Nothing too gory," she answers. "I'm guessing only stitches. Guy was helping his dad off a roof. Dad fell and took them both down. Melanie is treating the father." She grins and elbows me in the side, her voice changing into an annoying bubbly tone. "I stuck you with the son in case you're in need of some delicious eye candy … or a date."

I smack her shoulder. "You know it's frowned upon to date patients." *Not that I ever would, even if it wasn't.*

She winks. "I won't tell if you don't."

"Stitches. Got it." Stitches are easy-peasy.

"Ask him if he wants to grab some drinks with those stitches!" she yells to my back when I turn around.

I shake my head, blowing off her comment, and knock on the exam room door before entering. Work has taken my mind off Gage's being back, and giving people stitches is relaxing to me, like yoga is to some people. I got certified in suturing instead of learning how to meditate.

The voice on the other side yells for me to come in, and I don't hesitate before turning the handle and walking in, my self-proclaimed perfect nurse smile on my face.

My smile falls as I shuffle back. The door slams behind me, and I steady myself against it.

You've got to be kidding me! Is the universe against me this week?

Gage's shoulders stiffen when we make eye contact. I rub my forehead, my eyes catching his, and take a calming breath. A sleeve on his white cotton tee is ripped, and blood, grass, and mud stains decorate the front of it. His hand holds bloody gauze to his cheek, and minor cuts and scrapes are spread along his face and chin.

"For someone who despises my existence, you sure are going to extreme measures to see me again," I comment before taking a deep breath and moving away from the door to grab a pair of latex gloves.

"Funny," he mutters. "Trust me, it was not in my plan to see you today ... or ever if I could have it my way." A smirk hits his bloody lip. "I won't say I can complain about the view though. Sexy nurse and patient is my favorite porn. Shall we give it a go?"

I snap on the gloves and force a laugh while moving further into the room, which suddenly feels much smaller. "You know, this is your Karma for what you pulled yesterday. Don't count on any friendly bedside manner." I give him an innocent look. "It's tragic that I can't have fun and stick you with a giant needle or shove something up your ass. Would've made my day."

It looks like he's fighting pain to give me a challenging look. The dude is here for medical attention, and I'm giving him shit. *Not cool.*

This is my job, and I have to do it right, no matter our history ... or the fact that I'm terrified what emotions will be drawn out when I touch him.

He winces when I carefully pull his hand away from the gauze and peel the material back. I inhale the masculine scent of him—aftershave mixed with the outdoors. Like every muscle in his body, his scent has matured. His breathing quickens while I inspect the wound.

It's small. Not a deep laceration. Natasha was right about the stitches. It'll be an easy cut to close up.

"Wishing you could stick something up my ass doesn't sound like good bedside manner, Nurse Barnes. Doubt your boss will be happy, hearing you're discriminating against patients. Public service patients to be exact," he comments as I move away to gather my supplies.

"This might hurt," I say when I'm finished and back at his side.

"Shit!" he says through clenched teeth when I start to irrigate his wound. "You could've warned a dude."

"I did."

He flinches, a slight hiss escaping his lips, while I work. I take my time, making sure the wound is meticulously irrigated, and clean the dried blood off the scruff of his cheek.

"I'm discriminating against assholes, by the way," I finally correct, my attention on his cheek. "Not patients."

He snorts. "I'd love to see your boss's face when you use that as your argument. It's not smart to get canned from work when you're homeless."

I shrug. "He won't do anything."

His brow lifts when I pull away and start throwing my trash away. "You seem too cocky, Nurse Barnes. You sleeping with your boss?"

"Something along those lines. Fucking him. Sleeping with him after." I pat his arm. "Tattle all you want. It'll only make him want to screw me more. I wouldn't be surprised if he drags me to the supply closet and gives it to me there."

His jaw clenches.

Exactly my goal.

So what if it's not true?

"Your dad okay?" I ask.

We're in need of a subject change before he continues his interrogation and catches me in my lie.

He clears his throat before nodding. "He's in the next room. Luckily, we fell in the grass. I took the biggest hit, and even though he seemed fine, I insisted he get checked out."

The sharpness of his voice guts me. My words hit him harder than his physical wound. Our banter dissolves, and he doesn't give me another look while he lies back, and I start dragging out my supplies. A knock on the door causes us both to look at it, and I grin at the sight of Jay walking in looking handsome in his blue scrubs. Jay isn't only a great doctor. He's also great looking.

Hopefully, he doesn't catch on to who this patient is.

"Hi, Gage," Jay says, walking into the room and extending his hand. "I'm Dr. Whitman. I heard you and your father had a fall."

Gage looks at Jay with uncertainty before shaking it, and I wish I could read his mind. "Could've been worse."

Jay snaps on gloves, and I scoot out of his way to give him room to inspect Gage. I bite into my lip at the sight of Gage's jaw clenching when Jay touches his cheek.

"Cut isn't too deep, big guy," Jay says, glancing back at me. "Good job on irrigation, and thank you for having the anesthetic ready. I'll give it to him and let you fix him up."

I nod. "Sounds good."

Jay goes to his tray and grabs the needle. "This might hurt for a second, but it'll feel much better when I'm done, trust me."

Gage grits his teeth but doesn't let out a sound when the small needle hits the opening in his cheek.

Jay hands me the needle to dispose of and pats Gage's shoulder. "Nurse Barnes will do your sutures." He holds his hand up and wiggles his fingers. "She has magic fingers. I'll be sure to check up on you when she's finished and get you set to discharge. If you need anything, don't hesitate to ask Nurse Barnes or me."

Gage nods. "Thanks, Doc."

Jay's attention turns to me while he takes off his gloves and tosses them in the trash. "I'll see you tomorrow night?"

I smile. Jay is officially my favorite person. "Wouldn't miss it. Clayton's, right?"

He nods. "Seven o'clock."

"See you at seven." I run a hand over my mouth in a *zipping* motion. "And my lips are sealed, so no one finds out."

Jay snaps his fingers and points my way. "And that's why you're my favorite woman."

He shoots Gage a final look before leaving the room. Gage's breathing turns heavy when I move back to his side, and his hands are balled into fists. He seems in more pain than he was before we treated him.

"Was that not enough to numb you?" I ask, tilting my head toward the door. "I can ask the doctor to give you another shot or maybe some pain medicine."

"No need to do that," he snaps, not looking at me.

"Okay," I draw out. "Let me know if you change your mind. It's no problem."

The air seems thicker, and his anger over my supposed affair with my boss is stronger. I sigh while grabbing the needle holder and move next to him. He doesn't say anything when I help him lie on his back, and the room is quiet while I start stitching him up.

It's the first time I've treated someone I've been intimate with.

Not to mention, it's Gage.

My Gage.

Well ... used to be my Gage.

I should've walked out and told Natasha I couldn't treat him.

Conflict of interest.

It is a conflict when the patient hates you, right?

I'm almost finished when he finally speaks, "That your husband?"

"Nope," I answer.

"He was wearing a wedding ring."

I look down at him with a gentle smile. "Was he? I've never noticed."

If he could pull away from me, he would.

Disgust covers his features. "Never thought you'd go so low as to sleep with a married man."

I don't answer him as I tie the last suture. Nor do I when I inspect my work or when I clean up my mess and help him up. It doesn't come until I throw my gloves away and grab the door handle.

"I wish you a speedy recovery, Officer."

I shut the door and stalk to the restroom, controlling my tears until I hit the first stall and let them out.

FOUR

Gage

MY NERVES ARE SHOT to hell, and I hold myself back from busting out of this exam room and doing something stupid, like confronting the bastard doctor using Lauren as a side chick.

I tip my head back.

Dude was wearing a wedding ring.

She wasn't.

She's a mistress.

Where the fuck is the girl I fell in love with years ago?

She's gone. That much is clear.

My attention goes to the door at the sound of a knock. As bad as I don't want to, I hope it's Lauren on the other end.

My wish isn't answered.

My nostrils flare when Dr. Whitman walks back into the room.

Fucking douche bag.

Dude looks smart, rich, like he has his life in order, except for the whole cheating thing, and I bite back the urge to demand he get out of my face. Problem is, I'd look like a dumbass.

Lauren is no longer mine. She can do whatever ... or whoever ... she wants.

That doesn't mean I'll be happy about it, nor will I be happy for her.

He smiles like he isn't fucking the girl who owns my heart. "Nurse Barnes said she stitched you up. You got lucky, having the nurse with the best hands, although I'm surprised at how fast she was with you. She might've broken a record."

"I'm sure she's a busy woman," I grumble. I want to rip this fucker's arm off.

He inspects my stitches and removes his gloves. "That she is. We see a fair number of patients for a smaller hospital. I'll send the discharge nurse in. Hopefully, I'll have you and your father out before the game comes on."

I can't help but laugh. "He tell you he was leaving if you didn't?"

"Sure did."

I stop him when he turns around to leave. "You married, Dr. Whitman?"

He twists his ring with a smile filled with memories. "Yes."

Don't kill him. Don't kill him.

"Nurse Barnes is a lucky woman."

He flinches. "Excuse me?"

"Nurse Barnes is your wife, correct?"

He cocks his head to the side. "Mr. Perry, I'm not sure where you got the idea." His eyes widen when I crack my knuckles. "I'm confused on where you're going with this."

"How would *your wife* feel about you having an affair with a nurse? Treating Lauren as a side piece to get your rocks off while going through some midlife crisis?"

He shakes his head while processing what I said. "Lauren is not my wife, nor is she my side piece. I'm very happily married to my husband, Alec. Alec is one of Lauren's closest friends. The invite was to my husband's surprise birthday dinner. I apologize if any behavior led you to believe there was an inappropriate relationship between us."

I'm rarely lost for words. This is one of those moments.

Fuck. Lauren's lie made me look like an idiot.

Dr. Whitman stares at me for a moment, blinking. "You're *him*."

I raise a brow.

"You're Gage. Lauren's Gage."

What? Has she talked about me?

"No. I'm just Gage."

"Not from what I've heard." He laughs. "Alcohol makes Lauren talkative."

"Can't argue with that."

Her nickname was Motor Mouth in high school.

"I wish you a speedy recovery, Mr. Perry." He lowers his voice. "If you are the Gage she talks about during our weekly happy hour, don't let her fool you. She still loves you."

My nails bite into my palms. "You don't turn your back on people you love."

He tips his head down. "All right then. The discharge nurse will be here soon with your prescriptions. Don't hesitate if you have any additional questions for me."

"Thanks."

I pull out my phone when he leaves.

Me: Do you have plans tomorrow night?

It beeps with a reply seconds later.

Phoebe: I'm free all night.

Fuck. Lauren had better not bail tomorrow night. Phoebe is a stage-five clinger. I'm risking my privacy for revenge.

Me: Dinner at Clayton's at 7:00?

Phoebe: Pick me up at 6:30. I'll bring an overnight bag.

I stop myself from telling her not to bother. She can't bail on my ass before I succeed in calling Lauren out on her lie.

I go check on my dad after I'm discharged. He's okay. No stitches or broken bones. On the way home, he will be receiving an earful from me about not doing stupid shit.

FIVE

Lauren

I NEED A DRINK.

Multiple drinks. Stat.

Sleep wasn't my friend last night—for an array of reasons. The first being that I was sleeping in my childhood bedroom, the second because of all the thoughts of what I'd done with Gage in said bedroom after he snuck through my window in high school, and the third was worrying about when I'd see him next.

In conclusion, the culprit of my insomnia was Gage Perry.

The hostess weaves through white-clothed tables while leading me, gift bag in tow, to Jay and Alec. Clayton's is an upscale restaurant complete with candlelit dinners, to-die-for shrimp cocktails, and expensive wine lists. The men set their drinks down when they spot me and wrap me into tight hugs before giving me cheek kisses.

Jay pulls my chair out, and I take the seat next to Alec, who's sporting a suit complete with a *Birthday Boy* pin clipped to it, his highlighted hair pulled back into a man bun. Either this wasn't a surprise dinner or Jay spilled the beans. I'm guessing the latter. It isn't easy to keep secrets from his husband.

Jay straightens out his suit before settling back in his chair and throws me a brooding look, motioning my way with his glass of red wine. "You're lucky the hospital was a madhouse yesterday. Otherwise, you would've received quite the interrogation."

"What are you talking about?" I ask, looking around for our waiter.

"Is there a reason you told the man you stitched up yesterday that you were my mistress?"

Oh shit.

Of course Gage questioned Jay about my hinting at having an affair with him.

"What?" Alec cuts in, glancing over at Jay with humor. "You switching teams again? I thought your experimenting days were over?"

I sigh. "He was hitting on me. It was the first thought that came to mind. Sorry."

Alec squeezes my shoulder. "Oh, honey, you can use my husband as an excuse anytime that happens."

"Nuh-uh. Don't you *oh, honey* her," Jay says, causing Alec's attention to flicker between his husband and me. "She's lying." His coffee-colored eyes level on me. "It's him, isn't it? He's back."

I gulp, nodding. "Unfortunately."

"Is it unfortunate?" he counters. "You don't think it could be fate? I watched him with you. I saw the lust, the love. He barely took his eyes off you, and I'm positive he wanted to murder me after you told him we were sleeping together. Why don't you explain why you did what you did, and you two could reconnect? If nothing else, be friends."

"He hates my guts," I answer. "There's nothing I can say or do that will restore what we had."

"Whoa, whoa," Alec draws out, holding his hands up. "I'mma need someone to catch me up. I'm out of the loop here, and you know it's always critical I am in the center of the loop."

I met Alec during our residency at the hospital after graduating from nursing school. We instantly clicked. Jay was our attending doctor. He and Alec hooked up one night after a holiday party and have been inseparable since. When the news broke that they were dating, Alec was moved to geriatrics, and Jay received two weeks of my silent treatment for taking my hospital bestie from me.

Spending time with them made me trust in love again. They ignore the snide comments and dirty looks and relentlessly love each other. Jay is the sensible one. Alec is the overdramatic. They balance each other out in a world where it's necessary.

"Gage," I breathe out. "He's back in town."

"Gage?" Alec shrieks, causing a few patrons to look at us. "*The* Gage?"

"The one and only."

"Hot damn, sweetie. Things are about to turn complicated for you." He squirms in his chair, and this gossip will mean more to him than the expensive birthday present I bought. "Now, you'd better tell me every detail."

He doesn't get any details until the waitress comes and takes my lemon drop martini order.

"ISN'T THIS QUITE THE SURPRISE?"

The sharp, familiar, and masculine voice startles me.

Chills shoot up my back as I jerk around to confront Gage. He's only a few feet away from me in the dimly lit and narrow hallway that leads to the restrooms, yet it seems like he's looming over me.

I don't respond right away. Instead, I give him the silent treatment while roaming my eyes down his six-foot-three frame of gorgeousness. Just because I hate the man doesn't mean he doesn't make my panties wet. Gage is and always will be the most attractive man I've ever seen.

I grew up with him sporting basketball jerseys and athletic shorts. This dressed-up version might compete with the sight of him in his police uniform. I've been pleasuring myself at night with the memory of how desirable he looked in it. Gage sporting black jeans and a sleek, tight gray button-up will sponsor tonight's self-given orgasm.

"Keep eye-fucking me, babe. It's satisfying, knowing I'm something you can no longer have."

His comment smacks me out of my eye-fucking trance, and I'm positive that this isn't a surprise to him. Gage is back, and it seems he's taken a new hobby of making my life miserable.

"What are you doing here?" I snap.

He smirks while strolling closer into my space. "Enjoying dinner. Word is, this place is the best for wining and dining. According to Yelp, the chance of getting laid after you leave makes it five-star worthy. What are *you* doing here?"

My hands go to my hips in frustration. "Are you following me?"

"Don't flatter yourself, babe. I'm on a date."

This must mean war. He brought a date here, knowing I'd see them.

I stay quiet while taking in calming breaths. His goal was to bring out the jealousy in me. That won't be happening. I'll easily drown out that jealousy with more martinis.

"Funny, you never mentioned coming here when Jay and I talked about it yesterday."

"Jay? You mean, the man you're 'fucking'?" He uses his fingers to form air quotes around the last word. "I noticed him when I walked in. Your man seemed preoccupied with someone else. Unless you're into some harem shit with mid-husbands, I say you're lying. Is that a new trait of yours now, too? You a filthy liar?"

"Uh-uh. I'm not doing this with you tonight." I've only had one drink. A conversation like this calls for more. "Enjoy your date."

I go to walk around him but am stopped when he snags my elbow and pushes my back against the wall, out of the light.

His cool, minty breath hits my lips when he presses into me. "What? You don't like getting called out on your lies? Why'd you want me to think you were sleeping with another man?" His fingers run down my sides, and he stops at the base of my hips, grinning.

I look down, shivering, and let out a light moan.

He squeezes my hips and rocks into me. "Now, answer my question honestly. You fucking anyone? Giving someone else your sweet pussy now since you no longer want my dick?"

I close my eyes, fighting myself not to move into his touch, not to thrust against his body to feel if he's as turned on as I am. The rise and fall of his chest hits mine. His hand inches up, moving along the bottom curve of my breast, and I'm using all my power not to rock against him.

"That's ..." I pause to catch my breath, my voice cracking. "That's none of your business."

He torturously teases me, his finger feathering over my nipple, causing it to stand at full attention. "It's a simple question, *Dyson.* Are you fucking someone, or did you say it to make me jealous?"

Dyson.

His old nickname for me.

An inside joke he started my sophomore year as a result of me giving him a massive neck hickey. He blamed it on the vacuum when his mom questioned him.

Hearing him call me that stills my breath as a rush of memories hits me.

I don't push him away even though I should. Instead, I'm aching for his touch while silently begging for more of him as my lips lightly brush against his.

"Would you be jealous?" I ask.

He smirks. "No fucking way, baby."

An embarrassing moan of desperation runs through me when his hand moves, and he pulls away.

His smirk curves into a menacing smile. "You have your fun. I'll have mine."

I straighten out my dress and work to control my breathing. "Don't you worry, *baby.* I have plenty of fun. Just ask Derrick."

The hell? Why am I lying again?

This is not a common trait of mine, and I have no idea where it's coming from.

"Wow." He takes another step back, bringing him more into the light, and is now looking at me in disgust, his hands in the air, as if he's pushing me away from a distance.

All I see next is his back as he walks away, shaking his head. It takes me a minute to compose myself, and when I walk back to our table, I scan the room for him. Nothing.

Did he leave?

I mindlessly pick at my dinner when it arrives and listen to Alec ramble about the Caribbean cruise they're taking to celebrate their anniversary.

It's not until dessert is dropped off that I spot him. Unlike me, he wasn't lying about having a date. Even though all I see is her bare back and long strawberry-blonde locks, I know it's Phoebe Jedson. The familiarity is a consequence of living in a small town.

I tighten my fingers across the stem of my glass and stare at him until his eyes meet mine.

I hate you, I mouth.

I'm glad, is his reply.

I throw him the dirtiest look I can when he tilts his glass my way.

The remainder of dessert is spent with our never-ending contact. His attention isn't on Phoebe, and I only nod, feeling like a shitty friend while mindlessly hearing Alec's stories from geriatrics. I stop the waitress when she passes and order another drink.

Ten minutes later, I order another as my second dessert.

Drunken Lauren will numb all thoughts of how delicious Gage looks tonight.

———

ALEC GRABS my arm and hooks his through it, keeping me stable from falling in my heels and meeting the ground while we walk out of the restaurant to the valet. "We're driving you home."

My words leave my mouth in a slur as I shake my head. "It's *waaay* out of your way, *aaand* it's your birthday. I'll call a cab, *oookaaay?*"

"Then, we'll wait with you until it arrives," Jay tells me, wrapping his arm around my shoulders.

God, what would I do without them?

"I can take her home."

I cringe, and my back goes straight at the sound of Gage's voice. "It's on my way."

Jay's attention darts between Gage and me until he finally settles his attention on the jerk from my past. "Whoa, dude, I don't want to know why you're here." His face fills with protectiveness, giving Gage a warning not to mess with me in his and Alec's presence.

Alec steps in. "While we appreciate the offer, I won't allow my best friend to catch a ride with some stranger. I've watched way too many murder mysteries, buddy."

Gage chuckles. "Trust me, we're not strangers."

I lose Jay's hold when he slaps Alec's back and gestures to Gage.

"Oh ... boy," Alec draws out. "I thought I wanted to be in the loop, but this loop seems pretty darn serious at the moment." He grabs my shoulders and brings me to him. "Is this the ex?"

"Sure is," I mutter before straightening myself up. "I'm taking a cab home." I stumble while attempting to pull my phone from my clutch.

Gage comes to my side at the same time Alec helps me. "Let me take her home. I promise I'll take care of her."

I snort. "Last time we went for a ride, I was handcuffed, and you tried to leave me stranded."

"Did I though?" he fires back.

I open my mouth to continue our spat but slam it shut at the sight of Phoebe coming to his side.

"Sorry, my makeup was in need of a serious touch-up," she comments, sliding a compact back into her bag before running her hand over his arm. She stops midway when her eyes land on me. "Lauren ... it's, uh ... nice to see you."

No, it isn't.

Don't get me wrong. I have no ill will toward Phoebe. We were never close in high school. Still aren't. Gage is a single man, who most likely asked her out. Slut-shaming isn't my game.

Gage ignores Phoebe and keeps his attention on me. "It'll take a cab at least fifteen minutes to make it here and cost you a hundo in fare. As you're someone who's now homeless, I doubt you want to throw your money away like that."

"I'm not homeless," I argue.

"Oh, really? You move back into your charred apartment?"

All eyes are on me, and I suddenly feel like a giant, drunken pain in the ass.

"Fine," I say around a groan. "But I still hate you."

"And the feeling is *still* mutual." A few seconds of silence pass until Gage points to the valet jumping out of an oversized, four-door black truck. "This is me."

Gage opens the passenger door, gesturing for me to slide in, and Jay goes to help me before I stop him.

"Shouldn't your date take the front?" I ask, more dramatic than necessary. "I'm sure you showed her a terrible time."

"Doubt she'll be saying that by the end of the night," Gage answers, winking.

I snarl while opening the back door and practically face-dive into the seat. Alec and Jay tell me good-bye at the same time Phoebe takes the passenger seat. Gage jumps in and tosses a water bottle back to me. I struggle to twist the lid off and gulp it down when I do.

We're five minutes into the ride when Phoebe clears her throat. "Before this becomes weird, is there something going on between you two? I'm not interested in some weird love-triangle shit."

"There is absolutely nothing going on between us," I blurt out, gaining control of my voice and finishing without any slurs. "You two have your fun. Hell, go ahead and jack him off up there if you want."

But, really, don't.

I'll jump into moving traffic if they even hold hands up there.

Gage snorts and turns on the radio instead of answering her or entertaining me. I collapse onto my back across the expansive rear seat and rest my head, knowing damn well, in the morning, I'll regret both drinking so much and taking this ride.

"I'm guessing you're dropping me off?" Phoebe asks when we make it into town.

"Probably the right thing to do," he answers.

"Thank you for dinner." She turns in her seat to look back at me when Gage parks in her driveway. "Have a good night, Lauren."

Since my thoughts are delayed at the moment, she's already out of the truck by the time I start to reply. Gage, like the stupid fucking gentleman he is, walks her to the door. And me, like the fucking stalker I am, rise up onto my knees to watch their exchange.

They hug.

Eh.

He kisses her cheek.

Gag me.

I wait for him to kiss her lips next, but no action takes place.

Thank God.

He doesn't walk away until she shuts the door behind her.

Meanwhile, I'm snooping around the truck before he comes back. It's clean. No evidence of anything interesting. New tan leather seats, a flat screen in the dash filled with countless music options, and a backseat equipped with enough room to keep my drunk butt comfortable. Although awkward, the ride is cozier than what a cab would've been.

Gage slams the door shut and turns down the radio before reversing out of the drive. "By the way, thanks for running my date off."

Is he serious?

I sit up in the back seat. "Are you kidding me? In case you forgot, *you're* the one who ruined my night off work *and* interrupted my friend's birthday. If you hadn't decided to be Creeper McCreeperson and show up where you knew I'd be, you would've gotten laid, and I wouldn't have had to experience a massive hangover tomorrow." I fold my arms over my chest. "And maybe *I* would've gotten laid."

"By who? The doctor married to your friend … or was there

another fake boyfriend I didn't see? Perhaps he was imaginary, like the fictional others you've tried to make me jealous of."

"Screw you," I hiss.

"Been there. Done that. Won't do it again. Now, which homeless shelter would you like me to drop you off at?"

Even though he can't see me, I throw him a glare. "Take me to my parents', please and thank you, or do you plan on dropping me off in the middle of nowhere again for shits and giggles?"

"I'm not dropping you off at your parents' while you're drunk off your ass."

I pull out my phone to text my mom and ask her to keep the door unlocked. "I have nowhere else to go, so sure looks like you are. You know them. They'll file a missing persons report if I don't come home. The people at the restaurant will say I went home with you, and your coworkers will be arresting *you* this time." I smile. "If I were to turn up dead, I'd love nothing more than for you to go prison for it."

He swerves over to the side of the road, causing me to fall back against the seat, and I throw my arms up.

"Oh Jesus Christ, here we go again."

The door flies open. He jumps out and opens the back door. My phone is plucked from my hand before I open the text app. As if it's not a big deal, he hops back into the truck and pulls back onto the road like he doesn't realize what invasion of privacy means.

"Excuse me? Rude much?" I mutter, making a grab for it, but he stops me.

"What was your birthday friend's name again? Your supposed mid-husband?"

"Fuck off," I snarl.

"Interesting name. I wish my parents were that creative." He snaps his fingers. "Alec, right?"

I don't answer.

"I'll take your silence as a, *Yes, Gage, that's it.*" He starts typing on my phone. "All your parents will know about tonight is that you were too tired to drive home and are crashing at their place."

That's what I should've done in the first place. "One problem with that. Where am I supposed to sleep?"

He doesn't say anything.

"Oh no, don't you think about it, Gage."

"You can take the loft above the garage."

"Not fucking happening." A shelter is sounding pretty delightful right about now. "I'm not spending the night with you. I can't take the chance of you smothering me in my sleep."

"How do you know I won't worry about you driving a stake through my heart again?" He glances back at me. "I'll sleep in the main house."

"Why are you treating me so nice? Is this the whole *keep your friends close and your enemies closer* type crap?"

"To be honest, I have no idea."

"You have no idea why you're being nice … or if I'm your enemy?"

"Both."

Memories knot through my thoughts when he pulls into his drive. The ranch home hasn't changed. My attention goes to the detached garage with the loft above it, which was built when Gage was in middle school. His dad gave him permission to stay in there when he turned sixteen, and it's where we spent most of our time together.

Surprisingly, I don't push him away when he helps me out of the truck, and I don't give him shit while he helps me up the stairs.

Endless questions crackle through my inebriated mind.

Why is he back? Where has he been?

We're strangers now.

I catch the scent of him when we walk in, and I look around when the light flips on. The alcohol has taken its toll on me, and I keep quiet while moving to the couch from my past. Nothing in this room has changed.

Gage moves in front of me when I collapse onto the couch and holds out his hand. "Your legs not functional enough to walk to the bed?"

I swat it away. "Under no circumstances am I sleeping in that bed." It's where I lost my virginity. "I'll sleep here."

He drops his hand and takes a step back. "The couch it is."

A blanket and pillow are tossed to me, and I close my eyes the moment my head hits the pillow. I fake sleep while hearing him move around the loft, and my breathing shudders when I sense his presence next to me.

I tense when he runs a hand over my cheek.

"Why did you hurt me?" he whispers. "Why'd you leave?"

I stay silent and hope he doesn't notice the goose bumps crawling over my skin, and a tear slips down my cheek when he steps away. The light shuts off, and I drift to sleep.

SIX

Gage

IF SHE WAKES UP, she'll kick my ass.

A dim light comes through the blinds. I lean back in the tattered chair that was once my mother's favorite and feel shame as I watch the woman I love and hate sleep.

She's still gorgeous, still my favorite view. Lauren is the only woman I've looked at and not seen through. I've seen her at her worst—drunk, ridiculous, breaking my heart, in tears—and there hasn't been one instance when I didn't think she was breathtakingly beautiful. She consumed me before I hit puberty. Breakup or not, you don't heal from a love that pure, that real, that deep.

The attitude, the smart-ass woman I fell in love with, still shines brightly. She's the same. I'm not. If she knew the torture I'd been through, she'd never look at me the same.

Years ago, I loved the fact that I was the only man to ever touch and kiss her. Sliding inside her was always a high. I no longer have that privilege. And, as much as I want to convince myself she has never been with another man, I know there's no way that could be true. She wanted—*needed*—sex regularly when we were together. My nails sink into the arms of the chair at the thought of it.

My thoughts are broken when she squirms, kicking off the blanket, and I gulp when her smooth, bare legs go on display as her dress piles up around her waist. Her heels are still on, her hair messier than what it was, and the sight of her black lace panties causes my dick to stir.

I lick my lips. *Damn, I should've given her something to change into.*

Not that she would've accepted it.

When I saw her walk across the restaurant in that black number, there was no way I could stay away. The dress was short and showed off her toned legs and plump, perfect ass. I finished my drink before standing and followed her into the hallway, not sure what my plan was when I reached my destination. Pushing her against the wall definitely wasn't it. Neither was my cock growing hard as a rock or bringing her home with me.

She receives one last glance, and I pray it's not the last one I'll have in a while as I pull myself up from the chair. The sky is dark, the full moon shining bright, when I walk to the main house, kicking my feet against the gravel drive.

My dad is in the living room, leaning back comfortably in his recliner, and he looks away from the TV at the sound of the door shutting. "I thought you were going out."

"I did. And, now, I'm home."

He grabs the remote and flips off the TV. "There a reason you're not sleeping in the loft?"

"Thought I'd spend some time here tonight. My childhood bedroom, complete with a Ninja Turtles comforter, is calling my name."

He nods in understanding and what looks like devastation. "She's on your mind, isn't she?" He sighs with sadness in his eyes when he realizes I'm not entertaining the conversation. "You ever think she regrets what she did?"

I gently knock my knuckles against the wall. "Doesn't matter anymore. She did what she did, and my life has been hell since. Sure, she might be sorry, but I can't give her the same man I was in high school."

"CARE TO TELL me what happened with you and your arsonist sweetie?" Kyle asks when I walk into the station. "No police report was filed on your behalf."

After arresting and dropping off Lauren at her parents' the other day, I went back and picked up Kyle. He briefly took some bullshit report from the landlord, fully aware I wasn't going to stick Lauren in jail, and pressed me for details about where my prisoner was. He didn't get shit.

I called in the next day, given I had a mild concussion from my father's roof incident, and yesterday was my night off. He's had a few days to come up with his interrogation, so it's going to be a long shift.

I'm exhausted after last night. This morning, from the kitchen window, I saw an Audi SUV pull into the driveway. Lauren jumped in before I could see the driver. A car that expensive doesn't frequently roll around our small Iowa town.

Is she dating a doctor?

There are so many things I don't know about her anymore, and I hate it.

"She swore she didn't set the apartment on fire."

I pour myself another coffee before we get in the cruiser, me in the driver's side.

"I know you're blinded by your dick and all, but you need to take a step back and reflect on how long you've been in law enforcement. *I didn't do it,* is a criminal's favorite sentence," he replies.

"Not thinking with my dick. I'm thinking with my gut."

"That goes down to your dick."

Kyle has been my best friend since elementary school. We kept in touch for a few years after I moved to Chicago and then eventually lost contact. I didn't want any connection with my life in Blue Beech. All it did was remind me of her.

I came back to town, expecting Kyle to give me the middle

finger when I walked into the station looking for a job. Instead, he slapped me on the back and announced I'd be his partner. He hates Lauren just as much as I do, given that he blames her for my fleeing the state.

"She didn't do it. If anyone brings her in for questioning, you tell them I'll do it, you hear me?"

"Aye, aye, Lauren lover. Although Douche-Bag Landlord isn't going to be happy."

"He can fuck off."

He points his coffee at me. "You're in trouble, man."

I raise a brow.

"Lauren Barnes was your weakness then, and there's no doubt she still is."

No fucking shit.

"That's the past."

He nods but doesn't believe me.

"So, what's on the agenda today?" I ask.

"Don't anticipate anything crazy happening. Your menacing ex's apartment going up in flames is the most exciting thing that's happened this month. This place will have nowhere near the crimes and arrests you had in Chicago."

"Less drama is what I need right now."

I moved back to clear my head, be with my father, and not have a station filled with my old coworkers giving me pity stares daily.

"You ready to tell me why you split and transferred?"

"My dad needed me."

"Got that part. Now, you ready to tell me the other reason you came back to a place you swore you'd never step foot into again? If I recall, you said your dad would be moving there when it was time he couldn't take care of himself."

"It would've been wrong for me to drag him out of the home he loves."

"Mmhmm." He grins over at me. "Some of us guys are going to Down Home tonight for some darts and beers. You game?"

I nod. "I could use a drink."

The radio calls in and tells us there's a kid stuck in a tree.

"I told you," Kyle says. "Crazy shit happenin' in this town."

There was a minimum of one shooting each shift in Chicago. I witnessed shit I'll never forget. I lost shit I'd thought I'd never lose.

The scars are there.

And I have scars here.

Two women ruined me.

One I gave my heart to.

The other who punished me for it.

SEVEN

Lauren

I'M STRUCK with a blast of air-conditioning when I climb into the passenger seat of Willow's luxury SUV. My head throbs, and I use my hand to shield my eyes from the sun's reminder of the idiotic choices I made last night.

"Please tell me you have a spare pair of sunglasses." My plea is wrapped around a groan, and a sigh leaves me when she tosses a pair in my lap. "You're my favorite person in the world."

Willow looks from Gage's house and then to me as I slide the glasses on. "Morning, sunshine. And whose home is this?"

The loft was empty when I woke up. The view of Gage's truck in the driveway sent my anxiety into overdrive. I had to get out of there in case he decided to make a visit and have a conversation about last night. Facing him hungover wasn't happening.

Not only was seeing him a problem, but what I felt was, too. I slept better on that old, ratty couch than I had in my own bed. That terrified me.

My phone on the coffee table reminded me that Gage had never given it back last night. When I grabbed it, I found he'd texted both my mom and Alec, letting them know I'd made it to my destination safely.

Willow was my first call, and luckily, she was available to save me.

"A friend's," I answer.

"A friend with a vagina or cock?"

I was well aware questions would be asked by whoever picked me up this morning. Everyone in my family knows my history with Gage and where he lives. Willow was my safest option. Sure, she'd ask if I had a one-night stand, but she wouldn't think it was with him.

Still, a subject change is in order.

"Thank you for the ride."

She shakes her head. "I'll let you evade that question for now since you look like you were ran over. I owe you for all the trips you made for me back and forth from the airport. Plus, your brother practically kicked me out of the house to have some me-slash-girls' time. He and Samuel are having a daddy-son day, and Maven is hanging out with your mom at some bake sale."

Willow and my oldest brother, Dallas, had a one-night stand nearly a year ago. He was having a hard time with moving on with his life after losing his wife to breast cancer. Somehow, Willow broke through his wall one night. Fast-forward a few months, and Willow was trying to hide her pregnancy from him. Her boss and best friend, Stella, is dating my other brother, Hudson, and he overheard Willow spilling the beans to her.

Now, Willow and Dallas live together and take care of Samuel, their new baby, and Dallas's daughter, Maven. Willow was a saving grace to Dallas and our family. She's cool as hell, so I scooped her up as a best friend.

"You're a kick-ass mom," I say.

Let's keep this convo on babies.

Her lips arch into a smile. "I don't know how great I'd be without your brother. He's an amazing father who doesn't mind changing diapers. I hit the baby-daddy jackpot."

Their happiness fills my heart with joy. Our family is tight-knit, and we always look out for one another. If one of us is hurting, we're all hurting.

She glances over at me. Her red hair is pulled into a messy bun, and her sunglasses cover nearly half of her pale and freckled face. "So, I have to ask, did you catch our apartment building on fire?"

"No!" I throw my hands up. "Jesus, how can people even question that?"

"You can't blame a girl for asking. If you did, I'd be one pissed chick. Some of my shit was still in there."

Willow moved into my building after my brother begged her to move from LA to Blue Beech. She refused to stay at his house until they worked their issues out. After moving in with him, she kept her apartment as a storage unit.

"Why are you getting blamed?" she asks. "They catch you with a match in your hand?"

"Ronnie is blaming me for revenge."

"Ronnie?"

"Old Man Willard's grandson. He inherited the building when Willard died a few months back."

"Hold up. Our landlord died?" she chokes out.

"Uh ... yes. You didn't know?"

She frowns while shaking her head. "Damn, I feel bad for not going to the funeral."

"Don't. They had it somewhere else. He had no living family in Blue Beech, so his body got shipped to them."

"That doesn't sound morbid or anything. So, why does the grandson want revenge?"

"For turning him down when he asked me out."

"Girlfriend, you need a boyfriend ... or at least some dick. Why not take him up on his offer?"

I grimace. "Gross. I'd rather hire someone to give me the business than screw him. Dude is a creep who wears expensive suits, which he tells me the price of every time we run into each other, and polished shoes daily—in *Blue Beech*. Now, I normally don't discriminate against people's fashion choices, given I sport scrubs almost daily, but a man with a big enough complex and ego who has to show off his money is a hard limit for me."

She nods in understanding. "Hurting a man's ego can be a dangerous thing."

That's no lie.

"Tell me about it. So, because I don't want to screw his pretentious, suit-wearing ass, he's trying to make me out to be some pyro." My upper lip tightens as I roll my eyes. "Trust me, I would've made sure I snagged all my cutest shoes had I caught that place on fire. Oh, and my scrubs because those things aren't cheap."

She laughs and, for the rest of the ride, she listens to me name off the endless number of items I need to replace.

"You ready to tell me why your car is here?" she asks when pulling into Clayton's empty parking lot. She parks and presses her hands together in a pleading gesture. "*Puh-leeease* tell me you had a one-night stand."

Now, I know how she felt when I was always nagging her for details about her and my brother. Not fun.

"Nope," I answer. "You ruined the idea of a one-night stand for me after you got knocked up from having one with my brother. Lord knows, my ass does not need to get pregnant."

"Eh, I see your point there." She clicks her tongue against the roof of her mouth before her lips turn into a bright smile. "Will you at least tell me who took you home?"

My hangover headache maximizes as I slump in my seat. "Gage is back in town."

She gives me a blank look. "Am I supposed to know who Gage is?"

Willow and I are so close that I forget I haven't known her my entire life and that she didn't grow up in Blue Beech. In our small town, I'm known as the lucky girl who dated Gage. And he's known as the dude who dated me. It's sad that you're labeled by your relationship, but it's the place where sixty percent of the population has married their high school sweetheart.

"He's my ex-boyfriend and the reason I haven't had a relationship in years."

Her mouth falls slightly open as a thought hits her. "I've always wondered why you don't date. You've been hung up on him."

"Negative. I've been too busy with my job to be hung up on anyone."

Her laugh echoes through her car. "Denial only makes it hotter when you have sex again. Trust me, I know from experience."

I wrinkle my nose and shove her side. "Please refrain from talking about having sex with my brother. It'll make me puke more than this stupid hangover."

Willow gives me a loaner bag of clothes before I get out of her car since mine are burned to a crisp, and I'm waiting for my online orders to be delivered to my parents' house. I kiss her cheek, thank her again, and think about Gage on my ride home.

I need to find out if he's home for good.

If he is, I'm not sure how much pain that'll put me through.

My new home search might be out of Blue Beech if that's the case.

———

I THROW my arms around the chest of my big brother, Hudson, and squeal. "Happy birthday, you old man, you!"

Yes, I'm curing my hangover by attending my brother's birthday party at the Down Home Pub. Even if I do feel like shit, I can't bail on his party. Down Home Pub is the only place to drink in Blue Beech, so if you're looking to have a good time, this is where you go. Even though it gives you a comfortable and homey atmosphere, you'll still always end up running into someone you hate.

Hudson squeezes my shoulders and narrows his eyes on me upon pulling away. "Old man? I still don't regret cutting off half of your bangs when you were six."

Hudson is the middle child between Dallas and me. He's a tough dude, a former Marine, and a part-time bodyguard to his fiancée, Stella Mendes. She happens to be TV's *it girl*.

At first, he didn't want to work for her, but he broke down and took the job after dealing with the reality that his high school sweetheart and my former best friend were screwing behind his back. The fuck-boy bestie married said cheating ho on her and Hudson's scheduled wedding day. Good thing he did take the job, considering his life is hearts and roses with a talented and independent woman.

Yes, our family is one big dating-confusion circle. It'd take hours to break down every relationship situation. It's hard for me to keep up with it at times. They all got name tags from me for Christmas.

I slap his chest. "Joke's on you, homeboy, because I'm the one who cut the heads off your G.I. Joes, which Mom didn't ground me for *or* tell you because she understood it was done in retribution."

He plops down on a barstool at the crowded table and pulls the one next to him out. "Waitress delivered our drinks before you got here, but I'll track her down to get you something."

I wave off his offer and stay standing. "I'll run up to the bar and order something from Maliki. This place is a madhouse. It'll take forever for a drink."

He picks his beer up. "Throw it on my tab."

"You're the birthday boy. I should be buying your drinks." I hold a finger up. "Nothing too expensive though. This chick is on a budget."

He takes a drink and wipes his mouth. "Exactly. You've lost everything you owned. Add it to my tab."

I shake my head. "Nope, you know us Barnes kids don't like people feeling sorry for us."

"I don't feel sorry for your evil, G.I. Joe–killing ass. I'm having a good night, and I already told everyone at our table that drinks are on me."

I tap his head while he takes another drink and then move around the table to complete my hugging and greeting duty to everyone, including Willow, Dallas, and Stella. That takes a good fifteen minutes. A crowd of people surrounds the bar, but luckily, Maliki skips over them and heads straight to me.

A smile beams on his dark-skinned face. "There's my favorite arsonist nurse. What can I get you? Fireball?"

I lean against the bar to smack his shoulder. "So hilarious, ass. There goes your tip."

Maliki and I had a thing for a few months last year. He graduated with Hudson, and neither one of us was looking for anything serious, so we didn't feel the need to tell anyone. Not an ounce of drama happened after parting ways when the flame dimmed. That's the kind of sex relationship I want.

Perhaps I should ask him to share his bed with me tonight to fuck out all the sexual thoughts I've been having about Gage.

I shake my head. *Nope.* That's a bitchy thing to do. I won't use someone to get back at my pain-in-the-ass ex.

Maliki grins, showing off his bright white teeth. "Your usual? Lemon drop martini?"

I tap my chin. "I might be in need of something stronger this evening."

"Rough week?"

"Considering I'm homeless, yes."

He goes to open his mouth, most likely about to offer up his spare bedroom, when someone wedges himself between us, stopping him.

"My tab, man."

Ugh.

Just as I said, you never fail to run into someone you hate.

And what's up with everyone offering to buy my drinks? This chick buys her own drinks. Period.

The smile I had for Maliki slips, and the headache from earlier is creeping back in.

"Really?" I grumble. I don't have to look to know who it is. Not only do I recognize his voice, but I also recognize the smell of him, the heat of his body brushing against mine. "Maliki, do not add it to his tab. I don't accept favors from douche lords."

"Can't have a homeless woman buying her drinks," Gage throws back.

I give him a glassy stare when I finally turn to look at him and blow out a series of breaths. He's wearing a blue button-up flannel and what appears to be jeans, but I can't exactly shove away the person behind me, blocking half of him from my view. A light scruff still covers his cheeks, and I wonder if that's his everyday look now. It saddens me that I'm not sure if every change in him is recent or if he's been doing it for years and it's only new to me.

Maliki holds his palms up and breaks my attention from Gage. "The nightly goal of every bartender is not dealing with patrons' drama." He snaps his fingers and points to me. "Something strong is coming your way." His focus moves to Gage. "You two work your soap-opera shit out before I come back."

"I think this proves you are stalking me," I grumble to Gage.

He rests his elbow on the bar and leans against it, facing me. "It's a small town, Dyson. Get used to seeing me around."

"Small town, my ass. You've been here for weeks without us running into each other. Now, all of a sudden, you're everywhere. I'm not about to become a star of *Dateline. Everyone loved Lauren ... and her ex-boyfriend loved her a little too much.*" I wisp my hand through the air. "Blah, blah, blah."

"Again, don't flatter yourself, sweetheart. I had no idea you'd be here tonight." He gestures to the door. "I can leave if it'll make you more comfortable." He lowers his gaze on me. "Or we can leave and fuck our hate toward each other away."

Whoa.

Maliki slid some blue concoction in front of me at the same time Gage said those words. His eyes wide, Maliki holds his hands up while retreating backward and walking away.

I shyly look away and catch my breath before managing to give Gage a cold stare while hating myself for the excitement rushing through me at the idea of *hate fucking.* I rub my legs together to ease the sudden tension.

Sex with Gage was incredible when we were younger. I can only imagine what it's like with him now that he's older and more experienced.

Damn. The mood is ruined now that I've thought about him with other women.

I turn around and lean back against the bar, my drink in my hand. "Screw you. You can stay. I don't want to be blamed for your lack of getting laid *again.*"

He raises a brow. "That an offer?"

"Absolutely not. That's a kind way of saying, *Stay out of my way, and I'll stay out of yours.* You're right. We're going to see each other. Let's not make a big deal about it during every encounter, okay?"

"I heard you were back in town, brother."

I freeze at the sound and sight of Derrick Howard, the man I lied about sleeping with. He slaps Gage on the back while smiling at him.

"Let me buy you a drink," he goes on.

Uh-oh.

Gage pulls away from him in disgust. "I'd recommend not touching me, *brother.*"

"What?" Derrick asks around a confused laugh before slapping his leg. "Come on, man. It's been nearly a decade. Let's bury that high school rivalry shit."

Gage tilts his beer toward me with what sounds like a growl coming from his throat. "It's not done when you're fucking her. When it comes to Lauren, it'll never be done."

Derrick looks at me in confusion. "What is he talking about? We barely speak."

"Nothing," I answer, and I grab Gage's arm. "We need to talk in private."

Derrick might be a dick, but that doesn't mean he deserves to get his ass kicked.

Gage slips out of my hold. "No, we don't."

"My sex life is none of your business," I snap.

"You're right. Just answer me this one question, and I'll stop. I won't talk to you anymore. I'll let you and Derrick fuck yourselves happy." His voice breaks. "*Please.*"

"Gage, I'm not fucking Lauren," Derrick says. "You two figure your shit out and leave me out of it." He turns around and walks away without waiting for a response.

"All I needed to know," Gage yells to his back and glances at me. "This a new hobby of yours? Lying about whom you're sleeping with?"

I bite into my lip, answering honestly, "Sort of."

"Why? Is your mission in life to piss me off?"

"To be honest, yes. It's revenge for arresting me."

"Let me get this straight. You left me. You walked away for some bullshit reason after I begged you not to. Then, you tell me you're sleeping with the dude I fought numerous times for attempting to fuck around with you. If anyone should hate anyone's guts, it's me who should hate yours."

He turns around and walks away before I can answer him. I stare at his back while he maneuvers around the crowd and heads to Hudson's table. Hudson slaps him on the back, and they start what looks like a comfortable conversation. Hudson doesn't seem surprised to see him.

Not fucking cool.

I grab my drink and stomp over to Hudson as Gage moves around the table to talk to Dallas.

"You didn't think it'd be cool to give me a heads-up that he was back in town?" I ask Hudson, pulling out the stool next to him with added force and falling down on it.

He and I are close and spent a lot of time together growing up. Gage and I double-dated with him and his ex all the time in high school.

"It's a sore subject for you," he answers. "Anytime his name was mentioned after you broke up, you would leave the room."

"You know what was also a sore subject? When I found out my best friend was cheating on you and I told her to never come near me again." I press my drink to my lips. "Apparently, you've forgotten what loyalty means."

He shakes his head while slowly running a finger through his short beard. "The situation is different. Gage didn't fuck around on you with someone else. Otherwise, he wouldn't be walking. I didn't tell you because I didn't want to hurt you. Something sour went down between the two of you, and I know you have so much going on. You didn't need any more stress."

I glance over at Gage at the same time he moves around the table to my side.

He leans down, his elbows resting on the wood, and lowers his voice. "You staying at your parents'?" he asks.

I clear my throat to gain some time to get myself together. The feelings I have when he's this close are embarrassing. "Kind of have no other option."

There's a hint of mint and beer on his breath. "You can stay in the loft if you want."

I scoff, "You're joking."

He shakes his head. "My dad is listing it for rent in the paper this week for extra money."

"Where would you stay?"

"In the house with him."

I look around to see if people's eyes are on us, and about a dozen are staring. Both of my brothers have all their attention on their girls, and a few women have their gaze on Gage, assessing the situation to see if we're back together.

"Don't you think that'd be a little weird?"

More along the lines of extremely weird.

"Think on it and get back with me." He grabs his beer and tilts it my way. "Enjoy your night. If you need a ride again, let me know."

I watch his back as he walks away, and he joins a group of men at a table in the corner of the room. I finish my drink and depart for another one.

More alcohol equals fewer feelings.

"I have to say, I'm pissed you're not in jail."

I turn around at the gravelly voice to find Ronnie standing behind me. He takes my frown as an invitation to move to my side. He's, of course, wearing a suit in this hole-in-the-wall pub. His blond hair is gelled to perfection, like he's still a frat boy bonging beers in loafers, and his arrogance reeks from here.

"Word is, your little friend over there never took you in," he goes on.

"File a report, Ronnie," I answer. "I didn't set the building on fire."

The strong scent of him hits me as he comes in closer.

"I'll leave this alone if you give me one date. *One.* That's all I'm asking."

"No. I've made it clear that I'm not dating at the moment."

I look around the bar for my brothers. If they see this jackass talking to me, they'll no doubt put him in his place. I don't see either one of them.

Ronnie inherited the building but didn't grow up in Blue Beech. He grew up in some big city, attended a prestigious school, and came into town thinking he'd impress people with his money and expensive cars.

"Come on. I have to be better than these small-town chumps around here." He flashes me a smile. "You work nonstop. I own *several* buildings and will take care of you."

I grimace and pull away when he runs his hand down my arm.

"And I can promise, it won't only be financially. I do magical things with my tongue. Come home with me tonight."

I've seen enough rape victims come into the ER to know this man is a threat. Pissing him off, turning him down, will only make him more persistent.

I order a water instead of an alcoholic drink from Maliki and fake a laugh when I look back at Ronnie. "I have an early shift tomorrow and am staying with my parents. They're giving me the same curfew I had in high school."

Please buy it. Buy it.

EIGHT

Gage

AM I FUCKING CRAZY?

Why in the living hell would I offer Lauren the loft? My loft?

Not only did I do that, but I also lied about it being available for rent.

It's not—again, because it's *my* motherfucking loft.

The *keeping my distance* plan with Lauren is deteriorating fast. That woman has been my weakness from day one, and that weakness fucked up my life in so many ways.

I straighten in my stool when I notice Douche-Bag Landlord meeting her at the bar. He runs his sleazy hand down her arm, and she pulls away from his touch with revulsion on her face.

I slide off my stool at the same time she steps away from him, grabbing the glass of water Maliki slid over to her.

Good girl.

I flinch when a hand hits my arm.

"Gage, man, don't do anything stupid that'll cost you your job," Kyle warns. "You might've gotten away with roughing dudes up in Chicago, but that shit won't fly here. You put your hands on that guy, and he'll demand you lose your badge. I had the displeasure of hanging out with him while you ran off to do who knows what with your girl of destruction. He went on and on about how much money he has, how many cars he owns, and the endless parade of chicks he bangs. Dude will press charges in a heartbeat and demand you lose your badge." He tips his beer to his lips and takes a drink. "Not to mention, Lauren's ass won't fall for his bullshit. That girl is fucking evil."

As much as I want to, I can't bring myself to sit back down. If he touches her again, fuck my badge, fuck my job. I rub a sweaty hand over my forehead.

She's not yours to protect any longer.

I have to pound that through my thick skull and broken heart.

My attention stays pinned on her as she maneuvers through the crowd, holding her water in the air, and goes back to her table. I sit back down and make myself comfortable, knowing she's surrounded by a layer of her brothers' protection.

She circles the table, hugging everyone, and finishes off her water before heading to the door. I start to relax—until she goes outside, and the landlord does the same minutes later.

This time, I ignore Kyle's protests as I stalk out of the bar and into the parking lot. It's close to empty, which surprises me. Patrons are usually gathered out here, smoking and shooting the shit.

I follow the sound of his voice.

"Come on, baby. One night. You won't regret it. Trust me."

"I told you, my parents are expecting me," she answers. "I already called and told them I was on my way home."

I round the corner to find Lauren standing in front of her pink Mustang with Douche-Bag standing in front of her, blocking her from opening the door.

He snags her around the waist, and she pushes him away. "Then we can go to my car and mess around. A quick fuck then I'll take you to dinner tomorrow."

"You couldn't pay me to touch you, asshole."

He grabs her arms and pins them above her. "Baby, don't tempt me. Money talks. It always does."

He turns her head to the side as he grows closer, and I yell at the top of my lungs while running toward them.

"How much will it take? A few hundred? I'm willing to pay thousands to get between your legs. Now that I think about it, you need a place to stay. My bed is always open."

The idiot is practically screaming out his assault.

"You'd better step the fuck away from her before I bash your skull in," I yell, finally catching his attention.

He releases her and holds his hands up. "No need to interfere. My girl and I are having a little spat. We'll be on our way."

"I'm not your girl, sicko," Lauren yells.

She pushes him, and he stumbles backward.

He stares at me, blinking, while I clench my fist in hopes that I can control it from hitting his face.

"You're the officer who arrested her," he says.

"No shit, and she wasn't your girl when you demanded I do that," I reply.

"I now see why I haven't been updated on any charges." He lets out a gravelly laugh. "Looks like I'm not the only man who wants a piece of her. It's always more tempting when you have to work for it."

Anger spirals through my veins, and I hold my clenched fists up. "I'm giving you five seconds to split before I bust your jaw open."

Pretty boy doesn't take it as an idle threat.

He swiftly glances at Lauren. "You have my card. Let me know when you're ready for some quality dick."

There goes my patience and trying to lay low.

I charge forward, and he grunts when I slam him against the car. "The fuck did I say? Walk away, shut your fucking mouth, and don't you come near her again. You hear me?"

He repeatedly nods until I release him. He slides against the car, away from me, and then arrogantly runs his hands down to smooth out the wrinkles of his suit, which is nowhere appropriate to wear at a run-down pub like this. "Let me know if you change your mind, sweetie."

"That'll be never," Lauren blurts out. "Some words of advice: go buy a sex doll because that's the only way you're getting laid."

He sprints away to the other side of the parking lot, and I erase the distance between Lauren and me.

"You okay?" I ask, running my hand down her face, checking for any marks.

"Just peachy." She slaps my hand away. "Don't touch me."

I step away at her request, and she takes a deep breath before letting it out.

"Sorry for snapping," she says, her voice level. "He had me all hyped up."

"No need to apologize." I tip my head toward my truck a few spaces away. "Come on. I'll give you a ride home."

"I'm fine. I only had one drink."

"I'm not concerned about you being drunk. I'm worried about your safety."

"I'll be okay." She fishes through her purse for her keys with shaking hands. "I'll be fine. You scared him away."

"I'll follow you home then."

I do a once-over of the parking lot before lowering my voice and dipping down to Lauren's level. "Landlord didn't go back into the bar. He walked to his car and hasn't left. My guess is, he's waiting for you to leave, so he can do something stupid. I'll be damned if I let that happen."

Understanding dawns on her face.

"You don't think ..." she mutters, stopping mid-sentence.

"Who knows how big his balls are? Regardless, I won't risk it." I hold two fingers up. "That gives you two options. One is I'll follow you home. Then tomorrow, we'll file a restraining order against the punk." I put down a finger. "The second option is you let me give you a ride, and we'll still file a restraining order."

It's her turn to do a nervous scan of the parking lot. "I'll ride with you."

I keep my hand on her back as we walk to my truck, and I help her in.

She slides her sandals off and rests her feet on the dash as soon as we pull out of the parking lot. "God, I remember these days. Your truck was older back then. Ripped seats. Smelled like your dad's old cologne."

"Ah, yes, his rusted beater," I say with a laugh, happy she's no longer shaking. "That front seat saw plenty of action."

"Plenty of awkward, first-time action."

"I won't deny that." I tap my hand against the steering wheel and curse myself for what I'm about to do. It'll ruin the comfortableness of our ride, but the question has been haunting me for years. "Why'd you do it?"

Her feet drop from the dash. "Huh?"

"Why'd you leave me?"

"Gage … I told you why."

"No, you gave me a bullshit excuse."

"And you'll receive the same one tonight. It was for the best."

I scoff, "Maybe it was for you, but it sure as fuck wasn't for me. You were my fucking life, Lauren. The reason I bled. Hell, I loved you more than my own life, my own breath, and you knew that. We had plans, and then one day, you changed your mind, out of nowhere."

She scrubs her hands over her face. "That was the problem, Gage. You can't make someone your entire life. We didn't know anything, except for each other. We never had the chance to find ourselves."

"I knew myself. Knew I wanted you. Knew who I loved."

It isn't until we pull into her parents' drive that I realize why she's kept her hands over her face. It's to mask the tears falling down her cheeks. The urge to reach out and comfort her rips through me, but I can't.

"Can we not do this? It's in the past. Let it be." Her voice breaks.

She's had a rough night, and my actions have only made it worse.

"You're right. You're over it. It's time I do the same."

She clears her throat. "Let's be friends, okay?"

"I can't be your friend."

"I understand."

She gives me a quick nod before opening the door, ending our conversation. She's gone, rushing up the sidewalk to the front porch before I have the chance to say her name. I stay parked until she disappears into the house, and my phone rings before I shift my truck into reverse. My stomach churns when I see the number, and I accept the call, though I know it's a terrible idea.

I've already hashed it out with one woman who ruined me tonight, so might as well do it with the other.

"You have a collect call from … Missy from the Cook County Department of Corrections."

My fingers fist around the phone at the sound of her voice.

"Do you accept the call and any charges that can occur?"

"I accept," I grit out.

I don't wait for her to mutter a hello when the call is processed. She doesn't deserve that. Hell, she doesn't deserve a second of my time.

"I told you to quit fucking call me."

"Gage!" she yells on the line. "Please! Please listen to me for one minute! I want you to hear me out for once."

"Nothing you say will ever make me forgive you. Don't call again."

Click.

The phone rings again. Same number.

Decline.

I whisper to the darkness, "I fucking hate you, Missy."

NINE

Lauren

"SOMEONE CAME HOME LATE." My mom slides me a glass of orange juice across the kitchen table before placing two Advils next to it. "You look like you had a little too much fun at your brother's party last night." Her hands rest on her hips. "I know you like to keep up with the boys, honey, but you're much smaller than them. Alcohol hits you harder."

I wave away her warning. "Psh, I can drink them under the table."

"That's my girl."

I grin at the sound of Dad's voice as he comes strolling into the kitchen.

"Where's your car, Laur-Bear?" he asks. "I planned on changing the oil today."

"At the pub," I answer. "I didn't feel like driving last night."

"The pub?" my mom repeats. "Who took you home?" The expression on her face tells me she already knows the answer.

My mother is the gossip queen of Blue Beech, and I have a love-hate relationship with that hobby of hers. It's all fun and games until the gossip spread is about you.

"I see you still excel at spying on your children," I mutter into my glass before taking a sip and popping the pills. "Even when they're grown." An omelet is placed in front of me next.

She sits down across from me. "It was Gage, wasn't it?"

I stop mid-bite. "Now, why in the world would you think that? Gage left Blue Beech years ago and hasn't come back, right?"

Her taking a sip of coffee hides her enthusiasm terribly. "Nancy just so happened to mention that he's back in town, working at the station."

My fork clashes against my plate when I drop it. "Are you saying you've known Gage has been home for who knows how long and didn't think it would be a stellar idea to drop that bomb on me, so I wasn't taken by surprise when we ran into each other?"

"From what it looked like, your relationship with him didn't end on good terms. You've been busy at the hospital, so I didn't want to stress you more. You want to talk about what happened between you two?"

"Nope."

Disappointment flashes across her face.

My mother is a fixer. There's a solution to every problem in her book.

"You're older, more mature and, sometimes, people need a break from each other to be smacked in the face with the truth. It could be a second chance at love. You and Gage were inseparable for years. You loved that boy, and he loved you."

"Don't you dare try this on me. If you and your little knitting club start plotting some scheme to force us to reconcile, I will not be in attendance for Christmas."

"No Christmas means no gifts."

I frown. "Fine then. I won't be showing up on Thanksgiving."

My dad laughs. "Unless you plan on having a Marie Callendar's frozen dinner, you'll be here."

I'VE NEVER UNDERSTOOD the phrase, Desperate times call for desperate measures, until I find myself walking into the police station.

And I'm lucky enough to come face-to-face with Kyle. I'm not sure whose look is dirtier toward the other—mine or his. He stares me down, waiting for my conversation starter, because he won't be the one to initiate it.

"Is, um …" I glance around to see if there's anyone else I can talk to who doesn't think I'm the devil. "Is Gage around?"

Kyle looks like he'd rather arrest me than let me near his best friend. "Sure, I'll go grab him, and I'm only doing this because it's my job. I'm not allowed to tell people to kick rocks here."

"How courteous of you."

"Nice is my middle name. Maybe you should give it a try."

He gives me his back before I can reply, and Gage looks surprised when he walks out. Kyle must not have given him a heads-up it was me asking for him. I lick my lips and a tingle rolls up my spine at the view of Gage in his uniform again.

Shit. Control your hormones, girl.

I ignore all the stares around us. "Can I talk to you real quick?"

"Sure." Gage motions for me to follow him and takes me into an office, shutting the door behind us.

"You have your own office?" I ask, turning around and looking at the door when I sit down. "Aren't you a newbie around here?"

"I held a high position in the force in Chicago."

"Wait," I interrupt, holding my hand up. "You lived in Chicago?"

"Yes." He scratches his cheeks and goes on before I have the chance to question him more. "There was an open position after Monroe retired, and I took it."

Any Chicago talk is definitely off the table for him. His demeanor changed when I repeated that city. It moved from hate to hurt to understanding and now indifference. Last night, Gage said he was over our past, and now he's going to prove that to me.

I'm not sure which Gage is worse.

The pissed off one or the sad one.

He sits down behind the desk. "You here to file that report against the land-dick?"

I shake my head. "Is the loft above your garage still available?"

His face is emotionless. "I believe so."

"Will you temporarily lease it to me?"

He looks as shocked as I am at my question.

I laugh. "Trust me, I wouldn't ask if I weren't desperate. I've called nearly every rental available in this godforsaken town. No one will rent to me in fear that I'll burn the place to the ground. My parents are too nosy, and both of my brothers are in the puke-inducing honeymoon phase with their girlfriends. No, thank you to intruding on their love-fests."

He opens up a drawer and pulls out a key. "Move your stuff in whenever."

"Thank you. I'll be out of your hair as soon as I find another place."

He tips his head my way. "Sounds like a plan."

I rise up to leave, but the sound of his whistling stops me.

"About that report."

"He was drunk."

"Has he hit on you before?"

I nod. "A few times, yes."

"If you're not going to file a report, let me know if he keeps coming around." His gaze lowers on me. "And no more walking through dark parking lots alone, okay?"

"I don't need protecting." I cross my arms. "Plus, you hate me, so why do you care?"

"My hate toward you won't stop me from making sure you're safe." He slides the key across the desk. "Loft is all yours. I have to get back to work."

TEN

Gage

"CARE TO EXPLAIN what the fuck that was about?" Kyle asks when I step out of my office an hour after Lauren left.

She came to me. That meant something.

Sure, she made it seem like she had no other options, but she did. Her parents would love for her to move back in, her brothers would always open their doors for her, and her mid-husband friends would no doubt give her a room at their place.

"Nothing of your concern," I mutter.

"You can't bullshit a bullshitter." He trails behind me as I walk through the station, out the door, and straight to the car. This conversation isn't happening for all of Blue Beech's ears. "The girl you love but wish you hated strutted her evil ass into your office. She leaves, and when you finally come out, it looks like she told you she was knocked up with another dude's baby. What gives, bro?"

His saying I look pissed doesn't surprise me. I'd set myself up for failure by inviting her to move in.

"She's crashing in the loft for a few weeks," I answer, unlocking the car door.

He would've found out sooner or later. Might as well have him call me a stupid shit now.

He spits his coffee out on the sidewalk, more dramatic than

necessary. "You shitting me? She's moving in with you? As a roommate or fuckmate?"

I get in the car, slam the door behind me, and wait until he's sliding in the passenger seat before answering, "I'll sleep in my old bedroom in the house."

"You sure are being nice to someone you supposedly can't stand." He whistles. "I wish my enemies were as considerate as you. Is Miss She-Devil moving in with you when you buy your new house, too?"

I've been on the hunt for a new place since moving back, but the market sucks. Most residents stay in their houses until they die, and then their kids inherit them, repeating history. My dad has tried to sign over the house to me countless times, but I won't allow it. He built his life, his family, and memories there. I won't take that away from him. He deserves to have that happiness for as long as he can.

"It's only temporary until she finds a new place," I say. "No one will rent to her."

"Can you blame them? The chick is a walking Firestarter, à la Stephen King."

I start the engine and settle my cup in the holder. "Shut up."

He puts his cup in next. "You're too damn soft for her, man. Pussy is a weakness for some men, and there's no doubt, Lauren's pussy is yours."

I shove his shoulder. "Watch your mouth. She needs somewhere to stay. That's it."

"The chick has family. She can rent another apartment out of town. There are plenty of options for Blue Beech's golden girl that don't involve shacking up with you."

"My dad can use the extra income."

"Bullshit," he coughs into his hand. "You won't take a penny from her."

"What's up with you in my business? You been watching Hallmark movies with your mom again? I don't question you about your women troubles."

His lips tilt into a grin. "Oh, so she's your woman now?"

"I still hate her."

"Perfect. I have a date tonight, and she's bringing a friend. Your uptight ass needs to get laid." He smacks my back. "Time to fuck that she-devil out of your mind."

———

LAUREN'S UGLY-ASS pink Mustang is parked in the driveway when I pull in.

It doesn't surprise me that she's still driving her first car. In order to buy it, she worked at the town diner for years to save up money. Her parents agreed to match whatever she came up with. I thought the car was hideous then, and I detest it even more now. The dudes on the basketball team loved giving me hell when she forced me to ride passenger while she drove around town.

I contemplate whether to head up to the loft and check on her but don't. Kyle was right about me needing to pull my head out of my ass and remember the pain she caused me. I can't let her step back into my life with her gorgeous smile, those beautiful brown eyes, and that contagious laugh and break down my walls.

It fucking killed me last time.

I wasn't as weak then.

It'd be worse the second go-around.

I snatch my phone up from the passenger seat when it beeps.

Kyle: You driving or want me to pick you up?

Me: Driving. Be there in 30.

Kyle: Bring an overnight bag. Bringing a date home to a loft you share with your ex most likely won't be a turn on for her.

Me: Fuck off.

Kyle: See you soon, assface.

I make it my mission not to look toward the loft when I head into the house. I shower and throw on jeans and a simple white tee. It takes a minute to find my duffel bag in the back of my closet. I lay it on the bed and stare down at it.

Should I?

It's been nearly five months since I've had sex. Pussy hasn't been on my mind since Missy did what she did. Maybe it's what I need. They say sex helps with stress. Let's test that theory.

I pack the bag, throw it over my shoulder, and say good-bye to my dad on my way out.

Lauren is skipping down the stairs with her keys in her hand while I head to my truck. She's sporting tight-ass yoga pants and a tank top that shows off her generous cleavage. Her tits have grown since high school, just like my hands—although they'd still cup them perfectly.

How many other ways has her body changed?

Is her pussy still as tight?

Are her weak spots still the same?

She stops and looks at me before I make it to my truck. "Your stuff is still in the closet."

I drag a hand through my hair. "I haven't had the chance to clear it out yet. It'll be gone by the weekend."

She crosses her arms, emphasizing her cleavage, and leans back against her car. "The loft was never going up for rent, was it?"

"Does it matter?"

A smile tilts at her lips. "I guess not, considering it's now my place of residence." She points to my bag. "Going somewhere?"

I hold it up. "I have a date."

What are your plans for tonight? is the question I want to ask her, but I don't.

"A date." She clears her throat, her face expressionless. "Well, you, uh … have fun with that."

"Don't worry. I'll have a blast," I say with a wink.

No, I won't.

———

"SO, YOU'RE KYLE'S PARTNER?" my date asks.

Her name is Susie … Sandy … something along those lines. I feel like an asshole for not paying attention to a word she's said all night. I'm comparing everything she does to Lauren, something I haven't done in years.

After we broke up, it was all I did with every woman I attempted to move on with. I compared the way they ate, how they talked, how they sucked my dick, the taste of their pussy. No one ever came close to her. Eventually, I stopped myself ... until now.

Kyle was right, goddamn it.

Letting her move in was a dumbass idea, but I can't ask her to leave now.

"A man in uniform has always been a turn-on for me," she goes on, her dark purple lips curving into a flirty smile. "Your place or mine for a nightcap?" she asks after I pay the bill.

"Yours."

Kyle grins and slaps my shoulder in celebration. "Attaboy."

My best friend was pro-Lauren years ago. He might hate her more than I do now. He blames her for my leaving, for his losing his best friend, for our falling out of touch. I've tried talking sense into him. She didn't force me to bail on everyone and everything I ever knew.

I was a big boy.

I made that decision.

And, now, I'm deciding to fuck Lauren Barnes out of my system.

———

I SHOULD'VE DRUNK MORE.

Shouldn't have stopped after two beers to make sure I was okay to drive home ... just in case.

Maybe then, I'd be more turned on, my dick would be harder, and I'd be into S ... something. Fuck, I feel like an asshole for not remembering her name.

I'm on her couch, wearing only jeans, and trying to focus on her grinding against my dick and doing her best to get me hard, and she eventually does even though neither my mind nor my dick is thinking about her.

My dick is hard because it's imagining someone else is on my lap.

A woman with a smart-ass mouth who could do amazing things with it.

I cringe, hoping she hasn't been honing in on those sex skills with someone else. *Did she find someone who could fuck her better than I did?*

I shut my eyes and let my imagination take over. If I can't have her, at least I can envision her, which makes me an asshole, I'm well aware.

"Fuck, Lauren, baby, slow down," I hiss, grabbing her hips and digging my nails into her dress that's pulled up around her waist.

The chick grinding on me stops. "Did you just call me Lauren?"

I grunt when she climbs off my lap and I go to grab my shirt, preparing to get kicked out of her apartment, but she drops to her knees instead.

"You want to forget about her?" she asks, licking her lips.

"Like no other."

"I'll fuck every thought of her out of you. You won't remember her name." She grabs my belt and unbuckles it. "You won't even be able to say your own name when I'm done with you."

ELEVEN

Lauren

I OPEN the blinds to peek out the window for what seems like the hundredth time.

"I'm officially a stalker," I say to Willow over the phone.

Does this mean I still have feelings for Gage?

That shouldn't even be a question I ask myself.

I'll always have unresolved feelings for him.

Jealousy ate at me when I caught him leaving for his date. He wasn't as dressed up as he had been for his Operation Make Lauren Jealous and Crash Her Dinner Party date, but he still put in an effort to look good for her.

Was it Phoebe again?

Ugh. Quit thinking about his date.

The worst part was the overnight bag. I stopped myself from asking him to hang out with me instead. To get my mind off him, I went to dinner with my parents, Hudson, and Stella and hoped Gage's truck would be here when I got back.

It wasn't.

I've been in freak-out mode since.

"I won't dispute that," she answers around a laugh. We've been on the phone for nearly an hour while I updated her on the whole Gage situation. "Although I do like seeing you like this."

"Like what?" I tiptoe from the window and fall back against the couch. I've done this dance all night. "A freaking creep?"

"All worked up over a man. You always seem so in charge of your feelings. It's a nice surprise."

I sit up. "Whoa, whoa. I'm not all worked up over Gage. Call it curiosity."

"Curiosity, huh? Curious if he's balls deep in another chick's vajayjay."

"You're making it sound like I'd rather he be balls deep in me."

"Hey, you're the one who said that, not me. Plus, I don't believe your lying ass."

"Looks like you don't know me as well as you think you do."

"Then, explain this to me. Why'd you move in with homeboy then? Rooming with your enemy isn't a common practice for most people. I'd never do it, for fear of getting shanked in my sleep or whatnot. So, why'd you do it?"

I groan. "For the millionth time, I needed somewhere to stay."

"Hmm … I recall offering you a room here. I have cable, a man who knows how to throw down in the kitchen—aka *free* meals—and a stepdaughter who enjoys giving free pedicures. Not saying they're good pedis, but they'll save you some dollars."

"Your house is too crowded. I need personal space."

"Personal space, my ass. You would've turned me down even if I'd offered you the house all to yourself. You're there because you want to be around him."

Am I that transparent?

I snort. "You're so wrong."

"The girl looking out the window, hoping he comes home and doesn't spend the night with his date—whom he's most likely banging at the moment—is telling me I'm wrong."

"Gee, way to make me feel better. Why am I friends with you again?"

"I told you befriending me was a terrible idea and that I was a disastrous mess, yet you kept showing up, uninvited, at my apartment, poking and prodding for details about my life."

"You were knocked up with my big bro's baby. It was imperative I made sure you weren't some weirdo. Although that's still yet to be determined."

"*I'm* the weirdo? You eat pickles on your peanut butter sandwiches."

"That's a delicacy in some places, you know."

"Where? Prison?"

"Dorm rooms for poor nursing students."

"Now, let's save the pickle-slash-friendship talk for another occasion because my time is almost up and I need a story more interesting about why you left him that's better than the Winnie the Pooh book I'm about to read to Maven."

"Don't get your hopes up on that happening."

"Did you run over his cat or something and can't look at him without feeling guilty?"

"No. What's wrong with you? I've never killed an animal."

"My ex killed my gerbil. Accidentally, but that should've been the first sign that dating him was a bad idea. Now, spill. I only have a few minutes to spare before the bedtime festivities begin."

"There's no story. It was for the best. We needed to find ourselves."

"Bullshit," she coughs into the phone.

"I was leaving for college. His only plan after leaving high school was to follow me and figure out his life from there. He needed to find out what he wanted in life without it revolving around me. I made the choice for him."

Crying erupts in the background. "That's not the truth, but I'll take it for now, considering my baby requires attention. Hold on a sec."

I yawn. "Attend to my niece and nephew and call me tomorrow. I have to wake up at the ass crack of dawn."

She says good-bye and hangs up, and I lean back against the couch, doing a once-over of the loft. It was a mistake, staying here.

I run my hand over the couch cushion and smile as a memory hits me.

Gage begged his parents for years to move into the loft, and they always said no. They planned on renting it out. That decision changed when his mother died. When he asked six months later, his dad Amos finally agreed even though I could see on his face that he wanted to say no. Amos feared to be alone, and only agreed because his heart broke for his son losing his mother too soon.

This loft is where we spent most of our time together. The bed is the one I lost my virginity in. This is the same couch where I gave him a blow job for the first time.

Memories surround me.

Yes, most definitely a mistake.

To put my mind on something else, I hop off the couch, open a cabinet, and unpack the bag of groceries sitting on the counter. I start making the only thing I know how to concoct from scratch. The asshole on a date with another woman is on my mind while I cut the chicken breasts. I wonder where he took her for dinner— hell, if they even had dinner—when I dice the peppers, and I curse them both while pulling out the Dutch oven.

———

I HATE myself for the relief I get when the headlights of Gage's truck shine through the window. No night cuddling and breakfast the next morning for his date. I inch forward and slowly peel the curtains back, hoping he doesn't notice me in stalker mode.

He looks up, meets my eyes, and grins.

Of freaking course.

I run away from the window, pause the TV, and shut the lamp off. Maybe he'll think I'm going to bed. The faint sound of a knock on the door echoes through the room, and I debate on whether to answer it. A groan leaves my throat while I pull myself up and check the peephole before answering, just in case his date is with him and he wants to rub it in my face.

"Can I come in?" he asks when I open the door.

I peek out, checking that he's alone, while he waits for me to invite him in like a vampire from a horror movie.

All clear.

No date.

No sex mate.

Unfortunately, he looks like sex. Smells like sex, too.

I should shut the door in his face, but dude is letting me stay in his loft, so I take a step back, a silent yes. I won't admit that the urge to hang out and question him about his date tonight is biting at me.

"You settling in okay?" he asks.

Yes, if you don't count my anxiety-induced cooking to punch out the thoughts of you with another woman.

He still looks good, but his shirt is wrinkled at the bottom, evidence that there was a hand pulling at it. His hair is rustled, the messy look maybe brought on by another woman.

"For the most part," I say, turning on the light and stepping into the kitchen. "Not that I have much to settle in. The insurance company is giving me a hard time since Ronnie is accusing me of arson. No money for me until the investigation is complete."

"I'll have a look and try to speed up the process." He looks across the kitchen, his head tilting up. "Is that gumbo?"

Crap.

"Yep."

Don't remember. Don't remember.

"You know that's my favorite."

Busted and mistrusted.

"Is it? I had no idea."

He raises a disbelieving eyebrow.

I didn't make it for him. Maybe, subconsciously, I did. Gumbo isn't my favorite dish. Hell, it's not even in my top ten. So, why is it the only dish I can make successfully without burning? It's the single meal I know how to make because it was the favorite of my boyfriend.

I shrug. "There's extra if you want a bowl."

He does, and I go back to my spot on the sofa and turn the TV back on. He plops down on the other side of the couch with a full bowl.

"This still the only thing you know how to cook?" he asks.

"Yes. For some reason, I haven't been able to master anything else without burning it."

He chuckles. "Perhaps you shouldn't admit to burning shit to anyone else for a while."

I smile. "Good idea."

He takes a bite and groans while pointing to the bowl with his spoon. "I appreciate you making sure your landlord is fed ... with his favorite meal."

I roll my eyes with a laugh. "Oh, shut up. I made it for myself. I'm sure you had plenty of food *on your date*."

"Food sucked. This is better. Everything you made was always better than anything I could pick up at a restaurant."

"Yeah, right. You do know every *good luck* cupcake I made before your games was burned or tasted like shit."

"Yet I still ate them, didn't I?"

"To be nice and not make me feel bad."

"Yes, to be nice, but also because I loved that you took the time to do something special for me. You didn't give up. You kept trying to make them better with each game, and I loved that. I missed those bitter-ass, burned cupcakes after you left."

"I'm sure you've met someone who doesn't burn everything she touches."

"I haven't met anyone who doesn't burn shit as well as you." He leans in. "And, honestly, I haven't been looking either."

My lips pull up, ready to smile, but the air drifts my way as he goes to take another bite.

"J'adore," I whisper. "Dior."

His spoon drops into his bowl. "Huh?"

"You smell like her."

At least he screwed someone with decent perfume taste.

The reminder of him with another woman ruins the moment, ruins the memories that were rushing into me like waves. He's questioned me about whom I've been sleeping with since he moved back, but he thinks it's okay for him to do whatever he wants.

I shake my head. "How's that for a double standard? Don't you dare question me about my sex life anymore." I want to snatch the gumbo from him and pour it over his head. "I'm going to have sex with whomever I want to have sex with, too. If I didn't have to work tomorrow morning, I'd have a collection of men here, an orgy, getting screwed in every position possible while hanging from the ceiling."

A hard laugh interrupts my rant. "Keep lying if it makes you feel better."

"I'm not lying. I've had experiences, *plenty* of experiences, with other men."

He leans forward to settle his bowl on the table and slumps down in his seat, looking defeated. "Well, that ruins a man's appetite. I'd appreciate your not going into details, please."

"Why are you here?" I question.

His arm stretches along the back of the couch, settling behind me. "I have no fucking idea."

He needs to leave. He needs to stay.

Jesus, what do I want him to do?

"So, you hit it and quit it?" I ask. His bringing up the fact that he was with another woman tonight might lead me away from wanting his company.

An exasperated sigh leaves his lips. "I didn't fuck anyone tonight, Lauren."

"Yeah, right," I snort.

"I tried to."

"Tried to? Is your cock broken now?" I'm silently calling *bullshit* with the dirty look on my face.

"I couldn't get … into it. I was thinking about someone else. I *called* her by someone else's name. She gave me a free pass and dropped to her knees to suck my cock. A trooper who was ready to rid me of my thoughts of the woman who didn't deserve them."

God, I don't want to hear this, but I have to.

I can't stop myself from interrupting him. "If a man said another woman's name while I was grinding on him, I most likely would've poured battery acid on his junk."

"Are you sure you should be in the medical field?" He kicks my foot with his. "Better yet, are you sure you should be around anyone's junk? I'm suggesting you change professions and seek employment at a convent."

I roll my eyes. "Go on. So, chick gave you a blow job to rid your thoughts of a woman you shouldn't be thinking of—aka, most likely me. How is that any different from me talking about my sex life?" *It's weird, sitting on the couch where I did the same thing with him.*

"I shouldn't be having this conversation with you."

"Nuh-uh. You started it. You come in, smelling like the perfume of an expensive hooker, and start this story. You'd better finish it." My tone changes from friendly to annoyed. "You fucked her, didn't you?"

"She stroked me twice, and I stopped her."

"Whatever," I mutter, rolling my eyes. "You don't have to lie."

"Trust me, Dyson, you have no idea how much I'd love to go into detail about fucking another woman to hurt you."

"Then, why didn't you have sex with her?"

"Because, every time I tried to go through with it, I would stop because I didn't want to fucking hurt you. I couldn't think about her lips wrapped around my cock while you sat in this apartment, alone. It would've been wrong for me to have her suck my cock when I wished she were you."

What the hell do I say back to that?

"I, uh … appreciate it, but don't think our situation has to stop you from having … sexual encounters. I'm looking for a new place, and I will be out of your hair as soon as I can." *That's a lie.* "Then, you'll be free to go back to screwing women in here again."

His brows scrunch together. "You're the only woman I've had in here. Never felt the urge to have anyone else." He lets out a stressed breath. "I'd appreciate it if you extended the same courtesy. Go to their place. Screw them in their car. Let's have a mutual understanding that this is a no-fucking zone."

"What about the bedroom at your dad's you're crashing in? Is that in the no-fucking zone?"

"Do you want it to be?"

Yes! Yes!

"You can do whatever you want, Gage."

My breath catches in my throat when his gaze locks on mine, and he goes quiet until our eye contact is strong. I want to close my eyes, cut off our connection, but I can't pull away. I feel this affinity in my core, and that's exactly what he wants.

"Do you want it to be?" he repeats, enunciating each word.

I shrug and play with my hands without looking away. "I mean, it'd be weird, knowing my ex-boyfriend is only feet away, screwing another woman, but that's what they make Xanax and headphones for."

"Then, my bedroom is also a no-fucking zone."

"Glad we could come up with an agreement of where the no-fucking areas are." I pause. "Have you … slept with an ungodly number of women since me?"

What girl wouldn't want to scoop him up and throw him into her bed?

"A few here and there. You?" He shakes his head. "I don't know if I want to know the answer."

"A few here and there," I say in the same tone as his.

"Were they as great as I was?"

I slap his shoulder. "Really?"

So not going there. If I share stories, he might do the same.

"I had to crack a joke. Otherwise, I'd want to kill any other man who'd touched you." He picks up the bowl and goes back to eating. "You know, back then, I thought I'd be the only man who ever touched you like that. The only man you ever made love to."

"I haven't made love to anyone else." I sigh, and my answer stops him mid-bite.

He keeps our eye contact, his spoon half in the air, and waits for me to keep going.

"I mean, I've had sex, but it's never been anything serious. What about you? You ever *made love* to anyone?" I don't bother asking if he's had sex. No way he's been celibate since our breakup.

"Made love? Only you."

Those are the same words he said the first time he slid inside me. The same words he repeated every time we had sex.

"Only you," he mutters again.

The bowl goes to the table again, and he turns, so he's facing me. I lick my lips, and the mood in the room drifts into something dangerous.

No, I can't get turned on right now.

The need to straddle him and see if he's still as good as he was then tears at me.

Does he still know every weak spot on my body?

No. Don't go there.

This crazy thinking must be a side effect of the lack of sex in my life. It's been months since I've gotten laid.

He moves in closer.

One time.

Maybe we can do it one more time and get that frustration out. I've heard hate sex is all the rage.

I close my eyes, waiting for him to make the first move, and open them at the sound of the bowl moving. He's up on his feet, gumbo in hand, and walking to the kitchen.

"Are you leaving?" I ask while he sets his bowl in the sink.

"I have to before I push you down on that couch and fuck you."

Wait! I want to say. *Please do.*

I don't have time to state an argument before he's gone, the door slamming shut behind him.

I told myself that Gage would never come back to Blue Beech after what I did.

That a second chance was never in the cards for us.

Maybe I was wrong.

.

TWELVE

Gage

AS SOON AS I walk into my bedroom, I rip out of my jeans and head straight to the shower, desperate to tend to my hard-as-a-rock cock. The water rains down on me while I settle one hand against the tiled wall and stroke myself using the other, the same way I have done for years while thinking about her.

Rough and hard and fast.

Anger and frustration mingled with lust.

Lauren was as turned on as I was.

She wanted to fuck, and so help me God, I wanted to fuck her more than anything. More than when I had been a horny teen, sticking my dick into her for the first time.

I pump my hips, imagining it's her hand instead of mine, her lips sucking my tip. Even if she had wanted it, there was no way I wouldn't be disgusted with myself for letting her touch my dick after Susie the Grinder had her hands on me.

"Fuck, Lauren," I grunt out. "Fuck yes."

My cum shoots down the drain as I catch my breath.

Letting her move in was a bad idea.

Letting her back into my head was a terrible idea.

This time, it'll be tougher getting her out.

MY HAND CLENCHES around my phone when I read the text my friend—slash—once partner from Chicago sent me this morning.

Luke: Missy applied for an appeal.

Motherfucker. That won't be happening on my watch. My hands shake as I type out my response.

Me: I'll die before I allow that to happen.

I have to stop myself from throwing my phone across the room.

Luke: I'm with you, bro. I'll ask around and collect as much info as I can.

Me: Appreciate it.

Luke: You doing okay?

Me: As good as I can be.

Luke: Take care of yourself. You have my number if you need anything.

Me: Thanks, man.

A text comes in with the link to Missy's appeal paperwork. My teeth grit, my shoulders turning tense, while I slowly read it, taking in word by word. I nearly drop my phone at the sound of a knock at the front door. I shove it into my pocket and kick my feet against the hardwood floor on my way to answer it.

My interest piques when I eye Lauren through the glass. She's moving from one foot to the other, and the sight of her wearing one of my high school tees helps ease some of the anger from Luke's revelation. I hope like hell our conversation will stop me from boarding the first flight to Chicago to raise hell.

"Hey," she greets when I step out onto the porch and shut the door behind me.

Her short blue pajama shorts, which stop mid-thigh and show off her toned legs, are an extension to one of my old T-shirts. Traces of her nipples cut through the fabric of the white tee.

Shit, don't stare.

Is she trying to kill me?

Her gaze shoots down my body the same way I did hers, but I

was more discreet about it. She's either clueless to how transparent she is or she doesn't care. My cock twitches in my shorts. She needs to quit looking at me like she wants me for breakfast before I have her pussy as mine.

I tip my chin up in response. "Morning."

She bites into her lip and looks past me, into the house. "Sorry if I woke anyone up, but something is wrong with the water. I can't get any decent water pressure in the shower. Hudson said he'd stop by sometime today to look at it, so I wanted to give you a heads-up he was coming."

"I'll take a look at it."

There's sleep in her eyes, exhaustion on her face, and her thick hair is pulled into a ponytail, loose strands moving with the morning wind. "You sure?"

"If there's a problem, it's my responsibility." I cock my head toward the loft. "Come on, let's take a look at it."

The sun is rising as I lead her to the loft, and I don't realize I'm not wearing a shirt until we make it into the bathroom. She's sans bra. We're both somewhat bare to each other. A bra is on the floor. Red. Lace.

So fucking sexy.

She kicks at it with her feet. "Sorry. I was planning on cleaning up before I left for work."

"I don't mind the new decor." I step into the tub and quickly figure out the solution. "Looks like the showerhead is clogged. I'll get a new one and fix it after work."

"Should've been the first thing I checked. I'm working a double today, so I won't be back until late. There's no rush."

"You can use the shower in the house if you want."

She shakes her head. "Dallas said he'd lend me his shower in exchange for me bringing diapers."

"I heard you were a second-time auntie."

"It's a big responsibility, you know." She leans against the counter and crosses her arms. "Giving them candy and sending them home on a sugar high. I'm the best aunt ever." She sighs. "In all seriousness, it did bring my brother out of the darkness. Samuel is one of the best things to happen to our family lately."

"Glad to hear that. Dallas is a good dude. Good things happen to good people." I step out of the tub. "I'll try to have it fixed by the time you're home tonight, so you won't be on diaper duty again."

"Thank you." She pauses. "We, uh ... never discussed rent."

"Let me talk with my dad and get back with you." *Not happening.*

Kyle was right when he said I wouldn't take a penny from her.

"Cool." She picks up her bra, tosses it into the hamper, and closes the lid before grabbing her bag.

I stop her before she leaves. "As your landlord, it's probably smart I give you my number—you know, in case anything else like this happens again."

"Fair point."

I rattle off my number, and she punches it into her phone. I'm tempted to ask for hers but don't. I can't go there ... can't risk texting her when I'm desperate.

I'm about to leave the bathroom when she stands on her tiptoes, grabs my chin, and pulls it to the side, examining my cheek. "How are your stitches? Any pain or irritation?"

"No pain, no irritation. They haven't been bothering me at all."

She keeps inspecting them. "They're healing nicely."

I smile. "Because they were done by the best, right?"

"Duh." She follows me out of the bathroom. "I'll see you, uh ... later. Thank you for fixing the shower."

"It's no problem." I clear my throat when she turns around. "And nice shirt."

She pulls at the bottom while hiding a smile. "My wardrobe is limited right now."

"Wear my clothes as much as you like. The sight makes my dick hard."

A blush fills her cheeks when I take one last glimpse at her before leaving.

———

"WHO TOOK the report on Lauren's landlord situation?" I ask. "It was reported to her insurance company that she might've started the fire, so they're trying to fuck her over on cutting a check."

"Oh, you mean, after you were supposed to bring her in and never did?" Kyle replies.

Pretty much.

"I questioned her. She didn't do it."

"You're believing criminal exes now?"

"The dude is pissed she turned him down for a date. He followed her out of Down Home the other night and gave her shit for not going home with him. Lauren hadn't started that fire. His dick is the one blaming her."

"Damn, does she have a golden vagina? All you men falling for her."

"You might want to shut your mouth if you don't want to be eating through a straw for the next six months."

"Yeah, yeah. She's your first love, your one and only, the other half of your heart."

"You need me to mention the straw part again?"

He opens the dashboard and pulls a straw out, opens his coffee cup, tosses the lid, and drops the straw in. He annoyingly slurps from it while taking a drink of his coffee. "Straw or not, I'll still drink like a motherfucker."

"I hate your ass, you know that?"

"Love you, too, brother. I'll have Sanders look into your arsonist sweetie's case."

"Appreciate it."

"You sleep with her yet?"

"Who?" I know whom he's referring to.

"Who the fuck do you think I'm talking about? Kim Kardashian? Have you slept with *Lauren* yet? The date who you not only bailed on but also called the wrong name called *my* date and told her about it after you left, interrupting us during sex. I love you, dude. I loved y'all together, but I don't like seeing you get fucked over—again."

"We're not screwing. That ship has sailed, and we both know it."

"Not yet."

I shoot him a dirty look.

"If that's the case, Tamra has another friend she can hook you up with. Quit pining over your live-in ex-girlfriend."

"She doesn't fucking live with me," I cut in.

"As I was saying, you two are only feet away from each other, and I'm sure you're dying to have her. Might as well let a hot chick help with that frustration."

"I'm too busy to worry about women at the moment."

THIRTEEN

Lauren

JAY SLAMS his tray down on the table and takes the seat across from me in the hospital cafeteria. "FYI, my husband is pissed at you."

I drop my fork in my salad. "What? Why?"

"He has yet to receive an update on the ex situation. It's imperative he knows if you've had sex with him yet."

"No," I answer around a groan. "There will be no us having sex. In case you've failed to remember, he had his date in the car with us!"

"And he couldn't have given a shit about her. He was at Clayton's *for you.* He took you home *for him.* For his own peace of mind that you'd be safe. I'll bet he dropped his date off and went home alone."

Not exactly alone. But I won't be divulging that information.

"Behind all of that pissed-off, hard facade, Gage is a caring man who'll always think about my safety. That's who he is. He's a police officer. It's his duty."

"True, but he also does it because he loves you." He sighs. "You loved him at one point. Those feelings were there, and from what it looked like at dinner, they still are."

"That's not true."

"When's the last time you went on a date?"

"My job is my boyfriend. Saving people's lives is my orgasm. This is where I spend all of my time. You know that."

"So, why not date someone who works here? The doctors talk. I know how many people in this building have asked you out."

"I'm not interested in dating, and FYI, I've slept with someone I work with, so I'm not depriving myself of orgasms," I lie. I've never even gone on a date with someone from the hospital.

"Who was it?" He stares at me. "Tell me it wasn't Pete from ortho."

I draw a line over my lips and fake zip.

It wasn't Pete from ortho.

It was Victor, my vibrator, courtesy of Amazon Prime.

———

I CANNOT WAIT to shower and sleep this shift away.

The lights are on at the loft when I pull into the drive.

Gage must've forgotten to turn them off after he fixed the shower. Unless I left them on, which wouldn't surprise me, given I'm supposedly a lousy tenant and all. If this place goes up in flames, I'm for sure getting locked up.

There's no sign of life in the main house, but Gage's truck is here, so he must be in bed. I walk through the front door and start stripping out of my scrubs. I didn't check myself in the mirror before leaving work, but I know my eyes are puffy, and hints of mascara are running down my cheeks.

I'm rubbing my eyes and yawning as I make my way into the bathroom and then let out a full-on dramatic scream.

Gage is standing in front of me with a smile on his face, wiping his wet hands off on a towel. I'm in my bra and panties. I repeat, I'm in my bra and panties in front of my ex-boyfriend, and they're suddenly more soaked than what I'll be when I get in the shower. He's shirtless, and remnants of water are running down his fit chest.

"What are you doing here?" I ask, catching my breath.

"Fixing your shower," he says, pointing to the tub. "Sorry, I didn't mean to scare you. I should've given you a heads-up that I'd be here, but I don't have your number. I had a long day, and this was the first free minute I had."

"It's no problem."

He hands me a towel. "Trust me, babe, there's nothing on you I haven't seen before. To be more specific, I've seen *much more*." He chuckles and licks his lips. "I also know what you taste like."

"I can say the same for you," I whisper.

He wipes the side of his mouth. "Kyle is convinced we're going to have sex."

"Kyle must have turned mental since we last talked." I give him a frustrated glare. "You know he hasn't talked to me since we broke up? I know bro code is real and all, but homeboy hates my guts."

"That's my boy."

"Gee, thanks. I don't remember forming a hate club against you."

"Never told him to hate you. He formed that opinion on his own, and I'm not sure how anyone could be pissed at me for your ending our relationship." He leans against the wall. "You know I would've never done that to you, especially the way you did it."

"Can we go back to joking about sex now? I'm too exhausted to talk about blame and people being mad at me."

He blinks at me a few times. "You're upset."

I nod, trying to stop myself from bursting into tears.

"Long day?"

"You have no idea." I slump down the wall and settle on the floor.

"What happened?"

A tear slides down my cheek. "We had a baby come in this evening who'd gotten into his mother's coke stash while she was passed out. He overdosed, and instead of calling for help or bringing him to the hospital, she called her mother. His grandmother brought him in because his mother was afraid she'd be arrested for possession. By the time he got to us, he was having seizures, and we knew it was too late."

"Fuck," he hisses.

"I was his nurse. Jay, his doctor." Another tear falls down my face. "We tried everything but we weren't able to save him. Two years old and no longer alive, thanks to his selfish mother. I had no choice but to let her see him when she finally got the balls to come to the hospital. God, I wanted to snap when she screamed at us to save her baby like it was our fault, and then she dared to say we didn't do enough to keep her baby alive." I sigh, the memory jerking through me, and clench my jaw. "They prep us for situations like these. I've watched patients of all ages die, witnessed people lose limbs and go through severe trauma. It's hard, but for some reason, this woman infuriated me. Her son died because she was irresponsible and negligent."

His face pales when he sits next to me and drags me into his arms. "There's nothing worse than a mom who purposely endangers her child. Any parent who does that is a self-centered piece of shit." It doesn't feel weird when he tilts his head down and kisses the top of my hair. Surprisingly, it feels comfortable and comforting. "What you do is extraordinary, Lauren. Hard on the heart but extraordinary."

"You do the same," I whisper, snuggling into his side. "You're just as upset as I am."

He squeezes me. "I'm not someone who likes people hurting others. Trust me, there are times I've had to hold myself back from snapping, too."

I want him to tell me more, but I also don't.

Police officers are a constant in the hospital, and some of their stories make my skin crawl.

I wipe my eyes and slowly pull away, sniffling. "Thank you for listening to me." I nod toward his tear-and mascara-stained tee. "And for letting me ruin your clothes."

"Anytime. You either ruin them or steal them. Nothing has changed there."

"For some reason, when you steal a guy's shirt, it makes it a hundred times more comfortable."

"You're welcome to them anytime." He stands up and helps me to my feet. "Shower is fixed and all yours. Is there anything else you need while I'm here?"

Pull me back into your arms.

Stay here with me.

I shake my head. "You're probably just as tired as I am."

He rubs my back. "Get your shower. It'll help you relax."

I undress, and the water pressure is perfect when I step underneath the hot water. My tears fall down the drain, and I wish it'd take the memory of today with it. These are the days I don't love my job, when I question if I went into the right field, and when I wonder if I should take another career route.

I made the decision to set my feelings aside when I decided to become a nurse. Caring for my patients is priority number one. At times, it is the hardest part of the job.

Not having emotions would be beautiful because pain is so ugly. Watching neglect and not having the freedom to scream about it at the top of your lungs is painful. It's hard, having a heart when people come in without one.

And that's what I feel like happened today.

My sobs grow stronger.

I fought for that baby.

At least, in the short time he was with us, he had people fighting for his life, for his safety, for his happiness.

The hard part was that we failed him.

His mother failed him.

The system failed him.

And those are the cases that are the hardest to fight at work.

I wash my hair while releasing all my frustrations and scrub my skin harsher than necessary when cleaning it. I shiver as I dry off and throw on my pajamas.

Gage is sitting on the perfectly made, untouched bed when I get out, and a glass of water is sitting on the nightstand next to it.

"You haven't slept in the bed yet?" he asks.

I shake my head. "I crash on the couch."

"Why?"

I shrug. "The memories. The sheets still smell like you."

"Do me a favor and make them smell like you, so I have something to look forward to when I move back in."

"What? You said the place was for rent."

I had been right. He never intended to rent it out. Gage loved this place, loved his space, and would never let anyone take it over. Even when he moved. Neither would his father.

Amos had numerous offers to rent it when Gage left and turned them all down, hoping his son would one day return.

"My dad was thinking about it but changed his mind. You're more than welcome to stay until you find a place though. He enjoys my company in the house."

I narrow my eyes his way. "I don't understand. Why would you give it up and let me stay here?"

"It's late. You've had a hard day." He kisses my forehead. "Catch some sleep. Let me know if the shower gives you any more problems, if you need someone to talk to, anything, okay?"

FOURTEEN

Gage

I GRAB my phone from the nightstand when it beeps.

Unknown: You up?

I start to text back, *Who's this?*, when another text comes through.

Unknown: It's Lauren.

Fuck. I was afraid of having her number.

Me: Wide awake. What's up?

Lauren: Care to give a girl some company?

Me: Can't sleep?

Lauren: No.

Me either.

Me: On my way.

I jump out of bed, fully aware it's a bad idea. I step into a pair of gym shorts and throw on a shirt before quietly slipping out of the house and into the warm summer night. Grasshoppers chirp as I stroll down the walkway and then up the stairs.

The door is unlocked, and she's on the couch, her legs brought up to her chest. Hair wet. Eyes swollen.

"You know," I say, walking into the room, "the chances of you falling asleep are higher in a bed than on the couch. I can almost guarantee that."

She pats the cushion next to her. "Hey, I find this couch comfy. I can't believe you haven't changed anything in here."

"I have yet to find the time to hone in on my interior design skills." And I want to keep the memories. Even though they haunt me like a motherfucker, I want them all. "I had nothing in Chicago that reminded me of home, so the recollection is nice sometimes."

Curiosity crosses her face, curiosity of what my life was like in Chicago, but she stops herself from asking those questions.

Not that I blame her for her interest. It's what every Blue Beech resident has wanted since I came home. Answers. A report of what I was up to. Questions of why their golden boy got dumped, moved thousands of miles away, and then never came back for years—not for holidays, not for reunions, not even for my father's retirement party from the electrical company. Instead of celebrating that with him here, I flew him to me. I kept in touch with no one, didn't join any social networks, and became a stranger to the place that had raised me.

She clears her throat. "You want to watch a show or movie?"

I'll do anything to get her mind off of her horror of a day. I collapse on the other side of the couch and keep my eyes on her while making myself comfortable. "True crime still your jam?"

"My jam. My peanut butter."

"Your pickles on your peanut butter, you mean?"

A flicker of a smile comes my way. "My pickles on my peanut butter."

Lauren is the only person I know who enjoys PPB & Js—pickles, peanut butter, and jelly. She's most likely the *only* person on the planet who does, considering I have yet to meet someone else with that indulgence.

"True crime it is then," I say. I dramatically shake my head. "You and your serial killers."

She snags the remote off the coffee table. "Blame yourself. You're the one who got me obsessed with all those documentaries. My nickname at work is Nurse Paranoid because I assume everyone is a serial killer."

"Those shows are what made me decide to go into law enforcement."

My mom was the ringleader in our true-crime obsession. I grew up watching them and, as Lauren and I grew closer and older, we shared our loves of different interests with each other.

I got her hooked on true crime, and she got me hooked on strawberry-banana milkshakes.

She messes with the remote and scrolls through the guide on TV. "See, something good did come out of our documentary binges. Do you have any new favorites?"

What I want to tell her is no, I don't because I stopped watching any shows involving true crime years ago. Not because it reminded me of her, but because it became my life. I've seen it firsthand—the murders, the bribery, all of it. I don't though because she needs this. Her mind deserves to venture into somewhere else, and if it means I have to sit through something that might give me flashbacks, so be it.

"The choice is all yours," I answer.

Her feet drop as she lies back on the couch and brings herself to the fetal position after making her selection. A thin blanket is wrapped around her shoulders, her head rests on a pillow, and her attention goes to the TV.

I stay in my corner, my feet crossed at my ankles, and I surprisingly stay calm. Maybe it's her presence. Maybe my attempt to soothe her has done the same for me.

Two documentaries later, she's snoring. We made no light conversation. It was all solitude as we sat in the dimly lit room. I quietly slide off the couch and tiptoe out of the loft even though all I want to do is stay there, drag her into my arms, and create more memories on that couch.

I don't bother turning on the lights when I make it into my room and fall on the bed. My heart feels lighter tonight, and a smile is twitching at my lips as I think about how great it is to be around Lauren again. It doesn't take long for me to fall asleep, which is out of the ordinary.

Too bad my nightmares still come back to haunt me, sucking away all the calmness she gave me.

It's the same conversation.

The same scene that plays over and over again.

"WHAT DID YOU DO, MISSY?" *My voice grows louder, angrier, more venom flowing with every sharp, nervous word spit out.* "What the fuck did you do?"

"It's all your fault, you know," *she fires back.* "If you had loved me right, none of this would've happened!"

"You did this out of spite for me?"

I move closer at the sound of sirens in the background. Determination thrums through me to get to her before they do, and I drop to my knees, prepared to plead if need be.

"Where is he?" *I stress, tears biting at my eyes.*

Her smile is wicked. "You'll never know." *Those four words kill me yet satisfy her as she sings them out.*

I'M COVERED in sweat when I wake up. I jump out of bed and throw my soaking shirt off. Then, I go to the kitchen for water and decide I'm in need of fresh air.

FIFTEEN

Lauren

"OH, COME ON," I mutter during attempt number five of starting my car.

Can anything else go wrong this week?

My apartment catching on fire.

Check.

Ex back in town.

Check.

Having one of the hardest shifts in my career last night that emotionally drained me.

Check.

My car playing the game of not wanting to start.

Check.

The sun beams down on me. It's the butt crack of dawn, which means it'll be an inconvenience to wake anyone up and ask for a ride. I grab my bag from the passenger seat and start to rifle through it, searching for my phone. I hope it's not too complicated for them to find a replacement for me at the last minute.

I unlock my screen at the same time I hear the sound of a door slamming. I look through the windshield to see Gage stepping off the porch, a coffee cup in his hand, and sweat trickling down his chest.

The TV was still on and Gage was gone when I woke up on the couch this morning. I don't know how much longer he stayed after I fell asleep, but if it weren't for him being there with me, I wouldn't have slept at all last night. He was there for me as I broke down and cried in his arms, and the memories of when he'd done that in the past haunted me while I got ready for work.

I drop my phone back into my lap as he hops down the steps and meets me.

"Car trouble?" he asks.

I cringe as I attempt to start my car again, and it fails. I dramatically grip the steering wheel. "Yep."

"You know what the problem is, don't you?"

"If I did, I would already be gone."

"It won't start as a result of its ugliness. It's decided that it's finally time to go to car heaven."

"Shove it," I grumble. "It's too early to hear you passing judgment on my car."

"You have to work?"

"Supposed to, but I was about to call off. I can't expect anyone to make an hour round-trip to take me back and forth to work."

"I can. My shift at the station doesn't start for another two hours and will most likely end before yours does."

I think back to what happened last night. The way he held me as I cried, how the memories of when we'd hung out crept back into my soul. Getting attached to Gage will only ruin me later. It's dangerous for us to get close again. He hates me. And what if he wants to know why I broke up with him? It'll kill him that I have to keep my secret.

Everything is moving too fast. We went years without speaking, and now, all of a sudden, we're talking daily.

"Thank you for the offer, but I can call off."

"Lauren, I don't have cooties."

"You have much more than that."

My heart. A cock I can't stop thinking about.

"In my truck now."

I lose sight of him as he moves and taps the hood of my car.

"Let me change real quick."

I jump out of my car. "You don't have to do this."

He turns around and starts walking backward. "It's no big deal."

"Why are you being so nice to me?"

"As I told you before, I've been asking myself the same question since I arrested you."

His truck is unlocked, and I throw my bag onto the floorboard. Gage comes back, dressed in jeans and a tee. Two coffee cups are in his hand.

"In case you want one for the ride," he says, handing it to me.

I take a drink and groan. "This is delicious."

"My dad likes that sweet shit, which I can't stand. I think the creamer is cinnamon roll flavor or some shit."

I sip the coffee and straighten my legs out while he pulls out of the drive. He hasn't turned on the radio or initiated any other conversation after the sweet-coffee talk. I can't stand silence. I'd rather face an awkward conversation than awkward silence.

"What have you been up to since ... you know?"

He glances over at me. "Since you dumped my ass?"

Well, shit. Maybe the silence would've been a better option.

"Since we broke up," I correct.

"I moved to Chicago, worked a job in law enforcement, and then decided it was time to come home."

"That's it? Anything else happen in all those years?"

"Nothing I want to talk about." He focuses on the road. "What about you?"

"After graduating from nursing school, I snagged a job in the ER at the hospital, moved back home, and my apartment caught on fire, which lead me to crashing at my ex's place."

"That's it?" he asks, throwing my words in my face. "Nothing else happened in all those years?"

"Hudson got engaged to Stella Mendes," I add, moving the attention from me to my family.

There's been nothing too exciting in my life. During college, I immersed myself in my studies, and now, all I do is work to keep myself busy, so I don't think about my high school sweetheart. I've been disciplined enough not to look him up, though the urge has hit me so many times.

Admission time. I did look him up twice when I drank too much. The first time was the day after I graduated from college. God, I wanted to share the news with him. He had known it was my dream. The second was a year ago when my sister-in-law passed away from breast cancer. She'd died young, in her early thirties, and regret hit me that day. I wanted to apologize for what I'd done.

I couldn't find anything on him. He had no social media accounts, nothing. Gage was a ghost to everyone I knew since we broke up.

"I heard about their engagement," he says. "News travels fast when a Hollywood celebrity gets engaged to a Blue Beech local."

"Lucy died," I go on, my voice lowering as my chest aches.

"I heard about that as well. My heart broke for your family when my dad told me."

"Dallas had another baby with Stella's friend and personal assistant."

"Damn, I have missed some shit."

"Care to share anything else personal about *you*?"

"Not much to me, Dyson. I've never been engaged to a celebrity or knocked anyone up."

I wait for him to elaborate, wishing on anything that he'll give me more, but he doesn't.

"One-sided conversations are so fun," I comment.

"The hell do you want me to tell you, Lauren? What do I owe you?"

This is not a conversation I want to have first thing in the morning before working a double.

I cross my arms and shift in my seat to look out the window. "I wish I had never told you anything. I should've moved on, gotten married, had fifteen kids, so I could prove to myself and everyone else that I could be happy without you."

"Yeah, well, I wish I could say the same shit, but my love for you, my fucking *obsession* for you, has never allowed that. My love for you has ruined my entire fucking life."

The hell?

"What did I ruin for you? You could've easily gotten married and started a family. Don't blame that on me. It was your stubbornness."

"I was married."

I suddenly feel like I'm suffocating. "Say what?"

"I got married."

"You're married?" I shriek like I misheard him.

"No, I got married and am now divorced."

"You're lying." The words sound like whimpers leaving my lips.

He shakes his head. "I'm not."

"You said you'd never made love to anyone else," I whisper.

"Never loved her."

My brain is scrambling. "Why would you marry someone you didn't love?"

"It's complicated."

"Good thing we have plenty of time."

"That doesn't mean I'm talking about it."

"You were married."

"Yes." The topic seems to frustrate him.

I play with the fabric of my scrubs. "Where is she now? Do you guys still talk?"

Is she prettier than I am? Skinnier? Smarter?

I'm jealous of a woman I've never met.

"In prison."

Okay, maybe not so jealous now.

"What?" I wait for him to tell me he's kidding, that it's some sick joke, but he doesn't. "Care to elaborate on that truth bomb?"

"No. We married for a stupid reason, she lost her goddamn mind, and I divorced her."

"Just to clarify real quick. Does the wifey work in a prison, or is she an *inmate* in prison?"

"She's incarcerated."

That doesn't tell me anything.

"What did she do to earn her trip to the pen?"

"She was fucking selfish."

"Okay," I draw out. "With your work in law enforcement, I'm sure it's no secret that you can't be given a cellmate for simply being selfish. You have to commit a crime to do the time."

"Cool. Thanks for the education. Still not talking about it."

This morning conversation has taken a wrong turn. A turn I don't like.

"My stuff will be out of the loft by the end of the week. Hopefully, before that, considering I don't have much. Don't worry about picking me up tonight. I'll find a ride."

He points to himself in amazement. "You're pissed at me?"

I throw my hands up. "Yes!"

"Lauren, you have no right to be angry with me."

"You married another woman!"

"And you left me, giving me the opportunity to marry her. Had we never broken up, you would've been the only woman I ever said *I do* to."

"It doesn't matter or change how I feel about it. You've been harboring this grudge, this resentment toward me, for breaking your heart, yet you married another woman." I snort. "Then, you lied straight to my face about never falling in love again."

"Never loved her. We were friends, and I married her as a favor."

A favor? Who marries someone as a favor? Not sane people, that's for sure.

"Bull-fucking-shit. Maybe you need to be locked up with her—for *selfish* reasons, of course."

"Lauren," he says in warning.

"Screw you, *Gage*. If you didn't love her, why did you feel the need to marry her, like it's a common courtesy or some shit?"

"Not going there, nor will I ever." He shakes his head. "I should've never told you. Forget I said anything."

"*Whoa*, pump those brakes, buddy. You can't throw that truth bomb and then expect me to *forget it*."

I have so many questions.

"That's where you're wrong. Just like you don't owe me an explanation of why you broke up with me, I don't owe you one about what I've been doing since then."

I stomp my feet against the floorboard when he turns into the entrance of the hospital. I need more time to drag admissions out of him. Although I doubt he'll be confiding in me about anything else.

"What time does your shift end?" he asks, shifting his truck into park.

"Don't worry about it. I'll find a ride. Go call your wife." I'm acting petty, I know, but I'm dizzy while processing that he moved on with someone else. I shouldn't be, given I'd pushed him into her arms, but it's the only reaction I can give at the moment.

"We're too old to play fucking games," he says, annoyance running through his words. "What time, Lauren?"

"Eight," I huff out.

"I'll be here."

I step out and slam the door.

He got married.

Said *I do* to another woman.

Gage Perry has no right to be angry with me.

SIXTEEN

Gage

TELLING Lauren about Missy was a mistake.

Her too-many-questions road-trip game defrosted my defenses. My admission clipped out before I knew I'd even been thawed. Lauren is notorious for bringing my every thought out into the light, but she'll never know *everything*.

That shit is going with me to the grave.

No one in Blue Beech but my father will ever know. That nightmare will stay in Chicago.

The story made local headlines but never went national. Missy grew up in a family with politicians hitting every branch in the tree. Their pockets were full of old money, and they were experts in writing checks to fix any blemishes on their reputations. They could erase any word in an article with the click of a pen, forming the dollar sign.

That was the first and only time I was grateful for their pocketbooks. The thought of *his* picture being dissected and on display for the world to see would've ruined me. From the first time I found him outside the station, I made it my job to protect him but failed miserably.

I sink my fingers into the leather of my steering wheel.

Moving here was my solution to take me away from the

memories of hell.

Chicago was nothing but a reminder of what I'd lost.

———

"DUDE, WHAT'S UP YOUR ASS?" Kyle asks, sliding into the passenger seat of our cruiser. "I told you this would happen. You bring the devil into your home; it'll turn into hell. You know, that's why her last building went up in flames … because she's an evil demon."

"It's too early to listen to your shit," I mutter.

The thirty-minute drive back into town had given me time to clear my head before going to work. I went home, showered, and skipped breakfast with my dad. He would've known something was wrong.

Swear to God, he and Lauren are better at reading me than I am myself.

Kyle takes a sip of coffee and sets it in the cupholder. "Dinner at Mom's tonight. Be there at seven."

"Can't," I answer.

"You *can*, and you *will*. You know how I feel about people bailing on my mother."

Not a lie. Kyle will throw down with anyone to defend her.

"I have to pick Lauren up from the hospital after her shift."

No doubt he'll find amusement in that.

"You her chauffeur now, too? Driving Miss Demon?"

"Her car broke down this morning. She needed a ride."

His green eyes light up in amusement. "Bring her with you."

I glance over at him before pulling out of his driveway, seconds passing, to verify he's the one in the car with me.

I snort when I realize he's not kidding. "That's a big fuck no."

"It's my mom's birthday dinner, bro, and she's been asking about you nonstop since you moved back. You've been blowing off every invitation since you've been home. Not cool."

Damn, I feel like an asshole.

He's not lying. I haven't done much of anything, except work and hang out with my dad.

"I'll drop Lauren off and then be there. That cool?"

"Not so fast. You opened up the can of worms. Bring her with you. I want to see with my own two eyes that you're over her. Prove it to me."

"And I want to kick your ass sometimes, but it doesn't mean it'll happen." I narrow my eyes at him. "I take that back. You keep talking shit about Lauren and me getting back together, and I'mma end up kicking your ass."

"Yeah, yeah," Kyle mutters, fishing his phone from his pocket before hitting a name and pressing it to his ear. "Hey, Ma. I'm with Gage." He pauses. "Yes, I invited him, but he declined." Another pause, and he shoves the phone into my chest.

"Gage, honey," Nancy says over the phone when I grab it. "Please come. Growing up, you were like another son to me, and I'd love to see you."

"Trust me," I say around a sigh, "I'd love to see you, but I wouldn't be able to make it until after eight. That's a long holdup for dinner."

"No holdup whatsoever," she replies in her sweet Southern voice. "I've been a night owl since retiring. I eat late."

"All right then. I have to pick up a friend from work, and then I'll be there."

"The friend is Lauren!" Kyle yells in the background and grunts when I press my fist into his stomach.

"Lauren Barnes?" Nancy asks. "I haven't spent time with that nice girl since my son shunned me from talking to her. I'd love to catch up with the both of you. See you tonight!"

The line goes dead.

I throw the phone into Kyle's lap.

"I can't wait for this shit," he says, rubbing his hands together. "It'll be the best excitement I've had—aside from your arresting her."

"Remind me to file a request for a new partner," I mutter.

Lauren is going to flip her shit when she finds out about this.

SEVENTEEN

Lauren

JAY WALKS in and leans against the break-room door, arms crossed, while I grab my bag from a locker. "Alec requests a full report on tonight's festivities with your ex-lover boy."

During our lunch break, I spilled the dilemma with my new roommate situation, and it's no surprise that he went and tattled to his hubby. Not that I can blame him. I would've done the same thing ... if I had a husband.

I let down my ponytail and brush my fingers through the strands. "There will be no story."

He grins, his bright white teeth on display. "You're rooming with your ex. There will never be a lack of a story."

"We're not *rooming* together. It's more like neighbors. I'm going home *alone*, eating canned soup, showering, and then hopping my tired butt into bed. Nothing exciting about that."

He steps away from the door and pats my arm. "Keep telling yourself that, love."

Trust me, I do.

"Have a good night, Jay," I sing out, throwing my bag over my shoulder.

He laughs. "And you have an even better one. Get laid! You deserve it for all your hard work!"

There's a text from Gage when I power my phone on that says he's in the parking lot and to let him know when I'm walking out. I reply, and he pulls up to the automatic doors as soon as I make it out.

In the back of my mind, I had wondered if he'd bail on picking me up. During every break, I checked my phone, waiting for him to tell me to call a cab, considering our ride this morning had been cringe-worthy. Tonight's goal is to make it bearable.

No ex-wife talk.

No past talk.

No breakup talk.

The weather and why NSYNC broke up will be the only conversations happening tonight, ladies and gents.

The masculine smell of aftershave and peppermint hits me when I slide into the truck.

"Long day?" he asks as I settle myself into the leather seat.

His midnight-dark hair is covered with a blue baseball cap, cloaking his forehead and showing me only a sliver of his hooded eyes. The thin white V-neck tee he's wearing shows off the tan and muscular arms that wrapped around me like a security blanket last night. Guys in V-necks are right there underneath guys with huge cocks in the What I Lust For list. He also looks as tired as I feel.

"You have no idea," I answer, strapping my seat belt on as he exits the parking lot. I thought I'd seen everything until I worked in the ER. "I appreciate the ride. Hudson said he'd have my car towed to the shop tomorrow to take a look at it."

My grandfather started Barnes Machinery and Equipment decades ago. When he retired, my father took it over, and now, my brothers are in charge. They specialize in fixing large machinery and typically don't take on pink Mustangs, but they're making an exception for their sister.

"I'll do it," Gage answers. "I hoped I'd have a second to look at it today but got caught up in some shit."

We are not friends. We cannot try to be friends.

Our trying to be friends would only produce more scars when he asks for what I can't give him.

"Don't worry about it," I say. "It's my problem, not yours." My words burst out more harshly than I intended.

"I take it, you're still pissed at me?"

No. Yes.

"I'd be lying if I said I wasn't, though I have no right to be."

Today's shift was spent working and digesting the truth bomb Gage had thrown on my breakfast plate this morning. My rationality finally returned three hours ago. I'm not too proud to admit when I'm wrong, and it wasn't fair for me to be angry ... or jealous.

I gave him the opportunity to fall in love with another woman, the green light to *marry* another woman, and I have no one to blame for my anger besides myself. I've dated and slept with other men since we've been apart, and my fear of commitment with someone else doesn't mean he had to do the same.

"I appreciate the honesty," he answers, tapping his fingers against the steering wheel.

Silence passes, and the only noise cutting through the awkwardness is the faint sound of the radio. I stare out the window but steal glances at him every few seconds, hoping he doesn't notice my taking in the way he bites into his lower lip when he's holding himself back from saying something he shouldn't.

He's done that for years. I've read him and picked up on his quirks, and I consider myself a specialist in body language. At this moment, I'm sure his lack of sharing whatever he's thinking is for the best.

I'm wondering how to move this conversation to my love of Justin Timberlake when he interrupts my thoughts by clearing his throat.

"By the way, you won't be thanking me for the ride when we make it back to town."

"Why's that? You planning on killing me and throwing my body in the woods?"

"Nancy invited me to dinner tonight," he answers. He presses his teeth to his lips again.

"Cool. Word on the street is, she makes a killer roast."

"You're about to find out for yourself."

"Such a sweet man to bring me leftovers."

"Let me correct myself. Nancy invited *us* to dinner. My mistake for the miscommunication, Dyson."

"Did you tell Nancy there was no *us* to invite?" My stomach growls, like it's fighting for its right to be pro-dinner at Nancy's. It wants something better than SpaghettiOs. I pout out my lip. "Leftovers will be both accepted and appreciated though."

"Have you eaten?"

"I managed to chow down a sandwich and an apple during one break. The other breaks were filled with chugging down coffee, so I wouldn't give a patient Viagra instead of antibiotics."

He cocks his head to the side. "That happened before?"

I shake my head. "Nope, thanks in large part to coffee."

"Doubt that's why. You know how to do your job. You've wanted to be a nurse for as long as I can remember."

His mother is the reason I became a nurse. Melody worked in the same ER years ago, and I'd sit at their kitchen table for hours, listening to her tell story after story while I threw millions of questions her way. Her passing away from congestive heart failure at forty only strengthened my passion. I wanted to pursue this career path in her memory.

He grabs his phone from the console when it rings and answers the call. "Yes, I picked her up, and we're on our way. I don't have to reply to your ungodly number of text messages for check-ins." He chuckles and sneaks a look my way. "I'll be sure to divulge that you can't wait to see your favorite person."

Oh, hell. He wasn't joking about dinner.

"Not happening," I tell him when he hangs up. "Call your pain-in-my-ass partner back and tell him I won't be in attendance." I squish my face together in a smug smile. "I wish y'all a happy dinner though."

He's still chuckling, and though it's directed at me, it feels good to hear laughter coming from someone who regularly looks like he has a stick up his ass. "I promise I did my best to stop it."

"You're a grown-ass man, and the last time I saw you naked, you had balls. Tell them no."

He smirks. "Balls are still intact, FYI. I can show you, if it helps."

"Nice to know. No need for evidence."

"I can't bail on Nancy," he says, blowing out a long breath. "It's her birthday, and she's excited we're coming. And Kyle obviously is, as well." He smirks again, unable to hide it at the mention of his best friend and Blue Beech's biggest asshole to me.

Kyle will taunt me all night. His invite isn't genuine. It is an excuse to drag me through hell.

"The last time I talked to Kyle, he gave me a ticket for a broken taillight and said he'd hate me until he took his last breath for running you out of town. I don't trust the fool around my food. He'll be topping off my drink with antifreeze."

"Chill, Dyson. He won't poison your roast." He shakes his head as I give him my best death stare. "How about this? You come, and I won't make you pay rent this month."

"Your way of convincing me to hang out with you is free rent? What am I? Vivian in *Pretty Woman*?"

"Don't say it like that."

"Is there a better way to say it?"

"It's different. Dude got laid in that movie. Doubt our night will end up with me screwing you on an expensive-ass piano."

"Don't hold your breath on that happening. You're a *married* man." Yep, my selfish ass still can't let that go.

"I'm a *divorced* man, sweetheart. We were married for five years, three of which were hell."

Five years?

His marriage wasn't a temporary thing or a favor. You can't be with someone for half of a decade and not have feelings for them. It just doesn't happen.

"Doesn't matter if it was for a day. You can't keep throwing the *I*

ruined your life bullshit in my face. You found love. You had a wife."
I throw my arms up. "Hell, you might have kids. Any Gage Juniors
running around that I should know about?"

The mood in the truck shifts, as if a surprise storm suddenly
rolled over us with the clench of his jaw. Instead of his fingers
tapping to the beat, they're now biting into the steering wheel.

"Nope, no kids," he grits out.

I'd hand him water if I didn't think he'd throw it out the window
with enough force to split the street. My question cut out a grim
memory lodged inside him.

Were he and his wife unsuccessful in having a baby?

"What did I just open up there?" I ask, the words falling from
my mouth slowly and carefully—a skill I mastered in nursing school
for better communication with patients.

"Nothing," he snaps. His attention is on the road, as if he were
waiting for something to run out in front of us.

"Okay," I draw out.

Don't push him. Don't try to get back in.

I went into nursing because I wanted to heal and help people.

The problem is, Gage is a lost cause because he doesn't want
either from me.

"I don't have to go to dinner," I say. "Tell Nancy I'll visit her
sometime this week."

"We're both going."

"Why? You look like you'd rather have your toenails ripped off
than have dinner with me."

"It's not you, I fucking swear it." He pauses to take in a few
breaths and calms himself. "If anything, you'll be the only person
capable of pulling me out of this funk, so I don't walk into that
dinner and act like a miserable dick."

"All right."

There's a new level of pain powering through this gorgeous,
tattered man. That teenage boy I fell in love with years ago has been
replaced by someone darker. I'll take responsibility for some of that
pain, but something else had ripped him apart harder than I had.

Whatever it is, it's something he doesn't want to have come out because it'll bring him to his knees. He needs someone to keep him standing, and I was thrown into his space just in time. No matter how shattered our relationship is, I'll never let him hurt alone.

Everything happens for a reason.

People can redeem themselves.

My redemption for breaking his heart will be helping him get through this dark time.

I shift around in my seat. "I am pretty hungry."

He tips his head down. "Thank you."

His fingers go back to tapping against the beat, and the rest of the car ride is limited to the sound of the radio. It's quiet yet comfortable, like we've thrown out and taken too much for one night.

————

NANCY IS happy to see me when we walk in.

Kyle, not so much.

I'm shocked he's allowed me to step foot into his parents' home. The shit-eating grin on his face confirms his invite is for research purposes only. He wants to study Gage and me together.

Nancy's warm arms wrap around me in a tight hug. The last time I saw her was when she brought in Kyle's younger sister with a broken leg from a cheerleading stunt gone wrong.

Her attention goes to Gage, his hug tighter, sadder, filled with more relief. She moved into the second-mom role after his mother's death, and I'm sure it hurt her just as much as it did Amos when he left town.

Did they still talk after he left?

"Lauren, honey, it's been so long," Nancy finally says after her hugging spree. She pokes Gage in the chest. "I'm not happy with you, young man. You haven't visited me once since you've been home."

Gage wraps his arm around her shoulders. "Sorry. It's been a busy month, but I promise I'll make it up to you. You can make me roasts anytime you like."

I'm the only one who notices the forced excitement in his voice. It's not that he's unhappy being here, but our truck conversation had stirred something hard inside him that won't be let out anytime tonight. I feel guilty that it will interfere with Nancy's time.

'Tis why I need to keep my mouth shut.

"Your father must be thrilled to have you back," she goes on, looping her arm through his. "Dinner is ready."

Kyle comes to my side before I move out of the foyer, arrogance splashed on his face, and I know this conversation is going to be a fun one.

"Satan," he clips.

"Asshole," I mutter.

"I see we're still fond of each other." He moves in closer, his voice falling to a whisper. "Don't fuck him over, you hear me? This is a new Gage, a darker man, and I won't let you hurt him again. I'll be running *you* out of town next time."

A long sigh leaves me. "Gage and I are only friends. There's nothing wrong with that."

He scratches his cheek. "Wrong. Gage will never see you as just a friend. He cares about you more than his own life. He'll never choose anyone over you, and he will sure as fuck never move on from you for some goddamn weird reason. You were his life then, and you're still his life, no matter how much he denies or fights it." He shakes his head. "I only hope to God the feeling is mutual."

My stomach twists like a coil. "We've grown up. You have no idea what you're talking about."

"Figure out what you want with him. If you plan to only be *friends*, you're doing nothing but hurting the dude. If there's a chance you can make shit right again, then I'll be Team Reconcile. He needs love, not heartbreak." He glances over to Gage in the kitchen, talking to his mom. "I don't know what's going on, but it's something deep."

We're huddled in the corner, and I'm surprised no one has called us out for looking sketchy. It helps that everyone's eyes are on Gage. Kyle's two younger sisters and brother are staring at him as if he owned the world, and Nancy keeps insisting he taste-test different desserts. Kyle's dad is nowhere to be found, which doesn't surprise me, given he's the mayor of Blue Beech.

"You don't know why he moved back to town?" I ask, watching over my shoulder, just in case Gage wants to come through and eavesdrop.

"No idea. Been trying to drag it out of him for weeks."

"Was it the wife?"

"Wife?" He scrunches his brows. "He was married?"

"You didn't know that?"

"Nope. Never mentioned a wife to me." He shakes his head in pain. "I promised myself I'd give him time to tell me what was going on before I went looking around for it. He can't lose trust in someone else."

"Good luck. Whatever it is, it's not leaving his mouth."

"You have a much stronger pull. If anyone can do it, it's you." He leans in. "You make him happy, and maybe I'll stop hating your selfish ass."

I give him the brightest smile I can manage. "Cool. I'll never stop hating you."

His hand goes to his chest, faking offense. "Me? The fuck did I do to you?"

"Pissed me off when you called me Satan and for pulling me over for stupid shit over the years."

"Prove to me you're not."

———

"WHAT MADE you come back to this boring-ass town?" Rex, Kyle's younger brother, asks.

We're at the dining room table with a spread of food in front of us. I can't believe I'm eating so many carbs this late.

"Language," Nancy warns. "Just because you graduated doesn't mean you can talk like a grown-up."

"I technically *am* a grown-up," he fires back.

"Not in this house. Here, you're still my child. So, keep your profanities to when you're hanging out with your friends."

Rex groans while putting his attention back on Gage. "Let me rephrase. Why'd you move away from Chicago? There's nothing to do round here."

That's the mystery of the year.

I grab my water, hoping Gage will give him a better answer than he gave me. Doubt that will happen. Gage has loosened up since our heated talk in the car, but there's still a wall built up in there.

"My dad needed me," is all he says, taking a sip of water.

"We're happy to have you back, and I'm thrilled you and Kyle are partners," Nancy cuts in, most likely to stop her nineteen-year-old son from blurting out personal questions. "I had no idea you were in law enforcement."

Gage wipes his mouth. "After I moved to Chicago, I went to school for a few years and did some security work, and that's when I decided that I for sure wanted to be a police officer."

"It's what we said we'd always do," Kyle chimes in.

Gage nods. "I guess the both of us still felt that calling."

"I bet you saw some traumatic shit around Chicago, huh?" Rex asks. "I've heard at least one person gets shot a night."

"Rex," Kyle says in warning.

Instead of joking like he did when Nancy reprimanded him, Rex shuts his mouth and leans back in his chair.

"It's a high-crime area for sure," Gage answers. "It could be hard at times."

"What …" Sierra, Kyle's sister, hesitates before going on, "What is the worst thing you've ever seen?"

I don't blame them for their curiosity. Blue Beech has one of the lowest crime rates in the country. Robberies are rare, let alone a homicide. Had I not worked in a hospital outside of town, where I saw more than they did, I would've been full of questions, too.

"I saw a woman kill her child," Gage answers. "The worst thing I've ever seen is a mother who murdered her son."

The table goes quiet. I drop my fork. A whimper falls from Nancy's lips.

None of us expected that answer. Sierra and Rex were anticipating some high-speed chase, something exciting, not this appetite-killing reveal.

And, with the click of a question, Gage's wall has returned, now stronger than ever.

His back is stiff against the chair, his fingers clenched around his fork, and from years of Gage experience, I know when he's close to losing it. Someone needs to take this conversation down a different path. Everyone is thinking the same thing yet not saying anything.

I take it upon myself to do it, racking my brain for a good conversation turner. "So, uh … I get puked on all the time at work."

Probably isn't the best dinner conversation either.

"That's gross," Sierra says, her face scrunching together.

She made it a point to tell Gage she was *all grown up* when she sat next to him at dinner. There's no doubt she's *all grown up*. She'd been in her early teens when Gage left and always crushed on him. Gage called it cute, but the way she's looking at him now is anything but *cute*. She recently turned twenty-one, and there's nothing not grown-up about her. To be honest, she's gorgeous.

And she's staring at him as if he's more appetizing than dinner.

Not that I can blame her.

I see a hint of a thank-you in Gage's eyes when he looks over at me, and Sierra and Rex start questioning me about hospital horror stories. I give them short ones that involve vomit and dealing with objects in places where no sane person would stick in certain areas. My job talk puts everyone at ease, and we enjoy Nancy's roast.

———

"SOOO …" Sierra draws out. "Are you and Gage back together?"

Jesus. Can we be in the same room without that question popping up?

She followed me into the kitchen after dinner while the others went outside. I can't stop myself from looking down at the sloppy outfit that I threw on after work, considering I'd planned on showering and throwing my ass into bed, and then look at hers. I've never been jealous of the chick, but she's dressed to impress tonight.

I shake my head. "We're trying the whole friendship thing."

She grins. "Perfect."

"What do you mean, *perfect*?"

She shrugs one shoulder. "Perfect as in he's single and you have no interest, which means it's okay for me to ask him out."

Am I okay with this?

I have to be. Might as well get used to seeing Gage with someone else now before we start enjoying each other's company and get hooked again.

"You can do whatever you want," I say, grabbing a water bottle from the fridge. "He can do whatever he wants."

She nods and walks out of the room, as if I've given her permission.

I've never wanted to tackle someone so hard in my life.

EIGHTEEN

Gage

SURPRISINGLY, I managed to keep my cool at dinner.

No breakdown happened when Rex asked me about the bad shit I had seen in Chicago.

As much as I enjoyed seeing Nancy, anxiety crawled through me with the need to leave so that I could clear my head. It's the same reason I've been avoiding people. Questions don't surprise me, and their curiosity can't be blamed. I was gone for years without a word. I'm a stranger to them now. A stranger they want to pick apart for entertainment.

On top of that, too much shit happened today.

Lauren knows about Missy, people wanted too many details about my life away from here, and Lauren's stepping in with the vomit talk helped buy me time to regain some of my composure. Her saving my ass doesn't do anything but drag out all the feelings for her I've tried to keep stored away. They're coming back harder and faster, hitting me while I'm weak.

The short ride back from Nancy's is filled with small talk about how delicious Nancy's meal was, and Lauren jumps out of the truck as soon as I park in the driveway. Her door slams, and she doesn't look back at me while going up the stairs to the loft, her bag thrown over her shoulder.

I step out and watch her when she makes it to the top stair.

"You're coming up," is all she says.

It's a demand, not an offer.

And I stupidly obey.

I toss my keys on the counter as she turns on the light.

"There's something you're not telling me," she says.

My hands slide into my pockets. "Don't know what you're talking about." It was a mistake, following her. I should've said good night and gone to bed.

"Don't lie to me, Gage Perry. I know you better than anyone. You're hurting. Something happened while you were gone."

No shit.

I steady myself and lean back against the wall. "Whatever you think you know, it's wrong. I'm tired. Fucking sue me for it."

She stomps her foot and drops her bag. "I know you, Gage!"

"No!" The word leaves my mouth louder than I intended. "You used to know me. You used to course through my motherfucking veins." I push off the wall and stand straight. "You left me. You left me, and I ran and got hurt worse than any girl breaking my heart could ever cause. It's not about you." I throw my arm out and gesture to the room. "Nothing going on in my life is about you anymore."

I expected my response to anger her, but it does the opposite.

"What happened there?" Her voice cracks in her question.

A rush of adrenaline flushes my cheeks. "It doesn't matter."

"What happened?" The words come out more confident this time.

And mine are harsher. "It doesn't fucking matter."

I stiffen when she takes a step into my space. "You're hurting."

I snort. "Since when do you give a shit about my feelings?"

She doesn't come any closer, but stops only a few inches from me. "Can we please move on from the past? My God, it was years ago! We were freaking kids."

"*Kids?* We were eighteen. Eighteen and making adult decisions!"

Sadness passes over her dark features. "What happened,

happened. Yes, we have a past, but that doesn't mean we can't be friends now. And, from the looks of it, you need someone to confide in."

I don't want her pity. "I have plenty of friends. Don't need another."

This is the moment she closes me in, not giving me an escape as she stands in front of me, and if I back away, I'll hit the wall.

"Then, what do you need?" she asks.

My answer leaves my mouth as if it's been waiting there on autopilot, ready for when the time came.

"You." I take my hat off and toss it to the side. Not another second passes before my hand curls around the back of her head, my fingers digging into her silky hair, and my lips crash into hers. "I need the girl I fell in love with. Fuck, I need her now more than ever."

The thought of rejection and her pulling away doesn't faze me. I'm lost in the moment of touching the girl who got away. Her mouth falls open, and our tongues dance together so easily when she slides hers into my mouth, like our years of separation never happened. My body reacts to the memory of her. Hers does the same.

When she steps closer, I don't stop her. I wrap my hands around her waist. Her chest hits mine, and I'm pushed back against the wall. A groan leaves her mouth into mine, and that's what pulls me away. My hands fall, and I use them to brush her fingers from my chest. A whimper leaves her when I slide along the wall to move away.

"Fuck," I breathe out, wiping my mouth. "I'm sorry. This isn't a good idea."

"Gage," she says in an attempt to stop me from reaching the door.

I turn around to show her who I am now, so she can see the evidence of a broken man. "Lauren, I'm not who I used to be. You don't want me. I'm destructive, dark, and unhappy. You're smiles and sunshine. We no longer go together, and I refuse to release my darkness onto you."

She repeats my name as I walk out and jog down the stairs.

———

AS IF MY timing can't be any worse, I walk into the house to find my dad in the living room. I give him a head nod as a silent good night, but he stops me.

He moves back and forth in his old recliner while keeping his eyes on me. "Everything okay?"

I scrub my hands over my face. "Peachy. Just need to hit the sheets."

His wrinkles become more prominent, the longer he stares at me. "Have you told her?"

That question only fuels the uncontrolled fire burning inside me tonight. "Nope, and I'm not planning on it, so keep it to yourself, okay?"

"Maybe she can …" He stops to take in a breath of oxygen from his tank. "Maybe she can help you get through it."

"No one can."

He only gives me a slow nod, and I leave the room. I don't bother turning on my light, changing my clothes, or taking off my shoes as I fall onto my old twin-size bed. Endless thoughts on an array of topics rush through me. I consider asking Lauren to move out, consider running back to Chicago until justice happens, consider telling her everything.

As much as it pains me to admit, Lauren might be the only person capable of bringing me in a few steps from the darkness, but I can't do that to her. I won't. It's not only for my protection from getting hurt again, but it's also to protect her from getting involved with someone so fucked up. I moved home, hoping to go back to the chill guy I had been before, and I'm waiting for that to happen.

Not sure if it ever will though.

My phone goes off, and I fight myself on whether to look at it.

I regret it as soon as I do.

Unknown Number: Hey, it's Sierra. I got your number from

my brother's phone. Let's get together sometime this week and catch up. ☺

My phone beeps again with a picture.

It's her in lingerie.

Shit.

I quickly delete it.

The last thing I need is Kyle being mad at me for fucking around with his baby sister.

Fuck this day.

NINETEEN

Lauren

HIS MOUTH FELT SO FAMILIAR.

Comfortable.

Warming.

I brush my fingers over my smiling lips. They feel different—plumper, lighter, more alive. His walking out on me shouldn't have me grinning like a cheeseball, but I can't stop myself.

Does your body remember someone's touch as intensely as your brain remembers your memories with them? Our kiss felt different from those I've had with meaningless men. My skin tingles, wanting more of him everywhere.

That cheeseball smile is still on my face when I grab my phone and flop down on the couch, fully prepared to call Willow and scream out my frustrations, but I don't. Instead, I open my texts and hit his name.

My heart races like I've been sucking down caffeine on a quick work break. Now that I've experienced grown-up Gage kisses, I want everything from him.

Is it desperate to text?

Yes, probably.

I should wait until tomorrow.

Do I care at this moment? Hell no.

His kiss lit my world on fire, and I need more. The problem is, what can I say that won't result in an eye roll ... or a possible restraining order from him?

My goal in my text will be to make him remember what we had.

Me: Your kisses are amazing. Good night.

I put my phone down and get up to make a cup of tea. My phone chimes as I'm walking back to the couch. I take a sip of tea before looking at the screen.

Gage: That kiss brought up everything I'd wanted to forget.

Cheesy smile growing.

Me: Maybe you should stop trying to forget.

Gage: Maybe you shouldn't have left me.

Cheesy smile gone.

Here we go again.

His answer has made it clear. Nothing more between us will happen from that kiss.

The more I'm around Gage, the more I want to fix him, and from the looks of it, that's the furthest thing from what he's looking for. Now, I understand why Gage stayed away for so long. The pit in my stomach is feeling the pain he must've felt from wanting someone he couldn't have. My breathing quickens, and from his response, I know I can no longer stay here.

Me: I'll be out by tomorrow. You won't have to keep fighting to forget me.

Is it an idle threat? I'm not exactly sure.

I walked away from Gage for a reason—a damn worthy one, one I saw as selfless. I gave away my happiness, so someone else could have light. Since he's been back, the urge to explain to him why has never been stronger, but I can't.

It'd ruin him.

It'd ruin someone else.

I slide out of the comfort of the couch at the sound of a knock on the door, and my bare feet stomp against the floor. I turn on the overhead light and peek out the window before answering.

It's Gage.

He's pacing back and forth.

His gaze fixes on me as soon as I swing the door open, and my heart sinks as I take a good look at the man in front of me.

Unease lines his handsome face as he presses his fist to his lips and blows out a long breath.

"Are you trying to fucking ruin me?" he bites out.

My lungs constrict. His words chill me to the core.

It's not me Gage is fighting.

He's fighting his fears.

The fear of my hurting him.

The fear of him hurting me.

Fear that rekindling our relationship will drive him out of Blue Beech again.

That means I need to bow out of our living situation.

"No!" I blurt out. "That's why I'll leave. We're only hurting ourselves, getting close, spending time together, and dragging out old feelings that should've died with our teenage years." I step out and cup his cheek. "I'll leave, so you don't have to again, and then it'll be easier for us to get over each other."

His chin trembles under my hand. "Get over you?" he scoffs. "Is that what you think I want, Dyson? You think I want to get you out of my head and lose you again?"

I pull away and throw my arms up. "Yes! We're playing a childish game. You push me away but not enough that I'm out the door, and then you pull me back in. We've been dancing to this song since you came back to town. I've grown up. My heart has grown. I'm more mature, and in that, I know when to stop following my heart and listen to my brain." I lower my voice. "I don't want us to end on bad terms again. Consider this saying good-bye mutually, and we'll both smile and wave next time we run into each other." I take a step back when the first tear falls down my cheek. "Good night."

"Don't leave," he says, nearly a whisper, and his arm darts out to stop the door from shutting.

I freeze in place, and his eyes are glassy when we make eye contact.

"What?"

"I've lost enough people in my life. I'm fucking terrified of losing you again."

I lose a breath when his lips hit mine again, rougher, pleading. I gasp when powerful hands grip my hips, and I'm pushed back into the loft. The door slams with the kick of his heel, and my head spins as I'm picked up and set on the table.

Oh, hell yes.

TWENTY

Gage

MY HEAD IS CURSING my heart, fighting with my dick, and screaming what an idiot I am.

This.

Her.

Us.

Has the ability to ruin me.

My dick throbs when she wraps her legs around my waist to pull me closer. I pause and force us to make eye contact before this goes any further.

"You're so damn beautiful," I whisper, skimming my fingers over her jawline.

She bites into her bottom lip after I brush a single finger over it and then smiles. "I don't want to sound like a cheeseball, but damn, you're beautiful, too."

I respond by tilting my head down and kissing her again.

Passionately. Brutally. Carnally.

A kiss that makes up for the millions we'd lost.

The sweet taste of her mixed with cinnamon hits me when she slides her tongue in my mouth, stroking it against mine, and I hiss when she rocks her hips, brushing her heat along my jeans-covered erection.

"It's been too long," she says, pulling away. "Please, Gage, I need you inside me *now*."

Desire pumps through my veins, but I force myself to shake my head. "We haven't had enough fun yet." For years, I've imagined the thrill of tasting and touching every inch of her body before sliding into her sweet warmth. A quick fuck isn't how I want this to go down.

"You inside me will be plenty of fun," she snaps. Her demanding tone only turns me on more. "Let's save the extracurricular activities for another time. I need this, Gage. *We* need this. Right now. It's been too long."

How the fuck can I say no to that?

She curls her hand around the bottom of my shirt and drags it over my head. It gets tossed on the ground at the same time I go for hers. My mouth watered when I noticed the faint tips of her nipples through my tee the other day. I've been salivating to taste them.

Her back arches when her chest and dark pink nipples are exposed to me. I tip my head forward and circle my tongue around the tight bud. She inhales a deep breath when I capture one between my lips and suck hard.

My knees feel weak when she goes to work on lowering my pants. My dick springs free, fully erect and aching for her. There's no missing her annoyance when I step back at the same time she reaches for my dick. I grip her ankles and run my hands up the soft skin of her tan legs.

"I've been waiting to see all of you again," I whisper.

"Gage," she gasps when I pull her ass to the end of the table and slide her shorts off. "Don't make this some dramatic, soap-opera shit. Screw me, and then we'll do the whole foreplay thing on another occasion."

Another occasion.

Is that a guarantee of another night together?

Excitement burns through me at this happening again.

Her petite body is on full display. A beautiful exhibit I'd forever pay anything to see. I'd give my money, my heart, and my sanity for just a glimpse of this every damn time.

She licks her lips and rubs her thighs together before I spread her legs.

"One lick, and then I promise you'll have all of me," I say, maneuvering between her hips and sinking my nails into her skin. I ignore her protests of disapproval while lowering myself and resting her thighs on my shoulders.

Her heels sink into my back at my first taste.

Well ... my first taste in years.

"Holy shit," she breathes out.

She tastes divine, sweet, like perfection, all wrapped in one. I plunge my tongue inside her while my finger goes to work on her clit. My one-lick plan has shattered.

Okay, maybe three licks.

Her frustration turns into pleas, begging for more of my mouth while she wiggles beneath me. I give her that and more by thrusting a finger inside her while still sucking on her pussy. She moans when I add another finger and reach up to play with her nipple again.

I don't stop until I feel her falling apart as her body shakes, and her pussy clenches against my fingers.

Her chest heaves in and out as she comes down, and determination sets on her face. "Inside me *right fucking now.*"

No more fighting this.

No more delays.

We've been holding out for too long.

I wipe my mouth and claim hers when I stand up, allowing her to taste herself before situating myself between her legs. I stroke my shaft, wrapping my hand around the head, and just as I'm about to give us what we both want, it hits me.

"No condom," I say with a groan.

"I'm on the pill. I'm clean." She slams her hips forward, her wet opening sliding against my dick, causing me to grunt.

"Me, too." I pause and chuckle. "Clean, I mean. Not on the pill."

She laughs. "I've already suggested the doctors start looking into that for men."

I arch a brow, my hold on my dick tighter. "I thought you needed me inside you?"

"I do."

I drop my hold. "Then, take me."

My head falls back when she grabs my dick in her hand, and I take a deep breath while staring at it, not wanting to miss a glance of her carefully placing my cock at her entrance.

"Slide into me," she says, tilting her hips up.

I tighten my fingers around her waist, and with one hard motion, I am inside her.

Hot damn.

She feels amazing.

She takes all of me in one thrust.

And, just like our kiss, we give in to each other and make love.

Passionately. Brutally. Carnally.

She feels like paradise, and her juices slip down my thighs as I pound into her.

"God, I missed you," I bite out, watching her tits bounce as she meets each thrust. "Missed this."

She runs her hand across my six-pack. "Me, too, baby. Me, too."

Surprisingly, I don't stop when she finds the mark on my side and runs her fingers along the scar tissue.

My response is to continue our game of giving and taking.

We fuck like we can't get enough of the other, and I get swept away, inside her. Inside us. I'm at the top of the world when I know she's close.

I have her on the brink again.

She's going to cum around my hard cock.

And I'll be doing the same inside her pussy.

Bare. Raw. Nothing between us, whether it be latex or problems.

Nothing matters, except our love and lust for each other.

Fuck. Did I say love?

All my thoughts shatter when her legs shake around my waist, and she lets out a long moan before screaming out my name. Perspiration covers my chest as I fuck her until my back goes straight, and I let myself go inside her.

It takes us a moment to catch our breaths.

Even longer for me to calm my heart.

She presses a kiss to my chest, and every muscle in my body tenses when she reaches down and brushes her hand along my scar.

"This," she says, her breathing still catching. "What's it from?"

I gulp and rest my forehead against hers. "Work accident."

She nods, and the room goes eerily silent.

"Everything okay?" I ask, tapping her temple.

"That was … impulsive." She blows out a breath. "I'm trying to figure out if we made a mistake."

She thinks this was a spur-of-the-moment, lapse-in-judgment fuck?

"You decide and let me know," I say against her hair before kissing it.

"That's your answer?"

"Dyson, anytime I'm with you is never a mistake. That's how I feel, but you have to make that decision on your own."

"You don't … you don't regret this? You hate me."

I pull away and rest my hands on her still-shaking legs. "I've *wanted* to hate you for years, but I can't. My heart won't allow it."

She grins, which causes me to grin back.

"And don't fucking smile like that."

She doesn't stop. "What?"

"You know what." I lightly tickle her side. "You always liked it when I was wrapped around your little finger."

"You were never wrapped around my finger. You were a good boyfriend. Nothing like my friends' boyfriends who would brag about every base they hit with them, and then the girls would get slut-shamed while the guys would get high fives. You kept everything we did between you and me. You respected me."

Yet she didn't respect me enough to be honest.

I hold my response in, and her legs are wobbly as I help her down from the table. Nearly every piece of furniture in here has been sex-broken in by us when we were teens, except this one until now.

I make sure she's stable and grip her hips when she leans back against the table. "You ready to sleep in my bed now?"

She reaches down to link our hands. "Only if you join me."

I allow her to lead me to the bed and watch as she rips the blankets down. She flips the light off, and we quietly slide into bed. It feels comfortable when I pull her into my side, like she's always belonged there and a missing piece of myself has been put back in place.

"That better than expensive-ass piano sex?" I ask, squeezing her side.

She laughs and snuggles in closer. "Much better."

TWENTY-ONE

Lauren

WAKING up next to Gage is a high I never want to come down from.

Sex might complicate our situation, but I don't regret it.

Sex with teenage Gage was amazing.

Sex with grown-up Gage is nothing like I've ever experienced.

That doesn't mean I'm not scared.

Sometimes, history shouldn't be dug up.

One thing is for sure; history repeated itself in the sex department.

Never have I felt something so intense and intimate as what I feel with him—*every single damn time.*

I turn on my stomach and rest my palm on his chest, looking up at him. "Good morning, landlord."

He chuckles and sleepily looks down at me. "Morning, beautiful."

"I have to say, I didn't think this would ever happen again."

He reaches down and cups my ass, sending shivers down my spine. "Never has a truer statement been made."

The sight of Gage, naked and in bed with me, is breathtaking. I would be a woman on top of the world if I could do this every morning. It sounds so easy for us to go back to what we were before, and I'm ready to take that step if he is.

Ready for this to become a lifetime thing.

I reach up and trail my fingers over the stubble on his cheek before inhaling a deep breath of courage and closing my eyes. I open them and stop myself from saying what needs to be said.

Not this morning.

Expectations ruin moods, and I want this good time to last for as long as it can.

"Was this … is this …a one-time thing?" he whispers, taking the words from my mouth.

Shit.

"Can we not talk about expectations and just enjoy this morning?" I ask, my hand venturing under the blanket and grabbing his erect cock. "I know of a better way to spend our time."

His hand cups mine, an attempt to stop my hand from pleasuring him. "Before we do, I need my breakfast."

Even though he's cut off some of my power, I stroke him the best I can under his touch. "You're a breakfast-in-bed guy, huh? In that case, you might need to run to your house because all I have is cereal here."

He flips me on my back. "You have exactly what I need."

I yelp when the blanket is torn off, and he crawls down until his face meets my thighs. I thought a beautiful sight was him next to me in bed in the morning, but dear God, his head between my legs might compete. My hands travel to his hair, and I grip the strands as he gives me the good morning I've missed for years without him.

———

CAPTAIN CRUNCH IS in my bowl, and I'm eating my breakfast in bed.

Gage is at my side, enjoying his second breakfast.

The man has definitely improved in the oral sex department.

There's been nothing but comfortableness with us this morning.

We've hung out, watched TV, and had light conversation. No mentions of where this is heading or of expectations.

Hopefully, it stays that way.

I want to relish this moment where no resentment or regret exists.

"What time do you go into work?" I ask, swallowing down a bite.

"I'll head out in about an hour," he answers. "You have the day off, right?"

I nod.

"Any plans?"

Other than agonizing about what happened last night on repeat?

It's a bummer that I'm not working. The hospital is the best place to tear me away from my problems.

"I'm hanging out with Willow and the kiddos."

Knowing Willow, I'll be answering questions about him all day.

"Sounds like fun."

Goose bumps run along my leg when he runs his hand down it.

He smacks a kiss on my cheek before sliding out of bed and grabbing our bowls. "Want to do dinner tonight?"

I bite into the edge of my lip. "It's our mandatory monthly dinner at my parents' house." I pause to take a deep breath. "If you're hungry, you can tag along."

He grins. "You asking me to meet the parents, Dyson?" The bowls clank when they hit the sink. He cleans them and starts tracking down his clothes around the loft.

I narrow my eyes at him. "Oh, shove it. Pretty sure you've met the parents."

He sits on the side of the bed, next to me. "So, are we going to do this? Try again?"

That's the question of the damn year.

"I mean ... I don't know." I wipe the sleep from my eyes. "What happened last night terrifies me but in a good way, if that makes sense?"

"As much as it doesn't, I understand because I feel the same way."

His face softens. "But, what I said last night about being a different man, I wasn't lying. It wasn't a ploy to keep you away from me. I am, Lauren."

"I know you have … history, what with having an ex-wife locked up and all." *And secrets. You have secrets. A shit ton of secrets.* I'll save that conversation for another day. "And, uh … more."

He stands and starts to get dressed. "Yes, more."

I break our eye contact and start playing with the blanket, hoping my words sound comforting. "Do you think you'll eventually tell me sooner or later?"

His gaze is downcast.

"I'm not asking you to spill out your past right now, but I'd like to understand what you're going through. Maybe I can help."

"We'll see." He kisses the top of my head. "Let's take things slowly, okay? You might come to the conclusion that you can't stand my ass anymore."

"And you might conclude that you actually *can* stand me."

"Already figuring that one out, babe."

My phone beeps with a message, and I snag it from the nightstand to see Willow's alert that they're about to pull into the driveway. I jump out of bed as if it suddenly caught fire and start throwing clothes on.

Gage follows me into the bathroom and leans against the wall, hands sliding into the pockets of his pants, while I start brushing my teeth. "About dinner tonight."

I spit out my toothpaste and rinse my mouth before answering —with an inner fear of rejection—"You know what? Don't worry about it. It's too early for something that serious."

He takes a step forward and wraps his arms around my waist, lightly pushing into me. "Ask Mama Barnes if there's anything I need to bring." His lips go to my cheek, causing me to blush as he kisses it. "I'll be there."

My cheeseball grin has returned as I look at him in the mirror. "Really?"

"Really." He whips me around and clasps my hands in his, holding them between us. "Let's see where this goes."

"I like that plan."

My phone fires off again, and I pull away to grab it.

Willow: Coming up! Any exes in the building I should know about?

"Oh shit," I hiss.

"Oh shit what?" Gage questions.

"Dallas and Willow are here."

He scratches his stubble-covered cheek. "That a problem? I thought you had plans with them."

"They're coming *up* here. As in right this second."

A triple series of knocks interrupts our conversation, and Gage goes to answer the door. I'm behind him, my chest hitting his back, when he opens it.

A bright smile pops on Willow's cherry-colored lips. "Well, well, look at what we have here." She points to Gage. "Bet me five hundred bucks I know your name."

"Willow, stop messing with him," I say with a groan.

She smiles. "And who exactly is *him*? He your milkman, your landlord, your *ex*?"

Gage holds out his hand. "I'm Gage, definitely not the milkman, kind of the landlord, and yes, the ex ... *for now*."

"I vote for you to keep him," Willow says to me.

We move to the side to let Willow in. Maven is next to her, their hands entwined, and Dallas is behind them with Samuel in his arms.

"Gage, man, good seeing you," Dallas says.

Gage nods toward Samuel. "Congratulations on the addition to your family."

"The little one is my daughter, Maven, and the loudmouth to her side is my baby mama, Willow," Dallas says, jerking his head toward them. "A heads-up, she wasn't born with a filter."

Gage laughs. "The good ones never are. I'd love to catch up, but I'm due for work soon." He kisses the top of my head. "See you soon."

"Gage, huh?" Dallas asks when Gage shuts the door behind him. "Can't say I'm surprised once I heard he was back in town."

Willow sighs, her shoulders slumping. "Man, this is one of those times I wish I had grown up here. I need some juicy dating history."

Dallas hands Samuel over to me at my request and gives his good-byes. He drove the tow truck to take my car into their shop. Even though Gage offered to look at it, I can't put that on him.

I sit down with Samuel in my arms and rock back and forth while Maven roams around the loft, loaded with curiosity. The girl might be only seven, but she's a nosy one. She must've inherited that gene from my family.

Willow points to my clothes. "This a new style of yours?"

I glance down at myself. I'm sporting a pair of Gage's shorts and a scrub shirt. "Thought I'd try something new."

She snorts. "Yeah, whatever. I can't wait to get you alone."

TWENTY-TWO

Gage

"AND GOOD MORNING to my best friend who finally got laid," Kyle calls out, slapping me on the back when I walk into the station. "Was it an exorcism with the ex?"

All eyes of my coworkers go to me, and I don't answer him as I take long strides to my office, him trailing behind me. I've already been a subject of gossip since I got home, and now, Kyle has sparked the curiosity in their heads even more. They'll be keeping their ears open for any information they can gather and spill out to their friends and family.

I expected him to give me shit eventually, but damn, am I that transparent when it comes to Lauren? Maybe it's easier for people to read us than it is for us to read ourselves.

I read Lauren this morning, and I saw the confusion and panic in her. It was a familiar feeling.

"How about you quit worrying about my relationship?" I respond when we reach my office, and he plops down in the chair in front of my desk.

Kyle has his own office, which he hardly frequents because he hates being alone. Blame it on growing up in a large family where there was always noise in the background.

His eyes crinkle at the corners. "Ah … so it's a relationship now?"

I rub at my tired eyes. "Why are you asking me these questions?"

"You look the happiest you've been since you moved back, which is a giant motherfucking dis to my ass, considering you haven't ever been that happy to see my smiling face."

"Shit, my bad. I wasn't aware you wanted a make-out session to celebrate our reunion."

He flips me off. "You could've at least brought a guy some flowers."

"Noted. Next time we have a spat, roses and champagne will come your way. Are we finished with this whole bro-bonding talk?"

"Hell no. I'm only getting started."

"Doesn't surprise me," I mutter.

"So what? You two back on?"

"We didn't talk about anything. It's fresh, and bringing up the future isn't a good idea yet."

I don't want what we had last night and this morning to be a one-time thing. If I could have it my way, I'd have her before we shut our eyes at night and the second we woke.

The problem is, between those times, it's more complicated.

"You two are a hot-ass mess," Kyle goes on.

"It only happened last night. Dragging up old memories and expectations is a dumb idea."

"I'm sure you didn't think it was a dumb idea when your head was between her legs this morning."

I grin. "I'd never think that's a dumb idea."

TWENTY-THREE

Lauren

MY DAY CONSISTED of strolling around downtown with a strawberry smoothie in my hand and then running around the park with Willow and her kiddos. The chaos of keeping up with them has distracted me from my thoughts of Gage and what happens from here with our relationship.

We had straddled the line and played games since our first run-ins, and it doesn't surprise me that we finally crossed it.

We had sex, although I'm not sure how we got there in that moment.

Maybe it was the hurt on his face that drew me closer to helping him.

Maybe it was the way he looked at me.

Maybe it was the fact that I'm still in love with him.

I'm back in the loft. Maven is sleeping off her exhaustion from the day on the couch, and Willow is feeding Samuel while we sit at the kitchen table. She's been waiting to get me away from Maven's ears to grill me about Gage.

"Dude is hot, especially with the after-sex glow. It's about time you got laid," she says. "Are you back together?"

As much as I don't want to partake in this conversation, I need to. Willow might be overdramatic at times, but she's logical and levelheaded when it comes to relationships.

"We talked briefly, but I don't know where his head is. The last thing I want to do is get my hopes up, and then it falls apart."

Gage made it clear weeks ago that he wanted nothing to do with me and that he hated my guts. Sure, I said the same, but I was lying.

So, what changed his mind?

"Why would it fall apart?" she asks. "It's obvious that he still has feelings for you. You love him. Maybe it'll work out this time."

"He was married." *Is this my way of talking myself out of giving us another shot?*

"But he's divorced now, right?"

I nod. "Yes, but he *got* married. That's a big step for someone. He gave another woman a ring, said I do, and was with her for years. And get this; no one knew about her, not even his best friend."

"Divorces aren't that uncommon. Maybe he thought marrying her was the right thing to do. Did he knock her up maybe?"

I shake my head. "He said he doesn't have any kids. He might've divorced her because she went to prison."

"Prison? Chick is in prison? Like murder prison or fancy *I didn't pay my taxes* prison? I need details, pronto."

"Trust me, I want details as much as you, but he won't give me anything."

She sets Samuel's empty bottle on the table and starts burping him. "You didn't check the internet? Hello? Google is the new private investigator. It'll save you time and money."

I shrug. "I thought about it, but it doesn't feel right to go behind his back. I want him to trust me enough to tell me himself."

"You are a patient soul. I would've already had the prison wife's entire family tree looked up, seen her middle school yearbook pictures, and known her blood type."

"I just"—I sigh—"don't want to break his trust."

"I understand, but let me know if you change your mind and need assistance in the stalking department. I excel at it."

I laugh. "Why doesn't that surprise me?"

"Are you inviting him to dinner tonight?"

I can't stop myself from grinning like a teenager who just scored her first prom date. "Already did, and he said he'd come."

As if his ears were burning, my phone beeps with a text from Gage.

Gage: Just pulled in. You up for some company?

His offering to hang out is a good sign.

Me: If you don't mind a baby, a napping kid, and a nosy future sister-in-law, come right up.

Gage: Sounds like a blast to me. I'll stay quiet.

I set my phone down and attempt to give Willow a serious look. "He's coming up, so please don't interrogate him."

She frowns. "You're no fun anymore."

Gage doesn't bother knocking before walking into the loft, and I can't stop myself from licking my lips at the sight of him in his uniform again. He could sport that every night when he comes home, and I'd still never tire of it.

Willow swoons when he kisses my cheek and pulls out the chair next to mine. I can feel my cheeks blushing. This is the first time we've touched like this in front of someone.

He tilts his head toward a cooing Samuel. "You've got a cute little man there."

Willow peeks down at Samuel and plays with the fat roll on his arm. She scoots her chair out, situates my nephew on her side, and stares at Gage. "Thank you. You want to hold him while I use the bathroom real quick?"

At first, Gage seems taken aback by her question, but he eventually nods. "Yeah, sure."

"I can take him," I blurt out, sliding my chair out from the table.

Willow glances away from him to me. "Was that too intrusive?"

Gage holds his arms out. "No, not at all. Hand the little guy over."

Willow carefully places Samuel in Gage's hold and makes sure he's steady before heading to the bathroom. I'm tempted to kick my foot out and trip her. Her question was a test of his character.

My mom always says, "You don't know someone's patience until you see how they act with a child."

"You sure you don't want me to take him?" I question.

He shakes his head. "I've got this, Dyson."

My heart tightens as I watch him stare down at Samuel with an expression I know all too well. I see it regularly at the hospital. It's emptiness. Pain. Disappointment.

What happened to him?

Whom did he lose?

My thoughts jump back to when I asked if he had kids. He said he didn't, but there's a longing there.

Did he and his wife have fertility problems, and that's what broke them apart?

Did he want children, but she didn't?

Did she miscarry?

Samuel relaxes as Gage rocks him in his arms. My stomach flutters, and I wish I could record them together. Everything in Gage changed in that small moment—his demeanor, his skin bunching up around his sorrow-filled eyes—and his face confessed I was missing something significant about his past.

"Wow," Willow says, causing me to jump at the sound of her voice. She moves back into the room with a smile on her face. "He takes to you, Gage. Lucky for Lauren, it looks like you'll make a great father one day."

Her last words are like an electric bolt smacking into a power line, shutting Gage off from me. His shoulders still, his body going tight, and the lost expression on his face fires through harder.

He holds Samuel out to Willow, and his voice turns cautionary. "It was a pleasure meeting you and your family. I have to go."

His hands shake as Willow takes Samuel from him, and as soon as their exchange finishes, he jumps up from the chair and rushes to the door. I'm on his trail, reaching him at the stairs, and I grab the back of his shirt to stop him.

"Hey," I say, unable to get him to turn around. "What's wrong?"

"Forgot I needed to shower," he clips before sniffing his armpit. "I had a long shift."

Liar.

Alarm rings through my mind. There's something wrong. This isn't the right time to question him. Even though I don't know why he's upset, his slumped shoulders and emotion-choked voice tell me the pain is deep. Trying to draw out the reasoning from him with Willow here is selfish.

"Are we still on for dinner?" It's not a serious question, but it feels like a thousand bricks hit me when I ask.

He moves down a step, and I expect him to walk away, but instead, he turns around to look at me. "Shit, I forgot I promised my dad we'd do pizza, beer, and the game tonight."

Liar.

He's a pro at faking; I have to credit him for that. He's absorbing the pain deeper, hiding it from me, with each passing second.

"Want to stop by when the game ends?" I ask.

He rubs his eyes. "Sure. Have fun."

With that, he turns around.

I don't head back into the loft until he disappears into the house.

"Okay, what just happened?" Willow asks when I walk back in. Her face is filled with guilt as she stands with Samuel on her hip. "Did I cross a line, asking him to hold Samuel? Does he not like kids?"

I shuffle back to my chair and sit down. "He needed to shower."

"Is he still coming to dinner?"

"I'm not sure that's a good idea."

"Maybe he thought he really did smell." She laughs while lifting Samuel up, smelling his diaper. "Maybe my little guy here had a dirty diaper, and he thought it was himself."

"Does he have a dirty diaper?"

She frowns. "Negative."

I blow out a long breath. "He just randomly shut down. I don't know what happened."

She plops back down in her seat. "Did you ask if he wanted a shower mate?"

A snort leaves me. "Really?"

"What? Sometimes, sex helps to figure out problems. He also might feel more open to discussing personal stuff post-orgasm."

I scrunch up my nose. "You want me to sex-manipulate him into sharing secrets?"

"Wouldn't hurt to try. Plus, shower sex is the best sex."

"Shut up," I whisper, standing up and snagging Samuel from her. I lower my voice and cover his ears. "There are baby ears in here, and ew, I'd rather not listen to you divulge anything sex-related about my big bro."

She points to Samuel and laughs. "That little nugget heard sex talk hotter than that when he was hanging out in my womb."

"Ugh, you've now been demoted to my second favorite brother-dater." I rock Samuel back and forth as an attempt not to assume the worst why Gage bailed on me. "Do you think this was his plan all along? For us to have sex, for him to draw my feelings for him back out, and then dump me like I did him?"

"I'm not the best person to answer that question, considering I don't know your history and all. Maybe talk to your brothers and get an opinion from a male mindset." Her tone is now soothing, like she's trying to put Samuel to sleep, but instead, I know it's an attempt to make me feel better after Gage's rejection.

"Yeah, not talking to my brothers about my sex life."

"It's worth a try. They went through a tough time that forced them to push the people they loved away from them. Maybe they can provide insight into what could be going through Gage's head."

———

DURING MY RIDE with Willow to my parents' house, I had to stop myself from pulling out my phone and reaching out to Gage countless times. The fear of coming off too needy is what stopped me. Call it pride, but I can't be the woman who fights for a man who doesn't want her.

Good thing I didn't give my mom a heads-up that Gage was coming. Otherwise, I would've been answering questions while I watched her work around the kitchen as she waved away all my requests to help her. The only job she gives me is setting the table and laying out the food in her perfect spread. Every dish has the same place it's had for years.

"Lauren, honey," my mom says next to me, mid-dinner, "you've been so busy. I feel like I haven't had the time to talk to you about where you're staying."

"Correction: you haven't had the time to interrogate her," my dad chimes in, resulting in a death glare from her.

"Did you find another rental?" she continues.

Dallas snorts. "Sure, if you count Gage's being her landlord."

I throw a dinner roll across the table at him. "Shut up, big mouth!"

My mother is weakly attempting to hold back her grin. "Have you two gotten back together?"

I take a long drink of lemonade before answering her while all eyes are on me, even Maven's. "Nope. Amos had the loft up for rent, and it was my only option until I find something else."

"You're roommates then?" my dad asks, his face unreadable.

"No, he's staying in the main house with his dad."

My mom straightens out the napkin on her lap and isn't camouflaging her smile any longer. "I think it's just wonderful that you two are spending time together again. His coming home was a great surprise to all of us."

Now is the time to take advantage of my mom's gossiping ways. If I can't pull it out of Gage, maybe she can give me even a crumb. Anything will do at the moment because, right now, I feel like I'm fighting against the unknown.

"Mom," I say, setting my fork down, "do you know why he moved back, by chance?"

"The word around town is, he was worried about Amos being sick," she answers.

"Amos is ill?" Dallas asks.

"COPD," my mom replies with a soft, concerned tone. "And an array of other problems, I assume, even though Amos is too proud to tell anyone what's going on with him."

Gage's dad is a prideful soul who isn't one to accept handouts. Even when his wife died, he never asked for help. He worked two jobs, was present at every game of Gage's, and did all the grocery shopping and cooking. The man lived for family, and it doesn't surprise me that he's still the same.

"Is that *all* you know?" I push.

What's the plus of having your mom be in the gossip crew if she doesn't give you anything juicy?

"Sorry, honey. I wish I had more. He's cloak-and-dagger about what happened in his life when he was gone, and so is Amos. Give him time. If you push, he'll only pull."

I nod, and luckily, Hudson changes the subject. He has the best intuition on when to cut a conversation short and move on to something new.

———

"HEY THERE, BIG BROTHER," I say, sitting next to Dallas on the porch swing after dinner.

"Hey there, my mischievous little sister," he replies.

The sun is setting. My dad is in the yard, playing with Maven, Willow is taking care of Samuel and his dinner business, and my mom is deep into final wedding arrangements with Stella and Hudson.

They're having the ceremony at my parents' house, which was a surprise to me. The fact that she'd trade out some big Hollywood nuptials for something small here made my heart warm.

"Can I ask you a question?" I ask.

"Asking permission has never stopped you before."

"It's not exactly a question, I guess. More like advice."

He chuckles. "I might be the wrong person to go to for advice. I'm the dude who has to get that from others."

"You give good guidance," I say, elbowing him. "Sure, you're not the best at taking it when it's your own life decisions, but you've helped both me and Hudson with our problems I don't know how many times. If it wasn't for you, Hudson and Stella wouldn't be together."

He nods. "I won't take all the credit for that one, but thank you for coming to me. So, what's up?"

I hesitate before answering for two reasons. The first being I'm not sure if I'm making a bigger deal than what it is, and the second being it might bring up painful memories for my brother.

"Gage ..." I pause. "He was married before he moved back."

"And?"

"That's a big commitment."

Other than my parents, Dallas is the only one in our family who's been married. He also is no longer with his wife. The circumstances are different since he had no say in his marriage ending. He became a widower too young.

He nods in understanding. "Committing to someone in the past can't stop you from loving another, nor does it mean you have to keep the person in your heart forever. Not that I can say from experience, but people divorce for different reasons. But one thing to remember is, your heart is big enough to give people pieces of it. You can scatter your love along as you proceed through life. Maybe Gage was married, maybe he did love another woman, but that doesn't mean he can't love you, too."

"He's a different man from who he was when we were younger." Something else Dallas can relate to.

"Yes, most people change as they get older."

I shove his side and laugh. "Shut up, big head. You know what I mean. It's like he's carrying something on his shoulders that he can't let go of."

"You think it was a bad marriage?"

"I have no idea what to think. It's so confusing. He said he didn't love her, and whenever I bring her up, there's nothing but hatred on his face. Maybe she did him dirty, and he can't accept it?"

"Could've been a messy divorce."

I stop myself from telling him about her being locked up. I'll save that for another time. "There's something I'm missing. He shuts down anytime I bring it up, and he does the same with Kyle." I gulp and stop to determine if he can handle my next question. "How did you heal ... you know ... when you were broken?"

"I fell in love again."

He tips his beer toward Willow. She's in the yard with my dad now.

"She's who healed me." He goes on after taking a drink, "If Gage is broken, be his Willow. Don't push him, because admitting you're hurting takes time and courage."

TWENTY-FOUR

Gage

"YOU'LL MAKE a great father one day."

I tried.

I fucking tried.

And failed.

I don't deserve to be a father.

Had that chance.

Fucked it up.

I stomp through the front door, chug down a glass of water, and rest my forehead against the cool countertop.

The five words that haunt me daily drift through my mind.

"What did you do, Missy?"

I throw my glass across the kitchen, hearing it shatter against the wall, hoping it does the same to those words crammed into my mind forever. I stare at the wall as if I'm stuck in a daze, wondering when the pain, the memories, the guilt will finally end.

Never.

My failure to protect *him* will haunt me forever.

I don't move until I hear voices outside. I creep to the window that overlooks the driveway. Lauren is strapping Maven into the backseat of the SUV while Willow concentrates on getting Samuel into his car seat. Lauren slides into the passenger seat and slams the door shut.

It's not until the car pulls away that I start to pick up the broken glass from the floor. Lauren has every right to be angry with me. I should tell her about *him*, but I can't.

Can't open those wounds.

She'd understand. She'd comfort me. She'd also look at me differently. I have yet to come to terms with what happened, so bringing someone else into it would only cause more damage. She doesn't deserve that in her life.

Doesn't deserve being around a broken son of a bitch.

———

"HEY, PA, HOW ARE YOU FEELIN'?"

I drop the box of pizza I carried out on the table and start dragging out plates.

I haven't talked to Lauren since I sped out of the loft as if I were on fire. There's no way my behavior didn't embarrass her. I'd finally gotten my girl back, had her in my arms, my bed, and I ruined it. I tried to handle my shit, but it was impossible.

Holding Samuel and hearing Willow say he was drawn to me was too hard on my heart. She was wrong. So fucking wrong.

"As happy as a tick on a big, fat dog," he answers, falling into a chair. He snags a piece from the box and takes a bite without worrying about a plate. He speaks as he swallows down his food, "You moving back into the loft with Lauren yet?"

I stay standing while grabbing a piece and throwing it on my plate. It won't get touched. I have no appetite, but if I don't eat, he won't either. "You getting tired of me already?"

He shakes his head. "Not even close." The room quiets while he takes a long draw of Coke before he shrugs his shoulders. "Just want to see you happy, is all."

Instead of grabbing a Coke from the fridge, I choose a beer.

Hopefully, it'll help calm these nerves. "Doubt that will be happening anytime soon … or ever."

He drops his pizza and looks at me with pain in his eyes. "You know you can talk to me, right?"

"I know, and you'll be the first person I see if it comes to that."

Luke is the only person I've talked to about what happened. He was my best friend in Chicago and stood by me through my fight. He saw the highs and the lows, and he understood. Luke joined the fight against Missy and has been as hell-bent on her paying for her crime as I have.

"She'd understand, too," he adds, slipping the words through in a low tone.

"Don't do this."

"Don't do what? Think about your future? I want to see my son happy. She'll make you happy. She's always been what makes you happy."

"A woman is not the basis of my happiness. Maybe in high school, yes, but shit changes when you grow up. Priorities change."

"She can help you heal."

I shake my head. "I need to get out of here."

————

I'VE BEEN NURSING my second beer for the past hour.

It'll be lukewarm and taste like piss if I take another sip, but I'd put money down on that not happening. Even though I walked into Down Home Pub with every intention to get ass-face wasted, I can't.

There's a massive fear embedded in me that always stops me from finishing my second drink. There's unease in the back of my mind of something bad happening. My phone could ring at any second with tragic news—at least, that's what I tell myself.

I wonder if I'll always have that uneasiness or if, eventually, it will fade away.

Will he fade away?

I shake my head and force myself to take another drink.

Yep, tastes fucking terrible.

"There's a handsome man I didn't expect to see tonight."

I peek over my shoulder to find Sierra pulling out the barstool next to mine with one hand while gripping a drink in the other.

Fuck.

Dealing with Kyle's kid sister isn't what I need tonight.

"Why do you say that?" I ask when she sets her drink down on the bar and makes herself comfortable.

"You never replied to my texts."

She doesn't appear to be pissed. It's more along the lines of annoyed. It's not a lie that Sierra has grown up and found her sexuality. She's attractive, fun, and most likely isn't looking for a commitment.

I move my neck from side to side, hoping to release the tension shooting up it but fail. "Not exactly a good idea to sext your best friend's little sister."

She flips her blonde hair over her shoulder. "Your best friend's *very legal* little sister." She holds up her beer. "Looky here, I'm even old enough to drink."

"Fair point."

Doesn't mean I'll be putting my hands on her. I've always seen Sierra as a little sister, nothing more. Even if I didn't, I'd never betray Kyle. That's a line you don't cross.

She swings to the side, so she's facing me, and she rests her elbow on the bar. "Care to be honest about why you ignored me? If you're not interested, I totally get it. Just be up-front with a girl."

"Don't think there's an easy way to say it without pissing you off." I'm not a dick. I don't want to hurt the chick's feelings.

"I'm not easily offended," she answers around a laugh, "but this little exchange answers my question." She turns to face the bar and bumps my shoulder with hers. "Don't worry, Gage man; I don't take it personally."

I nod. "Appreciate that."

"So … what girl don't you ignore?"

"Huh?" I'm halfway in this conversation with her. Half of me is listening while the other half is thinking about someone else.

"You're drinking in the corner of a bar, looking like someone ran over your dog. There's a story, and most of the time, this type of behavior is caused by someone's relationship problems." The happiness in her face falls, unmasking that Sierra isn't as playful as she puts on. "Trust me, I've been there."

"Not a specific problem. *Problems*," I correct.

"One of those problems Lauren?"

I shrug. Not about to seek relationship guidance from the youngin'.

She holds up her hand when Maliki looks our way. "Get my friend and me another drink."

Maliki nods and slides two beers in front of us while shaking his head at Sierra. "It's weird, serving your young ass here."

She grins. "I'm legally allowed to drink now, so no more kicking me out of this place and confiscating my fake IDs."

He laughs. "I'm sure going to miss that weekly occurrence."

She hands Maliki her credit card and glances over at me when he leaves to help another customer. "You want to talk about it? I'm a woman, so I like to think I'm good at giving advice about women."

I move my piss-warm beer to the side and grab the fresh one. *Here goes nothing.* "It's hard to … rekindle with the woman who fucked you over before."

She nods. "Understandable. I know what it feels like to love someone and not have him … or her, in your case."

I ignore her comment, hoping it wasn't directed at me.

She laughs. "I'm not talking about you. Even though I've had a crush on you since you and my brother have been friends, there are other men in this godforsaken town who like to play games. Not to say I wouldn't forget about them had you come to your senses and hung out with me."

"I'm the brother's best friend. Off-limits crush, huh?"

A playful smile hits her lips. "I'm so basic."

"It sucks that we can't help who we like."

"Or, in your case, it sucks that you can't help who you *love*."

"Little one, I came here to forget my problems." I gesture to Maliki for another round while finishing off my beer. *Fuck it.* I deserve to forget for a night. "So, if you want to keep a man company, let's chat about football, random shit, what you were up to while I was gone."

She salutes me. "Aye, aye, captain."

Our drinks arrive, and I sit back in my chair, drowning my thoughts, while she takes over the conversation.

TWENTY-FIVE

Lauren

THE PASTEL COLORS of the sunset are dissolving into the night when my dad drops me off at the loft.

Gage hasn't called or texted, the driveway is void of his truck, and he's not in the loft when I walk in.

What happened?

Does he regret having sex with me?

My thoughts go to the worst-case scenario.

Gage made it clear that he hated me when I got arrested, and though I thought we'd moved past that, maybe he hasn't.

Maybe it was for revenge, to make me fall for him, so he could then give me the big fuck you *for leaving him.*

No, he's not that spiteful.

Correction: the old Gage wasn't that spiteful.

This new Gage is different—a rougher version on the exterior yet more vulnerable inside.

I check my phone again in case I missed something and collapse onto the couch. I reach for the remote at the same time I hear a car door slam in the background. Lucky for me, the blinds are open, so I don't have to creepily peek through them.

The floodlights beam down on an unrecognizable four-door

sedan, spotlighting the young blonde getting out of the driver's side and circling around to the passenger.

Sierra's skinny frame leans down, nearly on her knees, to wrap Gage's arm around her shoulders, and surprisingly, she takes his weight.

He is wasted.

Can barely stand straight.

With another woman.

A combination of fear and confusion seeps through me, drowning out any thoughts that we could reconcile. Now I know our time together was nothing but a game to him.

He went to her. Drank with her. No doubt shared his problems with her.

She'd asked if he was single, and I'd stupidly told her to go for it.

I don't bother hiding my stalking while watching their every move.

I'm silently begging for him to see the disappointment and disgust on my face.

His head is tipped down, his view locked to the ground, his feet dragging against the ground on their way to the front door.

Look up. Look up. Look the fuck up.

My heart sinks when he finally does.

It's a fast look, brief, and it only lasts a glimpse of a second as his eyes catch mine, and they're void of emotion, shut out, out of order.

He lowers his head in shame, and I stay there, looking pathetic, while Amos lets them in.

It isn't until they disappear into the house that I throw my hands up and snatch a blanket to sleep on the couch.

Joke's on me.

———

NOW THAT I'VE spent time in the bed, Gage was right; the couch is nowhere as comfortable as the bed is. Not that I got much sleep. I tossed, turned, and contemplated marching into that house and kicking his ass.

Problem is, it's not smart to kick a police officer's ass even if he did break your heart. Jail time isn't how I want to spend the rest of my summer.

Instead, I'm going to choose which brother I'm moving in with, find a rental, and steer clear of Gage for the rest of my life … or until we awkwardly run into each other in a public setting.

I have my coffee in one hand, my bag on my shoulder, and my scrubs on when I hear my front door being unlocked. Gage comes through the doorway, big and broad and looking like shit, complete with red-rimmed eyes, arms hanging loosely at his sides.

He clears his throat and scratches his neck when he sees me. "You ready to go?"

I clutch my cup, silently staring, waiting for him to clarify what last night was about.

"Look, I'm sorry about yesterday." His apology is rushed, panicky, and regret is evident on his face—along with signs of dehydration and lack of sleep. If Sierra did spend the night, he must not have been a decent lay. "It was a bad day."

My bag slips off my shoulder, and I don't stop it from falling on the floor. "What are you doing here?"

"Apologizing for my bullshit behavior."

I assess him, the need to figure out what I'm missing rushing through me, but there's nothing there. All I see is a hungover man who doesn't care about anything right now. The same empty man from last night.

Broken people make for regretful actions.

Gage came home with Sierra and is asking me for forgiveness.

I can easily give him what he wants.

But I can't play games with someone who freezes me out and isn't interested in giving me his all.

"Don't you think it's rude not to take your one-night stand to breakfast?" I ask before scoffing. "Or wait, is that what you had for breakfast, considering that's your *favorite meal* and all? Looks like you have no preference of whom you get it from."

He slowly blinks at me. "What?"

"Sierra. Did you already kick her out of your bed this morning?"

"Sierra? She helped my dad put my drunken ass to bed last night and then went home."

I shake my head and snatch my bag up from the floor. Getting myself worked up before my shift isn't a good idea. "It doesn't matter. I have to go."

He stops me from moving around him to get to the front door. "I said I'm sorry. I had a rough day. Just hear me out."

I cross my arms. "Want to talk about it?"

"Nothing to talk about. It was a stressful day at work." His voice turns into a fake playfulness. "You know how those are. You've had them."

My smartwatch pings with a text message that was sent to my phone. "My dad is here. I have to go."

I'm grateful that my parents answer their phones at any time throughout the night. Two in the morning, my dad answered, no sleep in his voice, and didn't ask any questions when I asked for a ride.

"Tell your dad to go home. I'll take you to work. I already committed to it."

Commitment. Ha.

"Things change, Gage. I will no longer be needing any rides from you."

"Lauren." His false playfulness is gone. Since he walked through that door, Gage's mood has gone from regret to forced jest and now to desperation.

My heart breaks as I look at him, and I see this as an opportunity to fix him, to fix us. "I'll share a ride with you if you tell me what's going on."

He violently shakes his head. "I can't. Don't ask me to do that."

"Enjoy your day, Gage."

Even though he doesn't block me from brushing past him, he's on my tracks, and he waits at the top of the stairs as I hop down them, taking two at a time. I jump into my father's truck without looking back, slam my cup into the holder, and sigh.

My dad's gaze pings from Gage to me. "Rough morning?"

"You have no idea," I mutter.

He doesn't continue the conversation until we're miles from Gage's house. "Are you and Gage attempting to reconcile?"

I peek up at my dad in surprise. Sure, he and Mom had the birds and bees talk with me when I started dating Gage, but he's never questioned or commented on my love life. Maybe he knew my mom had that department covered. My father is a man of few words, but those words always have deep meaning to them.

He's a strong man and the mentor my family needs. He's also one of the most compassionate people in the world.

"I'm not sure," I truthfully answer.

There will be no bullshitting him. He can see right through me. What I do hold back from saying is, *We had sex, and now, he's closed off.*

"Do you still love him?"

"I do," I honestly answer again, finally admitting it out loud.

"Does he still love you?"

I hesitate before answering.

"I think so."

"Then, you'll figure it out. It might be a complicated journey to get there, but love conquers all, my girl."

If only quotes were solutions to real problems.

"That's easy for you to say. You and Mom have been in love since forever and have been inseparable ever since."

"That doesn't mean there weren't hardships. Love isn't easy for anyone. Your mother and I have had our fair share of problems, but it was *us* against those problems, not *us* against each other. Talk to him. See where his battles are, and join him in fighting those battles. Then, your love will be stronger."

I use my arm to clean the tears falling from my cheeks.

"You decide if his problems are worth the trouble. That's all you can do. If you can't, then it's better to move on. But, if you love someone, you fight those demons together and live happily ever after, as your mom and I have."

His questions about Gage end there. He moves the conversation to my work, to my apartment-hunting, to offering me my bedroom back at home. He fills the ride up with easing my mind, and it works.

"You have a good day," he says when he pulls into the parking lot. "I'll be back to pick you up, and Dallas said your car will be fixed soon."

"Thank you, Dad."

He stops me before I leave the truck. "And, Lauren?"

I peek back at him. "Yeah?"

"I'm proud of you."

"Thanks, Dad," I say around a giant smile.

Time with him is exactly what I needed. Sometimes, you need to talk to someone who lets you see from a different perspective because it's easy to get blinded by your own hurt and your own needs. I owe it to myself, to Gage, to our relationship to talk to him. Whether we end up in a relationship as friends or as nothing, at least we wouldn't have given up before finding out what the other was feeling.

I PICK MY PHONE UP.

Set it down.

Pick it up.

Set it down.

I've been playing this game since I sat down in the cafeteria for my lunch break.

Should I call or text Gage? See if he wants to talk tonight ... or give him time before I try to pull all his secrets out?

I'm shoving a bite of salad into my mouth when a voice clears in front of me. My spoon drops into the plastic container, and I have to tilt my head up to see the tall stranger's face.

I wait for him to speak, and when he does, his words come out smoothly, like a practiced politician.

"Excuse me. I'm sorry to interrupt your meal, but are you Lauren Barnes?"

I swallow down my food before answering, taking in his expensive suit and Rolex watch. "Uh ... yes."

"My name is Robert. I'm Missy Perry's father."

"Missy?"

I run the name through my mind. The hospital has been busy, but I try to remember my patients' names the best I can, and Missy isn't ringing any bells. And I would've remembered this man if he had been in the room with Missy.

"Is she one of my patients?" I ask.

He shakes his head. "No, Missy *Perry*," he stresses. "Gage Perry's wife."

Dizziness rocks through me. "Wife?" I repeat, and it's my turn to clear my throat. "I, uh ... thought they were divorced."

"My apologies, Miss Barnes." He doesn't look sorry. He said it for the shock factor. "His ex-wife."

This is a black hole I do not want to jump into.

This guy looks like he's either the head of the mafia, the president, or someone I should be terrified of.

I wipe my mouth with a napkin. "No apology necessary, *Missy's father*. Gage's business is not my business." That's a lie, considering I've done nothing but persistently ask him to open up, but I'm not going to let Missy's pompous daddy interrogate me.

He pulls out the chair across from me and sits down.

Looks like I don't have a choice.

"Do you have a minute?" he asks, clearly ignoring the fact that I'm uncomfortable.

Fuck no.

I look to each side of the cafeteria, trying to catch the eye of someone I know who can save me from this weird situation, but it's dead. Mafia politician dude was lingering around until the timing was perfect.

He doesn't wait for my response. "Missy asked that I speak with you."

"How do you know where I work?" is my first question.

"We hired a private investigator." He shows no shame in his answer, like it isn't creepy at all.

"What?" I say, fixing my glare on him. "You've had someone following me?"

"Of course not. All he did was find out where you worked and when you'd be here."

"That's disturbing and a complete invasion of privacy."

"Some might think that. I'm only here because my daughter is convinced that Gage has been in contact with you."

"I don't think that's your business or hers."

His chubby cheeks form a patronizing smile. "I see this isn't going to be easy. I understand you see this as intrusive, but please talk to Gage. Missy is filing an appeal. She was ill then and is making progress since she was diagnosed. We're expecting Gage to fight her release. My daughter made a mistake and deserves to be free. Please pass the message on."

I slowly digest his words and replay them through my head before answering, "I'm sorry, but I'm lost here. What happened?" I'm getting the sense that Missy isn't in prison for a minor infraction like receiving too many traffic tickets.

His blond brows squish together. "You don't know about Andy?"

I shake my head.

"I assumed he would've told you. Please relay the message." He pulls two pieces of paper from his pocket and slides them across the table. "Here's my business card and an incentive in hopes that you'll convince Gage to hear us out. If you accomplish this, there will be more coming your way." He smacks the table before getting up. "I'll let you get back to your job, Miss Barnes."

"Wait," I call out, causing him to turn around and look at me. "Care to tell me who Andy is?"

His face falls—the first sign of emotion he's shown since he interrupted my meal. "Not my story to tell."

———

A HINT of relaxation hits my body when I step out of the shower and tie a towel around my wet hair. My shift was long, hard, and busy. Hell, the last twenty-four hours have been long, hard, and busy.

Luckily, it kept my mind off Gage and Missy.

Her father was gone when I looked at the papers he'd left me. The first was a business card, as he'd said. It was simple—white with only a phone number and his first name. There was no associated business. The second item he'd handed me was a check from a law firm, not him, for five thousand dollars. His visit to my job was to bribe me to convince Gage to do what they wanted.

I was tempted to tear up the card and bribe money but decided against it. Not because I wanted the money, but because I was going to show Gage when the time was right. He needed to set the man straight that it wasn't cool to have someone follow me around for their own shits and giggles.

I pad through the loft, barefoot, wearing only a towel, as I head to the kitchen for a glass of water and a snack. I snag a granola bar and am on my way back to the bedroom to get dressed, but a knock on the door stops me.

Gage is standing on the other side when I peek out. He looks as tired as he did this morning, now wearing his uniform with a five o'clock shadow covering his cheeks and chin. It's not the time to talk about Missy's scary dad. I'll save that conversation for later.

He steps in as soon as I open the door and then leans back against it, arms crossed. I wait for the roaming eyes, given I'm in a towel, and that's what's to be expected when you're half-naked in front of a guy you've had sex with, but Gage's gaze doesn't move away from my face.

"How was work?" he asks.

Got a visit from your ex-father-in-law, bribing me with money.

I shrug. "It was fine." I shrug again. "Busy."

He takes a step forward. "About this morning … and yesterday … and last night—"

I hold my hand up, stopping him from continuing. "I'm tired. Let's talk about it tomorrow, okay?"

My answer surprises him, and I'm betting he'd thought I'd tell him to kick rocks.

"Yeah, of course," he answers, running his fingers through his hair. "You still have the day off?"

I nod. "You?"

"Yes. How 'bout I bring you breakfast?"

"That'll work but not too early. I'm exhausted."

My response grants a small smile from the both of us.

He takes a step closer and hesitates, waiting for my reaction, but I slowly nod, giving him permission. His arms wrap around me, and it's exactly what I need. I relax against him, melting into his warm chest, and rest my hands at the base of his neck.

His lips go to my hair. "Soon. I promise."

I nod at his words, the top of my head brushing against his chin, and hug him tighter, closer, as a silent thank-you.

That's all I've wanted.

Another layer of insecurity peels away when he kisses my lips.

"My shirts and the bed are all yours," he says, pulling away and running his hands down my arms. "Get some rest, and I'll have deliciousness coming your way in the morning. And it won't be too early."

"Good night."

He kisses my cheek this time, and my hand reaches out, ready to stop him when he turns to leave, but I don't. We might be okay right now, but the wounds from today are still fresh. We wouldn't be able to walk into that bedroom and go to bed after what happened in the cafeteria today. I'd have too many questions, and we're too tired for it tonight.

I eye the check on the bathroom vanity after he leaves.

Why would his ex-wife's father give me money?

It doesn't make any sense. Nothing makes sense anymore.

I go to his dresser and shuffle through a drawer in search of another one of his old high school tees. I embarrassingly hold the shirt to my nose and take in the smell of fabric softener and cheap cologne. I slide it over my head and pull it down to cover my hips, the tee fitting me perfectly.

A yawn escapes me, and I can't wait to hit the sheets. As I go to shut the drawer, something catches, stopping me. I attempt to push harder. Nothing. I grab an armful of shirts out of the drawer and toss them to the floor next to me.

I find the culprit. It's an envelope. My hands shake as I pull it out. It's shredded at the top, and a return address sits on the left from the Cook County Correctional Facility with Missy's name above it.

Her name is printed at the top with bright pink cursive handwriting—*Missy Perry*, complete with an I dotted with a heart. I examine the envelope like it has the answer to all my questions, looking at the front and the back, analyzing the swoops in her name.

It'll kill Gage's trust in me if I do what I'm thinking, but I can't stop myself. After his ex-father-in-law's visit, after that man expecting me to know about someone named Andy, after Gage shut down on me yesterday, I need answers, and as much as I want to wait for him to give them to me, it's like candy sitting in front of me. There's no beating this temptation, and I only hope he doesn't hate me when I find out what he's been hiding.

I grab my phone, deciding to Google his name and Chicago, but then set it back down.

Ugh. What do I do?

I'll sleep on it. Ask him about it over breakfast tomorrow.

I go to shove the shirts back into the drawer but stop when I notice the stack of pictures and envelopes in the corner. My attention goes straight to the picture at the top of the stack. It's of Gage with a baby in his arms.

Gage looks happy as he stares down at the baby wrapped in a

blue blanket and wearing a blue cap. All the blue leads me to assume it's a boy. The baby boy doesn't have Gage's olive skin tone. His is dark, and his eyes are wide and innocent. There's no familiarity in looks between them.

I might be able to hold myself back from reading bitch-face Missy's letter, but there's no stopping me from flipping through the pictures. I fall back against the dresser, and tears fall down my face. There are photos of him and the baby and photos of Gage and I assume, Missy holding the child up over a birthday cake that says *Happy Second Birthday Andy!* There's another one of them smiling while the boy, now looking a few years older, sits on Santa's lap. I look through memory after memory of their family ... of Gage's family.

What happened?

The pictures only amplify my curiosity. I've already opened Pandora's box. There's no turning back now. I pick up the envelope in shame and pull the letter out before I can change my mind.

It's the same pink writing. The heart trend staying and added to the margins of the lined and wrinkled paper.

I slowly read it, digesting each word.

My dearest Gage, my husband, the man I love,

Why won't you take my calls? My father says he will pay any collect call bills. I NEED to talk to you, to hear your voice. Why can't you understand that? I love you. I'd do anything for you. I will never leave you. Please visit me. Write me back. DO SOMETHING! Let me explain myself, so I can tell you why I did what I did and how I realize now that it wasn't the answer to our problems. I loved our little boy. We can give him a sister or a brother. You know he'd want us to be happy as his mom and dad. Let us remember him as husband and wife. Let us remember the baby boy we rescued years ago. LET ME MAKE THIS RIGHT!!! I am hurting without you, and I'd rather die than not have you in my life. Is that what you want? For me to kill myself?

I love you so, so, so, so much!!!

Your wife,

Missy Perry

(I will ALWAYS be Missy Perry!!!)
There's one last picture in the envelope.
It's the three of them.
Gage is sporting a shirt that says *Andy's Dad.*
Gage has a son.
Andy.

TWENTY-SIX

Gage

I CALLED THREE TIMES.

Texted five.

Picked up breakfast.

It's noon, and worry is setting in.

Lauren never sleeps this late.

I call once more before unlocking the loft and walking in.

Her phone is on the counter, and I set the box of doughnuts down next to it.

The couch is empty, which means she slept in my bed. *Finally.* There might be hope for us after all. She's most likely still asleep. She had a long shift yesterday and deserves a decent night's rest.

I was up all night, going back and forth with myself on what to do today. Lauren wants me to let her in, but I'm not sure how much to give yet. The two women I trusted more than anything both hurt me.

Once I tell Lauren about Andy, our relationship will change. She'll be getting more of me than my heart. She'll be receiving my secrets, my burdens, and my trust.

Trust is a precious treasure to hand someone. You're giving them a piece of you, unknowing of how they're going to play with it.

I stroll into the bedroom, expecting her to be passed out and snoring in my bed.

It's not what I get.

She's on the floor, curled up in a ball, wearing only my tee and panties.

My heart is ready to burst out of my chest as I take in the scene in front of me. Surrounding her are pictures, memories, all I have left of my son. The sight of Missy's letter next to his preschool picture makes me snarl. Her handwriting and her pleas only taint the memories of him.

Those pictures were not meant to be seen.

They were hidden, only making it out into daylight when I was feeling lonely or missing the only sunshine in my goddamn life.

The pictures gave both good and bad memories.

Brought both the light and dark out of me.

I take them in, one by one, while Lauren lightly snores in the background.

One of my worlds circling my other.

While I was nervous about giving her pieces of me, she went behind my back and invaded my trust.

And this, ladies and gentlemen, is why I decided never to let anyone in again.

She read Missy's letter. Saw my son. Most likely studied each picture.

It was what I prepared myself for all night. The questioning I knew was impending.

Do I walk away and tell her it's done?

No. She needs to know why I was hesitant to let her in.

"You went through my shit?" I ask through clenched teeth, regretting how harsh my voice sounds as soon as the words leave my mouth.

You can't blame her too much. You would've done the same.

She stirs, her eyes slowly opening, and she looks up at me. A brief smile passes her lips but drops when she takes me in. Recognition dawns on her when she looks around.

She probably intended to hide what she'd done.

She probably planned to put everything back in that drawer before I got here this morning.

"You went through my shit?" I repeat.

She scrambles to her feet with pity on her face. "No! I grabbed a shirt, *like you told me to*, and couldn't shut the drawer. When I tried to fix the problem"—she pauses, swinging her arm to gesture to the pile on the floor—"I found all of this."

"You went through my shit." Right now, those are the only words I'm capable of forming.

She blows out a long breath. "Was it wrong for me to snoop? Yes. But, after Missy's dad showed up at the hospital last night, I was so confused. I didn't go looking for this, Gage, I promise."

"What did you say?" My mind has jumped from the pictures to what she told me.

"You want me to repeat all of that?" She stressfully runs her hand through her hair and blows away the few strands in her way.

"Missy's father paid you a visit at the hospital?"

"Yes. He asked me to talk to you about not disputing her appeal … something along those lines." She holds up a finger and runs into the bathroom before reappearing with a paper and handing it to me, as if it's counterfeit money. "He gave me this."

I take a look at it, recognizing Missy's parents' attorney's signature. I've gone round and round with this guy, torn up checks, and told him to fuck off more times than I can recall. He's a fucking sleazebag attorney … and Missy's sleazebag-ass family loves to have him do their dirty work. He writes their checks. They keep their hands clean.

"The hell, Lauren? Why didn't you tell me about this last night?"

"I don't know! It was late, and I didn't want to fight with you." She grabs my hands, the check falling to the floor, and leads us to the edge of the bed. "Gage, please tell me what's going on. Let me help you."

Tears prick at my eyes when I sit, and memories flood me. I've never said the words out loud. Luke is the one who gave my father details. The only time I've said what little I know about what Missy did was when I gave my police report and then interrogated her for hours straight until her parents came in with the check-writing, sleazebag attorney.

"I don't want to bring you into my mess," I tell her.

"Your mess is my mess," she says softly. "They involved me, not you. They hired a PI to track me, showed up at my job, knew my schedule. I'd like to know why they're doing all of this. Let me help you. Let me know what *we're* dealing with."

"It's too much, baby," I say, unable to stop the tears now. "I won't bring you into the darkness with me."

"Who's Missy?" she asks, refusing to let me off the hook.

I shake my head.

"You don't have to answer that. I already know. She's your wife." The words sound spiteful, but her tone doesn't. She's upset, somewhat angry, but holding it together for me. She can sense my pain.

"She's my *ex-wife*," I clarify for what feels like the hundredth time.

Missy made it hell to divorce her and convinced her parents to hire the best divorce attorney by threatening to hang herself in her cell. I fought them, declined ungodly amounts of money, and eventually won in the end. I'd still be struggling had I not had a buddy who was one of the top litigators in the state.

I lose contact with Lauren when she gets up from the bed and snatches a letter I will always recognize from the floor.

"Wifey doesn't seem to realize you're divorced." Her arm falls to her side, the letter still clutched in her hand, and hurt is on her face. "You have a child with her?"

I scrub my hands over my face. *Had. I had a child with her.* "It's complicated."

"You hated me because I kept a secret from you about something as simple as breaking up, and you act like I'm Satan, but you've been hiding the fact that you have a child. Where is he? Why isn't he here with you? Do her parents have him? Gosh, I have so many questions. You think keeping a secret like this from me is okay?"

Anger is replacing her understanding as she paces in front of me.

The problem is, people don't think of the worst-case scenarios because they've only seen it on the news, seen it on true crime documentaries; most people don't know someone close to them who's lived through the hell of real-life *20/20* episodes.

I drop my head, take a few deep breaths, and then slowly look back up. "Missy was my partner in Chicago."

She stops her rambling and pacing, at my first admission. Her back is straight, and she's still. I can see her mind working, telling herself to come up with a question to get her as much information as she can.

"What do you mean, partner? Life partner … sex partner?"

"We were both police officers … partners."

Her eyes widen in understanding. "And then you started sleeping together? Isn't that against the code of conduct?"

"There were no rules restricting officers from having relationships with other officers. It's actually common. Partners understand each other."

"So you started sleeping with her because she understood you?" That hurt is back on her face.

"I'm not sure how it started. It wasn't planned. We were drinking at a friend's birthday party. One thing led to another, and we had sex."

"Only once?

I pat the space next to me, and she sits down.

"We had sex off and on for years."

"I'm so confused. You had sex off and on for years while you were married? Shouldn't that stay consistent?"

"It was before and during our marriage."

"You said you got married as a favor to her?" She points to the stack of pictures on the floor. "Not to be rude, but that little boy doesn't resemble either of you. Was Missy pregnant with another man's baby and you married her to help raise him?"

My story with Missy is one people wouldn't guess. It's complicated. The preacher who married us called it a kind gesture and said we were saints for what we did.

"The station was a safe haven," I say. "Someone dropped off a baby one night, and Missy and I were the ones who found him. We brought him to the hospital. He was malnourished, addicted to every drug imaginable, and filthy."

I'll remember that day for the rest of my life. We were ending a shift, walking into the station to finish up some paperwork, when we heard the loud cry ring through the chilly wind. We followed the sound to a set of steps, and as soon as he saw us, he stopped.

My voice breaks. "Three months old and an addict. We visited him in the hospital daily, and Missy fell in love with him. *I* fell in love with him. She got in touch with his social worker to adopt him. Since we'd slept together plenty of times, and we had a trustworthy relationship, she suggested we do it together and co-parent. I agreed, and we got married."

"Why couldn't you co-parent him without getting married?"

"They were giving Missy a hard time about being a single foster parent. The social worker said they'd consider placing him with a married couple over her, but he'd be in the system until then. We didn't want him put in the system, so we made the decision to become that married couple who could have him."

She nods for me to continue.

"The first few years of our arrangement ran smoothly. We lived down the block from each other and spent time together, and yes, we still did sleep together. I'd told her I wasn't looking for anything serious before we slept together the first time."

"You got married and adopted a baby with her. You can't say that's nothing serious."

"You're right. I realize that now, and I should've earlier, but it seemed so simple."

"Then, what happened? Why is she in prison?"

"I told her about you, about my life here, about why I'd left. It's easy to get personal with someone you spend so much time with.

Missy said she understood and agreed we'd never be a real married couple, but she started to change as Andy got older. She grew more protective of me. Called me nonstop. Showed up at my house at all hours of the night. Started drinking more. She got suspended from the force as a result of aggression with arrestees.

"We had keys to each other's places, and I came home with Andy one evening to find her in my bedroom. She'd found a box filled with pictures of you and asked if I still loved you. I answered honestly and said yes. Her next question was if I loved her, to which I also responded that I loved her as Andy's mother, but I had no romantic feelings for her. She had known I didn't love her when we got married. We'd planned to divorce after gaining full rights to Andy and to split custody fifty-fifty. That never happened."

"Why not?"

I choke back a sob and look at the floor while shaking my head. "Because Missy murdered Andy," I whisper.

TWENTY-SEVEN

Lauren

GAGE'S SHOULDERS hunch in pain.

I begged him for the truth, demanded it, but now, I wish I hadn't.

His truth is too powerful to take in all at once.

Andy was his son.

Missy killed him.

His then-wife murdered their child.

Jesus.

I didn't prepare myself for a truth bomb of that magnitude.

As an ER nurse, I've witnessed death—parents losing children, children losing parents, lovers losing lovers.

Watching people hurt isn't easy.

It's harder when it's someone you love.

His shallow breaths engulf the room, and sweat lines his forehead. I swipe my tears away before doing the same to his.

Am I ready for this?

Prepared to hear the details of his tragedy?

I spent all night reading Missy's letter and repeatedly looking through the stack of photos until my eyes couldn't stay open any longer. I never meant for him to find out that I saw them. That's my karma for snooping.

"I'm positive she suffocated him," he says, his voice cracking. An empty stare covers his face, and he chokes back more tears while I gently rub his back. "Andy died because she was angry with me."

I've only seen Gage cry only one other time—when his mother died. We were in his bedroom. He was in a similar stance—head low, eyes to the floor so that he could hide his hurt—and only seconds passed before he pulled himself together.

He inhales a deep breath before continuing while I shake my head in disbelief. "We never found his body."

"Then, how …"

"She left me a voice mail, admitting to sending Andy to heaven to be happy. Later, in the car on the way to the police station, she admitted to killing him and then dumping his body in an undisclosed location. When she was brought in and it was time for her to confess, she took it all back. Her family's high-profile attorney came in and cut off all her communication with us. In the end, she feigned innocence and took a plea."

My hand flies to my mouth. "Oh my God."

"I failed him," he cries out. "I failed him, and now, he's dead."

I violently shake my head. "No. Her selfishness took him away, not you." Guilt sweeps through me. Missy's resentment of me led to her rage. "If anything, I'm more to blame than you. Had you not been in love with me, maybe he'd still be alive."

It's his turn to shake his head. "Don't you dare put that on yourself."

I want to tell him not to place the blame on himself, either. He's suffering from the guilt of Missy's actions. This isn't what I expected. Fixing him isn't going to be as easy as I thought.

How does someone get over an experience that traumatic?

I shudder. I can't even imagine.

It's easy, blaming yourself in situations like his. People go back to what they might've done wrong, what they didn't do, and what they could've done.

"I'm sorry," I whisper. I might not be able to heal him, but I can give him something he's been asking of me. An apology. "I'm sorry for leaving and turning my back on you. I'm sorry you had to go through that alone."

He surprises me by falling to his knees and gripping my hands in his. Tears roll down his cheeks. "Tell me why you did it then. *Please.* For fuck's sake, I need someone to be honest with me for once!"

I sniffle, and my hands shake under his. "I can't. I'm sorry, Gage."

"Oh, come on, Lauren," he begs. "It's been years. Tell me. Whatever it is, it's in the past. We'll get through it."

Is that possible?

It'll make him lose someone else in his life.

My chin dips to my chest as I glance away from him. "I wish I could, but it's not my story to tell."

The skin around his eyes bunches together, and he pulls away. "Are you shitting me? I ripped myself apart and showed you my secrets and scars, and all I ask for in return is your goddamn honesty!"

I want to reach out and console him, but I don't know what his reaction would be. "I'm sorry. This breaks my heart, but I made a promise."

He flinches. "A promise? A promise to whom?"

"That's part of the promise."

"Stop bullshitting me." He brings himself up and snorts, looking at me in disgust. "You took it upon yourself to snoop through my shit before giving me the opportunity to confide in you. Thank you for clearing up where we stand with each other."

"I'm sorry!" I burst out, jumping up from the bed when he turns around to leave. I grab his arm and am surprised when he turns around.

"If you're sorry, tell me why," he hisses.

I don't.

Instead, I kiss him.

My mouth claims his, and I bite his tongue when he attempts to continue his interrogation.

In the back of my mind, I know, when the conversation ends, so will we. He'll leave me, like I did him, at my refusal. He grunts when I push him down on the couch, and he makes another attempt to keep up our discussion when I straddle his hips.

"Lauren," he warns when my mouth meets his again.

I press my finger to his lips, and my voice turns weak. "Please. We can talk about this after you make me feel good."

His erection slides against my core when I rock into him.

"After I make you feel good," I add.

Every move I make feels like I'm walking on eggshells. The chance that Gage could pull away at any second is clear as day, and I'm drawing out everything I can get from him. When tomorrow hits, I know we'll be over.

His arm tightens around my back, and he stands with me in tow. My mind spins with uncertainty.

Is he going to throw me out on my ass already?

His steps are fast and swift as he carries me to the bed and drops me down on it. "It's about time I have you in here again. Maybe I can fuck the truth out of you."

He stands in front of me and undresses while I do the same. There will be no intimate touches this time. No love devotions. It's sex at the wrong time, but in the back of my mind, I'm aware it's sex for the last time.

I hold myself up with my arms, and we're both panting while staring each other down. His face is filled with pain, his work-of-art chest giving away his stressed breathing, and his cock is swollen, creamy pre-cum at its tip.

"Is this how you want me to make you feel good?" he finally asks.

All I can do at this moment is nod.

I scoot up the bed and inhale the scent of him on the sheets as his hard body crawls over mine. A moan escapes me when his member nudges my entrance, and he slides inside me with no warning, sans condom again. His hands search for mine, and he intertwines them, holding them over our heads.

He stills, and his mouth goes to my ear. "Is this how you want to say good-bye because you're too goddamn stubborn?"

I stay quiet and tilt my hips up, a silent beg for more.

He doesn't oblige.

"Tell me," he demands.

"Please, Gage," I cry out.

"Please what? Give you this?"

He keeps his hands in mine and gives me what I asked for.

It's madness.

But so damn good.

"Fucking tell me," he begs.

"More!" I plead.

He lets out a devilish laugh and slams into me harder, my head slightly banging against the headboard. "It seems I'm always giving you more while you give me nothing."

He swiftly pulls out, hauls me up, and throws me on my stomach. In one breath, I'm on my knees, and he's kneeling behind me.

This is breakup sex. Hate sex. *The last time this will happen* sex.

The thought of that hurts, but my twisted soul will take it.

I push my ass up higher while he tortures me before sliding back in. The sound of him slapping my ass echoes through the room, and I don't have to beg for more any longer. He's already giving it.

My body burns with emotions, and my knees feel weak as all my blood races to my core. A whirlwind of eagerness flies through me when he reaches around and plays with my clit to finish me off.

As I come down from my orgasm, my goal is for him to explode inside me. I back up even more and meet his thrusts.

His hands dig into the bottom of my ass. "Fuck! Fuck! Fuck! Yes, take all my cum!"

He goes still, runs his hands up my back, and then collapses next to me. I do the same after I calm my breathing. We're side by side and unsure of what the next move is.

He clears his throat. "Did that convince you enough to tell me?"

"Gage," I croak out, "I told you I can't."

He rolls off the bed and grabs his clothes. "Good-bye for good this time, Lauren."

TWENTY-EIGHT

Lauren

EIGHT DAYS HAVE PASSED without a word from Gage.

They've gone by in a blur.

In Gage's eyes, the solution to our problem is simple. I confess why I broke up with him, he'll digest it and then understand, and then we can work out our problems. He seems to think that, once my truth is out, we'll heal.

He's wrong.

The problem is, if I do what he wants, it'll hurt him more and ruin someone else's life.

He's lost too many people.

I won't let it happen again.

History will repeat itself, and I'll put other people's happiness in front of my own.

After I realized our argument was final, I packed what belongings I had and called my dad to pick me up. I cried the entire ride. He asked if I wanted to talk about it and nodded when I shook my head.

I see the questioning looks from my mom each time I come out of my bedroom, but she doesn't say anything. She was there during my last breakup with Gage.

She knows the symptoms.

Knows when to stay out of it.

All I can think about is what Gage is going through. His losing his son and having no one to comfort him pains me.

I contemplated calling Kyle, but if there's anything I can give Gage now, it's my loyalty to keep his secrets.

To rid my mind of him, I've buried myself in working, searching for a new home, and clashing with my insurance company to cut me a freaking check.

Stella and Hudson's rehearsal dinner is tonight. Their wedding is tomorrow, so I plan to be the most proactive bridesmaid in history. Hopefully, it'll shield me from my thoughts of Gage.

There's nothing better than throwing yourself into a project while healing from a breakup.

Was it a breakup?

We never technically got back together.

We hung out and slept together a few times but never established anything. Never had the *what are we* talk.

Losing Gage this time hurts worse than before, but the first breakup prepared me for living a life without him.

TWENTY-NINE

Gage

MY ATTENTION MOVES from the paperwork sitting on my desk to my office door at the sound of a knock.

I've slept here for the past four nights.

I grew familiar with the excitement of pulling into my driveway, knowing Lauren was in the loft. She's gone now, and the reality of that smacks me in the face every time I pull up.

I could move on and forget about her leaving me. I've come to terms with what happened years ago, but I'll never be satisfied with the unexplained reason of *why* it happened.

Was it something I did?

Did she meet someone else?

Was she no longer in love with me?

Unresolved endings make you question if the late-night conversations, the spilled secrets, the love for you were real. I confessed my demons, opened my chest and bared it all to her, while she gave nothing in return.

The door flies open as soon as I yell, "Come in!"

"You look like hell," Hudson says, shutting the door behind him.

"And you look like a man who enjoyed his bachelor party last night."

Said bachelor party was held at The Down Home Pub. Hudson

texted and extended an invite my way, but after my argument with Lauren, I was a no-show.

I respect the dude sitting in the chair across from me. He could've celebrated his last party of singlehood at some expensive club, but he stayed here, true to his roots. It most likely didn't kill him to go home to his fiancée at the end of the night either.

"I assumed you'd be at my wedding after I sent you an invite over a week ago. Your RSVP must've been lost in the mail because, according to my expensive-ass wedding planner, it's nowhere to be found."

"Your sister and I aren't on speaking terms at the moment."

He crosses his arms and legs at the same time and leans back in his chair. "Heard something 'bout that." A sarcastic laugh drops from his throat. "How about you meet her by the swings and fix your problems over fruit snacks?"

If only it were that simple.

"Your sister is ... complicated."

"No shit." He sighs and runs his hand through his short beard. "She's not an easy nut to crack, but she's fucking loyal. No one knows what went down between you and her, but I promise you this; she didn't walk away for a bullshit reason. Since she was six, her life plans included you. Something changed her mind. Something serious enough that she'd ruin her life over it."

"That's the problem. She won't tell me."

"Try a different way of convincing her to open up."

"Any tips for a man? She's open with everything but *that*."

"All I've got for you is a good-luck smack on the shoulder and hopes that you'll figure it out." He pushes himself to his feet and extends a paper my way. Another invitation. "Wedding is this weekend if you're free."

———

"I FIGURED YOU'D BE GONE," my dad says when I step into the kitchen.

There was no sleepover in my office last night. My dad made ribs for dinner and insisted on not eating alone. He needed company. I needed company. We devoured our meal and spent the rest of the night watching old action movies.

I knocked down a few beers and convinced myself to sleep in the loft. It was a hell of a lot more comfortable than my office chair. The smell of Lauren on the sheets relaxed me and allowed me to fall asleep.

I snag a glass from a cabinet and fill it up with water. "Why's that?"

"Isn't the Barnes boy's wedding today?"

I chug down the water before answering, "Yes, but I'm not going."

He winces in offense like it's his wedding I'm bailing on. "Why not?"

"Bad idea."

"Something happen between you and Lauren? It sure looked like y'all were rekindling those sparks."

"My love life isn't any of your concern." My attitude borders on rude, but I don't want to talk about her, or where she's at, or what weddings she's attending.

"It's my concern when I want to see my son happy."

"My happiness left long ago, and I refuse to hand over all control to a woman who broke my heart. I'm a broken man, but I'm working on healing, and she's not interested in the same." I scrub my hands over my face in frustration … hurt … something. "I told her about Andy, Pa. And Missy, yet she won't even confess why she left me." A harsh laugh leaves my throat. "It sounds petty, but I'll never get over not knowing what I did wrong for her to end our relationship like she did. It fucked me up, and then losing Andy killed me. The only action I can do to stop losing people I care about is not to put myself in that position any longer."

Fuck. Am I whining?

"I understand, son. You lost the woman you loved and then

experienced a loss even greater. Losing a child can be a scary soul-sucker, and you'll never return to being the man you were."

An unfamiliar wave of fear passes over his face, and he grips the edge of the table to stand up. "There's something you should know."

"Yeah?"

"Lauren left you because of me." There's no hesitation in his answer. He was preparing himself for this confession.

I take a step back. "What did you say?"

"I'm the reason she broke up with you."

"What do you mean?"

"You ..." He pauses, his voice wavering. "You loved her more than life itself. When she enrolled in school hours away, I knew you'd follow her." His eyes water while he runs his hand down the back of his neck. "I was mourning your mother and terrified of being alone."

"Pa, what did you do?"

Remain calm.

My heart wants to explode from my chest, unleashing all the anger from me. My father's being involved in ruining my love life wasn't the answer I'd been searching for.

His hands shake as he grabs his mug and takes a drink, his Adam's apple bobbing before he sets it back down. "I couldn't lose you, so I went to the diner during one of her shifts and begged her not to let you leave me. I pleaded that she wouldn't take you away."

"You asked her to break up with me?"

Say no. Tell me I heard you wrong.

"She refused, and then I explained my reasoning. She cried and was angry that she had to break someone's heart. Either yours or mine. We went back and forth until I told her I couldn't live without you. That's when she promised she wouldn't take you away from me."

"You asked her to leave to make yourself happy?" I slam my hand against my chest. "What about my happiness, huh? You saw what a mess I was after she left." I'm using all my self-control to reel in my anger. "For years, you've seen me broken over her, and now, you're telling me this? You've had years to do it!"

He experienced the pain of losing my mom. Why would he want me to go through that same hell?

Guilt and hurt are etched along the wrinkles on his face. "I've wanted to tell you for years, but I was so angry with myself. Not only did you leave town and me, but you also lost her for my selfishness."

Don't snap. Keep it together. This is your dad.

"Lauren made me promise to never tell you what I asked of her," he adds. "She's been keeping this secret, so you and I wouldn't lose our relationship. Don't blame her for allowing me to have the only person I have left in this world."

I hold my hand up to stop him from continuing. "I can't do this right now, or I'll end up saying something I've never wanted to say to my father. I have to go."

"Are you going to her?"

"I don't know. I need to get out of here."

He nods, and there's a cold silence as I walk out the door, slamming it shut behind me. I stomp to my truck, kicking gravel, and swing the door open. I sit on the edge of the seat, my feet still outside, and allow my head to fall between my legs, hoping it helps ease the tension running up my neck.

I'm conflicted on whom to be angry with.

She left because he'd asked her to.

She broke my heart, so my father's would stay whole.

Do I hate her or love her for that?

My phone rings, and I debate on answering it. I lift my head and lean back before grabbing the phone from my pocket.

My stomach drops when I see the name flashing on the screen. His check-up calls aren't made until the evening when he's off shift. That means, when I hit the Accept button, my life might fall apart.

"Not a good time, man," I answer.

"There's a chance they found Andy's body," Luke says.

"I'm on my way."

THIRTY

Lauren

"YOU LOOK STUNNING," I tell Stella when she stands to show off her wedding dress to me as well as the other bridesmaids and my mother.

Sure, I saw it months ago when we flew out to LA to meet with her designer, but the wedding-day glow makes it even more breathtaking. It was custom-made to accentuate her curves. The sleeves are lace, the style is fit like a mermaid, and the train is short. It's classy yet casual.

Her dark hair is down in curls with a crystal headband on the crown.

Hudson hit the wife lottery with her, although she says the same about him. Their *coworker with benefits* relationship ended with them getting married. No-commitment promises always end up causing you to fall harder and faster.

No commitment is a way for us to get what we want when we're not strong enough to let our emotions talk. So, you agree to sex with no strings, but everyone knows sex doesn't come without complications.

Hudson and Stella's relationship is ending up in marriage. Willow and Dallas's sex ended up with a baby and a relationship. You penetrate the person in more ways than one. No matter what anyone says, when you have sex, you give a part of yourself to the other person.

"Thank you," Stella says. "Hudson invited Gage, by the way."

I scrunch my face up. "What? I thought you supported my decision that Gage was no longer a word to be said in my presence."

"To be honest, I hardly know the guy, but Hudson went to his work and asked him to come."

Gage has been Voldemort in the Barnes family since we ended things *again*. I don't want to hear his name. Don't want to think about him. Nothing.

Unfortunately, there's not much I can do to Stella or Hudson today. You can't exactly smack your brother on his wedding day. It'll fuck up his gelled hair.

"Why would he have done that? I told him we weren't on speaking terms. It'd be a major buzzkill for you to walk down the aisle at the sound of our arguing."

She sighs. "He identifies with the situation. Your brother and I had a hard time giving in to each other at first. We're both stubborn. If we had never admitted our wrongs, we wouldn't be here today."

———

THE WEDDING WAS BEAUTIFUL.

Small and intimate in my parents' expansive backyard, which surprised me, given Stella's celebrity roots. The only people present who'd graced the covers of magazines were her castmates and her supermodel sister.

The bride and groom had their first dance, and the bouquet was thrown. And, if you think I went for that thing, you're absolutely wrong.

That doesn't mean I didn't shove Willow to the front of the group and then jump up and down in celebration when she caught it. She and Dallas need to tie the knot.

This family deserves another fairy tale since mine is nothing but *Nightmare on Elm Street*–worthy.

I take another sip of my champagne, hoping it moves me into positive vibes, but something about weddings brings out the PDA craze in couples. All it does is remind me of how much I want to see Gage and smack him with some PDA.

I'm not sure which loss was the worse—the one when I was young and naive or the one when I was old enough to know better but couldn't break another man's heart. His dad's health was deteriorating. My conscience couldn't let me reveal our secret now.

I lick the buttercream frosting off my fork and am washing it down with strawberry champagne when Amos comes barreling toward me, looking frantic and carrying his oxygen tank behind him.

I jump out of my seat and sprint his way, meeting him in front of my parents' house.

"Amos," I say, grabbing his arm to make sure he's stable, "what's going on?"

He bends down at the waist to catch his breath. "You need …" *Gasp.* "He needs …" *Gasp.* "He needs you."

"Gage needs me?"

I've caught the attention of my family, and all eyes are on me. I notice my dad getting up from his table to see what's going on.

"It's Andy," Amos spits out. "Gage came charging into the house and said they … they found Andy's body. He packed a bag, left, and said he'd answer my questions later."

My heart sinks in my chest. "Oh my God. Where's he now?"

"On his way to the airport."

Gage never gave information on what had happened after Missy suffocated Andy, and I never exactly had the chance to ask any further questions.

I help Amos to the front porch and situate him in a chair. "Do you need a ride?" I rush out. "You can come with me. Let me grab a bag."

I don't think twice before running to my bedroom and throwing clothes into a carry-on. Amos is talking to my parents when I walk out. Their faces are sympathetic. I don't know how much Amos told them, but I can't imagine he would spill the news about Andy without Gage's consent.

"It's not exactly safe for me to fly," Amos says as Hudson and Stella join us on the porch. "I have my truck, a full tank of gas, and am not scared of getting a speeding ticket to take someone there."

I look at my family in torment.

What do I do? Ditch my brother on his wedding day or go track down the man I'm in love with, who's going through something unbearable?

"Go," Hudson says.

"I'll drive you two," my father adds.

"Do you know anything else?" I ask Amos when we get into my dad's truck.

He shakes his head. "He got the call, packed his bags, and left for the airport."

I grab my phone and hit Gage's name. It rings a few times before going straight to voice mail. I smack the glove compartment.

Shit!

I call him again. Voice mail.

This isn't the time to be angry with me, Gage Perry.

"No answer?" Amos asks from the backseat.

I shake my head.

"I told him," Amos says.

I glance back at him. "Told him what?"

He clears his throat as I silently stare at him. "What I asked you to do."

No. Why?

"Amos, you didn't have to do that."

"While I appreciate your word, it was time I did. I robbed my son of years of happiness, and I needed to own up to my actions. Had I not selfishly asked you to leave him, he would've never moved to Chicago, would've never met Missy, and would've never gone through this hell. Andy might've moved in with a different family and had a mother who wasn't mentally ill. My son wouldn't be bearing these burdens today. He wouldn't be on his way to see his dead son's body had I not asked you to do that. I knew it'd tear him apart, losing you, but I was selfish."

"Amos, none of those things can be blamed on you or Gage."

"I know what it feels like to lose someone you love too early. I was selfish and should be blamed."

THIRTY-ONE

Gage

MY MIND IS RACING.

My flight can't come fast enough.

Minutes feel like hours.

Luke has been regularly updating me, but there hasn't been much information.

A boy's body was found in the lake where Missy's car had been seen earlier on the day of Andy's disappearance, even though she has denied disposing of his body there. Her story changed dozens of times, and it was hard for police to keep up.

My little boy's body had been in that lake for all this time.

I shudder, wishing I could've been the one to go through that pain instead of him. Missy should've saved my little boy and taken me. Killed the person she was angry with, not a little man who was obsessed with Spider-Man and watched too many episodes of *SpongeBob Squarepants*. Man, what I would do to be hanging out on the couch, watching that with him.

Missy left him there to decay in a shitty-ass lake like the heartless bitch she is. She left his body for two fishermen to find early one morning.

Call me a bad dude, but she's a fucking bitch. Period. Point-fucking-blank. Missy is the only woman I'd ever call that name, and she deserves it. She deserves a stronger punishment than prison. I hope what she did haunts her until she takes her last breath.

I'll be present at every appeal her attorney files, fighting for my boy who never got a chance. Andy was my sunshine after Lauren left me in the dark. Those five years I had with him kept me going, woke me up, and made me look forward to the day, and in the end, I was his death.

"Missy's father booked you a private flight," Luke says when I answer his call.

I grit my teeth. "Decline. I want nothing from that motherfucker."

"Take it, bro. No doubt, I wanted to tell him the same and hang up on his ass, but my love for you stopped me. It'll get you here faster, and I know you want that more than anything."

"That's the problem!" My voice rises and breaks at the same time. "I'll never be able to be with him again."

Luke doesn't reply, not trying to push it and giving me plenty of time to calm down. He gets my pain. He knows no words will ever heal my grief. I've been waiting yet dreading this day since Missy admitted to hurting him. Finding him will at least give me the answers that have been killing me.

I went to that lake for weeks, dragging Luke with me, but we never found anything.

There will always be a part of me that knows I could've saved him, should've done more when the signs of Missy's breakdown started to come through, when I realized she hated me for what I couldn't give her.

"The flight leaves in five minutes. I'll text you the info."

I snatch my bags and follow the directions in the text.

Twenty minutes later, I'm boarding a private plan.

THIRTY-TWO

Lauren

"IT'S the only flight to Chicago," I tell Willow over the phone, nearly out of breath from walking around the airport in search of him. "Unless he's hiding out in the restroom, I can't find him." I do another scan of the waiting area. "Should I check in there?"

"If you don't mind seeing random men's cocks pissing in urinals, go right ahead," she answers. "Your brother followed me into the women's restroom there once."

"No details, please. I don't want a conversation that consists of cocks and my brother."

"Do you think Gage might've taken a private jet?"

"A private jet?" I snort. "Gage doesn't have access to those types of luxuries."

"You never know. Let me see what I can do, okay? I have connections with people who can look up flights. I did it for Stella all the time. Call you back."

"Thank you, Willow."

"And, whenever you're ready to talk about it, I'm here."

Willow has been my lifesaver and my new best friend since I lost mine to the cheating-on-Hudson scandal. We've been each other's rock during hard times.

My dad and Amos are on their way home. My mom has been

calling for updates every five minutes, and I know she'll be pressing my dad for as many details as she can get.

I'm unsure of where I'll go and what I'll do when I land.

Time for me to figure that out.

Guilt sweeps through me when I go to call Kyle next. I should've called him on my way to the airport, but all I cared about then was getting here. My phone nearly falls from my hand when it rings with an incoming call.

Perfect timing.

"Hey," I answer. "I was about to call you."

"The hell is going on, Lauren?" Kyle shouts. "Gage texted me, asking for time off for an out-of-town emergency and isn't answering his phone. Did something happen between you two? Did you break up with him again?"

"I wish it were that simple," I answer, grabbing my bag and walking down the hallway, away from eavesdropping ears.

"I told you not to make him flee," he grits out. "I lost my best friend once, and I won't let it happen again."

"It's not my fault." I clear my throat. "Did Gage ever tell you about his life in Chicago?"

"The man has been a sealed-up coffin about that shit." His tone lowers. "What do you know?"

I sigh. "It's not my place, but find me any information you can about where he might stay in Chicago. Maybe a friend he still keeps in touch with?"

"Answer me on why he left," he demands.

The severity of the question breaks me down. "Gage had a son who went missing and was assumed to be dead. They found his body today."

"Holy fuck. Give me a few minutes, okay?"

He hangs up, and I walk around the airport, looking for Gage and ignoring the silent and curious looks from people. I'm wearing my bridesmaid dress, sporting an updo, and my cheeks are stained with mascara.

I want to be there for Gage, wrap my arms around him, and

absorb slivers of his pain. My job and life are about healing and helping, and it's killing me that the person I most want to heal doesn't want it.

I'll be Gage's backbone while he's crumbling.

I redial his number.

No answer.

I'm grateful when Kyle calls me back and gives me what information he has.

I board the plane, knowing I'll be facing a broken man ... if I find him.

THIRTY-THREE

Gage

IT IS no surprise that Missy's parents are waiting for me when I land.

The private jet wasn't an act of sincerity. It was bribery.

I accepted the favor to get to my son faster.

Her parents didn't want Missy to keep Andy. He was dark-skinned, didn't fit into the perfection of their Christmas photos, but they took to him when they realized Missy wasn't breaking. They then made it their mission to scream to the world that their daughter had been such a humanitarian to take an orphaned baby into her home. They didn't make it as known after they found out she was a murderer.

I ignore her parents and stroll straight to Luke, who's waiting for me on the opposite end of the section. I see the dirty looks he's throwing her parents. He despises them as much as I do.

"Thank you for picking me up," I tell him.

His face is sullen, heartbroken. He was Andy's godfather. "I got you." He hugs me—our second one of our entire friendship. The first was after he arrested Missy. "My guest room is cleaned out and ready for you. Let's go."

Missy's mother yells my name at the same time I go to turn my back to them. She frantically scurries over to us, her husband on her trail, with stress and worry spread over her face like a rash.

Even though the distance is short, she's nearly out of breath when she makes it to me. "Please … we need to talk."

I bite the side of my lip to inhale the words I want to scream in her face. "Not right now. There's nothing I have to say to you." *Other than you and your family can step the fuck out of my face.*

Missy's mom, Janice, has always been an honest and generous lady, a stay-at-home mother with the full-time job of organizing charity fundraisers. She had my full respect until she defended the woman who'd murdered my child … her grandchild.

"Five minutes, *please*. That's all I'm asking for. Don't you think we at least deserve that?" she begs.

I toss my bag on the floor in frustration and rub at my temples before replying, "You aren't entitled to shit. When you stop sticking up and fighting for the woman who killed my child, that's when you'll *deserve* my time. I don't owe you or *her* anything. You want my time? My respect? Do the right thing and stand up for Andy. For the love you have for your grandson. Accept that she deserves punishment for what she did."

"I can't stop protecting my child. Nothing she does will ever change the love I have for her in my heart. I don't look at her and see her terrible actions. I look at her and see the scared woman I raised, and I wish I had instilled more strength into her. I look at her and see my heart."

"At least you get to see your child. That luxury got taken from me!"

This is the first time I've listened to Janice's words and taken them to heart. I hear her pain. She raised a daughter who did something horrible, and she's dealing with the guilt of that.

"Gage, let's go, man," Luke says, grabbing my elbow, but I pull out of his hold.

Robert is quiet as he stands next to her. A change from what I've experienced since the first time I met him. The loudest man in the room isn't used to being powerless.

"She'll never parole," I hiss. "You'll have to kill me before I stop fighting for my son."

"We loved Andy just as much as you did," Robert says.

I snatch my bag from the ground. "Fucking prove it then."

They get my back as I follow Luke out of the airport and to his SUV.

"You've got to calm down, dude. You know how powerful that prick is," he says.

Robert is the mayor of Chicago, and his family litters the political scene.

"He could be the president of the fucking United States, and I wouldn't give a shit. I moved away from this city, so I wouldn't have to look at them, think about them or the hell I went through here." I look out the window. "All I do is think about what happened. How I hadn't stopped it."

"There was nothing you could do."

I ball my hands into fists and hold them against my legs. "I don't know what type of hell I'm walking into." I stare at him with watery eyes. "Tell me what I'm walking into, man."

"You want raw or sugarcoated?"

"Fucking hit me."

"They're running DNA and dental records right now." He stares ahead. "You know, it might not be him. Maybe it's not over yet."

"They found the body in the same lake Missy was seen driving from. You wouldn't have called me and put me through this hell had you not thought it was Andy. You were at the crime scene. You *knew* my son. Tell me, do you think it's him? Tell me what you saw."

He tips his head down and lowers his voice. "The body wasn't … wasn't easily identifiable. It'd been there too long, but from the size, the details, and everything else I know about the situation …" He stops to look away from me. "I'm sorry, buddy, but I think it's him."

"Fuck!" I open the door and release everything in my stomach in the parking garage.

"Let's get you back to my place. I'll talk to everyone involved and provide any information. It'll be too hard for you. I've got this."

I shut the door and use the back of my hand to wipe my mouth. "No, I've got this. I want to know everything, so I can make sure that bitch goes down for what she did. I won't stop fighting for him until I'm fucking dead. She never gave me the chance to say good-bye. Now, I can."

He nods, hands me a fresh water, and we stay silent on the short drive to his house. Luke lives in the same South Side neighborhood he grew up in. A block deemed as the wrong side of town. Even though he has the means to move somewhere safer, he chooses not to.

———

LUKE SOFTLY KNOCKS on the guest room door. "Ready to head to the station? Detective Lewis is working on the case."

Andy is in good hands. Cory Lewis is the best homicide detective in the state and my friend of three years. I have faith he'll help me in every way he can.

"Don't think I'll ever be ready for this," I mutter.

I go to the kitchen and pour a shot of Jack when the doorbell rings.

Luke comes walking into the kitchen. "Someone is at the door for you."

Fuck!

The shot burns down my throat when I take it, and I march into the living room. "Swear to God, if it's the fucking mayor, I'll flip."

"Not the mayor, just the woman in love with you," Lauren says.

THIRTY-FOUR

Lauren

KYLE HAD PULLED through with helpful information by the time I landed. There was no certainty of Gage being at the home of his best friend and coworker in Chicago, but it was all I had to run with on short notice. No one has been able to reach him.

He looks tortured when I step to him. His dark eyes are glassy, his face drained of all color, and his chin is trembling. I wrap my arms around him as a shield of comfort. He shoves his face into my shoulder and pours every emotion onto my skin. I rub his back, using my hand to make small circles while sniffling away my tears.

Even though I never had the fortune to meet Andy, he's in my heart because Gage is in my heart. And, just like that little boy I couldn't save at the hospital, my heart aches that another innocent child was selfishly hurt by someone who was supposed to care for him.

Why?

How?

How could anyone hurt a child, kill a child?

Andy along with so many others were innocent souls taken too soon.

Gage's eyes are bloodshot when he finally pulls away, and silence envelops us while we make eye contact.

Please see the apology in my eyes.

He needs to know that I have his back as he prepares himself to endure days of hell. I have so many questions that I'm scared to ask.

Was it Andy they found? How? Where?

"So, you must be the infamous Lauren?"

My hand flies to my chest when the man steps away from the wall at the corner of the room. I forgot we were in someone else's home. He's tall and tan-skinned with a sleeve of tattoos.

I hug myself into Gage's side and nod. A soothing comfort wraps around me as he pulls me closer to him.

"I've heard so much about you." He holds out his hand. "Luke."

I shake it. "Lauren. Those are all good things you've heard, right?"

He uses the back of his arm to dust away the sweat on his forehead. "I'd be a liar if I said yes. They've all been bad."

No shocker there. It wouldn't be a surprise if Gage convinced the entire city to hate my ass.

I don't look at Gage. He had his reasons for being upset with me.

"Hopefully, you'll make me change my mind about you," Luke says. "I'm getting good vibes from your showing up here, and you have my gratitude for that. I'll give you two time to talk." He nods toward Gage. "Let me know when you're ready to leave."

Luke squeezes Gage's shoulder before walking out of the room.

I pull away and turn to face Gage. "If you have somewhere to be, I don't want to keep you."

Pain closes over Gage's face, and his voice shakes. "I need to go to the station and talk to the detective in charge of the case."

"Oh." The word pops out of my mouth.

Does he want me to leave?

He slides his hands into the pockets of his jeans. "You want to come with me?"

I wipe away my tears. "Of course. I'll be at your side whenever you need me." I point to my outfit. "You mind if I change real quick?"

He shakes his head and shows me to a bedroom down the

hallway. I set my bag on the bed next to another one that I assume is Gage's. He lightly kisses my cheek and leaves the room without saying a word. I have so many questions to ask him, but now isn't the time. I change out of my dress into a simple summer dress before going to the restroom to wash my make-up off.

Gage and Luke are waiting for me when I return to the living room, and Gage's hand stays on the base of my back when we follow Luke to his SUV. Gage slides in the backseat next to me, and I grab his clammy hand in mine after we buckle our seatbelts.

"I owe Hudson one hell of a wedding gift for your bailing to come here," Gage says.

I shake my head. "You don't owe him anything. They understand."

"Did you tell them about Andy?"

I swallow. "They know who Andy was, but the details aren't my story to tell."

He blinks. "Kyle?"

"He knows about Andy and helped me find you, but that's it. He needs to hear everything from you."

A stressed breath pulls from his chest. "I have some explaining to do. My dad … he told me why you broke up with me."

I squeeze his hand. "Let's not talk about that right now, okay? Our problems don't need to be fixed in one day."

My stomach curdles when Luke turns into a back parking lot of what I assume is the station. He slips out of his seat and meets us outside, and we walk in as a team with my hand in Gage's, and Luke's arm swung over his shoulders.

All eyes are on us, and I scan the room to find faces filled with empathy, pain, and fear. These people were coworkers to both him and Missy and also most likely knew Andy. Their hesitation is evident, and a few gain the courage to head our way and hug Gage.

We crowd into the detective's office, and he shuts the door behind us.

I sit down next to Gage, and Luke settles against the wall.

"I wish I had more for you," the detective tells Gage. "The medical examiner told me she'd call the minute the autopsy report was finished. You're my friend, so I promise to pass along all information as soon as it comes, okay? Give me a day, and I'll have more answers for you."

I expect Gage to fight for more information, but to my surprise, he only nods. I'm not sure if he came looking for answers or wanted peace of mind that the body hadn't been identified yet. He wants to know but doesn't. It would answer his questions but set him back.

When someone goes missing, there's still the hope of seeing them again. That faith ends when they're confirmed dead. Your wish turns into dust, and the fear that you'd never hug them again is validated.

I spot a mob of camera crews in front of the station when we leave to head back to Luke's, and it gives me a bad feeling in my chest. It doesn't hit me that the reporters were at the station for Andy's story until we get to Luke's house. News vans and reporters with microphones swarm Luke's front yard when we pull up. They want someone to answer questions about Andy.

That someone most likely being Gage.

Luke parks in the drive and peeks back at us with a distraught look on his face. "Looks like Andy's story went viral."

My attention moves from the crowd to Gage. Every muscle in his body is tense.

"You two going to be okay while I run errands and attempt to ward off these scavengers?" Luke asks.

I peek over at Gage for the answer.

He nods. "We're good. Thanks for everything, man."

Luke unbuckles his seat belt and fishes in his pocket before pulling out a key. "I'll be here for anything you need. I'd suggest going through the back. You know the way."

My heart races as we quickly slide out of the SUV. Our heads stay down, our gaze low, and Gage's hand finds mine as he leads me through the fence to the back door. I hear Luke warning the media scavengers to step off his property at the same time Gage unlocks the door. He bolts the door when we safely make it inside, and his hand is back in mine while I follow him to the bedroom.

I stand in front of him while he sits down on the edge of the bed in exhaustion. He groans and slowly looks up at me in pain when I run my hands through his messy hair.

"I need you, Dyson," is all he says before his hands venture up my summer dress, and he drags my panties to my ankles.

There's no hesitation before I pull my dress over my head, toss it to the floor, and drop to my knees. His lips part when I loosen his belt and pull his pants down. My job tonight is to help him forget about his pain—at least temporarily—and heal the scar tissue over his heart that Missy caused.

His cock springs forth, ready for me, and I draw him into my mouth. His breathing quickens when I pull away to lick him up and down. He grabs the comforter in his fists, and the muscles in his legs tighten as he uses his power to keep them straight.

He's restraining himself.

"Take me how you want," I say around him. "Fuck my face how you want."

My words flip the switch in him. His hand leaves the bed to wrap around my hair, tugging it back, and his dick falls from my lips. He hisses and yanks me back to him, my mouth open, and clenches his hands around my strands.

His hips tilt as he feverishly rams his erection into my mouth, going deeper with each stroke. I let him control my every move, stopping myself from gagging, and I give him what he wants. What he *needs*.

"Fuck, you suck me so good," he says between breaths. "Reach down and play with yourself."

I'm soaked, and my thighs are sticky with my juices when I do as I was told.

"How wet are you for me, Dyson?" he asks in a strained voice.

I stroke my clit one time before pulling away and holding my finger up to him. I'm surprised at how well I'm multitasking. I gasp and nearly fall back when his hand loosens on my hair, so he can lean down and suck my finger.

"So wet," he says. "So delicious."

I cry out at the loss of him when he pulls away again, and then I stare up at him, licking my lips, already missing the taste of his pre-cum.

He pulls his shirt off and pats his lap. "Come here, baby."

I climb on him and moan when his fingernails bite into the skin at my hips.

"Ride me, Dyson. Ride this pain from me."

And that's what I do.

I grip his shoulders while carefully guiding his erection inside me. He doesn't loosen his hold on me as he rocks his hips up to go deeper.

My body quivers as he fills me up, and I set a pace that borders the line of steady and hard. It's rough but intimate.

His large hand wraps around the back of my neck, and he pulls my face down to his. "Did you miss this cock, baby?"

I pull myself up and slam down on him harder. "God, yes, so bad!"

His nose nuzzles mine. "Mmm … I sure missed your pussy. I've been dreaming about being inside you again." He groans and pumps his hips up. "So fucking good. Bounce on me."

His eyes stay on me as our sweaty bodies move against each other's.

"Take me. Take it all," I moan out, dragging my nails along his back.

"Damn, I love you. I love you so damn much."

My stomach fills with sparks at his admission, and I can't stop myself from responding truthfully, "God, I love you."

His palm finds the roundness of my ass, and he slaps it. His mouth meets mine, and he gives me a different kind of kiss. It's filled with steam and intimacy but also trust and apology.

We ride out our orgasms together, and he holds his hand over my mouth as I scream out my release. I work on leveling my breathing when he brushes my sweaty hair from my face and strokes my cheek.

"Thank you, Dyson," he says, his voice dark and masculine.

He takes me with him while falling on his back and grabs my hand in his, guiding it to his chest. My fingers shake as he slowly drags it to his side, straight to the scar I asked about before.

"This scar ... it's from her," he whispers.

I run my finger over the scar again. "Huh?"

"It's from Missy."

I rise up onto my elbows. "She stabbed you?"

He nods. "After she was brought into the station for questioning. No one searched her, given her position at the station and who her family is. When I walked into the interrogation room, she snapped and stabbed me with a knife she had in her pocket."

I bend down and kiss the scar. "I'm sorry she put you through so much hell."

He pulls me into his arms, my chest against his, and his lips hit mine. "You said you love me."

I slap his chest and blush. "So did you."

"There's never been a time I didn't love you."

———

"YOU NEED TO CALL YOUR DAD," I say, turning on my side and nestling myself against Gage's chest.

It's late, and we're cuddled in Luke's guest bedroom after our second round of sex and a much-needed nap. The sound of Gage's phone ringing non-stop is what woke us up.

Reporters and news outlets had managed to get his cell number. He turned it off, gave the detective my number, and asked Luke to keep us updated regularly. He'd have details before anyone. We haven't turned on the TV in fear a story about Andy would pop up.

Gage has been keeping to himself, not bothering to call anyone. I've stayed in contact with his dad, giving him the little updates I have, and everyone in my family tree has texted me. They don't know the details, but they've given me nothing but words of support for Gage.

"The news hit Blue Beech yet?" he asks.

I nod.

"Figured it wouldn't stay quiet for long." He shakes his head. "This is what I was afraid of. I guess money can't cover everything up."

I run my hand over his smooth chest. "Are you ... are you going to have a funeral for Andy?"

Is it too early to ask that?

"We had one. An empty casket. In the back of my mind, I thought I'd never find him. I knew what Missy had done. At first, she'd admitted to killing him, but she wouldn't tell us where he was. He deserved a peaceful good-bye." A scoff leaves him. "I'd put a million dollars down that she and her family are pissing themselves at this moment."

"Do you think you'll visit her now?"

"Missy?" He shakes his head with a twisted sneer on his face. "Fuck no. No matter how many times she calls, I'll never visit that piece of trash."

I nod before resting my head on his chest. He's had an exhausting day. Sleep is what he needs because I'm not sure what kind of news will be coming our way tomorrow.

———

I JUMP and drop the water bottle in my hand when a light flips on.

Luke walks into the kitchen, shirtless and wearing only a pair of athletic shorts. "Shit, sorry. I just got back from the gym and didn't think anyone would still be awake."

It takes me a moment to catch my breath. "It's fine. I can't sleep, and not to mention, my work schedule has turned me into an insomniac." My shifts are ever-changing. In the past month alone, I've worked every shift available.

I step out of his way when he walks around the table to the fridge and grabs a bottle for himself.

He opens it before taking a giant gulp and stares my way, as if he's assessing me. "Are you back with him … permanently?"

If I had a single friend, I'd try to set her up with Luke, especially after seeing his six-pack and deep V that disappears underneath his shorts. It's not only his looks he has going for him, but I've also witnessed his character. He's been a good friend to Gage, and he was Gage's backbone when Andy went missing.

"That's my plan," I answer.

"I talked to his dad today. Amos said he's the one who asked you to break up with my boy."

I stare down at my bare feet and silently sip my water. Amos might've admitted to what he asked, but that doesn't stop the guilt from surfacing. I didn't have to agree and go through with it. Leaving Gage was ultimately my choice. I chose his father's happiness over his. I only wish the younger version of me saw it that way. I never thought about what walking away from Gage would do *to Gage*.

"Does Gage know Amos told you?"

"He said something about Amos telling him but I'm not sure how much. I'm nervous about bringing it up right now. He has so much going on and our relationship problems seem so small at the moment."

"You're a loyal one."

I glance back up at him. "What do you mean?"

"You don't throw people under the bus, and you keep your word. You think about people. Shit, from what it sounds like to me, you have a heart of gold."

If only.

"Not everyone would agree with that statement."

"Not everyone knows the real you."

I shuffle my feet. "I grew up in a tight-knit family. My parents taught me to have people's backs."

He nods, giving me a warm smile. "I like that. If only my mom had those same values."

"Bad childhood?"

"Grew up in South Side, Chicago. Dad left my heroin-addicted mom at the word *pregnant*. My grandma took care of me the best she could with the pennies she got from Social Security."

"I'm sorry," I whisper, my tone gentle.

"Don't be. It only made me stronger."

"How did you and Gage meet?"

He scoots out a chair, gestures for me to sit down, and takes the chair across from me when I do. "Funny story. First time I met him was at a bar. We got into some bullshit fight over a pool game and managed to give each other a black eye. And what do you know? I show up to training at the police academy to find him there too. We became friends, graduated from the academy together, and got hired at the same precinct." He chuckles, grinning at the memory. "We call it our fight to brotherhood. Gage was my partner for a short time until The Storm of Missy came riding through. Her daddy dearest donates a courteous chunk of change to the city annually, and she was rewarded with choosing her partner."

"She chose Gage."

"She chose Gage."

I shiver at that revelation. Missy got everything she wanted and still wasn't happy. "I'm glad he had you there for him when his world fell apart."

Luke plays with his bottle. "I was worried when he moved back home. He couldn't bullshit me. Sure, he had good intentions, going back for Amos and to clear his head, but I knew he was ultimately doing it for you. In the back of his mind, his heart, he knew you would be the only person who could heal him. And I fucking prayed you would."

"I'm not so sure about that. The first time I saw him in years, he arrested me."

He raises his brows. "I like that. It'll give you a good story to tell your kids one day."

His response steals my breath, and my heart falters. With all the chaos that has happened since Gage told me about Andy, I've never questioned his outlook on having a family—until now.

"Do you …" I stutter while searching for the right words. "Do you think he'll want to have kids after *this*?"

Luke doesn't answer until we make eye contact. "That's something you need to talk to him about. He never talked about having children until Missy came along, but then again, he never thought you two would have a second chance."

"Let me guess …"

The gravelly voice causes me to jump.

Gage steps into the room with sleepy eyes and yawns. "I'm the center of whatever you two are talking about."

"No way," I draw out. "We were talking about best-friend things."

Gage snorts. "You two best friends now?"

"Damn straight," Luke answers. "We're ordering our friendship bracelets tomorrow."

I nod. "They're going to be pink."

"Blue," Luke corrects before standing up. He squeezes my shoulder and then slaps Gage on the back. "I need to hit the shower. Good night."

We both say good night, and Gage waits until he disappears down the hall before falling to his knees in front of me.

"I'm not sure if I thanked you for coming here," he says, grabbing my chin and caressing it with his fingers. "But thank you, Lauren. Thank you for everything—for thinking of my dad, for thinking of Andy, for wanting me even though I was acting selfish."

A tear falls down his cheek and hits my leg.

"I'd follow you anywhere," I say around a sob. "And trust me when I say this, Gage Perry, I will never walk away from you again. Never. You're stuck with me now."

A small glimmer of a smile passes over his lips. "I wouldn't want it any other way."

My lips meet his.

He gets up to grab my hand, and I can't stop myself from smiling at the sight of the scratch marks on his back as he leads me back to bed.

THIRTY-FIVE

Gage

ANDY AMOS PERRY.

My son.

The sweetest and most badass kid I've ever met.

The tiny tot who wrapped his small fist around my heart and held on tighter as he grew up.

The boy who was just confirmed to have been found in the lake.

The phone falls from my hand after Cory breaks the news.

I run to the bathroom.

Vomit.

Slump down against the wall and cry, my knees to my chest.

I wish my life would end.

I didn't fucking protect him. I didn't do my job as a father.

I knew the moment Luke called me and said they'd found a body that it was my boy, but there was that unknown hope that Andy was still out there. Maybe Missy had dropped him off somewhere, like his birth mother had … or maybe she'd given him to someone else in order to hurt me.

Missy is as manipulative as she is beautiful.

It's no surprise when Lauren comes to my side and pulls me to her. She doesn't flinch at my sobs. All she does is hold me close and let me release my pain.

She'd take it on as her own if she could.

And I'd do the same for her.

Maybe that's when you know your love for someone is real. You'd gladly take every ounce of their pain and lift it onto your shoulders. You'd rather be the one to suffer, the one taking each stab to the heart, than watch them hurt. Loving someone means their pain is your pain, and you're there to carry them when they're down.

Right now, Lauren is ready to carry me wherever I need to go.

———

LAUREN AND LUKE tried to talk me out of coming here, but I can't accept the truth until I see it for myself.

Their love for me is what has them by my side as we walk into the police station.

Cory doesn't want to show me the pictures to identify the body. He suggests Luke do it for me, but I shake my head. It has to be me. I'll regret it as soon as the photo is put on display in front of me. My hands go to the desk to stop myself from falling when Cory shows it to me.

My worst nightmare is now my reality. I've seen plenty of crime scene photos. I knew not to expect his smiling face. But he was my son, and it tears me apart.

My little boy.

Correction: my little boy's body.

The decomposing corpse isn't the boy I played soccer with or the son who wanted to be a cop, just like his daddy, when he grew up.

All I have left of him now are memories.

———

"HEY," Lauren whispers, her voice shy, when I walk into the bedroom with a towel wrapped around my waist, post-shower.

I got in the shower the moment we got back from the station.

After seeing those photos and the autopsy report, I was hoping to wash away all the thoughts of how my son had suffered.

It was comforting to have Lauren by my side this time. I went through it alone when Andy went missing. Sure, I had Luke, but there's a difference between a lover and a friend consoling you.

I sit on the edge of the bed. "Can we talk about why you left now and how my dad admitted it was him who had asked you to leave?"

She lifts her hands up, and her brows gather in. "Gage ... I can explain."

I stop her from going on. "As much as I want to be angry with you, you thought you were doing the right thing for my father." I let out a heavy sigh. "So, for that, I don't know what I think about it." We've both made mistakes that we regret, and every time I look at Lauren, I see her regret for letting me go.

Her face softens, her eyes watering, and she gives me her back while she moves to the closet. She opens my bag and starts dragging out clothes. My chin trembles when she grabs my hand to help me up and then releases the towel.

"Will you tell me about Andy?" she asks, tossing it to the side.

My shorts are in her hand, and she helps me step into them while I share story after story about the little boy I wish she could've met. I don't stop while she helps me get dressed or when she drags me to the bathroom to comb my hair. She takes care of me while I give her my memories.

———

"I KNOW it's not exactly sane for a woman to suggest her boyfriend talk to his ex-wife, but in this case, I think it might help you heal," Lauren says from across the kitchen table.

Earlier, she gave Luke a grocery list, and he picked up everything we needed for gumbo. I sat in the kitchen and continued my Andy stories while they listened to every word. It felt good to share his memory since I'd hidden every part of him away while I was in Blue Beech.

"Boyfriend?" I ask. "Are we back to that?"

Luke left for work, so it's now the two of us … if you don't count the reporters camping in the front lawn. Most of them bailed after we shut the door in their faces and have retreated to Missy's parents' house.

"I mean … *friend*." She shoves her face into her hands and shakes her head. "Why am I embarrassed? I mean, we've been sleeping together, but what exactly does that mean? I haven't had a boyfriend since you, and come to think of it, we never had *the talk*. We both just knew what we were to the other. Not that I assume we're dating," she continues to ramble. "Let me reword this. It's not exactly sane for a woman to tell her fuck buddy to go talk to his ex-wife."

I lean into the table. "Look at me, Lauren."

She slowly pulls her hands from her face.

"No need to have that talk this time either. You're sure as hell not my *fuck buddy*. You're my girlfriend, the woman I love, my goddamn everything. Let's make that clear right now, okay?"

"Okay," she draws out, a smile playing at her lips. "Glad we got that covered."

"Ditto." My vision starts to go blurry, and my throat feels scratchy as I think about what I'm about to say next. "I think you might be right about the Missy thing."

She flashes me a surprised look.

Even though I can't stand Missy, we need this closure. When she contacts me, it only brings the memories to the surface. It needs to stop. Her name, even the thought of her, is a reminder of what I've lost.

"Thank you for understanding this situation," I tell her.

She stands and circles the table. I grunt when she pulls out my chair and plops down on my lap, wrapping her arms around my neck.

"You're welcome. Give me a call if you need some reinforcement though. I'd love nothing more than to shove my heel into her throat."

"As a man of the law, I'll act like I didn't hear you say that." I lean in to whisper in her ear, "Although I can't say anyone would stop you or arrest you for doing it."

———

IT'S my first and only time visiting her in prison.

A sour taste fills my mouth as I sit in Luke's car and wonder if I'm doing the right thing.

I want to forget about Missy.

After this, she's dead to me.

All evidence against her was circumstantial. She was charged with neglect, child endangerment, involuntary manslaughter, and assault for my stabbing. Her lawyers initially argued, no body, no trial. They claimed there was no cause or time of death, and we had insufficient evidence. Luckily, we had good prosecutors on our side.

They worked with what little evidence they had. They used the voice mails she'd left me. The first one that threatened to hurt Andy and the second that told me I was to blame for what she did to him. She had Googled different methods of suffocation on her phone hours before Andy went missing and none of the endless stories and alibis she told lined up.

Missy fought at first, of course. She claimed the birth mother had kidnapped him but that was disputed after Luke hired someone to identify and track down the woman. She'd been in an inpatient rehab facility at the time. Her second claim was that she had gone to shower, and he was gone when she came back, like Andy had wandered off and started a new life somewhere. In the end, her parents convinced her to take a plea deal. She admitted to suffocating Andy and said she dropped his body in a river close to her house. That river was searched for months and nothing was ever found.

She denied being near the lake where they found his body days ago, even though someone saw her there. I tried so many times to get it searched, but my superiors deemed it unnecessary since there wasn't enough evidence. The real reason was *her parents* didn't find it necessary because they knew there was a chance Missy was lying.

I grab my phone to listen to the voice mail. It's the worst time to do it, but I need to go in there with the right state of mind and fight for Andy.

My head feels like it's spinning, and my body goes cold at the sound of her voice mail. Her words are screamed out around cries.

"GAGE! Gage! You'd better answer my goddamn phone calls, you hear me? I saw them. I saw all the pictures you had saved of that whore. That stupid cunt you love so much who left you. I'm the one who loves you, Gage, not her. Me! I've stood by you and done nothing but try to please you. Me! How could you do this to us? Andy wants his mommy and daddy together with him every night. That's why we have him—to give him a family—and if you can't, then we're wrong for having him … If he can't have that, then he has no family. A boy shouldn't have to live without family … I'll end his hurt for him. I'll let Andy go to heaven where he can have a real family. Say good-bye to us, Gage, since you've decided we aren't worth it. Andy won't be here when you get home. Take that."

I SHUT my eyes to stop the tears. I'll never forget the day I first heard that voice mail. I was on a fishing trip and never expected Missy would go back to my house in search of more Lauren evidence. We had a key to each other's places for years. She'd started spiraling downhill the past few months. She'd begged me to move in with her, tried to talk me into giving Andy a sibling, and lashed out when I wouldn't take the bait.

I never expected her to hurt him. Me? Sure. But not him. She loved Andy.

Anger can blind love.

I called the station as soon as I got the message and raced to her house.

I was too late.

Even though they found his body, I'm not sure if my visit will change anything with her charges since she took the plea, but I have to try. I also want to hear her admit to what she did and how she'd sent us on a bullshit hunt for his body.

I'm close to throwing up that sour taste when she walks into the cramped room. Being here reminds me of the countless hours I interrogated her until her parents' lawyer stepped in and put a stop to it.

The door opens, and she strolls in with a smile on her face.

"Hey, baby," she greets. Her blonde hair is pulled back into two braids, and bright red lips stand out along her pale features.

There's no denying that Missy is beautiful. She's also sick, and I wish I'd recognized the signs of it before she did what she did.

I inhale a deep breath and run my sweaty hands over my legs. "Hey."

She plops down in the metal seat and inches forward, getting as close to me as possible. I have to stop myself from flinching and pulling away in disgust.

"You're sleeping with her, aren't you?" she spits.

"Who?" I already know the answer to my question.

"That cunt ex of yours." She slams a hand on the table. "My father hired a PI, Gage. I saw the pictures. She's the same woman who starred in your sacred box of first-love memories." Her tone turns mocking. "You don't forget the woman you despise."

It's becoming more difficult to hold in my anger. "That's what you're concerned about right now? That I'm back with her?"

Tears fall down her cheeks and smear her lipstick. "I gave you so much of myself, Gage! Let you take me any way you wanted, even when I knew she was whom you imagined. I did everything for you —bought you expensive gifts—"

"Which I didn't accept and told you to return them and buy something for Andy," I interrupt.

She tried buying my love with gifts, just like her parents did with her, but it didn't work. You can't buy love from someone who doesn't have it up for sale.

I tap my foot while controlling my anger. "I'm sorry, Missy. I'm sorry I couldn't do enough to make you happy."

Her demeanor changes with my apology. She perks up, and the anger disappears from her face. "You did make me happy, baby! You did. I'm upset with myself that I didn't make you happy. You never acted like I was your world."

Come the fuck on.

The tapping of my foot speeds up, and I wouldn't be surprised if I wore a hole into the floor. "I need you to do me a favor, Missy."

"Anything," she blurts out.

"Admit to what you did. *Please.*" My voice breaks. "For Andy. For your family. For *me.*"

"Tell me you love me."

I stare at her, blinking. "What?"

"Tell me you love me, and I'll tell you the truth and nothing but the truth."

I grit my teeth. "I love you."

Her fists hit the table. "Say it like you mean it!"

"I love you, Missy, so damn much."

She shuts her eyes and throws her head back. "It sounds so awesome to hear you finally say those words. I knew you loved me. It took you long enough to admit it though."

I don't fucking love her. Bile sweeps up my throat, and I can't wait to brush my teeth for an hour to wash away my words.

"Promise you'll write me," she goes on. "Promise you'll visit me. Some inmates earn conjugal visits. Maybe we can do that."

"Yes, maybe," I lie.

"And you'll leave her?"

"Whatever you want. Just give our son the justice he deserves."

My fake admission gives her hope, and she lets everything out.

I want to die as I digest her confession.

THIRTY-SIX

Lauren

"ARE WE BECOMING BEST FRIENDS?" I ask when I answer Kyle's call.

"Bite me, Satan," he replies. "I'm calling about your arsonist reputation. We found the cause of the fire."

"Please tell me it wasn't a sugar cookie–scented candle from my apartment."

"It was meth."

"Meth! In my apartment?"

The hell?

He chuckles. "No, it never started in your place. Another tenant took up the hobby of cooking it."

Great, so I was living in a meth lab. Cool.

"You're joking."

"Nope, and your creepy-ass landlord is smack dab in the middle of said meth ring. Turns out, phony rich kid has made some dough, selling drugs."

"Can't say it surprises me."

"He has quite the record, including assaulting multiple women. One of his men snitched on him, but we have yet to locate him. You need to be careful until we do. If you see him, call me right away."

Yep. My creep-dar is never wrong.

"I appreciate the heads-up. And can we not mention this to Gage right now?"

"Haven't said a word to him. Don't intend to until shit dies down."

"Thank you."

He blows out a stressed breath. "How's our guy doing?"

I wish I knew the honest answer to that. "He went to see Missy today."

The rational part of me knows this is what he needs even though the irrational half told me to stop him. No matter the outcome, whatever happens with Missy won't be easy. I only hope it clears things up for him. There's no doubt he feels guilt over entrusting Andy in the hands of the woman who killed him.

"Bitch-face, murderer Missy?" he asks.

"The one and only."

"You should've gone with him and beat her ass."

"I think suggesting violence is against the police code of ethics," I say around a laugh. "Although, trust me, there's nothing I would've loved more than that." I'd have been nice about it. Punch her and then, given my professionalism, stitched her up and sent her back to her cell.

"I like you at his side. You've moved yourself up two notches on the devil board."

———

"ANY UPDATES?" I ask Luke, walking into his living room after my shower with a cup of tea in my hand.

At first, I thought being alone with him would be weird, but he's done nothing but make me feel welcome.

No one has heard from or seen Gage.

Willow sent me a link to countless news articles. The media is having a field day with Andy's story, and Missy was a trending topic on Twitter this morning—#MonsterMissy.

Pictures of them are flooding the internet. Everyone wants

justice for Andy, and I'm nervous about how Gage will handle all this attention.

"Sorry," he answers, shaking his head. He snags his beer from the coffee table and falls back against the cushions, stress lining his dark features. "My friend works for the prosecutor's office, and according to him, Missy admitted to everything during her visit with Gage and gave him the answers he had been looking for."

I frown. "As bad as the situation is, I'm glad he got what he had gone there for."

He shakes his head and whistles. "The fucked up part is what Gage had to do to convince her to admit everything."

"What do you mean?" My legs feel weak, and I sink down in a chair before I lose my strength to hold myself up. Whatever is coming isn't good news.

"She insisted he declare his love for her—repeatedly—and that he promise to leave you."

My heart sinks. "What?" I stutter out. "Are ... are you serious?"

He sees the shock and terror on my face. "Lauren, he won't go through with it. He said what he needed to say. I only wanted to give you a heads-up in case you hear it from someone else who's not Gage and who doesn't know the entire story."

"Wow," I draw out.

He wouldn't for real do that, would he?

No way.

"That's the best word to describe it."

"No, I think *fucked up* is better," I say.

He leans forward to tap his beer against my cup. "Looks like we've found a winner."

I rise from my seat and yawn. "I'm going to attempt to get some sleep. Let me know if you hear from him, okay?"

He tilts his head forward. "Of course, and same goes for you. Good night, Lauren."

"Good night."

———

I CAN'T SLEEP.

I've tossed, turned, and checked my phone dozens of times.

Still no word from Gage.

My pulse races when the bedroom door opens, and a silhouette of a body moves through the darkness. I blink, adjusting my eyes, and watch him shed his tee. The moonlight shining through the blinds gives me a glimpse of his chest. He hastily shoves his jeans down and slides into bed, wearing only his boxer briefs.

I flip around to look at him. "Jesus, Gage, where have you been? You had me worried sick."

I sound like my mother.

Is this what it feels like, worrying about someone you love so much that you lose sleep?

He clears his throat, but his voice is still hoarse when he answers, "The lake. I had to apologize." His body shakes when I reach out to touch him and caress his shoulder. "Sorry I've been MIA. I needed time."

"No, I understand," I say.

His skin is warm as I slide my hand from his shoulder to his cheek, wiping away his tears.

I shiver when his hand swoops underneath my T-shirt, and he brushes a thumb against my nipple.

"I love it when you wear my tees," he whispers.

"You've mentioned that once or twice."

I move away to pull it off, but he stops me.

"Leave it. I want to make love to you while you wear nothing but it."

I moan when he rolls on top of me. He pulls my panties and shorts down and slowly slides his cock between my legs.

His lips go to my ear. "I love you."

———

"I'M SORRY. I tried, but no one could take your shift without hitting too much overtime, and you know how the hospital looks at that," Natasha tells me over the phone. "All I could manage was one more day."

"I understand," I say around a sigh. "I appreciate your trying."

I never call in sick. *Never.* Not only am I addicted to my job, but they also need me. Even though it's a small hospital, it stays busy. Normally, I don't have a problem with that, but Gage needs my support. This sucks.

I didn't question him about his meeting with Missy. He has no idea I know what she made him promise. There's no doubt in my mind that Gage loves me and wouldn't walk away from our love. I trust him.

Now, after the hell of a day he's had, I have to break this news to him. I stroll into the bathroom after hanging up and wrap my arms around his waist from behind while he dries off from his shower.

"Bad news," I say, pressing my lips against the damp skin of his back.

"Words I'd be happy to never hear again," he comments, reaching back to give my arm a gentle squeeze.

"No one can cover me at work," I say around a swallow.

His shoulders stiffen. "When do you leave?"

"By tomorrow."

My arms collapse when he turns around to face me, and I lose my breath when he tips my chin up with one finger.

"Mind if I stay a few days?"

"Stay as long as you need."

He cups my chin and brings my lips to his. "I'd better make this day count then."

I smile at his plan but hold my hand out to stop him. "You don't need to worry about entertaining me. You've had a rough few days."

"Spending time with you will help keep my mind off everything."

"Tell me your plan."

"Chicago time with Gage Perry."

"I like the sound of that already."

It is a good idea, and I hate that it's ruined when we walk out the front door. Cameras are in our faces.

"Just ignore them," Gage mutters, grabbing my hand.

I tug on his arm. "Let's go back inside."

"Gage!" a reporter yells. "Did you have anything to do with the disappearance of your son? There have been reports that you knew Missy planned on hurting him!"

I freeze up and clench my fists, holding myself back from smacking the asshole.

My chest aches, and I lose Gage's hold when he darts toward the reporter.

"The fuck did you say?" he screams.

Regret fills the middle-aged man's face. "I, uh …" He pushes his glasses up. "A source told us—off the record, of course—that you were aware that Missy was dangerous."

"Fuck your lying source," Gage snarls. "I loved my son and would've never let Missy near him if she showed one sign of abuse. I came as soon as Missy left the voice mail but was too late." He thrusts his finger in the man's face. "Don't come to me, hoping for a story that will make headlines. The only one you'll receive is that Missy stole my son from me and ruined my life. There's no need for you goddamn scavengers to throw it in my face." He grabs my hand. "Don't fucking follow us."

"Wow," I say as we slip into Luke's SUV.

"This is what I was concerned about," he grits out, his head falling against the steering wheel.

Their cameras follow us as he backs out of the drive and turns down the road.

There's no doubt in my mind, that guy won't be the only reporter we run into today.

"Turn around," I order.

He glances over at me. "What?"

"Turn around. We'll order some deep-dish pizza and watch movies in bed all day."

A portion of the irritation drains from his face. "I like that idea."

THIRTY-SEVEN

Lauren

EXHAUSTION IS MY MIDDLE NAME.

It's early in the morning when I pull into Gage's driveway, and I yawn with each step going up the stairs to the loft before tiredly unlocking the door. I can't wait to eat, take a quick nap, and then see Gage. His flight lands this afternoon, so I plan to catch some sleep and then pick him up with Amos.

We've talked regularly since I came home five days ago, and he's stayed strong. It helps that Luke is there with him, and he has the support from him and his coworkers. They held a memorial for Andy at the lake last night, and I'm sad I had to miss it.

I drop my bag on the table and grab a bottle of water from the fridge at the same time there's a knock on the door. Amos has been visiting me between my shifts and bringing me meals since I've been back. Now that our secret has come out, we've gotten closer.

"It's open!" I call out and snag another bottle for Amos.

"Hello, Lauren."

My hands start to shake as I drop the bottles at the sound of his abrasive voice. I inhale three deep breaths before turning around to face him.

"What are you doing here, Ronnie?"

I pause to take him in. He reeks of alcohol, his button-up shirt is soaked in what looks like more liquor, and his eyes are bloodshot and swollen. One thing Ronnie isn't is in the right frame of mind.

"Have you been following me?" I stupidly accuse.

The evil smirk on his face confirms not only that this is a stupid question, but also that something bad is about to happen. Instead of waiting for his response, I rush over to the knife block and miss my chance at grabbing one when he captures my waist. He swipes the block off the countertop with his free hand, and the sound of knives crashing to the floor masks my groans when he presses against me and shoves my face against the countertop.

I cringe when his wet lips hit my ear and his thick body moves against mine.

"Now, now, tenant," he says mockingly, "why are you making trouble for me? I only wanted to be a good landlord and check that you were okay after the fire."

I bite into my lip to stop myself from crying out and struggle to reach for a candle, anything, to protect myself from him but am stopped when he grabs my arm and pushes it back. A deep pain shoots through me, and I freeze up.

Don't provoke him.

"Ronnie," I say as calmly as I can manage, "I was going for the bottle opener to offer you a beer."

He laughs behind me, and the smell of his breath nearly gives me a contact buzz. "I applaud you for not being as dumb as most women I have to punish, but I'm not falling for your tricks, bitch." He twists my arm against my back, and I buck against him. "Keep doing that, sweetie. It'll only make my dick harder."

I still while taking deep breaths.

"Not so brave now that your little boyfriend isn't with you," he taunts, twisting an arm harder. "You know, no one would've questioned what happened in that apartment had you not been spreading your legs for cop boy."

I stop myself from crying out when he whips me around and pushes me against the counter, my back biting into the rough handle of the drawer. Nausea hits me when he spreads my legs and shifts himself between them.

All I have to do is raise a knee.

It has to be timed perfectly though.

"He was only investigating the fire because you blamed me, Ronnie," I grit out.

He thrusts his hips against mine. "Shouldn't have turned me down."

"Smartest decision I've made in my life."

My response only lights more rage inside him. I have to be smart about this. I nearly gag when I feel his hardness rub against my leg.

"Ronnie, you need to leave before the police come," I warn. "If you go now, no one will hear about this visit, okay?"

He scoffs, "There's a warrant out for my arrest, you dumb cunt. Either way, I'm going to jail." He rolls his hips. "Might as well have some fun before I do."

I try to push him away, but he's stronger than I am. "Please stop. You'll regret this later."

"Trust me, I won't regret this one bit. In fact, I'll relish it forever."

He looks up and meets my gaze for the first time, and I can't stop myself from spitting in his face. I'm a survivor, and I also take no shit. My head slams back against the cabinet when he smacks me across my face, and I taste blood on my lips.

"Now, I'm really going to make you pay," he says, taking a step back to unbuckle his jeans.

I see this as my opportunity and slowly start to lift my knee up, hoping I get a good shot.

We both stop and jump at the sound of Amos's voice.

"Hey, hey, you step away from her right now!" he screams, stalking into the room, moving as fast as he can with his tank behind him.

Ronnie wipes my spit from his face. "What are you going to do, you old man?"

Amos raises his hand. "I'm going to protect that woman until you kill me. Do you hear me?" He holds his phone up. "I also hit the emergency button on my phone, and the police will be here any minute."

Ronnie steps away from me and kicks Amos's oxygen tank. I grab the candle I was going for and bust it over his head at the same time he punches Amos in the face. Ronnie falls. This is what some might call my stupid moment, but I disagree. Instead of making sure Ronnie is down, I rush over to Amos's side as blood pours from his nose.

The front door slamming catches my attention, and I rush down the stairs to catch Ronnie, but his expensive sports car is already flying down the street.

I run back into the loft with disappointment and situate Amos on the couch and hold a towel to his nose.

"What the fuck happened here?" Kyle shouts minutes later, appearing in the doorway. "Amos called with an emergency."

"Ronnie decided to pay me a visit," I say, biting back tears.

"Oh, fuck me!" Kyle yells. "That dumb junkie!"

"Can we not tell Gage about this?" I ask Amos, standing up.

His glassy eyes meet mine. "Last time we made a pact like that, you two didn't talk to each other for nearly a decade."

"When it rains, it fucking pours," I cry out.

THIRTY-EIGHT

Gage

I HIT Lauren's name while making my way through the airport.

The call goes straight to voice mail.

Seconds later, Kyle's name flashes across my phone screen.

"Hey, man," I answer.

We've briefly talked since I flew to Chicago. I want to tell him everything in person.

"I have something to tell you, but promise you won't freak out," he says with caution.

The fuck kind of statement is that?

"Depends on what it is."

"There was a situation."

"What do you mean, situation?" I've had enough *situations* to last a lifetime.

His breathing is heavy on the other end. "Ronnie … he, uh …"

"The landlord?"

"The landlord."

"What about the fucking landlord?" The volume of my voice grants me looks from people passing by.

"The building fire was caused by him cooking drugs there."

How the fuck is that a situation for me?

I'm happy it gives us the answer we were looking for and that people will stop giving Lauren a hard time.

"Good. Lauren won't be blamed for that fire now."

"Too late. Ronnie blamed her for his getting busted and paid her a visit at your place."

My breathing falters, and I stop in place. "The fuck did you just say?"

"He came to the loft and assaulted her. Thankfully, your dad walked in and fought him off. They're both a little banged up, but everyone is fine."

"And the landlord? Is he in custody?"

"Not yet, but we're on it. Everything is fine. We'll get him. I promise."

"Asshole touched my girl and my father, so no, everything is not fucking fine." My jaw clenches. "And why am I just now hearing this?"

"It happened only a few hours ago, and you were on a plane."

I speed-walk through the airport. "I'm going to fucking kill him."

"Not smart to say, given you're surrounded by people."

I raise my voice. "I. Am. Going. To. Kill. That. Motherfucker."

"Point taken."

"Where is she?" I snag my bag from the baggage claim, throw it over my shoulder, and sprint out of the building.

"Her parents'. We offered to take her and your dad to the hospital, but Lauren fixed herself and your dad up, and they're okay."

"I'll be there as soon as I can."

I hang up on him and start looking for an open cab.

A blue truck swerves into the pedestrian lane and stops next to me.

"Get in," Kyle yells through the open window.

I shut the door behind me and meet his stare. "Motherfucker will pay for this."

———

THE RIDE to town feels like it takes ages, and I jump out of Kyle's truck as soon as we pull in front of Lauren's parents' house. I race through the front door to find Lauren and her family in the living room, and two fellow officers are standing in the hallway that leads to the kitchen.

I rush over to Lauren and take her face in my hand, holding it back and inspecting it, searching for any marks. "Are you okay, baby?"

Her cheek is bruised, her lips swollen, but other than that, she's in one piece.

Thank God.

The landlord won't be blessed with the same destiny when I get my hands on him.

Her brown eyes water as she stares up at me and nods. "I'm fine. Just a little shaky, is all."

Typical, strong-willed Lauren.

My lips smack into hers before I take another scan of the room. "My dad?"

"He's in the bathroom," Lauren's dad says, standing up from the couch.

Lauren's father, John, has his legs planted wide when he stands and loosens his collar. Rory, Lauren's mom, is next to her with wet eyes.

Kyle moves away from the corner of the room and smacks John on the back. "We'll get the dude. I promise you that, sir."

"The fucker will pay for it. *I can promise you that,*" I bite out, not caring about my language in front of them.

Typically, I'm a respectful dude but not when a man has hurt two people I'd die for.

Lauren's lips tremble, and she winces, like it pains her.

"We have guys out looking for him. You don't need to worry about this," Kyle tells me.

I help Lauren when she struggles to get up, and she wraps her hand around my arm.

"Let them deal with Ronnie, okay?" she says. "Please don't go after him."

"I'll never stop stressing over someone hurting my family."

He will pay, and he will pay at my hands.

She sighs and nods. It's not an agreement. It's a promise that we'll be having this conversation in private at a later time.

I kiss her cheek when my dad walks in, and I march across the room to pull him into a hug.

"Thank you," I say before doing the same inspection I did with Lauren.

As with Lauren, I can tell he's been roughed up, but he's okay. Physically at least.

We stayed in contact when I was in Chicago but haven't broached his admission that he was the one to ask Lauren to break up with me. That conversation won't be held tonight either. It will happen, but causing more chaos than we have going on isn't smart, and as pissed as I am, I can't get angry with him.

Who knows how much time we'll have to work out our problems?

We'll talk, but there will be no grudges held.

We stay at Lauren's until it grows dark, and Kyle drives us home. We don't go to the loft. It's part of an open investigation. Plus, I might snap if I see the evidence of the destruction Ronnie caused. I pace in the kitchen, and Lauren makes herself and my dad each a bowl of ice cream before they walk me through what happened with Ronnie.

Later, I do another inspection of her while we shower. My nails bite into my knuckles as I eye the bruises on the backs of her thighs and back. I help her dry off, and we sleep in my old bedroom.

Ronnie will go down for this.

———

"YOU SURE YOU don't want to stay home?"

I'm spread out on the floor next to Lauren in my childhood bedroom. The twin-size bed we started the night in proved not to be big enough for the both of us. After I rolled off twice, I moved to the floor. Lauren joined me after waking up to an empty bed. We ended up snuggling in a build-a-fort made of blankets and pillows.

"I'm positive I don't," she answers. "You know we're short-staffed."

"They'll understand if you explain to them that you were assaulted."

Not that she would tell them.

I know I've lost when she gets up and starts to rummage through the overnight bag she packed from her parents. "They'd absolutely understand, but sitting around, thinking about the suit-wearing creep putting his hands on me, isn't what I want to do today. Work will rid my thoughts of him."

We both shudder at the thought of Ronnie.

I lift myself up onto my elbows. "Then, let me take you."

She shakes her head and leans down to kiss my lips. "I'll be fine, babe."

I grab her elbow and pull her back down next to me. "The lunatic who assaulted you is on the loose."

I already feel like a piece-of-shit boyfriend for not being there to protect her the first time. It can't happen again.

The final decision is made during breakfast. News to me, Lauren arranged for my father to volunteer at the hospital when she worked. He'll assist people with directions and be with her if she needs anything.

My goal today is tracking Ronnie down.

———

I'VE BEEN STALKING Ronnie's recent transactions and GPS locations from his phone records since I walked into the station. He has multiple rental properties, and I plan to visit each one. If he's not there, I'll question the tenants.

My time is saved when I spot his most recent location is fifteen minutes out of Blue Beech.

Appreciate your making it easy for me, dumbass.

I stop by Kyle's office before leaving for my manhunt and knock on his door. "I need to run a quick errand. Be back in an hour."

He stands and snags his wallet from the desk. "I'm coming with you. I need some fresh air."

"Nah, I'm good." I hold my hand up to stop him. "It's a dry-cleaning pickup for Lauren. Nothing fun."

His lips press into a thin line. "Sorry, partner, but you're on the clock, which means, I'm by your side during every move you make. I'll maybe even follow you to the urinals today."

I turn around and walk away without saying another word, and he follows me to the cruiser.

Not another word leaves him until he's buckling his seat belt. "I know you got a hit on Ronnie's whereabouts."

Kyle can't be dragged into my shit. I can't have him losing his job if trouble arises with Ronnie. I'll be the only one facing the consequences of my actions. I need to find a way to blow him off and pray to God that Ronnie doesn't change locations before I do.

"You don't know shit," I mutter, failing to meet his gaze as I shove the key into the ignition.

"I beg to differ, liar face. Let me and the guys handle him, and I'll keep you updated. I fucking swear it, Gage. You're not in a sane state of mind to be handling this. I can't risk your doing something stupid, like killing the predator asshole."

"He'd deserve it," I grit out.

"Good point." He snags the keys before I can stop him. "Promise me you won't leave any marks on the dude, okay? Give me your word, and I'm your wingman."

"Can't do that, brother. I'm sorry."

"There goes that idea. Hopefully, Sierra will know how to cover up any bruises with all the makeup she has." He throws the keys into my lap. "Let's find this asshole."

———

RONNIE'S shiny red BMW is parked in the driveway of the rental.

The idiot couldn't even hide out from the cops right.

Even better, the front door is unlocked.

Guy might as well have left us a breadcrumb trail.

The entire ride, I attempted to talk Kyle out of coming with me, but there was no changing my best friend's mind. He has my back, no matter what, and the way he loosened his collar when we parked down the street told me he shared the same hatred toward Ronnie not only assaulting my family, but other women as well.

I don't see Ronnie as a threat, but my gun is still in my hand. And Kyle takes the same precaution. I carefully open the door, and he follows me in. It's quiet, and the place reeks of alcohol, drugs, and piss. The living room is clear. So is the kitchen … with the exception of the meth lab set up inside.

Kyle glances back at me with a glare and shakes his head, mouthing, *Piece of shit*, before we hang a left down the hall. With the amount of drugs, I'd expect to see more people here, protecting the supply.

Dumbest drug dealer in history.

We find him passed out, naked, in a bedroom that has the door torn off the hinges with a woman next to him in the same position.

Disgust spirals through me.

Did he drug her? Rape her? Is she here by choice?

Dirty needles and more drugs litter the nightstand. I stalk around the bed and watch him sleeping soundly with not a care in the world after he nearly destroyed my girl's and my father's lives. That seems to be the problem with so many people. They don't think of the impact their actions have on other people.

My anger takes over, and before I can stop myself, I snatch him from the bed. He grunts, and the wall shakes when his naked body slams against it. It's a sight I wish I could bleach from my eyes. My hand immediately goes to his throat before he even has the chance to open his eyes.

"Good morning, motherfucker," I say, spitting in his face.

He opens his mouth to talk back, but my grip is too tight. I get a rush of satisfaction at the sight of his face turning red. My eyes stay on him until his bedmate screams and covers herself with the sheet.

"Don't worry," Kyle assures her, stepping further into the room. "We won't hurt you."

Her attention flickers from him to the array of drugs in the room. She's worried about being busted for possession.

Ronnie no longer looks like the man I met at the apartment. His cheeks are sunken in. His pupils are dilated, and his body is frail. The drugs have taken the best of him. Not saying his best was much.

"Gage," Kyle finally warns at the realization that Ronnie is on the verge of passing out at my hands.

Ronnie grabs his throat while trying to catch his breath when I release him, and you'd think he'd be smart enough to keep his mouth shut.

His words only prove further that he's the dumbest motherfucker in the room.

"I see you're here about your cunt of a girlfriend," he says, spitting at my feet.

I respond by swinging my fist back and punching him in the face. He staggers back against the wall, but that doesn't stop his mouth from talking. Asshole must not value his life.

"Did she tell you how hard I rubbed my big dick against her?" he taunts. "She said it felt better than yours."

I grab him by the hair and throw him down on his knees. My gun goes straight to his temple while I grit my teeth and try to talk myself down from blowing his brains out. The chick screams while Kyle rushes to my side.

"Okay, that's enough!" Kyle cries out.

I'm conflicted about my next move. The gun stays in its place, biting into Ronnie's head, and the anger inside me can't dim enough to convince me to pull back.

I can't shoot him.

I'd lose everything.

It's also not who I am.

I'm not a killer.

"Goddamn it," I hiss when Kyle slowly takes the gun from me.

Seconds later, a deep pain thrums through my head when the naked junkie chick strikes me in the side of the face with a candlestick.

THIRTY-NINE

Lauren

"BARNES, your hunk of a police boyfriend is here," Jay announces, throwing open the break-room door and waking me up from my nap. A conflicted look flickers across his face.

I rub at my tired eyes. It was nice, being in Gage's arms last night, but our pillow fort was far from comfortable. "Huh?"

Am I still dreaming?

"Gage is here," he clarifies.

I jump up from the couch. "To visit me?"

He had a full shift at work today, so for him to be here this early means something is up.

"Nope. He's in the ER."

"The hell?" I shove past him and run down the hallway, my heart on fire.

Jay stays behind me while relaying information. "From what it looked like, he got himself into an altercation. There's blood but no broken limbs or trauma."

Of course he did.

"Even though he's fine," Jay goes on, "he's insisting you're his nurse. Word is, he and your landlord threw blows at each other." He pats my back. "He's waiting for you in Lavender."

I stop to look at him. "Lavender? We never send patients there."

Lavender is a room the size of a closet that wasn't given a second chance during the hospital's latest remodel. It got its name because everything—the walls, the decor—is a dingy purple. The overstock supplies are stored in there, and we only use it as a last resort, so I'm confused on why he's in there. We've been slow today and nowhere near crowded.

"Your man isn't in much need of medical attention, to be honest. Therefore, he was sent to Lavender." He shoves the iPad we keep our charts on into my hands. "I'll give you some time, and I won't come in until you call me and tell me it's safe."

"It's safe?" I repeat.

He elbows me. "In case he needs you to *care for him*."

I slap his arm. "I'm at freaking work, Jay! Not at some porn shoot!"

He walks away, laughing, and I run down the hallway to Lavender. I swing the door open to find Gage in a gown, sitting in a chair, holding a piece of gauze to the side of his face. His cheek is caked with blood, and his lip is cut. Other than that, he seems to be untouched.

A sense of déjà vu rams into me from the last time he came into the hospital.

"Jesus, stitches again?" I hiss, storming into the room. "What the hell happened?"

My question is dumb because I already know. There's no doubt in my mind that Gage hunted down Ronnie today. I could see the fury in his face when he left this morning but didn't think it'd end up with him in the hospital.

"Ronnie's junkie girlfriend thanked me for taking her sleazy boyfriend away by smacking me with a candlestick," he says.

"Are you nuts?" I screech. "Ronnie is a dangerous drug dealer. You could've been killed."

"But I wasn't. The fucker is weak sauce, Dyson. No one is scared of him. Hell, I had him pinned against the wall, and he didn't do shit. It was his fuckmate who took matters into her own hands." He stands and grabs me around the waist, no pain in his eyes. "Trust me, he looks worse than I do."

He pushes into me, and I shiver at the feel of his erection brushing against my scrubs.

"I came here for some TLC, Nurse Barnes."

I wrap my arms around his neck and laugh. "Oh, really?"

A smile tilts at his lips. "I told you my favorite porn was patient and nurse."

"That porn dream will have to wait unless you want to get off while I give you stitches."

He nuzzles my neck. "The stitches can wait."

My blood runs hot when I look down and see the length of his manhood under the thin gown.

"Right now, I have something else I want you to heal."

I expel a long breath. "I can get fired for this, you know?"

I untie the back of the gown, revealing his throbbing cock, before dropping to my knees. I'm not sure who's more turned on—him or me.

Gage's fingers wrap around my ponytail. "Jay said he'd give us plenty of time for you to make me feel better."

His dick twitches when I wrap my fingers around it and start stroking him.

"I'm so going to hell for this."

I grunt when I'm picked up and tossed on the ancient medical bed. He strips off my scrubs and climbs over me.

"If this is what brings you there, I'll be right by your side."

I take a good look at his wound while he tilts my hips up and places his erection between my legs. "I do need to examine your wound and most likely give you stitches."

"Examine something else first."

With one swift motion, he's inside me, and the bed creaks with our every movement.

FORTY

Gage

"ARE YOU GAGE?"

I lose my breath upon looking up from Andy's grave and seeing the woman standing next to me.

A single rose is in her hand while a tear runs down her cheek. She's a skinny thing, barely any meat to her bones, and her hair is pulled back into a sloppy ponytail.

I know who she is, but I'll let her do the introducing.

I stand up and wipe the dirt off the knees of my jeans. "Yes?"

"I'm Darla Long ... Andy's birth mother."

Darla Long is a mother to four other children who were put in the system. She has had six drug overdoses, has been admitted into three different rehab facilities over the course of ten years, and has a record a mile long, full of shoplifting, solicitation, and possession charges.

As much as I should hate this woman for abandoning Andy, I can't.

I can't because, just like her, I let him down.

She shoves her feet against the grass. "I'm sure you hate me for what I did. I was young, an addict, and his father kicked me out on the streets when he found out I was pregnant. Another homeless woman told me that my baby would be safe if I dropped him off at the station. I stood in the shadows when you picked my baby up and rescued him. I watched him from afar while you gave him a better life than I ever could."

"Yet I failed him." I scrub my hands over my face and sigh.

Pain strikes across her face. "We all failed him."

She's right.

She did. I did. Missy did. The system did.

Why is there no better way to protect our children?

"I want to thank you," she goes on.

Her words are like a smack in the face.

"For what?"

"For giving my son love for the time he was here. He had someone who put him first, who fed him and gave him a warm and comfortable home." Fresh tears stream down her cheeks now. "I wish I could've met him before he went to heaven."

My neck goes stiff, and my gaze turns watery. "I'm sorry you were never given that opportunity."

Anger surfaces over the hurt. "And, that woman, I hate her. As much as I want to be angry with you, I can't because I see your heart, and I know it was with Andy every day you had him. It's still there. I want to thank you for trying to save my son when others, myself included, didn't give a damn about him."

I nod, choking back a sob, and open my arms.

She doesn't hesitate before hugging me.

———

I'VE RECEIVED three letters from Missy since my visit, and each one has been thrown in the trash, unopened. The media attention has died off after no one was willing to give interviews, even for the vast amount of money they were throwing out for exclusive stories.

They brought more charges onto Missy after her admission to me at the prison, but she took a plea again and it never went to trial. Last night, Luke sent me a report, claiming Missy was diagnosed with bipolar disorder, and she was finally seeking treatment for it.

Who knows how long she's been suffering with it? But, with her parents' need to keep a clean appearance, I'm sure it's been for years. With her new diagnosis, she wants an appeal now that she is in the right state of mind.

That's the shitty thing about mental illness.

People are afraid to ask for help.

They're ashamed, afraid to be the brunt of a joke, and they feel weak. Not a day will go by that I'll forgive Missy, but the state of her mental awareness casts understanding in me.

I say my last good-bye to Andy's gravestone as the sun starts to set behind it.

FORTY-ONE

Lauren

"SOMETHING SMELLS GOOD," Gage sings out after walking into the loft. He starts to dance by the stove. "And my girl is making gumbo!"

Our initial plan was to buy a house, but we delayed the house-hunting in exchange for staying in the loft. Amos enjoys having us around, and we like his company just as much. It took time for Gage to fully forgive his father for what he'd asked me to do so many years ago, but they're working on strengthening their relationship.

Life is more relaxing when there are no secrets.

It took us a week after Ronnie's assault before we managed to walk into the loft without wanting to puke, but eventually, we put that in the back of our minds. Ronnie is locked up, and more women have come forward with claims that he assaulted them.

From what Gage says, the bastard will be spending a good chunk of his life in jail for the assaults and the apparent drug ring he had going on ... in my old apartment building.

I jump off the couch and snap my fingers to stop Gage from taking a bite from the pot. We finally broke down and bought a new couch ... *after* breaking our cherished, memory-holding one during a night of drunken sex. I still miss that ugly-ass thing though.

I swat his hand away when I reach him. "Don't you dare touch that! It's for dinner tonight."

Gage frowns and drops the spoon. "Anyone ever tell you that you're no fun, Dyson?"

I smack his stomach. "You didn't say that last night, and I doubt you'll be saying it when we get back from dinner with my family."

He pulls me into him and wraps his arms around me. "I love it when you play dirty."

Amos bursts into the loft without knocking. "You two ready to go? I have a bet with Hudson on the game, and you know how much I hate losing money."

Gage is in charge of holding the gumbo as we walk down the steps and get into his truck. Our monthly family dinners have expanded. Amos along with Gage are always invited. Kyle has also been known to make a few appearances. He claims it's because my mom makes great food, but we all know he likes me more than he puts on. I've graduated from the Satan nickname.

This dinner is important to us tonight.

I move around in my seat, unable to get comfortable, as excitement thrums through me.

Gage leans in before starting the truck. "How long are we waiting before we break the news?" he asks.

"As it's looking right now, about ten seconds," I answer.

———

I'M GOING to chicken out. I'm going to chicken out.

My breathing catches in my throat when I stand up and look at everyone sitting at the long outdoor table in my parents' backyard. Gage and I didn't have a plan on *when* we were breaking the news, but he said he'd wait until I made the first move.

All eyes go to me. My mom sets her drink down, and my dad drops the spoon in his hand. I feel like the main character in a movie who's about to announce a life-changing event.

Granted, I am making an announcement about a life-changing event.

I look down and glare at Gage, who's still in his chair next to me. I flick the top of his head, and he tosses his napkin on the table before standing up and clearing his throat.

There's a beaming smile on his face that hasn't left since we got the news. I nod, giving him the go-ahead, wanting him to have this moment.

He throws his hands up. "We're having a baby!"

The celebrations occur, and my family is already making bets on whether we'll have a boy or girl. All I want is a healthy baby and to be the best mother I can be. I have no doubt that Gage will fulfill the perfect father role. The light on his face when the doctor confirmed the nineteen tests we'd taken were for sure positive was something I wished I could take a picture of and keep forever.

I had held back from asking Gage if he wanted to have children. It was a sensitive topic I wasn't sure how to approach. Luckily, he came to me after *cumming* in me. He helped clean me up and then asked me what I thought about going off birth control and starting a family. Even though he asked it so casually, I knew it meant so much for him to say those words. I had no hesitation in answering him with a yes, but I questioned if he was sure. He nodded, took my hand, and we went to the bathroom together to toss my pills in the trash.

This is his second chance.

Our second chance.

As the evening turns into dawn, Amos is at our side, telling everyone good-bye. He wraps his arms around me and Gage and grins. "You *three* ready to go home?"

Gage

EPILOGUE

I GRIN as I stare at the screen.

It's our first ultrasound. I don't think either one of us managed to get a minute of sleep last night. We spent our time throwing out possible baby names and talking about nursery paint colors, and we discussed whether the baby would look more like her or me.

Lauren's face shines as she squeezes my hand, her focus on the screen as well. "Our first view of our little one."

"I can't wait to meet him or her."

We hold our breath and nod when the tech asks if we want to know the sex.

We nod.

It's a girl.

We're having a princess.

The tech consumes our attention while she shows us our daughter. She has an adorable face with my nose even though Lauren disputes that you can't see any facial features yet.

The photo stays in my hand the entire ride back to our new home. It pained us to leave the loft, but there wasn't enough room for our growing family. We're only minutes away from my dad if he needs anything. The ultrasound photo gets put into a frame, and we settle it between a picture of Lauren and me and one of Andy after his first soccer game.

I've begun dealing with my guilt over losing Andy. The pain of being unable to stop his death will always be there, but it's less frequent now. He's my son whom I lost too soon, a little man who crawled into my life and made it brighter each day. I hope I did the same for him during the small amount of time he had here.

I grab his photo and relax on the couch while wiping a single tear as I stare at my first child. He would've been a kick-ass big brother. Our little girl would have screamed at him for helping me warn off boyfriends, and I could've shown him Blue Beech. His smile would've lit our small town up.

Lauren plops down next to me, and I rub her growing stomach before placing the photo of him on top of it.

"This is your big bro," I whisper, leaning down so that my mouth is at her bellybutton, hoping our girl can understand every word even though it's doubtful. "I'll tell you all about him when you get older. He would've loved you so much."

Lauren strokes my hair as a sob leaves her throat.

She visited Andy's grave with me last month. We bought hot dogs at his favorite stand at the Navy Pier and took them to his place of peace, making sure we had an extra one for him. I now have to live off the good memories, so the bad ones don't pull me back into the darkness.

"Our little girl will be happy, knowing Andy is watching over her like a guardian angel," Lauren whispers.

"He'll be the best damn big brother ever," I muster out.

I kiss her stomach one last time before falling to my knees. The small box has been lodged in my pocket all day after I asked John for his blessing. I exhale while looking up into her curious eyes. Since I asked my dad for my mother's ring, I've been debating on whether to make it a private or public proposal. My mind wasn't made up until this very moment.

She says *yes*.

Giving someone a second chance is oftentimes frowned upon.

Sometimes a second chance isn't an option, but we were lucky enough to realize we're stronger together.

We're no longer exes.

We're going to be husband and wife.

We're going to be parents.

We're going to be happy.

KEEP UP WITH THE BLUE BEECH SERIES

All books can be read as standalones

Just Neighbors
(Kyle and Chloe's story)

Just Roommates
(Maliki and Sierra's story)

Just Friends
(Rex and Carolina's story)

BOOKS BY CHARITY FERRELL

BLUE BEECH SERIES

(each book can be read as a standalone)

Just A Fling

Just One Night

Just Exes

Just Neighbors

Just Roommates

Just Friends

TWISTED FOX SERIES

(each book can be read as a standalone)

Stirred

Shaken

Straight Up

Chaser

Last Round

STANDALONES

Bad For You

Beneath Our Faults

Pop Rock

Pretty and Reckless

Revive Me

Wild Thoughts

RISKY DUET

Risky

Worth The Risk

ABOUT THE AUTHOR

Charity Ferrell resides in Indianapolis, Indiana with her future hubby and two fur babies. She loves writing about broken people finding love with a dash of humor and heartbreak, and angst is her happy place.

When she's not writing, she's making a Starbucks run, shopping online, or spending time with her family.

www.charityferrell.com

FIND ME ON:

CPSIA information can be obtained
at www.ICGtesting.com
Printed in the USA
LVHW011644291021
701929LV00008B/891